SENTENCED TO TROLL COMPENDIUM 2

BOOKS 4-6

S.L. ROWLAND

ALSO BY S.L. ROWLAND

Tales of Aedrea

Cursed Cocktails

Sword & Thistle

The Halfling's Harvest

There Be Dragons Here

Pangea Online

Pangea Online: Death and Axes

Pangea Online 2: Magic and Mayhem

Pangea Online 3: Vials and Tribulations

Sentenced to Troll 1-6

Path to Villainy: An NPC Kobold's Tale

Collected Editions

Pangea Online: The Complete Trilogy

Sentenced to Troll Compendium: Books 1-3

Sentenced to Troll Compendium 2: Books 4-6

SENTENCED TO TROLL 4

CURRENT STATS

Chod, Level 24 Barbarian/Summoner Forest Troll
  HP: 5880/5880
  Mana: 5000/5000
  Rage: 0/100
  XP: 603,208/665,000

Strength: 41
  Dexterity: 24
  Constitution: 42
  Intelligence: 10
  Wisdom: 15
  Charisma: 6

+1 Strength and Constitution racial bonus per level.

+1 Ability point per odd level.

5 stat points available.

1 ability point available.

. . .

Abilities:

Bite. *Using your massive tusks and powerful jaw, you take a bite out of an opponent, dealing immense damage. Cost: 10 rage Level 2.*

 Claw. *You attack with sharp claws, swiping at an opponent and dealing extra damage. Cost: 5 rage. Level 2.*

 Intimidation. *You stare down your opponent, confusing them so that they are unable to attack for two seconds. Cost: 10 rage.*

 Berserker Rage. *(Ultimate) Attacks and physical damage build your rage meter. 5 rage per attack. Rage meter deteriorates over time when out of combat at a rate of 5 rage per second. Activating Berserker Rage fills rage meter. For 30 seconds, rage meter does not decrease, deal increased damage, health regenerates at 5x the normal rate, cannot be stunned, slowed or otherwise affected. Cooldown: 10 minutes.*

 I'm Always Angry *(Passive. Available at level 10). Once rage meter is at 50%, it will not deteriorate below 50% when out of combat.*

Increased Regeneration. *(Passive) Regenerate health at a faster rate. Level 2.*

 Rapid Regeneration. *(Passive) When below 10% health, regeneration is doubled.*

 Nightvision. *(Passive) Increased vision in darkness and low light.*

 Thick Skin. *(Passive) Take 10% less damage from physical attacks.*

 Savage. *(Passive) Ability to eat uncooked meat without consequences.*

 Camouflage. *(Passive) When out of combat and not moving for 20 seconds, trolls blend in with their surroundings.*

 Sweeping Slash. *Form a sweeping arc in front of you, dealing damage and knocking your opponent off balance. Cost: 5 rage.*

 Conceal (Passive). *Hides level from anyone who is not a guard on city grounds.*

Summon Horror (Passive). *Ability to summon a horror. Each horror grants a unique ability. For every horror active, gain 1% increased damage and health points. Horrors decay 10% for every minute outside of combat.*

 Horror of Power. *Summon a horror with 20% of your strength. Cost: 100 mana. Cooldown: 30 seconds. Bonus: Your next attack deals double damage.*

 Horror of Vitality. *Summon a horror with 20% of your health points. Cost: 100 mana. Cooldown: 30 seconds. Bonus: Opponents near Horror of Vitality are slowed by 20%.*

 Horror of Finesse. *Summon a horror with 20% of your attack speed. Cost: 100 mana. Cooldown: 30 seconds. Bonus: Your next attack heals you for damage dealt.*

 Sacrifice. *Sacrifice X amount of horrors to receive a temporary buff. Horror of Power: +1 Strength. Horror of Vitality: +1 Constitution. Horror of Finesse: +1 Dexterity*

 Kamikaze. *Sacrifice a horror to deal a burst of damage.*

Champion. *Summon a copy of the most recent enemy you have defeated. Decays 10% every minute out of combat. Cost: 50% of mana pool. Cooldown: 6 hours.*

Available Abilities *(1 ability point to unlock):*

Massive Bite. *Deals double damage. Cost: 20 rage.*

Claws. *Swipe at opponent with both hands, dealing extra damage. Cost: 10 rage.*

Multi Attack. *Bite and Claw at the same time. Cost: 20 rage.*

Iron Will. *Immune to slows and stuns for 30 seconds. Cost: 50 rage. 180 second cooldown.*

Perception. *For 10 minutes, gain increased awareness of your surroundings. Spot hidden objects, as well as unusual sounds, odors, and tastes. Cooldown: 6 hours.*

Cleave. *Your next attack causes bleed damage, dealing 1% of opponent's health per second for 5 seconds. Cost: 10 rage.*

Battle Cry. *You let out a ferocious roar, increasing rage by 20. No cost. 60 second cooldown.*

Current Items:

Item. Phoenix Feather. 10% resistance to fire-based attacks. *A very rare item, phoenix feathers can only be gathered if they are willingly given by the host. Feathers plucked from unwilling birds turn to ash.*

Item. Tiger's Eye Pendant. Removes one debuff. Cooldown: 10 minutes. *A rare stone believed to ward off evil and bring balance to life.*

Item. Petrified Staff. An enchanted staff capable of taking on the properties of up to 3 attached stones. +3 Intelligence. +3 Wisdom. Bonus: *While holding Petrified Staff, the user can cast ranged physical attacks once every 10 seconds.*

Item. Forlorn Scepter. +5 Intelligence. *Increases the range of summoned creatures by 50%.*

Item. Glouwseeker Venom. *When injected into the bloodstream, glouwseeker venom immobilizes target. Length of stun dependent on size of target, resistances, and amount injected.*

Item. Sea Scorpion. +3 Strength. *An enchanted trident capable of taking on the property of 1 enchanted stone. Bonus: deals splash damage.*

Legendary Item. Angel of Death Brandy. *When drinker falls below 1HP, a metaphysical event will occur, rewinding time for the user to two seconds prior to death.*

Item. Brimming Tankard. *A magical tankard that, once filled, will never go empty. Warning: Once filled, contents cannot be changed. Only works on beverages.*

Item. Expandable Satchel. *A bag capable of holding enormous content and only* *burdening the wearer with ten percent of its weight. Simply focus on the item inside and it will appear in your hand.*

　　Item. Destroyer. An enchanted warhammer capable of taking on the properties of up to three stones. +2 Strength, +3 Constitution. *This ancient warhammer was forged in the heart of a volcano.* **Bonus Ability: Inferno.** *With each consecutive hit, Destroyer grows hotter, allowing it to warp or pierce through even the hardest metals. Multiplier works when hits are less than five seconds apart. Cost: 10 mana per attack. Cooldown: 10 sec.*

　　Item. Spaulder of Swiftness. +1 Constitution, +1 Dexterity. *Lightweight, durable leather mail designed to protect the off-hand shoulder during battle.*

　　Item. Mysterious Green Egg. *???*

　　Item. Halite Shield. *A lightweight translucent shield capable of taking damage without reducing visibility.*

PROLOGUE

Valery sat alone staring into Chad Johnson's pod. He looked peaceful laying there, despite the chaos happening on the monitor above. The technicians responsible for monitoring player health had either gone home for the day or were asleep in the on-call bunks.

For the past five years, she had devoted her life to the lab. This was her pet project, after all. And now it had morphed into something far beyond what she'd ever imagined.

The lab was quiet except for the gentle whir of the machines. Machines keeping twenty-five men alive while their consciousnesses were fully immersed in a virtual world.

That in itself was a miracle so far removed from the days where gaming was nothing more than hitting a ball between two lines. But this, *Isle of Mythos*, was far more than just gaming.

She'd been sitting there so long that the automatic lights overhead had switched to low-power mode. The glow from the monitors and the electric blue nanites gave the pristine white lab an ethereal feel.

It was fitting.

Nearly two months had passed since Chad had first logged in. Getting a gamer into the trial had been the goal—an easy way to work out the bugs so they could move up the timeline—but he had changed everything.

When they'd discovered that he was the reason the game was crashing, she couldn't believe it. Somehow, the AI believed that he was a part of the system. An integral part.

Looking at his body lying peacefully inside the pod, there was no doubt that this was only the beginning.

The system was designed to rehabilitate. It wasn't as simple as going in and rewiring someone's brain to make better choices. That was impossible. The AI that ran *Isle of Mythos* was one of the most advanced of its kind. It presented the user with choices, evolving the world around them based on actions and reactions. While most programs struggled to accomplish this with any real results for a single user, this AI evolved the world seamlessly for dozens of users at the same time.

Valery had known she would face obstacles in bringing her vision to life. She'd seen the writing on the wall. The only way she could have gotten the funding to pull this off was by appealing to a company with deep pockets. A company like Mythos Gaming.

She believed that this technology could change the world.

What she saw before her sent terror into the depths of her soul.

Chad Johnson had climbed into that pod weighing one-hundred and twenty pounds, skinny as a rail with acne and a sunken chest.

The clear skin and superficial changes had been expected. The nanites cleaned the body better than a hot shower and steel wool.

When they'd first pulled Chad from the pod, he had looked leaner, more defined. That happened to most of the users. The nanites provided them with a perfectly balanced, nutrient rich diet.

What had happened in the weeks since then was anything but normal. Thompson had pointed out the discrepancy when it first became noticeable, and Valery had checked the stats on everyone else to compare.

Whatever was happening, it was only happening to Chad. She had combed over every move he'd made since logging in. She had theories. Theories she wanted to test, but that meant finding more volunteers.

That was easier said than done—especially knowing what she knew now.

Pretty soon, she was going to have to answer some very tough questions.

Like how Chad Johnson's body had managed to put on twenty pounds of muscle while in stasis.

1. READY TO RUN

"Are you sure this is going to work?" Taryn squints as he peers through the foliage, brushing several dreadlocks behind his ear. "It's the middle of the day. This still seems kind of reckless."

I duck a little lower, concealing myself behind a leafy frond that drapes across one of the canals carrying water to the bathhouses.

"It's not like we have a choice. The only time this guy comes out is during the day." My gaze shifts from Limery to the beastkin he's tailing. "It'll work. Limery is the best pickpocket I know. He'll be in and out before we know it."

I focus back on Limery as he hovers along the crowded street several meters behind his target. Massive beastkin walk leisurely through the stone streets of the market, furry humanoids with the heads of lions, tigers, bears, and a myriad of other creatures that occupy the city of Goldspire.

The center of the city is rife with activity, from shops to entertainment. Despite being closed off to lower-level NPCs and players, the city forum is thriving. Taryn, Limery, and I are some of the few foreigners currently on the continent, but my troll appearance doesn't stick out as much here as in Vanaria or Seascape.

Limery comes to a stop behind a beastkin with the head of a hippo.

Cornix Coinbearer
    Hand of the Emperor
    Level: ???
    Monk
    Beastkin

. . .

He wears a white canvas toga draped across his oily, slate-colored skin, and several amulets dangle from his neck. For his position, his clothing is surprisingly modest. Except for a golden key hidden among the amulets.

A key that will grant us access to the emperor's villa on the edge of town.

For the past three days, the emperor has been absent from the royal palace. Rumor has it he's indulging in his very own saturnalia of debauchery at his villa overlooking the Sapphire Channel. But time is of the essence, and we need to deliver King Orso's message so that we can be on our way.

The hippo leans forward, the necklaces dangling as he admires a selection of bright yellow fruit on a cart. In the shuffle, the golden key catches the light. Cornix lifts one of the melon-sized citruses to examine it, and Limery moves in.

Limery's hand burns a molten orange as he reaches for the chain holding the key. The golden chain melts against his long spindly finger and it slips off the hippo's neck, slinking into Limery's other hand.

The imp flashes me a demonic smile and zips through the air. The chain catches against one of the other amulets, jerking Limery back and tearing the hippo from his focus on the fruit.

There's a moment of startling realization on both their faces as the wide-eyed hippo stares at the bulbous-eyed imp.

Cornix shouts something, and I launch myself across the trickling channel, landing with a thud in the stone courtyard of the forum.

"Some pickpocket he turned out to be." Taryn grunts as he lands behind me. "He's going to get us all killed."

Limery darts through Cornix's legs. The hippo turns in a flash, extending a ki-powered punch at Limery. His impish speed saves him, but the force of the punch explodes the fruit cart, sending wood and pulp raining through the streets.

Limery speeds down a flight of wide, shallow stairs toward Taryn and I.

He hovers for a second, inches from my face. "We's needs to goes, Chods." He glances over his shoulder just as Cornix leaps through the air, nearly covering the distance in a single bound.

We don't waste any time putting our feet to the stone-covered streets of Goldspire. The fruit market empties into the main courtyard of the forum, where a beautiful mosaic depicts a colorful battle. Musicians and street performers cover the courtyard, playing for tips. Beastkin sit around fountains, and tall Corinthian columns rise into the air, their floral embellishments topped with statues of great warriors.

Cornix runs with surprising speed for a being so large. His big round eyes are slits of anger as he chases us down the city streets. I summon a Horror of Vitality, hoping for its passive slow to give us some breathing room. Cornix's fist moves in a blur, exploding the horror with a single strike without slowing even a fraction.

Damn, he's fast.

Goldspire citizens step back as we run, watching the chase unfold. In the center of the forum, Goldspire's namesake—a towering golden obelisk—juts into the sky.

Taryn casts Strong Wind, buffing our movement speed, but it offers little advantage. Cornix's stout legs take on a golden aura and he matches our speed once again.

"We need to lose him!" I point at a temple with ornate columns at the edge of the forum. "Through there."

I take the stairs into the temple several at a time. Taryn avoids the stairs entirely by transforming into his bird form, then returning to his dwarven form at the top. The temple is filled with statues of Goldspire's multi-limbed gods and goddesses. Scenes of divine magic plaster the vaulted ceiling, and even more detailed mosaics cover the floor.

I summon more horrors and send them toward the entrance to block our pursuer, but they meet the same fate as their predecessor, destroyed by the hippo monk's lightning reflexes.

We exit into another wide street that's littered with carts and merchants. Limery tosses a fireball at Cornix as he exits the temple, but the monk dashes to the right in a blur and the fireball leaves a scorch mark against the marble as it explodes.

I point to a bathhouse, and Limery darts ahead. As I pass through the wide, green marble arch, I bump into a tiger beastkin with a towel wrapped around his waist, nearly knocking him into one of the many rectangular bathing pools. All around us, dozens of beastkin soak in the water or sit on the tiered edges as attendants groom them and comb through their fur with lavish oils. The vaulted ceiling gives the bathhouse a spacious elegance as water drips and bubbles all around.

At the back of the bathhouse, I climb a spiral staircase that empties into a veranda overlooking a lush garden. Limery and Taryn once again take to the air.

A long crystal blue pool stretches the length of the garden, with two elephant beastkin fountains shooting streams of water from one to the other. Ornate topiaries run along the edge, forming their own menagerie of fantastical creatures. Large trees offer shade among the many patios scattered throughout.

The thud of hooves announces that Cornix is catching up, so I jump from the veranda, landing hard against the stone pathway. Another burst of Strong Wind sends me speeding down the garden path.

Cornix leaps from the veranda without hesitation, landing at a full sprint without so much as slowing.

Damn his monk abilities!

At the end of the garden, we pass through a set of triumphal arches, the entablature on top carved with gilded runes, and exit into another street lined with apartments.

Taryn summons a cluster of poison mushrooms under the arch, and I follow Limery as he takes to the right. A few seconds later, the monk passes through the mushrooms, setting off their poisonous gasses. Purple clouds waft through the arch, and a silver sheen covers Cornix's body, mitigating the poison entirely.

At the end of the row of apartments, we cut through an open-air theatre. Boos swarm us as we disrupt the performance of a plum-colored minotaur. He shakes his fist overhead in the throes of despair, replaying some tragedy for the crowd. A tomato splats against my face from some disappointed spectator.

We pass another row of buildings before the city wall looms before us.

"End of the line." For the first time since our chase began, Cornix slows to a walk.

I summon a round of horrors in front of me while I try to find us a way out of this. There's no way we can fight him, and I'd rather not spend the next few days locked away in the Goldspire dungeon. Cornix takes another step toward us, and Limery summons a fire wall in front of him.

Cornix smirks, revealing his massive cinderblock teeth. "Fire doesn't scare me." He steps into the flame wall and a dense silver sheen covers his lower body, reflecting the flames like he is made of metal. "My body is an unbreakable temple, crafted through years of discipline. Now, give me my key and be on your way. No one need get hurt. I'll chalk it up to the folly of heroes."

Taryn and I glance at each other. It's nice that he is offering us a way out, but to meet with the emperor, we need this key. It's the only way we'll be able to gain access to him. We can't wait however many days it takes for the emperor to decide to return to the palace.

Incoming Message (Taryn): *I've got a plan. When I give the signal, we run down the alleyway adjacent to the wall and cut through the basilica.*

Taryn steps forward, one hand raised in surrender with the other on his Sapling Staff. "You're right. It was a stupid mistake. If you'll just allow us to—"

The earth cracks and a stone wall rises between the buildings, Taryn's newest ability separating us from the Hand of the Emperor.

"Run!" Taryn shouts and we race down the alley, Strong Wind giving us added speed.

There's a loud crash of what I can only assume is Cornix smashing through Taryn's Stonewall with his mighty fists.

"I hope that wasn't your entire plan."

We pass the blacksmith, whose hammer and anvil echo down the alley, and I jump through an open window into the basilica, where two long rows of spiraled columns run under the vaulted ceilings.

The elegant hall is filled with merchants selling spices, wool, clothing, and ancient books. We don't have time to appreciate the beauty of the art or architecture of the building before we exit the other side into another crowded street.

A door slams behind us as Cornix bursts out of the basilica. Steam shoots out of his nose just before we turn another corner and I lose visual. A moment later, he's right on us again.

"Taryn…" There's only a matter of seconds before we are about to be pulverized by this not-so-gentle giant.

He lifts his staff into the air once more, summoning a twenty-foot wall along the width of the alley. There's a crash as Cornix barrels into it at full speed. It won't be long before he tears through it as well.

"Quick, in here." Taryn pulls open the door, ushering us inside.

I'm about to chastise Taryn for thinking we can hide from a city official when a welcoming voice calls from over my shoulder.

"Welcome to The Wilty Rose Inn. Would you like a room for the evening?" A falcon beastkin wearing a purple silk toga bows slightly to us from behind the bar.

I reach in my pouch, pull out a gold coin, and slam it on the counter. "Yes!"

Taryn, you bloody genius.

2. THE WILTY ROSE INN

I hold the small, golden skeleton key between my fingers. The handle is composed of elaborate metal knotwork with an encrusted ruby in the center. Funny how something so small caused us so much trouble. This key will give us access to the emperor, where we can plead our case on behalf of King Orso. With the power scale of those in Goldspire, having them on our side when the time comes could be the difference between victory and defeat.

"Close call." I hand the key to Taryn.

He lifts it and grins. "No kidding. I was not expecting him to move that fast. Or be that powerful. I thought monks just sat in silence all day." He flips the key over in his palm. "Talk about subverting expectations. Good job getting out of Dodge, Limery."

Limery peeks through the shutters, examining the streets below. "Limmy is too fasts for the hippo mans."

"But not fast enough to not get caught." Taryn takes a pillow off the bed and hurls it at the tiny red imp.

Limery dodges the pillow with ease, sticking his tongue out at Taryn. "Nobodies is perfect. Right, Chods?"

I can't help but laugh. Maybe my words are starting to sink in. "Right you are. It all worked out in the end, though. Thanks to Taryn's quick thinking."

Coming up with a plan to block off the road was a brilliant idea—especially considering we were running for our lives. One of the amazing things about inn rooms is that they are magically protected. While renting a room, heroes can set their spawn points inside. Even if Cornix had seen us enter the inn, we'd be safe inside our room until we decided to leave.

Thanks to Taryn's wall, we were able to disappear inside The Wilty Rose Inn, leaving the Hand of the Emperor none the wiser. No doubt he is scouring the streets of Goldspire looking for us.

Let's just hope we can make it to the villa without being spotted.

We spend the rest of the evening in our room, waiting for the sun to set while Taryn complains about us not taking his pets on our adventure.

He crosses his arms and frowns. "I just don't see why we can't ride them across the city. It's a long walk. And you know how Berry gets when he doesn't see me."

"Once we talk to the emperor, you can parade them through the city for all I care. But for now, we're trying to keep a low profile. They're well taken care of at the stables. Besides, they have each other."

Taryn lays back on the bed and pulls a pillow over his face. "It's like you're taking away my children."

"That's a little dramatic. But who knows, maybe after two days, Stompy will show you a little affection." I smirk.

He tosses the pillow at me. "Now, you're just being mean."

When the streets are dark except for the torches that light the stony corridors, we venture out into the inn.

There's a dull roar of chatter as we descend the stairs. Glass clinks as two satyrs toast one another, their glasses brimming with golden wine. Platters of grapes, cheese, and toasted breads cover the tables.

Compared to the raucous taverns of the dwarves, this inn has a certain sophistication to it.

"They're quite refined to be so brutish looking, don't you think?" asks Taryn.

I nod. "Everything does seem much more laidback here."

Since arriving in the city, it has seemed to move at its own pace. No one is in a hurry. The beastkin take time to enjoy the moment, and their fondness for sports and the arts is unrivaled.

"Fancy a glass of spiced wine?" a gentle voice asks from behind the bar.

The elegant falcon from earlier has been replaced with a slender fox beastkin who flutters her eyelashes in our direction. She wears a teal sash around her head, just below her pointy ears, and a yellow tunic embroidered with a wilted red rose. Several small golden hoops dangle from her left ear. When she steps out from behind the bar, her silky teal pants flow with her movements, and an ornate dagger hangs from her waist.

She picks up an empty glass off a nearby table and returns to the bar. There's something oddly alluring about her presence. I focus on her stats and am surprised to discover that the Goldspire bartender is level twenty.

We are so out of our league here.

"What's it gonna be, big blue?" She winks.

Limery flies over to the bar, reaching for a wine glass. "Limmy wants wines."

"When we get back," I manage to get out. "We have business to attend first."

She smiles. "I'll be here all night."

I force my eyes away and examine the rest of the inn. A brawny, bluish-black bear sits in the corner smoking a pipe. A lioness and minotaura lean in close at a nearby table, playing a game with black and white marbles.

Limery swoops in and snatches a piece of cured meat off the satyrs' platter without being noticed.

"Now he can pickpocket," Taryn mumbles under his breath.

"Ready to get this show on the road?" I ask.

Taryn pulls his hood over his head, concealing his features in shadow. "Let's do it."

I take the white-and-green shawl I purchased in Sandholde from my satchel and drape it over my shoulders, doing my best to conceal my identity. "Limery, it's probably best if you hide in here. You are a wanted man, after all."

Limery climbs onto my shoulder and nestles himself within the fabric.

I open the door and we step out into the cobbled streets. The moon shines bright overhead, casting the skyline in a silver glow. Every so often a torch crackles, illuminating the gray stone with hints of orange. From where we're standing, the golden obelisk of the forum towers above all, as if drawing in the light of the moon itself.

Further still, the royal palace, gladiatorial arena, numerous temples, and other structures look down from the hilltop.

A black minotaur comes lumbering down the street, a pike slung over his shoulder. Limery grows warm against my skin, and Taryn and I both lower our heads, avoiding eye contact. When he passes by, I let out the breath I've been holding.

"Where do you think Pressley is?" Taryn asks as we continue down the street.

We haven't seen the death knight since leaving the arena. I doubt we would be here now without him. He's a solo adventurer by nature, but when the time comes, I know we'll be able to count on him. "No idea. I'm sure he's around here somewhere, looking for gold and glory."

"Well, he certainly came to the right place. Marble buildings, golden statues. This entire city is a work of art."

We enter the forum, where braziers blaze all around, bathing the mosaics and sculptures in flickering light. The gentle gurgle of the canals puts me at ease.

Compared to most cities, Goldspire is surprisingly alive at night. With so many people still out, we easily lose ourselves in the crowd. Music carries through the open windows of the inns and taverns, and the open-air theatres are filled with crowds watching the evening shows.

The royal palace sits at the top of the hill overlooking the forum, but the imperial villa is located on the other side of the city with views of the channel.

We stop for a moment to admire a fire-breathing performance where a silver-furred wolf beastkin spews flames in a cone above the crowd. It reminds me of Hawkin and the Underground Circus.

I wonder what they're up to these days.

Two lion beastkin approach from across the way. Their eyes are piercing and alert as they scan their surroundings. Massive manes rest on segmented armor composed of metal strips that are tied at the front. A red sash drapes across their shoulders: imperial armor.

Gaurus Bladefur
Imperial Guard
Level: 34

Caius Timbertongue
Imperial Guard
Level: 35

I grab Taryn by the arm and pull him into an alleyway before they spot us.

"What the hell, Chod?" Taryn snaps.

I can tell by his stiff posture that he's scowling at me beneath his hood.

"Put your head down and just keep walking."

His shoulders relax, and he does what I say. Limery's claws dig into my shoulders, but the imp doesn't speak.

Once we pass through the alleyway onto another street, I finally breathe again.

"Want to tell me what that was all about?" Taryn lifts his hood and his eyes bore into me.

"Those two lions were imperial guards, both leveled in the mid-thirties. If they chose to focus on us, there would have been no hiding our identities."

He lets his hood drop, once again hiding his eyes. "Good looking out, but maybe be a little more gentle next time. We need to get to the imperial villa ASAP."

Taryn raises his staff and there's a lightness in my feet as Strong Wind takes effect. We move at a brisk walk that's more akin to a run. Before I know it, we're at the edge of the city where the high-walled estates conceal the rich and powerful from prying eyes.

The edge of the city along the channel has no walls, just a steep and unscalable drop-off into the roaring currents below. The views are splendid, but no one is going for a dip in those waters.

As the houses get bigger, we see fewer and fewer travelers on the roads. By the time we reach the stretch with the imperial villa, Taryn and I are the only ones on the street.

Fortune favors us as the moon disappears behind a thick layer of clouds, shrouding the streets in darkness. The rich and powerful prefer their privacy and keep the torches that light the streets to a minimum, leaving us with plenty of shadows to cling to.

Elegant villas with sweeping vistas of the Sapphire Channel surround us. The grandest among them is the imperial villa. A golden gate with two ornamental Fs back-to-back is all that stands between us and our mission.

I come to a stop in front of the gate. "Kind of eerie that it's so empty, don't you think?"

"These are the summer homes of the elite. Most of them are probably living it up at their mansions in the city's center."

"But we haven't even seen any guards." That's the part that concerns me.

Taryn shrugs. "Maybe the Hand pulled them all to the palace. At our levels, it's not like he's worried about us attacking the emperor. They're so powerful around here that I bet their stableboys could kill us. He's probably more concerned with us stealing some rare artifact."

He makes a fair point. I take the key from my inventory and insert it into the lock. As I twist the key, the keyhole glows a bright white and energy flares along the metal of the gate.

The gate opens at the middle, and the facade of an empty villa fades. Lively music comes to an abrupt halt, and dozens of eyes stare in our direction.

3. THE ROGUE EMPEROR

So much for not causing a scene.

My first instinct is to run, but it doesn't take more than a quick glance to know that if hands start flying, we'll be respawning back at the inn before we have time to blink. Except for Limery.

If nothing else, I have to play this cool for his sake.

My heartbeat pounds in my ears, and for the longest time, no one moves. The many beastkin stare at us with curious expressions. Some hold glasses of champagne, and others dip their feet into a pool with a vibrant purple glow emanating beneath its surface. Olive trees sway gently in the breeze. Many torches flicker around the edges of the property. A band, consisting of two foxes and a deer beastkin with massive antlers, play stringed instruments on a raised platform to the left.

The clank of metal cuts through the silence as two imperial guards, one a black-maned lion and the other a golden-skinned rhinoceros, step out from the back of the crowd. Their hands grip the gladius strapped to their waists as they walk with purpose.

"There's no need for that," a sultry voice speaks up from the back.

Several beastkin step out of the way, revealing a tiger beastkin sprawled on a daybed draped with furs. Two servants fan the tiger with massive leaves, and another holds a platter of grapes. In spite of the severity of our situation, I suppress a grin when I realize that all of the servants are mice beastkin.

I focus on the tiger.

Festa Forgetooth
  Emperor of Goldspire.

Level: ???
Rogue
Beastkin

I don't know why, but I wasn't expecting the emperor to be a woman. But even more interesting is the fact that she has a class. A rogue emperor. Neither King Orso nor King Favian had a class listed when I focused on their stats. Was it because they chose to conceal it?

Festa doesn't move from her position as she lifts a paw, stopping the guards in their tracks. Her fur is a deep black, with orange stripes that match her fiery eyes. She wears a single golden necklace, and a golden laurel crown that glitters even against the night sky.

She extends a claw, pointing it in our direction. "It's not often we get outsiders in Goldspire. Even rarer that outsiders would be of such a low level." She pauses, and it feels as though she is looking into my very being. "But most strange is not the fact that they have a key to my private estate, but that two of them are heroes."

Gasps travel through the group, followed by hushed whispers.

"Heroes—"

"Is it true?"

"It's been ages. What could heroes be doing in Goldspire?"

The emperor raises her paw, and we stand in silence once more. "Leave us be."

There are more whispers as guests begin moving inside. The band exits the stage, taking their instruments with them.

The black-maned guard turns toward the emperor. "Your Majesty, it is unwise—"

"Choose your next words carefully, Cinnius," she cuts him off. "Do I not command the wisdom to lead Goldspire?"

The lion bows. "You do, Your Majesty."

"And have you met anyone who could best your emperor in combat, armed or otherwise?"

"I have not, Your Majesty."

"Then you would do well to remember your place and leave the decision-making to me. Now, inside with the others, for I do not fear two heroes and an imp, curious as they may be."

The lion nods. He takes one last glance at us over his shoulder before following the trail of whispers into the villa.

The emperor sits up on the daybed, waving away her servants except for the two fanning her.

"Come, I wish to look upon your faces."

Taryn removes his hood, and Limery burns uncomfortably hot against my shoulder as I remove the shawl.

"You have nothing to fear, little one. At least not yet." She flashes us a dangerous smile, her fangs a brilliant white against her obsidian fur.

We approach with caution. I keep mana at my fingertips, ready to summon a horror at a moment's notice. Not that it would do me any good. I could use Champion to summon Dakota, the minotaur gladiator we defeated in the arena. Perhaps he could buy us time to escape.

"Have a seat." She motions toward a second daybed nearby. "I have a feeling this story is going to take a while."

We do as she says, and once again, we find ourselves sitting in silence.

The emperor lets out a sigh. "Is my presence that all-consuming or are the lot of you mutes?"

Limery is the first to speak. "Chods saids Limmy should be quiet when we comes to the emperor's house. He saids we don't want to get caughts." The words spew out like a waterfall.

A grin forms at the edge of her mouth. "Is that so? I take it you are Limmy. Now which one of you would be Chod?"

I raise a hand. "That would be me. I am Chod, hero of the forest trolls of the Isle of Mythos."

The emperor can see our levels and the wanted marks placed on us by Cornix, but she must not be able to see our names unless we are identified. Or is she toying with us?

"A blue forest troll, that's a first. And who would that make you, Mr. Dwarf?"

Taryn proudly puffs out his chest. "I am Taryn, hero of the dwarves of Seascape."

Gentle music resumes inside the villa. Festa glances over her shoulder and her eyes narrow slightly.

"Never mind them." She places her paws on the daybed as she leans forward, and several ebony claws protract with the movement. Claws that could rip us to shreds. "Now, tell me..." Her voice has a gentle purr to it as she speaks. "How did you get this key, and what are two under-leveled heroes doing in my city?"

For less than a second, Festa's orange stripes turn black, her entire being a shroud of darkness. A cold breeze passes over me, sending a chill down my spine, and the next thing I know, Festa is holding the imperial key. She moved so fast that I didn't even feel her take it from my hand. I get the feeling that that ability is only a glimpse into what she is capable of.

Her eyes linger on Limery.

The small imp squirms next to me. "We stole its."

Sometimes I wish I could tape his demonic little mouth shut.

He scoots closer to me, as if I can shield him from her impenetrable gaze. Little does he know of my own inner turmoil. Because if this goes south, I'm not going to be able to protect anyone.

"Curious. You know, Cornix is renowned for—"

I interrupt her before she decides on a punishment to fit the crime. "We had no choice. King Orso asked us to deliver a message. You haven't been at the imperial palace since we arrived in Goldspire, and we didn't know when you would return. We were tipped off that you would be at the villa, and that your Hand had a key to all imperial estates. We didn't mean any harm, but we did what we had to do."

Her eyes turn to slits, and for a moment, my body tenses and I worry she is about to pounce. "Interrupt me again, and you will regret the day you ever set foot in Goldspire, hero or not." She sighs. "As flippant as you may seem to the hierarchy and rules of my empire, I am not without understanding. Like all Goldspirians, I too was raised on the legends of the Age of Heroes. I find it strange that only the Isle of Mythos has heroes, but more may reveal themselves in time. If you are here, it is because a change is coming. Now, tell me, what is the message from your king?"

Taryn gulps before speaking. He tells the emperor of the portals, of the king's fears, his council with the other leaders, and the behemoth that came through Seascape's portal. When he finishes, I receive a quest notification.

Quest Alert. *You have completed the quest "First Contact: Goldspire." You have traveled into the lands of Goldspire and delivered King Orso Brightgaze's message to its leader.*

Reward: *Increased favor with Seascape, potential allies in Goldspire.*

The quest notification must boost Taryn's confidence, because he continues, "So, will you join us when the time comes?"

"I think not," she says matter-of-factly, as if the rise of the dark wizard is nothing more than a passing problem that can be shrugged off.

"B-but—" Taryn's eyes are wide. "—are you not worried about the dark wizard, about the safety of your people?"

A cool breeze washes over us once again, and Limery grows hot against my side. Festa returns to a shadow once more, and all around us, the torch lights go out one by one until only the soft purple glow of the pool and the moon overhead give us light.

When she speaks, even my night vision can't see the features of her face. "I do not fault a king who has only just gained access to the portals for being afraid, but Goldspire has nothing to fear. We have fought off invaders time and time again. The gladiators you faced in the arena were merely a test. A test to determine if you were worthy to even walk our streets. When our best enter the arena, we leave no opponent standing."

She may talk a big talk, but our fight with the warlock outside of Lynchton is proof enough that something bigger is at play. Something we all need to prepare for.

In the darkness, the shrouded emperor exudes power, but Taryn didn't get this far by cowering away. "Valmar Worren conquered the lands of Mythos once before. Who is to say he can't do it again?"

She scoffs. "Is that name supposed to frighten me? Do you know the history of Mythos, the history of Goldspire? I battled Valmar on the sands of the arena when he thought my empire would be a worthy addition to his cause. He left the same way he entered: a would-be conqueror. Goldspire has never been conquered, and it never will be."

"You fought the dark wizard?" I stumble to my feet at the knowledge. This is a game-changer! Someone who actually knows how the dark wizard operates. "Then you can help us with the knowledge to defeat him. Not many were alive at that—"

"I have heard enough. Tell your king that I wish him well, but Goldspire will stand as it always has—alone. He is welcome to come and plead his case himself if it suits him, but my decision is firm."

"Festa, please," I plead.

I know my mistake instantly. Her shroud fades and the orange stripes along her body blaze with energy. She's in front of me in an instant, her long, lithe legs making her nearly as tall as me.

Her whiskers brush against my cheek as she whispers in my ear. "Leave now, and I will forgive this insolence. You delivered your message. You have your response. I do not advise you to test my patience."

I want to stay, to try one last time to win her over, but Taryn tugs at my arm, telling me it's time to go. We completed the quest, but we failed in the end. Goldspire will not be joining our cause.

4. POUR ME ANOTHER

The only good that came out of that meeting is that our wanted marks are gone. As we walk in silence from the villa to the inn, I'm sure we're all feeling the same thing.

Failure.

"I just don't get it." Taryn's voice is strained. "She's fought Valmar before. Not only that, they were able to keep him from marching on Goldspire. How can she just keep that information to herself? What if he's more powerful this time?"

I place my hand on his shoulder, offering what little comfort I can. "I know, buddy. We tried and we failed. Now, we have no choice but to move on."

"Yeah." Limery hops from my shoulder to Taryn's and pats him on the head. "It's like Chods says. It's ain't overs til it's overs."

He gives us a half-smile. "So what now?"

"Now, we continue on. We level up, and we get stronger. We explore new cities and keep trying to win people to the cause. With so many portals open, it will be a lot harder to find other heroes, but that doesn't mean we can stop trying. Who knows what else is waiting for us out there?"

He nods. "You're right. Only a handful of leaders came to the king's council. Our work is far from over, but I can't help but feel like we are leaving a lot on the table here. I mean, if Dakota and the others aren't even their strongest fighters, can you imagine what having them on our side would mean?"

"I do. But who knows what the future holds? For now, I say we're lucky we get to live to fight another day."

Taryn looks over his shoulder in the direction of the villa and shakes his head. "Ain't that the truth."

We spend the next while speculating on the emperor's power. The way she moved was like nothing I've ever seen.

The streets are much quieter on our return. By the time we reach the forum, only stragglers remain. A handful of imperial guards patrol the area, but we walk with our faces revealed, no longer having to worry about being arrested.

True to her word, the fox beastkin is still tending bar when we arrive at the inn. The lioness and minotaura continue their game of marbles, but the rest of the guests have cleared out.

"You boys look like you could use a drink." She gestures at three barstools in front of her.

"You have no idea." Taryn plops down on the stool. "I don't care what it is but make it strong."

I analyze the bartender a little more closely this time.

Portia Swiftwill
Level: 22
Beastkin

Limery stands on his stool and leans against the bar. Portia takes three glasses from the overhead rack and places them on the bar, filling them with a golden wine.

She slides the glasses in front of us. "I know a rough day when I see it. Here, these are on the house."

"Thanks." I tilt my glass to her before taking a swig.

The wine is cool and refreshing. It's crisp as it goes down, dry and minerally, like licking a wet stone, but the aroma is floral and vibrant.

Limery cups the wine glass in both hands and guzzles it, wine streaking down his chin. "Yums."

Taryn downs his and asks for another. "What can I say? Goldspire knows how to make a fine drink."

"That we do." She winks, her green eyes mesmerizing against her orange fur. "So, tell me, what has a group of travelers like yourselves in such a fuss?"

Taryn takes a chug of his new drink, then sighs. "We were on a quest for the King of Seascape. We failed."

She reaches out and taps Taryn on the hand. "That's unfortunate. Still, it must be pretty exciting to live the life of a hero."

Limery sways back and forth, the wine already hitting him. "They's the bestest heroes."

"Have a seat before you fall on the floor." I laugh as I help Limery sit on the stool before turning to Portia. "Do you have anything he's less likely to spill?"

She hands me a regular glass, and I pour the wine into it. Sometimes, having Limery around is like babysitting a toddler. If that toddler could burn you alive without so much as straining a muscle.

I take a seat between Limery and Taryn, finishing off my first glass. My head begins to buzz at the edges, and I suddenly feel much more talkative. "Being a hero is exciting. There's always something to do and someone to save, but there's a lot of pressure that comes with the territory. People look to us for answers, and we don't always have them. There's a lot more to being a hero than just adventuring."

Taryn gently pounds his fist against the bar. "That's the truth of it. And now that the portals are open, there's more to do than ever."

"What do you mean?" Portia leans forward, her green eyes vibrant with interest.

Taryn's eyes meet mine for a moment, and I can tell he's wondering the same thing I am. How much should we tell her?

I nod to him to go on. If we can't sway the emperor, we can at least spread word among the people of what we're dealing with.

"A war is coming..." he begins, recounting everything that has happened since the portal opened.

By the time he finishes, not only is Portia leaning against the edge of the bar, but the lioness and minotaura have quit playing their game. They both are turned toward us, enthralled like children at story time.

For the longest time, the only sounds in the inn are Limery's slurps as he drinks his wine.

"You are certain he has returned?" Portia's face is set in stone.

I shrug. "Nothing is certain, but everything points in that direction. The portals flaring to life on the Isle of Mythos, the only place where heroes have appeared. The warlock and his beings from the shadowlands. The behemoth. Something is definitely up."

She bites her lip and exchanges looks with the other two beastkin. "The emperor's battle with Valmar is one of the most famous tales in Goldspire. I was not yet born at the time, but we beastkin live long lives and there are many who can still vouch for its accuracy. It is said that the battle shook the heavens. That it was the only time in Goldspire's history where it was feared the city might fall."

"Tell us about it." Taryn slides his glass forward for another refill.

She shakes her head as she empties a bottle of wine into Taryn's glass. "I fear I do not have the skill to do it justice. We have talked enough of dark matters for one night. What is next for you three?"

I finish off my own glass and the room starts to spin. "Somewhere far from here. We're not sure where, though. What do you know of the other portals?"

"Me? Not much. There's plenty of adventure in and around Goldspire for me. You know, there are ancient dungeons of great power outside the city walls. I'm sure they are a worthy challenge for heroes."

Taryn laughs. "That might be too worthy of a challenge. Goldspire is beautiful and full of adventure, but for now, we should set our sights on greener pastures."

"It is rare for beastkin to leave Goldspire. We take pride in our lands and our culture. But there are those, scholars mostly, who have explored distant lands for first-hand knowledge of other cultures. I know one who may help guide you on your adventures."

Limery's eyes grow heavy, and he slumps over. I catch him and his glass just before they tumble to the floor.

"I think it is bedtime for this one. When can we meet your friend?"

She takes our empty glasses and sets them aside. "Take the day to explore some of the beauty Goldspire has to offer. At sundown, meet me by the spire, and I will introduce you."

I pay our tab, and we head to our room. Looks like we'll be in town for at least one more day.

5. THE PRICE OF FREEDOM

We enjoy a more leisurely walk through the basilica now that we aren't being chased by a hippo capable of swatting us like mosquitos. Dozens of small shops and vendors line both sides of the hall. A white owl beastkin stands behind a counter selling perfumes and other concoctions. His head twists at an awkward angle as he eyes our approach.

Dozens of exquisitely-crafted glass vials catch my eye, each one filled with a colorful liquid. One glass is in the shape of a teardrop, another a flame.

I pick up a yellow flower-shaped vial and uncork it. The essence is strong and floral. I hold it out for Limery to sniff. He scrunches his nose and coughs.

"Limmy no likes." He shakes his head vehemently, pushing the bottle away.

I place it back on the table and pick up another one in the shape of a pyramid. "Before Taryn came here, he used to smell like this all the time. You could smell him before you ever saw him."

Taryn elbows me in the side. "That is so not true. My cologne smelled good." He turns to the owner of the perfume stand and lifts his hands in front of him. "Not that yours doesn't smell good. What I'm saying is—"

I nudge him in the side. "You might want to quit while you're ahead. Unless you want to get beat up by a perfumer."

The owl beastkin clicks his beak and scowls at Taryn from behind the table. His feathered arms bulge as he crosses them across his chest. Taryn mumbles his apologies as we continue down the hall, the owl's eyes following us all the way.

Taryn comes to a stop in front of a massive pillar. Flowers and vines are carved into the stone all the way up to a beautiful bouquet at the top where the pillar morphs into the vaulted ceiling.

He runs his fingers along one of the stone flowers. "I bet the dwarves back at Seascape would love this. Not their style, but the craftsmanship is superb." He turns back to me. "Want to get out of here now? I'm ready to pick up my pets so that we can get Berry some armor."

I let out a long sigh before responding. "We literally have all day until we have to meet Portia. Don't you want to explore the city some more before we have to start worrying about Stompy trampling someone?"

"It's been two days since I visited the stables, and I miss them. I don't like leaving them alone that long. Besides, think of how awesome he is going to look covered in armor!" Taryn grins from ear to ear.

I can't help but laugh at him. "You're going to be one of those clingy parents, aren't you?"

He stands there and frowns at me with his arms crossed.

I wink at Limery. "Fine, fine. Let's get Taryn to his babies."

"Limmy will leads the ways!" He tucks his arms and prepares to bolt.

"Hold up." I spot a table covered in thin round stones and wave them over.

Each stone has a hole in the center, just like the one around my neck. There must be dozens of communication stones here. Back on the island, these would sell for a fortune.

"How do you have so many?" asks Taryn.

Limery picks one up, examining it. He seems confused that there are so many spread out upon the table.

The elephant beastkin behind the counter stands from her stool. "We speak the common tongue in Goldspire nowadays, there's not much use for communication stones among our people."

I pick one up and compare it to my own. There's nothing remarkable about them, nothing that would signify how powerful they truly are. Just a light gray stone with a hole through the middle. There aren't even any runes on them.

I set it back down. "How did you get so many? I thought communication stones could only be given away willingly? Otherwise, they wouldn't work."

The elephant glances at Limery before looking away. "There is another way."

"How?" A sense of dread runs through me when I realize I already know the answer.

Her eyes look like they are straining as she attempts to hold eye contact with me. "If the owner dies, then they may be activated by anyone."

Limery runs his tiny fingers over the stone like it is a precious artifact.

A lump forms in my throat. "So all of these came from dead imps?"

Dozens of Limerys, Leos, Lilliths, and Bazels cross my mind. My chest tightens at the thought.

She nods. "I'm afraid so."

I place the communication stone back on the table. "What happened?"

Her trunk twitches as her eyes drift to the ground. For a moment, I'm not sure if she is going to say anything, but then she takes a deep breath. "When Valmar invaded Goldspire many years ago, he did not come alone. His army was powerful, and many on both sides lost their lives that day. It wasn't until much later that we learned the imps had been tricked into doing his bidding." Her eyes drift back to Limery. "We were fighting to protect our way of life. I'm sorry."

Limery's eyes glisten as he lays the stone next to the others. "It's okays. You didn't knows."

We leave the basilica with heavy hearts. Seeing all those stones laid out like that only reinforces how important it is to raise a force powerful enough to fight whatever comes through those portals. It has been hundreds of years since that battle and yet they still have so many communication stones. How many more were sold over the years? How many innocent imps were tricked into their deaths?

It's best not to dwell on it, so I try to cheer Limery up. "Hey, Limmy, what do you say we go get something to eat?"

He perks up at the mention of food, and soon we gorge ourselves on exotic meat kabobs from a traveling food cart.

The stables are located near the gated entrance into Goldspire. A gray satyr with a scraggly goatee greets us as we arrive. He brushes the coat of a massive beast covered in long, white, dreadlocked fur. Two short black horns poke through the fur on each side of its head, and the locs hide large black eyes.

Gloomsheep. *Level 24. While gloomsheep make formidable mounts and pack animals, their wool is highly prized for being soft yet extremely durable.*

Tayrn stops in front of the satyr. "I'm here to pick up my pets."

The satyr looks back up from the beast. "One moment and I'll have someone bring them out." He motions to a slightly smaller satyr cleaning out one of the pens before returning his attention to Taryn. "That's a mighty fine beast you have, the big one with the horn. Never seen one in Goldspire. He's got quite the attitude, too."

Taryn grins. "You must be talking about Stompy. Has he been behaving himself?"

The satyr grins. "I'd say so. The other two were inseparable, but Stompy, is it, well, he would sunbathe for hours. We tried to get him in the stable at nightfall, but he wasn't having it, so we let him sleep under the stars."

"That's Stompy." Taryn laughs. "He's got a mind of his own."

There's a loud grunt from the back of the stables and then a pattering of feet as Berry and Ruby race toward Taryn. The small straw-colored jackal jumps into his arms, long pointy ears pinned back as she buries herself in his cloak. Berry nearly knocks Taryn to the ground as he nuzzles against his leg. Stompy trudges out, huffing as he comes to a stop in front of Taryn. He snorts before turning the other way.

"Looks like someone is salty." I laugh at Stompy's stubbornness.

Limery flies over and perches on the moulhaug's horn.

Stompy huffs but allows him to remain.

Taryn pays the bill, and we're on our way. We travel much slower since Stompy takes up a lot of room, especially when we pass carriages or carts. Eventually, we make it to a more spacious main road.

When we arrive at the armory, we're greeted by the rhythmic clank of the blacksmith in the forge next door. Taryn ties Stompy and Berry to a post out front, and Ruby darts between his legs with each step as we head inside. She's so elusive that even though it looks like she'll be stepped on at every turn, it never happens.

The armory is long, with stone arches that run from one end of the building to the other. There are shelves with shields of various shapes and sizes, and bins stocked with a variety of weapons. Swords, axes, pikes, and spears. An assortment of daggers and other smaller weapons line the shelves. Whenever a breeze passes through, the plate mail hanging on racks clank together like windchimes.

A tall beastkin with the head of a panther steps out from behind the counter. Sleek black fur covers his entire body, and a pink scar cuts through one milky white eye. His muscles ripple with each step, and he wears a yellow toga with a black rope cinched around his waist.

"Good day, sirs. How may I assist you today?" His voice is gravelly as the panther beastkin dips his head slightly.

Taryn steps to the front. "I'm actually looking to buy some armor for one of my mounts. He's out front if you want to take a look."

We descend the stairs to where Berry waits patiently. His eyes follow our every movement while Stompy lays on the stone street without a care in the world. Several beastkin gather around pointing at Stompy, but the moulhaug pays them no mind.

The panther places a large paw to his chin. "Will you be requiring armor for both mounts?"

Taryn shakes his head. "Just for the bear. Stompy's hide is pretty tough on its own. Plus, I can't imagine the cost of armor for something that big."

"Very well." The panther squints as he examines Berry. "Bring him to the rear entrance and I will show you some of our larger armor."

Taryn unties Berry and rides him around while Limery and I follow the panther back inside. We pass through the main armory and down another set of stairs into a second open-air hall on the street level. Stacks of massive armor and weapons for mounted combat lie on the ground. There's plate mail the size of car hoods, lances, shields, saddles, armored carts, chariots, and carriages. Some of the chariots even have spikes extending from the axles.

The selection is impressive—even Vanaria and Seascape didn't have items like this.

"Do you sell a lot of these?" I make small talk as we wait for Taryn, pointing to the various chariots and carriages.

"A fair amount. The chariot races are a big attraction during festivals."

"It sounds like living here is one big party." I laugh.

The panther's face goes even more serious. "We have paid the price for our peace."

I wonder if the scar on his face was part of the payment.

Limery flies over and grabs the reins of one of the chariots, whipping them as he hovers. "Limmy likes to race. Limmy likes to go fasts!"

The panther's demeanor softens and his lip curls at the edge, revealing a sharp tooth. "Imps are renowned for their speed all over Mythos. I do not doubt you could put on quite the show."

With his ego stroked, Limery releases the reins and displays his blazing speed as he coats himself in fire and zips back and forth across the courtyard like a meteor. He nearly barrels into Taryn, riding Berry, as he and Ruby turn the corner.

"Oh, wow!" Taryn's mouth hangs open as his eyes take in the rest of the armory. "This is even better than I hoped."

He climbs down and starts looking over all the items.

The panther straightens himself and walks over to a large collection of armor spread out on the ground. "As you can see, we have many options depending on your needs. We have basic brigandine armor, a leather outer layer with dozens of individual metal plates set into pockets on the inside. This is the cheapest and also easiest to repair, as any individual plate can be swapped out with ease." He moves over to a stack of polished plate mail. "Next, we have traditional plate armor. Leather straps will hold the armor in place. On a beast like your bear, I would recommend covering the back, shoulders, and belly, as well as the forelegs and head. Many of our beastkin helms will likely fit your bear as well. Plate mail of this size is incredibly heavy and cumbersome, but extremely effective at blocking damage. With such large pieces of armor, repair will be difficult if you are not near a city with a large forge."

Taryn nods along to each word, but his eyes are already focused on a different pile of armor. Ones with intricate engravings and colored metals.

"What's this?" Taryn asks as soon as the panther finishes speaking.

The panther grins. "That would be our enchanted armor. Pricey, but worth its weight in gold. All enchanted armor comes with the bonus effect of fitting securely to whatever mount they are equipped. You could essentially switch them between both bear and moulhaug with ease." He runs his paw over a pile of seafoam-green plate mail with gold accents. "This one offers increased attack speed when fighting in snow or water. And this one..." He taps a set of golden armor with a lion head engraved on the shoulder pieces. "This one grants increased Strength and Constitution to both mount and rider."

"Nice! What about this one?"

At the very back sits a stack of charcoal armor with blood-red trim. Compared to the others, it's very sleek and minimalistic, but there is something about it that's intimidating. Not waiting for the panther to describe it, I focus on its stats.

Item. Armor of Darkness (Complete set). *50% noise reduction. When all pieces of Armor of Darkness are equipped, both mount and rider gain 90% stealth from dusk until dawn.*

"Holy shit!" I blurt it out without realizing, and they all turn in my direction. "Sorry." I grimace at my outburst and the panther returns to his description of the armor.

I'm amazed that something like this exists. Ninety percent stealth is practically invisibility at night, and for it to work on something as big as Berry, that's quite an advantage, especially when attacking. And the fact that the effect doesn't disappear when they attack is seriously OP. That's not even taking into account the noise reduction on a beast as large as Berry or Stompy.

"I'll take it!" Taryn shouts as soon as the panther finishes.

"Excellent choice. That will be one hundred platinum."

In the silence that follows, I swear we could hear a pin drop.

Taryn's mouth hangs open. When he tries to speak, he croaks like a frog. After struggling to gulp, the words finally come out. "One...hundred...platinum. That's, like, ten thousand gold. Who in the hell has that kind of money to spend on armor? Hell, who has that kind of money?"

No shit. That's some serious change.

The panther bows his head. "I'm sorry for the inconvenience, sir, but surely you must understand the value of a piece this exquisite. It was crafted many years ago by the emperor's very own enchanter. You'll not find another piece like it in all of Mythos."

Taryn's shoulders slump, and Berry nudges him in the side with his snout. "I get it, but we don't have that kind of money."

"No worries, good sir. I'm sure we can find something within your budget that is worthy of a hero."

In the end, Taryn is able to afford enchanted armor, but just barely. The simple golden armor offers Berry a ten percent bonus to his Constitution, but nothing to Taryn.

As we leave the armory, Taryn looks over his shoulder and shakes his head. "Bro, why would he even show me armor that costs that much? It's like trying to buy a used car but test driving a Ferrari. Only I didn't even get to take it for a spin."

I laugh. "We're heroes. Maybe he thinks we're ballers."

Taryn scoffs. "Nobody balls that much. Not even Pressley."

"At least you got armor, though. And you were right, Berry does look badass."

The golden armor stands out prominently against the umber bear's reddish-brown fur. The giant pieces of plate armor make him look even more formidable, especially with the helm. Considering how often Berry is on the front lines, I think it will do nicely.

We still have an hour or so before we're supposed to meet Portia, so we meander around the forum, checking out some of the quainter vendors.

A long, sonorous horn bellows across the forum, drawing our attention from a cart selling flamingo tongues. A second horn joins in and we turn to find out they aren't horns at all, but a group of broad-shouldered minotaur and buffalo beastkin gathering around the spire. Their chests begin to rise and fall as more join in, forming a deep melody that resonates within my chest.

Each member of the musical group has a part to play. Some repeat the same hum over and over. Others only chime in every ten or twenty seconds. Pretty soon, a crowd has gathered, and we climb on Taryn's pets, allowing us to see over the congregation of beastkin.

I'm always amazed by these simple moments where the action and adventure of Mythos fades away and we're able to experience something every bit as magical and beautiful as anything in the real world.

To my right, Taryn is enraptured by the performance as he strokes Ruby behind the ears. Even Limery has found a moment of calm. When the buffalo all come together for a deep hum that shakes the very streets, Stompy tilts his head back and lets out his own matching tune.

Pretty soon, the sun dips below the horizon, and the golden spire illuminates the forum with reflected moonlight.

And then a familiar voice calls over my shoulder, "You boys ready for an adventure?"

6. FIGHT CLUB

We follow Portia down a dark street at the edge of town. The tail of the fox beastkin swishes back and forth as she leads us to meet her mysterious scholar friend. Hopefully, he will have some insight on where Taryn and I should head next. Somewhere we can level up without getting our heads thumped in.

We're far enough away from the city's center that I can see the guards patrolling the perimeter wall with bows and crossbows tossed over their shoulders. It makes me wonder what lies outside of Goldspire. What threats are so dangerous that even these mighty beastkin require defenses from their attacks? Portia mentioned dungeons, and I fear what beasts lurk within their depths. The behemoth we battled in Seascape Square crosses my mind and I shudder at the memory.

Limery sits on my shoulder tossing a fireball from one hand to the other. "Is we theres yet?"

Portia looks back, grinning as the golden hoops in her fox ears catch the moonlight. "Almost, little one. It will be worth the wait, I assure you."

Taryn and I exchange glances. The way she says it makes it sound like this is more than just a simple meet-and-greet. Where could she be taking us?

A few minutes later, we come to a stop in front of a bath house. Atop many levels of stairs, a white marble building looms over us. Ornate columns form the arched entrance, and at this hour, the place is completely empty.

"I'd recommend you tie your pets out front. It'll be easier for us to travel inside without them."

Taryn ties Berry and Stompy to the posts outside, but Ruby follows us as we ascend the steps into the empty bathhouse. The floors are tiled with green marble. What little moonlight passes through the archways reflects off the gold veins running through the marble like tiny lightning bolts. Long fronds sway in the breeze and water trickles along the aqueducts, feeding the large, square bathing pools.

At the far back, one of the pools is drained and empty.

Portia stops in front of it. "Not many outsiders have the pleasure of seeing what you are about to witness. On the surface, Goldspire presents a face that is elegant and refined, but beneath that facade lies the true nature of the beastkin. While we are majestic and proud, the thrill of the hunt still pulses within our veins."

That sounds pretty ominous, doing little to ease my concerns.

She kneels beside the ledge of the pool and presses a slab of marble. It sinks in and grating stone echoes around us as the bottom of the pool transforms into a stairwell that leads into an underground tunnel.

Now I see why Berry and Stompy needed to wait outside. My head nearly scrapes the ceiling as we descend into the tunnel. Torches line the dusty walls, casting everything with tints of orange and yellow. As manicured as the aboveground is, this is the opposite. The walls and floors are uneven, and rubble crunches beneath our feet every so often.

Ruby runs ahead of the group and comes to an abrupt stop, her nose trailing against an invisible line along the wall and floor. If she's focusing on it, there must be something there. Her perception is so good that she was able to spot the entrance to the cave where Limery's father was trapped when none of us could see it.

"Perceptive," says Portia as she passes the jackal.

When I step past the spot where Ruby is investigating, it's like I've entered an arena. Shouts, laughter, and the clash of metal assault my ears from down the corridor.

"What is this place?" I pull mana to my fingertips just in case, ready to cast a horror at a moment's notice. Whatever this is, we're not the only ones here.

Portia must sense my concern. "No need to worry, all will be revealed soon enough." She winks. "Now, hurry up before we miss the show."

"Show?" asks Taryn. He taps his leg and Ruby abandons her investigation.

I shrug. This sounds like a far cry from meeting a scholar for information.

"Limmy wants to sees the shows." He takes off from my shoulder and hovers beside Portia.

As we travel further down the corridor, light begins to spill in from an opening at the other end. There are bodies with their fists raised, cheering at something. Whatever it is, massive frames block our view.

And then a body soars through the air like it was shot out of a cannon. A green-furred tiger with purple stripes hits the ceiling with a crash, and two daggers fall from his hands. I push my way through the crowd of beastkin to get a better line of sight, and Limery hovers beside me.

"What's going on?" Taryn jumps up and down next to me, trying to get a view. "I can't see."

"It's the monk who chased us. He's fighting."

Cornix Coinbearer, the Hand of the Emperor, is fighting in some underground fight club. He stands over the prone form of the tiger that just flew into the ceiling.

Cornix extends a massive hand and motions for the tiger to stand. "Get up! I was promised a challenge."

The tiger stands, spitting blood to the side, and clenches his fists as he settles into a boxing stance, having lost his weapons.

As the two square off, I scan the area. Dozens of beastkin surround a raised platform where the two beastkin battle. It's like a boxing ring, minus the posts and ropes. Tables line the walls of the cramped area, and a dog-like beastkin bartender pours drinks at the bar in the back. Torches offer plenty of light. Whatever this place is, it feels like a cross between a fight club and a speakeasy.

Taryn continues to jump in the air, moving between one beastkin and the other, but they take little notice of his antics.

"Dammit! Why do they all have to be so tall?"

"I'm only going to ask this once, but do you want me to pick you up?" I can see the disdain in his eyes before he even speaks.

After a few more failed attempts at getting a better view, his shoulders slump. "Fine."

I try to hold back the grin, but I can't. Grabbing Taryn around the waist, I lift him up and place him on my shoulder.

"If you speak about this to anyone," he whispers in my ear, "I'll smother you while you're sleeping."

I suppress my laughter. "Easy, killer. Just watch the show."

Cornix and the tiger circle around the platform. I'm kind of concerned that we are so close to the actual fighting. Cornix is strong enough that a wayward attack could probably do some real damage to any one of us. The beastkin surrounding me range anywhere from level fifteen to forty-two, and I'm confident Cornix out-levels them all.

He huffs and smoke billows out of his massive nostrils. The hippopotamus beastkin still wears the same canvas toga we originally saw him in. His oily slate-colored skin glistens in the torchlight, and amulets dangle from his neck—minus the imperial key.

I wonder if he's met with Festa since our encounter.

The tiger feigns a jab with his left hand and follows with a right cross. In half a second, Cornix deflects the punch to the side and his fist glows green as he counters with a punch of his own. The outline of an emerald dragon coats his hand, roaring as it connects with the tiger's chest and launches him across the ring directly toward us.

Both Taryn and I raise our hands to defend ourselves, and Limery darts out of the way, but there is a second crash as the tiger smashes against an invisible force-field along the platform's edge.

He falls to the ground, breathing heavily before raising a hand. "I yield."

The air around the arena shimmers. Cornix bows to his opponent, then descends the platform. The crowd erupts into chatter, and Taryn slides off my shoulder like he was never there.

Portia turns around and raises her eyebrows suggestively. "That was the Emperor's Hand. There are not many who can last more than a minute with him in the pits."

"We've, uh, had the displeasure of meeting him before." I grimace at the memory.

"How curious." She cocks an eyebrow. "Let's grab a drink while we wait for my acquaintance."

Portia orders us all a glass of a rich red wine that is somehow both tangy and spicy. We take a seat at a table along the room's edge. After a few sips, my fingertips have an electric sizzle to them.

Item. Dragon's Wine. *-2 Intelligence for one hour. Bonus effect: Grants dragon aura, replicating the fiery buzz of dragon fire.*

Portia grins. "It'll wear off in an hour or so, but it feels pretty good. Especially after you've downed a few."

"Ooh." Limery casts a fireball in his palm and lets it roll down his arm. "Limmy likes Dragon's Wines."

"Limmy just likes to drink. Try not to set us all on fire, please." I laugh at Limery as he snuffs out the fireball and tilts the glass back. I return my attention to Portia. "So, what is this place?"

She takes a long swig and then releases a pleasurable sigh. "This is one of Goldspire's fighting pits. Where the great fighters come to test their mettle against one another."

"Is this how you all get so strong?" I once again look around at all the beastkin out-leveling my party. This group of random beastkin could give the kingsguard of both Orso and Favian a run for their money.

"For some, this is how they grow stronger. For the majority of Goldspire, our strength is formed in the trials while we are young."

"The trials?" Taryn chimes in, nearly finished with his first glass. "What's that?"

Portia leans forward, excitement bubbling in her green eyes. "The trials have been a tradition since the most ancient of days. When we come of age, the young beastkin are sent into several of the lower-level dungeons known as the Trial Dungeons, where we are forced to fight our way out as a team. The strong survive and the weak go on to the next life."

"That's brutal." I place my glass on the table to keep from crushing it in my hand. "You just send your young into dungeons to die?" Not even the mountain trolls would do that, and they value strength above all else.

Confusion passes across her face. "No, we send them to live. Without strength of body and character, Goldspire would surely crumble. Many of the bonds I formed in those dungeons carry with me even today."

I start to argue, but Taryn grabs my arm, shaking his head. I almost shrug him off, but then I realize he's right. This is their culture, who am I to critique it? This is a different society, hell, a different world. They probably have more in common with the ancient Spartans than they do with me. I might be a tough troll in Mythos, but I'm really just a soft kid from New York.

A gong sounds and beastkin begin to shuffle back to the platform.

Portia finishes her wine and stands.

I hold up my hand. "Aren't we going to meet your scholar friend?"

A wicked grin spreads across her face. "As soon as he's done fighting."

"Fighting?" I stand up, nearly knocking over the bench we were sitting on. "I thought you said he was a scholar?"

She nods. "He is, and a very good one at that, but knowledge is not always freely given. Sometimes, it must be taken. Now come, it is always a treat to watch Jegaar."

Taryn just shrugs before following Portia toward the platform, with Ruby narrowly avoiding being trampled with each step.

Limery is still at the table, extending his pointy demonic tongue into our left-over glasses as he tries to lap up any remaining wine.

"Come on, wino." I scoop him off the table and sit him on my shoulder. "We've got a fight to watch."

7. OUTSMART, OUTWIT, OUTLAST

I push my way to the front of the crowd, where Taryn and Portia are already waiting. I guess Taryn had enough of sitting on my shoulder.

A magically-amplified voice echoes across the room, introducing the fighters, but I have no idea where the sound is coming from. "Our first contender's love for fighting is undying. He's battled in the arena as a gladiator and has cleared dungeons single handedly. He has strength, speed, and a never-ending desire to better himself. Let out a roar for Gladiator Bellator!"

A stout warthog beastkin steps out from the crowd, his powerful muscles rippling with each step up the platform. His neck is almost as thick as his shoulders and framed by a black leather vest covered in studs. Corded muscles contract as he surveys the crowd. Leathery, dark brown skin is covered with scars and scattered patches of rough hair. A thin black mohawk runs down the center of his large head, and his eyes are small and beady compared to the rest of his massive frame. Four dangerous-looking tusks protrude from his mouth. The two larger ones curl out from his upper mouth framing his snout, and two smaller, pointier tusks jut upward from his bottom jaw.

I'd hate to be on the business end of any one of those.

A silver nose-ring dangles from his pig-like snout, reflecting the crowd in distorted proportions. He wears a black leather loincloth that matches his vest, and two sleek vambraces that shield his forearms.

In each hand, he carries a gladius, spinning them twice alongside his body before dropping to one knee and sheathing both swords in a fluid motion. He clenches his fists, each one a wrecking ball of pure power, and steam shoots out of his nostrils to the applause of the crowd.

. . .

Bellator
> *Level 39*
> *Gladiator*
> *Beastkin*

He extends his arms and paces across the stage before the mysterious voice begins again. "Our next challenger is no stranger to the pits. It is said that knowledge is power, and if so, then Jegaar has it in spades. 'Outsmart, outwit, outlast' is his motto. Back from his adventures abroad, he's ready to test his mettle once again in the pits."

Bellator moves to the far side of the stage as a wolf beastkin ascends the steps. Jegaar's fur is a dirty tan, like desert sand, but it's so thick and shaggy that he looks more suited for a land covered in snow and ice than the temperate climate of Goldspire. His eyes are bright blue and alert. A thick tail swishes behind him as he walks, and his ears are tipped black at the ends, as are his paws. He wears a brown gladiator skirt similar to Bellator's and carries a buckler shield in his left hand. In his right, he holds a morning star. The metal club is tipped with a spiked ball, a brutal weapon for delivering extreme punishment, capable of both punctures and blunt force with a single strike. His paws are wrapped around the knuckles, which leads me to believe he's a decent fighter as well.

He's unlike any scholar I've ever seen.

Jegaar
> *Level ???*
> *Battle Scholar*
> *Beastkin*

Battle scholar? This will definitely be interesting. His level is concealed, no surprise considering he's a scholar, but I can't imagine he's a higher level than Bellator. He looks badass for a scholar, but his opponent is a gladiator. Bellator has dedicated his life to fighting.

Jegaar nods to Bellator and then falls back to the other side of the platform. Compared to the warthog, he's slender and lean, even with all the fur. I just hope Bellator doesn't rough him up too bad before we get some information out of him.

A gong sounds, and the fight begins.

The two circle around the arena, eyes fixed on one another. Bellator holds both swords at the ready. He positions himself sideways with one blade pointed straight at Jegaar. The second he holds overhead, his arm curved like a scorpion's tail, showcasing his training with every movement he makes.

Jegaar has the morning star tossed over his shoulder. He moves casually, as if he was taking a walk in the park.

The metal whistles as Bellator steps forward and brings the overhead blade down in a forward slash. Jegaar steps to the side, leaving the warthog swiping at air. The second blade follows a split-second later, but the wolf evades again. Bellator quickly pirouettes, and attacks with both blades in a simultaneous strike, faster than anyone that big should move.

Jegaar raises his buckler shield above him at the last second, and both blades deflect to separate sides. The deflected blows barely slow the warthog before he is on the attack again. He brings one sword down, and then another as Jegaar uses the small buckler to block attack after attack.

Bellator presses until Jegaar's back is at the edge of the platform. He slashes again, and the wolf rolls to the side without moving the morning star from his shoulder.

"What's he doing?" Taryn throws up his hands in frustration. "He's going to get himself killed before we learn anything."

"Just wait." Portia's green eyes radiate with excitement.

"Wait for what, Bellator to tire out?" If that's the plan, put me in the ring.

She laughs. "Bellator could fight for days without tiring."

Then what the hell is Jegaar doing? Because right now, Bellator clearly has the upper hand. I return my attention to the ring just as the warthog unleashes another flurry of attacks. He moves with the finesse of a dancer, despite being so big and broad-shouldered, his vest fluttering with each movement like a cape. But no matter how swift or powerful the attack, Jegaar finds a way to deflect the blow, sometimes moving so fast that I'm not sure how he's able to get in position. He's quick, but can he fight?

Finally, Bellator stops attacking. His chest heaves, and steam pours from his nostrils, coating the arena in a dense layer of fog. The barrier keeps the steam from spilling over the edge and into the crowd, so it accumulates in the ring until both fighters are covered to their chests.

Jegaar sniffs at the air. "Smoked pork. Now, that's the stuff."

A few laughs trickle through the crowd.

Bellator grunts before launching himself across the stage. He leaps with enough power that he crests the fog, leaving a trail of smoke behind him, tucking both knees and holding his swords in a reverse grip as he falls toward Jegaar.

At the height of Bellator's jump, the wolf crouches in the fog and disappears. Bellator lands with a thud, sending smoke shooting out in dozens of wisps that begin to dissipate.

He twirls the twin blades vertically by his side, blowing the steam like a fan. It rises into the air, forming a cloud overhead and revealing Jegaar sitting cross-legged in the center of the ring. He scrapes the sharp claw of his index finger over his canine tooth as if cleaning it. The morning star still sits on his shoulder.

Maybe it's more for show than practicality.

Bellator grunts again and charges at the sitting wolf. He's halfway across the stage in the blink of an eye, and I'm certain there is no way that Jegaar can dodge this attack. The warthog raises his blades and brings them down with dangerous speed.

And just like that, our best lead since arriving in Goldspire is about to be dead.

The blades are inches from Jegaar's head when he decides to act. In a flash, he removes the claw from his tooth and places his palm on the floor. Both legs uncross in a fluid motion. He extends one and sweeps Bellator off his feet. The warthog crashes to the platform, his blades clanking against the stone.

Jegaar follows through with the momentum from his leg-sweep and launches himself into the air, somersaulting before he lands.

Bellator rolls over and climbs back to his feet. He crosses his blades over one another and grinds the flats together. The resulting screech causes me and most of the crowd to grimace. Limery tucks his fingers in his ears.

"Quit playing games and fight," Bellator rumbles.

"But where would the fun be in that?" Jegaar once again rests the morning star on his shoulder.

"I'll show you fun!" Bellator cocks his arm back and slashes with enough force to split Jegaar from head to foot.

Jegaar lifts the morning star and swings it like an underhand pitch. It hits the blade with enough power that sparks shoot out and Bellator loses his grip. The sword flips end over end like it was shot out of a cannon and lodges in the ceiling.

"You son of a—" Bellator grunts as he follows up with his second sword.

The blade cuts through the air so loudly that it whistles. Taking a step back, Jegaar winds up again. The sword lands between the spikes of the morning star and sparks rain down again, but the result is no different. A second sword lodges in the ceiling.

Jegaar snarls. "You leave my mother out of this."

Without looking up, he flicks his wrist. His weapon goes flying and the morning star's spikes bury several inches in the stone ceiling between the two swords. "You want to fight? Let's fight."

Maybe I underestimated this guy.

He crouches into a fighting stance and raises both wrapped paws. When he motions for Bellator to come and get some, I swear we could hear a pin drop.

"Hell yeah!" I shout without realizing it, my deep voice echoing across the cavern.

The energy in the crowd suddenly shifts as someone else echoes my sentiment. Pretty soon, the roars and yells are thunderous as the two beastkin square off.

Now, we've got us a fight.

Bellator's fists are massive, easily twice the size of Jegaar's. The muscles in his forearms tense as he clenches them. His reach is shorter than his opponent's, but I've already seen that he is lightning quick to be so big. He holds each fist level with his face, right foot planted in the rear for power.

Jegaar is light on his feet, rocking from left to right. His long reach might give him an advantage, but are his hits as powerful?

A quick jab from Bellator starts the second round of action. The boulder of a fist moves in a blur and Jegaar leans to the side, evading the punch. Bellator follows up with a cross, which the wolf ducks beneath before landing a jab of his own to his opponent's gut.

Bellator grunts but goes on the attack again, just like he did with his swords. Jab, punch, jab, punch, jab. Each one misses Jegaar by a fraction of an inch. A cross nearly connects, but only grazes the tops of Jegaar's ears as he ducks again.

Every time there is an opening, Jegaar lands a blow of his own. Bellator grimaces for the briefest moment, but then quickly launches another onslaught.

So far, Jegaar is evading with razor-thin margins, but one hit could rock his world.

After another flurry of attacks leaves Bellator with nothing more than a bruised chest, he takes a step back, steam pouring from his nostrils.

"I've had enough of your games, Jegaar. Fight me like a beast."

Echoes of "Fight him" are chanted from the crowd.

Jegaar takes a step forward and raises his fists again. Satisfied, Bellator charges at the wolf, fist cocked back. An orange glow forms around his hand, distorting the air. He swings, but Jegaar steps to the side, extending his leg and tripping Bellator.

The warthog falls face-first onto the platform, sliding until he crashes into the invisible forcefield.

He stands up, eyes narrow with fury, and a silver glow surrounds his body. For a second, it looks like he's going into a barbarian rage. But instead of steam radiating from his body, his dark leathery skin takes on a metallic sheen. The mohawk running down his head and back forms into metal spikes, and soon his entire body looks like liquid mercury.

Except for his eyes. They burn a fiery red.

"There it is." Jegaar grins. "I knew you had it in you."

"What just happened?" I ask Portia.

She places her finger to her lips, silencing me. "Watch."

I'm dumbfounded. Somehow, he got so angry that his skin turned to metal. Now, he's more dangerous than ever. Why in the hell would Jegaar provoke him like this?

Bellator charges, now moving faster than before. When he punches, Jegaar's fur ripples as he barely evades. If he was toying with Bellator before, he's certainly not now. His blue eyes are focused. When he tries to counter, a hollow metallic ring reverberates from Bellator's body. Instead of grimacing as he takes the blow, he lifts his knee into Jegaar's chin. The clack of the wolf's jaws snapping shut is like a gunshot. The force of the attack sends him soaring across the platform, where he lands on his back at the far side of the ring.

He opens his mouth a few times, rubbing his jaw as he stands up. "I guess I had that coming."

The warthog runs at him like a raging bull. Surprisingly, Jegaar charges back. Bellator lowers himself, arms spread wide, and metal mohawk pointed forward as he prepares to spear the wolf, but Jegaar jumps at the last second, using Bellator's shoulders as a platform to launch himself into the air. He grabs the morning star stuck in the ceiling and pulls it free.

When he lands, his smile is full of mischief. Bellator charges with blind rage, and I can't distinguish his actions from a barbarian rage at all. He attacks with the power of a feral meteor, but Jegaar doesn't back down. He holds the morning star like a baseball bat and swings it with two hands at the charging warthog.

Sparks explode as the weapon makes contact, and a metallic gong reverberates within my chest. Bellator flips backward twice before crashing into the forcefield.

Unfazed, he crawls to his feet and charges again.

Jegaar examines the tip of his morning star, where several of the spikes have bent sideways. He adjusts his grip and swings for Bellator once again. The blow launches the warthog for a second time, but again he stands, red eyes full of hatred.

Half of the morning star's spikes are flat and useless, but Jegaar adjusts his grip and repeats the process.

It's like Bellator is in a blind rage, incapable of any cognizant thought other than mauling his opponent. I really want to know what his deal is.

By the end of fourth charge, the morning star is nothing more than a dull club. As soon as his attack sends Bellator flying, Jegaar turns and runs in the opposite direction. He leaps in the air toward the forcefield, digging his claws into the invisible wall and using it to launch himself toward the ceiling.

He grabs both swords and pulls them loose as he falls back to the ground.

Bellator's skin begins to lose its sheen as he lays on the ground, slowly fading to its normal dull brown. He props himself up on an elbow as he attempts to stand, but Jegaar places a foot on his chest, pressing him back to the floor. With a flourish, he tosses both swords at the ground and they cross in an X over Bellator's throat.

The gladiator raises two fingers into the air. "I yield."

The crowd erupts into applause. Taryn turns to me with eyes as wide as saucers, mouth hanging open.

Jegaar bows to the crowd before exiting the stage.

I'm still not sure what we just witnessed, but it was awesome.

8. WARFORGED

Portia taps me on the arm and points to the far end of the room. "Let's go. Jegaar will be waiting for us in one of the fighter pods."

The crowd shuffles all around us. Some beastkin head for the bar, while others discuss the fight. Slashing his arms in an X, a jaguar beastkin replays Jegaar's final move with the twin swords in front of his friends. Limery starts to join a group heading toward the bar with empty mugs, but I stop the little drunk before he can disappear.

"What in the hell did we just watch?" I squint at the platform as if it might give me answers as to what happened to Bellator.

Portia holds up a slender hand. "Save your questions for once we're settled. Now, hurry, there is probably already a line."

She pushes her way through the crowd and around the fighting pit. Taryn follows in her wake, and somewhere under the mess of legs, Ruby solves her own personal obstacle course.

We enter a tunnel. At the far end, there's another arena that's less crowded. Along the tunnel, there are a handful of rooms carved into each side.

Inside one of them, Jegaar sits atop a picnic table with a tall glass of white wine surrounded by a dozen other beastkin. He's in the middle of a story, but his blue eyes light up when he sees Portia. When his gaze drifts to Taryn and then me, he narrows his eyes quizzically.

His mouth hangs open for a moment, then he gestures to Portia. "Gentlemen, I'm sure you all know Portia. She's the finest bartender in the city." He winks at her. "I didn't expect to see you here tonight."

She grins. "That was quite the show you put on. I have a few new friends who could use some of your scholarly advice."

"Oh, really." He returns the grin. "Consider me intrigued. Could you give us a moment, gentlemen?"

Portia's ears tilt backward. "Actually, this might take more than a moment."

He turns back to the other beastkin. "Ah, well, I'll have to regale you all with my tales from abroad some other time. I can't turn down an audience with someone who saved my life on more than one occasion, now can I?"

They all look at Portia with shocked expressions. After witnessing Jegaar fight, I'm also curious how she managed to save his life.

The group leaves, and Jegaar motions for us to take a seat. "Shall I order some wine for us?"

Before any of us have a second to process the question, Limery is hovering, hands pressed together in excitement. "Oh, yes! Limmy loves the wines."

Jegaar snaps his fingers and a mouse beastkin steps into the room.

"A bottle of your finest for my new friends," he orders.

"Right away, sir." The mouse bows and exits the room.

"That's very generous of you." Portia bows her head slightly.

"Anything for you. Besides, fighters get a pretty steep discount." He climbs down from the table and sits on one of the benches. "What'd you think of the show?" He smirks as he asks. The wolf beastkin knows what he did was an incredible feat.

I take a seat across from him, with Taryn and Limery beside me. "It was amazing. I've never seen anyone move like that."

The mouse beastkin returns with the wine and pours us all a glass.

Item. Ice Wine. *-2 Intelligence for one hour. Bonus Effect: Grants a cooling chill all over the body.*

I take a sip and a chill runs through me. The sweat on the back of my neck from the crowded underground lair crystalizes, and goosebumps erupt along my arms.

Limery lets out a long sigh. I can't even imagine the effect it is having on his naturally hot body.

"Feels good, right?" Jegaar takes a long drink. "Imagine how it feels after being kicked in the chest by a fluid steel warthog."

"Fluid steel?" So that's what Bellator was. "How was he able to do that?"

"He's a rarity. Long ago, many generations before our current emperor, Goldspire soldiers consisted of a subclass of barbarians called the Warforged. The process to attain the class was said to kill more than half who attempted it. Once the class had been attained, it could be passed on to one's offspring, so the Warforged were carefully bred and monitored. When they entered a rage, their bodies turned to fluid steel, making them all but unkillable. On the battlefield, they were unmatched. But after Goldspire's enemies had been conquered, the path of the Warforged became less and less. Many of the soldiers were castrated to prevent passing on their trait. They were pure destruction, but uncontrollable during a rage. Now, the Warforged trait is all but gone, only surfacing in the descendants of the original Warforged on occasion. Bellator is one of three that I know of in all of Goldspire."

Warforged. The chaos I could cause if I were able to turn into metal when I raged. I'd be unstoppable. "How does one become Warforged?"

Jegaar stares at me for a moment before speaking. "I'm not sure. No one has attempted the process in hundreds of years. There may be records of it in the archives, but if our ancestors found reason to fade them out of existence, then there must have been good reason. Bellator is a formidable gladiator and a worthy opponent, but comparing him to a true Warforged is like comparing a cat to a lion."

Damn. It sounds like one hell of a class.

Jegaar grabs the morning star and looks at its dented spikes. "I've fought a lot of monsters with this weapon. Never so much as dulled a tip." He shakes his head. "It won't be cheap to repair."

He places the weapon under the table before I have a chance to analyze it. If what he says is true, and Bellator really is that strong, then what Jegaar did is even more impressive.

But it makes me wonder how dangerous these fights actually are. "Do you not worry about killing or seriously injuring someone in a fight?"

"It's not a concern." He shrugs it off. "I assure you that one does not accidentally kill a beastkin. Occasionally, an injury may occur when someone is too proud to yield, but we are stocked with potions and elixirs on the rare chance that it happens."

Taryn takes a calming swig and then leans forward. "Alright, I've got to know. How did Portia save your life?"

Jegaar grins. "Let's just say that Portia doesn't carry around those daggers for show."

Portia's ears tilt back, and she looks at the floor. "Oh, stop it. It was a long time ago. Long before you were the mighty Jegaar you are now."

"She does herself a disservice. Portia and I completed the trials together when I was but a pup. I never would have survived without her. I may be strong now, but there was a time when I was the runt of the litter. And my dear friend Portia took pity on me. After a disastrous battle, due to my ineptitude, the third member of our party was ready to cast me aside, but Portia refused. I was battered and bruised, and she stuck by my side the entire way until we eventually made it out alive."

"Don't flatter me." She pushed Jegaar in the shoulder. "You had a lot of fight in you even then. If you'd waited a year, you would have been fine. Once you were out of the trials, you never looked back. The fact that you were the first beastkin in three hundred years to rise from Acolyte to Battle Scholar is a testament to that."

"Now who's flattering who?" Jegaar smirks. "But enough about us. What I want to know is what brings a dwarf and a troll to Goldspire?"

I set my glass down. Finally, we're jumping into business.

"We're searching for allies," answers Taryn as he strokes Ruby between the ears.

Jegaar leans forward. "Allies?"

Taryn tells the story of the attack on Seascape and King Orso's meeting with the other leaders.

"That is most interesting." He scratches his chin, running his black claws through the dense fur.

"How so?" asks Portia.

"It certainly makes Cornix's outlandish requests make a lot more sense."

The conversation briefly halts as Limery slurps at the last remaining droplets of his glass of wine.

"What does Cornix have to do with this?" I ask.

Jegaar sets his glass down before launching into a speech. "The Scholars Guild reports directly to the Hand of the Emperor. We're responsible for the reports and histories of Goldspire, keeping detailed records and archives, maintaining valuable tomes and artifacts, and in certain cases, administering foreign reconnaissance. For the most part, we govern ourselves, following whatever leads interest us most to uncover the histories of the past. We report to Cornix, but he is usually disinterested." He taps his claw against the table in a rhythmic pattern. "However, recently, he's been spending more time in the archives researching ancient items and spells that were lost to the ages. Powerful items even by Goldspire standards."

Now, I'm even more interested. Items like that could be invaluable in the war to come. "What items?"

"That I'm afraid I'm not at liberty to discuss. But I can say that I just returned from a fruitless journey to find one of them. I spent months searching through ancient letters and accounts, only to find that someone raided the tomb before me. I'll be leaving in a few days to embark on my next mission."

Taryn and I exchange glances. I'm willing to bet anything I know who is responsible. Valmar, the dark wizard.

"So you think that Cornix is preparing for the return of Valmar?" I look down and notice that my hands are gripping the bench rather hard.

"It certainly seems so," Jegaar says darkly.

"But the emperor, she didn't seem concerned at all."

Jegaar laughs. "Why would she? You're foreigners. If she were concerned, do you think she would reveal her hand to you? Have you met anyone since you have arrived in Goldspire that has displayed even an ounce of weakness to you? If I had to guess, I would say this is Cornix's concern and his alone. There is no one better suited to defend Goldspire than our emperor, but it is Cornix's responsibility to look into all matters whether the emperor is concerned or not. While most races do not remember Valmar's reign of terror, there are many beastkin who fought on that day. Cornix will do everything within his power to make sure that if war does come to Goldspire, we will be prepared."

Taryn shakes his head. "Then why not form an alliance with the other kingdoms? There is strength in numbers."

Jegaar sighs. "I do not disagree with you. But the emperor's decision is law. Goldspire will not interfere in the wars of foreigners unless they fall on Goldspire soil." We sit in silence for a moment before he speaks again. "What is it I can help you with? As friends of Portia, I will do everything within my power to assist you."

"We were sent to Goldspire to find allies. Even though the emperor denied us, our quest has been fulfilled, and we can once again return to our own adventures. Portia told us that you were one of the few from Goldspire who have traveled abroad, so we were hoping you may offer advice on where we should go next."

He nods. "I have traveled extensively across Mythos, so I should be able to shed some light. Though if your goal is to continue to gain allies while also gaining power, I can point you in that direction as well."

"That would be great!" Taryn drums his fingers against the table. "Kill two birds with one stone."

"Two birds with one stone." Jegaar laughs. "I like that."

"It's a saying from back home."

"Interesting. I did not know that the dwarves were known for their proficiency with slings."

Taryn gulps. "We're, uh, full of surprises."

"Tell me, which portals had representatives at your king's meeting?"

I think hard on King Orso's council meeting, trying to remember the lands of the races that were present. "Well, there were the three kingdoms from the isle: Seascape, Vanaria, and the forest trolls. There were also the catfolk from...Antadale, I believe."

Jegaar laughs. "Ah, Antadale. We refer to them as lesser beastkin. They are cunning, small, and particularly skilled with the healing arts." He pauses, raising a hand. "Sorry for interrupting, please continue."

I look to Taryn. "Do you remember where the others were from?"

He runs his fingers through his beard. "The gnomes were from Pruxford, and then the centaurs from Wandermere. And what about the merfolk? It was a fitting name. Watertown? Waterville?"

"Mistville," answers Jegaar. "That's the only kingdom of merfolk I'm aware of."

"That's the one." Taryn nods. "The only other portals we know of are seafaring orcs of Blacktide and the dark elves of Mosstar, and I doubt we'll be going there any time soon. We could always go back to Seascape and learn more, but I'd like to return with some sort of good news."

"Very well. All of the above portals are certainly within your range and should offer you sufficient challenges. But if they have already allied themselves with your king, then I would advise you to go elsewhere. The lands of Ellynmylly are sprawling, perhaps the largest continent in all of Mythos. You will find it full of adventure with a myriad of races to match. Ellynmylly is known as the 'Melting Pot of Mythos,' where races from all other kingdoms used to come to trade with one another before the fall of the portals. Several kingdoms call the lands home, and vast forests separate their borders. There is a network of lesser portals for traveling among its kingdoms. If Ellynmylly is a melting pot, Frostmoor is quite the opposite. It is a frigid land of snow and ice where the mountain tribes dwell."

"Hold up for a moment." I lift a finger for Jegaar to give us a moment, and whisper in Taryn's ear. "When I logged out, I saw Glenn and Jude in a cave. Snow was piling at the door, and they were covered in fur blankets. They could be in Frostmoor."

Taryn shrugs. "It's worth a shot."

I return my attention to Jegaar. "What can you tell us about Frostmoor?"

He takes another swig of the ice wine and sighs as the chill courses through his body. "Frostmoor is a brutal land. Those who dwell there are forged from the ice like iron is from fire. Proud and mighty, the ice tribes govern themselves, each one with its own customs and histories. They value strength the same as Goldspire, and you will find it hard to tread on their lands unless you can prove your worth."

That sounds ominous. "Is Frostmoor the only portal covered in snow and ice?"

"There are mountain ranges among many of the kingdoms, but Frostmoor is the only place where society flourishes in the icy embrace."

This has to be it then. With so many tribes there, Glenn and Jude could have easily slipped away into a cave in the mountains. By now, he could even be up to his old tricks again. If nothing else, we can warn the tribes and at least try to convince them to join Orso's cause.

I look Jegaar in his icy blue eyes. "Frostmoor it is then."

He stares back at me for an uncomfortable moment, not speaking. The crowd cheers from outside the door as the next challengers are announced, followed by clashing metal as the next fight begins.

Finally, the wolf speaks. "Chod, it is not a common request, but would you humor a curious scholar and remove your veil?"

Veil? I frown at him for a moment before I realize he means Conceal. I deactivate the passive ability that hides my level, and Jegaar's gaze buries into me.

"Interesting." He looks lost in his thoughts for a moment. "Thank you, Chod."

Portia places a hand on Jegaar's arm. "Now that we've got that out of the way, would you like to join us at the inn? Drinks are on me."

Limery, whose head had been drooping ever closer to the table, suddenly perks up.

Jegaar places his hand on top of Portia's, dwarfing it by comparison. "I wish I could, but there is much work to be done." He lifts his hand and then stands.

The old trial partners embrace and Jegaar heads for the exit.

He stops in front of us and bows. "I hope that I have been of service to you all."

"More than you know." I stand and extend my arm.

Jegaar's firm grip clenches around my forearm. He squeezes and pulls me in close, whispering in my ear. "When you reach level thirty, come and find me. We will put the trials of the Warforged to the test."

My arm aches when he releases it, and before I can say anything, he is out the door.

"What was that all about?" Taryn looks at me curiously.

"Nothing." I rub my fingers over my bruised forearm. "Ready to get out of here?"

We grab Taryn's pets and make our way back to the inn. Portia tells us stories of her time with Jegaar. She has Taryn's rapt attention, while Limery bobbles lazily on my shoulder.

I barely hear a word of it, my mind consumed with dreams of a shimmery metallic body. It's time to grind.

9. NOTHING GOLD CAN STAY

Despite Limery's protest, we call it an early night once we return to the inn. We'll be leaving Goldspire first thing in the morning so that we have a full day to get our bearings in Frostmoor. From what Jegaar told us, getting to the villages will be the toughest part.

As we lay in our beds, Berry whines outside. Deep, sonorous groans come through the open window. Taryn elected not to take the pets to the stables to save time in the morning, but knowing that Taryn is so close has Berry acting especially petulant.

Taryn rolls his eyes. "He's an eight-hundred-pound baby."

"Says the guy who couldn't spend a day walking through Goldspire without him." I snicker. "You two were made for each other."

I can tell he's smiling when he speaks. "What can I say? I love them."

Limery nestles against my arm, resting peacefully from all the wine he drank. He's such a peculiar creature, and yet I care for him in the same way Taryn does his pets. How could anyone ever believe that he isn't real just because he doesn't exist outside of this world? Out of the corner of my eye, Taryn strokes Ruby as she perches on his chest, staring at him.

I roll over to face Taryn and the bed creaks under my weight. "Today was fun."

His mustache twitches. "Yeah, it was. It was nice to take it easy for once, but it's back to the grind tomorrow. How are you feeling about heading to Frostmoor?"

"I'm excited." I pull my mana to my fingertips, trying to remember the last time I summoned a horror. "It'll be nice to adventure again. I can't remember when we last had the freedom to roam around searching for monsters."

"You're right about that." Taryn stops petting Ruby and she paws at his hand. "It's been one fight after another since we left Lynchton."

A long, deep groan comes from outside and we both laugh.

Limery stirs against my arm, and I pop his snot bubble with one of my claws. "It's funny...If Limery had snatched Cornix's necklace without getting spotted, we never would have ended up at this inn. We never would have met Portia or Jegaar."

"Yeah, crazy how things work out. Speaking of Jegaar, what was it he whispered in your ear?"

I watch Taryn as he strokes Ruby and wonder how much I should tell him. Level thirty is a long way off. I'm only level twenty-four, and it will be a real grind to get there. Who knows how much the world might change between now and then? I could be forced to log out before I ever get the chance to meet up with Jegaar. It's probably better to focus on the things right in front of us, not lofty ambitions we might never reach.

Still, Taryn is my best friend. And as far as I'm concerned, this is my life now. I've felt more at home in Mythos than I ever have in the real world.

"Well?" Taryn interrupts me from my thoughts.

What the hell. "He told me that if I reached level thirty to come back here and we'd put the trials of the Warforged to the test."

Taryn sits up so fast that Ruby falls off his chest. "What?! Are you kidding me? He told you that you could not only be a barbarian summoner forest troll, but that you could take on an additional class and turn to metal when you rage, and you were going to keep it a secret?"

His eyes are so wide I think they might pop out of his head.

"I didn't think it was important. I mean, it's not like I'll be level thirty anytime soon. And you heard what he said, most of those that attempted failed. We've got bigger problems to deal with at the moment."

Taryn shakes his head. "You better believe that if somebody told me I even had a chance at a super rare and powerful class, I would be annoying the shit out of you about it day and night until I got it."

I laugh. "Then I pray that never happens."

He tosses a pillow and it hits me in the side of the head. "You've got to admit, you're pretty damned lucky. You sure you don't have a hidden luck stat or something?"

"Ha." I flash him a rude gesture. "I'll try to remember how lucky I am the next time I get my face stomped in."

"Seriously, though." His eyes focus on me, all playfulness gone. "As fun as all of this is, the fact that it feels so real means that we're going to have to deal with some heavy stuff from time to time. We can all feel that something is changing, and if history has taught me anything, it's that casualties are the price of war. When bad things happen, it'll be important to have things we can focus on outside of trying to save the world. Things we can look forward to."

His words hit me like a punch in the gut. Are these the thoughts that keep him up at night? But more importantly, he's right. Even if we win, not everyone will make it through what's coming. My gaze lingers on Limery. I'll need to be Warforged to protect him.

I do my best to deflect the sobering topic. "Like an impossibly difficult trial that could very well be the most painful thing I have ever endured?"

"I'm serious." He sighs.

I'm not sure where this is coming from, but I know he is. "And what about you? What are you looking forward to?"

He grins. "More pets." As if on cue, Ruby climbs back in his lap. "Even if they don't listen to me. Now, let's get some sleep. Tomorrow is going to be a long day."

I put out the candle, leaving the room in the silvery glow of moonlight. As I drift off to sleep, I imagine myself with a body of steel as blades and arrows bounce off me like they are made of plastic.

<hr>

"Rise and shine!" Taryn shoves me in the shoulder, then he pokes Limery in the stomach. "You too, little guy."

Limery sits up, bulbous eyes crusty and full of sleep. He sways back and forth before he focuses on me. "Mornings."

"Morning, drunkie." I rub his head gently. "We're going to have to muzzle you the next time we go into a bar."

"Oh, Chods." He brushes my hand away. "Limmy is fines."

He shakes his head and rises into the air. He does a backflip with none of the sluggishness he showed only moments before. I wish I could shake off a hangover that easily.

We gather our belongings and head downstairs. The falcon beastkin stands behind the bar, and I'm a little sad Portia isn't here to say good-bye.

"Good morning, gentlemen," Portia's seductive voice calls from the booth in the corner. "I figured I would see you off this morning. Make sure you don't get lost on the way to the portal." She winks.

"That's very generous of you." Taryn places his hands together and gives her a slight bow.

Portia looks at Limery with amusement. "This one doesn't miss a beat, does he? He was out like a candle last night."

Taryn laughs. "He drinks like a dwarf."

She stands up from the booth. "Ready to hit the road?"

"Ready," we all say in unison.

She opens the door, holding it ajar for us to begin our journey. "Enjoy the crisp Goldspire air while you still can. I'm sure Frostmoor will have a bit of a bite to it."

Berry nearly tackles Taryn to the ground once we're outside. Stompy sits in the center of the street paying us no mind, forcing pedestrians to pass him on either side.

Taryn wraps his arms around the bear's head. "Nobody forgot about you, you big goon."

"How could we, with all of that whining?" I mutter under my breath.

He hugs Stompy, but all he gets in response is a grunt.

In the early morning sun, the entire city takes on a golden luster. The spire in the forum glimmers against the blue sky, and carts rattle against the cobbled streets as the vendors from outside the city come to sell their produce.

When we make our way into the arena, I'm suddenly confused by the layout. If those entering Goldspire have to face off with the gladiators, then how are we getting out?

Portia must notice my confusion as I stop underneath the arched tunnel entering the stadium. "What's wrong, Big Blue?"

"Are we just going to stroll by a bunch of gladiators mid-fight to get out of here?"

She tilts her head back and laughs. "Oh, wouldn't that be funny? Gladiators battling for life and death, and we just walk by with a nod." Her grin stretches from ear to ear. "As great as that would be, Goldspire has two portals. The one you entered through is for newcomers. For native beastkin, or those who have survived the arena, there is a separate portal at the far end of the arena. When you return, you won't have to fight your way through unless you have newcomers in your party."

"That's convenient. But how does the portal know who's been here?"

She shrugs. "Magic."

We follow her up a stairwell into the stands. The seats are mostly empty and only two gladiators stand in the arena. I recognize one of them as Mordrir, the satyr we fought on our second attempt into Goldspire.

At the far end of the stands, we descend another set of stairs to the portal. From inside the floor of the arena, it can't be seen because of the high walls. The swirling portal sits at the back on a raised platform, with no walls obscuring its view over-looking the sea. Compared to Seascape and Vanaria's portals, it's practically empty. Only one beastkin stands on the platform sorting through a satchel in front of the portal.

Jegaar closes the satchel and notices us, but he doesn't stick around for small talk. He gives a mock salute. "To new adventures." He winks at us as he steps through the portal.

One of the runes flashes red and then he's gone. Probably off to face some challenge that could kill the rest of us with its eyes closed.

"Well." Portia gives us a warm smile. "This is it. I'd never met a hero before, but I'm happy to have made your acquaintances. Perhaps we will meet again one day."

I extend my arm, and Portia and I clasp one another around the wrist. "There's still one somewhere in Goldspire. If you hear word of a death knight walking the streets, he's one of us."

"Yeah." Taryn repeats the gesture with Portia. "Don't let his appearance scare you off. He's a decent enough guy once you get past the skull and dark energy."

Portia scrunches her face in confusion, and Limery flies over from my shoulder, embracing her. "Its was nice to meets you. Limmy loved the wines."

She beams as the tiny imp wraps his arms around her shoulder. "It was a pleasure to meet you too, Mr. Imp. Good luck on your journeys."

We ascend the platform and focus on the rune for Frostmoor. It glows red, and with a final glance at Portia, we step through the portal.

In an instant, everything goes white and an icy chill pierces me to my core.

10. FROSTMOOR

A gust of freezing wind assaults my face, and my trollberries shrink like raisins in the sun. In the bitter temperature, I'm keenly aware of Limery's warm body clinging tightly to my shoulder. Everywhere is blanketed in white, except for the nearby blotches of Berry and Stompy. Even their massive frames are concealed by the dense snowfall.

The icy wind is uncomfortable, but not painful. I hate to imagine what this would feel like without my troll hide. Even now, it feels like being stuck in a freezer, and I don't know why we didn't think to bundle up. Limery will be fine, I'm sure, but what about Taryn?

"Taryn!" I call in the direction of his pets, but the words get lost in the wind.

Behind me, snowflakes melt as they hit the portal's whirlpool of energy. It's the only thing in the area that isn't blurred and muted by the snowfall.

I take a step forward and my feet sink calf-deep into the snow. How are we supposed to find our way out of here when everything is indistinguishable?

"Limery!" I have to shout for him to hear me over the roaring wind even though he's sitting on my shoulder. "Can you melt some of the snow around the platform?"

"Limmy's on it." His claws dig into me as he launches himself into the blizzard.

A second later, a bright ball of flame springs to life in front of me as Limery takes to his molten form. He hovers near the ground, flying in circles until the platform is cleared of snow. Puddles fill the stone surface and each new snowflake melts against the warmed rock. He summons a flame wall in the center of the platform. The wind whips at the fiery wall but it withstands the assault, keeping the snow at bay long enough for Taryn and I to reunite. The warmth from the flames takes away the bite from the wind for a moment.

Suddenly, the wind fades, and the blizzard of seconds before stills to a light flurry. Without the wind, the snowfall is calm and peaceful. Silence stretches for miles.

A roar shrieks from overhead, and an icy-blue, winged creature the size of a barn soars by. Its wings spread like sails, and its underbelly is shrouded in shadow.

White Dragon. *Unique Monster. Level 35. Perhaps the greatest hunters of all dragon species, white dragons dwell in harsh climates with even harsher prey. While preferring to feast on mammoths, nothing is off-limits to these apex predators. Capable of spewing ice-flames that can turn flesh to ice in seconds, their frigid core is said to affect the climate of their immediate vicinity.*

Damn. To have that kind of power.

A chill runs down my spine that has nothing to do with the temperature.

As the dragon flies further away, the snowfall fades until it stops entirely. The sun peeks out from behind the clouds, igniting the landscape, and suddenly, every-thing is so bright it burns my eyes. I lift my hand to shield my view, waiting for my eyes to slowly adjust to my surroundings.

The snowfall fades and I find Taryn with ice crystals clinging to his beard. He gapes at the fleeing dragon from atop Stompy.

"Are you sure we took the right portal?" Taryn's gaze is still fixed. "Because that was a dragon that controls the weather, and I don't think we can survive a fight with that."

I watch the dragon until its icy scales blend into the sky. "If that's the toughest thing this place has to offer, then I think we'll be okay."

A level thirty-five monster could kill us no problem, but if it's the top of the food chain then most of the monsters have to be in the twenties. At least I hope so.

There's a soft thunk as Limery plops headfirst into a snowbank. Steam rises as the snow melts against his warm body.

Berry follows him, his golden armor glimmering in the sun as he stands at the edge of the platform eating mouthfuls of snow. Even Stompy seems intrigued by our surroundings.

"Let's hope you're right." Taryn shivers and pulls his cloak tighter. Ruby's ears poke out from underneath. "I thought we made a mistake for a minute there, but this isn't so bad." He looks around. "This is peaceful. Cold, but peaceful."

Towering mountain ranges surround us on all sides. Five trails spread out from the portal in different directions. Somehow, their pebbled paths are not covered in snow, and torches with blue flames mark each path every so often.

I'm surprised the torches still burn after the powerful gusts of the snowstorm. Whoever is in charge of keeping them lit must have quite the challenge on their hands, not that it looks like this place gets too many visitors. Maybe they're enchanted somehow.

I approach one of the torches, hoping to steal some of its warmth, but the fire is no warmer than the air surrounding it. I place my hand in the flame, but it radiates nothing but a dull energy.

"That's cool." Taryn climbs down from Stompy and sticks his hand into the blue fire. He jerks his hand back immediately. "Ouch! What the hell?" he yells, shaking his hand before shoving it in the snow.

He grimaces as he lifts his hand from the snow, his fingers red and inflamed.

Strange. I place my hand in the fire once more and feel the energy it produces. It doesn't burn, but it's a familiar sensation I've felt before. It takes me a moment before I remember where.

Back at the forest.

"These are mana flames." I run my hand across the fire, and my mind runs wild with questions. Who did this, and how were they able to infuse fire with mana?

"Yeah, well, they still burn like a bitch." Taryn kisses his tender skin. "How are you not affected?"

"Really?" I hold out my arms, displaying the obvious. "I used to be green. Not to mention that forest trolls are capable of touching raw mana without being burned."

"Right," Taryn says flatly. "You could have warned me."

"Sorry, I didn't connect the two until you decided to make dwarf sausages. The forest trolls don't have anything like this." Were the damage severe, I might be concerned, but it's only a minor burn. I reach in my satchel and pull out a health potion, removing the cork. "Here, drink this and you'll be good as new."

He downs the health potion and after a moment, the redness fades from his hand. "Much better." He sighs. "So which way are we going? I'd like to find an inn with a warm fire."

I pull up my map, but it offers me little to go off. Aside from the portal, there's nothing displayed other than the mountain ranges. There are no towns or paths marked, and they probably won't populate until we've made contact with the locals. We're flying blind.

"I don't know, but I'd like our chances a lot better away from the dragon. Maybe we start on the opposite side and work our way through each path until we find something useful?"

"Works for me." Taryn climbs on Berry's back. "You can ride the big guy if you want. I'd hate for your toes to freeze off."

I climb on the moulhaug's back even though my feet would be fine in the snow. The skin on my soles is so tough I could walk on a bed of coals and probably not feel it. But riding Stompy, I can sit back and enjoy the view as we head toward the mountain.

The amount of snow distorts my perception, making it difficult to gauge just how far away the mountains actually are. As we travel, trees become visible in the distance, scattered around the landscape and covered in a thick layer of snowfall. Limbs shake on one of them, and sheets of snow fall from the branches.

I immediately jump down from Stompy and summon three horrors while equipping Destroyer. I have all my weapons back since defeating Dakota in the arena, but Destroyer is by far the strongest for combat. The ancient warhammer fills me with excitement as I grip the shaft, feeling the weight of the enchanted weapon. It's been too long since we've had a real fight.

Berry growls as a dark snout protrudes from underneath the pine.

Frost Wolf. *Level 18. With a thick coat and a dense layer of blubber, the frost wolf has evolved to survive the frigid climate of Frostmoor.*

If not for its black nose, the wolf would be indistinguishable from its surroundings. Brilliant white and ice-blue fur blends against the snow seamlessly, making me wonder how many other dangers might be lurking within plain sight.

Its mouth curls into a snarl as it emerges from the trees, revealing its giant frame, far bigger than any of the wolves I faced on Isle of Mythos. At level eighteen, it shouldn't be a challenge at all. Not when I'm level twenty-four and Taryn and Limery are both level twenty-two. With Berry level eighteen and Stompy at level nineteen, Ruby is the only one under-leveled at sixteen, but she's not here to fight.

This will be a nice warm-up.

The wolf tilts its head back and unleashes a loud howl. It carries over the quiet landscape like a foghorn, echoing off the distant mountains.

Stompy grunts and shuffles his feet. He must be dying for a fight as well.

"Who wants to do the hon—"

Before I can finish the question, several resounding howls answer all around us. A moment later, we're surrounded by wolves on all sides, at least a dozen, with golden eyes and black snouts their only revealing features.

This just got a lot more interesting. I summon a second wave of horrors, and our narrow path starts to feel a bit crowded. The grumbling horrors respond to my command, venturing out into the snow, but I quickly realize they aren't suited for this terrain. The lightweight Horrors of Finesse have no problem traversing the snow, but both the Horrors of Power and Vitality struggle to move as they sink into its depths.

The wolves trek through the snow toward us, their long powerful legs propelling them forward.

"Limery, can you clear some of the snow around the path? We need room to fight."

Without hesitating, Limery bursts into flames, and soon we have a circle of muddy earth to each side of the gravel path.

"How do you want to play this?" I ask Taryn.

He glances at the wolf pack slowly encircling us. "Spread out. Try to fight them in bunches and not all at once."

He lifts his Sapling Staff and summons a line of poisonous mushrooms along the boundary where the snow melts. Bulbous brown mushrooms with purple spots sprout to life, and once the cooldown wears off, he summons more until the perimeter is covered with a ring of fungi.

He scratches Berry behind the ears. "Time to put that armor to use."

Taryn climbs down and mounts Stompy while Ruby paces nervously between the moulhaug's legs. Limery hovers in the air between us all, his eyes darting from one wolf to the next.

I summon a third round of horrors and position each group an equal distance apart. I should be able to get in one more round before the wolves make it to us, two if we're lucky.

We briefly go over our plan of attack, making sure we're all on the same page before battle.

The wolves wait at the border still camouflaged in the snow. At this distance, I can see the saliva as it streams from their mouths, their sharp teeth desperate for flesh. Several of them eye Stompy, sensing a meal for the taking.

Not today.

The first wolf leaps from the snow into the mud, setting off a chain reaction of poisonous mushrooms. Purple gas erupts, staining the wolf's fur. The beast wobbles as it lands, coughing out the toxic fumes.

Nearby horrors rush toward the wolf, but before they arrive, there's a crack of thunder that startles some of the other wolves. Lightning and fire hit the wolf simultaneously, and the lingering gas takes out the rest of its HP.

One down.

Several more wolves leap the border. Taryn casts Stonewall, blocking the approach of two wolves, and Limery's flame wall halts another.

Berry doesn't hesitate, armor clinking as he charges the closest wolf, his jaws wide. His paw is raised for an attack when my attention is diverted by the two wolves in front of me. One pounces at me, and I swing Destroyer horizontally. There's a sickening crunch as the warhammer connects with the wolf's jaw. The wolf yelps as it slides across the muddy earth into the snowbank.

The warhammer flashes red as it gains a stack of Inferno, the enchantment from being crafted in the heart of a volcano allowing the metal to grow hotter with each consecutive hit.

The second wolf snaps at my ankle but I step out of the way, leaving it chomping at air. A Horror of Power buries its tusks into the wolf's hind leg, eliciting another yelp. The wolf turns back out of instinct, sinking its teeth into the horror until the muscled summon combusts in a puff of smoke.

The distraction gives me enough time to land a hit against the wolf's ribs and gain a second stack of Inferno.

To my right, Stompy slams his horn into a wolf like a wrecking ball, knocking it away, deep into the snow. Taryn casts Stonewall in front of the beast, giving us time to deal with the others.

All around me, thunder crashes, fire sizzles, and both Berry and the wolves roar. The white wolves are now a mixture of purple, red, and brown, their fur painted in a mixture of mud, blood, and mushroom gas.

My horrors attack where they are needed, and I gain two more charges of Inferno. Destroyer glows molten red with every hit, singeing fur and burning flesh. Each time the wolves return, their thick fur grows patchier.

Between strategically-placed walls and raw power, it doesn't take long before a mound of corpses surrounds us. My muscles burn with the excitement of battle, and steam radiates from my skin even though I didn't have to use my barbarian rage.

"That felt good." I lean against one of Taryn's remaining walls. "Good job, everyone."

The wall fades into ether, and I tumble into the snow. For the moment, its cold embrace feels good against my skin. I catch Taryn's laughter right before Limery plops in the snow beside me.

"Limmy loves the snows!"

I cup a snowball in my palm and pelt him in the face with it as soon as his head peaks out. His bulbous eyes go wide for a moment before he erupts in demonic laughter.

"Limmy will gets you." He attempts to make a snowball of his own, but the snow melts in his hands each time he tries to pack it together.

"Sorry, dude. You're just too hot for this climate." I make another snowball and hand it to him.

Limery admires the snowball like a priceless artifact before throwing it at my face. I let him have his fun and allow it to hit me between the tusks.

"Nice one!" cheers Taryn as he finishes casting Restoration on Berry, healing his minor wounds from the fight. "That was a good fight. It won't be long until I hit level twenty-three."

I check my own experience and realize I hit level twenty-five during the fight. I've kept my notifications muted to keep them from distracting me during fights and didn't even think to check after the battle.

Twenty-five. Five more and I can return to Jegaar. I pull up my stats and examine them. With my racial bonuses to Strength and Constitution per level, they dwarf all my other stats. I still have six stat points I've been saving, and two ability points I'm not ready to use. None of my current available abilities are beneficial enough to justify using a point on them.

Underneath the level alert, there's a second notification.

Class Advancements. *Upon reaching level twenty-five, you have unlocked a class advancement. You may only advance one class at a time. A second class may not be advanced until completion of primary advancement.*

Barbarian Advancement.
Spirit of the Beast. Unlock for further details.

Summoner Advancement.
Dreadbeasts. Unlock for further details.
Dual Subclass. Unlock for further details.

I sit there in shock for a moment. This is big. I won't know how big until I make a choice, but I have a feeling that whichever route I take could seriously change my role in the group going forward.

For now, I forget about the Warforged. Spirit of the Beast sounds awesome. And Dreadbeasts, that sounds terrifying. I have a feeling it would upgrade my horror summoning in some way. Dual Subclass sounds good, too, and I'm pretty sure that one would allow me to take on an additional summoning class that I was offered when I first became a summoner.

I take a deep breath. This is too big of a decision to make right now. I'll need to—

A snowball hits me in the face, interrupting my thoughts.

"Earth to Chod." Taryn looks at me expectantly. "What's going on?"

I must have been pretty zoned out. I wipe the snow from my face and join Taryn back on the path.

"I got a notification for hitting level twenty-five. There's an option for class advancement and I have three choices." I go on to tell him about my options.

"Dude, that's awesome!" Taryn grins, and his genuine happiness for me makes me appreciate just how lucky I am to have him as a friend. "Do you think I'll get one when I hit twenty-five?"

"Considering I got one for both of my classes, I would think so."

"Nice! Let's get moving then. Maybe we'll run into some more wolves."

I lose myself in thought as we travel. Since gaining a second class, I've been able to balance my summoning and barbarian abilities pretty well together. They synergize in a way that's rare, with my race and barbarian abilities improving my horrors. But now it feels like I'll be forced to commit to advancing one class for the foreseeable future. Regardless of what I choose, my horrors will continue to improve as I level and grow stronger due to their passive buffs from my Strength and Constitution. I can't think of another class better suited to my stats as a troll. But if I invest in my summoning, whether it be furthering my horror class or taking on a second summoning technique, I'll have reached the peak of my barbarian abilities for now.

This is a big decision, one not to be taken lightly.

"Do you see that?" Taryn brings Berry to a halt, and Stompy stops as well.

Taryn points to a splotch in the snow up ahead, where an abandoned wagon is surrounded by bloodstained snow.

Stompy snorts, and I pat him on the side. "Yeah, let's approach with caution."

"I can take my bird form and investigate," Taryn offers.

I shake my head. "I don't like that. Not here. We don't know what we're dealing with, and you'll stick out like a sore thumb against all this white."

He strokes his beard. "I could use transform and turn into a frost wolf."

"Badass, but likely to get you killed if wolves caused this."

"Fair point. Let's take it slow then and hope it's not a trap."

The closer we get, the more this feels less like a trap and more like a crime scene. Whatever was pulling the wagon is gone, the reins broken and lying on the ground. Bloodstained snow surrounds the wagon, and a crimson trail leads across the snow and into the snow-covered forest.

Something moves behind the wagon, and I equip Petrified Staff. Its bonus ability allows me to cast ranged physical attacks. Taryn readies his own weapon, and Limery grows even hotter against my shoulder.

"Who's there?" I ask.

A broad-shouldered human with a dense blonde beard steps out from behind the wagon. He wears a thick layer of furs drenched in blood and holds a bow at the ready, arrow nocked and pointed in our direction. He grunts, and his eyes narrow. I can't tell if it's in anger or fear.

11. THE FIVE PEAKS

"Stand back!" the bearded man growls, the arrowhead swaying back and forth between us as he assesses which one of us is the bigger threat. "Gods as my witnesses, I will take one of you with me before I fall!"

His blue eyes flare with intensity as they dart between me and Taryn. Ice speckles his dense blonde beard. A massive axe hangs from his hip, and his stance shifts repeatedly, no doubt due to the adrenaline pumping through his veins.

I quickly analyze him before we find ourselves outmatched again.

Archard the Precise
Level 22
Human
Ranger

He's strong, but we could handle him. I'm more concerned about his moniker than his level, though. A well-placed arrow to the eye could send me respawning back at the portal before I know what's hit me.

I put away my staff and raise my hands, showing him I'm not a threat. "We're not here to fight. We're on our way up the mountain. What happened here?"

He loosens the tension on the bowstring slightly. "What business do you have in Whitgard?"

Whitgard must be the name of one of the villages. "We're looking for allies, and we bring news from abroad."

He lowers the bow a couple of inches and laughs darkly. "Allies. You must be a long way from home."

"Further than you could guess." Taryn lowers his staff. "What happened here? There's a lot of blood. Are you injured?"

He finally releases the tension on the bow and lowers the weapon entirely. "Only my pride. A pair of frost giants caught scent of my hunt and ambushed me. Took my oxen as well. They don't normally venture this far down the mountain until winter, so they caught me unaware."

I glance around at the snowy landscape. "You mean this isn't winter?"

He lets out a hearty laugh this time. "You are a long way from home," he says again. "This is a crisp spring morning."

Taryn pulls his cloak tighter, as if imagining colder weather. "If you'll guide us to the village, I'll have my moulhaug pull your wagon. Looks like you could use the help."

Archard kneels and picks up the reins that once held his oxen. His eyes follow the trail of blood that leads into the snow-covered forest. "I can't return empty-handed. You lot know how to hunt?"

Taryn nods. "We provide for ourselves. What's on the menu?"

After some convincing, Stompy lets us harness him to the wagon. He doesn't take kindly to being restrained, and the loss of influence for having more than one pet makes this more difficult than it should be. After some sweet-talking, Taryn's able to persuade Stompy to get moving. The wagon isn't big enough for me to ride up front with Archard, so Limery and I sit in the back while Archard steers the wagon from the narrow driver's seat. Taryn follows us on Berry.

The wagon bumps along as we travel in silence.

I clear my throat to get Archard's attention. "You said frost giants took your hunt? Are they common here? I once fought a mountain giant."

He grunts. "More common than we'd like them to be. You see that peak over there, the one that curls into the shape of a dragon's mouth?" He points to the nearest mountain range. "That's Icemaw. The frost giants call it home."

The peak is imposing, with massive icicles that give the appearance of teeth.

"How many live there?"

"Anyone foolish enough to attempt a count never lived to tell the tale. Could be a few dozen. Could be much more." Even with his back turned, I can make out the scowl at the edge of his brow. "You'd be hard-pressed to call them a tribe. They're more like a group of abominations that choose to dwell near one another. Sometimes their clashes can be heard in Whitgard on a calm evening. Hardly ever do they travel in more than pairs, and each giant is worth twenty men in combat."

They sound more dangerous than the giant I fought. If two of them ambushed his wagon, it's a miracle he's not dead. "How did you manage to survive them attacking you?"

He turns around and his blue eyes bore into me. "Fighting a frost giant is not bravery, it is a death sentence. You'd be wise to remember that. We avoid them at all costs, appease them when we can, and fight when it is the only option. I survived because I did what any smart man would do. I hid." His death stare dares me to contradict him.

Were I in his shoes, I have no doubt I would do the same. Facing off against something that strong with only one life to live leaves no room for error.

Taryn urges Berry closer until he's right behind the wagon. "I don't blame you. What was it you were hunting anyway?"

Archard sighs. "I spent three days tracking a mammoth, slowly wearing it down until I was finally able to finish the beast. Spent another day dragging it on a makeshift sled back to the wagon. And all for what?" he scoffs. "The moment I start to butcher the mammoth, the giants show up. That amount of meat would have lasted the village for weeks. Not to mention the oxen. We keep them in short supply, and it'll be a year to raise up another pair to replace them."

"Damn, that sucks." Taryn opens his cloak and guides Ruby onto Berry's back. "I'll take to the air, see what I can scout."

Archard whips the reins, but it does nothing to increase Stompy's speed. "There's a forest up ahead. Deer prefer the safety of tree cover."

There's a soft flutter as Taryn transforms into his bird form. As he soars through the white landscape, he sticks out like a ripe berry.

Archard's mouth hangs open as he watches Taryn fly away. "It's been many years since I have seen one blessed by the gods. It seems the dwarves spoke the truth."

He must be referring to the emissaries King Orso sent for the council. "There are more of us."

"Us?" He squints at me.

I summon a horror in front of me, and Archard nearly jumps from the wagon at the sudden appearance. "Heroes."

"And here I thought you were nothing more than a troll. I would love to hear your story, but I imagine Gherhardt will more so. Save it for when we return to Whitgard."

He certainly has more patience than I do. Archard is a man of few words, so we travel in silence, the only sounds are the crunch of pebbles beneath the wagon wheels and Stompy's occasional grunts or Berry's whines.

As we pass another torch with blue flames, I finally speak. "Where do the torches come from? There was a snowstorm when we entered. I couldn't see a foot in front of me but somehow the flames didn't go out."

"They've been there since before I was born, but the torches can give light in even the most menacing of storms. Before the fall, all of Frostmoor traded with the other portals. We had some of the best tinkerers in all of Mythos. We were once two mighty tribes, the Frozen Ash Tribe of Whitgard and the Snowwalker Tribe of Greypeak, and both of our societies prospered. We spread across four of the five peaks and rivaled many kingdoms in size. As the portals closed, our societies slowly crumbled and the knowledge we used to raise our people to prominence was lost to time. Greypeak was overrun by hobgoblins and the Snowwalker Tribe was forced to relocate to the remains of Boneholde. Now, we are but a scattering of villages doing our best to survive." His gaze lingers on the torch as we pass it. "On a clear night you can see their faint glow from the village."

The trolls aren't the only ones who have fallen from grace. All the more reason for these people to join the cause.

My notifications flash and I pull up a message from Taryn.

Incoming Message (Taryn): *Bro, bird form is amazing in the snow. I can pick out every little thing that sticks out. I found a herd of some weird deer. Follow my location on the map and I'll keep trailing them.*

I pull up my map and locate Taryn. He's in the center of a nearby forest. It's not too far, but it will definitely take us some time on foot.

Message (Chod): *Alright, we'll be there as soon as we can.*

I relay Taryn's message and Archard nods, though it's hard to make out his facial expression underneath the massive beard.

"That'll save us some time at least. Finding the trail is the toughest part." He whips the reins, but we move no faster.

Stompy tilts his head and huffs.

Eventually, Archard pulls the wagon to the side of the path. "We'll take the rest of the way on foot." He releases Stompy from the harness, but the moulhaug doesn't move. Archard looks him in the eye. "You're a mighty beast, I'll give you that, but I don't think even you would want to tussle with a frost giant on your own."

Stompy grunts, but then takes a few steps into the snow.

I'll be damned. "I think he likes you."

Archard pats Stompy on the hindquarters. "I've always had a way with animals, ever since I was a boy."

"Berry's the friendlier one." I scratch him behind the ears, and he nuzzles against my fingers. "But if you want to take your chances riding Stompy, be my guest."

To my surprise, Stompy kneels in the snow—something he has only ever done for Taryn. I've had to leap onto his back every time I've needed to ride him.

Archard climbs on his back, and I mount Berry with Ruby curling up between my legs. Limery perches on my shoulders, and I'm certain we're a sight to behold.

I lead the way, guiding Berry through the forest toward Taryn's location. Under the cover of the trees, there's a surprising amount of life. Ruby leaps from my lap in pursuit of a rabbit. A fox dives in a snowbank after some unseen prey. Occasionally, a bird will chirp in a distant tree or movement will send snow falling from branches.

I turn to Archard. "I had no idea so many animals lived here. Everything looks quiet and peaceful from far away."

The edges of his blonde mustache twitch. "Frostmoor is full of life if you know where to look."

Limery's body temperature suddenly warms, and I catch him staring at a nearby tree. A blue bird sits perched on a branch, its tender chirps carrying across the snow.

Limery licks his lips and pounces. Flames flare to life as he soars at the bird with breakneck speed. His fingers clench around the poor creature, and feathers flutter through the air as he ends its song abruptly.

I look away as he enjoys his snack. When he returns, he wears a devious grin.

"Limmy loves the birds." He picks a feather from between his teeth with a claw.

"A fine hunt." Archard winks at Limery.

The small imp blushes.

We travel for another hour before we near Taryn's location.

Incoming Message (Taryn): *About time you showed up. The deer aren't too far ahead.*

I squint my eyes to look through the forest, but I don't see anything—neither the deer nor Taryn.

"Psst." I wave my hands until I get Archard's attention, then I whisper. "Taryn says the deer are up ahead."

Archard slides down Stompy's side, equipping his bow as he lands softly in the snow. "We will pursue on foot. It is best if the animals remain here."

Berry listens obediently, sitting in the snow next to Ruby as she devours a rabbit she has been carrying in her mouth for the past hour. Stompy does little to acknowledge he heard anything.

Archard spots something in the distance and draws his bow. His vision must be better than mine because I still can't see anything.

"What is its?" asks Limery.

Archard points to a tree. "They passed through here. See the markings?"

I focus on the tree he's pointing at. The bark is scraped raw in several areas.

"And here." He points to a path of pressed snow. "Now we follow the trail."

He leads the way as Limery and I follow quietly behind. Archard moves like a ninja, his fur-covered boots barely making a sound. It makes the gentle crunch of snow beneath my own feet sound like thunder in comparison.

He raises a hand, telling us to stop, and then nocks an arrow. I follow the trajectory of the arrow but can't see what he's aiming at. Limery lets out a low "ooh" next to me just before I spot the outline of a solid white deer with icy-blue antlers emerging from behind a pine.

Frost Deer. *Level 16. The elusive frost deer blends in naturally with the terrain, making them difficult to spot for even the most seasoned of hunters. Their icy blue antlers* *are used to make weapons and are highly valued as jewelry due to the starburst pattern when cut open.*

"Pretties," Limery whispers.

Archard is about to take the shot when a red bird lands on the tip of his arrow.

He nearly falls down when Taryn returns to his dwarven form in a burst of feathers. Limery cackles on my shoulder, and the deer bolts away.

"What in the icy hells of Mythos are you doing?" Archard's face is red as a tomato. "You've gone and scared it away."

Taryn smirks, taking little offense to Archard's harsh words. "That's not the prize. Follow me."

A few minutes later, we stand on the edge of a clearing. A half-dozen frost deer lay in the center, soaking up the sun's rays. Two large bucks sit at opposite sides, their massive blue antlers casting elaborate shadows. These deer are bigger than any I have ever seen. The tips of their ice-blue antlers are translucent and seem to glow in the sunlight. They are truly magnificent creatures.

"Well done," Archard whispers.

Taryn equips his staff. "What's the plan? I can stun them with Lightning Bolt while the rest of you finish them off."

Archard places his hand on Taryn's arm, lowering the staff. "No need."

He draws an arrow from the quiver on his back and nocks it. I don't know what he's playing at, because as soon as he shoots the first arrow, the herd is going to bolt and we'll be no better off than if he had shot the solo earlier.

"Are you sure you don't want to plan an attack? My Horrors of Vitality can slow the deer and make it easier. The four of us can handle them no problem."

He ignores me, lifting the bow until the arrow is pulled right beside his ear. I have the urge to smack it out of his hand and talk some sense into him, but I hold my temper.

The arrow releases with a thwip, and before it connects, he's already nocked another and fires. He shoots two more arrows just as quickly without checking to see if the others hit.

The first four shots land with dull thunks, hitting each deer right behind the forelegs. The two does wobble for a second before their heads drop. Both bucks are hit as they rise to their feet, taking a few steps before collapsing.

The fifth arrow zips through the air, hitting a deer as it prances toward the tree line. Archard holds the sixth arrow, trailing the movement of the final deer as it bolts away.

I'm certain the deer will escape, its long strides propelling it across the clearing. Archard looses the arrow and the beast tumbles to the ground inches from freedom.

Wow. The entire scene unfolds in under ten seconds. Six well-placed shots and not a single one off-target.

"How did you do that?" I look on in astonishment. He doesn't even have any magical ranger abilities.

"Practice." Archard slings the bow over his shoulder and heads toward his prizes, checking each deer to make sure it's truly dead. When he's satisfied, he turns to me. "I hope you're as strong as you look."

We wait while Taryn flies back to gather his pets. When they arrive, we strap the two frost deer bucks to Stompy. With their massive antlers, they take up the majority of the moulhaug's back. We tie one of the does to Berry. Taryn and Archard pull one together on a makeshift sled, and I'm stuck carrying one on each shoulder. At four hundred pounds, the does are mighty in their own right and will provide a lot of meat for the village. Archard refuses to gut them in the forest so that the village can use the entire deer, letting nothing go to waste.

By the time we reach the wagon, I'm covered in blood and sweat as I sling the deer into the bed of the wagon. Without the bonus Strength and Constitution I've gained as I've leveled up, I doubt I would have been able to carry both for such a long distance. Once I've loaded the others, I use the snow to wash away the blood from my shoulders.

Taryn sits in the front of the wagon with Archard while I ride Berry.

He plays with the vines on his staff, making them grow and retract with ease. "That was some amazing marksmanship back there. How'd you learn to shoot like that?"

"My father was a great hunter and ranger." Archard stares straight ahead as he answers. "He taught me everything I know."

Taryn smiles. "He must be proud."

Archard shrugs. "I'll never know."

"Why not?" Taryn's brows scrunch in concern, a look I've seen many times.

"Frostmoor is not an easy place to live. Even more so for a ranger. He went on a hunt one day and never returned. I was still a year or two from being deemed a man, but I had the skills to do the job, so I filled his place, and I've been a ranger ever since."

I speak loudly so that my voice carries over the crunch of the wheels on the path. "I'm sorry to hear that. Do you know what happened to him?"

He shakes his head. "We never found the body, but that's how it usually goes when someone goes missing. Could have been giants, hobgoblins, or any number of creatures. Not that the land is any kinder."

The sun dips behind one of the peaks, and suddenly we're covered in shadow. We pass the stone ruins of a village. With the way the rocks have crumbled, it's evident no one has called this place home for some time.

"What happened here?" I ask.

"You ask a lot of questions, you know that?" His gaze lingers on the ruins. "Before the fall of Frostmoor, the villages of the Frozen Ash Tribe stretched all the way down the mountain. These are a solemn reminder of how far our people have fallen."

I can't imagine what it's like being forced to look upon these every time he descends the mountain for a hunt. "Are there still villages on any of the other mountains? I know you said that Greypeak was overrun, but what about the others?"

He turns around and stares daggers at me. "You know the best part about being a ranger? The peace and quiet. I'm grateful for your help, so I'll tell you what I know of the other peaks, and then I don't want to hear a peep out of you. Sound good?"

I nod.

He turns to Taryn. "And you?"

Taryn nods, then mutters under his breath, "Somebody is a grumpy goose."

For a moment, I'm certain that Archard is going to toss Taryn from the wagon, but he just sighs. "Long ago, when the Frozen Ash and Snowwalkers were at their height, we settled four of the five peaks. The Frozen Ash also held Icemaw, and in those days, we had the manpower to keep the frost giants at bay. The Snowwalkers expanded to Boneholde, and villages were built in the skeleton of some ancient beast."

He takes a deep breath. "Many of our men were sent to battle the dark one. Most of them never returned. When the portals closed, those left outside were lost to us forever. Without the able-bodied men to defend the villages, Icemaw fell to the giants. Sensing weakness, the hobgoblins that resided in the deep caverns of Greypeak attacked, killing many and forcing the rest to abandon their ancestral homes and relocate to Boneholde. A hundred years passed before Frostmoor opened to the world again, but by then, we had little to offer. Our numbers have dwindled little by little into what they are today."

Taryn sits on the edge of his seat. "Why did the humans never settle the fifth peak?"

Archard turns toward the center mountain. It is the tallest of the five, with the peak disappearing above a ring of clouds. Even though the sun is on the other side of the mountains, it ignites the side in blazing white. "According to legend, it was already settled."

"By who?" Taryn asks.

There's a long pause, just as an icy breeze blows down the mountain side. The chill is nothing compared to the one I get when he answers.

"Trolls."

12. LET SLEEPING TROLLS LIE

I lean forward so far that I nearly tumble off Berry. "What do you mean trolls?"

Archard shrugs. "It's a legend as far as I'm concerned. You're the first troll I've ever seen in Frostmoor, but you look nothing like the trolls from the old tales. If there ever were trolls on Hornryx, they're long gone."

I think back to my first day in game, trying to recall what the arctic troll looked like in the creation menu. The option to play an arctic troll was unavailable to me, but I remember that it was massive, rivaling the desert trolls in size. It had skin that was a muted black and thick white fur covering much of its body, reminiscent of a polar bear. If not for the tusks and pointy ears, it could have been easily confused with a yeti. Is it possible that there are still arctic trolls in Frostmoor?

"What did the legends say?" I urge Berry to stay as close to the wagon as possible. Any clue, no matter how small, could give me guidance. If the arctic trolls are here, then I need to find them.

He frowns. "They're old wives' tales, nothing more. Stories created to scare children into behaving. The trolls were said to have been so strong that neither frost giants nor hobgoblins would set foot on the mountain. Even to this day, no one ventures beyond the base of Hornryx. My nan would tell us stories about how the trolls could tell when a child wasn't asleep, and that they would slip into our rooms and devour us whole. I spent many a night unable to sleep, watching the shadows on the wall with my furs pulled up to my chin."

Taryn laughs. "Some things never change. My mom used to scare me and my sisters into going to bed with stories of the Boogeyman."

Archard scrunches his brow. "I have not heard of this Boogeyman."

I ignore their conversation, still occupied with thoughts of arctic trolls. Something doesn't add up. "After all these years, why has no one climbed the mountain?"

"What do we have to gain from venturing into unknown lands?" Archard tugs on his beard. "We have enough problems in Whitgard without adding the threat of trolls. Say they are nothing more than myth, there is still a reason we never summited Hornryx, a reason even the frost giants or hobgoblins have not claimed it as their own. It's an unforgiving mountain with steep cliffs and narrow passes. Snow falls heavier on Hornryx than any of the other peaks. If we managed to survive the climb and find that trolls do still dwell there, would it be wise to disturb them when they have left us in peace for so long?" He shakes his head. "No, if they do exist, it is best to let sleeping trolls lie."

I pester Archard for more information, but what little he does know is based on tales passed down through the ages. No one has seen an arctic troll since before the portals closed hundreds of years ago. Maybe they were on the same path as the mountain trolls, slowly fading to extinction high in the clouds. Or maybe they are thriving, alone and undisturbed.

To know for certain, we'll have to climb Hornryx before we leave Frostmoor. But for now, my focus needs to be on Whitgard and making sure I can convince them that forming an alliance with King Orso is in their best interest.

We failed in Goldspire. I can't afford to let that happen again.

"Ooh, looks!" Limery points to a dark blob moving across the snow, far bigger than any deer or wolf.

"Is that..." Taryn's words trail off and his eyes fill with greed.

"A mammoth," Archard finishes the sentence. "It will be a while before I dare to hunt one alone again."

Taryn's gaze follows the mammoth until we lose sight.

The temperature drops the higher we climb, causing goosebumps to erupt all over my body like a dense new armor. My troll body is holding up, but I'll need to find warmer clothes once we make it to the village.

Before long, night shrouds the landscape, and the temperature drops again. Howls of distant frost wolves carry far across the empty night, and occasionally something stirs in the depths of the snow-covered trees and bushes. I can't fight back the occasional shiver that courses through me, and I'm thankful for both Berry's and Limery's warmth.

The landscape is coated in a silver hue as the moonlight reflects off the snow. We pass several more ruins before a faint blue glow welcomes us up the mountain.

The enchanted path ends at the entrance to the village, where two blue torches flicker next to the gate. A wooden palisade wraps around the village for protection, but it obscures very little as buildings with thatched roofs scale up the side of the mountain. A second trail, snow-covered and no longer infused with mana, winds around the outside of the palisade and higher up the mountainside.

Archard pulls a bell from within his fur cloak and shakes it. A moment later, the gate cracks open and a fur-clad man with a thick black beard stands in the way. He watches Stompy warily, and his eyes narrow as his gaze shifts from the moulhaug to Taryn and then to me and Limery.

His eyes lock with Archard. "Explain yourself."

Archard's shoulders stiffen. "Did Gherhardt die and make you Head of the Frozen Ash while I was gone? Because that is the only way you'll get an explanation out of me. Now, open the gate."

"Gherhardt will not like this." The man slams the butt of his spear into the packed snow and pushes the gate open. "There have been too many outsiders within our walls as of late. It is unsafe."

Archard huffs. "Then perhaps we should send them down the mountain with the six frost deer they helped kill. You can thank these outsiders when you have a full belly tomorrow night."

None of us correct the fact that Archard single-handedly killed all six deer.

The man grunts before stepping out of the way.

Archard scowls at the man as we pass. "Warley has always been a coward, afraid of anything he doesn't understand. And for all of his cowardice, he believes his word carries weight. We will deliver the deer to the butcher and then I will find accommodations for you and your pets for the evening."

I silently will Stompy to move faster as another shiver courses through me. The streets of Whitgard are not quite what I was expecting from a tribal village. The buildings are more rustic and many are windowless, but they aren't that different from some of the smaller towns on Isle of Mythos. There is an assortment of buildings, all constructed from stone in a similar fashion to the ruins we passed. Only some of them have windows, with shutters pulled closed. Smoke billows from many of the smaller huts, and light peeks between the cracks in the door frames. The streets are empty, not that I would expect anything else at this hour.

We come to a stop in front of a square, stone building. Archard jumps down from the wagon and bangs on the door.

After a long moment, he bangs again. "Bernd, wake up, you old sod."

There's movement behind the door, and then it cracks open. A burly old man with wild gray hair rubs his eyes. "Archard, what is so important that it can't wait until morning?"

"I've returned from the hunt with six frost deer." He gestures to the wagon. "I figured you'd want to get started before they freeze."

Bernd does a double-take when he sees the rest of us, and the sleep vanishes from his eyes. "By the gods. Strange times. Strange times, indeed. First dwarves, and now this." He turns to Archard. "Unload them out back."

I unload the deer while Bernd watches me with curious eyes. A light snow begins to fall, and he pulls up the hood of his cloak. He mumbles something under his breath about trolls, but there doesn't seem to be any malice toward me, so I carry on.

Archard says something to Bernd I can't quite make out. Bernd nods and then we're back in the wagon.

We come to a stop in front of a long two-story building that resembles a barn. It has an arched entryway with two massive wooden doors.

"Stompy will have plenty of room in the stables." Archard turns to Taryn.

"These stables have been here since before the fall, back when Aubert the Mighty was known for his domesticated mammoths."

Greed flashes through Taryn's eyes again and I'm certain he's imagining adding a mammoth to his menagerie. With another animal that big, we might as well join the Underground Circus.

"They'll be plenty warm inside its walls." Archard hops down and leads Stompy into the stable by the reins.

I climb down from Berry, keenly aware of the lack of warmth as a chill hits me between the legs. He follows Archard into the stable, and a moment later, Taryn returns with only Ruby as she scurries between his legs.

Archard strokes his beard in front of the stable entrance. "We haven't had a working inn in ages—there's been no need—so you'll have to stay in someone's home. I'd let you stay with me, but I'm gone so much that my hut is on the smaller side."

"They can stay with me." A figure cloaked in white furs is almost invisible against the snowy backdrop. He removes the hood, revealing a weathered face and forked gray beard.

Gherhardt
Head of the Frozen Ash Tribe
Level 25
Human

"Warley wake you up?" Archard frowns in the direction of the gate.

Gherhardt nods. "Leave him be. He likes to feel useful."

"Little snake," Archard mutters.

Those two must have some deep animosity between them.

Gherhardt extends a hand. "It is not often we receive visitors in Whitgard, so most of the village doesn't know how to act around outsiders. However, the fault is with me. I should have known after the dwarves dared to travel to our gates that it was an omen of more to come. The Frozen Ash have been in dark times for many years, but we will offer what we can, starting with a warm meal and a strong mead."

Limery perks up at the mention of mead, wiping away a drop of drool that trails down his chin.

I clasp Gherhardt's hand in mine and am surprised by the firmness of his grip. "That's very gracious of you."

Taryn and Limery echo their thanks.

"We have always been the more welcoming tribe of Frostmoor. I trust you had a good hunt, Archard."

Archard's face goes stern. "I lost two oxen, and the mammoth I killed, but we did manage six frost deer. Would have come home late and empty handed if not for this lot."

"Perhaps it wasn't an omen after all…" His voice is barely audible. "Let's get inside. I can't tell if it's troll toughness or bravado that has this one nearly naked in the snow."

I offer up a grin that probably looks more like a snarl. "Maybe a little of both."

We follow Gherhardt back to his home, where he pours us all a mug of deep amber liquid.

Item. Arctic Mead. *-2 Intelligence for one hour. In harsh climates, it helps to dull the senses.*

We sit around a roaring fire, sipping arctic mead from clay mugs as stew boils in a metal pot over the flames. The mead is syrupy and sweet, not my preferred drink at all, but Taryn and Limery seem to enjoy it.

"Just a few more minutes." Gherhardt stirs the pot and returns to his seat, a large chair with a wide back and legs that appear to be made of mammoth tusks. A fur blanket drapes over his shoulders, revealing a broad chest covered in gray hair. His hair is short and curly, the color matching his beard and chest. Though his face is weathered, he exudes a youthfulness in his blue eyes.

He lifts his mug in our direction. "For your help with the hunt."

I tilt my drink back to him. "Thank you, but Archard brought the deer down without any of our help."

Taryn mumbles under his breath, "Not like I spent hours tracking the damn things."

Gherhardt grins. "Archard is the most skilled ranger Whitgard has known since his father before him. He's a force to be reckoned with, but not even he can pull a wagon loaded with six frost deer up the mountain."

Taryn takes a deep chug from his mug. "If it's so hard to find food, why don't you move further down the mountain? There are certainly enough ruins."

Gherhardt sets his mug down on a polished wooden table in front of him. "This is our ancestral home. It has been the heart of the Frozen Ash Tribe for as far back as our story goes. We would not abandon it unless we had no other choice. Gods know the Snowwalkers have paid dearly since abandoning their homes."

He walks over to a wicker basket hanging against the wall and removes a purple carrot, tossing it to Taryn. "We provide for ourselves. We farm. We raise snowhogs and chickens. We would survive without the hunt, but the meat from the wilds reminds us of who we are and where we must go."

"I'm sorry. I didn't mean any offense." He raises both hands, nearly spilling his mead.

Archard pats Taryn on the shoulder. "Don't worry. It had been so long since an outsider visited Whitgard prior to your brethren that I feared the world had forgotten us. I doubt many know of our ways abroad, but it is good to know we have not been entirely forgotten."

I hang on the words he doesn't say. If the dwarves are the only people to have visited Whitgard in some time, then Jude and Glenn aren't here. Where could they be then? I'm certain they were in a cave with a snow-covered entrance. Could they still be in hiding, or are they on a different continent entirely?

Taryn takes a bite of the carrot. "Oh, wow. This is amazing. You grow these here? In the snow?"

Gherhardt smiles. "We have our ways. I will show you tomorrow. For now, I'm sure you are famished."

He ladles the three of us a healthy serving of stew, and even fishes out a few pieces of meat from the pot for Ruby. The warm bowl in my hands is a welcome feeling, and my stomach growls as the smell overtakes me. Limery doesn't hesitate, slurping away at the piping hot broth.

Item. Gherhardt's Famous Stew. *+3 Constitution for one hour.*

I don't know if it's because this is the first real meal I've had after a long day of traveling, but the stew is so delicious that for a moment, I lose focus on everything around me as I devour the entire bowl. I thought Kea's stew from the troll village was good, but this is on a different level. The meat is soft and flavorful, yet the carrots and other vegetables have a crunch that adds complexity to the dish. There's a spiciness to the broth that packs a punch but isn't overwhelming. The Constitution bonus has my body feeling rejuvenated in seconds.

I tilt the bowl, letting the last drops of broth pour into my mouth. "This was amazing."

"I'll let the cook know." Gherhardt winks. "He carefully cultivates the spices for many of our signature dishes. Would you like some more?"

I enthusiastically accept, taking more time to savor the next bowl. Gherhardt watches us as we eat, the sounds of slurping and the crackle of fire filling the silence before he speaks.

"The dwarves that came here, they mentioned a council hosted by the dwarven king of Seascape. I'm assuming that's why you are here?"

I set my bowl down, ready to finally discuss important matters. "Partly. Many of the leaders have agreed to form an alliance. King Orso fears dark times are coming, and he wants us to be prepared."

"Dark times." He chuckles. "Times have been dark in Frostmoor for many years. Giants run free across the lowlands. The Snowwalkers have been displaced by hobgoblins. My ancestors sent our best to fight alongside the other portals once, and we pay the price for it now. Where was this alliance when Frostmoor suffered?"

I can't fault him for his views, but this is bigger than what happened in the past.

"A behemoth crossed the portal." Taryn sits up straight. "It took dozens of the strongest fighters in Seascape to bring it down. What happens if one comes to Frostmoor?"

Gherhardt crosses his arms. "All the more reason for our men to stay here."

Taryn huffs and leans forward, passion burning in his eyes. "I can't speak for what happened in the past. All I know is that King Orso is a good leader. The portal to Seascape was open for less than a day before he started making plans. If you need help in Frostmoor, he will send it. We can help with the giants and hobgoblins, so long as you aid us when the time comes. That is all we ask."

Gherhardt's joyous eyes are lost in thought for a moment. "He would do that?"

Taryn places a fist over his chest. "On my honor."

He nods. "Then I will consider your proposal. Now tell me, what other news do you bring?"

We spend over an hour telling Gherhardt about the other heroes, how we came to be here, our suspected connections of certain events to the dark wizard, and finally Jude and Glenn.

Gherhardt strokes the forks of his beard. "They haven't been here, but who is to say they haven't traveled to one of the other peaks."

Limery unleashes a belch so deep that I can't believe it came out of something so tiny.

"Sorries." He covers his mouth with slender red fingers. "Limmy is fulls now."

"It's about time." I gently poke his bulging stomach before returning my attention to Gherhardt. "If there is a possibility they are on the other peaks, then we will have to investigate. I can't leave here unless we know for sure."

Gherhardt frowns. "The Snowwalkers are a shadow of their former glory, even compared to us. I cannot say if they will welcome you or not. They have lost a great deal. As for the others, that is unwise, even for heroes."

"We'll take our chances. For what's coming, we'll need to grow stronger. We need stronger enemies to do that." I grin. "And it seems you could use fewer frost giants stealing your hunts."

His frown vanishes. "There is a truth to that. If you'd be willing, I am sure we can find use of your services in Whitgard before you leave."

Taryn downs the rest of his mead. "Say no more. We love a good quest."

"Excellent." Gherhardt claps his hands together and stands. "Then let me show you to your quarters. My ancestors had large families, so there are plenty of rooms to go around."

"And what about you?" I ask. "Do you have a family?" There's no evidence of anyone else here, but we did arrive late. Perhaps they are sleeping.

"I have no wife or children of my own. Maybe one day. There is enough for me to do in Whitgard without the added burden of a family. The village needs me." He leads us down a stone hallway and up a flight of stairs.

Taryn and I take adjacent rooms. We say our goodnights and I close the door. Wood knocks against stone as both Taryn and Gherhardt bar their doors. I follow suit. Better safe than sorry.

The room is simple, with a wood-framed bed covered in an assortment of furs. A table topped with a candle sits to one side and a dresser to another. A large hide covers the floor in front of the bed and a small fire crackles in a fireplace on the opposite wall.

The stone floor is cool against my feet, but at least the fire will keep us warm.

I crawl in bed, and Limery curls up underneath my arm like a small furnace. It's crazy to me how far he and I have come since my first days in Mythos.

"Did you ever think that after trying to steal my necklace that we would end up traveling together to other portals and seeing distant lands?"

He touches the Tiger's Eye Pendant hanging from my neck and lets out a demonic laugh. "Limmy never thoughts he would leave homes. But now he has traveled lots with Chods. Farther than Mommy or Theo or Daddy."

"Do you miss them?"

He scrunches his bulbous yellow eyes for a moment as he thinks. "Oh yes. Limmy miss thems all. But Limmy loves Chods and loves the adventures. Mommy and Daddy just wants Limmy to be happy."

My words catch in my throat as I think about my own family. I've lost count of how long I've been in Isle of Mythos, but I still haven't heard a word from them. I wonder if they've even checked in with Valery. Do they have any idea what I've been through? They arranged this, saving me from actual jailtime, but have they put in the slightest effort to find out how I'm actually doing? Do they even know I'm still logged in weeks after my sentence was over?

I'm pulled from my thoughts when Limery climbs onto my chest, his gaze fixated on me.

"Is yous okays, Chods?" His eyes radiate concern.

I snap out of my pity party. It doesn't matter what they're doing. None of it matters. Because everything that's important to me is inside Mythos.

"Yeah, buddy, I'm okay. Let's get some sleep. I'm sure we've got a big day tomorrow."

I close my eyes and let the crackle of fire lure me to sleep.

13. A DASH OF SPICE

A loud banging on the door wakes me. Limery groans as I roll over him to check who it is.

The room is chilly, the fire nothing more than embers as I lumber to the door. "Who is it?"

"Does it matter?" Taryn taunts me from the other side. "What do you have to be afraid of?"

He has a point. I'm a pretty scary-looking troll, so it's not like I'm going to get robbed at knifepoint while I'm half-asleep.

I lift the wooden beam from the door, where Taryn waits impatiently on the other side.

"Let's go. Breakfast is calling." Taryn turns to head downstairs, Ruby trailing at his heels.

Limery lands on my shoulder, suddenly wide awake and grinning. "Time for breakfasts!"

The smell of roasted meat wafts up the stairs as we descend to the first floor.

Gherhardt leans over the fire, prodding a pan filled with sausage and eggs. "We rise early around here." Ruby stands at his feet, nose sniffing at the pan. "Get your fill and then I'll show you around the village."

Once we finish eating, Gherhardt leads us outside. Frigid wind assaults us as we step out into a bright morning. The sky is cloudless overhead, and the sun ignites the landscape.

In the daylight, the town looks as rustic as ever. Dozens of slate-gray stone buildings pepper the landscape between the palisade and the mountain cliff. A handful of people move about, fur hoods concealing most of their faces. A few stop in their tracks as they see us. Several nod to Gherhardt as we pass. There are no signs detailing the function of each building, making it difficult to determine what services Whitgard actually offers.

"Follow me. In exchange for your services, we'll outfit you in clothing more suitable for these parts." Gherhardt leads us to a building with a bear head mounted on the door.

Inside, a middle-aged woman sits at a table sewing two fur pelts together. Several racks hold fur coats, and shelves have blankets in different colors and sizes.

Her eyes go wide when she sees us. "So it is true."

Gherhardt shakes his head, turning to us. "Word travels fast around here. I swear they all have one hand sewn to their ears trying to catch the next piece of gossip."

"Oh, Gherhardt, we're not that bad." She flicks her wrist at him. "What can I do for you?"

"These three will be helping out around the village. I'd like for them not to freeze to death in the process."

She abandons her project and steps closer, eyeing us up and down. She points to Taryn. "Some of the children's clothing should fit you nicely."

I cough to keep from laughing, but Taryn still glares at me.

"And for you..." She points to Limery. "Amara and Flint's daughter has outgrown her last set of furs. They should be the perfect size."

"It's okays, Limmy doesn't needs furs." He conjures a fireball in his palm and the woman takes a step back.

"Hmm, I suppose not." She focuses on me, her eyes wide with a mixture of caution and wonder. "How about you?"

"I'd be grateful for something warmer." I smile, but it does nothing to ease her tension.

She pulls a rope from her pocket and uses it to measure from my waist to my ankles. Her hands shake slightly when I crouch for her to take the rest of my measurements.

She grabs a few pieces of fur from one of the shelves and places it on the table. "Give me a few hours and I should have something for you. I don't keep anything on hand for someone of your size."

"That will be fine." Gherhardt pats me on the shoulder. "I think he can survive a while longer. Our next stop is indoors. Thank you, Maud."

Taryn changes into his new fur cloak and fur-lined boots. He loses the effects of the enchanted boots and cloak that he acquired in King Orso's vault, but for the time being, the new items are more practical, especially if we're going to be actually working in the snow.

I wrap my arm around him as we exit the tailor's shop. "It's adorable that you can still shop in the little boys' section."

"Shut up, Chode." He whacks me in the knee with his staff.

Pain sparks through my knee, but the joke was worth it.

With the sun out, the chill isn't quite as bad except for when a gust of wind comes down the mountain. We pass a forge, where smoke pours out of a chimney on top. A stout man with a braided brown beard wears a sleeveless fur tunic. He pounds a hammer against a piece of metal sitting on an anvil, a rhythmic clank echoing with each hit. His arms are nothing but thick, corded muscle and steam shoots out of his mouth with each heave.

He glances at us as we pass but doesn't skip a beat.

At the end of the row of stone buildings, there's a greenhouse filled with plants. It's hidden in the depths of the village, nestled against the towering cliff. Water trickles from the roof as snow melts in the sun.

"You guys have a greenhouse?" Taryn stares at the building in astonishment.

Gherhardt looks around, confused. "None of our houses are green."

"No, this." He points at the glass building.

"Ah, this is our growing barn." Gherhardt beams with pride. "A gift from the gnomes of Pruxford many ages ago. It has served our people well. The enchanted glass not only keeps the heat inside at a suitable temperature, but it is also unbreakable."

"Really?" Taryn taps the glass with his finger. "Unbreakable glass?"

"Truly. Go ahead, give it a try."

Taryn looks uncertain for a moment before he swings his staff at the glass pane. The Sapling Staff clinks against the glass. "Impressive."

"Now, you try." Gherhardt gestures to me.

"Are you sure? No offense, but I'm a lot stronger than Taryn."

"Brains over brawn," Taryn mutters.

I resist the urge to taunt him about his small cloak.

"Our growing barn has survived far worse." Gherhardt takes a step back. "Give it your best."

Limery hops from my shoulder, and I equip Destroyer, taking position next to the greenhouse. I shake my head as I lift the warhammer. There's no way that the glass can withstand my enchanted weapon. It seems silly that Gherhardt would risk his people's food supply for a demonstration. But I can tell by the look in his eyes that he's not taking no for an answer.

I swing and close my eyes as the hammer makes impact. There's a loud clink and the force reverberates up my arm. I take a deep breath, thankful that Gherhardt's word was true.

He laughs. "I hear that the capital city of Pruxford is filled with so much glass that it looks like it was carved from ice. Now, come inside. This is where I do my finest work."

I allow Taryn to walk ahead of me. "That sounds beautiful. Maybe we will adventure there someday."

"Ah, to be a hero with the freedom to travel wherever adventure calls and your heart desires. I relished the tales of great heroes as a child. Perhaps someday, tales of your great deeds will entertain young ones as they lay down to sleep."

"I like the sound of that." Taryn grins. "Why don't you visit Pruxford yourself?"

Gherhardt's face goes somber. "Being the Head of the Frozen Ash Tribe comes with many responsibilities. I do not have the luxury to follow whims, but I do take joy in my work in the growing barn."

"Uncle Gher!" A young woman with straw-colored hair peeks out from behind a bush covered in red berries. "Oh!" She gasps when she notices the rest of us.

"Don't be alarmed, Liyah. I'm just showing our guests around town. Everyone, this is my niece Liyah. She is one of our best growers."

She steps out from behind the bush, her gray tunic stained with dirt. "Don't listen to him. Uncle Gher loves the growing barn more than anything. If he didn't have to run the village, he'd never leave this place. His spice plants are like children to him."

"Spices?" I remember him making a comment about the spices in the stew last night. "Are you the spice master?"

He gives us a wide grin. "Guilty. Come take a look."

I activate my herbalism skill as he points out a variety of plants, and the skill quickly advances a level.

Congratulations! You have leveled up the skill 'Herbalism.' You are now a level 7 Herbalist (Apprentice). Increase your skill and learn advanced techniques for herbalism by finding an advanced herbalist (journeyman or above). Ranks: Novice, Apprentice, Journeyman, Expert, Artisan, Master, Grandmaster.

"These over here are strictly for flavor. The growing barn has been in use for ages, but the art of growing exotic spices and herbs were lost to our people. Until one day, many years ago, we found a bag of old seeds in one of our cellars, and Whitgard cuisine has never been the same. I've managed to harvest seeds from each crop and now provide enough spices for the entire village. Thanks to the power of the growing barn, we grow spices found all over Mythos."

He points from one plant to another, giving us details about the flavor profile of Desert Needle, Fire Mustard, Berry Pepper, Tartmint, and many more. He dishes out so much knowledge that my herbalism skill increases another level. If I were a chef or potion master, this knowledge would be invaluable.

He takes us to another section of the greenhouse where the produce grows. There's enough ripe fruits and vegetables to fill a farmers market.

"This is one of my favorites." He plucks a handful of red berries from the bush and hands one to each of us. "Torchberry."

I examine the berry. It's a vibrant red with streaks of orange running vertically.

Gherhardt pops one in his mouth and we all follow suit. Immediately, a warm sensation fills my throat, working its way down to my stomach. It's not spicy. The berry itself is quite sweet, but the warmth continues to expand inside of me.

"Whoa, that's intense." I hold up a hand as he offers another one.

Limery greedily accepts.

"They're the perfect cure for a cold day. They're also a key ingredient in Torchmead."

"This is amazing!" Taryn claps his hands together. "Your herbalism skill must be through the roof. What level are you?"

Gherhardt makes an attempt to be modest. "I'm sure you've seen many plants on your travels. I'm but a lowly artisan."

Artisan. That means his herbalism skill is somewhere between level thirty-one and forty. Only master and grandmaster are above him.

Taryn clasps his hands together. "I'm only a journeyman. If you will teach me, I'd love to learn more."

Gherhardt nods. "Help us around the village, and it shall be done."

He leads us deeper into the greenhouse when someone bursts through the door.

A young man with a patchy beard pants for breath. "Gherhardt! It's Alvyn. He's having a fit again."

Gherhardt brushes past me. "I'll be right there. Prepare the ice balm."

The young man's face goes a stark white. "We're out."

"What do you mean you're out?" Gherhardt grabs him by the tunic. "I told you to warn Archard when you were low and he would go acquire the necessary ingredients."

The young man's head sinks. "I thought we had more. I'm sorry."

Gherhardt slams his fist on the table, shaking several of the plants. "Sorry is not good enough. With no setbacks, it will take four days to summit Icemaw and return. That's with fair weather, little sleep, and no run-in with giants. Do you think Alvyn has four days?"

The young man shakes his head. "I don't know."

"Go and find Archard. I'll have him do what he can."

Under Gherhardt's stiff gaze, the young man looks more like a child. I'm certain he would vanish into thin air if he could.

"Now!"

The kid nearly bumps into a table of spices as he rushes out of the greenhouse.

"What's going on?" asks Taryn. "Is there anything we can do to help?"

Gherhardt sighs. "Alvyn is one of the village elders. He has a condition that requires a special elixir whenever he has a fit. One of the ingredients—arctic clove —only grows in one place in all of Frostmoor: Icemaw, the territory of the frost giants. It usually takes Archard a week to locate it in order to avoid detection. We'll do what we can, but I'm afraid we don't have that much time."

"Can you describe the plant to me?" asks Taryn, and I already know what he's thinking.

"I appreciate the offer." He grabs Taryn on the shoulder and squeezes. "But if Archard cannot make it in time, I fear no one can. He knows these mountains better than anyone."

"It's not about that." Taryn stares him down. "Describe the plant to me and give me a location. I'll fly there. I'll make it in a quarter of the time."

"Fly?" He scrunches his eyes. "Are dwarves made with wings now?"

Using Transform, Taryn turns into a red bird and sits on Gherhardt's shoulder. Liyah gasps, and her uncle curses under his breath. There's an explosion of feathers and Taryn returns to his dwarven form once more.

Taryn crosses his arms. "Now are you going to tell me what to do or not?"

Archard comes stomping through the door just as Gherhardt finishes describing the arctic clove to Taryn. "I've prepped the goat. I'll be back as quick as possible, but I doubt I'll be able to avoid detection. Things could get messy." He sighs. "One job. He had one job."

Gherhardt holds up a hand. "There's been a change of plans. Our dwarven hero will be flying to Icemaw in your stead. I've described the plant to him, but you'll have to tell him the rest."

Archard nods. "The arctic clove grows beyond the encampment of the frost giants, high in the peak. You will have to bypass the frost giants. But you must beware, there are other terrors beyond the giants. In your bird form, I fear for your safety."

"Limery will go with him," I interrupt, and they all turn to me. "If he wants to. I can't force him, but I remember what happened with the mountain trolls when you were shot down by goblins. If something happens, you need someone to look out for you."

Even though his bird form is small, he'll stick out like a beacon against the white landscape.

Limery grins. "Okays. I goes with Taryns."

My stomach feels uneasy at the thought of them both going into unknown territory. With me and Taryn's pets, I feel confident in our abilities, especially with my horrors. But the two of them against an angry group of frost giants that likely out-level them... I watched Taryn die once in Goldspire, and Limery... I would never forgive myself if something happened to him.

Taryn must sense my inner turmoil because he comes over and pats me on the arm. "Don't worry about it, big guy. We'll be back before you know it."

Archard fills them in on the rest of the details, and pretty soon, they're ready to go.

Limery wraps his warm arms around me as we stand at the gate.

"Take care of one another." I pull Taryn aside. "If it's too dangerous, promise me you'll turn back."

"Hey." His face is set in stone. "I'm not going to let anything happen to him. You just try not to let the place go to shit while we're gone."

I laugh at his poor attempt at a joke. "I'll do my best."

There's an explosion of feathers and then the two of them are soaring through the sky.

"Alright," Gherhardt calls from over my shoulder. "Time to put you to work."

14. WORK, WORK, WORK, WORK

We stop by Maud's, who has managed to sew a cloak capable of covering me from head to toe. With the hood pulled up, I look more like Bigfoot than a troll as I trek through the village, but I have to admit it does an amazing job of taking the chill from the wind. Maud even managed to sew me a pair of moccasins with slits for my claws to poke through. I much prefer the freedom of my loincloth, or battle skirt, and I'll be ditching these the moment we're in a warmer climate, but they do a lot for my quality of life at the moment.

I catch a few stares from the townsfolk after we drop Ruby off at the stables, but Gherhardt assures me they are all just confirming the gossip for themselves.

"There's not much to do in a village besides work and gossip. And the work is never done." He stops in front of a building at the edge of town. "You'll be working with Dando today. He's one of our village craftsmen. Don't let his age fool you, he's one of the best and brightest. Tomorrow is our annual goat race and we need the trail cleared. We had a heavy snowfall a few days ago, so it's probably tougher than usual. I'm sure he can use the extra help."

Quest alert. *You have been offered the quest 'Clear the Trail.' The Ascent is an ancient tradition of the Frozen Ash Tribe, and every spring, young men race frost goats along the mountain pass. Help remove snow from the trail and increase your standing with Whitgard.*

Reward. *Increased favor with the Frozen Ash Tribe.*

He knocks on the door before entering. Inside, a young man stuffs tools into a satchel. I'm surprised by how tall he is. He's well over six feet and lanky, with brown hair trimmed close, bright blue eyes, and a face as clean-shaven as a baby that only adds to his youthful appearance.

"Gherhardt, I was just heading ou—" He freezes in place when he sees me.

I should probably be used to that reaction by now.

"I brought you some help." Gherhardt gestures to me. "This is Chod. His companions are on another quest for the village. You might not tell it by looking at him, but he packs some muscle underneath these furs."

Dando lets out a nervous laugh at Gherhardt's joke. "Sorry for my rudeness, I've just... We don't get many outsiders around here. Nice to meet you. I'm Dando."

His honesty catches me by surprise. I forget that I'm not an alien to these people, just a foreigner. They are all well aware that other races exist even if they've never seen one in person.

"Don't worry about it. You can call me Chod." I extend my hand and we shake. "Ready to get to work?"

"The snow's certainly not going to shovel itself." He grins at Gherhardt. "Give Liyah my best, will you?"

"You gentlemen have fun." I'm not sure if Gherhardt intentionally disregards Dando's words for Liyah or not. "And, Chod, when you're finished, come find me. I'll have your next quest waiting."

Dando seems to loosen up once we are outside. "We'll stop by the stables to grab a pair of goats and then I'll show you the track."

"Sounds good. So, what's the deal with the race anyhow? And why goats?"

He laughs. "It's tradition. It's called the Ascent, and we do it every year to commemorate the tale of Umen the Steadfast's victory over Edrar Snowwalker. Legend says that Umen and Edrar were brothers born from the ice, and that when they cracked themselves free of its frozen embrace, they were tasked by the gods with settling the five peaks. Both of them wanted Whitgard as their home so they came to an agreement that the first one to climb the summit would claim the mountain for themselves."

We arrive at the stables, but Dando stops in front of the gate to continue his story. "Edrar had special boots that allowed him to walk on the snow without sinking, so he quickly outpaced Umen as they climbed the mountain. But Umen was cunning and had a way with beasts, so he captured a wild frost goat and mounted it. The goat ascended with ease, and by the time Edrar knew he was being overtaken, it was already too late.

"Edrar was a prideful man, and the thought of losing angered him. He nocked his arrow and fired upon the goat, piercing it several times. But frost goats are sturdy creatures, and the goat continued its ascent, leaving a trail of red in its wake."

Dando is so into the story that he begins acting out the scenes as they happen. "The goat collapsed as Umen reached the peak and claimed victory over his brother. He offered to roast the goat as a peace offering between the two. With his anger abated, Edrar agreed to settle one of the other peaks. No sooner had they taken their first bite when a shrill screech echoed from above and blue flames descended." Dando flaps his arms like wings. "A white dragon burned the trees they were using for cover and stole the goat for its own. And as Umen built the first home in the frozen ashes of that feast, so our tribe was named."

"Wow." I give him a round of applause for his storytelling. "Now that's a good story! Why didn't the other tribe get a cool name?"

He shrugs. "I guess Edrar was a sore loser."

As we enter the stable, a silver falcon swoops in to perch on top of the roof. It could probably pluck Taryn out of the air with no problem. I can't help but wonder what other dangerous creatures might be lurking outside the village walls.

Berry groans from the far end so I go and pay him a visit. He stands on his hind legs against the railing so that I can scratch him behind the ears.

"Don't worry. Taryn will be back before you know it. He's got Limery with him for protection."

Stompy leans against the stone wall of the barn, paying me no mind, with Ruby curled behind one of his massive legs. How she got here, I have no idea.

One of the stableboys ogles at me as he sweeps manure into a bucket.

"Are they behaving themselves?" I ask.

He gulps. "Yes, sir. They're well behaved, sir."

I leave the young man alone before he has a heart attack and go find Dando.

The young craftsman waits for me at the stable entrance with two goats unlike any I have ever seen. They have thick white fur, black faces with bright blue eyes, and black horns that curl around their heads. The horns fade from a deep black at the base to an icy blue at the tip.

Each goat is as big as a cow, and I can't think of any reason why Archard doesn't have them pulling his wagon. One of the goats steps closer to the other and there's a crack like a gunshot as the second goat rams its horns into the other's. The first goat rears on its back legs, and Dando grabs it by the reins, pulling it away.

"Hey!" His voice is stern and commanding. "Enough of that." He separates the two enraged goats like he's done it a million times and hands a pair of leather reins to me. "Here, take this one. Frost goats are powerful and graceful creatures, but they tend to butt heads, so to speak. They'll be the safest way to travel up the mountain, though."

I glance up at the peak that disappears among the clouds. "How far up the mountain are we going?"

He cocks an eyebrow. "To the top. How else are we going to properly honor the legend of Umen and Edrar if not by following in their ancient footsteps?"

Warley is on gate duty as we leave Whitgard. He stares at Dando with nearly as much hatred as he does me but says nothing as he slams the gate.

"What's his problem?" I ask as I climb onto my frost goat.

"Jealousy." Dando rolls his eyes. "We fancy the same girl."

I guess Liyah must be the catch of the town. "And Gherhardt, what does he think about all of this?"

"Gherhardt likes me well enough when I'm not making eyes at Liyah, but of course no one is good enough for his niece." Dando leans toward me, a bit of mischief in his eyes. "Warley would have better luck setting fire to a snowball. Liyah can't stand him." Dando laughs.

I grin at his antics. "I can see why. He certainly seems to have a chip on his shoulder."

Our goats are slow and steady as they move up the mountain. We make sure to give them plenty of space between one another to keep their bravado in check.

"I try not to hold it against him." Dando frowns as he looks out into the distance. "I'm sure he feels a lot of pressure to live up to his father's legacy. He manned the gate for thirty years."

Family issues are something I can definitely relate to. I'm sure I've done my fair share of dickish moves because of them, too. "What happened to his father?"

"A frost giant wandered up the mountain one night while the elder Warley was at the gate. The giant kicked in the gate. Elder Warley was able to sound the alarm, but at the cost of not being able to defend himself for a few seconds. Gherhardt and the others responded quickly, but it was too late for Warley's father. The giants haven't come to Whitgard since, but they give Archard hell every time he goes for a hunt."

"That's terrible. I'm sure he feels a lot of pressure to live up to his father."

Dando nods. "Archard and some of the others are less forgiving. I mean, he can be annoying as a hobgoblin, but I try to look past it."

I don't know why I'm so surprised by Dando's understanding, but I am. It's not often you find wisdom in someone so young.

It doesn't take long before the trail is obscured entirely by snow.

Dando climbs from his goat and opens the saddle bag. "We'll start here and work our way up." He tosses me a shovel. "Let's put those big blue muscles to use."

The work is slow going, shoveling snow off the side of the mountain. I can't help but think of how quickly Limery could have cleared this entire path if he was here, but I'm glad he's with Taryn. As long as they are smart, I doubt they'll get into trouble. Plus, Taryn can message me if something goes wrong.

After about five minutes of shoveling, I decide to work smarter, not harder. "Don't freak out, but I'm going to bring in some reinforcements."

He gives me a questioning look, and I summon a Horror of Power. The muscled golden horror appears in a puff of smoke and Dando's mouth drops open. The horror's barbed tail swings back and forth as it paces through the snow, its black mane swaying in the breeze.

There's a huff nearby just before one of the goats charges the horror, ramming into it and snuffing out its life in an instant.

"What the hell was that about?" I shout as Dando reins in the crazed beast.

He pets the creature on the nose until the rage leaves its eyes. "What did you think was going to happen? The frost goats are here for our protection."

"Protection? I thought they were for carrying tools up the mountain."

He places a hand over his eyes. "No disrespect, but I could carry a shovel on my own. Frost goats are not work animals. They are natural protectors capable of punting anything that might attack us straight off the mountainside. With one above and one below, we can work in peace."

I'm a little embarrassed I didn't think of that. Most of the Frozen Ash tribe is so strong compared to those on Isle of Mythos that I didn't think they would need special protection. But just because they're high level doesn't mean they're all natural fighters.

I scratch my chin as I try to find a solution. "Well, is there any way we can tie them up behind us? I can make this go a lot faster if they aren't killing my horrors."

He rubs his baby smooth cheeks. "And what if something comes for us?"

A laugh escapes before I can stifle it. "If it gets past me and my horrors, then your goats never stood a chance."

"Are you really that strong?"

I flex my arms, but the effect isn't as impressive when I'm covered in fur. "These babies aren't for show."

With the frost goats tied up further down the trail, I summon as many horrors as I can. They work their way through the snow, scooping it and tossing it off the mountainside. The Horror of Power shovels mounds of snow between its legs like a dog digging through sand at the beach. As the time begins to expire on each horror, I move them further up the trail and cast Kamikaze, exploding them and removing even more snow.

Dando stabs his shovel into the snow and leans against the handle. "Wow, I've never cleared the trail this fast before! We'll be done before dinner at this rate."

We take a break for lunch while the horrors continue to work. Dando pulls out strips of jerky, bread, and a bright yellow melon.

I take the bread and jerky but leave the melon to Dando. "Where do you get the meat from? I find it hard to believe that Archard is hunting enough to feed a village the size of Whitgard."

"Gherhardt didn't show you the caves?" My look of confusion prompts him to continue. "We raise snowhogs and chickens in the caves at the base of Whitgard. There's a natural mana source that keeps the cave at a stable temperature even on the coldest of nights, and it provides a special grass that grows without sunlight. It's the main reason we don't starve."

That's fascinating. If there's a ley line running through the mountain, I wonder if that means there are dungeons in the area. What I would do for a map of Frostmoor with all the ley lines marked like the one Chief Rizza gave me.

"This place is full of surprises." I take a bite out of the jerky. It has a spicy flavor I can't quite place, no doubt from one of Gherhardt's spices.

I explode two horrors and then summon more to replace them while Dando packs away the leftover food. He starts to stand, but then sits down on the boulder again.

He hesitates for a moment before speaking. "You know, I've always wondered what drives heroes to risk their lives for adventure. Is there a big blue lady troll waiting for you back home? Is that why you are doing all this?"

The question comes so far out of left field that I laugh. Dando immediately frowns, and I do my best to get a hold of myself. I can't even remember the last time I had romantic feelings for someone. Probably my last train wreck of a date.

"I'm sorry, no, it's just that that's about the last thing on my mind. With all the adventuring and quests, my priorities have been elsewhere."

He gives me a questioning look. "If you're not doing this for a woman, then what's the point?"

I sit there for a moment gathering my words. I get what he's saying, but I don't buy it. I remember, a few summers ago, binge-watching a slew of superhero movies with Taryn. There was almost always a love interest that would drive the hero to be stronger or better than they would be on their own. In the hero's moment of weakness, they would think of this person and get the power to go on.

I believe that love has the power to make someone strive to be better, to fight against the dark when all hope seems lost, but it doesn't have to be romantic love. It can be the love of a friend or family. Or a community. Hell, it can be for no other reason than because someone refuses to have their future dictated for them. But for me, why do I do all this? Why am I still in this game when I could have logged out a long time ago?

"I do it for my people."

He nods, his face solemn. "There are rumors around the village that a darkness is coming. That the dwarves brought grave news from abroad. Is this true?"

I don't know if it's my place to tell him or not, but I do it anyway. "Something is happening. We don't know the full extent yet, but we're warning who we can, gathering allies for when the time comes."

He clenches his fist. "If there's anything I can do to make sure this darkness doesn't spread to Whitgard, sign me up."

I appreciate his enthusiasm. I'm certain that he's thinking about Liyah the same way I'm thinking about the forest trolls. He'll do anything to protect her. And at level seventeen, he's actually pretty formidable compared to a lot of NPCs I've met on Isle of Mythos.

Still, it's not my place to recruit individual soldiers. "You can talk to Gherhardt about it later."

It's not the answer he wants to hear, but he accepts it. We return to work, and within a few hours, the tip of the peak is within view. The trail ends and a hundred yards of steep rocky terrain is all that stands between us and a stone platform surrounded by a ring of trees. Dense firs grow on each side of the rocky path, framing the final ascent.

"Wow, I still can't believe we've cleared the trail so fast. The rest of this—" He points to the jagged rocks that lead up to the platform. "—is where the race takes place. Wait until you see the goats climb it. It's really something—"

A howl erupts from above, echoing off the surrounding mountains. Dando takes a step back and I instinctively equip Destroyer while recalling horrors to my side.

A level-twenty frost wolf peeks out from the tree line. It steps forward, carefully navigating the rocky incline. A moment later, four more wolves exit the wooded area. Their blue-and-white fur conceals them well against the snow-covered trees.

"This is why we bring the goats." Dando's voice is higher-pitched than normal.

"Go untie them. I'll hold off the wolves."

Dando takes off running down the trail. The biggest frost wolf, sensing its prey escaping, leaps over the rocks after him.

A Horror of Finesse greets the wolf, but it chomps off my horror's head, destroying it in one bite. A Horror of Vitality slows the wolf with its passive, and a Horror of Power gores its tusk into the wolf's hind leg. The wolf yelps, and the rest of the pack leaps down to protect their leader.

There's a mixture of snarls and growling as my horrors swarm in a frenzy, but the wolves hold their own. It took our entire party and my horrors to defeat twice this number at the base. Taking five on by myself might not have been the smartest idea.

The wolves' health bars trickle down, but their incredible Constitution means they'll outlast my horrors in a sustained fight. Eventually, I won't be able to summon horrors quick enough to attack in force.

Time for me to turn the tide while I still can.

I cast Champion, and a clone of the frost wolf I killed at the base of the mountain forms in front of me. It snarls at the other wolves, and I unleash its fury on them.

Hooves trample against the cleared path behind me as the cavalry arrives. With the frost goats, along with my champion wolf and horrors, we should be able to take care of this handily.

The first goat passes me by, head lowered as it charges into battle.

It collides with my champion like a battering ram, and the unexpected force launches the wolf off the edge of the mountain.

You have got to be shitting me.

The presence of the horror grows less and less as it tumbles down the cliff before fading entirely.

The second goat plows into a group of horrors clinging to a wolf. The horrors shoot through the air like confetti and the wolf is knocked back. Several horrors tumble off the mountainside and the other wolves chomp at more as they fall back to earth.

Dando apologizes frantically behind me, but I tune him out. The second goat elicits a shrill yelp as it rams into the shoulder of a frost wolf. It then kicks out with its hind legs, knocking more horrors away.

The goats attack in a blind rage, not caring if they hit wolves or horrors, or occasionally each other.

I grip my warhammer and activate Berserker Rage. Steam shoots out from underneath my cloak and it pulls tight against my skin as my muscles bulge. If I want this done right, it looks like I'm going to have to do it myself.

I rush into battle, grabbing the first goat by the horn and pulling it away. It tries to ram me when I let go, but it meets the head of my hammer. Red streaks through the weapon as Inferno activates and the goat charges again. A second hit knocks the goat back further and its knees buckle.

It stands up, woozy, and Dando grabs it by the reins.

Just as I turn around, a wolf lunges at me. I sidestep, dodging the attack and landing a hit to the ribs that sends the beast over the cliff.

One down, four to go.

The free goat runs rampant, kicking and ramming, hitting horrors and wolves. Two of the wolves have squared off with the goat, and the other two have turned their attention toward me.

"Bring it!" I roar, and they answer the call.

The two wolves leap over the small mound of horrors standing between us. Steam rises from Destroyer like an erupting volcano as it grows hotter from each consecutive hit.

With the increased power from Berserker Rage, I hit the first wolf with enough force that it smashes into the second. The second wolf tumbles to the edge of the trail and rolls off without ever gaining its footing. The first wolf follows it, but rolls over at the last second, gripping the ledge with its front paws as it tries to climb up.

Three horrors tackle it off the ledge.

I'm down to a handful of horrors that do their best to avoid hurting the goat while also attacking the wolves. One wolf has pinned the goat to the ground and has its teeth sunk in the thick fur around the goat's neck. As far as I can tell, there's no blood.

Yet.

I leave them to their stalemate while I deal with wolf number four.

The wolf backs against the row of rocks that mark the beginning of the race. Icy blue fur arches in spikes across its shoulders reminiscent of icicles. I twist Destroyer's handle against my palm as I wait for the threatened creature to lunge.

When it does, I sidestep at the last second. It goes flying past me straight for Dando. His eyes go wide and he lets go of the frost goat. It rams into the wolf with pinpoint precision, propelling it off the ledge.

Berserker Rage ends, and there is only one wolf remaining. It still has the goat pinned to the ground, but no matter how much it adjusts its bite, the fur doesn't give. I can see now why they are such great protectors. Fast-twitch muscles for lightning-fast rams, hard heads, and fur that serves as natural armor and insulation.

The wolf eyes me as I approach, but it doesn't release. I switch to Forlorn Scepter and slide the end of the staff in the open space at the back of the wolf's teeth in order to pry its mouth open.

It releases, snapping at me before backing up defensively. The goat stumbles to its feet and shakes out its fur.

Our standoff only lasts a moment before the wolf bolts into the woods.

Dando runs past me, inspecting the goats matted fur for wounds. "That was nuts! You were... You were... That was crazy!"

I summon more horrors just in case something else shows up. "Are they okay?"

He pets one on the neck. "Oh yeah, these guys have saved my bacon more than once. Sorry about your pet wolf."

"Don't worry about it. The important thing is that we survived. With only one wolf left, I don't imagine it'll be causing problems anytime soon."

"Yeah, the wolves don't normally come up this high. I wonder what they were after."

I shrug. "Beats me. You ready to get out of here? I'm sure Gherhardt has more work waiting for me at the village."

After gathering up the tools and belongings that got tossed aside during the fight, we head down the mountain.

Ever since Taryn arrived, I've been more focused on fighting as a team than anything, but it's good to know I can still hold my own when I need to.

We're halfway back to the village when my notifications flash, telling me I have a new message.

Incoming Message (Taryn): *Yo, Chod. Can you let Gherhardt know we're not making it back tonight? Things got a little wild. We're stuck in a cave, but we'll be back as soon as possible. I'll tell you all about it when we get back.*

15. A WING AND A PRAYER

***Quest alert.** You have been offered the quest 'A Wing and a Prayer.' Alvyn, one of the village elders, is in dire need of a special elixir, but they have exhausted their supply of arctic clove. Time is running out. Fly to Icemaw, acquire the arctic clove, and return to Whitgard with haste.*

    ***Reward.** Increased favor with the Frozen Ash Tribe, and advanced herbalism training with Gherhardt.*

Taryn closed the quest notification for the tenth time since leaving the village. He'd been flush with quests after logging in at Seascape, but since grouping up with Chod and Limery, quests had been few and far between. He'd leveled up nicely fighting monsters and clearing dungeons, but there was something special about following a quest line to completion. At times, quest rewards were even greater than experience. Training with Gherhardt was an easy opportunity to dramatically increase his skillset. With a high enough herbalism skill, he could search for rare plants and either sell them at the market or use them for advanced potions and elixirs.

The latter sounded better. Their small group was pretty well-balanced, except for not having a healer. He had Restoration, but it only worked on his pets. If Taryn could level up his potion-making skill as well then that would be a major boost to their team composition.

For the third time since leaving, he and Limery stopped to rest on a tree limb. Unable to communicate with the imp in his bird form, he transformed back into a dwarf. Red feathers exploded around him, and the branch sank with the added weight. Snow fell, plopping against the ground.

His dwarven form was much warmer, and Taryn was thankful for the magical properties that allowed his clothing and items to remain on his body when switching between forms. Transforming from a bird to a naked dwarf in this weather would be a nightmare. The ability only allowed for Taryn to be in bird form for two hours at a time, so he was forced to return to his natural state before the countdown expired. His primary form didn't have a set cooldown, compared to an hour for other animal forms. This was the perfect opportunity to talk things over with the imp.

Limery wiped a bit of drool from his mouth and grinned. His bulbous yellow eyes watched Taryn intently.

Taryn was well-aware of Limery's fondness for birds, and he often wondered if the imp was imagining a dozen different ways to cook him up. Their first encounter often replayed through his mind—when Limery had pelted him with a fireball.

"Rest up, Taryns. We's still has a long ways to goes." He leaned forward, falling until he was hanging upside-down like a bat.

Taryn stretched his arms overhead, almost losing his balance. "I know, I know. Red birds weren't meant to fly long distances non-stop. I'll be ready in a second."

Constant flying took a lot out of his stamina. In his bird form, he was great at covering short distance and had amazing agility. But long flights were more suited to birds of prey than songbirds. Taryn had never seen Limery so much as break a sweat.

He had second-guessed his decision to make his mother's favorite animal his avatar before, but for all the inconveniences it caused, he still smiled every time he saw those red wings out of the corner of his eye.

He was doing all of this for them. And Chod.

Who was he kidding? He was mostly doing it because this was the opportunity of a lifetime. No one had access to this kind of tech. If he won the lottery, he'd never be able to repay Chod for this experience.

What was a little homesickness when he could literally fly?

"Alright, let's do this!" Taryn transformed into his bird form and took to the air.

Limery let go of the branch and fell face-first into the snow, melting an imp-sized crater. He giggled to himself before joining Taryn in the air.

Bird-eating antics aside, it was easy for Taryn to see why Chod loved the little guy so much. He was endearing in his own special way, like a cute puppy that could burn down a house with a flick of its paw.

He was a troublemaker, that's for sure. A gifted pickpocket with a love for shiny things. Taryn often imagined this is how humans would behave if they abandoned the ego and superego, giving in to the primitive desires of the id.

Limery slowed down for Taryn to catch up. They both knew where they were going, relatively speaking. Somewhere above the mouth of Icemaw, the arctic clove would be growing. Limery could have undoubtedly made it faster than Taryn, but he had practically no herbalism skill to speak of. He could probably have flown straight across the gap between the two peaks, but Taryn needed to recharge periodically, so they followed above the mountain path, resting when they needed.

Even so, they were making way better time than they could have possibly done on foot.

The enchanted path wound its way up the mountain, mana-infused torches burning every so often, but there were no travelers. They passed a lone giant dragging the carcass of a frost deer through the snow, but otherwise, the ascent had been pretty boring and didn't seem that dangerous.

Halfway up Icemaw, a heavy snow began to fall, obscuring the path and the torches. Even with his bird-vision, navigating became increasingly difficult. With no clear destination, they didn't have to worry about getting lost. As long as they kept going upward, they were heading in the right direction.

After a couple of hours of flying blindly, the downfall abated, leaving the world freshly painted in white. A warm sensation enveloped Taryn as hands plucked him from the air and pulled him to the ground. The heat quickly became unbearable, forcing Taryn to transform back into a dwarf.

"Limmy, what the hell?" Taryn shouted, but a hot hand pressed against his mouth.

"Quiets." He pulled Taryn behind a tree, incredibly strong to be so small, and pointed at the clearing up ahead. "Giantses."

Taryn squinted but saw nothing until a large figure moved against the mountainside. The level twenty-four giant was nearly invisible against his surroundings, its slate-gray skin streaked with patches of blue. White hair covered his shoulders and arms, matching the dense beard that hung from his bald head. The giants were bigger than the one they had fought in the Greystone Mountains. Was everything bigger in Frostmoor?

The giant pushed a massive boulder across the snow. It grunted, thick muscles bulging with every movement.

The longer he looked, the more giants he was able to spot. They blended in well with the landscape and ranged from level eighteen to thirty. A chill ran down Taryn's spine. If he and Limery were spotted, they were toast. Dozens of giants were scattered around the maw of the mountain, which was easily the size of a football field. It resembled a cave without walls, and icicles and stalactites hung from the roof of the mountain like giant teeth.

If one happened to fall, it could crush them like ants.

Many of the giants were sleeping, only the rising and falling of their chests indicated they were more than errant boulders. Two larger giants fought over the bone of some large beast. Strips of meat and tendon still hung from one end. A mother sat against an old tree stump feeding a young giant.

If Chod were here, he'd make a comment about it being as big as Taryn. He pretended those type of comments offended him to keep the banter going, but they both knew that this was temporary. The day he logged out, he would be six-feet tall and two-hundred pounds again, back to where his mere presence caused people to keep their distance or eye him warily whenever he entered a store.

Being a dwarf, it was nice to just fit in. An ebony dwarf was treated no less than an ivory, and they both agreed that there was something strange about the blood dwarves. How he looked didn't define him. His abilities did. When he did stand out, it wasn't because of his size or his skin color, it was because he was a hero. This was the first time in his life that strangers had treated him like royalty.

He wanted to hang on to that feeling for as long as possible.

A loud crash pulled Taryn from his thoughts. The two giants skirmishing over the bone had erupted into an all-out fight. One held the bone over its head about to swing. The other held his jaw and blue blood trickled from his mouth to the snow.

The injured giant grabbed a stalagmite by the tip and pulled. The large spear of rock cracked like thunder as it snapped, and the giant wielded it like a club. He roared something, but the words were lost in the wind.

The two giants swung for one another, and the stalagmite club shattered the bone club on impact. The battle reminded him of Chod's fight with Kronan after their run-in with the mountain trolls. Pure power and rage. A third giant rushed in, gesturing wildly at the other two, but the stalagmite-wielder swung for him as well.

Taryn turned to Limery, who watched with interest. "That's our cue to go. We don't want to get caught in a giant brawl."

They used the distraction to slip out the backside of the maw and up the mountain. The enchanted path ended at the maw, but there was a well-trodden path that led higher up. There was a clear area of devastation around the trail. Tracks of moved boulders, broken trees, and animal carcasses littered the landscape.

The maw was only about three-fourths of the way to the peak, so they still had plenty of area to cover, but they were getting close to where Archard had predicted they would find the arctic clove.

The plant thrived in the highest altitudes, and only grew on Icemaw. Gherhardt had tried to grow some in the greenhouse, and even attempted to relocate some to the area above Whitgard, but it refused to grow. Instead, Archard was forced to go search for more whenever Alvyn was running low.

Taryn laughed to himself. Being a ranger seemed a lot like being a glorified errand boy.

The mountain was clear of wildlife in the immediate vicinity around the maw. Any creature smart enough would give the frost giants a wide berth, which explained why the giants had been down far enough to catch Archard on a hunt.

As they flew higher up the mountain, the trail grew less and less noticeable. If not for the slight indentation, the fresh snow would have blotted it out entirely.

It spiraled around the mountain until Taryn was certain they were above the maw. Several caves tunneled into the mountain, and a dangerous-looking platform stretched out from the mountain into the clouds.

The sun was beginning to dip closer to the horizon. They only had an hour or two of daylight before it disappeared behind the peaks.

Taryn transformed into his dwarven form and walked out onto the natural platform of the maw. There wasn't much time to waste, but he basked in the beauty of his surroundings. From this high up, there were clouds floating beneath them. The portal into Frostmoor was nothing more than a speck against the white wilderness.

He went to find Limery, who had disappeared inside one of the caves, and activated herbalism so that he could spot any plants in the area.

A faint glow surrounded the plants he had learned to identify, many from the brief visit in the Whitgard greenhouse. They grew along the side of the mountain, an occasional sprig fighting through the snow. None of them were arctic clove, but he'd expected as much. Nothing was ever that easy.

"What are you looking for?" he asked Limery when he found him in the cave.

The imp landed and picked up a rock, examining it. "Chods saids that he found daddy in a caves. Limmy doesn't know what might be in the caves."

He rested a hand on the imp's shoulder. "Maybe we can explore some other time. Right now, we have a plant to locate."

Limery nodded and tossed the rock over his shoulder. It skipped along the cave, echoing several times over.

As they were about to exit, the ground shook and stone grated against stone from somewhere deep within the cavern.

Taryn equipped Sapling Staff and prepared for a fight. "What did you do?"

Had they awoken a giant sleeping in the depths of the cave?

Limery summoned two fireballs in his palms. "Limmy didn't do nothings."

Taryn pulled one of Jon the Enchanter's enchanted flashlight stones from his bag and activated it. Limery's fire was casting enough light to see by, but if he tossed them, they would be sitting in darkness. Taryn didn't have the night vision that Chod and Limery had.

He took the lead. "Let's check it out, but be cautious."

Part of him wanted to run up the mountain and get the quest over with, but he didn't want some unknown foe attacking them from behind. If they knew what they were dealing with, then at least they could prepare for it.

Taryn's heart raced. It was one thing to follow Chod and his horrors offering support. It was quite another thing entirely to be the front line of defense. Berry and Stompy usually had that covered, but they were a long way from helping. He had his mushrooms and Stonewall if they needed a quick exit, but he silently prayed whatever they had awoken would fall back to sleep.

Light played tricks on the eyes as they turned the corner, and the shadows of every rock or hanging strip of moss took on the appearance of an unknown threat.

His heart skipped a beat when Limery abruptly canceled his fireballs and bolted down the cavern.

Taryn rushed behind him as fast as his dwarven legs would carry him. Chod would never forgive him if something happened to the imp on his watch. He found Limery standing in front of an arch carved into the mountain. Fresh marks lined the floor where a door had opened, and runes glowed around the edge.

Icemaw Dungeon. *Would you like to enter?*

16. DUNGEONS AND DRAGONS SECOND EDITION

"But Limmy wants to sees the dungeons," the imp begged, hands clasped together in prayer under his chin.

Taryn sighed. "For the third time, we can't right now. There's a man whose life depends on us finding this plant."

Limery crossed his arms and huffed. "Fines."

Other than moss, Taryn was unable to identify any plants in the cave using his herbalism skill. Limery was intrigued by the dungeon, but considering they had no backup and the levels of the frost giants below, it seemed like an unnecessary risk even if they weren't against the clock.

They had wasted precious minutes already and the sun dipped further with every moment they waited.

After Taryn returned to bird form, the duo took to the air to hunt for arctic clove once more. With his herbalism skill active, the white landscape became speckled with green outlines. Frozen and snow-covered plants dotted the landscape. There was more life here than Taryn had ever imagined.

They turned another bend and an icy roar stopped Taryn mid-flight. It was a roar he'd heard before. He tucked his wings and dove for the nearest tree, returning to his dwarven form. Limery's warm body hovered behind him.

"What is its?" He peeked around Taryn.

Taryn gulped. "Dragon."

The imp's eyes flushed with greed. "Ooh, Limmy likes dragons. They's strong."

"Yeah, well, I'd like to keep roasted dwarf off the menu tonight. Let's creep around and see what the situation is." He lifted his index finger to his mouth. "Stay quiet."

The untouched snow gave a muffled crunch with each step Taryn took. He clung close to the mountainside, careful not to accidentally reveal himself.

Another shriek cut through the thin air, and Taryn froze. This was stupid. Suicide.

If they were spotted, what chance did he have of escaping a dragon?

He peeked around the corner and all thoughts of running fled his mind. Less than twenty yards away, a radiant white dragon clung to the edge of the mountain, teeth ripping into a giant gray bird with white-tipped feathers. He tried to analyze the bird, but since it was dead, he got nothing.

Even in the fading sun, the dragon sparkled. It was truly breathtaking, the most beautiful destructive force he'd ever witnessed. As it ripped a piece of flesh from the creature, Taryn was content to watch it for hours. The dragon repositioned itself, pressing a clawed foot against the bird's neck, and a patch of green flashed across Taryn's vision.

His heart raced. "That's it. That's the arctic clove," he whispered.

Limery didn't respond, apparently just as enraptured.

Taryn took a step closer and his foot slipped. He fell into the snow with a grunt.

The dragon's head whipped in their direction, and it unleashed a powerful roar. Snow plummeted to earth, and a blizzard erupted out of nowhere.

"Run!" Taryn yelled.

Limery bolted like a bat out of hell, instantly disappearing among the dense snowfall.

Dammit! Taryn cursed to himself as he transformed into bird form. *I finally found what we're looking for, and it's under a feeding dragon.*

Everywhere he flew, more snow followed. He wasn't sure how far the dragon's abilities spread, but he didn't want to risk being eaten alive. They still needed the arctic clove though, and the dragon couldn't stay there forever. All they needed to do was wait it out somewhere safe.

He kept close to the mountain, careful not to fly into open air. He had to go slower than usual to make sense of his surroundings at all. When he finally located the entrance to the Icemaw Dungeon cave, Limery was already waiting.

Taryn activated Jon's flashlight rock and walked deeper into the cave. "I thought I might find you here."

He grinned at Taryn. "Can we goes in the dungeons now?"

Taryn shook his head. "There's a dragon out there that could wipe us out with one attack, and you want us to go into a dungeon that could probably do the same?"

Limery nodded. "Yes, Limmy wants."

"No way. Not going to happen. We just need to wait out the drag—"

Something landed outside of the cave entrance, and Taryn's blood turned to ice. Frost crept along the cave wall toward them, spreading like an infection.

Taryn grabbed Limery's shoulder and ushered him deeper into the cave. The cave was spacious, but not big enough for the dragon to walk unimpeded.

Scales grated against the cave floor, and Taryn tried to walk faster without making noise. His feet pattered against the stone floor, and he wished desperately that he was wearing his cloak that concealed his movement right about now. Heavy breathing cut through the empty silence as the dragon sniffed at the air. It grunted and then its scales scraped against the floor once again as it crawled deeper into the cave.

Taryn tapped Limery on the shoulder and pointed to the entrance of the cave's dungeon. Limery nodded.

If they could enter the dungeon before the dragon saw them, maybe it would leave. But the dragon was getting closer, and they were almost out of time.

The prompt for the dungeon flashed across his vision.

Icemaw Dungeon. *Would you like to enter?*

Taryn accepted and everything turned black.

17. CONTENDERS

I try to message Taryn several times over the course of the evening, but I don't hear back from him. I'm not too worried, though. He said they are stuck in a cave, but that could mean anything. Taryn has always been more tactical than me, planning things out and taking precautions instead of running in blindly. Since he didn't seem panicked or ask for help, I'm taking that as a good sign. If something bad had happened, I'm certain he would let me know.

Gherhardt must sense that something is up because he places a firm hand on my shoulder. "It's tradition to have a feast on the evening before the Ascent. Come and enjoy the delicious food and entertainment. There is nothing you can do for your friends from here."

I nod, knowing he's right. I have faith that Taryn and Limery can handle whatever they are up against, so I need to quit worrying. I force a smile and try to push the thoughts to the back of my mind.

The silver glow of night paints the town as I follow Gherhardt through the moonlight to a long stone building. He opens the door, and chatter and music spill into the cold, along with a slew of delicious smells, once again reminding me of my night at The Underground Circus.

Since I've been in Whitgard, I have only seen people occasionally as they walk through the streets, but there are easily a few hundred people filling this building. Their thick fur coats are hung along the walls, and most of them wear some sort of wool or leather tunic. Even without all the fur, the Frozen Ash Tribe are still a large people, not nearly as big as a troll, but much taller and broader than the humans in Vanaria.

The fireplace combined with the body heat of so many people has me removing my cloak.

My blue skin is a beacon among the pale humans. One thing I've noticed about the tribe is that they are not a colorful society. Everything from their clothing to their buildings come in shades of gray or dull brown.

Two long tables stretch the length of the room. At the front, there is a platform where a band plays music. I spot Dando playing a drum. He sits on a stool with a large bongo-type drum cradled between his legs, tapping it with his fingers. Next to him, Liyah strums a stringed instrument with a short neck and round body. They both grin from ear to ear and occasionally steal a glance at one another. A dark-haired lady plays a second stringed instrument behind Liyah, and a young man shakes a tambourine vigorously as he dances across the front of the platform.

A group dances in the space between the stage and the table, swaying back and forth.

This reminds me of my first night in the troll village. No matter what a society looks like from the outside, there are always moments like this where they are able to unwind. Even when clinging to survival, art and culture are a reminder of what they are surviving for.

The music fades and hundreds of eyes turn in our direction.

Gherhardt raises a hand to the onlookers. "Yes, the rumors are true. We do have a forest troll in the village. Chod here helped clear the trail up the mountain for the Ascent, and other members of his party are currently on a quest to gather arctic clove for Alvyn's elixir. We owe them our gratitude. While they are here, I trust that you will treat these heroes with the same respect you do me."

"And what if I don't respect you?" Archard shouts from the center of the left table and laughter snakes throughout the crowd. He holds a massive mug in his hand and foam coats his mustache.

Gherhardt grins. "Ah, yes. And let's not forget the man responsible for the roasted frost deer we are all about to enjoy, Archard the Precise. Humble as always."

Clapping and cheering fills the room. Archard climbs on the bench and takes a bow, mead sloshing onto the table.

The music resumes and people return to their business. I catch several glances as people try to conceal their interest in me, and others who are not so discreet and openly point in my direction. Their reactions don't bother me. I'm probably more out of place in their village than if I showed up as a blue-skinned troll in the middle of New York City.

"You're going to be the talk of the village for some time once you leave." Gherhardt winks at me. "Shall we grab a bite to eat? I spent all day roasting the frost deer. I'm sure it will be unlike anything you have eaten in Mythos."

There's a buffet-style table on the far wall loaded with food. Plenty of bread and vegetables, and in the center, giant slabs of meat.

I stick to the meat, grabbing myself a platter Limery would be envious of and a mug of arctic mead.

Taking the massive slab in both hands, I sink my teeth into it. Juices explode in my mouth and an uncontrollable grunt of pleasure escapes my lips. An array of spices battle for supremacy as the smokey, fatty meat melts in my mouth. It's so tender that the strips practically fall off the bone. I close my eyes and let the flavor profile wash over me.

When I open them, Gherhardt is grinning at me.

I analyze a piece of meat to see what deliciousness I just ingested.

Item. Frost Deer Chops. *Food coated in Gherhardt's Secret Dry Rub offer 50% reduction to cold weather effects for 1 hours.*

"How did you do this?" I ask as I wipe juices from my chin.

"If I told you, I'd have to kill you." He smirks. "I've done a lot of things that I'm proud of in this life, but perfecting my dry rub is at the top of the list."

I'm going to have to see about getting some of that for the road. Food is food, but this...this is an experience. And the effect from Gherhardt's dry rub will be incredibly useful while we're in Frostmoor. Too bad Taryn and Limery are missing out.

The music takes a break and Dando joins us at the table, Liyah close behind.

She wraps her arms around her uncle from behind. "The venison is delicious, Uncle Gher."

"Yes, perfectly seasoned," Dando agrees.

"Save your flattery for someone who needs it." Gherhardt stuffs a piece of bread in his mouth, but it does little to disguise his smile.

Dando takes a seat next to me with a mug of mead.

I clink my mug to his. "You're a man of many talents."

He blushes. "Ah, this is nothing. Liyah does the hard work. I just bang my hands."

I lean in closer, careful not to talk too loud. "I see you're getting some one-on-one time, where's your nemesis?"

"Warley?" He laughs. "He's on gate duty tonight."

"What are you two whispering about?" Liyah tilts her head and flashes a mischievous smile.

Dando stutters for a moment before I save him from his misery.

"I was trying to get him to reveal Gherhardt's eleven herbs and spices."

Dando breathes a sigh of relief.

She laughs. "Good luck with that. Uncle Gher keeps his roasting recipes a secret. It's probably the only reason he's still in charge." She pokes Gherhardt in the side.

After a few minutes of small talk, the duo returns to the stage, where they play something reminiscent of folk music.

I try my best to be a wingman for Dando. "Dando seems like a good kid. Smart, funny, hard worker."

Gherhardt glances up at the stage. "He's certainly an asset to the tribe."

"Seems to have caught Liyah's attention, too." I grin.

His brow scrunches. "She'll never have a thing to do with him if I have a say."

"Well, you are the head of the tribe." I cross my arms and lean back. "Why do you want to make it so hard on him, though?"

He sighs. "Bah. The writing is already in the stars. They are both good kids. Hell, don't you dare tell him I said this, but if I were a father, I'd be proud to call Dando my son. And I know Liyah's a woman now. I just want to keep her as the girl who used to stand on my shoulders for as long as possible."

I sit in silence for a moment. Gherhardt has an entire village to look after and yet here he is dealing with the same kind of family drama as anyone in the real world.

"You know there's nothing wrong with your relationship evolving. Just because she's not a little girl anymore doesn't mean you lose her."

His gaze drifts to the stage. He smiles at Liyah before returning his attention to me. "Yeah, I know. But unless I have children of my own, Liyah will be the next Head of the Frozen Ash Tribe. That is a lot of responsibility, and her partner will have a part to play in the future of Whitgard. I'm not ready for that yet."

The music stops and then a quick succession of drumming calls our attention.

"That's my cue." Gherhardt wipes the specks of food from his beard and stands.

All eyes fall upon him as he takes the stage. He strokes both ends of his forked beard before speaking.

"It's always good to see the Frozen Ash Tribe gathered together. Minus Alvyn, his caretakers, and the few who have other duties, this is it. This is who we are." He clears his throat. "As far back as I can remember, we have commemorated the ascent of Umen and Edrar every spring as a reminder of where we come from. Our people were born from the ice, and one day we will all return to its frozen embrace. But just like Umen before us, we will hold off that fate for as long as possible. The Ascent is a celebration of life, of overcoming the harsh reality of our surroundings, and a reminder that even our ancestors could not escape the calamity of Frostmoor. So without further ado, allow me to introduce our competitors.

"This year, we will have three new contenders. Though he is not here tonight, Warley has protected our gates tirelessly over the years. This will be his first time attempting the Ascent."

There are a few groans, mostly from around Archard, but a few claps are scattered throughout.

"Our second challenger has been begging me to compete since he was a child. Though he may look like a summer babe, he's assured me he is of age to compete."

Laughter erupts through the crowd before Gherhardt reveals Dando's name. With bright red cheeks, he salutes the crowd before returning to his drum.

"The final competitor holds a special place in my heart, so just know that if anything happens to her, you'll have to take it up with me." His gaze narrows on Dando. "My very own niece, Liyah."

The entire building cheers for Liyah, and she beams as she waves to the crowd. She winks at Dando, but his mouth hangs open in astonishment. Clearly, he had no idea she was planning to compete.

Gherhardt raises a hand, and everyone quiets down. "Enjoy the evening. Eat, drink, and be merry. Tomorrow, we will pay tribute to our people's beginnings."

He rejoins me at the table, and for the rest of the evening, we share stories as we down glass after glass of mead. I tell him of my adventures, the different troll tribes, and other societies. He shares the ins and outs of the Whitgard, along with their challenges and accomplishments over the years.

By the time the building begins to empty, my head is buzzing from the mead. We stumble our way back to Gherhardt's. Before I crawl in bed, I send Taryn a final message, wondering what on earth they have gotten themselves into.

18. ON THIN ICE

"Shit. Shit. Shit. Shit. Shit." Taryn pressed his palms against his eyes, trying to clear his thoughts.

He'd panicked at the approaching dragon, and in a desperate attempt to make sure nothing happened to Limery, they were now in a dungeon with who-knew-what kind of monsters and traps.

Taryn opened his eyes to find Limery staring back at him. The imp's bulbous eyes were larger than normal as he watched Taryn.

He tried to reassure the imp. "Everything is fine. We'll just wait in here for a couple of hours and then go back into the cave. Then we'll get the arctic clove and fly back to Whitgard. Nothing else can enter as long as we are in here."

Limery frowned. "Limmy wants to see the dragons."

Taryn fought the urge to raise his voice, not letting the stress win. "We can see the dragon when it's not trying to eat us. Let's just chill out and rest for a bit while we can."

Now that he thought about it, Taryn couldn't recall the last time he'd really rested since entering Mythos. He leaned back against the cave wall and took in their surroundings.

The inside of the dungeon was vastly different from the outside cave. Where the cave had been formed out of rough gray stone, the dungeon had smooth, navy-blue walls with white veins that arced like lightning. The walls still had a natural look to them, unlike the intricately-detailed walls of the dwarven kingdom, but it was as if the room they were in had formed inside of some precious gemstone.

Straight ahead, a crack in the wall emanated a blue glow. It was big enough to walk through but cut sharply to the right, hiding what lay beyond. Ice crystals covered the ground beneath the chasm, similar to the frost that had formed inside the cave when the dragon entered.

Taryn didn't want to think about what kind of monsters might be lurking on the other side. This was a high-level zone after all. He pressed his ear to the door, but whether it was because the dragon had left or the door was magically sealed, he heard nothing from the other side.

When he turned around, Limery was gone. His chest grew tight as he rushed through the crevice in the wall. His feet slipped on the icy surface and he fell hard, pain shooting through his right shoulder as he crashed into the wall.

He tried to regain his footing, but it wasn't until he equipped Sapling Staff and used its viny appendages to form a support base that he could stand.

Taryn gasped when he saw the source of the glow. Translucent gemstones in a dozen shades of blue protruded from the ceiling and walls, each casting its own aura. The gems pulsed with a gentle energy. Some had a similar coloring to the flames burning along the enchanted pathway up the mountain, so he assumed they were mana-infused.

In front of him, a bridge of ice stretched across a deep pit to a wooden door on the other side. Light blue runes glowed dully on the door, but there were no handles for opening it. The reflective gleam from the surrounding gems gave the bridge an ethereal appearance.

Carefully, Taryn peered over the edge of the cliff into the depths below. Limery was nowhere to be seen, furthering his worry, but there were many more bridges that led to similar doors as far down as he could see. From what he could tell, the runes were different on each door. If only his communication stone translated written language as well, but reading runes was a skill in itself. The pit descended deep into the mountain, and hundreds of mana-infused gemstones protruded from the walls, pulsing like some alien hive.

The blue glow seemed to go on forever. Did this dungeon descend the entirety of the mountain? And more importantly, where was Limery?

A struggling grunt caught Taryn's attention just above the crevice he was standing in. Very carefully, he stepped onto the ice bridge to look above the pit, where he found Limery struggling to pull a mana crystal from the wall. Above him, a slew of dangerous icicles and stalactites descended ominously from the ceiling.

Taryn let out a sigh of relief. "You can't disappear on me like that. You nearly gave me a heart attack."

Limery let go of the gem and tilted his head. "You's heart attacks you?"

Taryn placed his hands on his hips. "It's an expression. It means you worried me. I didn't know where you were."

"Sorries." Limery flashed a demonic smile. "Limmy found the shinies."

The apology was clearly fake, but Taryn still appreciated it. "Let's get back to the entrance."

Limery frowned. "Waiting is boring. Limmy wants to explore."

Taryn understood his frustration. Waiting around was boring, but Taryn was trying to be responsible and put them in the least amount of risk as possible. They had been sent here to find the arctic clove, not to adventure. There would be plenty of time for that once they had returned.

But there was nothing they could do about the arctic clove until the dragon left, and they were in a dungeon filled with opportunity. With so many closed doors, this place was practically a gold mine if they played it right. He'd been fantasizing about the new classes he might be offered at level twenty-five, and he wasn't getting any closer by sitting around.

Every minute they wasted was a minute their enemies were growing stronger. Taryn wasn't an offensive juggernaut by any means, especially without his pets, but Limery was pure destruction and especially suited to wreak havoc on an area like this.

Limery hovered in front of Taryn with his long, spindly fingers clasped together. "Please."

Taryn relented. "Fine, but give me a few minutes to prepare. And the first sign that we are out of our league, we're coming back. Deal?"

Limery gave the gemstone another tug and grinned. "Deals."

If they were going deeper into the dungeon, Taryn needed to make sure his stats were properly allocated. He pulled up his character sheet.

Taryn, Level 23 Ebony Dwarf Druid
HP: 4592/4592
Mana: 3210/3210
XP: 485,679/525,000

Strength: 9
Dexterity: 13
Constitution: 41
Intelligence: 19 (+2)
Wisdom: 30 (+5)
Charisma: 12

+1 Constitution racial bonus per level.

+1 Ability point per odd level.

1 stat point available.
1 ability point available.

Racial Abilities:

· · ·

Darkvision (Passive)-Better vision in limited light, but not total darkness.
   Blood of the Mountain (Passive)- Resistant to poisons.
   Heart of Gold (Passive)- Increased chance to mine or loot rare materials.

Abilities:

Transform- Transform into an animal you have seen for up to two hours. Primary animal: Red bird. Upgrade for additional time. Cost: 100 mana. Cooldown: 1 hour for non-primary transformations. No cooldown for primary transformations.
   Lightning Bolt (Level-2)- Deals a massive burst of damage with a 50% chance to stun. Cost: 200 mana. Cooldown: 10 seconds.
   Strong Wind- Increases movement speed of those in your party by 50%. Cost: 100 mana. Cooldown: 60 seconds.
   Imbue- Increases the size of a summoned monster or pet by 100% for 10 minutes. Cost: 200 mana. Cooldown: 5 minutes.
   Restoration (Level 2)- Restores 100 HP to a pet or summon every 10 seconds while communing with nature. Cost: 10 mana per second. Cooldown: None.
   Nature's Aegis (Passive)- You are immune to elemental effects.
   Nature's Bulwark (Passive)- Animals will only attack you if they are provoked.
   Tame (Available at level 10)- Form a pet from any beast brought to 5% HP and within 5 levels. Cannot be used on Unique Monsters. For each additional pet tamed, tamer loses 5% influence over each creature. Cost: 500 mana. Cooldown: 24 hours.
   Current Pets (10% influence loss):

Berry- Level 19. Umber Bear.
   Stompy- Level 19. Moulhaug.
   Ruby- Level 16. Jackal.

Summon Fungus- Summon a troop of poisonous mushrooms. Cost: 200 mana. Cooldown: 30 seconds.
   Stonewall- Summon a wall up to 20' x 20'. Cost: 200 mana. Cooldown: 1 minute.

Available Abilities (1 ability point to unlock):

Barkskin- Strengthens skin as if it were made of wood, offering damage reduction. Cost: 100 mana. Cooldown: 60 seconds.
   Stoneskin- Strengthens skin as if it were made of stone, offering additional damage reduction. Cost: 200 mana. Cooldown: 120 seconds.

Insect Plague- Summon insects within a 50-yard radius to attack a target. Cost: 200 mana. Cooldown: 5 minutes.

Conceal (Passive). Hides level from anyone who is not a guard on city grounds.

Perception. For 10 minutes, gain increased awareness of your surroundings. Spot hidden objects, as well as unusual sounds, odors, and tastes. Cooldown: 6 hours.

Current Items:

Item. Boar's Tusk Staff. +2 Intelligence, +2 Wisdom. A staff fitted with an enchanted boar's tusk.

Item. Druidic Helm. +2 Constitution, +2 Wisdom.

Item. Sapling Staff. +3 Intelligence, +3 Wisdom. A living staff capable of sending out whip-like vines.

Item. Shadow Dagger (x2). With blades of shadow energy, this dagger bypasses armor and drains mana and life force directly without leaving physical wounds. Drains mana equal to user's Wisdom and HP equal to user's Intelligence with each attack.

Item. Cloak of Silence. A cloak capable of concealing sounds associated with movement.

Item. Smuggler's Boots. Boots that leave no tracks no matter the substance or terrain they step through.

Item. Enchanted Rock Light. This enchanted rock emits light for a limited distance. 92% power remaining.

Item. Ring of Insight. +1 Wisdom.

Item. Ring of Understanding. +1 Intelligence.

Item. Ring of Judgement. +1 Wisdom.

Item. Sage Amulet. +1 Wisdom, +1 Intelligence.

Item. Expandable Satchel. A bag capable of holding enormous content and only burdening the wearer with ten percent of its weight. Simply focus on the item inside and it will appear in your hand.

Item. Fur Cloak. Protects wearer from the effects of frigid temperatures.

Item. Fur Boots. Protects wearer from the effects of frigid temperatures.

He also had a fair amount of health and mana potions that they'd purchased in Goldspire.

Taryn had wanted to save his most recent stat point and ability point for when he unlocked his new class, but there was no point in hoarding it. He added a stat point to Intelligence. It would help increase the damage on the few offensive abilities he had.

So far, he'd sunk all his points into Intelligence or Wisdom, with the majority in the latter. Points in Wisdom increased his mana pool and decreased his cooldowns, allowing him to better support the group, but Lightning Bolt and Summon Fungus both drew power from Intelligence.

He'd relied more on the potential stun from Lightning Bolt than its damage, but sinking another point into Intelligence could mean the difference between life and death. With his natural dwarven Constitution, he was a far cry from a glass cannon and could still outlast a lot of opponents at his level even with minimal damage output—especially with his pets around.

Taryn stared at the five available abilities. Neither Barkskin or Stoneskin appealed to him. He wasn't a front-row fighter, and putting an ability point into either of those felt like a waste. Casting it on Chod or one of his pets could make them tougher, but they weren't here right now to benefit. Insect Plague could be useful, but not currently. There had to be insects in the area to use it and the frigid temperatures meant that was unlikely. Conceal had little appeal since he didn't really care about concealing his level from strangers. Chod had invested in that ability because he had needed to when he was traveling solo, but now that they were traveling together, it seemed trivial. Perception was useful, but when they were able to craft perception potions, it really felt like a waste of a good point, especially when Ruby was around to investigate.

There was still the option to further upgrade Lightning Bolt or one of the other abilities, but he was so close to level twenty-five that it made more sense to save it. A new class with new abilities meant he would be able to unlock two instead of one. That could be a game-changer.

Though Perception seemed like a good option, the six-hour cooldown steered him away. He doubted they would still be in the dungeon in six hours, so a ten-minute window of increased perception was all but useless. He made peace with the risks and rewards of holding onto the ability point and closed his character sheet.

The message icon pulsed slightly, and Taryn opened it to see he had three messages from Chod.

Incoming Message (Chod): Hey, haven't heard from you. Figured I would check in. They've got me clearing snow for some race they are doing tomorrow.

Incoming Message (Chod): It's me again. Just checking in to see how things were going.

Incoming Message (Chod): I'm sure you guys are fine. Just check in when you get a chance.

Taryn smiled as he read through all the messages. It was a side of Chod not many people got to see, the complete opposite of the sarcastic, rage-fueled gamer he portrayed online. He'd really found a place for himself in this world. Somewhere he could finally be his best self.

He knew that if he told Chod that he and Limery were in a high-level dungeon by themselves, it would only make him worry more, so he kept it simple, letting him know they wouldn't be back tonight, but everything was okay.

After sending the message, Taryn equipped his old cloak and boots and returned to Limery, who had finally given up on the gemstone he was trying to remove.

"We play this smart." He tossed his satchel over his shoulder and stepped out onto the ice bridge. "We're already on thin ice as it is, and we can't afford to make any mist—"

Limery pulled on a different gemstone and it moved as if it was a switch. The ice cracked beneath Taryn's feet, chilling him to the bone. Tiny fractures spread out beneath his boots, turning the transparent ice into a fragmented kaleidoscope.

He froze in place. Cracks snaked along the bridge, spreading further as the ice fractures battled for supremacy against Taryn's thundering heartbeat.

Limery's eyes looked like they might pop out of his head as he hovered helplessly.

Finally, the cracks stopped spreading, leaving them in uncomfortable silence.

Taryn released the breath he was holding, and the entire bridge shattered. Limery let out a yelp of surprise, and Taryn extended the vines of his staff toward the wall. They wrapped around a three-pronged gemstone, but the prongs broke and Taryn continued to fall.

His HP dropped a fraction as he shattered through a second bridge. Splintered ice rained down, clinking and bouncing off the walls and other bridges. Taryn crashed through three more bridges before he had the wherewithal to use Transform.

Feathers exploded and ice speckled him as he flew to one of the glowing gemstones and perched on top. Even in bird form, his tiny heart pounded quicker than usual. He waited a moment before moving, letting his heart rate slow and trying to comprehend what had just happened.

Limery hovered in front of him. "Is yous okays?"

Taryn tweeted his affirmation, then he extended a wing, pointing up top. He couldn't talk to Limery in his current form, and he didn't trust any of the other bridges to support his weight.

Limery nodded. "Okay. We goes up!"

Once safely back at the entrance to the dungeon, Taryn returned to dwarven form. "Man, that was scary as hell. I was so shocked by the bridge falling it took me a minute to transform."

"How did yous break the bridges?" Limery put a clawed finger over his lips.

Taryn crossed his arms and scowled. "Me? You triggered a trap. I think the different colored gemstones are our key to opening the doors. Pull the wrong one and something bad happens."

Limery grimaced. "Limmy didn't knows."

He couldn't blame Limery for being enthralled by the gemstones. Chod did a good job of keeping the imp's baser instincts in check most of the time, but he was still like a small child in a lot of ways, always chasing the shiny object.

His younger sister had been the same way when she was a toddler. At age twelve, Taryn was the de facto evening babysitter while his parents worked multiple jobs to make sure he and his siblings all got the educations they deserved. So from four to eight every night, Taryn was in charge of cooking, homework, and baths. By the time he had been old enough to work an actual job, he'd gladly shirked those responsibilities to the next in line.

He'd need to recall some of those skills to keep Limery from killing them both.

Triggering the gemstone had reduced the integrity of the bridge, or possibly all the bridges, since his weight had been enough to shatter the others. They would need to carefully test what other traps might be waiting for them.

"Okay, here's the deal." Taryn snapped his fingers to gather Limery's attention. "I have a theory that there's a connection between the gems in the walls and what happens in the dungeon. We're going to need to test them out to see what happens. We're lucky that we have an advantage others don't. Do you know what that is?"

Limery scratched his chin with a clawed finger. "Limmy makes fires?"

"Not quite what I was thinking, but that's definitely in our favor. What I was thinking is that we can fly. So, here's the plan."

Taryn explained his theory on how the gems worked and then transformed into his bird form. The gemstone Limery had triggered had returned to its place in the wall. He landed on it, and sure enough, his weight wasn't enough to trigger the effect.

He chirped at Limery, and the imp carved a mark into the wall next to the light blue gem. Next, Taryn perched on a gemstone the color of a deep blue sky. It pulsed with energy. The gem next to it, a vibrant turquoise, did not. Taryn chirped once again and Limery pulled on the cerulean stone. It triggered and the dungeon shuddered. Cracks echoed above them, and icicles broke free from the ceiling, falling like missiles. One shattered an ice bridge that had reformed, and several others plunged into the depths below. They crashed like a bull in a china shop until eventually fading to a trickle, and then silence.

With the icicles gone, there were gaps between the stalactites that remained, but the icicles were already reforming. Taryn was certain a separate stone triggered those.

Next, Taryn had Limery pull the turquoise gem, and just as he expected, nothing happened. While all the gemstones produced light, only the ones that pulsed seemed to have an effect on the dungeon. After marking both stones, they moved on to the next.

Limery pulled on an indigo stone. It moved, but it appeared to have no effect. Taryn was prepared to chalk it up as a decoy when a door unlocked somewhere beneath them.

The bridges and icicles began to recrystallize, and if not for his increased eyesight in bird form, he wouldn't have noticed the dozens of tiny creatures emerging from an open doorway several floors below.

The humanoid creatures were smaller than Limery, with light blue skin and sapphire hair. They reminded him of the salt fairies from the dungeon outside of

Seascape. Crystalized armor coated their bodies and snowflake wings fluttered behind them. Each one had horns made of icicles and blue orbs for eyes.

Ice Fairy. *Level 25. The most fragile of all fairies, what they lack in durability they make up for in elemental power.*

The fairies had set their eyes on Limery, snarling with an icy vengeance, and each of their hands glowed with white light. Frost formed in the air around them as they powered up attacks.

Taryn tried to yell, to warn Limery, but all that came out was a peep.

The fairies unleashed their attacks, streams of ice shooting in their direction.

Limery looked intrigued, but wasn't alarmed by the tiny creatures.

Taryn panicked. No matter how fragile they were, dozens of level-twenty-five fairies would be the death of both of them if they didn't act fast.

Not knowing what else to do, Taryn perched on the cerulean gem and returned to his dwarven form.

An ice blast hit him in the shoulder, numbing it on impact and dropping his health by ten percent.

"Kill them!" he shouted as he held on for dear life to the gem, his increased weight triggering the effect.

Spells exploded on the wall around him as half-formed icicles plunged from the ceiling. Limery sent a maelstrom of fireballs as the icicles fell. The heat from the fireballs was enough to melt several fairy wings, sending them falling to their doom or spiraling into the wall. The ones he hit directly turned to water instantly. Icicles impaled others, and a molten Limery finished the rest.

"Good job," Taryn grunted as he hung on for dear life, feeling slowly returning to his arm. "Going back to bird form now."

He let go and used Transform as he fell, flying down to inspect the door the fairies had come out of. It was still open, and Taryn was surprised to discover that the runes engraved in the door were the same shade as the gemstone that had opened it. He glanced at the doors above and below, and each one had a slightly different shade of runes.

Inside of the doorway, the room was small, barely ten-by-ten feet. In the center, a shimmering chest made of ice rested on a platform.

Taryn transformed back and called Limery to join him.

"Ooh, shinies." Limery licked his lips as he approached the chest.

"Easy." Taryn extended an arm to stop the imp. "We need to make sure it's not a trap."

He equipped Sapling Staff and spread the vines out across the room, making sure there weren't any hidden tiles or trip wires. Once the room seemed safe, they knelt in front of the chest.

The chest was made of thick pieces of translucent ice. Intricate patterns were carved into each side, with a thin snowflake-shaped latch over the center. Something silver gleamed inside, but the translucent ice distorted whatever it was.

The latch was cold to the touch, sending a shiver through Taryn as he flipped the lid. Inside, a small buckler shield with a snowflake engraved in the center gleamed in the dull light.

*Item. **Frosted Buckler.** **+2 Constitution.** A lightweight and small shield capable of deflecting blows as well as being used offensively. **Bonus Ability:** Physical attacks blocked with Frosted Buckler cut the attacker's Dexterity in half for ten seconds.*

Taryn picked up the shield. It was lightweight and cool to the touch. His first thought was of Jegaar, the battle scholar from Goldspire who wielded a buckler. Having a shield that could slow an opponent would only further increase his power.

He handed the shield to Limery for him to inspect. If the imp sat in it, he could practically use it as a sled. Taryn didn't want to give him any ideas, so he kept that part to himself.

Taryn strapped the shield to his arm for the time being, though he doubted he could use it to its full potential. Of their group, Chod was the only one who specialized in hand-to-hand combat. But if he didn't want it, maybe they could sell it for a good price in the next city.

Still, this was a great item even if it didn't fit their needs. Was it possible there was a chest behind each door? If so, this dungeon was even better than Taryn thought.

After returning to the top floor, they quickly discovered that gems of the same color triggered an identical effect if it occurred in the pit, but once a door had been unlocked there was no replicating the action. Which was unfortunate, because Limery could have destroyed the ice fairies a hundred times over.

The cyan gemstones caused one end of the bridges to lower, creating a slippery ice slide. The cerulean gems had been particularly troublesome, as they were actually the protruding abdomens of frost wasps. They'd had to barricade themselves in the entrance behind Stonewall and wait for the wasps to return to their positions.

Taryn had nearly run out of the dungeon when an ice spider had emerged from one of the doors. Its frozen abdomen was bigger than him, and it grated against the wall as it climbed with grotesque movements. He had triggered falling icicles, stalactites, and summoned poisonous mushrooms along the wall, all while begging Limery to burn it faster.

It eventually died, legs curling up as it fell into the abyss.

Taryn was hesitant to enter the web-shrouded room until Limery had sufficiently burned the webbing, leaving nothing but another ice chest in the center.

After opening the chest, they found a white pelt inside.

*Item. **Winter's Might.** **+2 Wisdom.** The pelt of the elusive snow fox grants the wearer immunity to the effects of frigid temperatures while also casting an illusory aura that blends them into snowy landscapes. **Bonus Effect:** Druids or shapeshifters in animal form are granted a winter coat while in sub-freezing temperatures.*

Taryn snatched the pelt out of the chest, equipping it over his shoulders. Now he could wear his own clothing and not the hand-me-downs of some overgrown child.

"You okay if I take this?" he asked Limery after the fact.

"You takes." Limery grinned.

To further test out the pelt, Taryn transformed into his bird form. Instead of the vibrant red feathers, he was covered in stark white. He'd be practically invisible while flying in Frostmoor. This alone had made it worth entering the dungeon, and there were still dozens of rooms they had yet to unlock.

But time was ticking by. They had already been here for a few hours at least—plenty of time for the dragon to have moved on if it was going to. Strangest of all was the fact that they hadn't found a gemstone that matched the color of the top door.

Was it possible that there were multiple entrances into the dungeon? Or were they missing the obvious?

They needed to leave soon. A man's life was hanging in the balance, after all. And maybe they could return with Chod once they were done in Whitgard. A long venture through the Icemaw Dungeon could put them both closer to their goals.

But one more room wouldn't hurt.

19. WORK SMARTER, NOT HARDER

When I wake up, the first thing I do is check my notifications. Still nothing from Taryn since yesterday evening. We've always been different in that regard. Back in the real world, I'm the type of person to respond to a message straight away, where Taryn might not pick up his phone for hours at a time.

I wonder if this was what life was like before location tracking and instant messaging, back when people had to leave messages on answering machines and wait to get a call back.

No offense to Taryn, but waiting for responses is for the birds.

For now, I'll take no news as good news.

Downstairs, Gherhardt once again greets me with a delicious breakfast. "The race won't be until later in the afternoon, and I believe Dando can manage the final touches, so I'll be putting you back to work if that's alright with you."

I stuff a boiled egg in my mouth, enjoying the delicious spices sprinkled on top. "I live to serve."

After breakfast, I'm introduced to a man named Oakley. He's more broad-shouldered than either Archard or Gherhardt and sports a cropped red-beard.

We load tools into a cart pulled by a single ox. Oakley drives while I sit in the back alongside various axes, saws, and pickaxes.

He eyes me suspiciously before returning his attention to the path. "Never met a troll before." His voice is deep and gravelly. "Always thought the lot of you were monsters. You don't seem so bad."

I'm not entirely sure how to respond. "I mean, we are monsters. That doesn't mean we're evil."

He grunts. "I suppose. You ever eaten a child?"

"What? No! Of course not. We're not that kind of monster."

He shrugs. "What do I know? Like I said, never met a troll before."

"Well, I can assure you we don't eat children." I lean a little closer. "Not even when we're especially hungry."

He glances over his shoulder, one eyebrow raised, and I can't contain my grin.

"So, what are we working on today?" I ask, even though I have a pretty good idea based on the tools.

"We need wood and ore. Gherhardt assures me you are worth ten men, so I aim to put it to the test while my men work on other projects."

"I see. So, I get to work hard so they don't have to." This must be how Taryn feels in the real world, always being asked to do the heavy lifting.

He laughs. "Smarter than you look."

"Same to you." I chuckle to myself as I lean back against the cart, feeling each bump as we roll along.

After about an hour, we detour from the main path, following a non-enchanted trail that leads through abandoned ruins. We travel until we come upon a grove of trees growing in the shadow of the mountain. A dark cave disappears inside.

"You'll be working over here." Oakley hands me a pickaxe and points to the cave. "Once you fill up two carts of ore, come find me. The cart is inside the cave."

Quest Alert: You have been offered the quest "Working for the Man." Fill two carts of ore and load them into the wagon.

Reward: Increased favor with Whitgard and the Frozen Ash Tribe.

Oakley's not one for detailed instruction, but I'm sure mining can't be that hard, so I toss the pickaxe over my shoulder and get to work. Just past the snowbank at the entrance to the cave, a small wooden wheelbarrow rests against the wall. I lay the pickaxe inside and push it down the well-trodden path. My eyes adjust to the dark, and pretty soon, only the faintest amount of light spills in from outside.

The cave goes deeper than I imagined, and before long, I'm in complete darkness. My night vision allows me to see unimpeded as broken axe shafts and rubble litter the cave, making it difficult to navigate the wheelbarrow.

I park the wheelbarrow at the end of the cave and equip the pickaxe. It's a little small compared to many of my weapons, but it feels natural in my hand. The Frozen Ash Tribe are a hearty people, so their tools are larger than most I've seen on Isle of Mythos. I'm not sure what I'm supposed to be doing, so I take my first swing at the cave wall.

A chunk of stone explodes from the impact, revealing a vein of rusty ore underneath. I swing again, further revealing the chunk of ore until I'm eventually able to pry it free.

Item. Iron Ore. A mixture of raw iron and minerals, which can be smelted and further enhanced for use in tools and weapons.

Congratulations! You have learned the skill 'Mining.' You are now a level 1 miner (Novice). Increase your skill and learn advanced techniques for mining by finding an advanced miner (apprentice or above). Ranks: Novice, Apprentice, Journeyman, Expert, Artisan, Master, Grandmaster.

As soon as I dismiss the notification, the cave is filled with translucent outlines marking iron ore veins along the wall. After half an hour, my mining skill reaches level two and the outlines become more detailed, now able to reveal iron ore that is a few inches beneath the surface. Before long, I have the wheelbarrow filled with ore.

A rhythmic clack echoes from outside the cave as I deliver my first load. Oakley grunts as he swings his axe, leaving a nice size gash in a towering pine.

He looks over as I dump the ore into the wagon and does a double-take. "Gods be good, you are a strong son of a dragon. It would take my men hours to mine that much ore."

"This is nothing." I finish dumping the wheelbarrow and stretch my arms overhead. "With an army of horrors, I could probably do it twice as fast."

He lets his axe fall in the snow. "You don't say."

"I do say. Promise not to piss your pants and I'll show you."

After lighting a torch, Oakley follows me into the cave. I can feel his eyes boring into me from behind. I'm sure a lifetime of stories where trolls are the boogeyman is hard to shake, but he seems open-minded enough.

We reach the end of the mine and I tell Oakley to stand back. "Wouldn't want you to get hit by any rogue projectiles."

He takes a few steps back. "You forgot the cart."

I wink at him. "We'll be running an assembly line for this next part. Now, try not to freak out."

I summon one of each of my horrors, and Oakley's eyes go so wide he almost looks like Limery.

"What madness is this?" His hand rests on the dagger strapped to his side. "Do you summon these beasts from the gates of hell?"

His question flusters me for a moment. I've never given it a second thought to where the horrors actually come from. They're not as intelligent as Limery, but they do have a sense of wherewithal about them, even if they do respond to my every thought. The shadow demons that Ethan the Warlock summoned outside of Lynchton cross my mind and I wonder if my horrors come from the same place or if they are nothing more than mindless creations.

"Uh, you know, that is a good question." I watch the horrors grumble about for a moment, lost in thought. "I'll have to get back to you on that."

Over the next ten minutes, I summon a total of sixty horrors, separating them in a single file line down the length of the cavern. They grumble and shuffle their feet as I wait to get started. It might just be Oakley watching, but I have every intention of putting on a show.

As the first horrors expire, I summon three more to replace them, positioning them at the beginning of the line and forcing the others to shuffle their way to the end.

I take off the thick fur cloak and lay it to the side. I flex for Oakley and get to work. With sixty horrors active, I have a one percent increase in damage and health for each one active. Each swing digs deeper than before and chunks of stone and ore fill the ground around me. My horrors sort through the rubble, tossing rocks aside and sending ore down the assembly line toward the wagon.

As soon as horrors expire, I summon more, never missing a swing or slowing. Sweat trickles down my arms and back as the cavern grows warm from my body heat.

Then I activate Berserker Rage. Steam radiates from my skin as my muscles bulge and increased power flows through my body. My swings grow easier, and the pickaxe snaps from the force. I quickly replace it with another propped against the cave wall and carry on. Dust and debris fill the air as I break through the cave wall like a troll possessed. Ore notifications fill my vision and each hit lands with power and precision, knocking more and more ore free.

After thirty seconds, Berserker Rage ends and I take a step back, admiring my devastation.

Oakley looks on in awe, eyes blinking rapidly and mouth hanging open. "Do you have any brethren?"

I pat him on the shoulder. "I do, but we have bigger fish to fry at the moment."

With more ore mined in two hours than he had expected for the day, I lend my talents to chopping trees. I level up my logging skill, becoming a level-three lumberjack, and by midday, the wagon is loaded to the brim with ore and lumber.

"Looks like we're going home early." Oakley rolls his shoulders and they audibly crack. "You surprised me, troll. Not only are you strong, but your work ethic is admirable. I dare say you have what it takes to survive in Frostmoor."

"Now that is a compliment I'm proud to take." I walk beside the wagon as it trundles up the mountain, since there is no room to fit in the back. "Are you excited for the race?"

He nods. "The Ascent is always full of surprises. I competed myself when I was younger, though I never won."

After making short work of the day's tasks, Oakley is more talkative on the ride back. He asks a lot of questions about the world outside of Frostmoor. Even though their portal has reopened, no one from the Frozen Ash Tribe has passed through since it began functioning again. With the harsh terrain and climate, they don't worry about invaders, but they have surprisingly little interest in venturing to lands on the other side.

The return to Whitgard takes much longer with a full wagon, but we arrive with plenty of daylight remaining. Even though it's cold out, the village is more alive than I would ever have imagined. Music echoes from the mountainside and villagers stroll through the streets with steaming-hot beverages like this is some sort of winter wonderland.

As we enter, Gherhardt greets us with a shocked expression.

He picks up a piece of iron ore and examines it. "The two of you managed all of this?"

"You were wrong." Oakley slaps him firmly on the shoulder. "This troll is worth more than ten men. Any chance we can convince him to stay?"

Gherhardt smiles. "I fear there's no amount of gold that could keep him here. His sights are set far beyond Frostmoor. Isn't that right, Chod?"

"As much as I would love to mine ore and chop wood all day every day, there are a great deal of people counting on us back home. I'll have to leave the skilled labor to the professionals."

"Well, if you change your mind, I'm sure my men would love a chance to rest their backs." Oakley extends a hand to me and we shake. "It was an honor to see what trolls are made of. You've earned a drink. Enjoy the festivities, and I'll unload the cart."

He leads the ox through the crowded street.

"You must have made quite the impression. Oakley's not one to offer unearned compliments." Gherhardt places a hand on my shoulder. "Come, let's get you a drink. I've worked you enough for the day."

In the village center, a large bonfire blazes. People stand around with steaming cups, while Dando and Liyah play music. A rowdy group of men, who I assume had the day off, sway back and forth singing a song about a great battle. Dando and Liyah wave when they see us. Warley stands alone nearby, a mug in his hand and eyes fixed on Liyah. He frowns when he turns to see who they are waving at.

I lean in closer to Gherhardt so I don't have to yell over the music. "You think Dando will give it his all against your niece?"

"I'd prefer if he didn't so she wouldn't be interested anymore." He laughs. "She'd lose respect if he held back even the smallest amount."

Nearby, there's a smaller fire under a large pot full of steaming liquid. Gherhardt fills a mug and hands it to me.

A scream echoes from down the street and a crowd rushes in our direction.

"Demon!" someone shouts. "Demons in Whitgard!"

My body tenses and I turn my gaze toward the screaming. The last thing we need is a demon attack right now.

Gherhardt drops both mugs and grabs the woman by the arms. His gaze is piercing. "What's going on?"

She looks over her shoulder with wide eyes. "There's a demon at the gate."

I equip Destroyer and summon horrors, eliciting more screams from the unsuspecting crowd.

"Calm down, everyone. I'll get to the bottom of this." Gherhardt tries to maintain order as he unsheathes the dagger strapped to his waist.

We rush down the street to find a crowd gathered around the gate. I push my way through and find Limery pressed against the wall like a scared dog, with a fireball in his hand as the villagers point weapons at him.

"Stays back," he whimpers. "Limmy doesn't wants to hurts yous."

The fear in his voice breaks my heart, and I unleash a powerful roar, startling everyone. "Back away, all of you!"

I know they are scared of what they don't understand, but anger floods my being. If one of them so much as lays a finger on him...

Archard pries his way through the crowd, pushing weapons down as he does. "Lower your weapons, you fools. He's not here to hurt you."

"It's okay, everyone." Gherhardt sheaths his dagger. "He's an imp, not a demon. And he's a friend of the tribe."

There's uncertainty in their eyes, but they lower their weapons.

Limery's eyes glisten as he wraps his arms around me. "I sorries, Chods. Limmy didn't mean to scares them."

I gently pet his back. "Don't worry, buddy. You didn't do anything wrong."

Gherhardt addresses the crowd. "Alright, everyone, back to the festivities. There's nothing to see here. Give them some space."

Once the villagers begin to disperse, he and Archard come over.

"Is he okay?" asks Archard.

"Just a little shaken up."

Archard wipes his face, holding a hand over his eyes for a moment in frustration. "Bloody dolts. The lot of them wouldn't know a demon if it smacked them in the face."

My anger subsides a little. It makes sense to me that they wouldn't recognize an imp, especially if he wasn't with me. Luckily, no one was hurt.

I'm suddenly aware that Limery is here alone, and my heart leaps into my throat. "Where's Taryn?" I blurt out.

"Taryns will be heres soon. He tolds Limmy to fly ahead."

I take a deep breath and some of the tension leaves my shoulders.

There's a flutter of wings and then a whistle as a small white bird lands on one of the posts of the palisade. The bird winks at me right before there's an explosion of white feathers and it transforms into an ebony dwarf.

Taryn reaches into his satchel and hands a bushel of herbs to Gherhardt. "Sorry it took so long, but here's your arctic clove. We had a bit of a run-in with a dragon." He looks around at the awkward situation. "What's going on here?"

Gherhardt takes the herbs. "Just a misunderstanding. I'd love to hear the story of your adventure, but right now, I need to visit Alvyn."

I turn to Taryn, wide-eyed. This was supposed to be a simple fetch quest. "Dragon?"

He grins. "And a dungeon. I'd love to tell you all about it, but what's a dwarf got to do to get a drink around here?"

"A man after my own heart." Archard claps him on the back. "Follow me."

20. THE ASCENT

Taryn downs the warm mead in a single gulp, and some of it lingers on his mustache. "That's the good stuff."

Limery watches everyone with suspicion from my right shoulder. He's still a bit shaken up by what happened. He could have easily fought the villagers off or escaped, but this was the first time in all our adventures that townspeople had outright attacked him. Imps weren't well-liked back on Isle of Mythos, but I don't think he ever experienced anything quite like this.

Archard returns carrying a massive stump on each shoulder and plops them on the ground next to the bonfire. He gestures for Taryn and I to sit. "So, you had a run-in with Nessie?"

"Nessie?" Taryn cocks an eyebrow.

He glances in the direction of Icemaw. "That's what I call the white dragon. Nesira means 'snow' in the old tongue."

I take a seat on one of the stumps. "Fitting. We saw one when we first came through the portal. How many dragons are there?"

"Just the one as far as I can tell, and she's plenty to deal with. Nessie flies all over Frostmoor, and a blizzard usually follows in her wake. She likes the three center peaks most, but it's smart to give her a wide berth."

"Has she ever attacked the village?" I ask.

Archard shakes his head. "Dragons are intelligent creatures. They usually don't attack settlements unless provoked. I've seen her fly off with a mammoth clutched between her talons, so I'd rather not see what she can do to Whitgard."

"She was something else." Taryn looks longingly back at the mountain. "What I would give for a pet like that."

I scoff at his idea of a pet. "I think we're all better off without a giant snowstorm following us around. So, what took you guys so long?"

Taryn tells us of their journey, of the frost giants and the dragon, and how they hid in a cave until the dragon found them and they were forced to hide inside the dungeon. "It was like one giant puzzle. Each of the gemstones activated an effect corresponding to the color. Had Limery and I not been able to fly, we never would have gotten anywhere."

"Speaking of flying, why was your bird form white?" I ask.

Taryn frowns. "Bro, I don't interrupt you when you go on one of your long monologues. Can you let me tell the story?"

I scowl at him. "You interrupt me all the time when I'm talking."

He clasps his hands over his heart. "I would never."

I have half a mind to throw a snowball at him, but I'm more interested in what he has to say. "Whatever. Finish your story."

He continues, telling us how Limery's fire attacks were especially effective on the enemies they came across. About fairies, and spiders, and other ice-themed monsters. "There were dozens of rooms to explore. I'm pretty sure the dungeon extended to the base of the mountain, but we were only able to open a few chests in the time we had. I got a pelt that mitigates the effects of cold weather, while also making me camouflage in snowy environments. And we got this for you."

He reaches in his satchel and pulls out a small shield with a snowflake engraved in the center. He hands the shield to me. "I know you don't normally use a shield, but with this one, it's small enough that you can use it offensively as well. I haven't tested it out, but hitting someone with the shield might also trigger the bonus ability."

Item. Frosted Buckler. +2 Constitution. *A lightweight and small shield capable of deflecting blows as well as being used offensively.* **Bonus Ability:** *Physical attacks blocked with Frosted Buckler cut the attacker's Dexterity in half for ten seconds.*

The shield is lightweight, with a strap that moves easily up my arm, so I could still wield Destroyer with both hands if I needed to. After watching Jegaar fight with a similar shield, I'm well aware of how dangerous a small buckler can be.

"Not bad. What else did you get?"

He grins, and there's mischief in his eyes. "We were running low on time, but we decided to check one more room before leaving. Honestly, I don't want to tell you what we went through to get it, but the loot was worth it. Don't you think so, Limery?"

For the first time since we sat down, Limery is aware that we're having a conversation. He looks to Taryn, confused.

"Never mind. Here." Taryn pulls a frozen orb out of his satchel and tosses it to me.

The orb feels delicate to the touch, like it's made from a thin layer of pure ice, but my warm hands do nothing to melt the frosty exterior. It radiates a cold chill, and as I wipe away the frost from the outer layer, several snowflakes flutter inside.

Item. Frost Bomb. *Frost bomb explodes upon impact, freezing an enemy in place for five seconds.*

"That's sick! How many do we have?"

He holds up five fingers. "You can have two, but you better use them wisely."

I don't know if it's possible to activate them accidentally, but I'm extra careful as I place them in my satchel. Crowd control abilities are what help turn the tide of battle, so these little orbs could save our lives one day.

"So what now?" Taryn asks.

Archard claps his hands together. "I'd say you two have earned some relaxation. We'll start heading up the mountain in an hour or so for the race."

"Race?" Taryn looks confused.

Archard fills him in on the history of the Ascent, albeit with a lot less enthusiasm than Dando.

When Archard finishes the story, Taryn makes a pit stop by the stables to check on his pets. While he checks in, I watch the stableboys prepare the goats for the ascent. They cinch the saddles and check the shoes tacked to each hoof. Limery clings to my shoulder, unusually quiet and observant.

As we leave the stables, Berry's whines carry through the town.

I shake my head. "You know taking Ruby is only going to make him more jealous."

Ruby winds herself between Taryn's footsteps, narrowly avoiding being stepped on as if she is one move ahead of him.

Taryn sighs. "I know, but I hate to leave Stompy alone. And Berry isn't the most compact. There's no way Gherhardt is letting me bring a bear into his house." His eyes light up. "But I can't wait for him to help me advance my herbalism. I told you my story, but what have you been up to while we were gone?"

We follow the procession of people exiting the town, and I fill in Taryn on all the work I've done around the village.

He laughs. "Talk about grunt work. I'm sure you're ready for a little excitement."

I open the cloak I'm wearing, revealing my chest and posing suggestively. "Even with this beautiful blue body, I was not born for manual labor. I'll take fighting monsters any day of the week."

Taryn snickers before mumbling, "Beautiful, my ass."

The climb is slow, but eventually, we make it to the top of the mountain. Villagers line the wooded mountainside above the path before the trail cuts inward straight to the peak. No one stands on the path itself. I'm sure they are all well aware of the risks that are posed by the frost goats.

Where the trail diverges, it becomes rocky terrain and trees grow along both sides all the way to the summit. Villagers are more densely packed in the second stretch, and some have even perched themselves in the trees.

A firm hand clasps me on the shoulder, and I turn to find Gherhardt slightly behind me and Taryn, a hand on both of us.

His shoulders relax. "I mixed the elixir and Alvyn is in better shape already. He doesn't have the energy to climb the mountain yet, but I owe you a great debt for your heroism."

Taryn puffs his chest out, and the clasps in his beard jingle. "It was nothing. We were happy to help."

Gherhardt smiles. "We'll discuss your reward later this evening."

Taryn and I take a spot midway up the raceway, where we can see both the beginning and the finish line. Gherhardt trudges up the rocky trail, taking his position at the finish line.

Several minutes pass as the last of the stragglers make their way up. Pulling up the rear are the goats and their handlers. Even though they are wearing blinders, the stableboys give each goat plenty of space, and so far, they remain calm. Three goats are about all I would be willing to risk on the path considering the width and the treacherous fall from the embankment. After seeing my horror head-butted off the side, I do not envy those racing. It would be a painful fall down the mountainside. The contenders will definitely have their work cut out for them.

Warley, Dando, and Liyah wait behind the stableboys as they wrangle the unruly goats to the starting line. Even with the blinders, the goats can somehow sense one another. Steam shoots out of their nostrils as they struggle and huff.

Warley stands to the side of the group, an outsider as Dando and Liyah joke around. Liyah pushes Dando in the shoulder, and he tilts his head back in laughter. I'd almost feel sorry for Warley if he wasn't such an insufferable prick. But I'm sure many people have said the same thing about me in the past.

Taryn leans in closer. "Who's your money on?"

I shrug. "I've never seen any of them race, so I don't really know. Dando spends a lot of time working with the goats, so that may give him an advantage, but they are so unpredictable that I'd say they all have a shot. Warley has a chip on his shoulder, so that makes him dangerous, and Liyah seems the type who has something to prove."

"Hmm, I'll take your word for it. Should be an interesting race."

A long, bellowing horn resounds from atop the mountain. Gherhardt stands tall with the last rays of sunlight setting him aglow from behind.

He clears his throat and the crowd quiets. "For many years now, we have celebrated our forebearers and their famous ascent up Whitgard alongside the return of spring. As the frigid winter becomes slightly less cold, it is a chance for the young and hearty to test themselves in the same way as Umen and Edrar did many years ago. For Umen, his prize was the very land on which you stand, a land we still defend and call home. For our contenders today, victory comes with the respect of the tribe, and in the ancient tradition, this ice wreath."

He holds up a crystal wreath that sparkles in the fading sun like a chandelier. As the sunlight hits the wreath from behind, rainbows sparkle on the trail below.

"This wreath has been with our tribe for many years, created by the last mage to be born in Whitgard, Proma of the Frozen Heart. Her beauty was said to enthrall the hearts of men and women alike, but her magic was known all over Mythos. She left in the great battle against the dark one, arming our warriors with precious enchanted weapons and emptying the troves. All that remains is this exquisite wreath, which is said to bring luck to those who wear it. May it serve the champion well." He pauses and lets the sparkles of the wreath fall over the crowd. "Riders, take your positions."

Warley, Dando, and Liyah climb onto their goats and take the reins. They each have about two feet of space between one another, but I don't know if that is enough to keep the goats in check. Each rider wears metal armor over their legs, probably to prevent them from being broken in the event that a goat rams them.

The stableboys remove the blinders, and Dando's goat rears back, nearly throwing him off. Warley's goat tries to headbutt Dando's in the hindquarter, but a quick tug by the stableboy avoids catastrophe.

A horn erupts from overhead. "Begin!" Gherhardt's voice echoes off the mountains.

The frost goats dart forward, thick white fur whipping around as they are spurred on by their riders. Warley clearly has the most aggressive goat, because it swings its horns at Dando anytime he gets close. After a few failed attempts, it charges Dando. Dando tugs the reins to avoid being hit off the mountain, narrowly dodging the charge as his goat spins in a quick circle.

Warley's goat speeds toward the edge from the momentum of the attack, but it regains its balance before toppling off, setting his sights on Liyah. Is he the type of person that would let her win to try and gain her favor, or does he see her for the feisty person she is? Her goat gallops up the mountain, putting distance between her and the others.

Dando is several paces behind after the spin, but he whips the reins and his goat moves faster.

Warley catches up to Liyah, his goat chomping at the bit as it tries to bite the other goat's stubby tail. Liyah steers closer to the mountain, and Warley closes the distance until they are side by side. The two goats crack their massive black horns against one another, and the impact echoes like a gunshot. Each goat stumbles, and they square off in the center of the path.

Warley tries to lead his goat away toward the finish, but it's a mistake. Liyah's goat rams Warley in the leg, denting his armor. He unleashes a pain-fueled groan that echoes time and again.

Their standoff allows Dando to catch back up, and he charges in at full speed. He steers his goat toward the mountain, but there's not enough space between the embankment and Liyah. He's going to plow right into her.

Her goat turns and lowers its head, ready for a fight, but Dando guides his goat toward the embankment. He whips the reins and his goat jumps.

The goat leaps at the embankment, hooves landing inches from crushing a villager's dangling feet. The goat springs forward, bypassing Liyah without incident as he takes the lead.

Liyah and Warley both abandon their scrap to chase Dando, but it's too late. He doesn't slow down as he enters the final stretch. The goat hops from one boulder to another, ascending the rocky finish to where Gherhardt waits.

Warley and Liyah are only halfway up the final stretch when Gherhardt blows his horn. Dando crosses the finish with his hands raised overhead.

"We have a victor! Dando is this year's champion of the Ascent!"

Dando takes the wreath and holds it over his head. It catches the final rays of light and looks like a glowing beacon as he pumps it in the air.

Cheers erupt from all around. I join in because I'm happy for the kid. He ran a good race, and that jump over Liyah was executed to perfection.

The stableboys, who have run along the trail following the race from start to finish, retake the reins. With heaving breaths, they lead the frost goats back down the mountain. Now that the entertainment is over, the villagers begin the journey back to Whitgard, but I keep my eyes focused at the top.

Warley extends a hand to Dando and the two young men shake. As Warley begins his long walk home, Dando hands the wreath to Liyah. She smiles for a moment before placing the wreath around Dando's neck, and they both laugh.

Looks like he won more than just the race.

"Chod?" Taryn pokes me in the ribs.

I'm startled back to the company at hand. "Huh?"

"I said that was wild. Those goats seem like a terrible choice to domesticate." He shakes his head in disbelief.

"They're actually really good guardians when they are alone, but I get what you're saying. Pretty cool tradition, though."

He grins. "Is it even a tradition if it doesn't have the threat of imminent death?"

The sun descends on the hike down the mountain, and everything is once again shrouded in a silver glow.

Limery hasn't made a peep on my shoulder since we got here. He watches everyone from my shoulder as if they are out to get him.

"You okay, buddy?" I tap Limery on the toe to get his attention.

He crosses his arms, brow furrowed in frustration. "Limmy doesn't likes it here."

I lift him from my shoulder and hold his small body in my palms so that I can look him in the eye. "That's okay. I know it was scary for you, but they didn't know who you were. They thought you were coming to hurt them."

"But Limmy doesn't hurt nobodies."

"I know." I stop walking and take a seat on an old tree stump. Taryn nods to me as he waits a few feet away. "Do you remember when you and I first got together, how we had to hide from all the humans because they wanted to hurt me?"

He nods.

"It's like that. They were scared of me because they didn't know me. But once they saw that I wasn't going to hurt them, they stopped attacking us."

That's a simple way of putting it. It's more like once they saw that I could destroy them but wasn't going to, they saw it was better to treat the trolls with respect than to anger them. But I'm trying to ease Limery's worry, not have him scare the villagers.

"We'll be leaving soon, so if you don't want to get to know them, that's fine. But you're a funny, loving imp, and I bet they would really like you if you gave them the chance. What do you say?"

He lifts a finger to his chin as he considers my proposition. "Limmy will thinks about it."

"That's more than enough."

21. LEAVE THE WORLD BETTER THAN YOU FOUND IT

After we arrive back in Whitgard, everyone gathers in the communal building where we'd eaten the previous night. Music blares and I immediately spot Dando on the stage with the ice wreath around his neck. He holds a mug in both hands and dances with Liyah to the folksy music.

Good for him.

Ruby darts beneath the long table on the left to scavenge for scraps of food that may have fallen.

"Might as well enjoy the mead while we can. There's no telling when we'll have access to more. Want me to grab you a drink?" asks Taryn.

"Yeah, sure. Give me a minute, though, I want to talk to Warley."

Taryn tilts his head, but then shrugs and walks away. Limery joins Taryn at the table brimming with food and mead. He seems to slowly be coming out of his funk.

Warley sits alone at the far end of the table staring into his mug. I'm surprised by how big he looks sitting there all alone. His shoulders are broad even without the fur coat, and his beard is full and thick, and yet he's around the same age as Liyah and Dando. Where Dando is youthful in appearance and attitude, Warley looks haggard and aged.

I tap my claws on the table, stirring Warley from his thoughts. "Mind if I take a seat?"

"Sure," he mumbles before taking a long swig of his drink.

I sit across from him. "Hell of a race today. I wasn't sure who was going to win."

"Pretty boy Dando wins again." He stares back into his mug. "Not that anyone is surprised."

I don't know why, but I suddenly recall a memory from my childhood. We were at a family gathering, back when they still happened. My mother's sister, Aunt

Susan, was there. She'd never had children, and from what I recall, she worked as a park ranger upstate.

I'd just tossed a soda can on the lawn like I'd seen my father do many times when she picked it up. When I'd told her the maid would clean it, she knelt in front of me and said, "Always leave the world better than you found it."

Man, that was so long ago. Those words meant little to me at the time, and I can't even remember the last time I saw Aunt Susan.

I tap my finger against the table until Warley looks at me with annoyance. "You know it's not always about winning, right?"

He looks me in the eye, searching for anything to tell him I'm messing with him. The way his fingers clench around the mug doesn't escape me. "What's it about then?"

Before I logged into Mythos, I doubt I could have given him this talk. I honestly don't even think I ever understood what Aunt Susan meant until now. But here I am, in a position to maybe do some good not just for Whitgard or the trolls, but for all of Mythos. I've been in Warley's shoes way too many times—angry about losing and blaming it all on someone else.

"Sometimes, it's just about showing up."

He scoffs. "What does a troll know?"

"More than you could possibly imagine. Look around, there are a lot of people in this village, and you were one of three who were chosen to compete. That's an accomplishment. Tell me, did your dad ever compete?"

His face softens, and he lets go of the mug. "What do you know about my father?"

"From what I can tell, he's pretty famous around these parts. Sounds like growing up in his shadow, especially with him not around, was a lot to live up to."

"He was a great man. Before he passed, he was my best friend. Taught me so much. He actually won the Ascent three times." Warley smiles for the first time since I've known him. "Probably could have won a few more if he were still around."

"Hey, I get it. We all live in our parents' shadows. The difference between mine and yours is that it sounds like your dad was a decent person. I'm sure he'd be proud of you."

"Are you saying there's truth to the tales of trolls eating children?"

"No, I'm not saying that." I laugh. "I'm saying that you don't have to live up to his image to be a good man. You didn't win. So what? You protect the gates of the village. You do your part. And you never know what part you may have to play in the future."

He sits in silence for a long moment. Music and chatter fill the room, but I can tell that his mind is elsewhere.

"It's really going to happen, isn't it?" He stares at the table.

"What's going to happen?" I ask.

"I've heard the rumors. No one has shown up in Whitgard for many years, and now dwarves, and then you. Whatever it is you're trying to prepare for, it will find its way to Whitgard."

I sigh. This conversation has taken an abrupt turn. "I hope not. I pray that Gherhardt will—"

"Excuse me," a young woman interrupts us, eyes locked onto Warley. "Sorry to intrude, but I was hoping you might want to dance. You did a great job in the race today."

Warley looks around, making sure someone isn't playing a joke on him, before he finally returns her smile. "Uh..." he stammers.

"Go on," I encourage him. "Show the lady a good time."

He takes her by the hand, and they disappear to the front of the building.

Even though I can't picture Aunt Susan's face, the words still resonate with me. *Always leave the world better than you found it.*

Maybe being a hero is more than just killing monsters and finishing quests after all.

After having a heart-to-heart with Limery and Warley, I think I've done enough good for one day. I can't help but wonder if I've really grown this much as a person since entering Mythos, or if the AI is partly responsible. Valery did say that it would have an effect on us. The hair on my neck stands up just thinking about it.

I close my eyes and take a deep breath. Those are concerns for another time. For now, it's time to find Taryn and get that drink.

The evening passes in a blur of delicious food, strong drinks, and laughter. The villagers sing and dance, and even Taryn and I join in for a few songs. Limery makes friends with a young girl, and soon he has his own crowd as he juggles fireballs in the corner. Warley's spirits lift immensely, and by the end of the night, he has his arm wrapped around the young woman who whisked him away.

Everyone is cheerful as we stumble back to Gherhardt's, except for Limery, who is passed out on my shoulder. A gentle snowfall muffles the sounds of the night.

"What a day!" Gherhardt wraps an arm around me, and I feel the brunt of his weight. "It's a good thing it only comes around once a year."

"I'd say. You drink like a dwarf." Taryn chuckles.

We turn the corner, where Dando has his arms wrapped around Liyah as they make out.

I abruptly change course, taking the next street over before Gherhardt has a chance to see what's happening.

We make it back to his place, and Ruby darts past us as we shuffle through the door frame, taking several attempts before unlocking our arms so that Gherhardt can enter first.

He plops down on a chair in front of the fire. "I'm just gonna...stay down...here...tonight."

His eyes flutter before he falls asleep. I toss a few more logs on the fire and cover him with a fur blanket. As we're going up the stairs, he calls out.

"Taryn...I...teach herbalism...mornin'." His words are jumbled, but we get the gist of what he's saying.

Upstairs, I lay Limery in bed and he starts snoring immediately.

Taryn joins me in the bedroom by the fireplace. "Once we're done with herbalism training, what's next?"

"We? That's your reward. I doubt I'll get in on it."

He laughs. "Don't be silly, I'm sure he'll let you join."

"We'll see. I'm sure it's more beneficial to you anyways. Herbalism probably goes a lot farther with being a druid. I've only got a handful of potions in my arsenal as it is."

He shrugs. "You never know what might be useful down the line. But seriously though, what's next for us? I was thinking that dungeon could be pretty lucrative."

"Maybe, but with me, Stompy, and Berry, I don't see us sneaking past the frost giants like you did. Not to mention if the dragon actually lives at the top of the mountain."

He strokes his beard. "Hmmm. I hadn't thought of that. Maybe there's a lower entrance."

"We need to go to Boneholde so that we can warn the others, but first, I'd like to take our chances with Hornryx. Even if nothing is there, there might be clues as to what happened to the arctic trolls."

"Yeah, strange that they just disappeared. Who knows, maybe they went through the portal when no one was looking."

We say good night, and I try my best to get some sleep. Tomorrow will be a long day of learning and traveling.

22. HERBAL T

Gherhardt moves around slowly the next morning, and the curtains are pulled when we head downstairs.

As usual, Taryn has no effects from the previous night's shenanigans, and compared to Gherhardt's, my hangover is minor.

"Morning, Sunshine." Taryn plops on the couch.

"Mornings, Sunshines!" Limery giggles as he joins the dwarf.

Gherhardt tosses a piece of sausage to Ruby and the jackal snatches it out of the air. "Old age has its pitfalls, let me tell you. In my youth, I could drink from dusk till dawn and still fit in the day's work. I hope I didn't embarrass myself too much last night."

"You were a drunken gentleman," I tease.

He laughs. "I don't doubt it. You'll have to serve yourselves this morning." He points to the bowls and takes a seat by the fire. "It's a good thing you were around to help Archard bring the frost deer up the mountain. The village devoured all of the venison in two days. The celebrations wouldn't have been the same without it, though."

Taryn enthusiastically scarfs down his meal.

"In such a hurry to be out of Whitgard?" asks Gherhardt.

"Not at all." Taryn picks a piece of egg from his beard and tosses it in his mouth. "I'm excited to learn enough herbalism that people will start calling me Herbal T."

"Oh, that." Gherhardt sighs, oblivious to the terrible pun. "What do I have if not my honor? A reward is a reward. Let me know when you're ready, and I'll brave the brightness."

After breakfast, we return to the greenhouse. Dando is leaving just as we arrive. I wink at him as he exchanges pleasantries with Gherhardt, and he returns a mischievous grin.

When they are done talking, he shakes my hand. "It was nice to meet you, Chod. Maybe our paths will cross again someday."

I grip his hand firmly. "No one knows what awaits any of our futures."

Taryn elbows me in the side. "Okay, Confucius." He shakes Dando's hand. "Congrats on the race." He leans in closer. "And the girl," he whispers.

Dando turns bright red as he heads to work.

"No one knows what awaits any of our futures," Taryn mocks me, moving his hands through the air like a mystic.

"Oh, shut up." I roll my eyes. "What would you have said?"

"Uh, something normal. Like, I don't know, 'I look forward to it,' or 'I hope so'."

I shove him into the snowbank. "Nah, doesn't have the same ring to it."

Taryn pulls himself up, snow covering his beard.

Limery bursts out laughing and dives into the snow next to Taryn.

Inside, Gherhardt leads us to the far end of the greenhouse. After a quick hello to Liyah, we get to work.

Gherhardt leans against the table. "I'm sure you already know this, but there is more than one way to increase your herbalism skill. Learning and identifying plants is the easiest way. You gain a certain amount of experience when you learn a new plant, and less and less each time you identify it in the wild. It will gain you quick levels and it is as far as most herbalists will go with their skills." He presses his hands together. "Why do you think that is?"

Suddenly, it feels like I'm back in school.

Taryn answers. "Because most people are only using their herbalism to find food or ingredients."

Gherhardt nods. "Exactly. But there is so much more to herbalism. To be a great farmer, gardener, florist, or proficient in any profession or skill where you will be growing your own plants, you will need to know advanced techniques. I have heard tales of druids capable of enhancing plants with deadly power and energy. Those skills are well beyond me, but I will teach you what I can today. To start with, I'll have you identify every plant within this growing barn. Thanks to me, we have quite the supply."

We spend over an hour with Gherhardt identifying plants. While we learn, Liyah harvests crops all around us, filling wooden boxes to be divvied up among the villagers. Limery helps, using his tiny fingers to pluck hard-to-reach fruits and vegetables. Ruby investigates the greenhouse, occasionally returning to check on us.

Gherhardt goes into great detail about each plant. Most are standard fruits or vegetables for feeding the village, but there is a good amount that have special effects. Fever grass is used in several potions and elixirs for various illnesses. A pinch of golden thorn will give any drink a metallic sheen, but at the cost of breath that reeks like death. Many of the plants do nothing on their own, but have profound effects when mixed.

By the time we are done, my herbalism skill is up to level ten.

"It is quite possible to reach beyond apprentice solely by identifying plants—

many wanderers and scholars have done just that—but the further one levels, the longer it takes to see results from this method alone. To truly gain insight into what it means to be an herbalist, one must not only learn to identify plants but to tend them and cultivate them.

"Each plant is different. Some need direct sunlight and lots of water. Others—" He lifts a curtain beneath the table where clusters of vibrant mushrooms grow. "—can survive in the depths of caves without ever seeing the sun. To propagate, some plants bear seeds, some must be severed at the root, and some only need to be plucked from the source and are able to sprout roots." He leads us to a thick bush with waxy leaves shaped like teardrops.

Taryn listens with wonder. "This is fascinating."

Maybe for him. I can see the use of identifying as many plants as possible, but I doubt I'll ever be growing my own. My skillset lies elsewhere.

Gherhardt looks at Taryn like a proud father. "For this next part, you won't see any noticeable increase in your level, but if you use this knowledge in the future, it will be invaluable. Cultivating plants takes time, but its possibilities are endless. Advanced herbalists are capable of breeding vastly different varieties, sometimes creating new species altogether." He grabs a pair of small shears off the table. "A pair of quality pruning shears are an herbalist's best friend."

For the next few hours, he instructs us on techniques for pruning plants for optimal growth, cutting off diseased areas, and how to tell if a plant is thriving or dying. We break for lunch before continuing our education, learning about repotting, splicing, and so much that I'm sure I could probably work at a greenhouse in the real world with the knowledge I've gained.

True to his word, my herbalism skill only goes up if I'm putting this knowledge to use on actual plants. While I find it mostly boring, Taryn is absolutely enthralled, asking questions and doing as much hands-on learning as possible.

I'm sure we could spend days here, doing nothing more than increasing our herbalism skill, but by early afternoon, it's time to leave. Gherhardt gives Taryn a large box filled with carrots for Stompy, and a vial of his dry rub to me. I'm sure it'll be gone in no time.

This herbalism knowledge may prove valuable one day, especially for Taryn, but being able to grow and identify plants will do little in the battle against Valmar and his dark forces. My time would be better spent leveling my mana infusion skill, if anything, not that there's easy access to raw mana anywhere outside of the troll forest.

What we need are warriors, and people willing to fight for what they believe in.

Gherhardt accompanies us to the stables to pick up Berry and Stompy and I make one last pitch for him to join the cause. "I appreciate your hospitality. As outsiders, we weren't expecting to be welcomed like this. I hope you will consider our offer. If nothing else, go to Seascape and meet the king in person."

He nods. "We offer hospitality to all who venture this far up the mountain. You are no longer outsiders to the Frozen Ash Tribe. I dare say you are friends." He turns to Limery. "I'm sorry for the confusion at the gate. I hope that you have seen that we mean you no harm."

Limery smiles. "It's okays. Limmy knows theys was scareds."

At the gate, Archard waits alongside Warley. The ranger has his axe strapped to his side, a pack on his back, and a bow on his shoulder. A surly frost goat stands behind him.

"Going out for a hunt?" I ask.

He taps the bow. "Not as far as last time, but we'll see what I can find. I'll accompany you a short way at least. Find out what you really think about Gherhardt when he's not listening." He winks.

"Nothing but kind words, I'm sure. Stay safe out there." Gherhardt gives us each a final pat on the back.

Warley opens the gate. As we're leaving, he steps outside. "Thank you. For the talk." He looks down and shuffles his feet. "I've been living in the past for far too long, holding on to what's gone, and blaming everyone else for not being stuck there with me." He lifts his gaze, meeting my eyes. "I can see that now. I've got big plans, and I'm certain our paths will cross again someday. Take care until they do."

I'm speechless. Last night, I spoke from the heart, but I never thought my words could have such an effect on him.

Warley extends his hand and when I move in to shake, he clasps me around the forearm, a gesture usually reserved for those considered brothers.

"Now that's how you say good-bye." Taryn grins as he climbs atop Berry.

I straddle Stompy, and we descend the mountain. Archard stays a healthy distance ahead of us. As powerful as that frost goat may be, I'll put my money on Stompy or Berry any day of the week.

The gate snaps shut behind us, and a fresh snowflake melts against my nose as we head to our next adventure.

23. PIGS AND A BLANKET

The snowfall continues as we descend Whitgard, covering the sprigs and patches of escaping greenery until the world is blanketed in white once again—everything except for the enchanted path that guides us down the mountain. Snowflakes melt as soon as they touch the trail.

Every so often, a mana-infused flame burns continuously, and I'm once again curious if ley lines run underneath the pathway or if they are pulling mana from some other source. Maybe the enchantment that keeps them burning is just that strong.

Up ahead, Archard pulls his fur coat tighter. "Every year, you think spring is finally here and then another snowfall turns it all upside-down. At least this isn't Nessie's doing."

"Does the snow ever truly melt away?" asks Taryn.

Archard grunts. "It clears around the portal and about halfway up the peaks. Summer comes and goes within weeks, but it's a beautiful sight while it lasts. Whitgard is rarely snow-free, but the trees and bushes shed their snowy coats."

I don't think I could handle a climate as unforgiving as this. Even in New York, I preferred the warmth of the indoors during the winter.

Whitgard is lucky to have the greenhouse. I wonder if the Snowwalker Tribe has something similar.

We pass the ruins where I helped Oakley mine and chop wood. Archard leads the frost goat off the path.

"This is where I leave you be. There's usually a fair amount of smaller game around these parts." He climbs down from the frost goat and adjusts the pack on his shoulders. "Time to see what beasts are lurking nearby. I wish you safe travels. Wherever you go, keep an eye out for frost giants."

We continue down the mountain, but I doubt we'll reach the base before nightfall. The sun is already slipping across the sky, and we got a late start.

Snow falls from the branch of a nearby tree, and Limery darts off in pursuit of whatever small creature made the disturbance.

"They were a nice group of people." The clasps in Taryn's beard jingle with each of Berry's steps. "More civilized than I expected."

"You mean aside from wanting to kill Limery?" I laugh half-heartedly. "No, they weren't half-bad."

"Yeah, but can you blame them? He can be a scary little bugger." He gestures toward Limery, who has feathers clinging to his cheek and fingers as he returns with a devilish grin.

Poor bird.

Truthfully, the Frozen Ash Tribe treated us better than I imagined they would. When Jegaar described them as mountain tribes, I expected something more along the lines of the mountain trolls. But these were salt of the earth people who kept to themselves. They are only a generation or two removed from trading with the outside world.

As good as this experience was, we must remember not to let our guards down. While they still held onto the civility of days past, that doesn't mean the Snowwalkers have done the same. We are outsiders. And that is always dangerous.

"I'm concerned if we'll be welcomed quite the same in Boneholde. Gherhardt says they're a more barbaric tribe. Especially since they were displaced."

"At least you're worried about something." Taryn rolls his eyes. "I'd say you should be more concerned with what lies up the mountain you're so intent on climbing."

"If there was anything worth worrying about, someone would have seen it by now. Even the frost giants come down from their mountain from time to time."

He sighs. "I hope you're right."

An hour later, we come across more ruins of Whitgard's past. Many of the houses are dilapidated, with roofs or walls long crumbled, but some of them still seem habitable. Stompy grunts as I force him to stop.

"Want to camp here for the night? I'm not sure where the next ruins are, and we don't want to be traveling at night."

Taryn looks around, frowning. "I'm going to miss that warm bed tonight." He rubs Berry behind the ears. "I hope you're ready to cuddle."

We find the ruins of an old barn and make camp. The walls are made of thick stone, but even so, there are gaps where the wind seeps through. It's the only place we find that's big enough to fit Stompy and still has four walls and a decent roof. This may be considered springtime for Frostmoor, but we're going to need all the warmth we can get during the night.

I gather logs, and Limery starts a fire, which eases some of the chill. After a quick dinner, I sleep against the wall, bundled up in my fur clothing and an extra blanket Gherhardt gave us. Limery's warm body curls up in the crook of my arm.

"Wake up!" Taryn shakes me. Even though he's whispering, urgency coats his voice.

"What is it?" I wipe the sleep from my eyes, but immediately discover what has him so alarmed.

Something grunts outside of the barn, and feet crunch through the frozen snow. A second later, another grunt answers.

Berry stands snarling in front of the door, hair raised. His growl is low and sonorous. I nudge Limery, and he frowns as he wakes.

Outside, it's still dark, and the dull glow of the night seeps in through the cracks in the slatted roof. A shadow passes across the gap in the door frame and the creature on the other side sniffs at the door. Dust shoots across the floor as it snorts again.

A wooden beam holds the old barn doors in place, but I don't trust it to keep whatever's on the other side out if it really wants to get in. It was more for peace of mind than anything. The hinges are rusted from years of disuse and are likely to break with the least amount of pressure.

"I'm going to check it out," Taryn whispers.

Without waiting for my response, he transforms into his bird form. Thanks to his new item, he's a brilliant white in the cold climate. He flutters up to the ceiling and disappears between a crack barely wider than he is.

More shadows pass over the door, and the snorting continues. Limery climbs onto my shoulder, and his hot claws dig into my muscles. Whatever's outside, they know we're in here.

Mana rages at my fingertips, and I summon my horrors. If whatever's outside breaks down the door, they're in for a rude awakening.

Incoming Message (Taryn): *This could definitely be worse, but there are four iceback warthogs outside the door. They're pretty big, with nasty tusks, some kind of frozen armor on their backs. All level twenty.*

Four level-twenty warthogs. I'm positive we can take them, but we'll probably tear down our shelter doing so.

Message (Chod): *Get back inside. I say we wait it out. Maybe they'll leave, and if not, we fight them at daybreak.*

Tiny claws scratch against the roof as Taryn squeezes back through the crack. He transforms into a dwarf just as I summon another round of horrors.

The sniffing gets louder as what I assume is all four of the warthogs pressing their snouts to the bottom of the door. Berry continues to snarl, but Stompy rests against the back of the barn like he doesn't have a care in the world. Ruby stares silently at the door.

"I don't think they're going anywhere." Taryn strokes Berry on the shoulder in an attempt to calm him.

"Yeah, well, neither are we."

Taryn fills me in on a more detailed description of the warthogs as we wait, and over the next hour, I keep a steady supply of horrors. With sixty of them crammed into the barn, there's enough body heat that it actually feels warm.

We use the time to come up with a plan, and once the first rays of sunlight pass through the slits in the roof, all hell breaks loose.

We cram against the back wall, using Stompy as a shield while Taryn casts Stonewall inside the barn, pinning my horrors between his wall and the door. My horrors are crammed together like stuffed animals in a claw machine.

Taryn hands me his Sapling Staff and flies through the crack in the roof to ready the next stage of our plan. The vines from the staff crawl through the slim space between the top of Taryn's wall and the roof, descending and wrapping around the wooden beam that bars the doors in place.

Footsteps thud overhead, and the wood groans as Taryn returns to his dwarven form.

I adjust the grip on the staff and turn to Limery. "Ready?"

"Readies!" He grins.

Taryn stomps twice, giving the signal that the cooldown for Stonewall is up.

With a heave, I pull on the staff, removing the beam from the door. There's a crash as the warthogs trample into the barn. If this works, then he should be summoning a second wall where the doors used to be, pinning the warthogs inside.

"Now!" Taryn shouts.

I cast Kamikaze, exploding all sixty of my horrors in a single blow. The explosion is so powerful that it shatters Taryn's wall. Stompy's massive hide shields us from the blast, and he bellows as he loses a chunk of health to the debris.

Limery summons a wall of fire in the wreckage, and warthog squeals pierce through the dawn. With the doors blown off, light floods into the barn.

The warthogs, gashed and bleeding, are the most ferocious-looking pigs I've ever laid eyes on. Their skin is a light blue with stripes of white that are stained red. Where a normal warthog would have a strip of coarse hair running down its back, these have shards of jagged ice. Two piercing icicle tusks jut up from their lower jaws, though some look to have been broken or chipped in the blast.

They thrash around in slow-motion as their health ticks down in the fiery rubble. Then one locks its eyes on us.

The passive slows from the Horrors of Vitality fade and one warthog squeals as it charges.

I toss the staff aside and equip Destroyer as I vault over Stompy. As soon as I land, I swing at the charging beast, and Destroyer connects just above the front shoulder. Red flashes through the weapon as the warthog spins, flying into the barn wall with a thud, and Berry pounces on the downed creature.

I hit the second warthog with an upward swing. Its jaws clack and a tusk breaks at the base as it flips backward into the third warthog.

I can't get my weapon down in time before the final warthog buries a tusk into my leg. The tusk pierces my flesh like a toothpick through warm butter, and shooting pain is all I can focus on as I'm bulldozed into Stompy.

There's a flash of bright light as the roof explodes and a deafening thunder rattles my bones. The pressure vanishes from my leg, and I'm launched against the wall. Somewhere, Limery's voice calls out to me, but it's quickly drowned out by the ringing in my ears.

I attempt to stand, but my left leg doesn't support my weight and I collapse against the wall. It's been a while since I felt this kind of pain. Without thinking, I pull a health potion from my inventory and down it. Immediately, the world comes back into focus.

Limery's warm hands press against my cheeks and two bulbous eyes blot out my vision. "Chods, is yous okays?"

I'm suddenly aware of the smell of roasted pork, and my mouth waters involuntarily. "Yeah, I'm okay."

His tiny shoulders relax.

Next to me, Taryn kneels over Stompy, casting Restoration, and the two are shrouded in a golden glow. The potion slowly stitches the wound in my leg back together and I'm able to stand by the time he is finished. Four warthogs lay scattered around the barn among rubble and smoking wood.

I take a deep breath. That was a lot harder than I expected.

Taryn presses his boot against one of the warthogs, checking to make sure it's dead. "That went well."

I stretch my neck from side to side. "Easy for you to say. You didn't have a foot-long tusk stabbed into your leg. I don't even know what happened at the end there."

He grimaces. "Yeah, that looked rough. Once I saw they were making Chod kabobs, I figured it was time to step in. You and Limery took out about three-fourths of their health in those first few seconds. My lightning bolt finished off the one you smacked in the face and stunned the other for Limery to take out. Stompy sideswiped you with his horn. It got the beast off of you, but it looked like it hurt."

I walk over and pat Stompy on the shoulder. "Thanks for looking out, big guy. You hit like a sledgehammer."

He huffs in response.

Taryn offers him one of Whitgard's carrots and he chomps it with vigor.

I kneel by one of the warthogs and slice off some of the meat with my claw. It's fatty, with a smoky flavor. "Loot what we can, but we need to get moving. We caused quite a commotion and we don't want any big scaries getting scent of this roasted meat while we're around."

Most of what we loot is meat for our journey. Gherhardt gave us eggs, bread, and vegetables, but meat was in short supply. I also manage a few warthog tusks. If we had time, I would have skinned them for their armored hide, but we want to be as far away from this place as we can.

I don't know how far a frost giant can smell, but I most certainly do not want to find out.

24. AIN'T NO MOUNTAIN HIGH ENOUGH

Our journey back to the portal is uneventful. Even though I'm sure we pass the areas where Archard lost his hunt and where we battled the frost wolves, all evidence has been hidden by the snow.

When we arrive at the fork where the five paths meet, the view is daunting. Hornryx towers above the other peaks. A ring of clouds surround it where most of the other mountains reach their summit, obscuring its apex. The mountain is still wide at that point, so there's no telling how much further up it goes.

"You sure you want to do this?" Taryn squints as he stares up at Hornryx. "We could travel to Boneholde in the time it would take us to reach halfway up this one."

"I need to go. It's going to suck, but I need answers. There's no way I can go back to Chief Rizza and the others knowing I was this close to the home of one of our people and didn't at least check it out, you know?"

"I know." He sighs. "Damn it to hell."

"Damns it to hells." Limery scowls up at the mountain.

I push Limery off my shoulder, and he falls into the snow. "You two have been spending too much alone time together."

He pokes his head up from the snow, giggling. I think the little devil has discovered that copying Taryn is a good way to annoy me. I hope he hasn't just entered the annoying teenager phase of imphood.

We carry on traveling, and by twilight, we've only just reached the base of Hornryx. There are no ruins or caves for us to make camp, so we have to get creative.

"We could try to make shelter between those two trees." Taryn points to two massive pines not too far from the trail.

I'm all for sleeping outdoors, but not in freezing temperatures. "How long does one of your walls last?"

He shrugs. "No idea. I've never actually tested it. The ones from our battle with the wolves were gone, so I'm guessing they decay at some point. Either that or something destroyed them."

"I guess there's only one way to find out."

I summon enough horrors to clear a large patch of snow. Once the area is cleared down to the frozen grass, Limery summons several flame walls, drying away the moisture. His attacks leave the ground barren and charred, but that's better than wet and cold.

Once a big enough space is cleared, Taryn casts Stonewall. After each cooldown, he summons another wall. Before boxing us in with the final wall, we gather wood for a fire.

The opening above us is too big to tie any of our blankets together for a roof, so the cold air still creeps in, but with a roaring fire and tall walls, the frigid breeze is kept at bay.

Stompy lays against one wall, and Taryn bribes him with more carrots so that we can use his broad belly as a pillow. Taryn cuddles against Berry as Ruby curls up in his lap. Limery nestles in my arm.

The moulhaug's chest rises and falls with each boisterous breath, and the wind whirls overhead. It's kind of comforting.

"This was a good idea." Taryn gently strokes Ruby from head to tail. "You're not such a dumb brute after all."

"You know it." I laugh. "I've got brains and brawn."

"You must have learned from the best." He smirks.

"Maybe once upon a time, but now you're more like brains and scrawny."

"Pssh, it's called being stout." He crosses his arms.

"Okay, Mrs. Teapot." I put one hand on my hip and extend the other like a spout.

He shows me a rude gesture. "Either way, we're a pretty good team. Good night, guys."

"Good night, bro."

"Good nights, bros." Limery tosses a final flame at the fire before tuckering out.

From where I'm lying, the mountain takes up the entirety of my view of the outside world. The clouds have a silver glow as they hug the mountain, and I can't help but wonder what lies within their depths. Trolls? Dungeons? Monsters? Or nothing?

It could very well be that the first race of trolls has gone extinct from the world. All the more reason why we must fight like hell to protect what we have.

A cold gust of wind wakes me up as one of Taryn's walls disappears. Stompy stirs, agitated, before Taryn calms him.

"On it!" He sounds half-asleep as he summons a new wall to replace it. Over the next few minutes, the other walls fade from existence, and he immediately replaces them. Once our new fortress is in place, Limery stokes the fire and we're back to sleep.

In the morning, we roast some of the boar meat over the fire. When we're ready to leave, I use the water from Brimming Tankard to douse the fire. Even though Taryn can cancel Stonewall himself, I equip Destroyer to break through just to test it. While it has the strength of stone, the wall itself has no magical properties and it breaks easily enough under the enchanted weapon.

We load up the animals and begin the slow crawl up the mountain. Snow falls all around us, concealing everything but the enchanted path. Occasionally, we pass frost deer and even a few wild frost goats as we ascend. The higher we climb, the more dangerous the monsters become. We do our best to avoid them when we can.

At one point, an icy blue spider with spiked crystalline legs clatters out from a cave, but a well-placed flame wall from Limery sends it skittering back inside.

"Never going in a cave again." Taryn shivers, shaking his head in disgust. "Nope."

Wolves howl nearby, but we're unable to see them. With their white fur, they could be anywhere and with the way the wind is blowing, it's hard to tell the direction the howls are coming from. I'm not sure if they are following us or not, but I summon horrors just in case.

We'll need to keep watch tonight.

By nightfall, we can't be more than a few hours from the ring of clouds. The closer we get, the heavier the snowfall.

Now that we're near the ring, I notice that the clouds are actually rotating around the mountain at a pretty fast pace. I watch them, mesmerized. "I'm excited to see what's beyond the clouds."

"Just please don't let it be spiders." Taryn grimaces. "That's all I ask."

He summons his walls and we make camp for the night. Tomorrow morning, we'll know if this was all worth it.

The high walls obscure the light from our fire, but I still don't feel safe without one of us keeping watch, especially after our encounter with the spider. Who knows what else could be creeping around the mountain at night?

I take the first watch, staring up at the sky as snores erupt all around me. The fire crackles, basking my toes in warmth and sending the occasional ember drifting through the air.

Sitting against the wall, I wonder how this space compares to a prison cell. It's not lost on me that this could have been my fate had I not been able to log into Isle of Mythos. As shitty as the situation feels knowing I haven't heard from my parents, I still owe them for getting me here. I could have been stuck in a cell with a less-promising view.

I can't even imagine how I would have dealt with that, with people like Glenn or Jude. Pressley and Jon seemed normal enough, but even they are from worlds vastly different than my own.

A chill runs down my spine.

Something taps against the other side of the wall, startling me, and I fight the urge to scream. In a flash, I'm on my feet with Destroyer clenched tightly in my grip. Ruby shuffles in Taryn's lap at my sudden movement. Her ears twitch, and she's wide awake staring at the same spot on the wall where I heard the sound.

Wind whooshes overheard like a whirlpool, making it impossible to hear anything on the other side of the walls for that moment, but I know something is out there. I heard it through the stone.

I wait for another scratch or tap, but it doesn't come.

My heart pounds in my chest, the fear of the unknown running wild in my mind. Spiders, wolves, it could be anything on the other side. I take solace in the fact that if it was Nessie, she would have destroyed us by now.

Maybe this was a bad idea.

After several long minutes, Ruby rests again. That puts me at ease a little. Her perception is incredibly high after all, but I keep a hold on Destroyer just in case.

The hours pass slowly before it's Taryn's turn to take watch. I tell him about the noise as I settle down against Stompy.

"Maybe it was a tree branch?" His gaze drifts upward, toward our only view of the outside world. "Or it could have been the antlers of a frost deer passing by."

I shrug. Whatever it was, I pray it's long gone by now.

I wake briefly in a couple of hours to a chill as Taryn's walls fade and he summons more. Luckily, there's no monstrous beast waiting to kill us on the other side, and I'm able to return to sleep with only the vaguest recollection of being awakened.

Once morning comes, we pack up and I summon a full army of horrors as we journey toward the clouds that bar our view of the top. I don't know what waits beyond, but I'd rather be safe than sorry.

A silver falcon perches in a tree, watching us as we gather our belongings. Limery eyes it greedily, but then it disappears into the clouds.

The snowfall steadily increases the closer we get until eventually, we can't see more than a dozen yards in either direction. It's like when Nessie passed over the portal, only never-ending. The only warmth comes from Stompy's hide between my legs, and Limery clinging tight against my shoulder. His heat permeates the fur cloak.

I send half of my horrors to lead the way and have the other half bring up the rear, using them as bumpers against the fog of snow. If something happens to them or their presence goes missing, I'll be able to tell right away.

Taryn pulls Berry to a halt and turns around. Ice crystals cling to his beard. "How are we supposed to find anything in this blizzard? It's only getting worse."

Shivers run through my body as cold wind seeps into every open crevice of my fur clothing. "I don't know. I'm hoping it clears up once we get high enough."

He squints in my direction. "We can barely see the trail as is. If we leave it, we're screwed."

"I know. So, don't leave the trail."

A half-hour later, Taryn stops again. A thick layer of snow has gathered on both Berry's and Stompy's backs. The snow comes down faster than it can melt away. My breath comes out as thick steam, causing a layer of ice to coat my tusks. Limery is the only one not covered in ice and snow.

"What is it this time?" I shout above the wind.

"End of the line!" His voice is soft in the snowfall.

I climb down from Stompy to see what Taryn is talking about. Sure enough, the enchanted trail ends abruptly against a mound of snow. A single mana-infused torch crackles against the wind.

Fuck.

Berry groans beside me, his displeasure mirroring my own.

"What now?" Taryn calls from the bear's back. "Should I scout ahead?"

I shake my head. "Too dangerous. I don't want to risk getting separated. We've made it this far. Let's push a little farther."

He stares at me intently. "If we push much farther, we're not escaping this blizzard tonight."

Icy dread rests on my shoulders. I hope like hell we make it to the other side.

Stompy and I take the lead, using his massive horn to bulldoze a path for Taryn and Berry to follow. My horrors pick up the rear, no longer able to scout ahead without slowing us down.

With every step, I'm more and more certain this was a bad decision. The reason nothing comes down from Hornryx is because nothing can survive this type of environment. This was nothing more than a fool's errand. I should have listened to Taryn. Now, I've wasted precious time that could have been spent elsewhere. We could be in Boneholde by now, presenting our cause to their leaders. Then we'd be off to somewhere new, some place where my ass cheeks wouldn't be frozen together.

One of my horror's presences vanish.

I turn around, but I can't see past Taryn in the snow, much less to any of my horrors. In these conditions, it could have fallen off a cliff for all I know.

"One of my horrors went—"

Taryn's black eyes go wide, and he points a stumpy finger over my shoulder. As I turn around, I'm keenly aware as several more horrors vanish.

Frost spreads across Stompy's hide. There's a loud crack as it thickens and forms into ice. His body freezes in place.

The frost spreads, creeping up my legs. I try to move but I'm stuck. It inches up my body, rapidly freezing me in place before I can escape.

"Chods!" Limery yells as he presses warm fingers against my neck.

For the first time, his touch feels anything but warm. The ice crawls up his arm and his bulbous eyes bulge with panic.

I try to tell him it's going to be okay, but my jaw locks in place.

For the longest time, the world is a swirl of snow. My eyes lock with Limery. He's scared, and it's all my fault.

As we look upon one another, I try not to think about the fact that this might be the last time I'll see him alive.

I've fucked us all. And for what?

I struggle against the ice, but it doesn't budge.

I'm a second away from activating Berserker Rage when a hulking white figure steps into view. My hesitation dooms us all because before I can activate my ability, my eyes freeze shut, and everything goes dark.

25. ARCTIC STROLLS

I've never been so cold. Not even the time I locked myself inside the freezer at one of my parents' business galas. I was only eight or nine, and so bored out of my mind that I wandered around the event space. I ended up in the kitchen because it seemed more exciting. After shutting myself inside the walk-in freezer, I panicked, not knowing that the doors opened from the inside as well. I had frosted tears on my cheeks by the time a server came in to retrieve the desserts.

Everything is dark and hazy. I can't move, but uncontrollable shivers still somehow manage to snake through my frozen body.

Figures move across my blurred vision. I have no idea what's happening, where I am, or who or what is responsible. The last thing I remember is the hulking figure and everything going dark as ice covered my eyes. I pull up my notifications.

Alert! *You have been frozen. You are unable to move for the next thirty seconds.*

More than thirty seconds has passed but I still can't move. I might not be technically frozen by whatever ability hit me, but I'm guessing I'm stuck in a block of ice.

The ice cracks around my forehead and shards break away from my eyes. The rush of sunlight is blinding, but all I can do is squint.

I have access to my abilities, but I don't want to waste Berserker Rage without knowing what the situation is. Even though it makes me immune to stuns, slows, and effects, I don't know if being stuck in a block of ice counts as an effect. Or if it just means I'm trapped. The heat that accompanies my bulging muscles might be enough to break through, but I can't be certain. If it was enough to freeze Limery, then I doubt I have any chance of breaking out. Whatever did this is more powerful than we are.

So I'll need to be smarter.

My eyes finally adjust to the daylight, and two large bright blue eyes stare back at me. My heart jumps, but the ice keeps me in place. Even my startled scream stays constrained within my chest. The eyes are so close to my face that I can't see beyond them.

I attempt to look around, but my neck and jaw is still frozen. I have no idea if Taryn, Limery, or the others are with me or not.

"You are either incredibly brave or incredibly stupid." The voice is deep, even with layers of ice muffling my hearing. "It has been a long time since someone attempted to climb Mount Hornryx. We normally kill those that make it to the ring. Usually, it's an adventurous hobgoblin, or a frost giant that has forgotten its place in the world, occasionally, a greedy tribesman, but imagine my surprise when I find a troll leading a party of misfits onto my lands."

He leans back, revealing black skin the color of a faded charcoal. Two short tusks poke through the hair of his thick white beard. White fur covers the majority of his body. All except for his hands and a large patch on his stomach, both areas are the same faded charcoal black as his face. I take a second to analyze him.

Chief Laojin
Level: ???
Druid
Arctic Troll

My chest tightens, and it feels like it could crack through this frozen prison. An arctic troll! I was right. I found one, and now it's about to be the death of me. I struggle against the ice, but it is unforgiving.

"What I really want to know..." He leans in again, blocking my view. "Is why there's a lone forest troll on my mountain?"

There's a long pause before he speaks again. "Senzala, can you do something about this ice? I'd like to talk to him before we decide whether or not to kill them."

Chief Laojin slides off the side of Stompy's neck and lands in the snow, revealing a second troll that was standing behind him.

Senzala
Level: ???
Shaman
Arctic Troll

Another troll shaman. She's the only one I've seen besides Jira. She's more slender, almost half the width of the male troll. She doesn't have a beard, but she does have an ample amount of fur-covered bosom above a patch of hairless black skin on her midsection.

She waves her hand in my direction and ice falls from my face.

"Where's my party?" I shout. "If you hurt them, I swear I'll—"

As quickly as it disappeared, ice reforms over my mouth.

"You'll do what, exactly?" Senzala laughs mockingly.

Laojin climbs back atop Stompy, a frown plastered on his ugly face as he sits backwards in front of me. "You have no power here. Look at me." He presses a thick finger against my forehead, and rage boils inside of me.

Once I break out of this ice, I'm going to show him what real power is. I bring my eyes to meet his.

"That's better." His mouth curls into a snarl. "You're only alive because I am a curious troll. Let that sink in for a minute. We could have killed you in the ring. We could have left you there to die slowly and painfully. We could have pushed your frozen bodies off the cliff and watched you break into a thousand pieces as you fell down the mountain. We could have fed you to the dragon. There is no end to the number of ways we could have caused you to suffer, ways we can still make you suffer. Make no mistake, you came into our lands and you will deal with the consequences of those actions. We live in peace because we stay hidden. Because one cannot bother what they don't know exists. But now here you are, so I will ask you one time and one time only. Why?"

He nods to Senzala, and she removes the ice from my mouth once again.

They both stare at me with a bone-chilling intensity.

I choose my next words carefully. If there's a chance Limery and the others are still alive, I need to talk my way out of this.

"We—no, I—I was looking for you."

He places his hands together, and his blue eyes fill with mischief. "Continue."

"It's a long story."

He holds up a finger, telling me to wait a second as he slides off Stompy's ice-covered hide and disappears from my view. Senzala watches me with cold eyes.

A moment later, I can barely see him out of the corner of my eye as Laojin pushes Berry's frozen body. It's like the bear is sliding on a conveyor belt as his stiff legs glide across the snow. Taryn sits atop him, face petrified mid-yell, his right arm outstretched with the Sapling Staff still frozen in his grip. Ruby's snarl is carved in ice.

If I weren't a troll ice cube, I'm certain I would collapse from relief. They're still alive, which must mean Limery is still on my shoulder. I don't know how they were able to freeze his hot imp body, but at least I have a shot at saving them.

Laojin lifts Taryn's frozen body from Berry and tosses him into the snow like he's nothing more than a toy. I clench my jaw, fighting the urge to yell as he does the same to Ruby before he climbs on Berry's back and faces me. If I lose my cool, we're all dead.

He leans forward. "I've got nothing but time."

I take a deep breath, and recount my adventures since entering Mythos. "It all started when I woke up in the forest..."

Laojin listens with rapt attention, hanging on to every word as I tell him of my adventures since arriving in Isle of Mythos. Aside from the times I logged out, I tell him everything. He doesn't interrupt, but he does make comments to himself as I tell the story, mumbling "interesting" or "curious" all the way until I get to us reaching the ring around Hornryx.

Telling the story, my origin story, reminds me of all the people and places I have experienced in this world. From my first encounter with Gord until right now, this world has shaped me, and continues to shape me, into the hero I am. That in itself is worth fighting for.

By the time I finish, the sun has set and we sit in a silver glow. There's been no snowfall since the ice was removed from my eyes, and this high up, the moonlight seems to shine brighter. Or maybe it's because there are no clouds blocking its reflection.

"This has been a fascinating tale. I am glad we didn't kill you on sight. It is good to know our brother and sister tribes have not yet perished." He runs clawed fingers through his beard. "You have told us how you came to Hornryx, but you haven't answered my question. Why are you here? You didn't know what awaited you past the ring, so what were you hoping to find?"

I sit in silence for a long moment, not sure that I have an answer. "I don't know. Hope, maybe. I've gone from one society to another, having to convince everyone but the dwarves at Seascape that this world is worth fighting for. I guess just once I was hoping to find someone who didn't need convincing, a troll society that wasn't on the brink of collapse or afraid of the outside world."

"I am sorry, but you will find none of that here." He turns to Senzala, and she nods. "While I do not agree with your path, you are a troll after all, and I believe that Chief Rizza was correct in supporting you. A troll hero still means something; therefore, I will allow you and your party to stay in Hornryx for the time being, and we will help you with what knowledge we have. After that, I will send you on your way and you will forget you ever saw this place. We will have no part in the wars that plague men, dwarves, elves, and the like. Understood?"

I nod. It might not be what I hoped for, but it's something. "Understood."

"Release them."

A white aura surrounds Senzala as she slashes her hand through the air. Ice cakes off my body like I stepped out of a mud bath, and everything devolves into chaos as my companions unfreeze all at once.

Stompy bellows and thrashes his horn. Limery yells, and ice sizzles and turns to steam as he goes molten. Taryn looks up from the snow, confused while Ruby rushes to him, licking his hand. Berry thrashes about, tossing Laojin from his back.

The druid chieftain lands with one knee pressed to the snow and extends his arm as a shield of ice materializes just as Berry swipes at him.

"Everyone, calm down!" I roar.

Taryn crawls to his feet. "What the hell is going on? Where are we?" He holds his staff ready to attack the two arctic trolls. "Who are they?"

"Later!" I shout. "Call off your pets, Limery, back to me."

Limery's flames fade and he lands on my shoulder. He stares at the two new trolls with uncertainty. Berry returns to Taryn's side, still snarling, and Stompy huffs in agitation.

Taryn stabs his staff into the snow. "Will someone tell me what the hell is going on here?" His gaze shifts between me and the other trolls. "Where are we? And who are they?"

Laojin smiles as he looks at Taryn. "It has been too long since I have met another druid. And a feisty one at that." He motions up the mountain. "Come, follow us to the village and all will be explained."

"Another druid?" Taryn's eyes light up as he analyzes Laojin. "You're a troll druid! I am so confused. The last thing I remember, we were being attacked in the blizzard."

Laojin nods toward the shaman. "You can thank Senzala for that. Her totem grants her the ability to cast the ring."

I stop in my tracks. "The entire ring? You have the power to cast a spell that strong constantly?"

Her level must be through the roof.

Senzala gives me a blank expression. "The closer I am to my totem, the more powerful my magic."

Just like Jira. His attacks were powerful in the forest, but when the phoenix was nearby, they took on another level.

I fall back in line and follow them up the mountain. "What's your totem?"

She smirks. "Nesira, the guardian of Frostmoor."

"Nesira." I stop in my tracks as the realization seeps in. "Do you mean Nessie? Your totem is a white dragon?"

"Nessie?" She laughs. "You've seen her around?"

"You could say that." My mind runs wild for a moment. With the arctic trolls having a dragon, Jira's phoenix, and the three wyrms the forest trolls have, troll society isn't looking as fragile as it once was.

But everything feels like it's resting on a razor's edge. The difference between a thriving kingdom and extinction rests on the fate of impending war.

It rests on my shoulders and the rest of the heroes.

Laojin leads us up the mountain, while Senzala brings up the rear. Taryn and I walk on foot with his pets following us.

Limery sits on my shoulder complaining. "Limmy was colds. So colds. Limmy never knows what the colds is like, but now he knows. No likey."

"Now you know what it's like for the rest of us," I tease. "We don't all have a furnace inside of us."

"Are you sure we can trust them?" Taryn leans in close and whispers. "They literally froze us."

"I don't think we have much of a choice. If Senzala really does control the entire ring, there's no telling how strong she is. She has the power of a white dragon behind her, and there's no way we're making it back down without them. Besides, if they wanted us dead, then we wouldn't be here right now. They want to help us, and where else are you going to get one-on-one training with a high-level druid?"

Taryn tilts his head forward, eyebrows raised. "Uh, seriously? How about Seascape?"

I cock an eyebrow. "If that were the case, then why did King Orso send us away to train? Why not train us at the castle?"

Taryn purses his lips. "Hmmm. Good point."

"I know it's a good point. It's because he wants allies more than just two strong heroes. This might be a way for us to get both."

"Yeah, yeah. I guess your instincts were right after all, but I wouldn't count your chickens just yet. Our track record has been pretty shitty for gathering allies."

He's right, but that doesn't mean we have to give up.

As we climb the mountain, I can't help but notice how quiet it is. We haven't seen any other trolls or animals since coming out of the ring. Are the arctic trolls barely holding on to life this far up?

I catch up to Laojin, who seems unconcerned with whether or not we can keep pace. Ahead of him, there are only two sets of tracks in the snow, both leading down, so they obviously don't come down this far very often, and they must have been confident enough that the two of them could take on whatever threat we presented.

Or they were the only two capable of fighting.

Laojin comes to a stop and raises his right arm for us to halt. "Welcome to Hornryx, home of the arctic trolls. While you are here, you will be treated as honored guests."

Taryn and I exchange glances. Has Laojin been living alone in the mountains for so long that he considers the wild terrain his village?

"Uh, it's beautiful..." Taryn lets the words trail off as he looks around.

And then I see it: a faint shimmer in the air. One that I've seen before.

"You have a protective barrier." Now that I've spotted it, I can see more ripples in the air. The same type of forcefield that kept strangers from approaching the forest troll village.

Laojin puffs out his chest. "Remnants of a different time, but you can never have too many defenses."

"What's he talking about?" Taryn scrunches his eyes in confusion.

Ruby passes through Taryn's legs, stepping through the barrier. For a second, her body is distorted, until it vanishes entirely.

26. HORNRYX

"Ruby!" Taryn chases her through the barrier, the frozen clasps in his beard jingling like a cat with a bell around its neck.

I call for Taryn but it's too late. He's already stepped through.

Laojin makes a noise that's somewhere between a grunt and a deep chuckle. He steps through, and I follow him. On the other side, Taryn stands frozen, Ruby squirming in his grip.

My chest tightens for a moment before I realize Taryn isn't actually frozen. My jaw drops wide open as I take in the surroundings, just as awestruck as he is.

Before me, a frozen jungle spreads up the mountain, a fusion of plant and ice. There's more greenery here than I've seen in every other part of Frostmoor combined. Yet at the same time, there's so much ice that the entire place shimmers in the moonlight, like a garden carved from colored glass. Plants grow tall and vibrant even though many are encased in ice.

The sun has already set but I don't need my night vision to see. This high up above the clouds, the sky is filled with streaks of green and purple, reminiscent of the Northern Lights. This must be what it's like to live in Alaska during the summer when it never goes completely dark.

Trees and vines form the foundation of a handful of buildings, while thick, translucent ice blocks make up the walls—like a cross between an igloo and a treehouse. Vines cross over one another, forming windowpanes with ice so thin they appear as clear as glass. Frozen flowers cover many of the roofs, and some of the trees grow frozen fruit.

Pathways wind through the village. Vines run along the edge of the paths like a sidewalk, and the ground between is free from snow just like the enchanted paths from the portal. The land where the village is located is relatively flat and recesses back into a deep crag in the mountain. Each path leads to a different cave in its depths. Some are small, while others are tall enough to drive a semi through. To the left and right of the village, trails disappear higher up the mountain.

"You infused all of this?" I kneel and examine the vine-work of one of the structures.

Laojin nods. "The mountain provides all we need."

Through the window of the nearest building, salted meat rests on several racks. A large cauldron filled with some sort of stew bubbles over a low fire, reminding me of Kea's delicious stew in the forest. Steam rises out of a small chimney made of ice.

I'm impressed. This place is even more beautiful than the forest troll village.

As I continue to survey the area, I notice two guardian trolls standing sentry beyond the buildings where the paths lead to the caves. Their bodies are translucent from using Camouflage while not moving. Unlike the forest troll guardians, who normally crouch while on watch, these stand like soldiers, and each one holds a massive sword made from ice, each one taller than Taryn. Serrated edges cover one side and sharp ice the other. The sword tip sticks in the snow, and the trolls rest their hands at chest-height on the pommels. The guardians watch us with interest, but neither move. Aside from them, the village is eerily empty.

"Where is everyone?" I ask.

"It is late." Laojin glances at the moon. "I am sure you are tired. We will find you a place to sleep and introduce you to everyone in the morning. Then we will begin training."

"This place is crazy," whispers Taryn. "No offense, but it's way cooler than the forest."

As we approach the caves, the guardian trolls step back, canceling Camouflage and revealing their location to the non-trolls. Taryn jumps back, nearly falling into me.

"Tits on a pig!" He takes a fighting position, looking around for more trolls. "Where the hell did they come from?"

I laugh to myself before nudging him in the back. "Camouflage. It's a troll passive, remember?"

He stands up straight, relaxing his shoulders. "Right." He nods to the two guardian trolls as we pass, but they are stoic as ever in their new positions.

They must be incredibly disciplined, because it's unlikely they have ever seen a dwarf or forest troll, yet they show no reaction to our presence. The only explanation I can imagine is that they have absolute trust in Laojin and Senzala.

That's one thing I appreciate about trolls—not just here, but everywhere I've encountered them. When they believe in a leader, they will follow them to the ends of the earth.

Laojin pulls Taryn aside as we continue along the path. "Do you prefer your pets to stay with you or with the others?"

"Wait, you have pets?" Taryn looks at him incredulously.

"Am I not a druid? While I may have focused on the elemental path of druidism, we are all called by the wild. Come." He gestures for us to follow him.

He leads us to the first cave on the left, where a massive chasm disappears into the mountain, big enough for even Stompy to follow. A rumbling sound grows louder as we step inside, and Limery's claws dig into my cloak.

The cave is cast in a dull blue from mana-infused torches that burn along the walls. This sparks more questions, but for now, I'm interested in what Laojin is about to show us.

We follow the cave a short way before it opens into a wide cavern, tiered with natural formations and indentations along the floor and walls. Dozens of animals are scattered about, all sleeping. Snores rumble like a gentle thunder. A gargantuan mammoth rests against the far wall, its belly heaving with each bellowing snore erupting from its snout like a trumpet.

"Bro." Taryn elbows me in the side. "They have a freaking mammoth."

"Don't get any wild ideas." I grab him by the shoulder and force him to look elsewhere.

In the far back, several white bears lay huddled together. There are wolves, foxes, and a few snowy owls perched near the ceiling.

Little white creatures hanging from the ceiling catch my eye.

Frost Bats. *Level 18. These small, winged creatures are prized for their ability to scout without light. Native to Frostmoor, in the past, many were trained as guides to adventurers exploring the shadow lands. Their blood is a key ingredient in advanced Intelligence and Wisdom potions.*

"This is amazing," Taryn whispers. "How do you control them all?"

Laojin lifts his arm, and one of the owls flies down from its perch. "They are not all pets. I have bonded with many, but others have arrived of their own accord. This is a sanctuary of sorts."

Taryn's eyes widen. "Wait, you can do that?"

"You have only touched on what druids are capable of. Here, raise your arm." Laojin nudges the owl to hop over.

Berry grunts and moves in closer, prodding Taryn in the leg with his snout.

Taryn leans into Berry. "Oh hush, you'll always be my first."

The owl twists its head backward, watching Taryn with golden eyes. The owl is pristine white except for speckles of black along its legs and wings.

Limery's body grows warm against my shoulder and he smacks his lips.

"Don't even think about it," I order before he gets any wild ideas.

Taryn gently strokes the owl. "So, where's Nessie?"

"Nesira is not a pet!" Senzala snaps. "She is my totem, and she possesses powers you could only dream of."

"Sorry." Taryn raises his free hand in apology. "I didn't mean any offense. Nessie—I mean, Nesira—is an amazing creature. Beautiful, powerful. She has my respect."

The scowl fades from Senzala's face. "Nesira goes where she pleases. As my totem, I borrow from her power, but I have no influence over her."

Laojin extends his arm, and the owl jumps back onto his forearm. "I'm sure you are aware that there is a limit to the creatures we can tame. Unique monsters can only be bonded with under special circumstances, they cannot be tamed as pets."

Taryn instructs his pets to stay in the cave for the night. Berry is reluctant, but eventually curls up against the wall with Ruby. Stompy leaves them to go deeper into the cave, where he sits beside the mammoth.

Taryn shrugs. "He has a mind of his own."

After leaving the pet cave, we go deeper into the gorge to a cave in the far back. Two more guardian trolls wait outside the entry.

With only four guardian trolls watching over the village while the others sleep, either they are very confident in their protections, or their society is on the brink of collapse, perhaps even worse than the mountain trolls.

Compared to the human and dwarven cities on Isle of Mythos, the entirety of troll society barely rivals a town. I don't know why I expected one of the harshest climates to be any different.

Briefly, the lone desert troll we came across outside of Sandholde crosses my mind. How many of them are left? Or was it a lone survivor?

Laojin leads us past the guardian trolls, and Taryn remains oblivious to their presence. This cave is more narrow, but it has the same mana-infused torches along the wall.

At the end of the long tunnel, the cave opens into a cavern once again. It looks like the cavern is covered in shag carpet before I realize that the white carpet is hundreds of arctic trolls sleeping together. Since camouflage only works when a troll is awake and purposefully standing still, their bodies are all visible. There must be three or four hundred trolls scattered about.

I stand there for a moment, taking it all in. Maybe I was wrong. Maybe the best thing for trolls is for them to hide away and rebuild their numbers. Whatever the arctic trolls have been doing seems to be working.

"That's a lot of trolls," Taryn whispers. "This is like a bear cave."

Laojin steps between us. "We still keep to the old ways. Every night, we all gather in the cave to sleep."

"Maybe you're used to sleeping in castles where you're from—" Senzala walks past, kneeling between two large trolls. "—but in Hornryx, everything we do is for the tribe, for its safety."

Laojin gestures toward the mess of trolls before us. "Go ahead, make yourself comfortable."

Taryn takes a deep breath and navigates his way through, careful not to step on any outstretched arms. "I just hope they don't stink."

I follow him, and we find an open spot in the back against the wall. At least this way, we're only surrounded on three sides.

I take off the fur cloak and use it as a pillow. With so many trolls, their body heat keeps the cave warm enough that I don't need the furs. I lean against the wall, and Limery takes his usual spot in the crook of my arm.

As I lay there counting the white-furred trolls like sheep, I eventually drift off to sleep.

27. KNOWLEDGE IS POWER

I wake up surrounded by trolls. They hover around us, a wall of white with icy blue eyes that watch us with curiosity. A young troll, no more than two feet tall, grabs my toe with its small fingers.

"Hey, there." I raise my hand slightly to wave.

The small troll jumps and hides behind the leg of an adult female.

"Hellos." Limery waves at the young troll and grins.

The young troll peeks her head between the adult's legs and gurgles, not the least bit terrified of the imp's demonic smile.

Another young troll, this one slightly taller than Taryn, tugs on the adult's fur from behind. "Are you sure he's not a mountain troll? Grago said forest trolls were green." The voice is surprisingly childlike.

"He's a special troll." Taryn sits up, rubbing the sleep from his eyes, and they all gasp. "One of a kind."

"Doesn't look special to me." A tall, broad-shouldered, level-twenty-five troll with a deep voice crosses his arms. "What's he doing here anyhow?"

A female troll answers, "Chief Laojin and Shaman Senzala brought them here. Says they are heroes."

They continue their conversation like we're not even present.

"Very strange." The tall one scowls at us.

"I agree. In all my years, they have never brought an outsider to the village. Something is up."

"And what about the two little ones? Are we supposed to eat them?"

"Whoa, whoa, whoa." Taryn backs against the wall, extending his arms. "Nobody is eating anybody. We're here to train."

The large troll scratches his chin. "Hmm. Never had dwarf before. Or imp."

I rise to my feet. All the trolls take a step back except for the big guy. He's several inches taller than me, but I look him straight in the eyes.

"They're not food. They're my companions."

He frowns. "If you say so."

"Rhaz, that's enough." Laojin makes his way through the group, and they all step out of his path. "How many times must I explain we don't eat the other races?"

"But you said—"

"What I said was that many races fear us because they believe we will eat them. We're nothing more than monsters to them."

Rhaz stomps his foot. "But they don't even know we exist. How do they fear us?"

I answer. "People fear what they don't know. But they are learning."

Laojin rests a hand on Rhaz's shoulder. "That's enough questions for now. You all have work to do, and I would like to speak to Chod and his companions with the council."

The trolls disperse. A few of the young ones crane their necks in our direction as they walk away.

I wave at the young girl who pulled my toe, and she waves back. "There are so many of you. How?"

"So many?" Laojin snarls. "How far have we fallen that filling a cave with our people is seen as some great accomplishment? There was a time when trolls roamed all of Frostmoor. A time when we may not have been respected, but we were feared. That fear still runs deep, even if we are nothing more than legends."

I understand his frustration. I've felt it myself during my time in Mythos. It's not easy being a troll. "The world is changing. There is a place for trolls once more."

He shakes his head. "Maybe for a hero. But I will not risk the fate of my people because there is something out there more scary than a troll. Now come."

Taryn leans in close. "Who peed in his cereal this morning?"

I narrow my eyes at Taryn. The last thing we need is to piss off the chief.

We follow Laojin out of the cave. In the daylight, the village is even more resplendent. The ice-covered buildings and trees sparkle in the morning sunlight.

Trolls are on the move all about, some heading out toward the buildings, others disappearing into various caves, a few carrying weapons. Laojin leads us into a smaller cave without speaking.

After a short walk, it empties into an oval room with a rectangular stone table in the center. Four trolls sit at the table in stone chairs, a male and female on each of the longer sides. One of the males is overweight, with a potbelly. If not for his broad shoulders and chest, he could pass for a pregnant female. The other male is the prototypical arctic troll, muscled underneath a mound of fur. One of the females is much older, at least according to her withered face and saggy bosom, but that is all that gives away her age. The second female has longer fur and hair than any of the other trolls, nearly concealing her charcoal features. They all have shorter tusks than any of the other troll races.

A throne-like chair sits at the far end and there's an empty seat closest to us.

Laojin sits at the head of the table. A moment later, Senzala arrives and takes the final seat, leaving Taryn and me standing.

The chief clears his throat. "In all the years since the ring of Hornryx was forged, our council has gathered in this cave to discuss the fate of our tribe. We make the difficult decisions that keep our tribe safe. I have already informed them of your position, that you would have us risk our lives to join our brothers and sisters in battle. That will not be happening." He pauses, locking eyes with me.

I clench my fist, not allowing my face to show the disappointment washing over me.

Laojin continues, "However, we respect the path of the hero. A path often imperiled with difficult choices. It is no coincidence that you have found your way to Hornryx just as you have the other tribes. We do not fault you for fighting against darkness. As a hero, we recognize your duty is greater than one tribe. You fight for all trolls. While stories of troll heroes are rare, there have been a few in our history. You may check our library if you are inclined to learn of their deeds. But for now, we are here to discuss what we can offer you."

Typical speech, and nothing I haven't heard before. At this rate, I'd be more surprised if someone actually decided to join us. Whether trolls, humans, or beast-kin, it's always the same. Everyone feels betrayed and let down by the other kingdoms. They have all suffered in the past and are reluctant to risk their people for a cause when those old wounds still sting.

But the fact that my own people turned me down is somehow more disappointing. Still, I can't say that I don't understand it. We'll take what help we can get, and then we'll travel to the next village.

I meet the chief's eyes. "And what is it you can offer?"

He shrugs. "You tell us. If you have questions, we will answer what we can. Our library is yours while you are here. We are strong believers that what you know is as important as what you can lift. Our dungeon is yours to train in. Show us your weapons and abilities and we will share what knowledge we have of them."

Taryn raises his hand before speaking. "Hold up, you have a dungeon? And a library? None of the other tribes have libraries. And what's the deal with the frozen plants? And what can you teach me about being a druid?"

"Easy there." Laojin laughs. "One question at a time. Tzane maintains our dungeon. He can enlighten you."

The pot-bellied troll huffs before speaking. "We have one of three known dungeons on Frostmoor. Hornryx Dungeon provides us with enough food to feed the village and keeps our bodies strong. It is an ancient dungeon, so while it does not provide loot, it is rich in mana and provides a steady supply of spawn."

Interesting...so it's like a hack-and-slash dungeon. Now, that sounds like fun.

"And the library?" I ask. "Why do none of the other tribes have them?"

Laojin gestures to the older female troll. "Oyana."

She taps her clawed, black fingers against the table. "It doesn't surprise me that none of the other tribes have chosen to preserve our histories. The forest trolls were always too proud for such things, thinking their kingdom would live on the lips of men forever. The mountain trolls were too brutish, caring for strength above all else. And the seaside trolls, I always feared that a stiff breeze could blow them across the ocean. Here in Hornryx, we value knowledge. Knowledge is in itself a power. I am saddened that we have not added to our collection since removing ourselves from the world, though your news from abroad will be added soon."

"What about the desert trolls?" I interrupt. "You didn't mention them."

"Theirs is a sad story for another time. You may find it in the library if you wish, but it will not help you on your journey. To answer your question, why do we have a library when the others do not, we must go back many ages. Before the fight with the dark wizard and the closing of the portals, before our retreat into the mountain and the forging of the ring, we had a chief by the name of Titamora. She was a sorcerer troll, the only one known to have ever existed, and she prized knowledge for the powers it could grant her. Heroes roamed Mythos during this time, and her power rivaled the strongest among them. She traveled far and wide, gathering tomes from different kingdoms and creating a vast library for us to use."

Limery leans forward on my shoulder, enraptured by the story. "What happeneds to hers?"

"She perished. It turns out there is some knowledge too great for even a sorceress."

That sounds like a fascinating tale for another time. For now, we need to take advantage of the situation we find ourselves in.

"How can you help us get stronger?" I get right to the point. Libraries and frozen villages are nice, but we need to get stronger. No matter how many kingdoms we gather, the heroes will be the ones on the front lines. We can make the biggest impact. At level thirty, I hope to unlock the Warforged class. And right now, I have the option to further advance my summoner or barbarian class.

"That depends on what you are after." Laojin taps his claws against the stone table. "If you only want to grow stronger, the dungeon will provide. If you are looking to make the most of your class and abilities, then that will require a more specialized approach."

I pull up the notification that I received for class advancement after hitting level twenty-five.

Class Advancements. *Upon reaching level twenty-five, you have unlocked a class advancement. You may only advance one class at a time. A second class may not be advanced until completion of primary advancement.*

Barbarian Advancement.
   Spirit of the Beast. Unlock for further details.

Summoner Advancement.

Dreadbeasts. Unlock for further details.
Dual Subclass. Unlock for further details.

I've been letting it marinate in the back of my mind for days, but I still have no clue which one to choose. I'll take all the advice I can get on my class options.

"What do you know about class advancements and multiple classes?" I ask.

The group exchanges a look before Oyana speaks. "Class advancements are common once someone with a class reaches a certain threshold. It seems heroes are always blessed with a magical class. For the rest of us, it comes down to the will of the gods. Laojin and Senzala are the only ones with magical classes within our tribe. Having multiple classes is known to have happened occasionally among heroes, but it is very rare among the rest of us. Many who are blessed with a class never reach the level of advancement. Why do you ask?"

"I was granted a second class after the mana explosion, but now I am being offered the choice of three class advancements."

Taryn eagerly steps in front of me. "And I'm only two levels away from my own class advancement."

"Wait your turn." I playfully shove him out of the way. "I was hoping you could give me some insight on what to pick."

"You two are heroes from different cultures, yet you bicker like brothers," Laojin laughs. "There is no need to worry. While it is our duty to help a hero of the trolls, I have taken a special interest in you, young druid."

Taryn blushes before stepping back beside me. "Thank you."

"What abouts Limmy?" The imp bats his eyelashes.

"It seems these two would not be where they are without your help. We will do what we can for you as well." Laojin winks. "But perhaps we should nourish our bodies before we begin planning your futures."

Limery offers him a grotesque grin in appreciation.

After checking on Taryn's pets, we follow the council to the buildings out front. The door is open to one of the buildings, where an elderly male troll stirs the massive pot of stew. I make a comment about how Kea has a similar pot boiling in the forest troll village.

Tzane rubs his potbelly like a pregnant woman. "I am glad to hear the forest trolls have kept something of the past."

"I'm not sure what stories you have heard, but the forest village is not that different from your own." I take the bowl of stew that is offered to me and say my thanks.

He frowns. "Maybe so. Too much time has passed since the troll tribes last gathered. I doubt any living troll was alive at the last grand council."

We all take a seat at an overlook near the entrance to the village. From this high up, we can see over the clouds, over the ring around Hornryx, and even the peaks of some of the other mountains. It's like we're looking out from a plane window.

The stew is meaty and delicious. There's a gaminess to it I haven't tasted before, probably from some animal they hunted in the dungeon. It has less spice than the food from Whitgard, but there's something about it that nourishes me on a deeper level.

Taryn bites into a bright-red fruit that he plucked from one of the ice-covered trees. "Oh god, this is so good. It's like biting into a slushy."

Laojin smiles. "The fruits are a favorite among the young. They are not so appetizing once our tastes shift."

"More for me," Taryn mumbles between bites.

Limery slurps down his stew between us.

"Can I ask you something?" I say to none of the council in particular.

Oyana answers. "You have a thirst for knowledge rare among your people. Go ahead."

"Why are there arctic trolls in Frostmoor and not on Isle of Mythos?"

Oyanna looks around at our surroundings, as if taking it all in for the first time. "The answer to that lies in our first story, the origin story of all trolls."

Two female trolls lead a group of young ones from the caves to the stew building, but Oyanna waves them over.

"Have a seat." She gestures. "It is important that the young ones remember where we come from."

One of the young trolls crosses her arms. "But Gran, we've heard this story a hundred times. I'm hungry."

"Our people's history is food for the soul." Loajin's voice booms as he displays his authority. "And you will hear it a hundred more times if it pleases your gran."

The young troll takes a seat quietly, pouting.

Oyanna clears her throat. "In the beginning, when all of Mythos was still one land, the mother of Mythos birthed five troll sisters from the earth. With gray skin and short tusks, they were sent out into the world as a blank canvas. The first of the sisters was playful and quiet, so she made her home by the sea. As time passed, her skin began to mirror the ocean she loved, and her hands and feet formed webs so that she could be as nimble in the sea as on land. The second sister took to the mountains, for she loved the thrill of the climb. Her skin took on the purple hue of the mountains at dusk, and muscles formed from her hearty adventures. The third sister was bold and reckless, and she set out to travel far away to the volcanoes on the coast to view their power and destruction. The mother warned her of the dangers, and that if she crossed the desert she would never return."

Several of the young trolls gasp at the revelations, and I find myself equally enthralled by the origin of my people.

"But the third sister wouldn't listen. The journey was long and perilous, and after days of travel, she thought she would die to the sands. However, the mother was not without mercy, so she granted the sister salvation in the form of an oasis. The sister made her home in graceful defeat, and her body adapted to the harshness of the sand.

Oyanna locks eyes with me. "The fourth sister traveled to the forest, for she loved the frenzy of the hunt. Under the trees, she grew fast and wild, a deadly blend of speed and strength, and soon all of the forest bowed before her. The fifth sister watched as the others traveled and waited for their return, but they never did. She waited until her heart grew cold. Her cold spirit spread like wildfire until the ground was frosted and mountains rose from the earth, fracturing a piece of Mythos into the sea. As her sisters floated away, she climbed the mountain. The world around her grew colder, and fur erupted along her body as she climbed higher and higher to catch a glimpse of the others as they drifted across the sea." She offers me a sad smile. "And that is why there are no arctic trolls on the Isle of Mythos. Now, go on, children. Have your stew."

"And fruits," her grandtroll says excitedly.

A genuine smile returns as Oyanna turns to the young trolls. "Yes, and your fruits."

Listening to Dando describe the history of the Frozen Ash Tribe, and now this. I'm once again amazed by the depth of this world. Every race, every kingdom, every person has their own history. And now I am a part of it.

I tilt the bowl, finishing the last of my stew. "That was quite the story. It's the first time I've heard it."

She slurps at her own stew now that the story is over. "I'm not surprised. The forest trolls lost a great deal when their kingdom fell. I can only wonder what we could have achieved with our tribes together."

"You can still find out. The mountain troll tribe has already relocated to the forest."

"Enough of that." Laojin's voice is stern but not angry. "Our decision is final on the matter."

I can make another push before we leave, but for now, we need to make the most of our time here. If I anger them, they could cancel all of this and send us packing.

I nod. "Understood."

The chief stands. "Good. Now, if you would like to follow me, your training can begin."

28. CHOOSE YOUR OWN ADVENTURE

A Horror of Vitality sits in the center of the library, a furry finger stuck up its nose. Chief Laojin, Senzala, Tzane, and Oyanna watch it with great interest, poking and prodding it and observing it from every angle.

After lunch, the other two council members had matters to attend to while the rest of us go to the library. Taryn and I have been describing our abilities to the council so that they can help us decide where to go from here.

For a troll village high in the mountains, the library looks like it belongs in a castle. There are hundreds of leather-bound books, rolled parchments, and scrolls stacked from floor to ceiling. The shelves are carved into the walls and the cave stretches deep into the mountain. Cobwebs coat many of the nooks and crannies. Some of the books are so old that the leather binding is barely holding the pages together.

Blue mana flames light the room in an ethereal glow. Half a dozen intricately-carved chairs are spread around the cave, and several stone tables with matching stools are scattered throughout. Ladders are propped against the wall for reaching items on the higher shelves. Limery perches on the top rung of one of the ladders.

Laojin taps on one of the horror's horns with his claw. "You are a special troll, indeed. With enough of these, you're practically a tribe all by yourself."

"Maybe, if they didn't puff out of existence whenever I'm not in combat." I summon a Horror of Power and it prowls around the library like a lion. "They get stronger as I do, but they don't last nearly long enough in an extended fight."

"Then you need to be stronger," he says matter-of-factly.

Senzala scratches the Horror of Power behind the ear and its leg twitches in pleasure. She offers it a rare smile.

"Don't get too attached. It'll be gone in ten minutes," I chuckle.

She gives the horror another scratch and then takes a seat in one of the leather chairs. "So tell us, what are your options for class advancements?"

I pull up the notifications again. "I have one path for my barbarian class and two for my summoner class. Is it strange that I only get one for barbarian?"

Laojin answers, "It depends on the advancement. No two classes are guaranteed the same advancement path. Some are offered multiple path options because each path is rigid. Others are offered a single path capable of multiple branches. What is your barbarian path?"

"It is called Spirit of the Beast."

The other council members nod approvingly.

The chief grins. "And the two summoner paths?"

"One is called Dreadbeasts, and the other is Dual Subclass."

Oyanna disappears deeper into the cave. A minute later, she comes back with a thick book and places it on the table. The cover is a deep black with a golden inlay of runes and geometric shapes.

She blows the cover and a thick layer of dust puffs into the air. "This may be of use."

Taryn stands on his tiptoes to try and get a view. I can't read the words as Oyanna flips through the book, but there are plenty of pictures. I spot images of imps and goblins, and many creatures I've never seen or heard of. Finally, she comes to a stop.

A grotesque monster snarls out from the page. Even on paper, the creature looks dangerous with its powerful muscles, barb-covered joints, and jagged teeth. She flips the page to a second monster, this one with barbed ram horns. It has thick hooves on all four legs and tusks that jut upward from the lower jaw.

"Look familiar?" she asks, flipping to the next page.

This one is tall and slender, with sharp claws and pointy ears. It walks on two feet and a shadow trails behind it.

"Are these horrors?" I lean in closer, examining the details of each image.

"They are similar. These are dreadbeasts. They come from the same plane of existence as your horrors, but where your horrors might be the cub, these are the mother bears."

I gulp at the thought. My horrors are scary, but these are the creatures of nightmares. No one would ever come near me with an army of dreadbeasts.

"So you're telling me that if I choose the dreadbeast path, I can summon them? Will I still be able to summon my current horrors?"

She shrugs. "I can't answer that for you. This is one of our oldest tomes. Even before the fall, summoners of horrors and dreadbeasts were a rarity. I'm sure you can imagine why. If I had to guess, judging by their appearance and since it is an advancement, choosing this path would improve your current horrors by turning them into dreadbeasts." She closes the book. "I'm sorry I don't have more info, but I can tell you how the Dual Subclass works."

"I think I have a pretty good idea on that one, but go ahead."

She nods. "It's pretty simple. Many classes have it as an advancement option, allowing for a wider array of spells and abilities. For summoning, whatever option you had when you picked your class, you will be able to choose a second. What are your options?"

I pull up my notifications from when I first unlocked the summoner class.

Class:

Summoner. *Magic users capable of summoning magical beings to fight on their behalf.*

Subclass:

Elemental. *Summon golems created from the elements.*
Brood. *Summon insects that evolve.*
Horror. *Summon monstrous creatures. Requires 20+ Strength and Constitution.*
Techno. *Summon robotic beings. Requires 20+ Intelligence.*
Undead. *Summon undead creatures from nearby bones.*
Champion. *Summon one powerful creature at a time.*

I tell her each of the classes that were available to me, and then add, "I have something similar to Champion already, but it only allows me to summon a copy of the most recent monster I killed. I imagine the Champion subclass works differently?"

"That is correct. Champion summoners were well-known among the elite in ancient times. Upon killing a beast, a champion summoner could choose to have it as a member of their stable, calling it to battle whenever they wished. A champion summoner could claim three champions at a time. This led to grand adventures with massive parties designed to procure the strongest champions for the kingdom. One of the Pruxford gnomes was said to have claimed three dragons as champions. But those days are long gone." She watches my horrors as they puff out of existence. "You made the right choice. While the other classes are worthy for certain races, the horror class is especially suited for trolls. If only more of us were blessed with mana in our bodies." She sighs. "Nonetheless, if you choose to embark further down the summoner path, I would advise you to stick to what you know."

"That makes sense. I'd like to hear about the Spirit of the Beast path. My summoner abilities have made up for our lack of allies, but it has always been my barbarian abilities that have proved the difference. So, if this is a barbarian path, it should be well suited for trolls, right?"

She smiles, looking at the other members of the council. "He is smart for a forest troll."

At least she has a sense of humor for an old bag of bones.

Taryn snickers behind me, but I pay him no mind.

Laojin rests a heavy hand on my shoulder. "You are in luck. As it happens, my predecessor walked the Spirit of the Beast path. He was a true barbarian, meaning he could go into a rage at will, not under intense situations like the rest of us."

My hands practically tingle with excitement. "What can you tell me?"

He gestures for me to take a seat at the table. "The Spirit of the Beast advancement is rooted in nature, just like trolls themselves. It's not that different from the shaman and druid classes. This path blends nature with magic."

I tap my foot as I wait for him to get to the point. Just tell me what awesome abilities it unlocks, already.

"Embarking down this path will change your body—" He looks at my blue skin. "—but that is nothing new for you. There are five stages to the Spirit of the Beast path. First is the Spirit Inquiry. To achieve this you must locate your spirit animal."

I furrow my brow. "Uh, how do I do that?"

"That is for you to discover. A spirit animal is similar to a totem, but vastly different. While a totem is a singular creature that grants power to the shaman, a spirit animal is not one particular animal. It is an animal that resonates with you, that feeds your spirit. My predecessor went on a pilgrimage for weeks to discover his spirit beast."

I clench my fist, wishing I had something to smash. "There's a war coming. I don't have time to get lost in the woods."

"You put too much pressure on yourself." He sighs. "The war is unlikely to start tomorrow. But even if it did, you are not the only one who will be fighting. You are a piece of the greater puzzle. Not everything will always line up as you wish, but if this is the path you choose to take, then you must embrace it."

I take a deep breath to calm my raging hands. "I know you're right, but there are a lot of people counting on me."

He rests his massive hand on top of my own. "That is the burden of the hero. But it is still your choice. Nothing comes easy."

I nod. "What else can you tell me about this path?"

"Once you locate your spirit beast, it will influence what comes next, but the path remains the same regardless of the beast. After Spirit Inquiry comes Spirit Embodiment. You will need to find an amulet that connects you to your beast. Once you have done so, a change will happen in your body that connects you to your spirit beast. Then comes Spirit Enhancement, where you will gain a passive ability based on the animal. Fourth is the Spirit Guide, where you will be able to summon a spirit version of the animal for guidance. Lastly is the Spirit Power. Here, you will gain a powerful active ability from your spirit beast."

So essentially, I'll gain three new abilities, the same as the dreadbeast path. While it would be useful to have some abilities that weren't directly related to smashing shit, there's no way to tell what those abilities might be, especially since I don't know my spirit beast.

I close my eyes and massage my temples, hoping the answer might present itself, but I'm still not sure which to pick. Stronger horrors would be nice, but they already grow stronger with each level I gain. Even though Oyanna advised against it, having a second summoner class could be beneficial, but considering how low my Intelligence and Wisdom are compared to the rest of my stats, would they be anything better than cannon fodder?

I open my eyes to find Laojin watching me with amusement. "Your predecessor, what was his spirit animal?"

Laojin grins. "Erato was a fierce warrior from a young age, but to find his spirit beast, he had to learn patience. For the first two weeks of his pilgrimage, he searched high and low for a spirit to connect to. It wasn't until he gave up searching that the spirit came to him. After three days of waiting in the snow at the peak of Mount Hornryx, a lone frost wolf sat down in front of him."

Taryn's eyes light up at the mention of the wolf. "Dude, we could be beast brothers."

I roll my eyes. Taryn's enthusiasm is a major knock on the Spirit of the Beast path. I don't think I can handle any more animal puns than we already have.

I ignore the comment, returning my attention to Laojin. "What abilities did he gain?"

"Once he found his amulet, his fur took on a blueish-white color, matching the frost wolves. For his passive ability, his senses were heightened and he could move twice as fast while tracking the scent of an enemy. His active ability was a howl that confused enemies and rallied allies. They were all fitting attributes for a leader of the tribe."

"I'm going to need time to think," I confess. This is a big decision, and with how slow levels are coming now, who knows when or if I'll be able to do another advancement.

He nods. "I've often found that a walk through the snow does wonders for the mind. Go, clear your head. I have much to discuss with the dwarf."

29. BIRD PEOPLE

Taryn licked his lips at the prospect of actual alone time with the chief. Well, the chief and three-fifths of the council.

Druids were not common in Seascape. Most dwarves blessed with a class were either clerics, paladins, or warriors. Mages were rare, druids rarer. And now not only did he have a powerful druid to learn from, but also a library that spanned ages. Not just the history of trolls, but the history of Mythos. Taryn had a million questions.

"What kind of class advancement do you think I'm going to get? What's yours? What abilities do you have? I saw the ice shield thing, but what else can you do? Can you transform into an animal? Which one? Did you use your druid abilities to make the ice plants? Can I do that? What about—"

"Easy there," Laojin laughed. "Slow down and take a breath. I can only answer one question at a time."

Taryn bowed his head. "Sorry. I know I still need two levels, but I can't wait to see what happens."

"Do not worry. I have a plan for you, but first we must wait for Chod to make a decision."

"You have a plan for me?" Taryn blushed. He'd known the chief was planning to help him, but he'd assumed Chod was the featured artist on this track.

"You are a special dwarf to have allied yourself with a troll. Most dwarves care only for the material things of the world. I sense that you give much of yourself to those you care for."

Taryn found himself at a loss for words. Were the NPCs of this world that perceptive or was the AI feeding the chief these lines based on what it knew of Taryn? He very rarely put himself first, in life or in this game. That was just how he was built, a natural caretaker. A pillar of support. He'd taken on one responsibility after another since he was a child. Whether it was watching his siblings while his parents worked or picking up a part-time job to help his mom and dad make ends meet so that he and his sisters could have a quality education, he did what needed to be done. Even with Chod, while they had a ton of fun together, it was always Taryn helping to put things in perspective for his best friend. If there had not been pay involved, Taryn wasn't sure he would have taken the time off from school to play this game. There's no way he would have put the added stress on his family.

He put a lot of himself out there, but it was also what kept him fulfilled. That was just how it was.

"You're right. I do."

Laojin's icy blue eyes bored into Taryn. "That is the nature of the druid, to nurture and protect, but that doesn't mean always putting yourself second. Making yourself a priority at times allows you to better support those that you care for."

Once again, Taryn was speechless. He felt more like he was in a therapist's office than a troll library.

He scratched his chin. "How do you do that?"

The chief grinned. "Follow me." He turned to the other council members. "If Chod returns before we do, entertain him with a story."

Taryn waddled behind the chief, his short legs practically jogging to keep up with Laojin's long strides. They left the library cave and entered a smaller tunnel barely wide enough to fit the massive troll.

After walking a long way down the narrow hall lit by mana torches, they came upon a spiral staircase carved into the mountain. Chief Laojin took the stairs up three at a time while Taryn's heart raced as he hurried behind. Riding his pets everywhere had been terrible for his cardio. His breathing was so ragged he couldn't even manage to ask where they were going.

They climbed for what felt like an hour before the chief stopped. If not for his discomfort, Taryn might have been amazed that a stairwell was buried this deep in the mountain. Architecturally, it was something even the dwarves of Seascape could respect. Instead, he grimaced as he sucked in air.

"How...much...further?" he asked between breaths.

With the way the staircase spiraled, it was impossible to tell how far they'd come or how much further they still had to go. He didn't even want to think about the climb back down.

If this was Laojin's idea of taking care of himself, Taryn wanted no part. A strong ale in a crowded tavern suited the dwarf just fine.

The chief reached back and patted him on the shoulder. "The journey will be worth it. Not much further now."

Sure enough, after about a dozen more stairs, bright light flooded the stairwell. The stairs emptied into a long hallway where white light spilled through an open doorway.

Taryn squinted as a cold wind blew past him, jingling the clasps in his beard. Once he stepped through the doorway, his eyes adjusted to the brightness, revealing a stone platform that extended from the side of the mountain. There were no walls or railings, just a flat platform floating in the air.

Cold wind whistled around them. Chief Laojin walked to the edge and Taryn joined him. As he looked down, the summit of the other mountains seemed small, barely peeking above the clouds.

The view was beautiful, but Taryn was more confused than ever. Was this where the chief came for alone time? To meditate? It was peaceful, but how was this making anyone a priority?

The chief sat, letting his legs dangle from the edge. He patted on the ground next to him for Taryn to join.

Taryn scooted toward the edge, keenly aware of how high they were. This would be a hell of a fall.

"Who made this?" asked Taryn.

As far as he could tell, the trolls weren't well known for their craftsmanship and this stairwell had to have taken a lot of time to carve into the stone.

"My ancestors, long before I was born. They used to force their prisoners to make the climb and then toss them from the ledge." Chief Laojin leaned forward, looking into the depths below.

Taryn instinctively scooted back. Had Chief Laojin brought him all the way up here just to toss him off the edge? Maybe he'd misread the whole situation. Clearly, the arctic trolls had no love for the outside world. If the chief killed him, there was no way he was making it back past the ring without them knowing. Senzala had been able to sense their presence the first time. His pets and Limery would be at the arctic trolls' mercy. Chod would do his best, but what could he do against an entire village?

Laojin stood, and Taryn's heart threatened to burst from his chest. If Senzala was capable of forming the ring, there was no telling how powerful the chief was. What could Taryn do against that kind of power?

"I use it for a different purpose now."

Taryn let out a sigh of relief just before the chief grabbed him by the cloak and tossed him from the ledge. He flew high into the air like he had been launched from a cannon. There was a moment of panic before he remembered his bird form.

He could fly down and find Chod before the chief could descend the stairs. But first, he would need to sell the fall.

As gravity took hold of Taryn, Chief Laojin exploded into feathers, his troll form replaced by a silver falcon that quickly dove past him.

No fucking way. He's a bird guy, too!

Taryn laughed as he used his own ability, transforming into a small white bird.

Chief Laojin dove through the air, and if not for Taryn's heightened eyesight, he might not have seen the bird of prey barreling toward the clouds below.

He dove after the chief.

Tucking his wings, Taryn darted toward the clouds. He'd never been interested in sky-diving, but if the rush felt like this, he'd leap out of a plane the first chance he had. This was the fastest he had ever flown, and he still wasn't catching the chief.

The silver falcon dove like a missile. He spiraled, doing barrel-rolls with unimaginable grace for something so fast.

Just when Taryn was certain the chief would leave him in the dust, the falcon's wings extended and he soared up, doing a massive loop that brought him closer to Taryn.

Taryn flapped his own wings, and the two slowed until they were floating on an air current. Laojin's falcon form was beautiful. His silver feathers were tipped with navy, and black slits cut through the icy blue eyes. The falcon outsized Taryn's bird form by nearly the same ratio as the troll did the dwarf.

The falcon unleashed a piercing screech and dove once more. Taryn followed. Laojin was clearly holding back, occasionally extending his wings to slow his acceleration.

This was a hell of a way to unwind.

They barreled through a layer of clouds and all of Frostmoor became visible once again. The ring circled Hornyx, hiding the majestic village above its cloudy depths.

Laojin shifted course, flying back to the mountain and perching on the limb of a snow-covered pine. He hopped to a few lower branches before landing in the snow and returning to his troll form.

Taryn changed forms as well, electing to remain on the tree branch. It sagged with his new weight and snow plopped against Laojin's shoulder.

He expected a reprimand, but the chief gave him a mischievous smile. "What did you think?"

"That was amazing." Taryn beamed with delight. "I don't know if I've ever felt so free."

The chief wiped the snow from his fur. "Protecting a village is a great responsibility. The council is invaluable, and they each have their own responsibilities, but there is still enough trouble to drive one mad. This is how I take care of myself and clear my mind. Plummeting through the clouds has a way of putting things in perspective."

"I bet." Taryn narrowed his eyes. "But did you really have to throw me off the mountain?"

Laojin's laughter echoed off the mountain. "Your face was priceless. I will carry it with me for all my days."

Taryn joined in. He had always found it amusing when something so big and scary showed its playful side. Like watching lions play like kittens, or Berry's obsessive need for attention. The trolls had their quirks, but underneath it all, they weren't that different from the other races.

"So, what now?" he asked.

"The flight up will not be as quick with those tiny wings of yours."

30. SPIRIT INQUIRY

Cold wind assaults my face, and I pull my cloak tighter. I've narrowed my decision down from three to two, but I still have no clue what class advancement to pick.

With the dreadbeasts, I know what I'm getting, and I already have experience with summoning horrors. It seems like the smart choice.

Spirit of the Beast is more like a lotto ticket. It could pay off big time with the right abilities, but if I end up with a snow bunny as my spirit animal, I could be screwing all of us over.

Still, something about it calls to me. I lucked into being a summoner when I fell into the ley line. My horrors have saved my ass more times than I can count, but I came into this world as a barbarian. The Spirit of the Beast path has a place among the history of trolls. It feels fitting. Natural.

As far as I know, I'm the first troll summoner to ever exist. But does that mean I shouldn't pursue summoning to its highest power?

I sigh as I kick the trunk of a pine tree. Its branches whisper as snow collapses on my head.

I could walk this entire mountain and I'd have no better understanding of what I should choose. Closing my eyes, I kneel and rest my back against the trunk.

Maybe I'm making all of this unnecessarily complicated. I'm not alone here anymore. I don't have to be a one-man army, and all of this isn't resting solely on my shoulders. We might not have had luck abroad, but King Favian and King Orso are doing everything within their power to unite as many people as possible. There were at least half a dozen kingdoms at his council meeting. The forest trolls and mountain trolls have joined forces. They have wyrms and goblins on their side. We're not alone.

Hope isn't lost.

I don't need to overthink this. I can be a piece of the puzzle and let everyone else play their part. That's how we will win this war. I've made it far with the abilities I have right now. Abilities that will continue to gain power as I do. Dreadbeasts are awesome, and I'm sure that one day I'll witness their power. But for now, the best thing I can do for myself is to unleash my inner beast.

As I return to the village, I'm nearly clobbered by two birds speeding toward the caves. A silver falcon explodes in front of me, and I equip Destroyer out of instinct before I realize it's the chief. A moment later, Taryn appears in a flutter of white feathers.

I narrow my eyes. "What have you two been up to?"

Taryn grins. "You wouldn't believe me if I told you."

Considering all the weird stuff that's happened to me in this game, I doubt that.

A loud groan echoes from a nearby cave, followed by the patter of footsteps. Berry comes tottering out of the cave like an excited puppy followed by Ruby, two foxes, and a turtle with a translucent shell that looks like ice.

Stompy slowly brings up the rear next to a massive mammoth, proof that the big guy loves Taryn just as much as the others even if he doesn't show it.

Berry tackles Taryn to the ground and he licks him vigorously.

"Did you miss me?" Taryn talks to him like a baby as he wraps his stubby arms around the bear.

"Looks like they've made friends. Even Stompy." I laugh as the moulhaug huffs over Taryn, blowing his dreadlocks aside.

Chief Laojin strokes the mammoth behind the ear and the beast wraps its long trunk around his arm. Each of the mammoth's tusks rivals Taryn in size.

Watching a troll ride a mammoth into battle would put fear in anyone.

The chief turns to me. "I take it you have found some clarity?"

I nod. "I have."

"Good." He pats the mammoth on the side. "Let us return to the council."

After escorting the pets back to their cave, we find ourselves in the dimly-lit library where three of the council members are already waiting. Limery has curled up on one of the highest shelves and snores loudly. Laojin stares at me expectantly, and Taryn sits on the edge of his seat.

I feel like I'm about to give a press conference. *Tune in for the latest on Chod's Decision.*

I clear my throat. "I've decided to take the Spirit of the Beast class advancement."

"A worthy choice of a hero." Laojin walks over and extends a hand. "But there is no time to waste. Bonding with a spirit beast is different for everyone. It could take days or weeks, so it's best to have you on your journey at once. Now, remove all of your items and hand them to me."

He nods to Tzane, and the pot-bellied troll disappears out of the cave.

I unhook my satchel and give it to Laojin. Nearly everything I own is in that tiny bag. I remove the phoenix feather from my hair and the Tiger's Eye Pendant around my neck.

"And that." He points at the communication stone hanging from my neck. "You won't need it where you're going." He stares at the fur cloak from Whitgard and grunts. "Keep it. This is all for nothing if you freeze to death."

It suddenly feels like I might have bitten off more than I can chew.

Laojin grabs me by the arm. "Come." He turns as we exit the cave. "Have the others ready upon my return."

Everything is suddenly happening so fast. I stop walking, pulling my arm from Laojin's grip. "What in the hell is going on?"

He raises an eyebrow. "You have chosen to embark on the Spirit of the Beast path."

I stand firm. "I don't know what that means. Or why you're having the others get ready. What are they getting ready for?"

"You do ask a lot of questions." He sighs. "I am glad you have chosen the advancement you did. It is fitting for a troll, but your path is yours alone. Once you embark, there will be nothing I can do for you until you return. You must find your own way. For the others, there is still much we can offer but it will take time. Which is all the more reason for you to be on your way. Do this right and you will all leave here stronger than you came."

That still doesn't answer any of my questions, but I suppose it's better than nothing. I give a final wave to Taryn as we leave. I want to say good bye to Limery, but he looks so peaceful with his closed eyes and expanding snot bubble that I leave him be.

Outside, we travel up a snow-covered path that winds higher up the mountain. Laojin stops once we can no longer see the village.

"This is where I leave you. Travel far and lose yourself. Once you are ready, select your class advancement. It will give you all the information you need to find your spirit beast."

I clasp him around the forearm. "And what about you?"

He winks. "The dwarf and I have a dungeon to clear."

Stupid. Stupid. Stupid.

This idea was so fucking stupid. I could be summoning dreadbeasts right now, but instead, I'm knee deep in snow, freezing my balls off, with no idea of where to go.

I've been walking for at least a few hours now. Far enough that there is nothing reminiscent of troll society out here. No fancy ice plants, no broken trees from troll antics. This high up, there isn't even a trail to follow. Nothing but wilderness.

Cold wilderness.

The sun is nearly below the horizon, but there is still plenty of light to see by. Not that I need it with my night vision.

I pick up a handful of snow and toss it in my mouth, letting it melt into water. With my satchel gone, there's no more Brimming Tankard, no jerky. Everything that I'll need to survive, I'll have to find out here.

This far from the village, I should be good to choose my advancement, but before I do, I need to eat. Once I start the search for my spirit beast, I don't want to have to slow down to hunt.

I find an open area between two pine trees. Tiny tracks trail across the snow, so I'm certain there are animals around here.

I sit down, waiting for Camouflage to take effect. When it does, the reaction is worlds different from the troll forest, where it would spring to life with birds and insects the moment I was no longer visible. For the longest time, all I hear is the wind.

But then suddenly, there's a crunch. If not for the overwhelming silence, it would normally go unheard, but in this climate, it sounds like an iceberg breaking into the sea.

There's movement beneath the snow at the base of the pine tree as something burrows out from underneath. A tiny pink nose breaks through, followed by a white head.

Snow Bunny. *Level 15. Maddeningly quick. Although small, their hind legs pack a ferocious kick.*

The bunny crawls from the snow and hops around, sniffing at the cool air. It hesitates for a moment, cocking its head to the side and looking in my direction.

Too late.

I use Intimidation, roaring at the bunny and confusing it for two seconds. It stumbles back and forth, eyes glazed over. With a quick snap of its neck, I have my dinner before it knows what's happening.

Thanks to my Savage passive ability, I don't need to cook the meat before eating. I skin the bunny with my claws, tossing the pelt aside since I don't have my satchel. The meat is not nearly as enjoyable as something roasted over an open fire and covered in spices, but it gets the job done.

Once I'm done eating, I pull up my notifications and select the class advancement for Spirit of the Beast.

Alert! You have selected to advance the Barbarian class. New class option available.

Barbarian. *Savage warriors capable of using basic weapons and entering into a berserker rage.*

Subclass:

Spirit of the Beast. *Bond with a spirit animal to gain new abilities. The Spirit of the Beast path is composed of five phases.*

. . .

Phase 1: Spirit Inquiry. *A spirit animal is a guide from the spirit world, possessing traits similar to those of the individual. Unlocking one's spirit animal leads to a better under-standing of the self and one's place within the world.*

Completion: Locate your spirit animal. Further phases will become available upon completion.

That's it? Talk about finding a needle in a haystack. There are no instructions, no guide points, just "go and find the damn thing."

I sure hope Taryn is faring better than I am.

I ball up the bunny's pelt and toss it as far as I can down the mountain to keep whatever predators are lurking at bay. Without my weapons, it's just me and my horrors against whatever is out here.

For someone supposedly helping me, Chief Laojin has done a shit job at preparing me for this. He practically kicked me out of the village with an attaboy. I spend several hours walking through the snow. Not knowing what I'm looking for, my frustration builds with every step. I don't even know how I'm supposed to bond with an animal. Do I have to kill it? Tame it? Blow it a kiss? Laojin acted like it was simple, but this is anything but.

Compared to Whitgard, Hornryx is severely lacking in monsters. I imagine it takes a lot of food to feed so many trolls, so it makes sense, but I remember the chief saying they hunted their food in the dungeons. Why couldn't I find my spirit animal in there?

An owl swoops down nearby, plucking a small rodent from beneath the snow. I take off running as it flies to a nearby tree.

The owl watches me with large round eyes as the rodent squirms within its beak. A leg twitches and a long white tail jerks back and forth.

"Are you my spirit animal?" I feel like an idiot even asking. Like the owl is going to magically start talking.

The owl crunches the rodent in its beak and the twitching stops. With a few quick motions, the rodent slides down the owl's throat until only the tail is remain-ing. A second later, the tail disappears in the owl's beak like a spaghetti noodle. The owl extends its wings and puffs out its chest, hooting softly before flying higher up the mountain.

"I guess not."

I continue my search over the next few hours, coming across bears, a lone wolf, and even a sleeping mammoth. I sit near the mammoth for a while, hoping that it will become my spirit animal, but nothing happens.

Eventually, tiredness wins out and I carve myself a makeshift cave in the snow. I take one last look at the beautiful streaks of blue and green across the sky before settling in my cave. Before I fall asleep, I send Taryn a quick message.

. . .

Message (Chod): *I hope you're having better luck than me. It feels like I'm walking blind out here.*

I wait a few minutes for him to respond, but he doesn't. Leaning against the cold packed snow, I'm more aware than ever of Limery's absence as I drift off to sleep.

I wake up screaming as something cold and wet presses against my cheek. A small, white, cat-like creature hisses at me from the corner of my snow cave. I summon a Horror of Power and it pounces on the cat, pinning it to the ground. I quickly summon two more horrors to help.

Arctic Bobcat. *Level 18. Smallest of the Frostmoor predators, the arctic bobcat is fast and agile while packing a dangerous bite. Solitary creatures, they are known to have fought off predators three to four times their size.*

The bobcat screeches so loud that I wince as my Horror of Power latches its jaws around the bobcat's neck. The cat kicks out, hitting the Horror of Finesse and launching the blue, gangly horror at me. It rakes its back claws across the Horror of Power, ripping into its flesh. After a flurry of quick kicks, the horror dissipates. The bobcat is on its feet in an instant, lunging for the Horror of Vitality.

The cat buries its sharp claws into the horror before biting it on the nose with enough force to kill it. The bobcat's hair stands on end as it arches its back. The Horror of Finesse runs in, but a quick swipe across the face ends it.

The bobcat hisses at me and makes a noise like a demon caught in a blender before bolting out of my snow cave like a rocket.

I rush out behind it, shouting. "Wait! Are you my spirit animal?"

31. DUNGEONS AND DRUIDS

Taryn kept to himself as several more trolls entered the library. From the looks of it, these were the biggest and strongest trolls in the village. With Chod gone, what were they up to?

Taryn gravitated toward Limery, leaning against the cave wall next to the bookshelf. The imp's snores were like a dull saw cutting through wood. A bubble of snot expanded to the brink of bursting with each breath.

Tzane, the pot-bellied council member, barked orders at Rhaz, the troll who had expressed an interest in eating Taryn and Limery earlier in the day. Rhaz carried a bag over his shoulder that was filled with weapons.

Taryn gripped his staff a little tighter. He wanted to know what was going on, but the less attention he drew to himself the better, at least until the chief returned. It wasn't that he didn't trust the arctic trolls, but he was still a level-twenty-three dwarf, and he didn't quite feel he could call these trolls friends yet.

When the chief finally returned, his eyes flared with excitement.

He knelt before Taryn. "Do you wish to advance before Chod returns?"

Taryn nodded. "I want to advance as soon as possible."

"Good." He flashed Taryn a smile. "It will be difficult. It will be exhausting. You will be pushed to your limits. But it can be done. Shall we begin?"

Taryn stood. There was no point waiting around while Chod was already out on his quest. "Let's do it."

Laojin's gaze fell on Limery, who was oblivious to the world. "Wake the imp."

With Limery awakened, and extra grumpy because Chod didn't say good-bye before leaving, they all gathered around Chief Laojin.

The chief raised his hand and all eyes fell upon him. "It has been a long time since the thrill of adventure has swept over Hornryx. Many lifetimes have passed since heroes and outsiders have set foot in these caves. We have worked hard to keep ourselves hidden, yet Chod still felt the call of our tribe. I, for one, am glad he came. While he travels through the wilderness searching for his spirit beast, we are tasked with a quest of our own." He gestured to Taryn and Limery. "The world below Hornryx is dangerous, and dark tidings whisper from abroad. While we have fortified ourselves behind the safety of the ring, these two heroes and their companions aim to meet the darkness head-on. I'd like to see them stand worthy of the challenge."

He looked from Rhaz to Tzane and the others before continuing. It felt as if the speech was as much for the other trolls as it was for Taryn.

"I've gathered our strongest trolls here for one purpose: to delve deeper into the dungeon than we have gone in many years. We have used the higher levels for food and sustenance since the days of old, but it has been too long since we tested our bodies against the threats that lurk deeper. Our guests are not strong enough to face these threats alone, so we must accompany them so that they may grow stronger. Now, who's ready to rage?"

Rhaz beat a fist against his chest. A second later, Tzane joined in, then another troll and another, until all of them, even the elderly Oyanna, sounded like they were ready to tear the mountain down.

Chief Laojin tapped a fist to his own chest. "Good. Choose your weapons."

The trolls riffled through the bag, picking out all manner of brute-force weapons: axes, warhammers, maces, and more. The weapons were fine quality. Some had runes carved into the handles, and others had settings for stones. It was clear the trolls knew how to do one thing.

Smash.

Chief Laojin held a silver staff made of a sleek metal that was tipped with a clear blue gemstone. Wherever the weapon was from, it wasn't troll-made, that was for sure.

He tapped it on the ground three times to gather their attention. "Rhaz, Tzane, you will accompany me alongside the dwarf and imp on the first team. Senzala, Machu, and Fiero will be second team. When the three of us tire, you will support our guests."

They all nodded in affirmation.

"Why can't we all go in?" Taryn asked.

"Too many of us will cut into your experience. We need enough in the party to survive, but not so many to where you gain nothing."

"Do I get to bring my pets?"

The chief frowned. "Normally, yes. But by splitting the experience further, it will only prolong the process."

Taryn crossed his arms. "But they are going to be with me in every battle going forward. Shouldn't they be as strong as possible?"

Laojin sighed. "Yes and no. I know you can't stay here forever. The hero's journey is far from stationary, and as soon as Chod returns, you will be on to your next adventure. There are many paths for a druid, and wherever you are when you choose to advance will determine the paths you are offered. If you advance here, you will be offered paths not available through the other portals. The choice is yours. If you want your pets to level with you, we will still help, but there is no guarantee you will advance in time."

Taryn racked his brain. There had to be a solution that would help keep Berry and Stompy on pace with him. The bigger the gap in their levels, the more danger he put them in in every fight.

"What if we took in one less troll. Stompy and Berry can make up the difference, and I can fight in my natural style, using my pets."

The chief ran his fingers through his beard before nodding. "Spoken like a true druid." He looked around the room. "We will make it work."

"Will Limery get a class advancement?" asked Taryn as they waited outside of the entrance to the dungeon.

The group had to wait for the trolls currently hunting for food inside the dungeon to exit before it would allow anyone else to enter. Only one party was allowed in the dungeon at a time.

Chief Laojin shook his head. "Imps do not progress in the same manner as other races. They are beings of raw power and do not take on classes. Limery is a special case, though."

Limery sat on Stompy's snout with his back against the moulhaug's horn, but he perked up at the mention of his name. "Limmy is?"

"You are. Imps were never known as great adventurers or for their ambition. Most were messengers. Others took jobs as servants or apprentices. They did not need to reach high levels to unlock their power or speed. You—" He tapped Limery on the foot, eliciting a giggle. "—you are one of a kind."

"I don't think we could handle two of him." Taryn laughed to himself.

Limery had never spoken about his class or his abilities to Taryn. Maybe Chod knew more, but Taryn had no idea if Limery had an interface or not. It was clear that many of the NPCs could access their stats and abilities, at least the ones with classes, but whether they could allocate points and choose their abilities, or received predetermined stats, he had no idea.

Either way, Limery was pure offensive firepower, and ridiculously strong for his size. He didn't need a second class to make his presence known. He was a pint-sized wrecking ball, and Taryn knew he could count on the imp in any situation.

Stone grated against stone as the dungeon entrance opened. Five male trolls, levels twenty-five to twenty-eight, exited carrying dead animals over their shoulders. One carried a boar. Two others held opposite ends of a giant frost deer. The other two carried large rabbits with unicorn horns.

As they left, the dungeon entrance closed. Taryn was greeted with a prompt.

Hornryx Dungeon. *Would you like to enter?*

Taryn glanced around at his party. Rhaz held a massive axe across his shoulder. He looked ready for a fight. Chief Laojin spoke a few words to the troll hunters as they exited the cave. Limery mesmerized Stompy with a fireball that he kept tossing from one hand to another. And then there was Berry, his oldest and most loyal pet.

Ruby wasn't a fighter, so she didn't need the levels like the rest of them. She would wait with the council until their dungeon run was over.

Taryn took a deep breath. "What are you chumps waiting for? Let's go."

Chief Laojin tapped his staff on the ground. "You heard the dwarf."

The entrance to the dungeon groaned as it closed behind them. With both Berry and Stompy, the tunnel felt extremely tight. This dungeon was a more natural formation than any other Taryn had been in. The walls were rocky cave walls, nothing was polished or carved. It was no different than any other cave aside from the mana torches that continuously blazed along the walls.

Rhaz led the way with Laojin not far behind.

The chief turned to Taryn. "The first few levels are not difficult. They can be cleared once per day, but they provide more than enough to feed the village. Today, we'll be going deeper."

The first level was empty. Several corpses of the unicorn bunnies lay scattered around the room. Rhaz walked past them without stopping, entering a crude stairwell with uneven and misshapen steps. Stompy barely fit through the spiraling tunnel. On level two, blood covered the floor. Skid marks, from where corpses had been dragged across the dungeon, painted a gruesome picture on the floor. Only a lone warthog remained, its thick body gashed along the side with claw marks. Taryn finally understood how they could feed so many trolls this high up the mountain.

Judging by the scene, the dungeon may have provided for the arctic trolls, but that didn't mean it was easy pickings. The stronger trolls had been forged inside this dungeon.

Taryn hoped the same would happen to him.

The third floor was not much different, with the warthogs replaced by frost deer. A couple of detached antlers lay on the ground. They clattered as Rhaz kicked them aside.

He stopped at the next stairwell, looking to the chief for instructions.

Laojin stepped forward to where he could face them all. "This is the boundary for our hunts. Those empty rooms we passed have taken our hunters all day to clear. The next few levels offer no sustenance, so it's normally not worth the energy or danger to press forward. But today, we will go as far as we can."

"Whats is downs there?" Limery hung onto Stompy's horn like a pirate in the crow's nest.

The chief smirked. "You're about to find out. Follow me."

Laojin took point, with Rhaz close behind. He held his axe firmly with both hands, ready for action. Taryn followed next on Berry, and Limery and Stompy pulled up the rear.

As they descended the next stairwell, frost clung to the walls reflecting the light of the torches in a glimmering sheen. Laojin tore through a spiderweb that blocked the entrance to the next level.

Taryn stopped Berry in his tracks. "Not spiders," he whispered to himself. "Please, not spiders."

The room only had a single torch burning. Stalactites hung from the ceiling and much of the room was hidden in shadow. Webbing draped across the cave, and something chittered up above, raising the hair on Taryn's neck.

"Limmy no likes." The imp conjured a fireball in his hand.

More chittering erupted, drowning out all other sounds. It was like a swarm of cicadas had descended on them. Laojin shouted something and pointed at Taryn, but the words fell mute.

Prickly legs wrapped around Taryn like a straightjacket, pinning his arms to his sides and ripping him from Berry's back. Stompy bellowed nearby. Taryn struggled against their embrace, but the long legs were unforgiving. Their sharp barbs penetrated his cloak, slowly dropping his HP. Several spiders descended from the ceiling like this was some sort of Halloween spectacle. Rhaz split one in half with his axe, the force of the blow spraying a line of green ichor across the wall.

Laojin raised his staff, and a spike of ice shot up from the ground, impaling another spider on a frozen skewer.

Limery tossed a fireball in Taryn's direction, and he suddenly plummeted to the floor. His chin smacked against the hard ground. Stars danced across his vision, but the legs still held firm around his midsection. His body jostled as someone or something fought the spider holding him in place.

There was a loud crunch, and then cool slime dripped down Taryn's back and neck. Berry nuzzled him, his face covered in green goo from his attack on the spider. Taryn crawled to his feet as battle continued to rage all around him.

A spider lunged for Taryn, but Stompy's massive hoof squashed it inches from his face. Green guts exploded into his beard and eyes.

He didn't have time to be grossed out by spider guts. More arachnids appeared by the second.

Laojin formed an ice spike on the end of his staff, using it as a spear to pierce the barbed abdomens of spiders as they lowered themselves from the ceiling or skittered across the floor. A half-dozen butchered spiders lay around Rhaz. Limery tossed fireballs, severing webs so that Stompy could crush the fallen spiders with his hooves.

"Alright, boy, let's do this." Taryn climbed on Berry's back and joined the fray.

He extended the vines from Sapling Staff, forming a makeshift cage around his body to keep any spiders from prying him off again. If there was an opportunity, he cast Lightning Bolt, but with how crowded the room was, those chances were few and far between.

A spider landed on top of the viny cage and it pressed its head against the bars, its mandible clacking as a toxic substance dripped from the pincers. The spider pried at the vines, desperate for Taryn's flesh.

He equipped one of the Shadow Daggers in his off-hand, and a blade of shadow energy erupted from the hilt. He stabbed the spider's face through the cage. The dark shadowy blades bypassed its tough exterior, depleting the spider's life and mana directly.

The spider shrieked as it recoiled, right into Laojin's ice spear.

One by one, they finished off the spiders until the chittering was replaced by the group's heavy breathing.

"I see why you don't come down here." Taryn retracted the vines back into his staff, freeing himself once again.

Laojin snapped off the green-tinted ice from the end of his staff. "This is only the beginning."

32. THAT'S THE SPIRIT

Incoming Message (Taryn): Bro, I hope you're having fun out there, because you are missing out. This dungeon is legit! I hit level twenty-four earlier today. The chief thinks I might hit twenty-five tomorrow morning.

I close the message. Two days freezing my ass off in the wilderness is not what I would call fun, but I'm glad Taryn is leveling up while I'm away. They must be really grinding to get those kind of results so quickly. Hopefully, when we meet up again, we'll both be stronger than ever.

Having a high-level druid showing him the ropes can't hurt. Then we can make a quick stop by Boneholde and be off to warmer climates.

After searching for tracks, I sit down and wait for dinner to appear. Snow bunnies have been easy enough to catch once I'm in Camouflage. I've eaten so many that I'm ready to give up the hunt for my spirit beast just so I can have a real meal again.

Swallowing the last of the stringy raw meat, I climb higher up the mountain to make camp for the night.

A snow fox scurries away in the distance, but I pay it no mind. I assume I'll receive some kind of alert or notification once I've found my spirit beast. If that's the case, I've eliminated a majority of the wildlife on Hornryx already: snow fox, snow bunny, arctic bobcat, frost deer, mammoth, various owls, wolves, and bears. I've seen a lot of animals while I've been sitting around waiting.

Waiting and freezing. My tough troll skin and cloak have kept me from suffering any damage from the cold, but I've been in discomfort almost non-stop.

With my luck, my spirit animal is something either incredibly rare or incredibly stupid. I swear if my spirit animal is some kind of arctic skunk, I will log out before I go around blasting stink gas out of my ass.

As I prepare for my second night alone on the mountain, my horrors and I dig a large burrow in the snow. When we're done, I hunker down in my snow cave wrapped in the cloak from Whitgard.

I decide not to message Taryn back. I'm in a grumpy mood from finding no leads, and hearing about his awesome adventures will only make me more jealous that I'm not there.

I close my eyes and wait for sleep to come.

A clack like a gunshot wakes me. I reach for my weapon before remembering that all my items are back at the village. Instead, I summon a round of horrors and peek my head out of the entrance to my cave.

The mountain basks in the light of early morning, the one part of the day where birds can be heard actively chirping. Another gunshot echoes from higher up the mountain, and I shift my gaze upward.

Two glowing frost goats lower their heads, pawing at the ground with their hooves. These two are much bigger than the goats in Whitgard. Their thick white fur isn't as clean and groomed as the domesticated versions, and the horns that curl around each side of their heads are much larger, fading from deep black at the base to icy blue at the tip. Blue eyes stand out predominantly from their black faces.

A smaller female with nubs for horns stands to the side watching the battle unfold.

The two rams rise onto their back legs, almost hovering in the air for a moment before charging one another with concussive force. Their horns clash, the violent collision echoing off the mountain. The force separates them, where they paw at the ground before charging again.

The brutality of their collisions is awe-inspiring, but I'm drawn to the orange aura that surrounds the males. I never saw anything similar on the goats in Whitgard. Are they in some kind of goat rage, or are they—

A notification alert flashes in the corner of my vision.

Alert! *Spirit beast located. Subdue the beast in order to bond and unlock phase two.*

As lame as saying my spirit beast is a goat sounds, the creatures before me are impressive. Raw power and stubbornness rolled into one. Not all that different from me. The goat's muscles ripple as they crash into one another again.

I'm far from disappointed, but how in the hell am I supposed to subdue an angry goat without killing it? It's not like I can tame it like Taryn. I've seen what these things can do in Whitgard, and those were domesticated. How much more dangerous are wild ones? Judging by the sound of their collisions, these hit like a wrecking ball.

Both male frost goats are level twenty-five, and the female is twenty-three. I'm sure I could take them one on one, but if I run in guns blazing, they could forget about their beef with each other and focus on me. Without my items, I'm not a hundred percent certain I could win that fight. Especially if the female joins in.

I summon more horrors into the back of my cave just in case. Then, I watch.

I've been searching for my spirit beast for two days. What's a little more time?

The goats ram each other for what feels like hours, and their health barely drops. They're fighting in a display of dominance, not to actually kill one another. Still, their health trickles down with each collision, but the Constitution it takes to endure such repetitive attacks means their health recovers just as quickly. There can't be an animal on the mountain who hasn't heard their ruckus.

The orange outline covers their bodies like someone sketched over them with a watercolor. If my instincts are correct, then I should be able to subdue either one of them. This gives me an idea.

I watch and wait as the goats square off again and again, wondering if they are ever going to stop fighting. When one of the goats takes a hard fall upon impact, he's slow to get up. The other ram looms over him, steam pouring from his nostrils. He lands a few hard kicks against the downed goat before leaving with the female.

The loser eventually stands, and after a few agitated huffs and angry paws at the ground, he stalks away in defeat.

Sixty of my horrors and I set off in pursuit. To anyone below, I'm sure we look like a blotch on the mountainside.

The frost goat quickly ascends the rough, snow-covered terrain, and if I don't make my move quickly, he'll be gone before I have a chance to subdue him. So, I grab a Horror of Vitality by the horn and chuck it at the goat with all my might. It tumbles through the air, screaming its disapproval, and I activate Berserker Rage.

My legs move faster through the snow as my body flexes with rage. The horror hits the goat, its passive ability slowing the creature momentarily. The frost goat headbutts my horror, obliterating it with one hit, but I already have a second horror flying through the air.

After three horrors descend on him from the sky, the goat finally notices our approach and charges in for a fight. I run toward him at full speed, and the goat lowers his head.

At the last second, I jump, twisting in the air as the goat barrels into my army of horrors, turning a handful into smoke instantly. The others swarm the beast as I land on his back, hands gripping firmly around his horns. I pull back with all my strength as my ultimate ability continues to pump through my veins.

My horrors attack the goat's legs, dropping him to his knees. Horrors of Finesse claw while the Horrors of Power gore the goat with their sharp tusks. His health ticks down more rapidly than it ever did in the fight with the other ram. My muscles burn as I continue to pull back on the horns, giving the goat nothing more than his legs to attack with.

The goat falls to his side with ten percent health, each breath ragged as he kicks out. My horrors are depleted by half, but I have them pile on the goat thirty strong.

Berserker Rage ends, but the goat has given up the fight. The orange glow fades around his body, and I receive a new notification.

I release the goat and take in a deep, cooling breath. Phase one complete. The creature kicks out and then stumbles to his feet. I stand, ready to fight if I have to, but the goat lowers his head, huffs, and then runs up the mountain as his health begins to recover.

Once I'm out of combat, more horrors fade away as their timers expire. I pull up my new notification.

Alert! *Spirit of the Beast Phase One: Spirit Inquiry complete. New class option available.*

Phase 2: Spirit Embodiment. *Bonding with a spirit beast is only the beginning of the Spirit of the Beast path. By finding an amulet that connects you to your beast, the bond between the two will grow stronger, unlocking further advancements.*

Completion: Find an amulet that connects you to your spirit beast. Further phases will become available upon completion.

I gather myself and set off after the frost goat once again. If I'm going to find an amulet, it has to be connected to the goats somehow.

But at least I don't have to subdue it again.

The black specks of the frost goat's horns grow smaller and smaller as he climbs the mountain. I wish Taryn was around to cast Strong Wind right about now.

With each step, my anger continues to simmer. The goat is now so far away that I can't even hit him with a horror if I tried. It took three days to find my spirit beast and now I'm about to lose the only clue I have.

I'm about ready to scream when I pass a cave emitting a familiar orange glow—the same shade of orange that the goats had when they were fighting.

I summon more horrors and step inside the cave. If this isn't a clue to finding the amulet, then I just fucked myself over big time. But it can't be a coincidence that they are giving off the same aura.

The cave is long, and the glow grows denser the further in I go. When the tunnel empties into a large cavern, it's practically a sea of orange. Bones litter the cavern floor. Hundreds of them.

This is a graveyard.

A frail frost goat lays against a pile of bones in the far corner. When he sees me, he fights to stand. His legs tremble and then he collapses to the ground, rattling the bones and stirring up a layer of dust. His horns are bigger than either of the goats that were fighting earlier, and his eyes are a faded gray.

Poor guy. He must have been a hell of a fighter in his prime.

I carefully approach. Even though the goat is on his deathbed, his eyes burn with the same intensity as his brethren. He huffs, stirring up bone dust before resting his head on the cavern floor.

The bones surrounding the dying goat are coated in the same orange watercolor outline that the goats had earlier. I pick up one of the skulls and the aura of the cavern instantly fades.

My head pounds with a splitting headache and stars dance across my vision. The ram's skull dissipates in my palm, and orange energy floods into my chest. Skin tears at the side of my head and I fall to my knees in intense pain. It feels like someone is drilling into my head for about five seconds straight before the pain stops and the tip of two blue ram's horns appear in my peripheral vision.

I receive a new notification, but I ignore it for now. The giant horns sprouting from my head have all my attention. I trace my fingers from the tip of each horn as they widen, curling around and connecting to the side of my head. The tips are the same translucent blue as the frost goats, so I'm certain that they fade to black at the base as well.

Holy shit! I'm a troll with ram's horns.

I rap my knuckles against the horns but feel nothing. Giving them a firm tug, they don't budge. They're literally fused to my skull. If they are a fraction of the strength of the real thing, then I just got a hell of a lot tougher. I quickly pull up my notification.

Alert! Spirit of the Beast Phase Two: Spirit Embodiment complete. New class option available.

Phase 3: Spirit Enhancement. *Just as your body has undergone a change reflective of your spirit beast, your spirit may be enhanced in the same manner. Gain a new passive ability based on your spirit beast.*

Completion: Unlock using one ability point. Further phases will become available upon completion.

That's it? All I have to do is use an ability point and I gain a new passive? I knew I was hanging on to the ability points for something great and this is exactly it. I don't hesitate, using my ability point on Spirit Enhancement. Immediately, I'm flooded with new notifications.

Alert! Spirit of the Beast Phase Three: Spirit Enhancement complete. New ability and class option available.

Ability: (New)

Ram Rage: *Barbarian rage now lasts twice as long. Physical attacks deal splash damage.*

. . .

Phase 4: Spirit Guide. Your body and spirit have undergone great changes, but your bond with the spirit world is only beginning. Summon your spirit beast as a guide. Spirit guides are capable of leading you through darkness and guiding you to locations you have previously visited, even if you do not know the way. Spirit guides may be absorbed for a 50% increase to Wisdom for 10 minutes. A spirit guide may not be summoned for 24 hours after absorption.

Completion: Unlock using one ability point. Further phases will become available upon completion.

I could do without the darkness guide thanks to my night vision, but the other part is pretty cool. It's like I'll have my own personal GPS.

I use my final ability point to unlock phase four and more notifications appear.

Alert! Spirit of the Beast Phase Four: Spirit Guide complete. New ability and class option available.

Ability: (New)

Spirit Guide: Summon a frost goat spirit guide. The spirit guide may lead you through darkness and guide you to locations you have previously visited, even if you do not know the way. Spirit guides may be absorbed for a 50% increase to Wisdom for 10 minutes. Cooldown: 24 hours after absorption.

Phase 5: Spirit Power. The path of the beast is not for the faint of heart, and those who complete all five stages are blessed with a mighty power from their spirit beast. Gain a new active ability based on your spirit beast.

Completion: Unlock using one ability point and the Spirit of the Beast path will be complete.

Of course they save the best for last. A new active ability. My mind races with possibilities of headbutts with my new horns, powerful kicks, or the ability to climb mountains with ease. Whatever it is, I'm sure it'll be awesome. But I won't know the real ability until I hit level twenty-seven. Talk about anticipation.

I can't be mad, though. I've unlocked two new abilities and went through a transformation over the span of a few minutes. I doubt even Taryn is having that kind of luck right now.

The frost goat groans, drawing my attention away from my interface. He rests his head on the cave floor and looks up at me with knowing eyes, the fire all but gone. This is it. He came here to die, and it will all be over soon.

I kneel and rest my hand on his head. Surprisingly, he doesn't fight me. Gently, I stroke the patch of rough white hair between his horns. If only Taryn were here, he could cast Restoration and maybe buy the goat some more time.

Taryn might not be here, but maybe there's still a way to help this goat. It's not like he'll be any worse off if I fail.

I scratch the goat behind the ear. "What do you say, big guy, want to go on an adventure?"

The goat groans as I struggle to lift him onto my shoulder. He must weigh two or three hundred pounds, but nothing I can't handle. The bigger issue will be making it down the mountain in time. I've been wandering for three days and have no idea what the quickest route is.

Luckily, I have just the answer. I cast Spirit Guide and a ghostly frost goat appears in front of me, its body made of an ethereal white-and-orange aura. The spirit goat puffs out its chest and paws at the ground, head raised high.

"Lead us to the village."

33. THE GRIND

Taryn brushed a chunk of ice from between Berry's ears and it clattered against the floor. The remains of shattered ice golems littered the dungeon. Nearby, steam radiated from Fiero's fur as he pulled his spiked mace from a block of ice that had once been the head of a golem.

Watching the arctic trolls rage felt different than when it happened to Chod. His was a controlled burn, devastating but directed, while theirs was like an all-consuming wildfire.

True to the chief's words, Taryn was exhausted. He'd barely slept for the past three days, rotating between the three groups of trolls. Loading up on potions and elixirs, he kept going with one group while the others rested, and Restoration kept his pets in good health. The first team was Chief Laojin and Rhaz. Second team consisted of Senzala and Tzane. The third and his current team was Machu and Fiero.

Machu took in deep breaths as he leaned on his warhammer like a crutch. They'd been clearing levels for a few hours now, and it was almost time to switch teams again.

He'd reached level twenty-four early in the morning the previous day. With a little luck, he could hit level twenty-five before the day was out.

Taryn put away his staff for the moment. "You two can go on and rotate. I'll wait here for the next team."

Fiero patted Stompy on the side. "This one is formidable. I have enjoyed witnessing his power."

Stompy huffed as he leaned his weight against the large troll while he munched on a carrot. The moulhaug had stomped and smashed his fair share of monsters the past few days.

"Good fortune with the bats." Machu nodded as he and Fiero left the room.

"Thank you for your help!" Taryn shouted after them.

He knew what was coming for the next few levels. They'd made it further on day two than day one, and they were on schedule to go even deeper into the dungeon today. Knowing what to expect meant they could go in with a game plan. After the ice golems, frost bats awaited.

Limery splashed around in a puddle that had once been an ice golem before he'd melted it like ice cream on a hot summer day. His fire abilities were especially effective against anything ice-related. He was now level twenty-three and part of the reason they had cleared so many levels already.

Taryn healed his pets and popped a mana potion as he waited for Laojin and Rhaz to arrive. While Laojin and Senzala were the only members of the tribe that had mana in their bodies, the trolls were rather adept at making mana potions. Their access to the mana well and the potion recipes in the library allowed them to concoct enough potions to keep Taryn going until he advanced.

If they had any left over, he'd make sure to pack some for the road. The ones in Hornryx felt more potent than any he had purchased in other cities. Perhaps it was the proximity to the source.

Taryn lay on Stompy's back while he waited, making shapes with the vines of the Sapling Staff until he heard footsteps approaching.

Chief Laojin grinned as he entered the room. "No time to waste, young dwarf. No time to waste."

A change had come over the trolls as they cleared the lower levels of the dungeon. Even though it was dangerous work, they seemed more relaxed between battles. They laughed. Occasionally, they even joked. After so many years of only clearing the upper levels for food, it had to feel good for them to really test themselves.

The chief held up a hand just outside the entryway to the next level. "Same plan as before."

Taryn and Rhaz nodded. Limery cackled.

Laojin rushed into the room and raised his staff, the tip flashing with a blue aura. Dozens of large bats, each one two to three feet tall with an even wider wing-span, hung from the ceiling. As soon as the group entered, the bats began to stir.

The chief's attack took hold, and a thick layer of frost formed across the ceiling. It spread over the feet of the hanging bats, down their legs, and across their bodies until they were frozen in place like icicles.

The group didn't have much time, so Taryn rushed into action, casting Stonewall beneath a row of frozen bats. The wall erupted from the cave floor, stretching all the way to the ceiling and crushing five bats in one go.

Limery zoomed through the air, flames coating his hands as he melted the ice around the feet of the others one by one. The frozen bats crashed against the floor, ice shattering from their bodies upon impact. The beasts stumbled around like they had just woken up from a deep sleep.

Rhaz's axe hit one with so much force that it split the bat in half and sparks flew as the blade gashed the cave floor. Stompy's massive hooves flattened two bats into pancakes, and Berry mauled a third. Chief Laojin took out the rest with some well-placed ice spikes.

Taryn's experience bar shot up once again. It wouldn't be much longer before he was finally the same level as Chod, then he could give him a hard time for the foreseeable future. He already had a few jokes brewing.

After a short wait, they readied themselves for the next floor. It had nearly done them in the previous evening, leaving their party battered and bruised.

From the entrance, they counted six gargoyles statues around the room. The surprise of them coming to life had been part of their near-downfall. These were not as intricately carved as some that might be spotted in Seascape or other cities with great architecture. Instead, they had the look of a statue that had endured the elements for many years. They had the appearance of some winged creature, but the features were hard to define. They could have been carved from the cave itself, whittled away by someone with only the most primitive tools.

Six on six should have been a fair fight, but the gargoyles were nearly impossible to kill. They had tough stone skin, and when not moving, they received an additional buff making them near invulnerable. They'd learned that the hard way.

The group entered the room and twelve orange eyes suddenly opened. The gargoyles stood silent, waiting for the intruders to make the first move.

Taryn cast Stonewall, summoning a wall that divided the cavern in two, keeping three of the gargoyles at bay temporarily. He'd talked it over with Laojin, and they thought they had a better plan for this second attempt. Divide and conquer.

He equipped Sapling Staff in one hand and a Shadow Dagger in the other. Vines extended from the staff, wrapping around the closest gargoyle. The monster didn't struggle against the binding, not until Taryn plunged the Shadow Dagger into its heart.

The weapon bypassed the gargoyle's natural stone armor, its formless blade of energy depleting health and mana directly. Vital areas like the heart and head drained HP and mana more quickly. The gargoyle convulsed from the sudden disturbance like its heart had been jolted with electricity. Its health dropped rapidly as it struggled against the entangling vines.

The gargoyle roared, stretching the vines to their limits, and the other two gargoyles stirred. Thuds echoed from the other side of Taryn's stone wall.

The vines snapped from the tension, and a stone fist punched Taryn in the chest, knocking him across the room. Taryn collided with the wall, losing only a sliver of health due to his high Constitution, but he felt every bit of it. He sucked in air and his vision flared in and out of focus as all hell broke loose.

Frost spread across the ground as Laojin froze the other two gargoyles in place. Rhaz chopped at one of the stone beasts with his axe and sparks exploded from the impact. Meanwhile, Stompy pinned the third gargoyle to the ground with a massive hoof while Berry mauled it and Limery pressed molten hands against the gargoyle's head, slowly draining more HP.

That's it. If Stompy can pin them down, I can drain their health.

Taryn grimaced as he crawled to his feet. His staff and dagger were scattered somewhere around the room, but he still had a second Shadow Dagger.

The two nearest gargoyles broke free from their ice prison, keeping the two trolls' attention.

Taryn shouted at Laojin as he ran past. "New plan! Keep the others busy while Stompy holds one in place and I drain its life."

Limery and Berry had whittled the gargoyle down to a quarter-health by the time Taryn arrived. He plunged the dagger into the monster's head. Its health dropped more rapidly than ever, and a few seconds later, it lay still.

"One down, five to go."

Stonewall exploded as the other gargoyles broke through, sending rubble across the cavern.

Chief Laojin cast an ice wall, but the gargoyles smashed through it in seconds. A blue aura surrounded his staff as he raised it in the air. When he slammed the butt of the staff against the floor, ice spread out like a shockwave, turning the cavern into an ice rink.

Rhaz slipped and fell, his axe clattering against the floor. The gargoyles slid across like butter on a hot pan, unable to gain their footing. Taryn dropped to all fours to keep from falling. Only Stompy seemed to have no trouble standing.

A gargoyle slid into the moulhaug, and he swung his horn like a wrecking ball, knocking the monster against the back wall.

One of the gargoyles punched the ground, splintering the ice. The others followed suit and soon the ice was nothing more than slick gravel.

Taryn cast Lightning Bolt. The accompanying thunder was deafening in the packed cavern as it stunned the closest gargoyle in place. Laojin seized the opportunity, summoning a stalagmite-like spear of ice that pierced the monster from underneath. Taryn leapt for the gargoyle while it was still stunned, plunging the Shadow Dagger into its face. The critical hit drained health rapidly, and there was only a sliver left when the stun faded.

A sliver too much.

A powerful fist launched him across the room for the second time, dropping his health once again. His entire body ached as he struggled to stand.

"Twos downs!" Limery's voice carried above the chaos while he hovered over a downed gargoyle.

Rhaz took a beating as he traded blows with one of the former statues. Blue blood trickled down his nose, staining his fur. Laojin held his left arm out, a shield of ice protecting him as he stabbed with his staff, an icy spear on its end. One of the gargoyles glowed red as Limery summoned a flame wall underneath it. When the flames faded, Laojin hit it with an ice blast, slowing the gargoyle. A powerful strike from Berry sent cracks forming all along the stone creature before it crumbled.

"Hit them with fire and then ice!" Taryn shouted. "It weakens them."

He grabbed a Shadow Dagger laying on the ground as he ran toward Stompy, who had another gargoyle pinned to the ground under his massive weight. The gargoyle swung its arms desperately, but it was no match for the moulhaug's weight. Taryn effortlessly drained the creature's health with the Shadow Dagger he'd recovered.

They made short work of the final three, taking two out with a fire-and-ice combo, and draining the last as Stompy sat on it.

Laojin leaned against his staff, breathing heavily. "Gargoyles: strong, slow, and difficult to kill."

Rhaz puffed out his chest. His white fur was stained blue in several areas. "We showed them." He grimaced as he raised his axe overhead.

Taryn took a deep breath as he cast Restoration, healing the lacerations across Berry's snout before moving on to Stompy. Even with the chief on their side, that had been a difficult fight. But he was so close to leveling up.

With the pets healed, the rest of the party downed potions to restore their health, minus Limery, who had escaped unscathed. The gash on Rhaz's nose rapidly sealed itself, leaving only crusty blue blood in its place.

Taryn gathered the dagger and staff he had lost during the battle and placed them back in his inventory.

He paced with nervous energy. The final grind was upon them.

⸻

Taryn lay on his back, the soft corpse of a shadow fox draped across his face. His heart pounded as he pushed the body to the side and sat up. Notifications flared in the corner of his vision, but they would have to wait.

Berry groaned as he collapsed to the floor. His claws and snout were coated in a thick layer of blood. Rhaz leaned against the wall, a chunk of fur completely missing from his forearm. Laojin leaned over Stompy, who had taken the brunt of the damage, whispering encouragement.

Limery lay on the ground, his arms and legs splayed in an X formation. "Limmy is tireds," he whispered.

Taryn gathered the last of his strength and huddled over Berry. Energy from the mountain passed through him and into the bear as he cast Restoration. Once finished, he moved on to Stompy.

Since Taryn had been so close to hitting level twenty-five, Laojin had wanted to stay for one more battle even though they were low on potions and scheduled for a team switch.

They ran out of potions in the middle of the fight. In addition to being lightning quick with sharp teeth and claws, the shadow foxes left a trail of dark energy in their wake that drained health and mana from anyone who stepped into the shadows. The foxes could also hide and travel in the shadows, attacking the group from multiple angles without warning. Stompy had been too big to avoid the shadows, but in the end, they'd scraped by.

Barely.

With his pets healed, Taryn pulled up his notifications. He'd have to tend to his own health once they were back aboveground.

Congratulations! You have reached level 25. +1 stat point to distribute. +1 Constitution racial bonus. +1 ability point to distribute.

Class Advancements. *Upon reaching level twenty-five, you have unlocked a class advancement. You may only advance one class at a time. A second class may not be advanced until completion of primary advancement.*

Druid Advancement. *(Choose one)*
Shadow Druid. Unlock for further details.
Druid of the Dawn. Unlock for further details.
Ice Druid. Unlock for further details.

Taryn was so lost in the notifications that he didn't notice Laojin standing over him until a firm hand squeezed his shoulder.

"I see you have succeeded." There was a look of pride on the elder troll's face. "You have the heart of a troll within you. What advancements have you unlocked?"

Taryn couldn't quite explain it, but he suddenly felt overcome with emotion. His cheeks grew hot, and he blinked rapidly to fight back the tears. The way Chief Laojin looked upon him with a sense of pride reminded him of his own father.

His father had been a star athlete in high school. He'd even gotten a scholarship to play for a small college in upstate New York, but a knee injury his freshmen year and lingering medical bills had put an end to any dreams beyond that. He'd always been proud of Taryn for choosing academics over sports, even though Taryn had inherited his father's physique and work ethic.

He took a deep breath and recentered himself, pulling up the notifications again and reading them aloud to the chief.

"Interesting." Laojin stroked his beard. "You have been blessed with quality selections. The Shadow Druid draws his power from the night, with spells that harness the moon and darkness. Druid of the Dawn is quite the opposite, harnessing the power of the sun. And then there is the Ice Druid—" He grinned "—which you may have guessed is my own path."

Taryn scratched his head. They all sounded like good options. "Which one should I choose?"

Laojin frowned. "That is not for me to decide, but I can offer you some guidance. The path of the Ice Druid has favorable crowd control. Slows, freezes, and the ability to make the terrain slick and difficult to battle on are only some of its benefits. It also possesses a fair number of offensive abilities with bonus effects. The path of the Druid of the Dawn is more common, using the sun for light-based attacks and healing. The Shadow Druid is a rare path, powered by the moon, it is devastating at night and in the shadow realms. It offers a balance of offense, defense, and subterfuge. Each has its strengths, but you must decide which one is right for you."

Taryn nodded, and Berry nudged a blood-stained snout against his hand. He had a lot to think about.

Each advancement sounded awesome in its own right. He'd seen firsthand the power that an ice druid had. The ability to freeze enemies in place was advantageous, especially considering the synergy it could have with Chod and his horrors, and not to mention the fire-and-ice combo with Limery.

Then there was the Druid of the Dawn. If Taryn could offer more healing to the rest of the party, and not just his pets, he'd be even more valuable as a support, especially once their party grew. They did most of their fighting during the day, so that would lend to making the most of the source of his druid powers. It seemed like a no-brainer.

But something about the Shadow Druid called to him. Maybe it was what Chief Laojin had said about it being more powerful at night and in the shadow realms. They'd gone head-to-head with demons and behemoths from the shadowlands already. And unless the dark wizard attacked them first, at some point they would be doing battle there. Wouldn't Taryn want to be at his best when it mattered most?

He sighed. Maybe it was possible to have too much of a good thing.

Who was he kidding? There were worse things than having to decide between three awesome class advancements in the most fully-immersive game on the planet. He thought deeper about his choices and what Laojin had said. The word 'devastating' kept replaying in his mind. Taryn loved being the support of the group, but there might come a time when he needed to be more. When that time came, he wanted to be devastating.

Taryn stood straight and spoke with confidence. "I'm going to advance Shadow Druid."

Laojin nodded his approval.

Taryn selected the class advancement, and a flurry of notifications appeared.

Alert! You have selected to advance the Druid class. New class option available.

Druid. *One with the natural world and the elements, druids take their power from nature itself.*

Subclass:

Shadow Druid. *Blessed by the moon, shadow druids draw power from its light and the darkness.*

. . .

Available Abilities *(1 ability point to unlock):*

Moonbeam: *Cast a beam of radiant energy. 50% increased damage at night. 100% increased damage against the undead. Cost: 100 mana. Cooldown: 60 seconds.*

Scry: *Using a personal item of your intended target, channel the power of the moon to locate their presence on your map. Cost: None. Cooldown: 24 hours.*

Mind Warp: *Corrupted by the darkness, a targeted enemy will attack its allies for 30 seconds. Cost: 200 mana. Cooldown: 30 minutes.*

Tidal Wave: *By harnessing the pull of the moon, cast a tidal wave from a nearby body of water. Cost: 200 mana. Cooldown: 120 seconds.*

Shooting Stars: *A celestial barrage of stars falls from the heavens, dealing damage. 50% increased damage at night. 100% increased damage against the undead. Cost: 100 mana. Cooldown: 60 seconds.*

Shadow Cloak (Passive): *While enabled, shadow druids have increased stealth at night or in the shadows.*

Endless Night: *For 30 seconds, shroud an area in a veil of impenetrable darkness, obscuring the sight and smell of those within. Cost: 200 mana. Cooldown: 1 hour.*

Taryn rubbed his hands together, giddy with excitement. "Oh, this is good! This is really good."

He had his ability point from reaching level twenty-five, but he also had the point he had saved from level twenty-three. He knew he was saving it for something great, and this was it. The only problem was choosing which two to spend his points on.

There were three active abilities: Moonbeam, Shooting Stars, and Tidal Wave. Tidal Wave was cool, but since it had to be near a body of water, it was best to put it on hold for now. Moonbeam and Shooting stars were similar abilities, and their bonus damage against the undead would likely be a huge benefit in the future. Moonbeam was more of a directed attack, while Shooting Stars covered a larger area and was capable of hitting more enemies. He would be choosing one of those, for sure, but would it be better to hit one enemy with a powerful attack or to spread that damage over several enemies?

The choice between the final four would be tough. The ability to locate someone as long as he had one of their items seemed extremely powerful, especially with the portals opened. But how often would that situation arise?

Mind Warp could offer some interesting possibilities, effectively giving them another party member for thirty seconds.

Shadow Cloak would be great for recon and stealth, but Taryn could accomplish most of those feats while in his bird form, so he eliminated that one for now.

That left Endless Night. It reminded him of a better version of the Infernal Darkness Potion, which they had wasted during their first fight with Dakota upon entering Goldspire. While Endless Night only lasted half as long as the potion, it could be cast every hour.

Taryn took a moment to describe the abilities to Laojin.

The troll ran his fingers through his beard. "You have quite the decision ahead of you."

Taryn nodded. With seven available abilities and only two ability points, it would take him ten more levels to unlock them all. He'd been lucky with power-leveling the Hornryx dungeon, but once they left the village, he'd have to earn the upcoming levels the hard way.

All the more reason to get this right.

He'd pick an offensive ability for now, and then discuss the other options with Chod once he returned. Who knew, if he took much longer, maybe Taryn could grind out another level or two.

After careful deliberation, he placed his first ability point into Moonbeam. It added more direct firepower to their arsenal.

Taryn raised his staff and activated the ability toward the center of the room. Shimmering silver light blasted from the ceiling, momentarily casting back the darkness. The beam sizzled for a second against the cave floor before fading away. Aside from that, it was completely silent, a far cry from the accompanying thunder of Lightning Bolt. This attack could kill without ever making a sound.

"Shinies." Limery stared at the area the moonbeam had hit, where a silvery residue coated the ground.

Rhaz looked impressed as he crossed his arms.

Chief Laojin slightly raised his eyebrows. "Very nice. Now, let us return to the village. If you wish, we may continue tomorrow."

Taryn laughed. "I'll take all the free levels I can get."

"Free?" Rhaz frowned, lifting his hairless, blood-covered arm. "Your levels were paid for with my blood."

Laojin laughed.

"You're right, Rhaz," Taryn conceded. "I couldn't have done it without you."

Rhaz stood a little taller after receiving the compliment.

They made the long journey up to the dungeon entrance, bypassing their carnage from previous fights along the way. Having completely cleared the food levels three days in a row, the village was well stocked on meat for the next few weeks.

As they exited the dungeon, a group of people had gathered in the crag. It was far later than Taryn thought, and darkness reigned overhead. Taryn thought maybe they had heard he'd advanced somehow, but they were all facing the opposite direction.

The group parted in front of the chief, revealing a ghostly image of a frost goat that approached from outside the village. The beast's body looked to be formed completely from some ethereal energy, and a hazy orange outline surrounded it whichever way it moved. The goat stopped, turning sideways and looking over its shoulder.

There was a grunt as a large figure emerged from the night. Everyone was suddenly silent, and Taryn could hear the heavy breathing of the creature even from so far away. The figure was as tall as a troll, but with much broader shoulders and black horns that curled around its face. A large fur cloak covered its shoulders.

Taryn stared at it for a minute, sensing something familiar but unable to place it. Suddenly, all the pieces came together. "Chod? What the hell happened to your head?"

Chod fell to his knees. He struggled to remove the fur cloak, and Taryn realized it wasn't a cloak at all. It was a frost goat he'd been carrying on his shoulders. How far had he traveled like this?

Chod leaned over the frost goat's body. "Please, I need your help."

34. GREATEST OF ALL TIME

With my last bit of energy, I lift the dying frost goat from my shoulders and collapse to the ground. A multitude of arctic trolls watch with shocked expressions. Some stare at my spirit guide, its glowing body a beacon against the night. Others look at me warily, no doubt unsure of what to make of a blue forest troll with horns sprouting from his head.

I search for a friendly face, anyone to ask for help, but find no one. When the crowd parts, Taryn and Chief Laojin step through. Taryn shouts something, but I can't hear him over my thundering pulse.

My hands rest on the frost goat as it struggles for breath. "Please, I need your help."

Limery closes the distance in an instant, his warm hands clutching my shoulder. His bulbous eyes are ripe with worry. "Is you's okays, Chods?"

"Yes...need...Taryn."

"Taryns!" Limery yells, but the dwarf is already running in our direction.

He and the chief kneel beside me when they arrive.

I meet their eyes. "I'm fine, just heal the goat."

Taryn exchanges looks with Laojin as he places his hand on the goat. I wait for the familiar glow of Restoration, but it never comes.

He curses. "I'm sorry, but I can't heal animals that aren't my pets." He turns to Laojin. "Can you?"

The chief shakes his head. "I'm afraid I reached my limit for pets long ago."

"Then make him your pet, Taryn," I snap—whether from panic or exhaustion, I'm not sure. All I know is that I didn't carry him all the way down the mountain just to watch him die.

He frowns. "I don't know. I can't just—"

I grab Taryn firmly by the arm with what little strength I have left. "Please. I'll explain everything later, but for now...just, please, help him."

I don't know why this goat means so much to me. He was going to die anyway through no fault of my own. Maybe it was finding the connection to my spirit beast, and the stubbornness that frost goats represent. If I can't save my own spirit beast, what chance do I have against the dark wizard?

He nods. "Okay."

Taryn places both hands on the goat, and a green aura surrounds him. The creature is so weak that he's practically ripe for taming. Taryn's hands glow yellow, and energy spreads out from his palms, coating the frost goat in a similar aura. After a moment, the goat's breathing steadies, and then his health begins to trickle in the other direction.

When the aura fades, Taryn takes a step back. The goat rolls over, his hooves clacking against the ground as he stands. He lowers his head, and I wonder if I've made a mistake, but then the goat slowly steps forward, pressing his horns gently against Taryn's chest.

Taryn smiles and scratches the goat between the horns. "Hey, buddy. It's all okay now. Wait until you meet your brothers and sister." He turns to me. "You've got a lot of explaining to do, but first, we need to get you some health potions."

Laojin wraps my arm over his shoulders and helps me to my feet. Another troll takes position on the other side. I've pushed my exhaustion to the limit, nearly to the same point as I did after Ismora was stabbed so long ago. Back then, I'd passed out when we made it back to the forest and had to recover for almost two days. Luckily, this won't be as bad.

They lead me into a cave and sit me down on a bed covered in fur blankets. A table against the wall is filled with vials and clay pots. The next thing I know, a health potion is being pressed against my lips. An elderly female troll shakes her head as she looks down at me. She knows I pushed myself too hard, but I'm a hero, it comes with the territory. Immediately, a warm tingle spreads through my body and my energy returns fraction by fraction.

Laojin watches me intently, and Limery sits on my stomach. I smile at the imp, and his small shoulders relax.

A moment later, Taryn enters the cave. "I just put Michael Jordan with the other pets. I was worried he might attack them, but he seems much calmer than the ones we saw in Whitgard. Stompy actually acknowledged him."

I lift my head off the bed, certain that I must have misheard him. "Did you just call him Michael Jordan?"

Taryn gives me a devilish grin. "I was thinking Mikey or Jordy for short. I haven't decided."

The exhaustion must be playing tricks on my brain. "Why Michael Jordan?"

Taryn's grin grows wider. "Because he's the G.O.A.T."

I roll my eyes, not even willing to dignify his statement with a response.

Laojin looks at him with a confused expression. "Is Michael Jordan a dwarven name?"

Taryn's smile fades. "No, it's, uh, you know what? It's not important." He turns his attention to me. "Want to explain to me why I now have another pet and a twenty percent chance that they won't obey me? Stompy is stubborn enough. It's bound to rub off on little MJ."

"Oh, come on. He'll make a great pet. And you said yourself it's not like they'll refuse to listen, they just might be a little more creative in how they do it. Don't sweat it." With more of my energy replenished, I sit up on the bed. "I'm famished. What's for dinner?"

After three bowls of stew and an entire boar leg, I finally feel like myself again. Taryn and Limery both slurp at their bowls beside me. When we're finished, we'll meet Chief Laojin and the others in the council room.

I catch lots of glances and outright stares from the villagers. A young troll stalks around like a monster, his two hands mimicking horns on his head. None of the looks are hostile, but I'm sure I'm quite the sight to them, especially when I didn't have these monstrous horns a few days ago.

I toss the bone from my boar leg to Berry. He snatches it up and lumbers away.

"What have you two been up to while I was gone?"

Taryn wags his finger at me. "No, you're the one who stumbled in here with a damn ghost leading the way. I don't care how awesome my news is, and it is awesome, you owe us an explanation."

"Yeah," Limery echoes, his mouth full of food. "Yous owes us an explanations."

I give them my best pleading look. "Come on, you know I'm going to have to tell this story to the council. Can't you wait five minutes?"

Taryn narrows his eyes. "Fine. Go ahead and analyze me."

I do what he says, focusing on him until his gamertag appears.

Taryn Jones
   Level 25
   Shadow Druid
   Ebony Dwarf

"Holy shit! You hit level twenty-five already. And what's a shadow druid?"

Taryn smirks. "Yeah, and Limery is level twenty-four. We've been busy while you were frolicking through the snow. Even Berry and Stompy leveled up nicely." He tilts his bowl, finishing the last of the stew. "Shadow druid is my subclass. I'll tell you more about it later when we can really talk it over, but I think it will be good for us. I still have one ability point to use and can't decide what to spend it on." He stands up. "Alright, let's get the interrogation over with."

After taking Taryn's pets back to the cave, we go to the council room. The council is already at the table when we arrive, in the middle of a heated discussion.

Laojin slams his fist against the table, rattling the empty bowls. "It is no coincidence that—" He cuts his words short when he sees us, and his glare softens. "Chod, Taryn, Limery. We were just discussing you."

Sounds like that was going well. My shoulders stiffen. If they are talking this heatedly about us behind our backs, it can't be good.

"The horns suit you." Senzala winks at me.

I drop my gaze to the floor, and heat rushes to my cheeks. I've never done well with compliments on my appearance, and I'm suddenly aware that in spite of being a troll, the shaman has incredibly feminine features. Her eyelashes are long and wispy against her piercing eyes, and the way her short tusks peek above her lips gives her a mischievous look.

When I sneak a peek at her, she's still staring at me with a wry smile.

"Thank you," I mumble.

Taryn nudges me in the side, and I shake my head to clear my thoughts. Now is not the time to get flustered by a pretty girl.

The chief clears his throat. "Congratulations on finding your spirit beast. The frost goat is a respectable creature. One full of strength and determination. They are not easily intimidated and attack their opponents without hesitation of defeat. I trust that you have found the knowledge to continue down your path?"

I nod. "It was a process, but I'm happy with the results. Thank you for all of your guidance."

Oyanna straightens out a piece of parchment and holds a feather quill in her other hand. "I would like to record your adventure for our library. There is nothing better for scholars than a firsthand account of advancement."

I tell them my story, which consists mostly of me waiting around and staring at animals until I found the frost goats. Her pen moves rapidly, and though she doesn't have an inkwell, it never runs out of ink.

When I get to the part where I find the dying frost goat, Senzala raises a hand for me to stop.

"It is strange to help an animal that has already resigned itself to its fate. Why did you do it?"

I shrug. "I've been asking myself that a lot. It would have been easier to leave it there. But I don't really know. I guess maybe because I thought I could, that if I could bring him here then his story didn't have to be over."

She smiles, and my cheeks grow red again. "I think his story is just beginning."

"Speaking of stories..." Laojin sets my satchel on the table and pulls out the green egg I took from the vault at Seascape. "I'd like to know how a troll came into possession of a dragon egg?"

35. MYSTERY LOVES COMPANY

"Dragon egg?" I exchange looks with Taryn, who seems just as surprised as I am, before returning my attention to the chief. "How do you know?"

Chief Laojin frowns. "Do I look like the type not to recognize a dragon egg when I see one?"

I picked the egg up in King Orso's vault because I thought it looked cool and its stats were nothing more than question marks. I thought it was a trinket, some item that would prove useful in the future. Not once did I consider there might be an actual living creature inside. Every time I analyze it, it just says Mysterious Green Egg. I focus on it again, but this time, there is a description.

Item. Green Dragon Egg. *Green dragons rule with impunity over the forests they inhabit. They are the most territorial of all dragon species and capable of spewing toxic gas in lieu of flames. Wherever a green dragon calls home, a dense fog is said to follow. Green dragon eggs may only be hatched in the heart of an ancient forest.*

Wow. I've been carrying around a dragon egg all this time and had no idea.

"How do we hatch it?" Taryn blurts out, his eyes filled with greed.

Laojin laughs. "You have eyes for it already."

He lifts the egg, admiring its beauty. The egg is slightly larger than Limery's head, bright green like freshly-mowed grass. Thick, diamond-shaped scales lap over one another like a pine cone.

Laojin places it carefully on the table. "Green dragons can only be hatched in the heart of an ancient forest, where the life aura can infuse it."

I pick up the egg. It's so lightweight that it's hard to imagine it ever being something as big as Nesira. "Where can we find an ancient forest?"

Limery reaches over my shoulder for the egg, tracing his claws along the scales.

Chief Laojin's expression is unreadable. "There are only two that I know of. One is in Wandermere, home of the centaurs."

"And the other?" asks Taryn.

The chief's face goes serious. "Mosstar."

Taryn's eyes go wide. "Wait, isn't that—"

"Home of the dark elves…" He pauses for a long moment. "And birthplace of Valmar Worren, the one you call the dark wizard."

Everywhere we go, it's a constant reminder of what's coming. I don't know much about ancient forests, but if they have the power to hatch a dragon egg, there's no telling what Valmar has waiting on the other side of those portals.

I take my satchel from the table and place the egg back inside. "Considering the portals are still closed to Mosstar, I don't think we'll be going there anytime soon. But there's no way we can turn down the possibility of having a dragon on our side." I lock eyes with Senzala. "Which I'm sure you understand. So, after Boneholde, we will set our sights on Wandermere."

Laojin strokes his beard. "Very well. I hoped we would have more time with you, but you have an opportunity few in Mythos ever experience—to witness the birth of a dragon." He turns to Taryn. "Another day in the dungeon is little compared to a dragon on the battlefield. I advise you to leave for Boneholde at dawn. Tonight, we will celebrate your good fortune."

Tzane rubs his belly, a massive grin on his face. "I'll have them prepare the sweetwater."

***

Taryn lifts his cup of sweetwater in the air. "To dungeons."

"And dragons!" I shout, tapping my cup against his and we both take a large gulp of the famous troll brew.

"And Limmy!" The imp hovers before our faces, holding his mug with both hands.

"And to Limmy," Taryn and I both echo, toasting him in turn.

The sweet, frothy liquid burns as it trails down my throat. It tastes just like I remember at the troll village. Even though the tribes are different in many regards, it's nice to know some things remain the same.

I can't help but think how far I've come since then, back when my top priority was not getting killed by other heroes.

Trolls spill out from the caves, and the village looks like the site of a yeti festival. Drinks flow freely, and drums echo off the mountain. Pets roam the village, and I'm surprised by how social MJ has become. He's like a completely different animal compared to the frost goats in Whitgard. Stompy lays next to the mammoth at the entryway to the caves sharing his carrot. Every time they finish one, he returns to hover over Taryn until he gets another.

"This is the last one you get tonight." Taryn pulls a carrot from his satchel. "Tell your girlfriend to mooch off someone else."

Stompy snorts as he heads away, and Taryn grins like a proud father.

Laojin has made an ice slide for the children to play on that descends from the caves down into the village. It even has a loop in the middle and a ramp at the end that launches the children into a snowbank that Senzala created. Young trolls run from the snowbank at the bottom back to the caves to slide again and again.

"Limmy wants to slides." The imp finishes his sweetwater and zooms toward the top of the slide.

I'm glad he's having fun.

Across from us, Senzala and Laojin stand side by side. The chief whispers something in her ear, pointing to one of the children as the young troll comes to a stop against the snowbank at the end of the slide. Senzala laughs, spilling some of her drink in the snow.

Taryn elbows me in the side. "You gave me so much shit about Lady Brollen when we were in Sandholde and look at you, swooning over some hairy titties."

I shove him away. "Dude, it's not like that. She's just, I don't know, I think she's kind of cool."

"So that's your type?" Taryn smirks. "I thought you didn't have time for women."

"I don't." I focus on the children playing to keep from looking at Senzala. "We'll be gone in the morning, off to our next adventure."

Taryn scoffs. "All adventuring and no play makes Chod a dull boy."

A loud roar draws our attention as Rhaz beats his chest in the center of the village. "Who will challenge the mighty Rhaz?"

There's chatter before a deep roar answers, and Tzane emerges from the crowd with a mug of sweetwater in each hand. He chugs them both back-to-back before tossing the mugs aside and slamming a fist against his own chest. "A few days in the dungeon and you think you are king of the mountain." He cracks his knuckles. "Let's see what you've got."

Cheers and roars echo as a circle forms around the two challengers.

Rhaz and Tzane lock hands, to the delight of the crowd, each one pushing with all their might as they try to overpower the other. The two trolls grunt, their muscles bulging as they hold each other at a stalemate.

After several minutes of neither one giving an inch, steam starts to rise from Tzane's body. A few of the onlookers catcall as the challenge shifts in Tzane's favor. He grunts louder, and Rhaz starts moving in the other direction. His feet dig into the earth, but the pot-bellied troll keeps pushing. Tzane unleashes a mighty roar and shoves Rhaz onto his back.

Tzane flexes for the crowd and asks for another mug of sweetwater, and then he extends a hand to Rhaz.

Rhaz slaps it away. "No fair, you raged."

Tzane shrugs. "The mountain favored me today. A worthy fight."

"Hey, look. Now's your chance." Taryn points across the way to where Senzala is standing alone drinking her sweetwater. "Bro, live a little. It's just a conversation. It's not like you have to worry about her dragon biting your arm off or anything." Taryn steps behind me and pushes me forward.

Well, I hadn't been worried about that.

I know Taryn won't shut up until I talk to her, so I concede. As I walk over, I feel the same nervous energy I used to get when I was called to the front of the class, keenly aware of every step and afraid I might fall on my face. I don't know why I'm so nervous. We've talked before, but we've never just chatted, and I'm no good at small talk. All I can think about is how stupid this is.

"Want some company?" I ask, thankful for the cold air against my warm cheeks.

She smiles. "Sure. Are you enjoying yourself? The little one certainly is."

I take a large swig of sweetwater and let the burn wash over me. "You mean Limery or Taryn?" I laugh. "I'm having a good time. I love a good troll party."

She runs her hand along one of my horns, letting the tip poke against her finger. "Too bad you're leaving soon. We'll be having our spring festival before long. Now, that is a party you don't want to miss."

My pulse races at how close she is to me. "Sounds like fun, but we have a dragon to hatch." I pull the egg from my satchel, admiring its beauty. "Want to hold it?"

"It's beautiful." She lets go of my horn and takes the egg, admiring it like some precious jewel. "You have no idea how lucky you are to have this. Dragons are a true wonder. Nesira is my totem, but she will never be mine. She lends me her power and allows me in her presence, but she has a mind and will of her own. I never got to see her as a hatchling, back before she realized the world bowed before her."

"You could come. See the dragon hatch and join us on our travels. We could use someone with your power for what's coming."

She shakes her head. "A shaman belongs with her people, no matter how tempting the offer. Plus, the ring wouldn't hold with me being so far away."

Everywhere I go, there's always a reason for inaction, a reason for people to stay stuck in their ways. "Don't you think your tribe deserves more than hiding away in the mountain?"

She frowns, handing the egg back. "What I think doesn't matter. It is not my decision to make."

I put the egg away before I crack it in frustration. "But you're on the council."

She sighs. "I offer guidance and wisdom when I can, but our place in this world is a matter that was settled long ago."

"Wheeeee!" Limery shouts as he speeds down the slide, interrupting our conversation and eliciting laughter from the crowd.

He launches off the end, but instead of plowing into the snowbank, he flies into the air, his molten form a beacon in the sky.

"Showoff!" Taryn shouts. "If you think that is cool, watch this."

He lifts his staff and a beam of silver energy shoots down from the sky, exploding against the snow. The way he wobbles back and forth, I can tell he's feeling the sweetwater. For several seconds, the moonbeam radiates sizzling energy, melting a crater in the snow before eventually dissipating.

The crowd cheers in response to his theatrics.

I decide to let our conversation fade, summoning my spirit guide and letting it run through the crowd. Michael Jordan runs over to the spirit goat, lowering his head in respect. A drunken Taryn gives me a thumbs-up.

The trolls playing the drums increase the rhythm, beating in rapid succession until everyone quiets. Chief Laojin starts a slow clap as he walks up the pathway to the ledge overlooking the village. Several male trolls follow him, joining in with clapping.

Once at the top, the others continue to clap as they fall in behind him until there are at least thirty trolls standing behind the chief. The drums beat louder and faster. The claps fall in sync until it all sounds like a rapid rumble.

Chief Laojin raises his staff in the air and the village goes silent. "Tonight, we celebrate the accomplishments of our guests, and knowing that whatever role they play in the future of Mythos, we had a small part in that. Tonight, we will send them off in style."

The chief slams the butt of the staff to the ground, and the ice slide crumbles into a million tiny shards. It sounds like rain as they pitter-patter down the mountain.

There's an audible inhalation just before the trolls unleash a thunderous roar that has my hair standing on end. In perfect unison, they all stomp with their left foot, clap, then stomp with their right. They lower into a squat and roar again, making faces that would keep children up at night.

Then they perform their tribal dance, a beautiful display of grace and power. Stomps, roars, and thunderous claps echo across the night. Senzala grabs my arm as she watches, and I'm thankful she can't see my blushing face. I lose sight of the performance as I focus on the warmth of her touch.

Their final chant brings me back to the world as they all tilt their heads back and a brutal scream escapes into the night. The scream ends, its echo calling back to them again and again.

And then the dragon answers.

A powerful gust of wind blows across the village as snow pours from the heavens. In a matter of seconds, the clear sky is a whirlwind of white. Nesira's shrieking roar cuts above it all, and though I can't see her, I can feel her presence.

Senzala squeezes my arm. "I think the celebration is over."

36. ON THE ROAD AGAIN

The next morning, we say our good-byes to the tribe before Senzala and Laojin escort us down to the ring. I'm surprised that Taryn seems more well-liked by the arctic trolls than me. He and Limery both have a crowd of trolls wishing them well on their journey.

It feels like the chief and Senzala are the only ones I've really connected with since being here. Even though I got my class advancement, I can't help but feel like I missed out on an amazing experience inside the dungeon.

Taryn balls his fist, teaching Rhaz how to fist-bump. The muscled troll then tests out his new greeting on Limery. He bumps a little too hard, sending the imp somersaulting through the air, before tilting his head back in raucous laughter. I guess the best bonds really are forged on the battlefield.

Stompy nudges Taryn in the side, almost knocking him over.

"Fine." He pets the moulhaug on the snout before pulling a carrot from his bag. "They won't last forever, you know."

Stompy takes the carrot and drops it at the feet of the mammoth. She grabs it with her trunk and tosses it in her mouth.

Taryn puts his hands on his hips. "They grow up so fast."

Oyanna loads us up with health and mana potions, and after Taryn struggles to get Stompy to leave his new mammoth girlfriend behind, we set off down the mountain.

I take one last look at the village in all of its icy glory. The fresh layer of snow from Nesira makes it more picturesque than ever. I take a mental picture, because in all likelihood, I'll never set foot here again.

"Alright, Jordy, lead the way!" Taryn slaps the frost goat on the hindquarters, and he trots to the front of the party, snorting at Berry and Stompy as he passes.

Limery swoops down, landing on the goat's back. Taryn climbs on Berry, and I elect to stay on foot with Senzala and the chief.

"Is that what you settled on? Jordy?" I ask.

"Yeah, Mikey just didn't have the same ring to it." He grins. "I can wait to see him in action."

Laojin grunts. "You will have many opportunities on the journey to Boneholde. But beware the hobgoblins of Greypeak. What they lack in intelligence, they more than make up for in numbers and tenacity. They have a certain fondness for ambushing unsuspecting travelers."

"I thought the hobgoblins stayed hidden in the mountain?" I ask.

He nods. "They do, but there are always hobgoblin scouts roaming Frostmoor, so be wary."

"Let them try and ambush us." Taryn puffs out his chest. "They aren't the only ones who can scout ahead."

Taryn and Laojin get lost in talk of pets, scouting, and all things druid, so I walk beside Senzala. We haven't spoken since our time together was cut short by Nesira. I open my mouth half a dozen times to say something, but I can't seem to find the right words.

I know I have bigger priorities, but I did enjoy her company. It's a shame it has to end so soon.

"You know, I never got to see you in action," I finally manage to say.

She smirks. "Consider yourself lucky."

"Oh yeah?" I can't help but grin. "Why's that?"

"You'll understand when you hatch your own dragon."

If it weren't for our promise to King Orso, I'd be tempted to head straight to Wandermere without even visiting Boneholde, but maybe we can end our stay in Frostmoor on a strong note. We've made friends in Whitguard and Hornryx, but what we really need are allies.

The conversation flows smoother the rest of the journey, and before I know it, we're only a few hundred yards above the ring. The massive snowstorm rages around the mountain, obscuring our vision of what lies below.

"I'm glad I met you, Senzala." I extend a hand.

She grasps me around the forearm. "As am I. Perhaps one day, we will meet again." She winks, and I feel like there is more to those words than she is letting on.

"Travel safely." Laojin places a hand on my shoulder. "I sense great things from you all. Let the other tribes know that we have not perished. If they wish to find us, then you know the way."

I shake my head. "If you want the other tribes to know you remain, then it is you who must find them. I respect you, but I will not be your messenger."

The chief narrows his eyes. I can't tell if he's surprised or angry, but he nods. "Very well."

I summon my spirit guide, and it takes position next to Jordy, ready to lead us into the depths of the ring.

"Good-byes!" Limery shouts as the snow swallows us whole.

"Hell yeah!" Taryn shouts as Moonbeam finishes off a wild boar. "That's what I'm talking about."

"Congrats, you're finally useful," I tease as I start skinning the boar for our dinner.

He flashes me a rude gesture. "No need to be salty because you have to wait for your new active ability. Speaking of which, I still need to allocate my last ability point."

"Hey, I'm not salty." I use my claws to separate the skin from the meat. "My spirit guide has already proven useful. And now that my attacks deal splash damage, I can probably sell or trade Sea Scorpion at the next town we get to. It should get a nice price." Taryn squirms as I pull the skin from the boar's body. "So, what ability were you thinking?"

He scrunches his brow. "I don't know. I've narrowed it down to four, but they all seem so useful. Scry could be good for tracking our enemies. Mind Warp can help turn a fight in our favor. Shadow Cloak gives me more utility, especially for sneaking around. And then Endless Night can really turn things on their head."

"If it were me, I'd think about which one is going to be the most useful right now. Tracking our enemies is cool, but do we have need of it at this moment? Do we even have anything to use to track them with? I'd save that one for the future, but keep it in mind going forward." I point to Limery, who is clearing an area for a fire. "We can finally put his greedy little hands to use for good."

Limery looks up from his work with a devilish grin.

Taryn scratches his forehead. "If we want to look at it like that, then Endless Night is the easy choice. I can use it offensively to blind the enemy while we bombard the area with spells, or we can use it as a quick getaway if things get hairy."

"Sounds like a good plan." I finish gutting the boar and empty the innards into a large pot from my inventory. "Summon us a shelter for the night and I'll get our meat cooking."

Our little shelter is more crowded than ever now that Jordy has joined the mix, but it still beats sleeping in the open air. The goat tucks his legs beneath him, sandwiched between Berry and Stompy. Ruby sits in front of the fire next to Limery, eyeing the meat as it sizzles.

At the base of the mountain, the ring that hides the arctic trolls once again towers above us. Tomorrow, we will abandon the enchanted trail and cut through the snow toward Boneholde. It will probably take us at least two days to reach the Snowwalker Tribe, and that's with Taryn casting Strong Wind.

Taryn reaches for a piece of meat and jerks his hand back. "Ouch! Hot!" He kisses his fingers gingerly. "First mana flames, and now food. Why does everything have to be so damn hot?" He grimaces at the puffy red skin. "You really think we're going to be able to hatch a dragon?"

I shrug. "Who knows, but I figure it's worth a shot. Not like we have anywhere important to be once we leave here."

Limery sticks his hand into the open flame, grabbing a piece of meat and tossing it straight into his mouth. "Limmy wants to sees the baby dragons."

Taryn places his hands on his hips, and Limery mirrors his expression next to him. "Look, it's thirty seconds. If we want to use my abilities to their limits, then we need to test them."

I summon more horrors so that we can properly test the effects of Endless Night. "Fine, let's get it over with."

The next thing I know, everything is pitch-black. I can't see. I can't hear. Not even my night vision can penetrate the darkness. I can sense my horrors' presences, but I can't even begin to guess their location. It's unnerving to feel so helpless. So lost. I summon my spirit guide, but even it can't cast light through Taryn's spell.

When the darkness fades, Taryn looks at me expectantly. "Well?"

I use my hand to shield my eyes from the sudden brightness. "It's OP. No sight, no sound. Nothing. I can think of a handful of ways to use this to our advantage."

After an hour, the ability is off cooldown, so Taryn casts Endless Night on himself and his pets. The darkness fades again, and Taryn grins from ear-to-ear. "This is good."

We discuss strategy as we walk, testing out new theories every hour as the ability becomes available. As we get closer to Greypeak, Taryn and Limery take turns scouting ahead for any signs of hobgoblins.

As the sun begins to set, we pass the enchanted path that leads up to Greypeak.

"Want to go beat up on some hobgoblins?" Taryn gestures up the mountain.

I shake my head. "I want to hit up Boneholde and get out of here. It might be a good idea to scout the area before we camp."

"Aye-aye, Captain." He mock-salutes me. "You and Limery get dinner ready, and I'll scope out the area."

An hour later, Taryn returns. "I flew up to some of the ruins. There's no signs of hobgoblins anywhere."

I hand him a piece of roasted boar. "Maybe they're all inside the mountain."

The next morning, Taryn scouts the area again, but there's still no sign of the hobgoblins. As cold as everything is in this climate, I'd probably be content to hide away in the mountain as well. At least it's one less thing we have to worry about.

By midday, the features of Boneholde begin to come into view. It's the shortest of the five peaks, and the skeleton of some ancient beast can be seen half-buried around the base of the mountain. Long ago, the hobgoblins made their homes in the shadow of the skeleton. Now, it belongs to the Snowwalkers.

Eventually, we come across the fifth enchanted path, and we're on a straight shot to the village. As we get closer, I can make out smoke rising from the massive bones. Judging by the positioning of the sun, it'll likely be dark when we arrive, but I think I have a plan that will get us a warm welcome.

"Think anything will come of this?" asks Taryn.

"I don't know. Gherhardt says they're more tribal. I don't want to judge them before we meet them, but I doubt that will work in our favor."

The sun finally sets, and small orange dots appear along the mountain. The Snowwalker Tribe has made their home much lower than Whitgard, so the fires can be seen burning from where we are. These guys must have a flare for the dramatic, because the eye-holes in the massive skull glow ominously from above the village.

"That's not foreboding at all," mumbles Taryn.

"Ready to let them know we're here?" I ask.

"Go for it."

I summon my spirit guide, and the ethereal frost goat lights the way as we approach Boneholde. I'm hoping the spectacle gains us at least a little favor with the natives.

We must be a sight to behold as we make our way up the mountain—with the glowing frost goat leading the way, followed by Jordy, with Limery holding onto his horns, then Taryn and Ruby riding Berry, and finally me lording above them all on Stompy's back. All we need is some whacky music and a little dancing to set the scene.

A slight incline leads up to the village, where a wooden palisade forms the boundary. Inside the walls, the ancient skeleton towers above all. Wooden huts are built along the bones, using them for structural support, and some of the buildings are several stories tall along the rib cage.

At the gate, two massive pyres burn, casting the figures watching us from the lookout in a shadowy silhouette.

I halt my spirit guide about fifty yards from the gate. Something definitely feels off about this.

Mana pulses at my fingertips, but I fight the urge to summon my horrors. The villagers might not be welcoming, and I don't want to give them a reason to attack.

"What business do you have in Boneholde?" one of the shadowy figures asks.

"We come seeking allies on behalf of King Orso of Seascape," I shout.

The two figures laugh, and it chills me to the bone.

"You just won't stop, will you?" There's something familiar about the way the man spits the words out. "You should have stayed in the forest where you belong."

My hair stands on edge as the pieces fall into place.

"We need to go," Taryn whispers.

"I'm surprised you found us, but you made a big mistake coming here. There's no one to save you this time. You're finally going to pay for all the damage you've done."

The man takes a step back, and the light of the fire reveals his face. Jude Duggan, the hero who has had it out for me since Vanaria. Shaggy black hair falls just above his dark eyes, and his lip curls up in a snarl.

If that's Jude, then the other figure must be—

"Good to see you again, troll." Glenn smiles as he steps into the light, but the smile doesn't reach his eyes. His cheery disposition is nothing like the monster underneath.

He's as plain-looking as ever, and his mismatched armor has been replaced by leather and fur. If I didn't know any better, he'd look exactly how I'd imagine a tribesman to appear.

He pulls out a dagger with a bone hilt, and the blade catches the light of the flames. "I think we have some unfinished business."

Taryn inches Berry backward, but I hold my ground. I refuse to be intimidated by these assholes.

"What are you doing here? I demand to speak to the Head of the Snowwalker Tribe."

Jude cackles madly. "You hear that? He demands to speak to the head of the Snowwalker Tribe." He lets out a sigh of pleasure. "Oh, that's good. Well, go ahead. I'm listening."

"I'm not here for your games, Jude," I snap, urging Stompy forward. "We're taking you back to Seascape to face your crimes."

Glenn shakes his head. "Stupid troll. You don't understand. You have no power here."

I take a moment to analyze both, just so I know what we're getting into.

Glenn Orickson
> _Level 21_
> _Warrior_
> _Human_

Jude Duggan
> _Level 24_
> _Fighter_
> _Human_

Whatever they've been up to, they've been busy. At those levels, they are definitely dangerous. There's no telling what abilities they've unlocked. And if Glenn has somehow convinced the Snowwalker Tribe to follow him... I clench my fist, trying not to think about how they earned those levels.

Regardless of how strong they are, we're still stronger. I'll carry them back to Seascape on my shoulders if I have to.

"We can't leave," I whisper to Taryn. "I've seen what Glenn is capable of. First with the townspeople of Lynchton, and then the dwarves at the portal. Jude might just be an asshole, but Glenn is dangerous. We can't let him do anything to these people."

Taryn frowns. "What can we do? They're already inside the wall."

"Then we lure them out." I jump down from Stompy and equip Destroyer, waving it in the air at the two heroes. "Why don't you come and fight me like a man?"

Jude leaps down from the lookout. He lands with one knee to the ground like a superhero. "Don't mind if I do. Then I can mount your head on the gate like all the rest."

All the rest?

"Dear god," Taryn whispers.

That's when I notice the heads mounted along the palisade.

Dozens of heads top the spikes that make up the wall of the village. Men, women, and children stretch for as far as I can see. So many lives gone forever. How did I not notice until now?

Fresh rage consumes me. "Why?" My voice cracks when I ask, though I'm not expecting any reasonable explanation from these two.

Glenn jumps down, landing next to his demented partner and flashing me an unsettling smile. "Don't worry, Boneholde is in good hands now."

"Enough talking." Jude touches his palms together and four shadow doppelgängers spread out from him, two flanking each side. "Let's fight."

He pulls two daggers from his waistband, and the clones wield shadowy weapons of their own.

Glenn grins with delight. "You heard the man."

His body erupts with a golden glow, and he charges at us.

37. BONEHOLDE

A wave of shadow and light washes over us as Glenn charges alongside Jude and his four doppelgängers. The two heroes are dressed similarly in fur clothing and wield blades with hilts made from bone. Jude has several daggers and knives strapped along his body. Glenn grips a shortsword.

I turn to Taryn. "You and Limery take Jude. Glenn is mine!"

Taryn's face is set in determination. "I don't like this. It feels like a trap."

"Look what they've done!" I snap. "How many more have to die before they're dealt with? We can end this now."

He bites his lip, then nods. That's all the confirmation I need to summon horrors as I rush into battle.

Sparks run along Glenn's arm as he slashes his sword at me. I raise the frosted buckler that Taryn looted from the dungeon to block the blow.

His dagger connects and lightning explodes. Electricity courses through my body and jumps from me to my horrors, stunning us in place. For a moment, I can't move. Glenn stabs for my throat, but I quickly activate my Tiger's Eye Pendant, cleansing the stun from myself but not my horrors.

I block Glenn's attack with the buckler, and he raises his sword for another swing. With his Dexterity cut in half thanks to my buckler, he thinks twice. Instead, he takes a few steps back and smirks.

My horrors press onward, but he makes short work of them with his sword.

"Big, bad troll, always pretending to be the hero." He keeps smiling. "Pretty soon you'll all be food for the worms."

I ignore his comment. I'm not here for a conversation. The only thing that matters is making him pay for all the people he has hurt.

Lightning crashes nearby, where Taryn and Limery have the upper hand against

Jude. The fighter is on the defensive, along with his doppelgängers, as they dodge fireballs and the whipping vines of Sapling Staff.

Jude somersaults backward with his clones mimicking his every movement. When he lands, he swipes his arm in front of him, and three shadow blades shoot toward Taryn. The doppelgängers each shoot three of their own, sending a barrage of dark blades.

Stompy steps in front of Taryn and Berry, taking the brunt of damage as fifteen shadow attacks bury themselves in his flesh. He bellows in pain, and anger flares in Taryn's eyes.

Limery yells, hitting one of the clones with a fireball and setting it aflame. A simultaneous Lightning Bolt and Moonbeam disintegrate another doppelgänger.

Blood pours from Stompy's wounds as he favors his left front leg, but the stubborn moulhaug refuses to quit, charging toward Jude.

Glenn attacks while I'm distracted, but I see him out of the corner of my eye. I swing Destroyer up in time to meet his blade. The force from the warhammer is enough to knock the weapon from his grip. It flips end over end, landing point down in the snow.

I press the attack while he's weaponless, and he equips a small shield made from the skull of some monster. He parries my first attack, backpedaling as he reaches for his weapon. I bring my weapon down on his head with all my momentum, but a silver dome forms around him at the last second, absorbing the blow and reflecting it back to me. The reverberation launches me like a cannon blast.

I crash to the ground twenty feet away, crawling to my feet as Glenn kneels to retrieve his weapon. Jordy rams into him at full speed, drilling Glenn in the chest and tossing him like a ragdoll.

Nearby, Taryn and Limery still have the upper hand. Jude uses some sort of shadow-step, leaving a trail of blurry figures as he barely dodges consecutive fireballs. He pauses for half a second too long as he casts more doppelgängers, and a fireball hits him in the chest. He loses a chunk of health but manages to get the spell off, and more doppelgängers appear.

"Time to finish this!" I shout.

Taryn nods, but a loud bellowing note blares over everything. I turn to see Glenn with a horn pressed to his lips.

He removes it, and his smirk is more punchable than ever. "You're right. It is time to finish this."

Jude falls back, laughing hysterically as he does.

A dull rumble forms from inside the village, and snow cascades from the roofs of buildings.

At first, I think he's learned how to summon an avalanche—until I hear the growls that accompany the unmistakable trampling of feet.

There's scratching on the other side of the wall, and then dozens of round heads with pointy ears climb over the heads mounted along the palisade.

Hobgoblin. *Level 20. Full of more anger and rage than traditional goblins, hobgoblins do not bow to those with greater power. They trample them.*

They leap from the palisade without fear, landing in the snow and setting off at a sprint. Each hobgoblin is about three feet tall, with dull gray skin, putrid yellow eyes, hooked noses, and long pointy ears.

It all makes sense now. The reason there were no hobgoblins in Greypeak is because they were all here.

"Run!" I shout.

Taryn is already leading Berry in the other direction as I summon more horrors and send them at the hobgoblins to buy us some time. Ruby and Jordy sprint ahead of the group, but Stompy is slow to follow with his wounded leg.

More hobgoblins spill over the wall by the second, and the gate shakes as countless more beat against it from inside the village.

Taryn's eyes are full of panic as he casts Strong Wind. I immediately move faster, but Stompy continues to limp noticeably.

He glances over his shoulder at the influx of hobgoblins. "Hold them off while I heal him."

He casts Stonewall, forcing some of the hobgoblins to leave the path and go through the snow. This slows them some, but they continue to climb the palisade. Meanwhile, Glenn and Jude retreat toward the village.

I meet the hobgoblins in the snow, smashing them with Destroyer until it is molten hot. Limery peppers them with fireballs and summons flame walls. I try to keep them as close together as possible. With my new passive, every hit deals damage to those around my intended target.

Jordy joins the fray, headbutting, stomping, and kicking hobgoblins to death. Berry rips one's head clear off.

Taryn leans over Stompy, casting the moulhaug in a golden glow, when a black dagger stabs him in the shoulder. The aura of Restoration fades.

"Not so fast," laughs Jude.

Taryn grimaces as he tries again, but another dagger hits him in the back.

The gate to Boneholde bursts open, and countless hobgoblins spill through. These carry stone clubs, bones, and other blunt force weapons.

"We have to go now!" I smash Destroyer into another hobgoblin, caving its head in. "I'll clear what I can but get moving now."

I activate Berserker Rage, using the increase to my stats to fight off goblins as we retreat. Stompy moves a little faster with some of his wounds healed, but he's a long way from healthy.

Taryn summons another Stonewall, separating me from the horde. "Let's get out of here."

He lifts his staff, and a cloud of darkness forms over our pursuers. Strong Wind hits me again, and my feet move faster.

By sheer numbers, the hobgoblins push through Endless Night, looking dazed and confused as they emerge from the dark cloud. More and more continue to pour out of the village like ants.

Glenn blows the horn again and the hobgoblins refocus on us once again. My heart pounds in my ears as I sprint after Taryn and the others. Even with Strong

Wind, the hobgoblins are gaining on us. There's no way we'll escape if they continue to pursue.

"The Frost Bombs! Toss them!" I shout.

I pull both frost bombs from my inventory and toss them at the horde. They explode upon impact, freezing a dozen or so in place, but more hobgoblins trample over their frozen brethren.

Taryn hits more with his own frost bombs, but it's not enough. There are just too many.

I summon horrors and watch them get swallowed by the horde. There are so many hobgoblins that Horror of Vitality's slow can only affect a few at a time.

Stompy comes to an abrupt halt, and I crash into his backside.

I pat him on the leg. "Come on, boy. Let's go."

He snorts, turning to face the horde.

"Uh, Taryn!" I yell over the approaching chaos.

He brings Berry to a halt. "Stompy, let's go."

The moulhaug huffs, taking a step toward the approaching hobgoblins.

"Stompy! Now!" Taryn yells. His face is contorted in confusion and anger.

I grab Stompy by the reins and pull hard, but he refuses to budge. He paws at the ground, pulling against my grip with all his power. I pull back just as hard.

The reins snap, and he charges back toward the horde, leaving me holding the torn leather. I'm at a loss for what to do.

"Stompy!" Taryn pleads.

In all my years, I've never seen Taryn with such a pained expression.

He jumps down from Berry, running after the moulhaug.

I step in his way, wrapping him in a bearhug. "We have to go."

He struggles against my grip. "I can't... Stompy... I can't!"

Stompy swings his horn from side to side like a battering ram as he collides with the horde. Hobgoblins fly in every direction like bowling pins. For a moment, he wreaks devastation on the smaller creatures like a bull in a china shop, but they continue to swarm him as a steady stream continues to pour through the gate. They pile on him until there's nothing but a mound of hobgoblins.

Taryn's struggling fades, replaced by heaving sobs. I lift him onto Berry's back.

Limery hovers in the air with a look of grim confusion.

I squeeze Taryn's leg. "We have to go now."

Tears stream down his face. He looks at me, but it's like he can't see me.

I grab him by the cloak. "Now, or we all die!"

His eyes focus, and he glares at me as he whips the reins.

38. THE ULTIMATE SACRIFICE

We walk for hours, and no one says a word. Empty silence, aside from Taryn's occasional sniffle or Berry's groans, and the crunch of gravel beneath our feet. Limery clings silently to my shoulder. Even he is at a loss.

I look over my shoulder constantly, but nothing follows us, at least as far as I can tell. Either way, we won't be resting any time soon. I've already reached the point where my stamina is waning, but how can we rest knowing that there are hundreds of hobgoblins out there?

I still can't wrap my head around what happened. Not just losing Stompy, but all of it. The last time I logged out, I remember watching Jude and Glenn lying in a cave through the monitor, but I never would have suspected this. Glenn must have used the hobgoblins to overtake Boneholde.

An entire village wiped off the map. And Whitgard could be next.

I need to warn them. Maybe it will be the push they need to talk to King Orso. Maybe not, but they need to know what they are up against.

The arctic trolls can hold their own. They have the ring. They have a dragon. No one even knows they still exist.

"Limery," I whisper. "I need your help."

He looks up at me with bulbous yellow eyes. "What is its?"

"I need you to fly to Whitgard. Tell Gherhardt what happened and then meet us back at the portal. We can't stay here, but they need to be warned."

He nods, and tears well up around his eyes. "Chods."

"What's up, buddy?"

"Is Stompys coming backs?"

The words hit me like a punch in the gut. The moulhaug's last moments replay over and over in my mind. That look of stubborn defiance as he snapped the reins from my grip. He was loyal until the very end, sacrificing himself for the person he loved more than anything in this world.

I blink back tears. "No, he's not."

He wraps his warm arms around my neck. "Limmy will miss hims."

Yeah, we all will.

Limery says good-bye to Taryn before taking off into the night, but there's no response.

Taryn continues to cast Strong Wind whenever it's available, but he hasn't said a word or even acknowledged my presence. I give him his space. I can imagine what he's going through, what it would be like if I lost Limery, but I'll never really know how it feels unless it happens.

I pray that day never comes.

Jordy, who normally leads the way, clings next to Berry. The two walk so close together that there's barely any space between them.

After a few more hours, I finally break the silence. "Taryn."

No response.

"We should probably rest soon."

Silence.

"Hey, man, I know you're hurting right now, but if we pass out from exhaustion, then we're screwed."

There's an angry sigh as he guides Berry off the path. He leads the bear toward a group of trees, where he casts Stonewall. During the time it takes him to summon three more walls, he never looks in my direction. His posture is stiff as a board.

Without Limery, there's no fire. Taryn sits against Berry with Ruby in his lap. Jordy attempts to nuzzle Taryn, but he ignores the goat.

I sit against the opposite wall aimlessly cleaning my claws. "You know you can talk to me, right?"

He glances at me, and I don't know if I have ever seen so much hatred in his eyes. I know he's upset, but I don't understand why he's taking it out on me.

"What?" I snap. "You're not the only one upset. I cared for Stompy too, you know! I tried to get him to run. I fucking tried!"

Taryn is on his feet in an instant, pointing in my face. "I told you I had a bad feeling about that place but you didn't listen. And if you hadn't brought that stupid goat down the mountain, this never would have happened. I didn't want to make him my pet. If I hadn't added another pet, then maybe Stompy would have listened to me. Maybe he would still be alive right now. You—" He presses his finger against my chest. "—You caused this."

I smack his hand away and jump to my feet, towering over him. "Don't you put this on me." My vision blurs, and hot tears run down my cheeks. "No one forced you to do anything. I'm not the reason Stompy is dead. Neither is Jordy. Stompy had a mind of his own, regardless of what your stupid stats say. He never listened to anyone unless he wanted to. You want to know why he ran back in? Why he didn't listen?"

Taryn continues glaring.

I clench my fist, but the tears keep flowing. "He did it because he loved you. He sacrificed himself so that you could live. So that we could all live. If you want to hate me, go ahead, but you know I'm right."

He looks up at me, brow furrowed, and for a moment, I'm sure he's going to hit me. Then his lip quivers and his shoulders collapse. He grabs my cloak and buries his head into my chest. "I just miss him so much. I didn't even get to say good-bye," he wails. "This isn't fun anymore, Chad. Games aren't supposed to make you feel like this."

His body shakes violently between sobs, and for a moment, I just wrap my arm around him and hold him tight.

When his sobs fade to sniffles, he lets go. "They are going to pay for what they've done?"

I wipe away the ice crystals that have formed around my eyes. "One day, but right now, we need to worry about getting to safety."

He nods, wiping his nose on his sleeve, then he reaches into his pocket and pulls out a black leather glove. "We'll get them when they least expect it."

I analyze the glove, but it's nothing more than a simple garment. "What's that?"

His eyes narrow as he stares at the glove. "I took it off Jude during the fight. Once I unlock Scry, they're both dead."

After a short rest, we're back on the road. We're a far cry from normal, but some of the tension is gone.

Taryn reaches into his satchel and pulls out a carrot. He leans down from Berry's back and offers it to Jordy. "I'm sorry I called you a stupid goat. None of this is your fault."

Jordy takes the carrot from his hand.

"How many of those do you have?" I ask.

"Gherhardt gave me an entire box before we left. I used to give them to Stompy —" He chokes up, and there's a long pause before he clears his throat. "I used to give them to Stompy as treats."

Jordy crunches the carrot in his powerful jaws. When he's finished, he bleats, and the wavering cry carries across the night.

We elect to rest in short doses, never camping for more than a few hours before moving on. One of us is always on alert, watching and waiting for any sign of trouble. During my watch, I keep a full army of horrors ready at all times, just in case something shows up. Eventually, the sun spills over the horizon, setting the snow ablaze with light and allowing us to see for miles in every direction. The coast looks clear, but it does little to ease my worry.

Taryn slows his pace until we are side by side. "What are we going to do about Whitgard?"

"What can we do?" I shrug. "We don't have the forces to fight that many hobgoblins. I sent Limery to warn them. We can make sure they are prepared, but that's about it."

"Maybe we should stop in Seascape before going to Wandermere. We can tell the king what happened. Maybe he'll send his forces to capture Jude and Glenn, or at least offer protection."

I scrunch my brow. "You wouldn't want to join?" After everything that's happened, that doesn't make sense to me.

He shakes his head. "It's too raw. I know for certain that if I saw them now, I would do something stupid." He pulls Jude's glove from his pocket. "When the time comes, they'll get theirs."

I pat him on the back. "I'll be right there with you."

He suddenly lifts his hand to his forehead and squints in the direction of Horn-ryx. "What the hell?"

A dark splotch moves along the enchanted path toward the portal. I curse. They're going to try and stop us from leaving Frostmoor. The hobgoblins must have had time to flank us while we were resting.

I search the sky for Limery, hoping he might arrive before they do, but I see nothing. Not that I'd be able to pinpoint his small frame against the sea of white.

I turn to Taryn. "You should fly through the portal in your bird form. The king will send help if he knows we're trapped. I'll go stay with the trolls until you return."

"Don't be crazy." His eyes are focused on the approaching hobgoblins. He says it so nonchalantly that I'm worried where his head is at right now.

"Don't be crazy?" I throw my hands in the air. "We can't win this fight. You just said you aren't ready."

He stares into the distance. "It doesn't matter."

I grab him by the cloak, causing Ruby to jump and nearly pulling Taryn from atop Berry. "What do you mean, 'It doesn't matter'? I know you're grieving, but there's no need to be stupid."

He pushes my hands away. "It doesn't matter because those aren't hobgoblins. They're trolls."

I do a double-take, but I can't make out anything for certain without enhanced eyesight. "What are they doing this far down the mountain?"

He shrugs. "Your guess is as good as mine. Want to go find out?"

Taryn flies ahead in his bird form to check on the situation, leaving me with his pets. Berry whines the entire time, but by the time we arrive at the portal, Taryn and Limery are waiting along with the entire population of arctic trolls, including all of Chief Laojin's pets.

Berry, Jordy, and Ruby pile on top of Taryn, tackling him into the snow. For the first time since the battle with Jude and Glenn, he laughs.

Rhaz frowns when he sees us. "Where is the big one?"

"He— Stompy didn't make it. We were attacked in Boneholde." I go on to tell them about Glenn and Jude and their army of hobgoblins.

Chief Laojin kneels next to Taryn, placing a hand on his shoulder. "He was a fine pet, and a strong warrior. I am grateful for the time I shared with him."

Taryn blinks back tears. "Thank you. That means a lot."

I don't want to cut into their moment, but I still don't understand why the entire tribe is at the portal. "What are you all doing down here?"

Laojin sweeps his arms in an arc, gesturing to the tribe. "Fighting alongside Taryn in the dungeon awakened something in the trolls. We have decided it is past time we reunite with our brethren."

"Really? That's great." I look over my shoulder at the distant mountain. "But what about Boneholde?"

He scowls at the mountain. "If your words are true, then this dwarven king will send his army to Frostmoor. And if not, that will be a matter for the council to decide."

I turn to Limery. "Did you warn Whitgard?"

He nods. "Limmy did. Theys was not happy."

"Yeah, I don't imagine they would be." I take one last look up the mountain. "Alright, let's get going. I can introduce you to both King Orso and Chief Rizza when we get to Seascape."

Senzala steps forward, shaking her head. "Nonsense. We can make our own introductions." She grins. "You have a dragon to hatch."

"But we need to tell them what happened in Boneholde." I extend my arm in the direction of the village.

"Do you think us incapable of delivering a message?" She touches my arm. "Go where you are needed. Let the forest heal your broken spirits."

I place my hand on top of hers. "I like the sound of that."

She winks. "I'm sure our paths will cross again."

Chief Laojin is the first one through the portal, riding atop his giant mammoth. The council follows next, and then one by one, the rest of the tribe steps through to Seascape.

"You think they'll be okay?" asks Taryn.

I wrap my arm around Taryn and stare into the maelstrom of energy. "I do. Now, let's get out of here."

I focus on the runes for Wandermere, a triangle with a V that cuts through it. The runes ignite, and we step through to our next adventure.

EPILOGUE

Valery sat in the corner of the break room staring into her cup of steaming coffee. Her head pounded, but that was nothing new these days. Time was running out, and she needed to decide what to do about Chad Johnson.

Footsteps echoed down the hall just before Thompson entered. The technician sighed, tossing his tablet onto the table, oblivious of Valery.

He sat down, placing his head in his hands. "Fucking Glenn."

He kicked one of the chairs so hard that it rocketed across the room. It crashed into the wall, startling Valery. She yelped.

Thompson looked over with wide eyes, immediately standing up. "I am so sorry. I didn't see you over there." He picked up his tablet. "Sorry. I'll get back to work."

She waved a hand for him to stay. "Don't worry about it. I know it's a little tense out there right now. What's bothering you?"

He looked at the floor. "Oh, it's nothing. Really."

She softened her expression. "Thompson, talk to me. You're normally so calm and collected, that's why I hired you. So how about you tell me what has you so upset?"

He stood there for a moment like a deer in headlights. Valery wondered if he might run out the door and never come back.

Thompson sighed, then he took a seat at Valery's table. "It's Glenn. I don't— I just don't get it. We're letting him run around and hurt people, and we aren't doing anything about it. I thought this program was supposed to help him?"

Valery smiled. There were a lot of things she didn't have answers for at the moment, but this wasn't one of them. When it came to Glenn, she knew exactly what she was dealing with.

"He's something else, isn't he?"

Thompson's eyes narrowed. "He's a monster."

She nodded. "He has compulsions to do things most of us never experience. Do you mind if I ask you a few questions?"

He nervously tapped his tablet. "Uh, sure."

"You've been watching Glenn's progress since he was immersed, correct?"

"I have."

"Do you think he's changed at all?"

"No. He slaughtered an entire village earlier today. If anything, he's getting worse."

"I can see why you might think that. But you have to remember, those villagers are NPCs."

"Does he know that?" asked Thompson.

"I think he knows it far better than you do." She sat up, taking a sip of her coffee. "Let's take a look at him for a moment. In the months since he's been in Mythos, he has made it his mission to destroy a monstrous race. While his methods might not be ideal, he has not directly killed any of the human NPCs without provocation. This village he killed, they attacked his army first. The only living player he has attacked has been Chad, hero of a monstrous race. He's made an ally in Jude. He is doing exactly as the AI has intended. What we're working with here, it's not a quick fix. It's not a fix at all. It's a reframing of how these individuals interact with the world. Glenn is the hero of his own story. And so far, his violent tendencies have been directed at NPCs. I'd say that is a step in the right direction."

Thompson sighed. "It'd be a lot easier if they didn't feel so realistic."

"If they weren't realistic, this wouldn't work."

He scooted back in his chair. "I suppose you're right. Sorry again for my outburst."

"Don't worry about it."

He'd done what she'd felt like doing on many occasions.

He stood and started to leave, but then turned around. "Can I ask you a question?"

She smiled. "Go for it."

"What are you going to do about Chad Johnson?"

She froze. That was the million-dollar question, and everybody knew it. "I don't know."

SENTENCED TO TROLL 5

CURRENT STATS

Chod, Level 25 Barbarian/Summoner Forest Troll
HP: 6235/6235
Mana: 5000/5000
Rage: 0/100
XP: 673,291/735,000

Strength: 42
Dexterity: 24
Constitution: 43
Intelligence: 10
Wisdom: 15
Charisma: 6

+1 Strength and Constitution racial bonus per level.

+1 Ability point per odd level.

6 stat points available.

0 ability points available.

. . .

Abilities:

Bite. *Using your massive tusks and powerful jaw, you take a bite out of an opponent, dealing immense damage. Cost: 10 rage. Level 2.*

Claw. *You attack with sharp claws, swiping at an opponent and dealing extra damage. Cost: 5 rage. Level 2.*

Intimidation. *You stare down your opponent, confusing them so that they are unable to attack for two seconds. Cost: 10 rage.*

Berserker Rage. *(Ultimate) Attacks and physical damage build your rage meter. 5 rage per attack. Rage meter deteriorates over time when out of combat at a rate of 5 rage per second. Activating Berserker Rage fills rage meter. For 30 seconds, rage meter does not decrease, deal increased damage, health regenerates at 5x the normal rate, cannot be stunned, slowed or otherwise affected. Cooldown: 10 minutes.*

Increased Regeneration. *(Passive) Regenerate health at a faster rate. Level 2.*

Rapid Regeneration. *(Passive) When below 10% health, regeneration is doubled.*

Nightvision. *(Passive) Increased vision in darkness and low light.*

Thick Skin. *(Passive) Take 10% less damage from physical attacks.*

Savage. *(Passive) Ability to eat uncooked meat without consequences.*

Camouflage. *(Passive) When out of combat and not moving for 20 seconds, trolls blend in with their surroundings.*

Sweeping Slash. *Form a sweeping arc in front of you, dealing damage and knocking your opponent off balance. Cost: 5 rage.*

Conceal (Passive). *Hides level from anyone who is not a guard on city grounds.*

Summon Horror (Passive). *Ability to summon a horror. Each horror grants a unique ability. For every horror active, gain 1% increased damage and health points. Horrors decay 10% for every minute outside of combat.*

Horror of Power. *Summon a horror with 20% of your strength. Cost: 100 mana. Cooldown: 30 seconds. Bonus: Your next attack deals double damage.*

Horror of Vitality. *Summon a horror with 20% of your health points. Cost: 100 mana. Cooldown: 30 seconds. Bonus: Opponents near Horror of Vitality are slowed by 20%.*

Horror of Finesse. *Summon a horror with 20% of your attack speed. Cost: 100 mana. Cooldown: 30 seconds. Bonus: Your next attack heals you for damage dealt.*

Sacrifice. *Sacrifice X amount of horrors to receive a temporary buff. Horror of Power: +1 Strength. Horror of Vitality: +1 Constitution. Horror of Finesse: +1 Dexterity*

Kamikaze. *Sacrifice a horror to deal a burst of damage.*

Champion. *Summon a copy of the most recent enemy you have defeated. Decays 10% every minute out of combat. Cost: 50% of mana pool. Cooldown: 6 hours.*

. . .

Spirit of the Beast. *The Spirit of the Beast path is composed of five phases.*

Phase 1: Spirit Inquiry. *A spirit animal is a guide from the spirit world, possessing traits similar to those of the individual. Unlocking one's spirit animal leads to a better understanding of the self and one's place within the world.*

    Spirit Animal: *Frost Goat*

Phase 2: Spirit Embodiment. *Bonding with a spirit beast is only the beginning of the Spirit of the Beast path. By finding an amulet that connects you to your beast, the bond between the two will grow stronger, unlocking further advancements.*

    Spirit Embodiment: *Ram Horns*

Phase 3: Spirit Enhancement. *Just as your body has undergone a change reflective of your spirit beast, your spirit may be enhanced in the same manner. Gain a new passive ability based on your spirit beast.*

    Spirit Enhancement: *Ram Rage: Barbarian rage now lasts twice as long. Physical attacks deal splash damage.*

Phase 4: Spirit Guide. *Your body and spirit have undergone great changes, but your bond with the spirit world is only beginning. Summon a spirit guide of your spirit beast.*

    Spirit Guide: *Summon a frost goat spirit guide. The spirit guides may lead you through darkness and guide you to locations you have previously visited, even if you do not know the way. Spirit guides may be consumed for a 50% increase to Wisdom for 10 minutes. Cooldown: 24 hours.*

Available Abilities *(1 ability point to unlock):*

Massive Bite. *Deals double damage. Cost: 20 rage.*

    Claws. *Swipe at opponent with both hands, dealing extra damage. Cost: 10 rage.*

    Multi Attack. *Bite and Claw at the same time. Cost: 20 rage.*

    Iron Will. *Immune to slows and stuns for 30 seconds. Cost: 50 rage. 180 second cooldown.*

    I'm Always Angry *(Passive. Available at level 10). Once rage meter is at 50%, it will not deteriorate below 50% when out of combat.*

    Perception. *For 10 minutes, gain increased awareness of your surroundings. Spot hidden objects, as well as unusual sounds, odors, and tastes. Cooldown: 6 hours.*

    Cleave. *Your next attack causes bleed damage, dealing 1% of opponent's health per second for 5 seconds. Cost: 10 rage.*

Battle Cry. You let out a ferocious roar, increasing rage by 20. No cost. 60 second cooldown.

Class Advancements. *Upon reaching level twenty-five, you have unlocked a class advancement. You may only advance one class at a time. A second class may not be advanced until completion of primary advancement.*

Barbarian Advancement.
Spirit of the Beast. Unlock for further details.
Summoner Advancement.
Dreadbeasts. Unlock for further details.
Dual Subclass. Unlock for further details.

Current Items:

Item. Phoenix Feather. 10% resistance to fire-based attacks. *A very rare item, phoenix feathers can only be gathered if they are willingly given by the host. Feathers plucked from unwilling birds turn to ash.*
Item. Tiger's Eye Pendant. Removes one debuff. Cooldown: 10 minutes. *A rare stone believed to ward off evil and bring balance to life.*
Item. Aquatic Boots. *Allows user to walk on water.*
Item. Petrified Staff. An enchanted staff capable of taking on the properties of up to 3 attached stones. +3 Intelligence. +3 Wisdom. Bonus: *While holding Petrified Staff, the user can cast ranged physical attacks once every 10 seconds.*
Item. Forlorn Scepter. +5 Intelligence. *Increases the range of summoned creatures by 50%.*
Item. Glouwseeker Venom. *When injected into the bloodstream, glouwseeker venom immobilizes target. Length of stun dependent on size of target, resistances, and amount injected.*
Item. Sea Scorpion. +3 Strength. *An enchanted trident capable of taking on the property of 1 enchanted stone. Bonus: deals splash damage.*
Legendary Item. Angel of Death Brandy. *When drinker falls below 1HP, a metaphysical event will occur, rewinding time for the user to two seconds prior to death.*
Item. Brimming Tankard. *A magical tankard that, once filled, will never go empty. Warning: Once filled, contents cannot be changed. Only works on beverages.*
Item. Expandable Satchel. *A bag capable of holding enormous content and only burdening the wearer with ten percent of its weight. Simply focus on the item inside and it will appear in your hand.*
Item. Destroyer. An enchanted warhammer capable of taking on the properties of up to three stones. +2 Strength, +3 Constitution. *This ancient warhammer*

was forged in the heart of a volcano. **Bonus Ability: Inferno.** With each consecutive hit, Destroyer grows hotter, allowing it to warp or pierce through even the hardest metals. Multiplier works when hits are less than five seconds apart. Cost: 10 mana per attack. Cooldown: 10 sec.

Item. Spaulder of Swiftness. +1 Constitution, +1 Dexterity. Lightweight, durable leather mail designed to protect the off-hand shoulder during battle.

Item. Green Dragon Egg. Green dragons rule with impunity over the forests they inhabit. They are the most territorial of all dragon species, and capable of spewing toxic gas in lieu of flames. Wherever a green dragon calls home, a dense fog is said to follow. Green dragon eggs may only be hatched in the heart of an ancient forest.

Item. Halite Shield. A lightweight translucent shield capable of taking damage without reducing visibility.

Item. Frosted Buckler. +2 Constitution. A lightweight and small shield capable of deflecting blows as well as being used offensively. **Bonus Ability:** Physical attacks blocked with Frosted Buckler cut attacker's Dexterity in half for ten seconds.

PROLOGUE

The elevator opened with a gentle swish, and every head in the laboratory turned in that direction. Valery scowled at the disturbance. Nobody was scheduled to visit today, and she wanted her team focused. The last thing they needed were distractions.

Polished leather shoes clacked with each step as a broad-shouldered man wearing a custom-tailored suit exited the elevator and stepped into the lab. Valery's lips curled down at the edges as she noticed the thin twenty-something blonde falling in step beside him.

"Back to work, everyone," she ordered.

There was stilted movement as eyes darted between Valery and the head of Mythos Games.

"Daughter." The man came to a stop in front of Valery, unnaturally white teeth flaring with his smile. His purple eyes gazed into her own.

"Father."

He winked at Valery. "If you keep frowning like that, you'll end up with wrinkles like your mother."

Bastard. Valery gave him the fakest smile possible, doing little to conceal its disingenuousness. "To what do I owe this unexpected visit?"

His smile widened. "I've been following along with your little project."

Valery felt her chest tighten. This was her project, and the last thing she needed was her father meddling.

"And?" She tried to sound as calm as possible, but she knew her father could read her like a book. That was one of his strengths—the ability to figure people out with ease and use that information to play them like a fiddle.

"Don't worry." He winked again. "Your little secret is safe with me. I love what you've done with the game—creating your own lore and integrating it into the real-time evolution of the game-world. It's beautiful. Especially the trolls, they might play a bigger part in this story than anyone imagined."

Her father might be a dick and a shrewd businessman, but he still had a child-like fascination with lore and world-building. But there was no way in hell he was here with his new side-piece just to tell her this.

She gave him a knowing look. "Should she be here?"

The young woman pursed her lips but said nothing. This entire lab was highly classified among the company. Aside from the general details of the program, none of this was public knowledge, and she doubted her father had made the woman sign an NDA. Bringing an outsider into the lab was asking for trouble, but as the head of Mythos Games, no one could stop her father from doing as he pleased. Not even Valery.

He laughed. "Oh, it's not like that. Let me introduce you to Miss Dorothy Jordan. I expect you'll get to know each other very well in the coming months."

1. WANDERMERE

A heavy fog spreads across the forest floor of Wandermere. The name is fitting because we've been wandering aimlessly for almost two days. There's been evidence of centaurs—well-trodden paths and empty outposts—but it's like they've abandoned the forest.

The entire vibe of this place sits uneasy with me. All around us, birds chirp and bugs rattle, but it's hard to see clearly for more than ten feet in this fog. In every direction, massive trees tower over us in perpetuity. Each tree trunk is wide enough to carve a car-sized tunnel through it.

But aside from wolves and warthogs, every animal we've come upon has bolted, even from Taryn.

"I get that it's ancient, but I thought there would be a little more action," I say to no one in particular. Living in New York City, I know what it's like to feel small among buildings that touch the sky, but this is different, somehow peaceful and terrifying at the same time.

"It's beautiful." Taryn tilts his head back, staring into the canopy overhead.

Taryn hasn't been very talkative as of late, especially toward me. Since losing Stompy, most of our communication consists of things we see or which direction we should take rather than actual conversation. I don't press the issue, though, hoping that giving him space will heal things between us.

There's a sparkle as two small, brightly-colored fairies peek out from behind a tree and point slender fingers in our direction. When they speak, it sounds like wind chimes, their language clearly not translated by my communication stone. Before I have a chance to point them out to the others, they bolt away into the forest.

We come across a small stream, and Berry walks down to the edge for a drink.

He grunts before returning to Taryn's side. Ruby has her eyes focused in the direction the fairies disappeared, while Jordy stands stoically on Taryn's other side.

Even though it's midday, the forest feels like twilight. The massive leaves are easily the size of my head, and their branches tangle and intertwine, forming a canopy that nearly blocks out the sky, only allowing light to penetrate in small doses.

There's a loud caw as a massive golden bird takes flight. Limery grows warm against my shoulder before bolting into the foliage overhead.

"Be careful!" I shout behind him, but he's already out of range.

As I gaze at the towering trees of this ancient forest, I imagine this is what it feels like to be an ant walking among giant blades of grass. How do they navigate being stuck in a towering world without a map?

I just hope that if we run into any real monsters that they aren't proportionate to the gargantuan trees. Occasionally, wind hits the canopy and piercing beams of light give the forest a magical quality, like the heavens are reaching down with radiant fingers. When the light hits the fog, it glows gently, giving the appearance of dozens of troll-sized wisps.

While we walk, I pull the green dragon egg from my satchel and examine it for the hundredth time, hoping it might give us some inkling of direction.

Item. Green Dragon Egg. *Green dragons rule with impunity over the forests they inhabit. They are the most territorial of all dragon species and capable of spewing toxic gas in lieu of flames. Wherever a green dragon calls home, a dense fog is said to follow. Green dragon eggs may only be hatched in the heart of an ancient forest.*

The egg is slightly smaller than my fist and bright green even in the dull light. Thick, diamond-shaped scales lap over one another like a pinecone. It could be my imagination, but it seems slightly warmer than before.

Maybe we're getting close to the heart of the forest.

I place the egg back in my satchel. A week ago, I had no idea that it was a dragon egg. Now, it's the entire reason we're in Wandermere.

But we'll need to find the heart of the forest if we want any chance at hatching the dragon.

With the fog obscuring everything that isn't directly in front of us, it's almost impossible to make an educated guess. I assumed this would be a foggy area based on the egg's description, but the reality is beyond anything I could have imagined.

I cast Spirit Guide, and a frost goat formed of orange and white energy appears in front of us. Its presence pushes back the fog for several feet in all directions, revealing ground covered in wet leaves, moss, and rich dirt. Small creatures scurry back into the foggy depths.

My guide makes the immediate vicinity clearer but does little to help our navigation. Watching it walk like a beacon while pushing back the fog is a beautiful sight, though. There's also comfort in knowing that no matter how lost we get, it can always guide us back to the portal.

Taryn's own frost goat approaches my spirit guide, lowering his head in a show of respect.

I turn to Taryn. "Looks like mine is the top dog."

"When it comes to pets, I'll take substance over style," he says flatly.

He rolls his eyes as he pats Berry's back for Ruby to join him. The jackal leaps into his lap with surprising finesse and curls up between Taryn's legs.

After everything that has happened over the past few days, my jokes don't seem to have the same effect that they used to. Taryn brushes them off more times than not. I don't expect him to get over losing Stompy any time soon, but I think staying busy will help. If we can ever find anything worthwhile in this sprawling maze of trees, we still have objectives to complete.

It might be a while before things are truly normal again between us. I know it's selfish of me, but I miss goofing around with my best friend. I've replayed what happened in Boneholde a hundred times in my head, wondering what we could have done differently. I've always been itching for a fight, and even though Stompy made his own decisions, I know it was my choices that put us in a bad situation to begin with. That's something that will never change. Taryn's grief will take time, but I just want to keep it from consuming him in the meantime.

I give his shoulder a firm squeeze as we look out into the murky beyond. "Do your druid senses tell you if we're getting closer?"

"Do I look like a GPS?" He sighs. "Judging by the size of the trees, this is a giant forest, and we've barely populated any of our map. Without a village or manned outpost to give us directions, we can't even fill in the markers on our map. The heart of the forest could be anywhere."

I summon a few more horrors and we continue our journey through the woods. I wish we had done more research before coming here. I bet the troll library in Hornryx probably had information on Wandermere. We followed the most well-traveled path out of the portal, but it's possible we went in the wrong direction. All I know right now is that this is one of the few ancient forests in Mythos. Supposedly, it's the home of the centaurs, and most likely a scary green dragon as well.

Limery returns after a few minutes wearing a mischievous smile.

"Find anything good?" I ask.

He lands on my shoulder. "Limmy likes this place. The birds is bigs." He wipes a string of drool from his chin.

"Just don't get yourself eaten. We don't want Limmy being bird food." I poke the bulge in his stomach, and he cackles.

By early afternoon, we come upon an underground spring that empties into a bubbling pool. Fog gathers at the edge of the water like there's some unseen force keeping it at bay. In the center of the spring, there's a giant stone with a jeweled sword buried nearly halfway up the blade. A stream of sunlight breaks through the canopy, igniting the jeweled pommel in a dazzling display against the surrounding trees.

Limery's bulbous yellow eyes fill with greed.

"Hold up." I raise my hand in front of the imp before he has a chance to fly over. "There's no way we're this lucky. Let's play this smart."

Taryn gives me a look that I can't quite make out, like a mixture of sadness and uncertainty. Maybe my sudden caution is a painful reminder of how things could have gone in Frostmoor.

He turns away. "I'll scan the area and make sure it's not some kind of trap."

Before I have a chance to argue, he transforms into a red bird and flies away. His feathers are no longer white now that we're in a more temperate climate.

I ignore his brash behavior and step closer to the pool. The bubbling spring is relaxing. If we weren't searching for the heart of the forest, I could see myself losing hours soaking my feet in the cool water.

There's no telling how long the sword has been in that boulder, but it looks to be in pristine condition. When I try to analyze it, all I receive are question marks. If this isn't a trap, then we could have stumbled onto a pretty powerful weapon.

I stare into the spring. Tiny ripples distort my reflection, but I can still make out the massive horns that sprout from my head. A gift from my Spirit of the Beast path, I trace my finger from the black base to the icy blue tips. They are practically identical to the horns on Taryn's frost goat.

I tap the tip of my left horn. It's not sharp, but it could still do some damage, though they would be more effective smashing than goring. It looks cumbersome in the reflection, but I hardly notice they are there most of the time. Sleeping on them was a bit of an adjustment, though.

Somehow, I've managed to look even more badass. I can't wait to see Gord's face when we return to the troll forest. No doubt he'll be jealous of my new look.

There's a flutter of red feathers as Taryn returns, transforming back into his dwarven form. "I didn't see anything. There are some paths nearby that look like they were recently traveled by something with hooves, but that's it. I went up high, but the forest goes on forever. If there's a town or village anywhere near, it's hidden beneath the trees. And if someone is waiting to ambush us, their Camouflage is on par with the trolls."

I'm not sure if I should feel comforted by that or not. "Trolls are the only race I know that have Camouflage as an ability, but we don't really know much about the races outside the Isle. I've always been able to see trolls as translucent figures when they have it activated, but I doubt it would work on another race. Ruby's perception should spot anything out of the ordinary, right?"

He nods. "In theory."

I place a hand on his shoulder. "You cool with this?"

He sighs. "Yeah. I think it's going to be a bit before I'm back to myself, but that doesn't mean we should stop adventuring. I owe it to Stompy to make sure his death means something." He turns to face the sparkling sword. "It looks like a good sword. Go ahead and see if you can pull it out. We'll keep watch."

I wade into the spring, where the water is even colder than I imagined. Goosebumps erupt over my entire body.

Surprisingly, the pool is only waist deep when I reach the boulder.

I glance at Taryn before wrapping my hand around the hilt. He nods, and I give the weapon a hearty pull. It doesn't budge, so I grab it with two hands, plant my feet, and yank.

Water sloshes in the pool just as a massive boulder slams into my side. Several of my ribs crack, and pain flares through my midsection as I'm rocketed from the spring. I crash into an unforgiving tree and fall to the ground, stars dancing at the edge of my vision.

I grunt as I fight against the shooting pain to stand, unable to see above the fog. "What the hell was that?"

Limery hovers in front of me saying the words I've heard all too often. "Is yous okay, Chods?"

"Ungh. Yeah, I'm fine." I grimace as I equip Destroyer and use it as a crutch to stand, searching the area for enemies.

"It's not a treasure, it's a monster." Taryn guides Berry back from the spring, and I notice what he means.

A golem-like creature stands in the center of the pool, its arms and legs composed of several boulders stacked on top of one another like those little rock statues I would always see in Central Park. Only I think it will take more than a stiff breeze to knock this guy down. One giant boulder forms the golem's body, which is also where the sword is buried. The blade gleams in the ray of sunlight as the monster thrashes about.

Sword-wielding Stone. *Unique Monster. Level 32. An enchanter of great renown, Kathwyn the Benevolent traveled far and wide across Mythos hiding her enchanted objects in challenging locations where only the brave and worthy could retrieve them. The Sword of Repercussion was tested by many, but none proved capable of removing it from the stone she had placed it within. As the portals closed and the sword was lost to time, its enchanted properties began to fuse with the life aura in the heart of Wandermere. As life aura passed through the stone to the sword, the stone grew sentient and has been seen wandering the forest ever since, searching for rays of sunlight to bask in.*

The faceless golem reaches with fingers formed of stacked pebbles and pulls the sword from its backside. Even though it has no eyes, it points the sword in Taryn's direction. At level thirty-two, this might be more of a challenge than we bargained for. A sword that has feasted on life aura for years and years—there's no telling what abilities a monster like this has. With a name like The Sword of Repercussion, they can't be anything pleasant.

Jordy lowers his head and paws at the earth.

"Easy, buddy," Taryn orders as he guides Berry a few more steps backward. "I'm not sure you want to headbutt this monster."

I touch my tender ribs, still feeling the discomfort. "We're off to a rocky start, but I think we can handle it."

Taryn frowns at my attempt at humor, but then his face softens. "Yeah, but I've heard it's best to let sleeping stones lie."

I laugh at his pun and try to keep it going. It's been too long since we've bantered. "Maybe, but I thought dwarves were boulder than this."

He shrugs, smirking. "Your call, but don't cry to me when you're stuck between a rock and a sharp blade."

I summon a round of horrors and gather them at the edge of the spring while

Limery hovers next to me. The sword-wielding stone stands in the center of the bubbling pool, but it hasn't attacked. Not yet.

"Would you like to do the honors?" I gesture toward the monster.

Taryn raises his staff and a bolt of lightning rips through the trees. Thunder rumbles as the bolt hits the spring. Electricity arcs along the golem's body, and I'm certain that it's stunned in place.

I charge in with my horrors to get in a few free hits, but the golem shudders and the tiny arcs of electricity are absorbed into its stone body. Two of Limery's fireballs explode against the monster's chest, leaving scorch marks but barely doing any damage. A yellow aura surrounds the sword, and electricity trails from the hilt down the blade. At the tip, the electricity merges together and three massive bolts arc in our direction.

Limery zips out of the way, avoiding the attack, but one of the bolts catches me straight in the chest. My insides vibrate with energy as I'm stunned. I hold off on activating my Tiger's Eye Pendant. If the monster isn't attacking, then there's no point in wasting it.

Taryn grunts as he jumps from Berry's back and disappears beneath the fog. The bolt meant for him zigs by and explodes against one of the massive trees.

A moment later, Taryn crawls into the fogless area around my spirit guide. "What was that?"

Once again, the stone warrior stands sentry in the spring. It's not aggressive, but it packs a hell of a punch.

I grimace at the charred flesh on my chest. "It has to have something to do with the sword. If the life aura has made it sentient, then I bet the enchantment from the sword has morphed into some kind of ability for the monster. It must absorb the attacks and send them back."

He frowns. "Then what do we do?"

I grip Destroyer even harder. "We crush this rock into rubble."

Hooves pound against the earth behind us and I take a defensive position, ready for another fight. Three centaurs, two male and one female, come to a halt a dozen feet away, their weapons raised in our direction. They stand proud, mighty warriors that rival me in height. The males both have broad shoulders and thick torsos, with their equine halves reminiscent of powerful draft horses. The female is more slender, with the lower half of a racing horse.

The two fairies I saw earlier peek out from behind the centaurs and chimes once again fill the air.

The centaur on the left has a dark chestnut coat on his lower half, with matching hair that drapes over his shoulders and olive skin. Runic tattoos cover his shoulders and arms, and he wields an ornately-carved wooden bow pointed in our direction. The centaur in the center has a charcoal coat, hazelnut skin, a forked black beard, and braids similar to my own. A massive ornamental shield tattoo covers his chest, swirling around his pecs and onto his shoulders. He holds a long spear tipped with a carved tusk. The female has a palomino lower half that's tan and speckled with white splotches. Her ivory skin is much paler than the other two centaurs, making the blue tattoos that run down her arms much more prominent. Flowing auburn hair drapes across her ample chest. She also wields an ornate bow with an arrow pointed at Taryn.

My grip tightens around Destroyer, and I call the horrors to my side, not sure what to expect.

The middle centaur raises a fist and the other two lower their weapons.

He rests the butt of his spear on the ground. "That's not a fight you'll win. Come with us if you're looking for a worthy challenge."

2. DARK TIDINGS

"Dude, quit staring," I whisper as I nudge Taryn in the arm.

He shifts his gaze from the female centaur to the trees overhead, not the least bit inconspicuous. "Sorry, it's just that this is not how lady centaurs look in games. She's a little...distracting."

He has a fair point, but he could still be a little less obvious about it.

The female centaur watches us with curiosity while the two small fairies hover around her shoulders. Not much smaller than Limery, the fairies stand out in sharp contrast against the muted tones of the forest. At first glance, they look adorable. One is pink and the other purple, they both have translucent lacy wings, and a trail of glitter follows wherever they move.

There's something unsettling about them, though. They're almost angelic in appearance, but their arms and fingers are spindly, not unlike Limery's. While their eyes are proportionate to their faces, the lack of pupils makes their beautiful faces almost creepy, like a wolf in sheep's clothing. They murmur melodically to one another, laughing and pointing.

I focus on one of them and a description appears.

Celestial Fairy. *Level 21. Though not native to Wandermere, celestial fairies have thrived in the aura of the ancient forest. When an adventurous party of gnomes perished while searching for gold and glory, their fairy companions were left to their own devices. They quickly reproduced, becoming an invasive species and overtaking much of the forest. With sufficient numbers, the celestial fairies waged war on the native woodland fairies, eradicating them from the forest. Wandermere is now home to the largest celestial fairy population across Mythos.*

I blink rapidly as I read the description over once more. I've never pictured fairies as conquistadors, especially ones looking like they just slid down the rainbow bridge. But I should know better than most not to judge solely on appearance. Limery might be mischievous at times, but I get the feeling that these two are always up to something.

I gesture toward the two fairies. "Did these two warn you we were here?"

The female centaur smirks. "There are many eyes throughout the forest."

"That's not ominous at all," Taryn mumbles as he narrows his eyes.

The bearded centaur laughs. "I doubt you have what it takes to scare a forest troll, Sylvie." He turns to Taryn. "The dwarf on the other hand..."

Taryn scowls in their direction. "I'm sorry, but aren't you the ones who just asked for our help? Who are you all, anyway?"

The bearded centaur places his hands together and bows slightly. "Apologies. We meant no offense. Our leader, Swift Thundercrest, told us a tale of encountering a blue forest troll traveling with a dwarf while he was in Seascape. He said that heroes have returned to Mythos once more. While he made no mention of horns, the pairing is such an oddity that we had to assume it was you two. Were we misguided?"

I think back to the council meeting with King Orso. I never spoke with the centaurs, but they were there along with a half-dozen other races. If we can meet with this Swift Thundercrest, maybe he can help point us in the direction of the heart of the forest so that we can hatch the dragon egg.

I shake my head. "No, it was us. I'm Chod. This is Taryn, and this is Limery. We're here on a bit of a time-sensitive mission. Any chance we can meet with Swift?"

He nods. "Very well. I am Thannis Smokehoof. This is Daimun Stonewhisper." He gestures toward the chestnut-colored male wielding the bow. "And this is Sylvie Redmane. The two fairies are Starlight and Sunbeam. Together, we scout the forest for threats and—"

Water splashes behind us, and I look over my shoulder where the stone-wielding golem has retaken its slumbering position in the center of the spring.

"Do not worry about the Wanderer." Thannis follows my gaze. "It is a powerful but simple creature. Unless provoked, it will spend the entirety of its days basking in the sunbeams."

Taryn scoffs. "Sounds like a cushy life."

Thannis's eyes narrow. "It is a peaceful life, more than I can say for the centaurs of late."

The demeanor of the other two darkens, and Starlight and Sunbeam chime in agreement from behind.

"What do you mean?" I focus on Thannis intently, uneasy about what news he may have.

"There have been dark tidings from abroad, and mysterious occurrences within the forest. It is no longer safe to travel at night in Wandermere."

Taryn and I exchange nervous glances before I speak. "We've been out of contact while on our travels. What's the news from abroad?"

Thannis's hooves paw at the ground, his tail flicking in agitation. "There have been more sightings of dark creatures. A handful have now made their way through various portals even though Mosstar, the shadowlands, and others remain closed on our end."

A chill runs down my spine. If Valmar is able to send monsters through the portals without risking invasion into his own, that puts us at a major disadvantage.

Taryn looks over his shoulders as if searching for threats. "And what about the forest? Why is it no longer safe?"

Daimun huffs, his body language mimicking Thannis's as his fingers tap against the bow nervously. When he speaks, his voice is deep and boisterous. "Mysterious holes have begun appearing across the forest. Holes that are too small for centaurs to explore and too dangerous for fairies. The fairies who have ventured into their depths have not returned. We don't know what resides within, but shadowy figures have been spotted moving through the forest after twilight. Many centaurs and fairies have gone missing at night, to the point where Swift has ordered us all to stay at camp after nightfall."

Taryn strokes his beard and the clasps jingle against one another. "Is that why all of the outposts were abandoned? We've been traveling for almost two days without seeing anyone."

Sylvie is angry when she answers. "The forest is too big to patrol without our outposts. By forcing us to retreat to our camp, we are cutting our legs out from under us. The shadows are expanding, and if we don't act soon, I fear we will face a battle we cannot win."

"What's your plan?" The plight of the centaurs isn't lost on me. It wasn't that long ago that the trolls were in a similar predicament.

Thannis scans our party. "That depends on whether the mighty heroes will offer their assistance."

I step forward and extend my hand. "If you will help us locate the heart of the forest, then we will help you in whatever way we can."

Thannis nods as he grips me firmly around the forearm. "It will be done."

Sylvie whispers something to the fairies, and they dart off deeper into the forest leaving a whimsical trail in their wake. After a few moments, the fairy dust dissipates.

"Follow me," Thannis orders as he turns in the opposite direction of where the fairies disappeared.

Our party falls in line behind Thannis along the well-trodden path, while Sylvie and Daimun bring up the rear. The fog grows thicker as we walk. My spirit guide pushes back the fog around us but offers little additional visibility. The centaurs are tall enough that they can see above the fog with ease, but I have a feeling they know these paths well enough that it wouldn't hinder them if they were buried in fog.

We walk for half an hour in near silence before Thannis comes to a halt. He reaches into a pouch strapped around his lower abdomen and pulls out a bronze talisman in the shape of a starburst. A yellow stone glows gently in its center. Thannis places the talisman around his neck and a moment later, a gust of wind explodes from his body, pushing back the fog for close to thirty yards in all directions. Leaves and dirt tumble away toward the edge of the boundary, revealing an assortment of holes several feet in diameter.

"That's cool!" Taryn grins, eyeing the talisman. "What is it?"

Thannis grabs the amulet by one of its points and holds it toward us. The stone in its center now glows brightly. "It is an Amulet of Sight. At night, it will cover the area in light. In areas such as this, it keeps the fog at bay. But come here." He motions toward one of the holes in the ground.

Taryn climbs down from Berry and we both join Thannis at the hole's edge. It reminds me of my battle with the mana-infused wyrm, only these holes are filled with pure darkness that not even my night vision can penetrate. I pull one of Jon's enchanted rocks from my satchel and activate it, but the light has no effect against whatever is causing the shadow. It's unsettling how the darkness can persist even in the presence of light.

I kneel and shine the light closer with no success. "You have no idea what's in there?"

Thannis shakes his head. "Some shadow creature, but we know nothing more than that. We've not been able to catch one out in the open, and anyone who has seen one up close has not returned to tell the tale."

A raspy sound comes from within the hole, like someone straining for breath. "Shh." I hold up a hand for the others to quiet and lean a little closer, tilting my head sideways to hear better.

"Chod," Taryn whispers.

I brush him away, closing my eyes to better make out the noise. It sounds almost like words.

Limery grows warm against my shoulder, and Taryn calls my name again as I try to make sense of the words.

"Chod." Taryn pulls at my elbow.

"What?" I snap and turn to see what the problem is. "I can hear something in there."

He points into the hole and my gaze shifts to the darkness where two orange eyes are staring back at me.

3. THE HIDDEN VILLAGE

A thick, black, slime-covered tongue lashes at the air, and I dive out of the way. Limery squawks, conjuring fireballs in both hands, and I equip Destroyer as I crawl to my feet.

The tongue disappears as quickly as it came, but when I shine Jon's enchanted light into the hole, the glowing eyes are nowhere to be seen.

"What the fuck was that?" I turn to Thannis for answers, my heartbeat pounding in my ears.

Daimun and Sylvie have their bows pointed at the hole, faces grim, but their leader stands stoic.

"Your guess is as good as mine. Whatever they are, these creatures are not native to the forest." Thannis shakes his head and purses his lips. "But at least we have a clue as to what happened to the missing fairies. Whatever foul monsters lie within these holes are multiplying, but whether it is from their own accord or some parasitic infestation, I don't know."

My grip tightens around Destroyer. "You think they could be turning other monsters into these shadow tongue things?"

Thannis nods. "It is a possibility. They could also be using the life force of those they kill to power their replication. We don't have enough information to know for sure. What matters is that they are stopped before they overtake the forest."

Taryn creeps toward the edge of the hole. "If that was its tongue, I'm not sure I want to see the body."

I take a step back, and Limery returns to my shoulder. "We'll do our best to help you with these monsters, but we require something in return."

Thannis raises a brow. "If it is within my power, it will be done."

I put away my weapon and pull the green dragon egg from my satchel. Its vibrant exterior gleams in the aura of Thannis's amulet.

Daimun and Sylvie both gasp when they see the egg, but Thannis is more reserved.

He watches the egg intensely before speaking in a low voice. "Where did you find that?"

I pull the egg closer to my chest. "That doesn't matter, but we were told that it could only be hatched in the heart of an ancient forest where life aura is most concentrated."

He nods, his eyes never leaving the egg. "You were told correctly. This is a rare and powerful item indeed. I cannot recall the last time a dragon egg has entered Wandermere." He slowly extends both hands. "May I?"

I hesitate for a moment before letting him take the egg. If they were going to rob us, they could have done so far easier when we were fighting the Wanderer. The way he stares at the egg, I'm not sure if it's greed or reverence, or maybe a little of both, but we need his help if we're going to hatch it at all.

Thannis holds the egg like it's the most precious object in Mythos, and the other two centaurs gather around him like kids on a playground.

Taryn leans in close and whispers, "I have a feeling King Orso might not be happy you took that."

I shrug. "I'm pretty sure he has bigger problems at the moment. Besides, he gave us full access to his treasures. It's not our fault if his advisor wasn't paying attention."

Thannis hands the egg back to me. "I hope you understand the power that lies within this egg."

I think back on Senzala's totem—Nesira, the white dragon from Frostmoor—and the abilities it granted her. How it shrouded everywhere it went in a blizzard. Even the mana-infused wyrm from my first quest displayed immense power. There's no telling how big the three in the troll forest have grown by now. "I think I've got an idea."

Taryn steps past me to shine one of Jon's flashlights into the hole again. "So, what's the plan here? Make a few bombs, toss them in, and call it a day?"

"The shadows can wait." Thannis flicks his tail. "Swift will want to hear of the dragon egg. First, we will take you to our camp."

Even with Taryn casting Strong Wind, I have to sprint to keep up as the centaurs gallop across the forest. Berry traipses along fast but clumsily, his golden armor clinking, while Jordy charges in sync beside him. Limery flies next to me, my shoulders too jostling for his comfort.

Before long, I'm completely lost among the towering trees with no way of telling which direction we came from or where the portal is located. Only my instincts keep me calm, assuring me that this isn't a trap.

My mind wanders as we travel, and when Thannis comes to a halt, I nearly barrel into his hindquarters.

The fog here is denser than anywhere else in the forest, and without Thannis's amulet to keep it at bay, it forms a towering wall in front of us.

The charcoal centaur turns toward us. "Very few outsiders have been granted access to our ancestral home. I hope you respect what an honor this is."

Taryn bows slightly. "We appreciate the honor."

I nod in agreement.

"Very well. Welcome to the Hidden Lake." He gestures toward the wall of fog, and both Daimun and Sylvie step back, taking sentry positions. "Follow me."

He steps between the two centaurs and through the wall of fog. Taryn follows close behind, and I pull up the rear.

For a moment, the fog is so dense that I can't see anything, but then it clears to reveal a vibrant village bustling with fairy and centaur activity. Several fairies chime overhead, watchful guardians among the trees. Compared to the rest of the forest, this is like an entirely different world. The trees are spread much further apart, with sprawling fields full of lush grass in between. There are gaping holes in the canopy where sunlight spills through, and trails of glittering dust follow dozens of fairies as they zoom around.

Several hundred yards away, there's a village of mostly stable-like structures that are fitting for centaurs, almost like an outdoor flea market. There are no doors on the entryways between buildings, and everything is big enough for a full-grown centaur to move through with ease.

Next to the village, a sparkling blue lake shimmers in the sun. In the center, large bubbles erupt from beneath the surface, bursting to emit smoke that travels in wisps toward the wall of fog surrounding the village.

This place isn't all that different from the troll village. There must be some powerful ley lines running beneath the lake if it's the source of all this fog.

In one of the open fields, two centaurs spar with wooden spears. Several more take aim with bows at a nearby target, where two pink fairies retrieve the arrows once the quivers are emptied.

I join Thannis on his right side. "This place is amazing! Do you not need guards to protect the boundary?"

He huffs. "Normally, we have scouts posted throughout the forest, but Swift has ordered them all to remain within the boundary of our village until we have a plan. The fairy patrol keeps a constant presence at the border concealed within the fog, but it is no longer safe for them to venture out alone. Only certain of us are permitted to leave, and only to where we can make it back by nightfall. That is the only reason we were fortunate enough to come upon you." He turns to face the wall of fog. "We are safe while within the boundaries of the Hidden Lake. While we do not worship in the ways of men or dwarves, this is sacred ground among centaurs and all those who roam the forest. Only once we leave do we become susceptible to the creatures that have invaded our forest."

I brush my fingers through the wall of fog. It reminds me of the barrier around the troll forest that casts illusions to keep trespassers from entering the village. The fog flows around my hand as I move but whatever I displace is immediately filled by more fog. "Does the barrier protect the village from outsiders or is it simply for concealment?"

"I have heard of the protection surrounding the troll forest." Thannis smiles. "Though ancient, that is a different type of magic. Centaurs cannot work with raw mana in the same ways as trolls. Our barrier conceals us, but the grounds within are its real power. They were blessed many years ago to protect the heart of the forest from corruption. No creature of shadow or death may set foot within our boundary without suffering a terrible fate."

Taryn gulps. "What about shadow druids?"

Thannis's hooves pound against the earth as he laughs heartily. "It is one thing to practice magic formed by darkness. It is quite another to be forged from it. You will be fine."

Sylvie coughs as she attempts to conceal her own grin.

"What?" Taryn leans forward. "It was a fair question."

A stampede of approaching centaurs draws everyone's attention from Taryn's embarrassment. A half-dozen fairies hover around them, one for each centaur.

I recognize the largest of the centaurs from King Orso's council. He's stout with a silver lower half and a matching gray beard trimmed to a point. A massive broadsword hangs from one side of his body and a bow on the other. His chest is covered in a detailed tattoo depicting a dragon curled around the base of a towering tree.

He raises one eyebrow as he takes us in. "We've not been formally introduced. I am Swift Thundercrest, leader of the Wandermere centaur herd. You've changed since I last saw you." His lips curl as he stares at my horns. "It is a mighty look befitting a hero troll and one that will strike fear into your enemies. Finding you here bears even more credence to the claims of King Orso."

Thannis clears his throat before I have a chance to respond. "There is something you must see." He turns to me. "Show him."

I once again pull the egg from my satchel, and it definitely feels warm against my fingers this time. The centaurs surrounding Swift gasp, but Swift's expression doesn't change. His eyes move from the egg to me and then back to the egg.

"I see." His right hand trails up his side, resting on the dragon tattoo covering his midsection. "You wish to hatch it here?"

My fingers trail over the warm scales of the egg. "Is this the heart of the forest?"

His hand falls back to his side and his expression is once again jovial as if laughter is on the edge of his lips. "Mighty, but still with much to learn. Come with me. Time may be of the essence, but some things are worth an explanation." He nods to the other five centaurs surrounding him. "I will be in my private quarters with the heroes. Thannis, Sylvie, Daimun, I trust you can make the necessary arrangements?"

Thannis nods before galloping off toward the lake with his companions. The other centaurs disperse, and we follow Swift toward the village.

Swift grins at me as we take the well-trampled path through the village. The architecture boasts a primitive design combined with modern items and fairy magic. While most of the buildings are stables with open-air walls on at least one side, there is a forge, a tavern, a tannery, and shops not that different from what I would find in Lynchton or some other small town. There also seems to be a maze of stables for sleeping throughout the center of the village. One of the stables has a massive grill where two fairies cook meat and vegetables. My mouth drools at the smell. All around, fairies zip to and fro, completing tasks that the centaurs are incapable of.

We pass by the tavern, and I have to physically restrain Limery from darting to the bar. "I'm sure there will be time for a drink before we leave."

"But Limmy is thirsties." He gives me his best pout.

Swift laughs. "Centaur brew is not for the faint of heart."

"I can assure you, Limery has more courage than the lot of us combined." Taryn winks at Limery, eliciting a blush from the imp.

Swift catches me as I slow to watch a fairy grinding herbs at the potion shop. "I'm sure the village is a sight to behold for an outsider. When the celestial fairies began reproducing, they changed the trajectory of the herd. We were a simple people in many aspects, content to live our lives among the trees, but by working together, we've become a force all over Mythos."

The fairy notices us and chimes at Swift. I'm still surprised that their language isn't advanced enough for my communication stone to translate.

I wave at the tiny creature, and it sticks its tongue out. Limery mimics the fairy, blowing a raspberry of his own.

I fight not to laugh. "How does that work?"

"We look out for one another. Centaur bodies are built for strength and power, but it comes at a cost. Fairies are smart, cunning, and industrious. Their magic allows them to do many things that their size would not. We harvest materials, they put them to use, and we trade with the other kingdoms across Mythos. They are more than just companions; we coexist. We give them a purpose and protect them from those that would do them harm...until recently. Now both of our races are in danger of isolation from the outside world."

He stops in front of a stable and gestures for us to enter. "My private quarters."

Taryn starts to climb down from Berry, but Swift stops him.

"You may enter with your pets. All are welcome here."

Taryn grins as he guides Berry into the building, scratching the bear behind the ears. Ruby sleeps peacefully between Taryn's legs and Jordy trots behind them, head held high.

We pass through a wide hall that empties into a sprawling open-air room. The walls give privacy while still feeling at one with nature. There's no roof, and the sky is unimpeded save for a few fruit-bearing trees that grow within the room. Tiny hammocks stretch between several limbs, probably for the fairies to sleep in.

Small blue melons with purple dots dangle from the branches. Swift plucks one and tosses it to Taryn. Juice explodes across his beard as he takes a bite, followed by a loud groan of pleasure.

Taryn wipes the juices from his beard. "Wow, that's so good. Like a blueberry and a grape had a baby."

I focus on one of the melons until a description appears.

Item. Twilight Gusher. *+1 Constitution for 1 hour. A hybrid melon found only in Wandermere, the Twilight Gusher was cultivated by celestial fairies and has become one of the most sought-after treats in Pruxford and Antadale.*

Swift offers me one, but I decline. Going into battle, I might eat one just for the stats, but not here.

"Trolls don't have much of a palate for sweets."

Taryn takes another bite and speaks with a full mouth. "Dude, you're missing out."

Berry snatches the gusher from Swift's hand but quickly spits it on the ground, apparently not a fan of the sweetness either. Jordy doesn't waste any time eating it off the floor.

"Don't worry," Swift laughs. "We have an assortment of meats that are sure to be more to your liking. But first, let us get down to business. I would offer you a seat, but we don't get many two-legged visitors."

A pile of hay rests in one corner, but the remainder of the floor is nearly empty aside from a handful of spears and other weapons propped in another corner. Shelves line every wall and are filled to the edge with potions, scrolls, books, and trinkets. Everything is at least four feet off the floor, making it easy for a centaur to reach.

"It's no problem. We're used to standing." I lean in close to Taryn. "Good thing you're on Berry or you might miss all the action."

He rolls his eyes. "You used to be such a good trash talker. What happened?"

I search for a witty retort, but the words don't come, leaving my mouth gaping like a fish. I can tell by the smirk on Taryn's face that he knows he got me.

"Fair enough. My jokes have been rather short-sighted as of late."

Taryn smirks. "I'm sure you'll have plenty of new ones inside that big, empty head of yours."

Swift's tail flicks as he watches us. "I used to bicker with my brother in much the same way. It is a blessing to have such a bond."

I give Taryn's shoulder a soft squeeze. "What happened to your brother?"

Swift stares off into the treetops for a moment, eyes distant as he relives some memory. "Draydon was an adventurous spirit, even for a centaur. Where action and adventure awaited, he answered the call. He explored far and wide, and when Wandermere offered no more secrets, he traveled through the portals. He became a fan of prize tournaments, competing against the best warriors for gold and glory. He won many, but he perished in a tragic accident when a broken lance caught him in the chest. The gnomes honored him with a glass sculpture outside of their tournament grounds."

I grimace at the thought of taking a lance through the chest. "I'm sorry to hear that. He sounds like an amazing competitor."

"That he was." Swift clears his throat. "But that is enough idle chat. The night grows ever closer, and we have urgent matters to discuss. I'm sure Thannis has informed you of our situation?"

"The formless monsters with glowing eyes and super-long tongues," Taryn says dryly. "Yeah, we've seen them."

My skin crawls at the memory. "You want us to find a way to kill them. What have you tried already?"

"Not enough, I am afraid." He sighs. "Since the disappearances, I have ordered everyone to return to the village after nightfall. Limited scouts go out during the day, but that is when the creatures are hidden. We've discovered the holes but have no understanding of how deep they go or what lies within. We can't fit inside, they are impenetrable to light, and the fairies who've investigated never returned. Once we witnessed a tongue snatch a fairy from the air, we haven't risked their safety since. We've tried dropping fire and fairy explosives, but with no luck. I feared our only option was to meet the monsters at nightfall, a fight we are most assuredly not prepared for."

I trace my horn as I think, running its pointed tip beneath my claws. "That's something to work with. We'll do what we can."

Swift nods slowly. "That is all we ask. While you are here, you will have access to any of our items, elixirs, and explosives."

Limery claps his hands together at the last part.

Swift grins at the imp. "In exchange for your help, we will hatch your dragon."

As soon as he finishes, I receive a notification with a quest alert.

Quest Alert: *You have been offered the quest "Tit for Tat." Shadow monsters are overtaking Wandermere, and mysterious disappearances have occurred throughout the forest. Identify the threat and eliminate it, bringing peace to the forest once again.*

Reward: *Increased favor with Swift Thundercrest and the Wandermere Herd.*

Bonus: *In exchange for your efforts, Swift Thundercrest will guide you through the process of hatching a green dragon egg.*

When I accept the quest, Swift releases a sigh of relief.

I remove the egg once more, and it's still warm to the touch. "Chief Laojin of the arctic trolls said that we needed to hatch it in the heart of an ancient forest. How far are we from there?"

Swift laughs again, the same as the first time I mentioned the heart of the forest.

I raise an eyebrow. "What's so funny?"

He lifts his arms, spreading them wide as he gestures at the surroundings. "The Hidden Lake is the heart of the forest. It is our ancestral home and has the highest concentration of life aura throughout Mythos."

Taryn raises a finger, a confused look on his face. "I thought there was supposed to be an adult green dragon living here."

"You are correct. For over one hundred years, Verdaria has slumbered in the depths of the Hidden Lake. The life aura nourishes her while in her stone form, and the fog that coats the forest is thanks to her."

Taryn's mouth hangs open. "So, you're telling me there's a dragon sleeping at the bottom of your lake that has been there for over a hundred years?"

Swift nods. "And if your dragon egg belongs to her, it is all the more miraculous that no one has attempted to hatch it until now."

I keep the fact that it belonged to King Orso to myself. "What do we have to do to hatch it?"

He smiles. "Tell me, are trolls known for their patience?"

Taryn snickers, and I hold back a groan. The trolls might have patience, but it's certainly not my strong suit.

4. WHAT DREAMS ARE MADE OF

Word travels fast and there are hundreds of centaurs surrounding the Hidden Lake by the time we arrive. An equal number of fairies dart through the air, and some dive low against the lake, letting their spindly fingers trail against the water's surface. One sprinkles fairy dust onto the dragon's bubbles, and glittery fog wisps through the village toward the wall.

This place must be even bigger than I thought because I only saw a few dozen centaurs when we first entered the village. I wonder just how many of them used to be spread across all of the forest. Their tails swish and hooves paw at the ground, and I get the feeling that this is a once-in-a-lifetime opportunity for them.

The forest has darkened since our arrival, and the sun lies hidden somewhere beyond the treetops. Dozens of torches blaze around the edge of the lake, and occasionally, pink embers soar into the air. Night will come soon and with it our promise to find out what exactly has overtaken the forest.

Thannis and Sylvie stand back from an open space where a large raft rests on the lake's edge. The raft is made from freshly-chopped trees roped together with vines, and leaf-covered branches protrude in a few areas, giving it a more natural look than anything built by humans or dwarves. In the center, there's some sort of altar where vines intertwine into a cradle for the egg.

The herd goes quiet when they notice our approach, but the chiming of fairies still carries across the lake. Swift leads the way, followed by Taryn and Ruby riding Berry. Jordy flanks his right, and Limery and I pull up the rear.

Limery adjusts himself on my shoulder. "Limmy is exciteds for the baby dragons."

"I think we all are. A dragon can't be more trouble than you, right?" I gently poke him in the stomach.

"Limmy isn't troubles." He cackles. "Limmy will shows the baby dragons how to makes fire."

Just what we need, a wild and powerful imp teaching an untrained dragon how to breathe fire in the middle of the forest.

"How about we discuss that when the time comes?"

When we arrive at the raft, Swift pulls a horn from his satchel and blows. Deep sonorous notes echo through the forest and even the fairies quiet.

He speaks, and his voice is amplified across the gentle waves of the lake. "A shadow has loomed over the forest of late but today, we have reason to see the light. For when we are at our darkest, the forest has brought two heroes into our village."

"And me's," Limery interrupts.

"And a brave imp." Swift winks at Limery before returning to his speech. "While the heroes will fight to push these monsters of shadow and death back to whence they came, we are granted something even more miraculous—the opportunity to witness the birth of a dragon."

Whispers and gasps start around the lake as the rumors are finally confirmed.

Swift raises a hand and they quiet once again. "None of us here have witnessed Verdaria in her living form. For over a hundred years, she has slumbered, and it has been two generations since a dragon was last hatched in Wandermere. But the winds of Mythos are changing and today, we will play a part in that change."

As if on cue, a gust of wind rips across the village. Branches shake violently and waves spread across the lake.

"Now that's spooky." Taryn looks around for the source of the gust, but there's nothing there.

Swift speaks in a low voice. "Chod, please place the egg on the altar."

When I remove the egg from the satchel, the wind dies down immediately. I can't help but wonder if the forest can sense the power within the egg? Or perhaps Verdaria's presence extends beyond the bottom of the lake. Whatever the reason, the egg is warmer than I have ever felt it, and the green scales are as vibrant as fresh grass. We're definitely in the right place. The altar cradles the egg perfectly as I set it down.

Swift nods to Thannis, Sylvie, and Daimun before continuing. Each of the centaurs steps forward with an item.

"Hatching a dragon takes time, but we have gathered some items that should help boost the concentration of life aura around the egg."

Sylvie holds a plain gray stone in her palm. A dull rune is etched across the top of the stone, and it's small enough that it could fit into one of the sockets on Destroyer or one of my other enchanted weapons.

She kneels and places the stone at the edge of the raft closest to the water. "This is a Regeneration Stone. It increases the healing and health regeneration of whoever holds it. It can also transfer its properties to enchanted weapons when equipped."

Item. Regeneration Stone. *Increases health regeneration by 20%.* **Bonus:** *When* *paired with Shield of Vigor and Renewal Spear, user will be granted a ten-foot aura that provides 20% increased regeneration for companions within its radius.*

That's a hell of an attachment, especially combined with the full set. By having all three pieces, it's basically like the entire party has a Regeneration Stone. I wonder if the aura would work on my horrors to keep them from dying when out of combat? Even if it kept them at one percent health, the amount of health they have doesn't matter when casting Sacrifice or Kamikaze. I'll need to talk to Swift about these items when this is all said and done.

Next, Daimun holds up a dull gray shield. The shield is massive, with a shimmering green tree engraved into the front, eerily similar to the tattoo on Swift's chest. In the center of the tree, there's a socket that's the perfect size for the Regeneration Stone.

He places the shield in the bottom left corner of the raft. "The Shield of Vigor increases the overall health of whoever wields it. When paired with the Regeneration Stone, healing and health regeneration are increased even further."

I quickly examine the shield.

Item. Shield of Vigor. *Increases HP by 30%.* **Bonus:** *When paired with Regeneration Stone and Renewal Spear, user will be granted a ten-foot aura that provides 20% increased regeneration for companions within its radius.*

Now, this is an item I would love to have. A thirty percent health increase combined with the bonus from my horrors would make me pretty tough to kill. Not to mention the Rapid Regeneration passive I already have when below ten percent health. With these items, I could fight with low health for even longer. I could even bait opponents into continuing a fight by playing weak before exploiting the rapid healing.

Thannis showcases the final item, a spear in the same dull gray color as the other two items. The weapon is tipped with an emerald spearhead.

He holds it in our direction. "The Renewal Spear is the final piece of the set. On its own, the spear gathers aura while not in use, but it also saps life force when it touches a living being. The aura is stored within the weapon and can be transferred to the wielder on command. When all three items are combined, they produce an aura that buffs companions within a ten-foot radius."

Item. Renewal Spear. *Capable of holding life aura equivalent to 500 HP. The Renewal Spear gathers aura passively while equipped and can steal health from enemies during battle. Life aura may be absorbed by the wielder at any time.* **Bonus:** *When paired with Regeneration Stone and Shield of Vigor, user will be granted a ten-foot aura that provides 20% increased regeneration for companions within its radius.*

This one makes me giddy with excitement. I can already see a hundred different uses for the Renewal Spear. It would synergize with the passive from my Horrors of Finesse perfectly. Part of me wishes that we could use these for our quest to clear the forest, but if Swift is putting them on the altar, there has to be a good reason.

Thannis places the spear in the bottom right corner of the raft, forming a triangle around the altar. As soon as he releases it, a trail of energy zips from one item to the other, forming some kind of magical current that produces a deep green aura. The runes along all three items pulse with energy, and the aura travels up the altar to where green ghost flames surround the egg.

"These items will further increase the already potent aura in the lake." Swift moves to the front of the raft and picks up a rope attached to both corners.

Stepping into the lake, he hauls the raft in. It bobbles for a second before resting on the calm water. With a final tug, the raft floats gently toward the center of the lake. As the daylight continues to fade, the ghost flames reflect on the water's surface and add an eeriness to the bubbling fog, making it look more like a cauldron than a lake.

After a few final words, the rest of the centaurs begin to disperse.

"What now?" I ask.

"For the dragon, we wait. For you, we must gather provisions for your quest."

Inside the armory, I place an ornately-carved spear back into its bin. "Do you have any more item sets like the one on the altar?"

The centaurs have well-made items in their armory, but very few of them are enchanted, and not at all suited for either mine or Taryn's playstyle and abilities. The spear is sturdy and beautiful but offers me nothing that I don't already have with my trident, but even Sea Scorpion's enchantment no longer provides much value thanks to the passive from Ram Rage that allows me to deal splash damage on all physical attacks.

Swift runs his finger over the tip of the spear I just passed over. "We make fine bows, arrows, and spears, but we have little need for the weapons of the two-legged. Very few of us prefer plate armor, and we aren't built to be agile sword wielders. This one—" He grips the hilt of the broadsword hanging from his side. "—was a gift to our herd long ago. Our blacksmith primarily forges arrowheads and shoes for our hooves. The item set on the altar was a gift from abroad."

"Makes sense." I stop in front of a rack of intricately-designed arrows displayed on the wall. They are made from a variety of materials—some wood, others metal, and the feather fletchings come in various sizes and colors. I'm sure Archard would have a field day testing out how they all work. "I prefer a more in-your-face approach, and Taryn has leaned into his druid abilities more and more. We're magic and mayhem. Bows and spears just aren't a good fit for us right now."

Swift motions for us to leave. "Do not worry. Our fairy companions should have some items to help you with your quest."

The next stable we enter is coated with enough glitter that it could pass for the backstage of a drag show. A half-dozen fairies scurry about. Up close, they're somehow both beautiful and terrifying at the same time. Each fairy has flawless skin and perfectly proportioned features, but their spindly arms and fingers seem out of place, and there's something unsettling about their eyes. They're opalescent and without pupils, so it's impossible to tell if they are watching me or not. Each one is a slightly different shade of pink or purple with lacy wings that look like they could blow away in a stiff breeze.

Two stand together mixing a potion in the corner. One holds the container while the other stirs it with a long stick. Colors swirl together, and I catch the faint aroma of cotton candy. Another ladles the contents of a completed batch, carefully measuring each scoop as it pours the vibrant liquids into vials.

On the other side of the stable, another fairy looks drunk as it stumbles across a raised platform before lying down on a small pile of straw. Three others already lie there asleep. A second fairy looks about to pass out as it clenches its palm over an empty vial. A moment later, a sparkling pink powder appears in the vial.

It takes me a moment before I realize what the others are up to. "Are you harvesting fairy dust?"

Swift cups the dazed fairy in his palm and strokes it between the wings. The fairy nuzzles against his thumb and chimes so softly it almost sounds like a purr.

He places the tired fairy on the straw pile next to the others just as two new fairies fly in and take their seats. They chime with delight as they clench their fists and streams of fairy dust fall into the container.

"They've been working overtime since the invaders appeared. The males produce Dream Dust, and the females produce Sleep Dust. It's a draining process for them to provide so much dust, but we are well-stocked even though we haven't had the opportunity to use them yet."

"What do we have here?" Taryn lifts a vial filled with a purple, glittery substance. As he tilts it, the substance moves like sand.

Swift grins. "Celestial fairies have some of the most potent dust of all the fairy races. Where other fairy abilities are often tied to the elements, celestial fairies are known for their sparking trails and the magical dust they produce. This—" He taps the vial in Taryn's hand. "—is Dream Dust. A few sprinkles of this can lead to vivid dreams while sleeping. An entire vial can make one experience dreams as if they were real."

"So, like hallucinations?" I pick up a vial and give it a shake.

*Item. **Dream Dust.** A powerful, potent substance capable of unlocking hidden realms of the mind. Effects are dependent upon amount ingested.*

Swift nods. "Exactly, those affected are unable to distinguish dream from reality until it wears off. We have no idea if it will affect the shadow monsters, but it was our next course of action before you arrived."

"It's worth a shot." Taryn adds a few vials to his satchel, and I do the same. "What else are we working with?"

"While the Dream Dust may disorient an opponent, Sleep Dust is capable of immobilizing them outright." Swift points to a collection of vials containing a light pink substance. It's less vibrant than the Dream Dust and much less glittery.

*Item. **Sleep Dust.** Often mixed with liquid and drank as a tonic, Sleep Dust offers effects ranging from drowsiness to instantaneous deep slumber.*

"Now, that could be useful." Even if we don't use it here, you never know when you might need to sneak past a guard or bypass a dungeon mob.

Swift showcases some of the other items containing fairy dust before we leave. Small amounts are mixed into potions, elixirs, and tonics. Some offer increased or modified dreams; others help with relaxation. There seem to be countless options for using these two types of dust depending on how they are brewed. Before the shadow monsters invaded Wandermere, these concoctions were the herd's most-traded items with other kingdoms.

We load up on as many vials of Dream and Sleep Dust as we can find, but most of the other items are unlikely to help us in battle. Still, we pack a few more that might prove useful once we find ourselves back in a city again. While we still have some gold from our time on the Isle of Mythos, we've spent more than we've earned lately so we might need to trade soon.

The fairies return to their glittery escapades, and we follow Swift to a row of empty stables at the edge of the village. From our vantage point, the torches blaze around the Hidden Lake. In the center, the raft sways gently and the green aura from the three items reflects off the calm surface.

Swift's tail swishes as he watches the raft. "The days always pass too quickly of late. For your safety, I would wait until daybreak before beginning your quest. The less time you spend under darkness, the better. We have plenty of open stables for you to sleep in, and if you wish, you may watch the ceremony as one of our colts is branded a stallion."

Taryn shifts his gaze to the ground. "That is a generous offer, but I'm going to call it an early night. We have a long road ahead of us tomorrow."

I'm sure he's not in a partying mood, but it would probably do him some good to be around others for a while.

"Oh, come on." I squeeze Taryn's shoulder. "We've never been known to turn down a good party." I laugh.

He doesn't answer, guiding Berry into one of the open stables. I offer Swift a shrug before joining Taryn. Maybe he just needs a little convincing.

Swift nods his understanding. "Very well. Settle in. You will find the herd down by the lake if you choose."

Limery smiles devilishly. "Oh, yes, Limmy loves to parties."

At least he won't take any convincing.

5. THE SCARS OF LIFE

Taryn fluffed the pile of hay before collapsing onto it. Berry nestled beside him, jostling Taryn as the bear positioned himself until his head rested on his owner's lap. Jordy tucked his legs and sat down on the druid's other side while Ruby cuddled in the warmth of Berry's rust-colored fur.

"What?" He raised his head to meet Chod's eyes. "Can't we rest for just one night?"

Chod frowned. "Bro, come on. When are we ever going to have the opportunity to party with centaurs again?" He knelt in front of Taryn, his massive horns making his threatening presence even larger. "I think it would be good for you."

Taryn clenched his jaw, fighting the urge to snap at his friend. Chod was only trying to help, but comments like that always made him sound like a dick. Taryn didn't need anyone telling him what was good for him, especially the person who was a large part of the reason things felt so shitty. He took a deep breath, letting the moment pass.

"I've got everything that's good for me right here." He scratched Berry on the head, eliciting a groan. "Isn't that right, Berry?"

Chod sighed, but it wasn't from disappointment. It was more like a sigh of failure, and it matched his sunken shoulders as he shook his head. "Alright, suit yourself. Limery and I are going to see what all the fuss is about."

"Yeah, Limmy wants to parties!" The imp threw his hands in the air and pumped them, a move Taryn had taught him not long ago.

Taryn smiled. "You show them how it's done, little dude. I'll be here if you guys need me."

As the two were leaving, Taryn called after Chod. "Thanks for trying."

Chod gave him a half-smile before disappearing into the village.

Taryn stared at the empty space where Chod had stood. Underneath all the rage and wise cracks, he was a good person—it was part of the reason they'd remained friends for so long—but Taryn wasn't ready to put himself out there just yet. He'd exchanged a few wisecracks with Chod earlier, but everything was still raw. Too raw. Like someone had scraped out his heart with a rusty spoon.

He wasn't ready to let his guard down again. Not yet.

He laid back against the straw. It wasn't the same as a bed at the inn, but since the hay was piled on soft earth, it was surprisingly comfortable. Plus, it was always more enjoyable to lay next to his pets, something Berry and Jordy wouldn't be able to do once they were back in the cities.

Taryn imagined the duo clamoring through a busy tavern, Berry knocking chairs aside with his massive size and Jordy's hooves clacking against the wooden floors. They'd be kicked out in a heartbeat.

He pulled the last of the carrots Gherhardt had given him in Frostmoor and fed it to Jordy. The frost goat crunched on it loudly, his jaw moving back and forth as he ground it against his blocky teeth. He'd been on death's doorstep when Chod first brought him down the mountain. Jordy was old, but since they'd bonded, it was like the goat had turned back the clock.

Good, because Taryn couldn't handle losing another pet.

He scratched the bridge of Jordy's nose, and the goat lowered his head in a show of respect. He was an interesting creature—stubborn and proud, but not in the same way that Stompy had been. More like if Berry's affectionate qualities and Stompy's heroic qualities had been combined.

"He would have liked you a lot." Taryn wiped a tear from his cheek. The two pets had only spent a handful of days together before Stompy passed.

He closed his eyes and leaned back to keep from crying. At least he was alone. Chod felt bad enough without seeing Taryn's inner turmoil. As upset as he might be, what was done was done, and he didn't want to hold a grudge against his best friend.

Squeezing his eyes tighter until they started to tingle with pain, he focused on the world around them. Anything to distract himself from what was happening inside his head. Distant chimes told of fairies coming and going. Owls hooted somewhere high in the trees. Branches hissed in the night, and faraway laughter could be heard.

Hooves clopped through the village as a latecomer raced to join in the fun.

Then a wet tongue licked Taryn on the nose. He opened his eyes to find Jordy's nose inches from his own. Jordy snorted, followed by another slimy lick as his outrageously-long tongue darted for Taryn.

He moved out of the way, leaving the frost goat licking at air. "Fine. We'll go down for a few minutes."

Berry and Ruby were on their feet in an instant. Berry's stump of a tail wagged like an excited dog and Ruby paced between Taryn and the stable entrance.

Taryn placed his hands on his hips. "Message received. How to tell me I'm a party pooper without telling me I'm a party pooper."

They came to a stop at the edge of the village, and Taryn inhaled deeply as he took in their surroundings. This truly was a beautiful place. The way the torches and dragon altar reflected off the lake was mesmerizing. Not to mention the fairies that zipped around, blurs of bubblegum and lavender against the night sky with trails that sparkled in their wake.

Down by the lake, a large fire blazed. Several deer roasted on three spits constantly rotated by a group of fairies.

Chod's hulking frame was noticeable immediately, even next to the large centaurs. He held a slab of meat in one hand and a drink in the other. Limery swayed in the air, both hands wrapped around a beverage much too big for him.

"Oh, man." Taryn laughed. "I really hope we aren't turning him into a delinquent." He turned to his pets. "Go on and have some fun. It's safe here. You don't have to stick around me all night."

Berry nuzzled Taryn's leg before frolicking off toward the lake with the others in tow.

For the moment, Taryn wanted to sit and observe. He'd go talk to the others when he was ready. While there were plenty of centaurs feasting and drinking, there were other activities taking place all around the village.

A group of younger-looking centaurs were tossing spears to see who could throw one the farthest. Dozens of spears stuck in the ground over a hundred yards away. Every time a new record was set, cheers echoed across the forest. Another group practiced archery, they shot at a tree playing a game where the goal was to shoot an arrow directly above the previous shot. A trail of arrows zigged and zagged halfway up the towering oak.

"I sense there is great trouble within you."

Taryn jumped at the sudden sound, turning to see a dark-skinned centaur with a forked beard only feet away. He'd been so focused on the centaur games that he hadn't heard Thannis's massive hooves approaching from behind.

"It's been a tough week." Taryn sighed.

"I do not doubt it. Dark times are ahead for all of us, I fear." He placed a hand on Taryn's shoulder. "But for now, we still have nights like these. Come, I will show you how some centaurs have made peace with the pain inside their hearts."

Taryn couldn't explain why, but he followed Thannis. They took a roundabout way, sticking close to the village but bypassing Chod and the most raucous of the herd.

They stopped next to a smaller fire, where a few centaurs sat on their haunches. It was an odd sight, seeing them sitting. Several more stood around the fire chatting and drinking. Sylvie and Daimun were both there, and Taryn tried his best to avert his gaze from her exposed chest. The duo tilted their mugs to him as he passed.

Closest to the water's edge, an older centaur with a bluish-gray coat and long gray braids appeared to be chiseling into the chest of a much younger centaur. Upon closer inspection, he could see the outline of a tattoo. Almost all of the centaurs had tattoos, and this one looked to be the outline of two spears crossed over the young centaur's chest.

He took a moment to examine some of the other's tattoos.

The elder was covered more than any of them, from his neck all the way down to his waistline. Trees and flowers, weapons and shields, even runes and designs that seemed to only be decorative; he'd left no space empty.

Sylvie had blue tattoos along both arms. They swirled into wispy ends like gusts of wind. Daimun also had tattoos along his arms, but his were intricate symbols and runes. Thannis had an ornate shield over each pec with ornamental embellishments that ran onto his shoulders and a quarter of the way down his arms.

Thannis placed a hand on his chest as if feeling his own tattoo. "Armun has etched the bodies of every centaur on their name-day for as far back as I can remember. And now, young Danetro has joined our ranks."

Danetro grimaced as Armun tapped the end of a short metal needle with a hammer, slowly moving it across the young centaur's chest.

Taryn had watched documentaries on traditional tattoo design. There was usually a trail of blood and ink as the design took shape one dot at a time, but Danetro's body was healing as soon as the needle was removed.

Taryn scrunched his brow. "How is he healing so fast?"

Armun raised the needle, and Danetro immediately relaxed. "The life aura from the lake increases regeneration, allowing the body to heal almost as fast as the ink is applied."

Danetro groaned as Armun resumed the tattoo. "It still hurts like a banshee."

Taryn stepped closer. "You do amazing work. So much detail for only using a single needle."

Armun's tail swished. "That is high praise coming from a dwarf. Dwarven craftsmanship and attention to detail are the finest I have had the pleasure to witness. I would love to see their skill with a needle."

Taryn smiled at that. "I can't say I've ever seen a dwarf with a tattoo, but maybe now that the portal to Isle of Mythos is opened that will change. Is there a reason you all have tattoos?"

Armun stopped again, giving the young stallion a moment of reprieve. "The reason is different for each of us. In ages past, the tattoos depicted great victories or tallied enemies defeated in combat. Swift's brother, Draydon, held onto that tradition and would return to the forest after every tournament to mark his victories. There was a time when those tattooed would ingest Dream Dust and watch the scene play out as it was etched into their bodies. Nowadays, some choose to honor their history, others their goals and ambitions, some choose to honor those they have lost. While others do it for no other reason than to honor the history of the herd."

Taryn choked up for a moment. *Some choose to honor those they have lost.* There was something beautiful in that sentiment.

He cleared his throat. "When you are done, I would be grateful if you would tattoo me."

"You're doing what?" Chod stood up so quickly that his drink sloshed over the edge of the mug. A pile of bones sat at his feet, remnants of the roasted boar.

Taryn straightened, his conviction set. "I'm getting a tattoo."

Chod stared at him for a moment, body swaying from the effects of the centaur mead, before extending a fist. "Badass! What are you getting?"

"I don't want to ruin the surprise. Just thought I would let you know what was happening in case you went looking for me." Taryn looked around, where centaurs were drinking and laughing. "Is the party everything you thought it would be?"

Chod placed a hand on Taryn's shoulder more forcefully than he would have when sober. "It's great! I'm next up in the spear toss, and Limery has made friends with the fairies. They're putting on quite the show."

He pointed over the lake where Limery and a handful of fairies hovered over its surface. Limery held a fireball in each hand. When he tossed it, the fairies threw up a handful of dust. As the fireball passed through the dust, it exploded into a colorful blaze of light that crackled like fireworks.

Taryn laughed. "I'm not sure I want to know how they discovered that trick."

"Chod!" Swift yelled from the field where nearly twenty centaurs had gathered to toss spears. "Time to show us some of that barbarian troll strength."

Taryn slapped Chod on the side. "Good luck with the spear toss. Time for me to go get stabbed repeatedly with a needle. They tell me it's fun."

<hr>

Danetro stood proudly, shoulders back to push out his chest as he showed off his new tattoo. He trotted like a show-horse, tail swishing as he spun in a circle. It had taken hours, but the tattoo was finished. Finely-detailed spears that had been painstakingly designed one dot at a time.

The two spears crossed over one another in an X, taking up the majority of Danetro's chest. Taryn had learned that they represented the young stallion's role in the tribe—a hunter during times of peace and a warrior in times of unrest. One spear was uneven and knotted in places, with a stone spearhead lashed together with leather and adorned with feathers—a symbol of the past. The other was polished wood, sleek and perfectly balanced, fitted with a metal spearhead—a symbol of the present. Both played their part in centaur society.

"It looks amazing." Taryn gaped in awe. Soon, he would have his own tattoo. "You really killed it, Armun."

The elder centaur dipped his head. "Practice leads to perfection. Now tell me, what tattoo is worthy of a hero dwarf?"

Taryn cleared his throat. "I would like to honor the pet I lost in Frostmoor."

Armun's brow furrowed as he focused on Taryn's words. "Tell me about this pet of yours. Tattoos tell a story in themselves, and the better I understand your connection to the tattoo, the better I will be able to uncover the story within you."

Taryn took a deep breath. He'd known this moment would come. If he was getting Stompy's memory tattooed onto his flesh, he should be able to talk about him. But it wasn't just talking about what had happened at Boneholde that was hard. Since that day, anything that reminded him of Stompy was also a reminder that his pet was no longer around.

A strong hand rested on his shoulder.

"Not all tattoos are created equal." Thannis's gaze lingered on him with a soft expression that contradicted his powerful appearance. "My tattoo honors those I lost as well. These shields that cover my chest are my promise to defend the Hidden Lake so that it never happens again. Dream Dust helped me to make peace with the demons in my head."

Thannis looked to Armun and the elder nodded. Reaching in his satchel of tattoo supplies, Armun pulled out a vial that swirled with a purplish-brown liquid.

*Item. **Manifestation Potion.** Brewed with Dream Dust and psychedelic mushrooms, this potion has the ability to intertwine the subconscious with reality. **Warning:** Highly potent. Do not use while working or operating contraptions.*

Armun lifted the vial for Taryn to see. "Take this while I am tattooing you and whatever you choose to focus on will revisit you once again."

Taryn reached for the vial, but Armun pulled it back. "But first, tell me about your pet."

Taryn steeled himself. He could do this.

"His—" Another deep breath. "His name was Stompy. He was a moulhaug, the most stubborn creature I've ever met, but he was mine. He saved my ass on more than one occasion. He died saving my ass."

Armun's face was grave. "He sounds like a very loyal companion, but I am afraid I'm not familiar with, what was it, moulhaugs?"

Taryn's chest tightened. If Armun didn't know what a moulhaug looked like, then how was he supposed to tattoo it?

He would try his best to describe it. "They're native to the Isle of Mythos. I guess with the portals being closed, it makes sense you wouldn't see them here. He was big, easily two to three times as large as a centaur, with gray skin that had patches of green so that he looked like a moss-covered boulder when sleeping. He had a massive horn on the tip of his nose, kind of like a rhi—"

Taryn stopped himself. Of course, they wouldn't know what a rhino was.

Armun sighed. "I'm sorry, but I am not familiar. Perhaps if there is something that reminds you of him, that is all that truly matters. Tattoos are a symbol, after all, nothing more."

Taryn closed his eyes. He could get a horn, but there was no telling if it would look like Stompy's. Maybe he should just give up on the idea. It had been worth a shot, but it didn't sound like this was meant to be.

Something hard pressed against Taryn's side.

He opened his eyes to find Jordy with his horns lowered. Berry and Ruby stood behind him. They were always there when he needed them.

"Your pets have great affection for you." Armun petted Berry behind the ears, and the bear groaned in pleasure. "They can sense when you are in distress."

Taryn lifted Jordy's chin until their eyes met. "Thanks, Jordy," he whispered. He turned back to Armun, grinning. "I think I know just what to get."

6. BITTERSWEET GOOD-BYE

Taryn rested on a raised platform lying on his back. He clenched the Manifestation Potion in his palm as he lay there shirtless, staring at the night sky. He would take the potion soon, but he wanted to feel these first few pokes.

Armun leaned over him, needle in one hand and the small hammer in the other. "Ready?"

Taryn nodded and then focused his eyes on the starry sky overhead. Many a night he had gazed up at the same sky as he rested on Stompy's tough hide. Somehow, it felt appropriate.

He winced as the needle jabbed into his chest. The pain flared but dulled almost immediately. Half a second later, the next tap came, followed by more pain.

He'd chosen to have the tattoo over his left pec, over his heart. It might have been cheesy, but he didn't care what anyone else thought. This tattoo was for him and him alone.

His family had never had any pets growing up, there was precious little money to go around as it was. Bonding with Stompy, Berry, Ruby, and now Jordy, he'd made up for lost time rather quickly. In the same way Chod had bonded with Limery, he'd found a real connection with these bits of data that rivaled any relationship he'd had outside the game. Their companionship and vastly-different personalities filled a void in his heart that Taryn hadn't even known he'd had.

As each successive stab of the needle built on the last, Taryn embraced the pain. He let it course through his body, mingling with the suffering already inside him. The more he embraced the pain, the less intense the emotional hurt seemed to feel, until he came to appreciate the physical pain. Was this how people felt about tattoos in real life? He'd never once thought that physical pain could help heal emotional wounds.

Armun stopped for a moment, and Taryn felt invincible at the brief reprieve.

"How are you holding up?" the centaur asked.

"I'm good." He lifted the vial. "Time to see what this is all about."

Taryn downed the potion, and it tasted like candy that had been dropped in the mud, simultaneously sweet and disgusting. It only took a few seconds before the world went hazy.

The pain of the needle resumed, but it felt distant. He sat up and was surprised when a ghostly copy of himself rose from his own body, leaving the corporeal version under the needle and hammer of Armun's experienced precision.

The world swirled around him in a watercolor tide of purples and pinks. Aside from the immediate vicinity around his body, all shape and form left the world.

He hovered over Armun's shoulder, watching the tattoo come to life. Laughter coursed through his chest unbidden at how silly the design was.

A deep bellow echoed behind him, the sonorous tones reverberating in his chest.

Taryn froze, and whatever ghostly version of a heart he currently had halted as well. A second bellow erupted, much closer now, followed by a massive snout resting on his shoulder.

He refused to move, refused to turn around in case this was all some clever trick. There was a snort, and a warm gust of air huffed against the side of his face. When Taryn turned, Stompy watched him with large moss-colored eyes.

Taryn wrapped his arms around the moulhaug, burying his face into the creature's side. "I'm so sorry, boy." His body shook with waves of emotion.

Stompy huffed again, his nostrils flaring before taking a step back. When Taryn tried to follow, Stompy lowered his horn, blocking Taryn's approach.

Their eyes locked again.

"What?" Taryn's voice cracked. "I didn't mean for any of this to happen. I tried to get you to come with us, but you wouldn't listen." He clenched his fists. "What do you want from me?"

Stompy lowered his head, sniffing at Taryn's leg. Suddenly, there was something firm in his pocket that hadn't been there before.

"Of course." Taryn laughed when he reached inside. "A carrot. Is this my dream or yours?"

The carrot glowed with energy as he held it out to Stompy. The moulhaug snatched it up, grunting as he crushed it between his sledgehammer teeth. When he was finished, Stompy lowered himself to the ground so that Taryn could climb on his back.

Taryn settled in, and Stompy kicked off from the ground, floating into the air as the world shifted around them once again. The purples and pinks shrunk back, revealing a star-speckled vastness. Far away, Taryn could faintly feel the prick of the needle against his skin.

Stompy soared through the heavens like some god-powered beast. Scenes began to appear around them, ghostly holograms depicting events from Taryn's time in Mythos.

The fight with Stompy where they'd first bonded. Their travels through the Greystone Mountains. Relaxing by the beach in Sandholde.

Stompy slowed, groaning softly at the image of them soaking up the sun.

Then there was chaos as a scene showed Stompy smashing through the stable in Seascape and running through the streets to find Taryn and Chod battling Glenn outside the portal.

One by one, Taryn revisited the memories he had created with this magnificent beast, all the way up until the gates of Boneholde.

Stompy slowed down.

"Don't stop," Taryn whispered softly. "I can't watch this one. Not again."

Stompy snorted, lingering in front of the image as the hobgoblins spilled over the gate.

"I said no!" Taryn yelled, and his voice echoed through eternity.

Stompy responded with a bellowing trumpet of his own, bucking Taryn from his back. He turned on the druid as he hovered in space, steam pouring from his nostrils and fire blazing in his mossy eyes.

He bellowed again, as if telling Taryn this was not an option.

Taryn forced himself to watch. He watched as Chod tried to slow the horde down with his horrors. Watched as Stompy turned back. He witnessed his own face contorted in desperation, and Chod's bulging muscles as he pulled with all his might to try and turn the moulhaug around.

For the first time, he saw the mirrored desperation in his friend's face as Chod realized he'd finally met his match in a battle of wills.

Stompy wasn't scared as he ran into the horde of hobgoblins. He was mad as hell and determined to make sure his master made it away safely.

Tears streamed down Taryn's face as he watched it all unfold, but he finally understood why Stompy had brought him here. It didn't matter if Chod had been reckless. In the end, it was Stompy's choice to sacrifice himself—not just for Taryn, but for Berry and Ruby and Jordy. For Chod and Limery. He'd done what family was supposed to do—look out for one another.

The scene faded and the starry night morphed back into the forest of the Hidden Lake. Taryn saw himself lying on his back as Armun finished up the last lines of the tattoo.

There wasn't much time, and Taryn didn't want to waste a second of it. He leaned forward and wrapped his arms around the moulhaug's side, listening to the slow heartbeat for the last time.

7. HUG IT OUT

The fairies and centaurs are equally fascinated with my horrors as the grumbly creatures scurry around the open field. Horrors of Power and Finesse grunt and groan as fairies poke and prod at them.

Limery seems to be having fun with a group of rowdy fairies over by the lake, and occasionally, streaks of flame zip across the night or an explosion rains down a trail of colorful sparks.

"I expected more from a hero troll," Swift goads me. "But I guess technique is more important than strength for spear throwing."

The centaurs are pretty good trash talkers, and they've been gloating all night. They must get a special pleasure from beating a hero at something.

I finish my drink and toss the mug aside. "I wouldn't count your dragons before they hatch."

Compared to all the centaurs competing in the spear toss, I've been in the middle of the pack each turn. But little do they know that I have a few tricks up my sleeve.

I pull one of the spears from the ground and ready my throw, calculating the best angle to release. Taking a deep breath, I cast Sacrifice, and all my horrors vanish in a puff of smoke. My muscles bulge as the added Strength and Dexterity floods my being.

I cock the spear behind my shoulder and take three steps, launching the weapon through the air. It arcs high into the night sky before sticking into the earth with a wet thud, some twenty meters further than the next closest.

Several centaurs murmur behind me.

I flex my muscles, giving my bicep a kiss before winking at Swift. "You were saying?"

He laughs. "Well done. Well done indeed."

"Thanks for the competition," I tell the group. "I might have won this bout, but I don't think there's any chance of me winning a footrace against any of you."

Several of them laugh and offer me congratulations before Swift and I step aside.

"I'm going to check on Taryn and call it a night. We'll head out first thing in the morning."

Swift leans in a little too close, and I can tell the mead has him feeling good. "If there is anything you need before you go, ask and it shall be done."

We grip one another's forearms, and then I head back down to the lake while the fairies retrieve the spears from the far end of the field.

I find Taryn at the edge of the lake, engaged in conversation with a group of centaurs. His pets sit around him in a circle like something out of a children's fairy tale. Three of the centaurs I recognize as Thannis, Daimun, and Sylvie, but the other I haven't met. He has gray fur and matching braids, much older than the other three. His torso is covered in tattoos, and he gives off an air of power and wisdom.

They all look in my direction as I approach, and it feels like I'm intruding.

I lift my hands to apologize. If Taryn doesn't want me around right now, I understand. "Sorry, I can come back later if I'm interrupting."

Taryn is the one to answer. "Nah, it's all good. We just finished up. I was actually about to come track you down to see how your spear throwing was going."

"Uh—" His casual tone catches me off guard, leaving me speechless for a moment. "Let's just say I did the trolls proud."

He says good-bye to the others and stands by my side. "There's something I wanted to talk to you about."

I'm not sure why, but it makes me nervous. After waving to the others, I follow Taryn a few paces away.

When we stop, he just stares at me, eyes focused like he's trying to find the words, but the uncomfortable silence wins out, forcing me to speak.

"So, what'd you ge—"

He wraps his arms around me and squeezes. I'm not sure what's happening or where this is coming from, but I return the gesture, gently patting him on the back until he releases.

"We're good. I just wanted to let you know." He lets go and wipes his eyes, unleashing a deep breath as he pulls down his tunic to show me the tattoo. "What do you think?"

A massive grin spreads across my face, and Taryn mirrors my expression. "Nice."

A bright orange carrot rests over his heart. The black outline is thick and pronounced, while there are fine details accented with blue and green ink.

"It looks amazing. Did it hurt?"

His smile spreads even wider, revealing his pearly white teeth. It's the most genuine smile I've seen from him in a while. "It hurt, but it was one of the most amazing experiences of my life."

We grab a drink and walk around the perimeter of the lake while he tells me about the tattoo and the potion that reconnected him with Stompy. "It was hard to watch, but Stompy forced me to. In the end, I think it helped."

I offer him a half-smile. "I know I can't relate to what you're going through, but I'm glad you were able to find some semblance of closure. He was a great pet."

"That he was." Taryn takes a long swig, leaving beads of mead in his mustache when he's done. "But now it's time to focus on the present, clearing the forest and finding our way back to a big city. Maybe finding some adventure that doesn't revolve around psychopaths trying to kill us."

"I second that. Let's try to pry Limery away from his new friends and get some rest. I have a feeling tomorrow is going to be a hell of a day."

The next morning, I wake up to the squawk of some demonic-sounding birds. Their shrill call cuts through my restful sleep like a jagged blade. Sunlight spills through the open roof in streaks between the tall canopy.

Limery sits up on my chest, one eye still shut and the other halfway open.

"Good morning, party animal." I grin, scooping him up and setting him on the ground. "You enjoyed yourself last night."

Taryn peeks out from beneath his cloak, dreadlocks concealing most of his face. "Let's be real, Limery enjoys himself every night."

Limery shakes his head, and his body goes molten for half a second. Pieces of hay catch fire, but the imp looks as fresh as ever.

That's one way to cure a hangover.

I pat the flames and quickly extinguish them. "Let's not burn the village down before we leave."

He rubs his belly. "Limmy hungries."

We quickly gather ourselves and set out, the smell of roasted meat luring us through the village until we find a group of centaurs eating breakfast. Half a dozen fairies cook over several small fires. One pan crackles with what looks like bacon. Vegetables roast in another. A fairy cracks open a green speckled egg, and a matching green yolk falls into the pan.

Berry hovers too close to the fire, drool dripping from his mouth. Ruby sits on the bear's back, and Jordy clings to Taryn's side.

There's a chime as one of the fairies brings over a plate loaded with food and hands it to Limery.

Taryn throws up his hands. "What about the rest of us?"

Deep laughter comes from behind us. "Someone has made himself a friend of the fairies." Swift smiles as an equally big plate is handed to him. "How did you all sleep?"

I stretch my arms overhead and my back cracks audibly. "Surprisingly well, though your alarm isn't the most pleasant."

He laughs again. "Ah yes, the screeching pheasants can be...intense on the ears. But they lay the most delicious eggs." He stabs at the green eggs with a two-pronged fork before taking a bite. "I hope you are well-rested for your quest."

I say thanks to the fairy as it hands me a plate, and I take a seat on the ground. "We're excited to see what we can do to help."

The eggs are surprisingly good. There's a spice I can't quite place that's somewhat sweet and savory at the same time. The eggs give me a Wisdom bonus for one hour, but the real delight is the warthog bacon, which gives me a nice Constitution bonus.

Item. *Screeching Pheasant Eggs.* *+1 Wisdom for one hour.*

Item. *Warthog Bacon.* *+1 Constitution for one hour.*

Not a bad buff just for eating breakfast. The fairies must be doing something to give the food the added bonuses.

After breakfast, Taryn shows off his tattoo to Swift and some of the others. After seeing so many centaurs at the lake last night, the village feels almost empty this morning. Even though it's surrounded by a wall of fog, the village has to stretch further into the forest than I imagined with its sprawling fields, tall trees, and lush vegetation. I'm not even a hundred percent sure that this is the only village within the boundary.

Before we head out, Swift meets us back in our stable as we gather our belongings. "Before you leave, I have a final gift to help you on your quest. I do not share this information with just anyone, so use this knowledge wisely."

I wait anxiously as he touches me on the temple. There's a flutter of energy from his fingers, much the same as when Chief Rizza gave me my first quest, and then dozens of dots populate on the map in the corner of my vision.

He touches Taryn in the same manner. "These are the holes we have discovered. They spread by the day, but this should give you a starting point."

I rub my hands together in excitement. This is a game-changer.

I zoom in on the map until it takes up the majority of my vision. Where before, only brief sections of the forest were visible, it's now as detailed as a blueprint. The entirety of the hidden village, the lake, and all of the herd's outposts are marked all the way to the forest boundary. There are also veins that stretch out from the lake marked in a light blue. They snake throughout the forest but are most concentrated within the village. Those must be the channels of life aura.

"Wow." Taryn's eyes are distant and unfocused. "This will be super helpful."

I hear hoofbeats down the path outside before Thannis pokes his head in. "I must be heading off soon to scout our boundaries, but I wanted to offer you a parting gift while you complete the quest. I believe you will gain more use from it than we will currently."

He pulls the amulet he used in the forest from his satchel and hands it to me. It's surprisingly heavy for being so small. The yellow stone glows gently in the center of the bronze starburst.

Item. *Amulet of Sight.* *An amulet capable of revealing surroundings for thirty yards in all directions for a total of two hours per day, however, it is incapable of bypassing celestial or infernal obstructions. Remaining Sight: 120 minutes.*

I place the amulet around my neck and feel its warmth against my chest. "Thank you, Thannis. I'm sure this will prove valuable with our quest."

"I wish you all good fortune." His tail flicks as he turns around. "I must be going now. The work never ends."

On our way to the boundary of the village, we make a quick stop by the lake. Smoke continues to bubble and plume from the center of the lake, where the faint green aura can still be seen surrounding the raft containing the dragon egg. I count eight centaurs standing sentry around the edge of the lake, spears or bows held at their sides.

Swift heads to the wall of fog. "Do not worry, the egg will be well-guarded while you are away."

When we step through the barrier, I understand what he means. Every hundred yards along the boundary, a centaur stands guard. There is no way anyone or anything is making it into the village without them noticing.

I raise my brow. "All of this for a dragon egg?"

Swift's face goes stern. "A dragon can turn the tide of any battle. They can lay siege to castles and have been the rise and fall of kingdoms. Do not forget that. Good luck with your quest. The fate of Wandermere lies with you all."

There's nothing to say to that. With a final look at the centaur and the fog, we set out in the direction of the closest marked hole.

8. WHAT LIES BENEATH

I pull up the map, focusing on the locations Swift has marked while Taryn does the same. "You seeing what I'm seeing?"

The longer I stare at it, the more confident I am that there's a pattern to the hole formations. There's a sizable gap from the portal to the first set of holes, which I can't quite explain, but then they spread out in an arc. After the initial holes, they all seem to be expanding in the direction of the Hidden Lake, almost like a triangle. There are a few sections that break off midway as if they weren't sure which way to go, but then the trend continues toward the village.

The distant look fades from Taryn's eyes, and he focuses on me. "Yeah, it looks like they're expanding in our direction."

I run my finger over my tusk as I ponder on what might have caused this to happen. "I'm guessing that once the centaurs retreated from their outposts, the shadow monsters could sense the movement. Either that or they're being drawn to the life aura of the lake."

Taryn strokes his beard, the clasps jingling slightly. "Makes sense. Regardless of the reason, I say we meet them head-on. If we can manage to push them back, I think it will be a lot easier."

I equip Destroyer and give it a twirl in my palm. "Sounds like a plan. Want to hit us with a little druid speed boost?"

Taryn raises his staff and a moment later, Strong Wind takes effect, increasing our speed as we travel through the foggy forest. I cast Spirit Guide and allow it to lead the way, clearing our sight for at least a few extra feet in front of us. With only two hours of visibility from the Amulet of Sight each day, it seems smarter to save it for when we might really need it.

As long as we stay focused, traveling is easy, but taking my eye off the path for even a moment results in a surprise branch to the face more than once.

I keep a full army of horrors ready just to be safe, summoning replacements as soon as they expire. Limery disappears occasionally, soaring into the treetops after an unfortunate bird. Knowing where most of the holes are, I'm not as worried about him now, especially if he keeps to the air—not to mention I think he'd be pretty spicy for anything bold enough to try and eat him.

After a couple of hours, we arrive at the first hole. It has the same impenetrable darkness as the ones Thannis showed us. I'm careful not to lean too close over this one and risk French kissing whatever waits inside. About fifty feet behind it, there are two more.

Once we check the surroundings, I send a Horror of Finesse down into the hole. Being the smallest of the three horrors, it should have the easiest time exploring. It's inside for about two seconds before its presence vanishes entirely.

"Something's definitely in there." No sooner have I finished the sentence before a puff of smoke wafts out.

"What happened?" Taryn holds his staff at the ready in case something climbs out.

I shrug. "No idea. My horror was in there, and then it vanished."

"Hmm. So do we want to try to lure it out or kill it inside?"

I take a quick peek into the hole and then step back. "We don't even know what we're dealing with or how many might be in each hole. I think we've got to lure it out in order to know for sure."

He raises his eyebrows. "And how exactly do you propose we do that?"

The twitching leaves on Taryn's Sapling Staff give me an idea. "Do you think you can send the vines on your staff in there and get a gauge of how deep the hole goes?"

"Ugh, it's a good idea, but I don't like it." Taryn frowns. "Playing tug of war with a giant tongue trying to steal my staff doesn't sound like a good time."

I shudder at the memory of the tongue. "I have a feeling we might be doing a lot of things we don't like before this quest is completed."

Taryn climbs down from Berry and gets into position about six feet from the edge of the hole. He takes a deep breath, then the vines on his staff slowly extend into the darkness.

After about thirty seconds, the vines quit growing. "That's as far as they will go. Either the holes are connected or that hole is at least thirty feet deep. Whatever's in there doesn't seem to care about inanimate objects, though." The vines begin to retract back into his staff.

I walk over to the other two holes and look inside. They're just as dark and ominous as the first.

I summon more horrors. "Alright, let's see if we can flush it out. Can you summon your fungus around the other two holes to alert us if anything exits? If these holes are connected, we don't want to be attacked unaware."

A minute later, Taryn gives me the go-ahead and I send my ten oldest horrors into the hole. The first one vanishes from my awareness. As soon as it does, I cast

Kamikaze on the rest. The ground vibrates for a second before the entrance to the hole collapses on itself from the horrors' explosion.

For a moment, the forest is quiet, and then I hear the gassy release of Taryn's poisonous mushrooms.

"Get ready, both holes just activated," Taryn yells.

"That's what she said!" This isn't the time for crude humor, but the opportunity was too good to pass up.

I send my horrors out into the fog surrounding the other two holes, and several of them vanish immediately.

"We need visibility now, Chod!" Taryn shouts.

I don't hesitate, activating the Amulet of Sight. A gust of wind rushes out from me, pushing back the fog for thirty feet in all directions. Leaves and dirt blow away, but there are no monsters in our immediate vicinity.

"To the other holes." Taryn urges Berry forward, and I follow beside him. The fog pushes back with each step I take.

I can hear whispers up ahead, the same ones I heard at the first hole when the tongue attacked me. Gripping Destroyer tightly, I press forward until a shadowy presence comes into view at the boundary of the amulet.

Three giant orbs of smoke hover in the air.

My heart beats faster as I take another step. The amulet pushes back the smoke surrounding the monsters, revealing them in all their grotesque glory. The core of the monsters are veiny, jelly-like sacks composed of nothing more than a mouth and claws. Each mouth is full of razor-sharp teeth and a long black tongue that nearly drags against the ground.

"Oh noes," Limery whispers.

Berry's low growl echoes the sentiment, and I completely agree. Goosebumps prickle along my arms.

Mesmer Wisp. *Level 24. Molded in the depths of the shadowlands, these wisps are far more deadly than their light-based counterparts. Mesmer wisps lure enemies with enticing whispers, putting them into a trancelike state before absorbing them into their amorphous bodies. After reaching peak size, wisps split in two, forming a collective with a hive mind. Underneath their shadowy silhouette, these wisps sport powerful claws used for digging interconnected burrows and a long, powerful tongue capable of subduing victims until they are ingested.*

The whispers call to me, and my grip on Destroyer slackens. The wisps aren't fast, but they approach with ominous intent. I take a step toward them. Distantly, Limery and Taryn call to me.

With each step, drool drips from the wisps' monstrous mouths, their veiny bodies pulsing like some alien spawn.

Lightning crashes between them, and their bodies glow with electricity for a moment before the whispers fade and my mind suddenly clears. I step back, sending my horrors at the creatures.

"Chod, what the hell?" Concern radiates from Taryn.

I shake my head to fully clear my mind. "It's some kind of enchantment. Don't get too close to them."

The mesmer wisps pluck my horrors with their tongues like frogs catching a fly. I cast Kamikaze on the rest of my horrors before they are devoured, but it has little effect on the wisps. Limery hurls fireballs that are slightly more effective, taking out their health in minuscule chunks.

Taryn casts Moonbeam, and the stream of silver light coats one of the wisps. Its jelly-like orb of a body sizzles upon contact, and an ear-splitting shriek leaves my ears ringing.

When I'm able to focus again, I notice the wisp that took the blow lost a third of its health from that one attack. Its once-pulsing body now seems shrunken and drained.

My spirit guide stands by my side, its pupilless eyes radiating cold anger as it paws at the ground. Streams of ethereal energy blast from its nostrils.

My ears quit ringing and I take a fighting stance, ready to smash these wisps into jelly. "Your Moonbeam must be extra effective on them."

Enraged by the attack, the wisps press forward, but they halt when they enter the radius of my spirit guide's light, hissing at the goat before retreating.

The three wisps disappear into the fog, but we don't pursue. We need to regroup and plan now that we have more information.

"Holy shit." I crouch and take a deep breath. "Those things were creepy."

Limery frowns in the direction of the retreating wisps. "Oh yes, Limmy no likes the scary monsties. They whispers for Limmy to come play, but Limmy no wants to."

Taryn grimaces. "That's probably a good idea, little man. How do those things even float in the air? The tongue is bigger than the body."

I shrug. "I have no idea, but your Moonbeam seemed to be the only thing that did any real damage."

He scrunches his brow for a moment, deep in thought. "They seemed wary of your spirit guide, too. Do you think they count as undead? That would explain the extra damage my attack did. Too bad it's not night, or I would get an even bigger bonus."

That's right, Moonbeam deals double damage to undead and fifty percent additional damage at night. "You think there's any way we can use that to our advantage?"

"Probably, but then that means we're fighting these bastards at night, where they probably have some advantages of their own." He looks up as if tracking the daylight left, even though the sun barely breaches the dense canopy.

"Right, we still have a lot of day left. Let's see what we can find out about their burrows." I stand and walk over to the two holes we didn't destroy, deactivating the amulet to conserve its power. With the wisps gone, I can see directly into the tunnels with no issues for the first time. "Limery, want to go on an adventure?"

Limery's bulbous yellow eyes flash with excitement. "Oh yes, Limmy loves adventures."

His grin fades when he finds out what the adventure entails.

I send him down into the holes to figure out how far they go and if there are any offshoot tunnels that connect to more of the mesmer wisps. After a couple of minutes, Limery pops out of the second hole covered in dirt.

He coughs before going molten and burning the dirt and debris from his skin.

"What'd you see?" I ask.

"The tunnelses only has two holeses. Limmy thinks theys was three but Chods exploded its."

"Good job." I turn to Taryn. "If all of the tunnels aren't connected, just the ones close to one another, then they likely travel in pods. If we can figure out how to hurt them, we can take them out one pod at a time."

Taryn nods. "I like it. A lot less dangerous than trying to fight too many at once."

We make our way to the next closest set of holes. Once again, there are three within a relatively close vicinity, and I can't help but wonder if there is some significance to that.

I take a quick peek into the hole, where the same impenetrable darkness stares back at me. Soft whispers call to me before I take a step back. "They're definitely in there. Whether they're the ones from before or a whole new batch, there's no telling."

Using the amulet for only a moment, I activate it to push back the fog and leaves. When I deactivate it, there's about a thirty-second break before the fog comes rushing back in. It's a good way to get a look at the area without wasting much power.

I point to the holes in the back. "If there was a way to block off those two back holes, then we could try to flush the wisps out of the front entrance."

Taryn climbs down from Berry and walks over to the two furthest holes. He moves his fingers through the air as if measuring something out. Then a mischievous grin spreads underneath his mustache, curling it up at the edges. "I think I've got a plan."

9. WHISPERS

I send a horror into each of the furthest two holes from where we approached, keeping a careful perception on their presence as they crawl into the tunnels. It doesn't take long before one vanishes, soon followed by the other. I wait a moment before testing again. This time, I have the horrors wait just inside the entrance. They sit there undisturbed until I instruct them to go deeper into the holes. Each time, the horrors vanish once they go deeper, but the wisps never attack those at the edge.

Only when I approach the holes do the wisps seem to move closer to the entrance. It's as if they can sense my body but aren't attracted to the horrors.

I step back to where I believe the wisps can't sense me. "Looks like the wisps are hanging out about ten feet from the entrance to each hole."

Taryn summons a ring of poisonous mushrooms inside the first tunnel and then moves to the next. Once the cooldown is up, he summons mushrooms inside the second hole, rotating between the two until fungi surround all edges of both entrances.

While he does this, I equip Forlorn Scepter. I used it with great success back in the troll forest when we were fighting Glenn. The weapon's passive ability gives me fifty percent increased range for summoning.

It allows me to summon horrors inside the tunnels just out of reach of Taryn's mushrooms and far enough away not to disturb the wisps.

Taryn casts Stonewall over one entrance and then the other, leaving the front entrance as the only viable exit. The rest of the group—spirit guide included—all stand guard at the one open hole. I continue summoning horrors but only make it to four in each tunnel before I feel one of them vanish.

"Showtime!" I call to the others as a chain reaction of disappearing horrors goes down each tunnel.

I cast Kamikaze on the last remaining horror in each tunnel. The ground shakes slightly and purple gas seeps around the edges of Taryn's walls as his mushrooms activate. I run back to the others, equipping Destroyer just as a loud shriek echoes underground.

A thick ball of smoke emerges from the tunnel, and I quickly activate the Amulet of Sight. A gust of wind pours out, ripping the smoke from around the monstrous jelly being. It snarls before lashing its tongue at Limery.

Jordy charges, ramming into the wisp just as the dangerous tongue whips inches from Limery's face. The wisp barely budges as Jordy slams into it. Instead, its jelly exterior wraps around the frost goat. Ripples surge through the wisp's body, burying Jordy's head and neck inside its gelatinous membrane while the goat's hind legs thrash.

Taryn yells as Moonbeam cuts almost silently through the air, hitting the wisp dead on. Its translucent skin sizzles under the silver beam and its health plummets, forcing it to release Jordy as its mouth contorts with a violent scream.

My ears ring from the wisp's anguished cries. I take a step forward and bring Destroyer down on the wisp, expecting it to explode like a water balloon. The warhammer has little effect, lodging inside the gelatinous blob. The monster's tongue snakes down the handle of the weapon and up my arm before I have a chance to let go, gripping me with surprising strength. It continues to writhe up my arm, wrapping around my shoulder as I try to free myself. Pain flares along my arm and hundreds of needles stab me all at once.

Limery's yelling sounds distant as he peppers the wisp in fire. I lose focus as whispers surround me and two more mesmer wisps emerge from the tunnel.

A second tongue wraps around my neck as I continue to struggle with the first. It squeezes, cutting off my air supply until my vision darkens at the edges. I dig the claws of my left hand into the tongue but it only clenches tighter, while my right arm has gone completely numb. Sharp pain pierces my side as claws rake against my ribs, then a cold substance spreads over my hand and along my midsection. Panic flares through me as I realize that the second wisp is trying to absorb me into its body.

The more I struggle, the weaker I feel. The pain in my ribs grows more intense, but there is nothing I can do. It's like I'm trapped in a riptide, unable to escape.

Then, the pressure suddenly fades, and the tongue releases me from its embrace. I fall to the ground, gasping for air.

Limery hovers next to me, completely covered in silver goo. His bulbous eyes are full of worry, but his mouth is set in firm determination. He says something, but my ears are still ringing.

Two tongues lay motionless on the ground next to me, and the final wisp snarls at Taryn between lashes. My spirit guide steps forward, and the wisp unleashes another ear-splitting screech. Limery turns, body going molten as he darts into the wisp's open mouth. A Moonbeam hits the wisp at the same time as Limery flies down its throat. The jelly-like surface of the wisp erupts into boils, and a second later, it explodes.

I collapse to the ground, and pain pulses along my ribs while the ringing in my ears slowly fades.

A warm tongue licks me on the cheek, and I open my eyes to see Berry hovering over my head.

Taryn finishes casting Restoration on Jordy and then kneels beside me, examining my arm. "Are you okay? Those things really got a hold of you."

I sit up, and Limery perches on my shoulder, examining the dozens of tiny puncture marks that run up and down my right arm where the wisp's tongue was wrapped around me. Gashes cover my tender midsection.

Limery frowns. "Chods needs to bes more careful."

I gently press against my ribs before downing a health potion. "I'll be fine. I think Jordy and I both learned that we aren't going to power our way through this. How did you two manage to kill them, anyhow?"

Taryn kicks one of the tongues and it curls in on itself like a dead snake. "Moonbeam hits them like a knife through warm butter. The only problem is the cooldown. Limery's fireballs aren't that effective against their outsides, but he basically boiled them alive from inside, so I'm guessing they have some kind of magical resistance to their exteriors. I'm not sure what the deal is with your spirit guide, but whenever it gets close to them, it's like the wisps are in pain. They lose focus on whatever they are attacking until they are out of its range."

I cancel Amulet of Sight and crouch next to one of the tongues. Upon closer inspection, each tongue is covered in suction cups, almost like an octopus tentacle, except the edges are serrated. That explains the stabbing sensation. If these creatures are able to consume living beings by absorbing them through their bodies and can also drain them directly using their tongues, then they're even more deadly than I originally thought. It's like their entire purpose is to feed.

Jordy and I are lucky to be alive right now. If not for Taryn, Limery, and my spirit guide, we might not be. They're going to be integral to completing this quest.

I shiver at the memory of the tongue entangled around my neck. "Maybe we can find a way to use the spirit guide to our advantage. Once I'm healed enough, let's take what we learned and use it on the next pod, since we've still got a couple hours of daylight left. I'll be sure to stand far enough back next time."

While my wounds heal, I summon more horrors. By the time we arrive at the next set of holes, I have thirty horrors ready to go. The holes are spread out in the same triangle pattern. They remind me of a beehive with the way they all seem perfectly positioned to one another.

I send ten horrors into each hole. Once the first one vanishes, I explode the other nine in each tunnel. The tunnels collapse, blocking the exits and trapping the wisps in the center until they use their claws to dig straight to the surface.

The ground caves in near the center, and two claws poke through. Taryn catches the first wisp with a sustained Moonbeam as it squeezes through the small hole, killing it before it ever completely emerges. The cooldown allows the other two time to crawl out. They slowly climb through Limery's Firewall but only lose a fraction of their health. My spirit guide flanks the wisps, keeping enough distance to scare them away but close enough to prevent them from escaping into the fog.

The wisps screech and snarl when they get too close to my spirit guide, but they refocus on us as I feed the wisps horrors to keep them engaged until Moonbeam is ready to go again. It's a game of patience but eventually, we take them all out.

We try several tactics over the next few hours, with some having more success than others. For my horrors, Kamikaze is the only attack that deals any damage, and it's the least effective of our party's magical attacks. I switch to Petrified Staff and use the gnarled staff's passive ability to shoot ranged physical attacks, but it's about as effective as flies attacking a crocodile.

Limery's fireballs and Firewall do minimal damage to the wisps' exteriors, but attacks to an open mouth are effective. These creatures have an insane magical resistance and their jelly-like bodies combined with a lack of internal organs make physical attacks almost useless. Any physical attacks to their bodies lodge inside like they are trapped in quicksand. Even removing a tongue from a wisp does little to hamper it because they can still absorb my horrors through their bodies.

For the first time, Taryn seems to be the strongest one in the group. His Lightning Bolt is more effective than Limery's fire, but Moonbeam is the star of the show. However, the cooldown on Moonbeam forces us to kite the wisps for far too long each time.

And then there's my spirit guide. It doesn't directly damage the wisps, but something about it causes them to retreat. Maybe because it's the antithesis of their shadowy nature. We lose several wisps to the depths of the forest due to my spirit guide getting too close, but anytime we're on the verge of losing, I'm able to call it in to save our asses.

Wherever the runaway wisps go, we're unable to track them. There are never more than three wisps in each pod, so they have to be going somewhere. I get the uneasy feeling that they'll all catch up to us again at some point.

We manage to clear ten pods before nightfall, but there are still dozens more spread across the forest. As we make camp for the night, settling inside a fortress made from Taryn's Stonewalls, one thing I notice is the distinct lack of animal noise in the area. Far away, owls hoot and wolves howl, but there's nothing in our immediate vicinity aside from the whispering leaves.

I point it out to Taryn as I lean against the cool stone. "Strange, right?"

He rests against Berry, using the bear's belly as a pillow. "Either the animals are staying away from the wisps, or they've all been absorbed."

I grimace at the thought. "Do you have to put it like that? Absorbed. The mental image is enough to give me the creeps."

His expression mirrors my own. "I'll be glad when we're done with this. I don't want to be the token Black guy from every horror movie that dies to the monsters in the woods. Get me to an inn with crackling bacon and flowing drinks."

"Limmy wants drinks and bacons." Limery rubs his hands together.

The thought of bacon and drinks has me salivating as well. Not to mention a comfortable bed. We can make do in the wilderness, but there's something about the city's amenities that makes life much more interesting.

I take the first watch while the others sleep. My spirit guide is extra bright in the enclosed space, so I cancel it for the time being to keep from waking the others.

Limery snores softly in the crook of my arm, a large snot bubble inflating with each breath. His demonic features look peaceful as he slumbers.

Leaves hiss as they rub against one another in the night breeze, and then I hear something else. Whispers. They're soft at first, but they grow louder until they surround us on all sides of our small fortress.

My pulse quickens, but I stay still. The walls are high enough to keep the wisps at bay. They might hover in the air, but I've yet to see one fly higher than a few feet off the ground. That doesn't mean it's not possible, so I keep my focus overhead.

For hours, the wisps call to me, whispering words I can't quite make out. But this time, it feels different. Maybe it's the wall that separates us, but I don't feel the same compulsive urge to join them.

The night drags on, and the whispers multiply until it's almost torturous. How many are out there, waiting for an opportunity to strike? Even though they aren't luring me the same as before, their whispers are causing a different reaction. I'm weary and on edge. I don't know if it's an effect from the wisps or if listening to half-formed words for several hours is slowly driving me insane.

At this point, I'm not sure how long they've been outside, but I don't know how much more I can handle. I lay Limery to the side without jostling him and crawl over to wake Taryn.

I tap him on the shoulder at the same time as one of the walls expires. Fog floods through the opening and conceals everything in sight, all the while the whispers grow louder, luring me out into the forest.

10. ONE STEP FORWARD, TWO STEPS BACK

Everything is distant and dark as I crawl through the opening where the wall used to be. Right now, the only thing that matters are the whispers calling to me, beckoning me into the comfort of darkness.

"Chod, snap out of it!" Taryn shouts.

A firm hand smacks me on the side of the head, bringing me back to my senses. I activate Amulet of Sight and both light and wind explode from my chest, revealing more wisps than I can count lurking outside our camp. Dozens of long tongues and spindly claws lash out, their grotesque bodies pulsing with dull energy.

The whispers call to me again, but they're cut off abruptly as Moonbeam hits a cluster of wisps and fireballs sail past my shoulder. Berry growls ferociously behind me.

In the moment of respite, I summon my spirit guide. Shrieks immediately echo across the forest from all directions as the wisps scatter into the darkness.

A second wall fades before Taryn has replaced the first, leaving us boxed in.

Limery and I stand guard in front of Taryn's pets. I summon more horrors in front of us, not that they can do much damage, and Limery hovers next to me, two fireballs in his palms.

We're still protected on two sides, but Taryn needs to get his walls up fast. My spirit guide circles our enclosure, a sentry of light, while Taryn replaces the walls one by one.

Limery's warm body presses against my shoulder. He grimaces. "Limmy no likes the monsties."

Taryn leans against the wall once he's finished and shudders. "There were so many of them. What the hell have we gotten ourselves into?"

I clap him on the shoulder. "Just another day in paradise."

"If this is paradise, I'm ready for the vacation to be over." Taryn shakes his head. "You need to rest, though."

"There's no way I'm sleeping after that."

"Take this." He grins as he pulls a vial of dull pink dust and tosses it to me.

Sleep Dust.

I laugh. "I guess that's one way to do it. I'll pass on the Dream Dust considering what's fresh on my mind."

"Look at you. Maybe there are some brains in that giant skull of yours." He winks as he strokes Ruby. "Limery and I will keep watch." He points a stubby finger in my direction. "You, get some sleep. I'm sure our new friends will be waiting for us in the morning."

This time, I leave the spirit guide outside our camp. I doubt the wisps will come anywhere near us with it around. I just wish I knew why they hated it so much.

All it takes is a pinch of the Sleep Dust, and I'm out like a light.

When I wake up, the walls are gone and I'm sprawled across the forest floor, groggier than I can ever remember being in-game.

"Chods is ups!" Limery calls from the tree above me.

A moment later, Taryn appears. "Might want to go easy on the Sleep Dust next time. There's no waking you up until it wears off. You don't even want to know the things we tried to get you up." He smirks.

Limery hovers in the air next to me. "Oh, yes. Chods had a big sleeps."

I stretch my arms and try to clear my head. The after-effects of too much Sleep Dust feel about the same as when I would get too much sleep back in the real world. My dad called it a sleep hangover, and he said it was a luxury of having too little ambition.

After a quick breakfast consisting of dried meat and bread from the Hidden Village, we head back toward the wisp burrows to start the day's work. The lack of animals in the area does have me slightly concerned about what we'll eat when our rations run out. The forest is still certainly full of life, but the question is how far will we have to travel in order to hunt?

Taryn curses, bringing Berry to a halt.

"Something wrong?" I ask.

He has a distant look in his eyes. "Pull up your map."

I look over the map carefully, double-checking to make sure my mind isn't playing tricks on me. "You've got to be shitting me."

Yesterday, we took out ten pods over the course of the day. A few wisps managed to escape due to my spirit guide's overbearing presence, but we cleared ten burrows. After they were cleared, a red X replaced the circles that had marked them on the map.

Looking at it now, half of the Xs are gone.

I turn to Taryn. "How is that possible?"

He shrugs. "I don't know, but we need to check it out."

He casts Strong Wind, boosting our speed, and we arrive where we were supposed to start today's work a short while later. A dark haze shrouds the entrance to the burrow, where the wisps wait inside.

We follow the path back to the previous burrow, the one that should be empty. When we arrive, the upturned earth and destruction from our battle remain, but not even twenty feet away, a new burrow has formed.

"Fuck." I kick a loose stone and it tumbles into the fog.

Taryn presses his fists to his eyes. "Could this be any more annoying? We spend half the day clearing these bastards out and they retake half their land back overnight. This is some grade-A bullshit."

Limery leaps from my shoulder, clenching his fist as he hovers in the air. "Yeah, this is somes grade-A bullshits."

Taryn looks up, a wide grin plastered on his face, but he doesn't say anything. He just gives me a knowing look.

I shrug. What's a curse word in the grand scheme of things? Limery drinks like a sailor and is fire made flesh. I just hope Lillith doesn't blame me for his bad behavior when all is said and done. I do not want to be on Limery's mother's bad side.

"I guess we go back and clear it all again. We've got a better understanding of how to deal with them this time. Plus, I've got an idea for the Sleep Dust."

By noon, we've retaken the lost ground, but we still have very little understanding of where these new wisps came from. We stop for lunch in a clearing, my spirit guide pushing back the fog for several feet in all directions.

Taryn rips off a piece of bread and gestures with it while he talks. "It's strange. If the wisps aren't leaving any of the burrows empty as they advance, and none of the ones we've cleared have had more than three wisps, then it means they're only expanding once they have new wisps. We know they are all connected, and their description said they split at peak size, but what does that really mean? Can they split at will or did they go out for a massive feast last night?"

I wish I knew the answer, but I think the only way we'd find out is if we're out in the open when they do their midnight marauding. So, with each wisp we defeat and burrow we clear, I keep my mind on the end goal, the reason we're out here to begin with—hatching a dragon.

After lunch, we get back to work. I pull up my inventory to see how many vials of Sleep Dust and Dream Dust I have.

I take one of each and display them in the air, shaking them in front of Taryn. "I've got ten vials of each, how about you?"

In addition, I also have several elixirs and potions, but I doubt their liquid state would work for what I have planned.

Taryn's eyes go vacant for a second before he answers. "Eleven vials of Dream Dust. Nine vials of Sleep Dust. What'd you have in mind?"

"I've got a few crazy ideas. We don't have the stock to use them at every hole, but if they work, it will be good to have them in our bag of tricks."

Taryn grins. "Alright, magic man. I'm sure this will be interesting."

I summon a Horror of Finesse and hand it an uncorked vial of Sleep Dust. I position it tilted in the horror's hand so that a small trail of dust falls out as it moves, then I send the horror into the tunnel.

Once my horror vanishes, I turn to Limery. "Will you do the honors?"

He summons a small fireball in his palm and tosses it at the trail of Sleep Dust. The line of dull pink glitter crackles to life, sending a streak of flame into the tunnel, followed soon after by an explosion that shakes the ground. A notification flashes in my vision, but I ignore it for now.

Two wisps emerge from the far holes, but the third is nowhere to be found. We finish them off much quicker than when we faced three at a time.

Now that the fight is over, I pull up the notification.

Congratulations! You have unlocked the skill 'Demolition.' You are now a level 1 Demolitionist (Novice). Increase your skill and learn advanced techniques for demolition by finding an advanced demolitionist (Apprentice or above). Crafting Ranks: Novice, Apprentice, Journeyman, Expert, Artisan, Master, Grandmaster.

Now that's a cool skill to have. I wonder what techniques I could learn at the higher levels.

At the next burrow, I do the same thing but use the Dream Dust.

Limery sets the glittery purple dust ablaze, and the explosion is twice as loud as the first. It's powerful enough to cave in the area around the explosion and send purple smoke pluming out of the other tunnels. Only one wisp survives this time, and Taryn quickly dispatches it with Moonbeam. I receive a second notification telling me I've leveled up my demolition skill again.

Taryn looks at me with wide eyes. "Bro, that was awesome. How'd you come up with that?"

"After you gave me the Sleep Dust last night, I remembered the fireworks display Limery and the fairies put on at the lake party. I figured it was pretty flammable, and it turns out I was right. I even unlocked a new skill for blowing shit up. We're saving this for emergencies, though."

Over the course of the day, we clear twenty-one burrows, more than double the previous day. Five of them we cleared for a second time, which feels like wasted progress, but at least I didn't get wrapped in killer tongues today.

When we make camp for the night, I station my spirit guide outside our enclosure to keep the mesmer wisps away. Taryn takes first watch, allowing him to replace his walls before waking me for my shift.

"Any whispers?" I ask as I rub the sleep from my eyes.

"Barely. Your spirit guide seems to be doing the trick. I can hear them out there, but they sound way more distant than last night." He snuggles in next to a snoring Berry. "By the way, you should really come up with a name for it. It's kept us safe enough to earn one."

"Heh, you might be right. I'll give it some thought."

He pulls his hood down over his eyes. "Glowy has a nice ring to it."

I roll my eyes. "Dude, go to sleep."

In a matter of minutes, Taryn is snoring in rhythm with Berry. Ruby lies curled up in his lap, and Jordy has his legs folded so compactly that he looks like he could be stuffed in a box and shipped.

Limery lies sprawled out along Berry's side, oblivious to the world.

Despite all of the pain and hardships of the last few weeks, I can't help but feel incredibly lucky to be here. The longer I get away from the real world, the less desire I have to ever go back. Mythos has plenty of challenges, but it has become my home, and everyone within these four walls are a part of my family.

I will do whatever it takes to protect that.

A gust of wind blows overhead, snapping a branch that crashes to the ground outside of our camp. Limery stirs and his bulbous yellow eyes squint open.

For a moment, I'm not sure if he's actually awake, but then he wipes his eyes and flies over to my shoulder.

"Time for watches," he grumbles.

"You can go back to sleep if you want. I think I can handle it tonight."

He looks up at me. "It's okays. Limmy likes to stays up with Chods."

"Good, I like staying up with you, too." I gently poke him in the stomach. "Can I ask you something, little man?"

He nods. "What is its?"

"When this is all over—when we've fought all the bad guys and things go back to normal—what do you want to do?"

He scrunches his brow while he thinks, tapping his lips with a sharp claw. "Hmm, Limmy likes adventures. He wants more adventures with Taryns and Chods."

"Don't you miss your family? Your mom and dad and brother."

"Oh yes." He clasps his hands together. "Limmy misses thems very much. Maybe one day Leo will comes on adventures with Limmy."

My mind wanders back to my earliest days in Mythos, back when I spent some time with Limery's family in their burrow. Leo had a fiery personality, that much I recall, but by the time Limery and I had returned from my quest, Leo had set off on his own grand adventure. I wonder what he's up to now.

"The world better watch out the day that happens." I laugh, and Limery grins. "Taryn thinks I need to come up with a name for my spirit guide. What do you think about that?"

"Limmy thinks the spirit guides needs a names. What does Chods want to names hims?"

"That is the question." I lean back against the wall.

Anything but Glowy.

Limery flies to the top of the wall and looks down at what I assume is my spirit guide. He scratches his chin before rejoining me. "Limmy doesn't knows what to names hims."

I wish I had Taryn's confidence to create the dumbest name and just roll with it. Back when I used to stream, picking a name at character creation was always the hardest part. I'd spend twice as long deciding on a name as I did picking out every minute feature on my character because I wanted the name to mean something.

Meanwhile, Taryn would play a paladin named Pete. His most popular character was a cleric named Bert McHealy.

For my spirit guide, I can finally make up for the fact that I had no say when the AI named me Chod.

I rack my brain thinking of names that conjure meanings of light or ghosts, from mythological names like Apollos and Hades to more quaint names like Aurora or Raiden. There are so many options, but in the end, one stands out above them all.

In school, I was a bit of a history nerd. I remember when our class studied the Seven Wonders of the Ancient World. Students gave presentations in front of the class about the Great Pyramid of Giza, the famous Hanging Gardens of Babylon, the Statue of Zeus, the Temple of Artemis, the Mausoleum at Halicarnassus, and the Colossus of Rhodes.

I was the final presentation that week. With a cracking voice and shaky hands, I told the class about the seventh wonder of the world. A lighthouse in Alexandria that served as a beacon to guide ships along the Mediterranean Sea. For centuries, it was one of the tallest man-made structures in the world. The lighthouse itself was located on a small island called Pharos, where the structure became so well-known that the name of the island was now synonymous with beacon or lighthouse.

And that's what my spirit guide is: a beacon of hope in dark times. A guiding force that can always lead us back home.

"Pharos," I whisper. "I'll call him Pharos."

11. FORGOTTEN QUESTS

"I still like Glowy better." Taryn crosses his arms, and after a moment, he smirks. "But this beats hearing you say 'spirit guide' a hundred times a day."

I roll my eyes at him and then pull up my map as we follow Pharos through the fog. Just as we anticipated, nearly half of the burrows we cleared yesterday have been retaken by the wisps. At this rate, we'll spend half of our time retaking lost ground.

We're three days in, and I can't help but wonder if there's been any progress with the dragon egg back at the Hidden Lake. The prospect of having my very own green dragon excites me every time I think about it. Isn't it every nerd's dream to have a pet dragon? And I might actually make it happen.

Strong Wind passes over me, and my legs move a little faster. A few streaks of light break through the treetops, like golden arrows piercing the dim underbelly. We make our way to the beginning of the reclaimed burrows so that we can eliminate those first. We want to keep the wisps as far away from the Hidden Village as possible, and if that means retaking lost ground every morning, then so be it.

At least the wisps are sticking to a predictable pattern. They never leave more than a hundred yards between burrows, and they never skip ahead to retake what they lost. We just need to clear the burrows faster than they can spread.

Over the course of the day, we manage to clear twenty-five burrows. Each day, we get a little better and quicker at eliminating the creepy monsters. Once we find a decent routine, it's all about kiting the wisps and keeping them engaged so that Taryn and Limery can damage them while also preventing them from retreating into the fog.

This time, we only manage to lose one wisp due to Pharos' getting too close.

Each day feels like a grind, but we make steady progress until we are clearing thirty burrows a day. After over a week, the end seems like it's finally in sight.

When we make camp for the night, I check the map again. "With a little luck, we might clear the last of them tomorrow."

Taryn shakes his head and the clasps in his beard jingle. "There's about thirty burrows left, not to mention that we'll have at least a dozen or so retaken by morning. I think we're looking at at least two more days, and then we can all get the hell out of here."

"Yeah, thens we's can gets the hells out of here," Limery echoes.

"Not without a dragon." I grin.

"Oh, yes. Limmy wants to play with the baby dragons. We can makes fires and fly high in the trees and chase all the birdses." His bulbous eyes flare with excitement.

"Ha, whatever you say, little man." I lean back against Taryn's wall once our camp is set for the night. "You guys get some sleep. I'll take first watch tonight."

The nights have gotten more peaceful since our first encounter with the wisps that wanted to cuddle us in the dark. Thanks to Pharos's nightly patrol around the encampment, the whispers sound further away than ever. Soon, they'll be gone altogether.

My mind wanders as I watch the others sleep until a loud scream carries across the forest.

"Help!" a deep voice yells. "Spawn of the shadowlands! Oh, gods, help! Heee—"

The words cut off, leaving the forest in silence aside from the pounding in my ears.

I crawl over and shake Taryn awake as fast as I can. "Get up, there's someone out there that needs our help. It sounded like they were attacked."

He gives me a confused look. "What are you talking about?"

I grab Taryn by the shoulders and shake him until the sleep fades from his eyes, waking up all of his pets and Limery in the process. "Listen to me. I heard a man screaming for help. I don't know why they would be out here at this hour, but I can't stand by and do nothing. Cancel your walls so that we can go check on him." The memory of my body entangled in the wisps sends chills down my spine. "If the wisps have him then we don't have much time."

Limery must sense my urgency because small flames sprout along his body.

"That way!" I point in the direction I heard the screaming. "Fly ahead with Pharos. We'll be right behind you."

Limery and Pharos take off into the fog, and Taryn and I follow close behind. Branches smack me across the chest as I run blindly through the forest.

"You sure this isn't a trick by the wisps?" he asks.

After getting entranced by the wisps on more than one occasion, I'm far from certain. But if there is someone out there, we have to help, so I keep my doubts to myself. "I'm sure. There was definitely someone out there."

"Chods! I found hims," Limery calls from up ahead.

He hovers high in the air next to a green cloak that's crumpled on the ground. Two large clouds of fog surround the lump, long tongues wrapped around it like snakes constricting the life from a mouse.

Pharos charges into the wisps, his ethereal body passing through them and dispersing the smoke that conceals them. Blood-curdling shrieks claw at my ears, but the wisps release their victim and disappear deeper into the fog.

Pharos stands protectively over the unmoving figure, his eyes glaring intensely where the wisps vanished.

With so much fog, even my night vision is unable to penetrate across the forest. I activate Amulet of Sight to clear the area, and wind and light pour out from me. At the edge of the boundary, the amulet reveals the grotesque features of a half-dozen wisps. Their tongues lash and claws grasp in our direction.

Pharos charges a few steps, and screams rip through the night as the wisps vanish into the darkness.

"Ungh." There's movement under the cloak and a large red head pokes out with a braided beard that drapes across the ground.

Emrak Stonebraid
Level ???
Ivory Dwarf
First Ranger of Seascape

The ivory dwarf's clothing is in tatters, and scrapes and scratches run along his arms and neck from the wisps. His leather armor is caked with blood from where the wisps raked their claws across his midsection. Strands of hair escape what I imagine is normally an immaculately-kept beard, and there's dirt smudged across his brow and clothing. He grunts as he stumbles to his feet, face stricken with worry.

"Oh, gods," Emrak says weakly, looking back over his shoulder.

Taryn climbs down from Berry and pulls a health potion from his satchel. "Here, take this." He hands the vibrant red potion to the dwarven ranger. "What the hell is a dwarf doing in Wandermere? You're a long way from home."

Emrak's eyes go wide when he notices Taryn, then he gulps down the potion. "Gods, you're a tough lot to catch. I've been tracking you all the way from Goldspire."

"What for?" I ask.

"I've a message from the king." He looks over his shoulder. "What in the dwarven hell are those things doing in Wandermere? I thought these lands were protected by the centaurs. Those monsters nearly sucked the life out of me." He shivers as he finishes the potion.

Taryn takes the empty vial and stuffs it back in his satchel. "Those monsters were mesmer wisps. They lure their victims with whispers and then drain the life from them. From what we've heard, shadow monsters are appearing through various portals all across Mythos. These wisps have spread across Wandermere like a parasite, and we're on a quest to eliminate them."

I pat the dwarf on the back and shoulders, wiping some of the dirt from his cloak. "I had a pretty close encounter myself not too long ago. The potion should heal the wounds from their tongues in no time."

He squints as he takes me in, his eyes lingering on my horns. "You've changed quite a bit since you were in Seascape. I hope it wasn't something you ate."

I don't remember meeting Emrak personally while I was in Seascape, but there were more dwarves than I could count in the city for the king's quest. Being First Ranger, he might have even been in the castle.

I decide to have a little fun with him regardless, so I reach up and touch my horns, gasping as if I didn't know they were there. "Where did these come from? It must be a side-effect from the wisps."

His eyes look like they are about to bulge out of his head before Taryn and I burst into laughter.

"I'm kidding. You said you had a message from the king?"

He scowls at both of us as he pulls a piece of rolled parchment from inside his cloak. "As First Ranger for King Orso, I am often sent abroad to deliver messages to those who don't want to be found. Before the portals opened, that meant the lands below the Greystone Mountains. In light of recent events, my skills have been tested further." He turns from me to Taryn. "No offense to our dwarven hero, but this message pertains to Chod, Hero of the Forest Trolls."

"Ands the mountains and arctics trolls," adds Limery.

"Very well," acknowledges Emrak. He hands me the scroll.

A wax seal depicting an axe and warhammer crossed over one another remains intact. I break it and unroll the parchment, wondering what kind of message the king could have for me but not Taryn.

Chod,

I hope your adventures find you well. There has been barely a moment to catch my breath since the portal opened in Seascape Square. Your actions in opening the portal are precisely why I have sent my most trusted ranger, Emrak Stonebraid, to hand-deliver this message.

In the ensuing chaos of the portal's reopening, certain promises and rewards have remained unfulfilled. I promised a dwarven keep and all attendant lands to whoever managed to complete the quest to open the portal. You held up your end of the quest, and it is high time I did the same. Therefore, I am awarding Chod, Hero of the Forest and Mountain Trolls, the keep at Tawdrybluff.

Traditionally, one would be granted dominion over all attended lands within its borders, answering to Seascape in stately and legal matters. You would be responsible for taxes, and to provide those of fighting ability in times of war. However, you are not a dwarven citizen and these are not normal times.

In your absence, a large force of forest and mountain trolls now reside in Seascape as we make preparation for what is coming. If you accept, I would propose that they be given Tawdrybluff Keep to rule in your stead as a sovereign nation until you return. This will cement an official alliance between dwarves and trolls, and allow the trolls to have a societal outpost in the north. Chief Rizza and her council have given their consent, but the final word is yours. Please give your response to First Ranger Emrak with haste.

-King Orso Brightgaze

A notification flashes in the corner of my vision, but I read the letter three times before acknowledging it. I'd completely forgotten about the reward for King Orso's quest. Hell, I thought since I activated it accidentally that I wouldn't receive anything at all. It wasn't like I thought jumping into the portal would trigger the forest troll's blessing and open the whole thing up. It was pure dumb luck.

I pass the letter to Taryn and pull up my notification.

Quest Alert. *You have completed the quest "Open the Portal."*

Reward: *Dwarven keep and all attendant lands.*
Please return to Seascape to claim your reward from King Orso Brightgaze.

As Taryn reads through the letter, his eyes get wider and wider. When he's done, he stares at me, his mouth hanging open.

"He gave you a castle," he says dryly.

"Well, technically, it's a keep." I grin.

"Don't give me that. The keep is the heart of a castle, and you get all the attendant lands. That means lands necessary to keep it functioning. So unless there is a keep out in the middle of nowhere with no walls and no buildings inside those walls, then you are getting a fucking castle." He rubs his fingers through his dreadlocks and sighs. "How are you this damned lucky? It's like you're the protagonist in a fantasy novel."

I gently pat him on the back. "Don't worry, bud. Your time will come."

He pushes me in the side. "So, you gonna do it?"

I stare off into the darkness as I ponder his question. When I first logged in, the forest trolls were on the verge of extinction. They were hunted on sight and never left the boundary of the forest. And now here we are, being offered a castle and an alliance with the dwarves. How could I possibly turn that down?

"Yeah, I'm going to do it." I turn to Emrak. "You can tell King Orso I accept his proposal, but I would advise you to camp with us tonight for your own safety."

12. MONEY CAN'T BUY HAPPINESS, BUT IT CAN BUY ITEMS

I have a hard time falling asleep once we set up camp again. My head is filled with visions of a castle where a massive dragon perches on the watchtower. Calling it excitement would be an understatement. Things are definitely looking up for old Choddy-boy.

Will my new achievements open up more opportunities or will it put an even bigger target on my back?

If I'm able to give out quests, then maybe I could use it as a recruitment base to gather more heroes. Only time will tell.

Pressley the Death Knight briefly crosses my mind. He wanted a castle so bad that he partnered with that shady cleric to get one. I wonder what he's up to right now. Is he still in Goldspire, or has he set his sights on treasure elsewhere? Wherever he is, he's going to be jealous once he discovers I got a castle before him.

I open my eyes and notice Emrak is having a hard time sleeping as well. It probably has something to do with the ordeal he just went through, so I offer him a pinch of Sleep Dust. I take one for myself and in a matter of seconds, it's lights out.

When we wake up, Taryn has a small fire going with eggs roasting in a pan. Considering I don't feel as groggy this morning, I think I did a much better job with the Sleep Dust.

Taryn waves his spatula at me. "Limery thought you all deserved a proper breakfast. He flew deep enough into the forest to find some eggs."

"I'm in your debt." Emrak bows slightly. "I've been eating nothing but bread, cheese, and dried meat for the past week."

Taryn laughs. "Must be a hard life."

Emrak smiles. "I know I sound like a spoiled elf." He takes a seat around the fire. "No one tells you that you get used to the finer things in life. You become soft and you forget what it took for you to get there to begin with. I might be stronger and more accomplished than I ever was, but in my younger days, I traveled far and wide. My reputation was forged in the fires of adventure. Every meal I hunted with my own hands." He balls his hand into a fist and squeezes. "I drank swill with the common folk, not from barrels that cost more than they'd ever hope to earn in their lives. I would have killed for a block of cheese and stale bread on some of those trips, and now here I am complaining about it."

Taryn hands him a plate with a fried egg. "Awareness is half the battle."

He shrugs. "Doesn't make it any less true. If you want my advice, don't settle down just because you have a castle now. It'll be waiting for you when you're old. There's far too much of the world out there waiting to be adventured. There's a reason politics are an old man's game."

I take a seat next to him, and Limery brings me a plate of food. I offer my thanks before returning to Emrak's conversation. "I'll keep that in mind. Don't be too hard on yourself. If you worked for everything you have, then you have a right to enjoy it. No one is promised tomorrow."

Emrak bursts out laughing and pieces of egg fall into his beard.

"What's so funny?" I ask.

"Wise words coming from a hero. You lot have more lives than an alley cat. How many times have you died now?"

His words catch me off guard. Of course, it's not the same for me. I might come back, but every death takes me further from my objectives. Being here in Wandermere has made that even more apparent. How long would it have taken the wisps to overtake the entire forest had we not shown up when we did? The centaurs and fairies could have possibly fortified the Hidden Village, but how long could that hold when access to the portal would be closed off? By the time they would have formed a plan to fight back, it'd be too late.

Threats like this are why heroes exist.

I suddenly lose my appetite. "I've died too many times already, and I can't afford to die another."

Emrak eats the rest of his meal in silence. When he's finished, Taryn takes the plate.

"Don't mind him. Sometimes he needs to brood." He lets Berry lick the plate before stuffing it in his bag.

True to Taryn's words, I do sit and brood. I give myself five minutes to dwell on how impossible this all seems, and then I put it to the back of my mind. Those thoughts will always be there, but I can't let them control my every moment.

As Emrak is packing up his things, I'm struck with an idea. One that might help us clear the last of the wisps before nightfall.

"Hey, Emrak. How would you like to get a little payback on those wisps before you go? I'd love to see the First Ranger of Seascape in action."

He looks up from his pack, grinning. "I don't see why you lot should have all the fun."

Emrak digs into his satchel, pulling out a change of clothing and more leather armor, as well as a variety of weapons and vials of brightly-colored liquids.

After changing from his tattered clothing, Emrak looks like a new dwarf. The greens and browns that he wore before are replaced with vibrant shades of red accented with silver. He wears a red tunic covered by a deep crimson leather armor. Two embroidered silver arrows cross over one another across his chest, and a maroon cloak drapes from his shoulders. Silver vambraces cover his forearms and a matching clasp engraved with runes dangles from the end of his fiery beard.

He definitely can pull off the look of a renowned ranger when he wants to.

Next, he pulls out an ornately-carved bow. The bow is made from a material as black as night, and the string glows a piercing silver even in the dull light of the forest. A warthog head is carved just above the grip, its tusks jutting outward and serving as the shelf for arrows to rest upon. A quiver hangs from his waist on one side, filled with a variety of arrows with different colored fletchings, and a dagger with a jeweled pommel rests on his other hip.

Taryn gawks at him with dwarven pride. "Badass!"

I step closer, taking in all of the small details on the bow. "Definitely badass, but just so you know, physical attacks aren't really effective against the wisps."

He winks as he taps his quiver. "That shouldn't be a problem. One doesn't become First Ranger without learning a few tricks."

I'm intrigued to see what the old dwarf has up his sleeve. Archard was a superb ranger and expert marksman, but he had no abilities outside of his own skills. I get the feeling that's not the case with Emrak. We fill him in on the wisps as we travel to the first burrow, explaining our strategy and how the wisps operate during the day versus at night. According to our map, there are forty-two burrows that we need to take out.

Emrak grumbles. "Those bastards might have caught me unaware in the darkness, but they'll have a much tougher time singing me to sleep while there's daylight."

At the first burrow, we show him our technique, using Stonewall combined with my exploding horrors, Taryn's Moonbeam and Lightning Bolt, and Limery's fire to make short order of the wisps.

"Not bad." Emrak nods approvingly. "You all fight as one. That is a crucial advantage in most situations—the ability to rely on your party to cover your blind spots and act in predictable ways."

Taryn laughs. "That's only because we've been at this for a while. I don't want to say any names, but the big guy with the horns has a way of doing the unexpected."

I shrug. "What can I say? I'm a barbarian."

Emrak scouts the next burrow, examining each hole and surveying the surrounding area. He mumbles to himself as he walks around, occasionally tapping one of the arrows in his quiver.

When he's finished, he returns to where we are waiting. "There are several options I could take, but after last night, I feel I should take a little pride in myself. Could you be so kind as to lure the wisps out into the open?"

We do as he says, blocking off the two furthest entrances with Stonewall. Then,

I have Pharos approach from between them, and though it doesn't deal any damage, his presence alone penetrates through the ground, funneling the wisps out of the lone exit.

Violent shrieks pour out of the tunnel as they try to escape.

When the first wisp emerges, its tongue lashes out, and drool flings across the forest. I activate Amulet of Sight, and its smoky shroud rips away.

Emrak grunts as he nocks an alabaster arrow with a golden tip and matching fletching. It contrasts starkly against the dark-colored bow. As he pulls it back, the arrow floods with white energy, and the warthog's obsidian eyes flare a deep red. White energy swirls around the shaft as he takes aim. A second and third wisp emerge, and then he releases.

Melodic notes sing from the arrow, and sunlight pierces through the treetops as it sails. A beam of light follows the projectile as it soars across the forest. The blinding white arrow penetrates the first wisp, tearing through its flesh. The gelatinous exterior explodes like a water balloon captured in slow-motion. The skin rips apart, curling into ribbons as fluid bursts forth. Light continues to follow the arrow as it punctures and gashes through the final two in a similar fashion.

In a matter of seconds, all that remains are three writhing tongues and a puddle of liquid.

"Holy shit!" Taryn and I say in unison, both of our eyes wide with shock.

"No." Emrak smirks. "Holy arrows."

"Whatever it was, it was awesome." I kick one of the tongues back into the hole. "With abilities like that, we'll have this cleared in no time."

He shakes his head. "That was a combination of an ability and a very rare item. Blessed arrows take a cleric a month just to enchant one arrow. They are incredibly time-consuming to create and equally expensive to purchase, but as you can see, they wreak havoc on dark-aligned creatures. I don't have enough Blessed Arrows for all of the burrows, I'm afraid." He taps his quiver. "Though I do have quite the arsenal."

"We wouldn't want you wasting something so precious out here anyways. The wisps are dangerous, but not worth that kind of expenditure." Taryn purses his lips. "Do you have any spells, or do you rely only on enchanted arrows?"

"A little of both. Most of my abilities enhance my tracking and fighting prowess. Though I'll be honest, my buffs are mostly geared toward fighting monsters that pose a physical threat, not those from the shadow realms. I can move through the forest quieter than a fox, and my senses are on par with your bear companion. My supply of arrows makes up for any deficiencies I may have."

"What happens when you run out of arrows?" I ask.

He grins. "I'll let you know if it ever happens. Here, take a look at this."

He takes off his quiver so I can analyze it.

Item. Quiver of Holding. *A quiver capable of holding an enormous supply of arrows. Simply focus on the arrows you desire, and they will appear in the quiver. Quiver of Holding can be linked to other expandable items for even greater inventory.*

"Wow, that's impressive." Taryn looks on in astonishment. "So, if your quiver's inventory is full, you can have it pull arrows from an expandable satchel? Talk about an unlimited ammo cheat."

Emrak slings his bow across his back. "Not unlimited, but I'll perish before I ever pull from an empty quiver. I have arrows for all occasions, some much more valuable than others, as you have seen."

I pat him on the back and head toward the next burrow. "No point in waiting around all day. Let's see what else you've got in your bag of tricks."

While nothing is as devastating as the Blessed Arrow, the variety of arrows in Emrak's arsenal is incredibly impressive. He has arrows that explode, tracking arrows, arrows tipped with small vials of holy water, electric arrows, and many more.

We learn the effect of ice against the wisps when he hits one with a frozen arrow. The gelatinous wisp freezes solid, falling to the ground with a thunk. Jordy rams into it with his powerful horns, shattering the wisp into hundreds of shards.

The day winds on and we make amazing progress, but as dusk approaches, there are still ten burrows left. Emrak could make the portal by nightfall, but not with the wisps still about.

"Taryn, do you still have your Dream Dust?" I ask.

His eyes go distant as he checks his inventory. "Eleven vials. What are you thinking?"

"We can restock when we head back to the village." I flash him a devilish expression that would make Limery proud. "I say we use everything we've got and go scorched earth on their slimy, jelly asses."

"Dream Dust?" Emrak raises his eyebrows. "Back in my younger days...Well, let's just say I liked to experiment. Some of the parties King Orso threw, he'd kill me if I told you." He smiles mischievously at the memory. "How exactly do you plan on killing a wisp with that stuff?"

My grin matches his own. "Not *a* wisp. All of them."

13. TICK TICK BOOM

Between Taryn and I, we have twenty vials of Dream Dust and seventeen vials of Sleep Dust to use among the ten remaining burrows.

I plan to use every last one of them.

Taryn looks up from the pile on the ground. "This is never going to work. The burrows are too far apart, and there's no way to ignite all of the vials at once even if you do manage to get them inside each tunnel. Let's just take them out one at a time."

"Dude, aren't you tired of doing this day in and day out? I'm going to rip my horns off if I have to spend another day twiddling my thumbs while I watch you and Limery do all the work. If we play this right, then we can be back in the Hidden Village tomorrow." I turn to Limery. "Limery, you used to build contraptions back home. Do you know any way we can rig together a fuse of some kind? We don't have enough dust to make a trail like we did last time. Not from burrow to burrow."

Limery scratches his chin. "Limmy will thinks on it."

After a few minutes of silent pondering, he leaps into the air with excitement and hovers as his words spill out a mile a minute. "When Limmy was littles, he liked to make bombses, but when Limmy blows ups the kitchen tables, Mommy doesn't let Limmy make bombses anymore. Limmy still remembers, though. If we has strings and waxes, then we can use the Sleeps Dusts to make the fuses."

I search through my inventory, where I have about twenty feet of rope, but that's not nearly enough for what we would need. "I've got about twenty feet of climbing rope, but I think it's too thick for what we want. What about you two?"

Taryn shakes his head. "Climbing rope, but that's it, sorry."

Emrak laughs to himself as he digs in his satchel. "I guess you lot are lucky I showed up after all. Not only do I have rope, I have string. A good ranger never leaves home without it."

I clap my hands together, startling Ruby who is curled up near a tree trunk. "Awesome, how much do you have?"

"A good ranger is always prepared for the unexpected." He grins even wider. "But me, I'm a great ranger. I have enough that I'll never even need to think about buying string again."

Taryn pumps his fist in the air. "If you weren't so ugly, I'd kiss you, old dwarf."

"Dammit!" I curse as a new realization dawns on me, killing my excitement as quickly as it came. "We still need wax, and I have no idea how we're supposed to find it. Do you have any candles in that bag of yours?"

Emrak pulls out a large spool of string from his satchel. "I'm sure myself or the bear could track down a beehive if need be, but lucky for you, my bowstring is already waxed. It protects it from the elements and keeps it from snapping as easily. A little heat and it should melt enough for you to do whatever it is you need to do."

What else does he have hidden away in his expandable satchel?

My hands tingle with anticipation. We just might pull this off. "Alright then, we don't have much time. Let's get to work."

By the time everything is in place, twilight can't be more than twenty minutes away. A heavy silence settles across the forest. If this doesn't work, then the time we spent setting all of this up has probably added an extra day to our quest.

A slew of fuses stretch out before us, thirty in total. Limery used his natural body heat to soften the waxed string without melting it, then we coated the string in Sleep Dust. It took seven vials to coat thirty strings in enough dust to make a working fuse.

Each fuse runs to a separate entrance at one of the ten remaining burrows, where a horror stands ready and waiting with a vial of Boom Dust. One vial of Dream Dust was enough to explode an entire burrow by itself. For this, we elected for overkill. By mixing the twenty vials of Dream Dust with the remaining Sleep Dust, each burrow is about to be hit with more than double the explosive power as last time. My hard work creating the mixture manages to gain me an extra level in Potion-making during the process.

I double-check with my horrors one last time, making sure they're all in position.

"We ready?" I ask the group.

Taryn and Emrak nod.

"Readies." Limery summons a fireball in his open palm.

"Once the fuse is lit, cover your ears and open your mouth until it's over. The explosion will be big, and we don't want anyone bursting their ear drums." I give Limery the go-ahead, and he lights the fuses.

The strings ignite like sparklers on the Fourth of July, quickly burning away into the fog. Once they're out of sight, I pray that the fuses stay lit as I send my horrors descending into the burrows, a trail of Boom Dust spilling out with each step. A moment later, their presences begin to vanish.

And then we wait.

We're at least fifty yards from the first burrow when it explodes. The ground shakes and dirt erupts into the sky like a volcanic blast. Fog is pushed out of the way like a tidal wave, revealing a pink-and-purple mushroom cloud pluming into the trees. A heartbeat later, a shockwave hits me like a sledgehammer, flinging me into a tree as debris peppers me like a shotgun blast. My entire body burns and aches as my vision darkens at the edges.

I crawl across the forest floor, trying to regain my bearings enough to find the others when the explosion cracks like a sonic boom, reverberating in my chest and nearly crippling me. A second explosion follows, trailed quickly by a third and then a fourth. Over the course of ten seconds, all our homemade bombs detonate.

I search for the others, coughing as debris rains down around us. Between falling dirt and the dissipating smoke, I can't see more than a foot in front of me. Notifications flash in the corner of my vision, but I push them away.

"Is everyone okay?" I shout.

I bump into Berry, and he grunts his annoyance. The fog is gone for the moment, but a heavy layer of dust hangs in its wake, making it equally impossible to see.

"Ungh, we're okay. A little bruised, but otherwise fine," Taryn answers from the other side of Berry. "Limery? Emrak?"

"Limmy is okays."

"I'll live. Gods, remind me to never piss the three of you off." A hand grabs me by the side as Emrak steadies himself. "Oh, there you are. I haven't seen an explosion like that since Brannia Bravefall, a powerful young pyromancer mage, went mad and tried to explode Seascape portal many years ago."

By the time the smoke and dust clear enough for us to see in our immediate vicinity, it's well-past nightfall. We're all covered in so much dust from the explosion that we look like we stepped out of a sepia photograph.

Luckily, I have enough juice left in the Amulet of Sight for us to survey the damage.

Taryn grimaces as the amulet reveals the area. "We're going to be in so much trouble."

A crater the size of a house sits where the burrow once was. The damage is so extensive that the amulet can't reveal it all within its radius. As we walk to the next burrow, the edge of the first crater overlaps the second. The trees that surrounded the burrow are gone, and there's a gaping hole through the canopy from the explosion, revealing a full moon among the starry sky.

When all is said and done, our explosion has formed a crater big enough to be a small lake. The hair on the back of my neck stands on end. We're lucky to be alive. If we had been any closer, we might not be.

"Yep, we're so screwed." I sigh. I just hope this doesn't affect the deal we made with Swift.

"So screweds," murmurs Limery.

Emrak pats me on the lower back. "Don't sweat it. They asked you to eliminate the wisps. Unless they specifically said to not blow up a large portion of the forest, I think you'll be okay. Just tell them to request a water mage from King Orso, and they can call this the 'Not-So-Hidden Lake'."

Taryn grins. "You'd make a good lawyer."

"There's no need for lawyers when there is a king. His majesty's word is the law. Speaking of which, now that I've delivered the king's message and you've fulfilled your quest, I'll be taking my leave come morning."

I extend my arm, and we shake. "You have our thanks. There's no way we could have done this without you."

"Maybe not this." He nods toward the giant crater. "But you would have cleared the forest of wisps just fine. I'm glad to have played a small part. This will be a story worth telling over a large mug of ale when I return."

"I remember ale." Taryn groans. "Let it know that its sweet taste still lingers on my lips."

"Okay, Casanova." I squeeze Taryn on the shoulder. "How about you summon some shelter for us and then you can dream about your frothy mistress without creeping the rest of us out."

We make camp near the crater, and even though the wisps are gone, we still use Taryn's walls for safety. I elect to leave Pharos outside as well, just in case. After the past week, a little peace of mind goes a long way.

As I rest against the wall, taking first watch, I finally pull up my notifications from earlier.

Quest Alert: You have completed the quest "Tit for Tat." Mesmer wisps haunt the forest no more, and soon peace shall return to Wandermere.

Reward: Increased favor with Swift Thundercrest and the Wandermere Herd.

Bonus: In exchange for your efforts, Swift Thundercrest has agreed to help you through the process of hatching a green dragon egg.

Please return to the Hidden Village to claim your reward from Swift Thundercrest.

Congratulations! You have reached level 26. +1 stat point to distribute. +1 Strength and Constitution racial bonus.

Not bad. A quest completion and a new level. I also get three more levels in my Demolition skill from the epic blast, putting me close to becoming an apprentice. It feels like I leveled up much quicker than I have been the past few weeks, but I guess we did a lot of fighting, especially by clearing most of the burrows more than once. Maybe I got some kind of bonus for taking out so many in one go last night. Either way, I'll take it. It puts me even closer to level thirty and the exclusive Warforged class Jegaar told me about.

With this newest stat point, I now have seven that I haven't distributed. I'm anxious holding onto them when they could be benefiting me, but I keep waiting for something to offer guidance on how best to allocate them. My racial bonus makes it a waste to put them in Strength or Constitution. Dexterity makes the most sense to keep my speed matched with my power and toughness, especially now that I deal splash damage with each attack thanks to the Ram Rage passive from my Spirit of the Beast path. But there's no telling what leveling up Intelligence or Wisdom could do for my summoning abilities.

The one thing I know is that I don't want it in Charisma. I still don't understand why that particular stat works so much more differently than it does in other games, but I've done just fine without it and don't want to ever feel that reckless again while I'm in Mythos. There's too much on the line.

I analyze the others while they're sleeping. It seems everyone leveled up from the quest, but it's impossible to tell with Emrak. With his level hidden, there's no telling how strong he actually is. Judging by his attacks, he's definitely stronger than us.

Taryn and I are both level twenty-six now. Limery is close behind at twenty-five. Jordy is twenty-three, Berry twenty-two, and Ruby eighteen. It's been so long since we ran into any other heroes outside of Glenn and Jude that I'm not sure where we stand in comparison. Sometimes I feel like Taryn and I are the only ones trying to make a difference in this world while everyone else is out there having fun.

When my watch is over, I nudge Taryn on the shoulder. "Wake up. It's your turn to take watch."

He grunts as he sits up. "I can't wait to be back in a city where we can get a full night's sleep again."

"You and me both, buddy. Looks like we all leveled up today. You think Limery unlocked anything like we did for hitting level twenty-five?"

Taryn shrugs. "He didn't say anything. But he never said anything when he unlocked his molten form either. Maybe it's not the same for imps. He doesn't exactly have a class, does he?"

It's my turn to shrug. "Who knows? I'm still not one hundred percent sure how things are different between us and the NPCs. Anywho, I'm beat." A yawn overtakes me as I lie down. "See you in the morning."

After such a long day, I'm asleep as soon as my head hits the ground.

I wake up to the sound of birds chirping. With the wisps gone, it doesn't take long for nature to return to the area.

"Sleeping Ugly has arisen," Taryn jokes as he prepares breakfast.

"Mornings, Chods!" Limery perches on my shoulder as I sit up. "Do we gets to sees the baby dragons today?"

His excitement warms my heart. "If we're lucky. I have no idea how long it takes to hatch a dragon." I look to Emrak, but he just shrugs.

"I can't recall the last time a green dragon was hatched." He shifts his gaze to the forest. "But I can't think of a more potent location for life aura."

After a quick breakfast, we pack up our things. In the daylight, the devastation our bombs left behind is even more apparent. Without the tree cover, the sunlight spills through, pushing back the fog in the immediate area. The tree branches cling to debris like an overzealous spiderweb, and a thick layer of dirt covers limbs and bushes. We really did a number on this section of the forest.

"What's next for you all?" Emrak asks as he tosses his satchel over his shoulder.

"We were planning to go to Pruxford, but now that I have a castle, I guess we should probably head back to Seascape once we're finished in the Hidden Village and check in with King Orso. With the arctic trolls joining the forest and mountain tribes, I should probably help them get settled as well."

"What did I tell you? The castle will be waiting when you return." Emrak narrows his eyes. "Do you not trust Chief Rizza to maintain the peace and hold order until then?"

I lower my head like a scolded child. "I do."

"Then go and explore Pruxford. The gnomish council supports King Orso's efforts against the dark wizard, but they are not as concerned as they ought be. Their annual tournament still stands, and some of the greatest warriors across Mythos will try to showcase their skill." He grabs me firmly by the arm. "It is said that the council showers the winner in favors. King Orso has sent messengers to the council time and again, but they are not concerned with the mounting threats. You may have better luck yourself. Win and you will have an opportunity to speak to the council directly. If you truly want to make a difference, that is the way."

I ponder on his comments for a moment. Competing in a tournament could give us the platform we need to bring in more powerful allies. If other heroes have been sticking to major cities, they've likely heard about it. This might be the best chance we have to meet other heroes. There are still a great many we haven't met, and if they are looking for gold and glory, then my castle can wait. I trust that Chief Rizza can manage until I get back.

"What kind of tournament?" asks Taryn.

"I can't say for sure. The last time a Seascape dwarf competed was before the portals closed. We can't afford to part with our strongest warriors with times being as they are, but King Orso and King Favian have encouraged heroes to enter. Prux-ford is known as the City of Glass, named for the Crystal Palace and its amazing arena carved from towering gemstones. It's primarily gnomish, but many races live among one another in relative peace. Our histories from before the portals closed describe wondrous battles between warriors and mages in their tournaments. Heroes competed against one another in ancient times. From what I recall, a field of combatants eliminate one another in single combat until a lone victor remains." He makes eye contact with Taryn and me in turn. "If my time among you is any indica-tion, then either of you have a shot."

Taryn and I exchange glances, but his face gives away nothing.

Taryn runs his fingers through his beard, making the clasps jingle slightly. "I don't want this to come across the wrong way, because I know how important your relationship with the trolls is, but if Chief Rizza has shown us anything, it's that she's a great leader. Even Kronan has given up his own power to follow her lead.

Chief Laojin is a wise leader as well. Between the three of them, they can run a castle until you return." He nods at Emrak. "Emrak is right, and I think you know it. This is an opportunity not only for us to test ourselves against some of the greatest warriors across Mythos, but I'm sure there will be other heroes there. Heroes we can recruit. To save the trolls and the dwarves, we will need every ally we can get."

"Yeah, I think you're right. This is too good of an opportunity to pass up." I wink at Taryn. "Besides, finally getting to go all out against one another might be pretty fun."

He flexes a short stubby arm. "Maybe you haven't noticed, but I can carry my own weight nowadays."

"Believe me, I've noticed." I'm reminded of how useless I've felt for most of this quest. We're long past the days of mindlessly farming just so he can catch up on experience. With his pets and new abilities, Taryn is a formidable opponent.

We say our good-byes to Emrak, and the ranger disappears into the foggy depths of the forest. Pruxford awaits, but first, we have a dragon to hatch.

14. THE WAITING GAME

The forest seems livelier than ever with the wisps gone. Birds chirp overhead, and Limery disappears among the trees several times over the course of the journey. There's constant movement in the underbrush, even though the source of the disturbance is often concealed by the fog.

I can't help but feel a sense of pride that we did all of this.

I share those sentiments with Taryn. "It's pretty crazy what we've been able to accomplish as a group. Between Limery, your pets, and my horrors, we've become a pretty formidable party. I think we could hold our own against a group of four or five heroes no problem."

Taryn scoffs. "I'd rather not test out that theory any time soon. I'm all for adventure, but nothing good ever comes of meeting other heroes."

"That's not true," I say flatly.

He narrows his eyes. "Hmm, let's see. Glenn and Jude? Murderhobos. The warlock and his posse we met in Lynchton? Servants of the dark wizard. The cleric? Trouble follows him like a baby duck. Not to mention the run-ins you told me about before I got here."

"Oh, come on. It's not that bad. What about Pressley? Or Jon? They both turned out alright."

He laughs dryly. "Key word is 'turned out.' They were a headache to begin with, too."

I shake my head. "Who peed in your mushroom soup this morning? You're the one who said we should go to Pruxford."

He sighs. "I know. I know. It's just... Ugh, I don't know. Everywhere we go, you've got a target on your back, and by extension, I have one on mine. That means my pets do as well. It's one thing to know going to this tournament is the smart decision. It's another thing to think about what it might cost us."

I slow my pace, and Berry does as well. "Believe me, I know. But we can't stop fighting for what's right. I made a promise to the trolls. We both made a promise to King Orso. We're in the thick of this. Maybe back in the re—" I catch myself before I say 'real world.' "Maybe back home, we don't have the power to affect great change, but here, we do. And you know what they say about great power."

He chuckles at the reference. "Yeah, yeah. With great power comes a high electric bill."

I shove him in the arm a little too hard, and he nearly falls off Berry's back before catching himself on the saddle. After that, Taryn's shoulders relax, and he seems more at ease. I never really thought about it much before coming to Mythos, mostly because I always kept everything bottled inside until it finally erupted into a rage-fueled tirade, but sometimes just talking about your worries can make them feel less oppressive. Funny how it took me embodying a raging monster to find a little inner peace.

Even with Strong Wind buffing our speed, it takes us most of the day to make it back to the Hidden Village. Thanks to Pharos, we don't need to use our maps, and his passive ability guides us back without issue.

A dark-colored stallion stands sentry at the village boundary, holding a spear in his powerful arm. He looks around as if making sure the coast is clear before disappearing into the fog.

Taryn casts me an uncertain look as we approach.

Something definitely feels off, so I cancel Pharos and we advance quietly. After a short moment, the centaur returns. A minute later, he looks around before disappearing into the fog barrier once again. This happens twice more as we watch from behind a large bush.

"Everything okay?" I call out once he returns.

The young stallion nearly jumps out of his skin at my words.

He raises his spear but lowers it once he identifies us. "Gods, you startled me. I'd be grateful if you didn't tell Swift," he pleads, looking at me sheepishly. "I'm on guard duty tonight, but this is a once-in-a-lifetime event. I don't want to miss it."

"Miss what exactly?" I raise my eyebrow.

His front hooves tap against the earth in his excitement. "You should really see for yourselves. I don't want to spoil the surprise."

I shrug at his vague answer and step through the fog barrier.

On the other side, I stop in my tracks. The village looks nothing like it did when we left. An eerie green glow stretches across the village, covering everything in a spectral radiance. Hundreds of centaurs stand around the Hidden Lake as it pulses ominously. Fairies zoom across the evening sky, their chimes ringing through the air. Toxic-looking bubbles burst around the altar in the middle of the lake, spewing ghastly fog into the sky. The aura from the altar is brighter than ever, a dense chartreuse that's almost sinister in its brightness. In the center, the dragon egg shimmers, nearly double the size it was when we left.

Limery gasps in awe above my shoulder, and a chill runs down my spine. How is it possible that the egg has grown bigger?

Taryn gulps. "This is creepy as hell. What have we gotten ourselves into?"

"I don't know." My hands tingle, and I clench my fists several times until the feeling fades. "Let's go find Swift and see what the deal is."

The eerie silence as we make our way down to the lake has my skin crawling with goosebumps. Aside from the chiming of fairies, and the gentle bubbling in the lake, the otherwise quiet is unsettling.

Every centaur is focused on the lake. It's almost like they are in a trance as we squeeze between their massive frames. I spot Swift down by the water's edge next to Thannis and Sylvie. His silver hair reflects the bright glow of the lake.

He doesn't so much as turn in my direction when he speaks. "Forgive us for not showing you a hero's welcome, but as you can see, we've been a bit preoccupied."

I glance around, wondering if I'm missing something. A hidden reason as to why the centaurs are behaving so weird. "What exactly is going on?"

His tail swishes, but he still doesn't look away. "Can you not feel it? That gentle pull at your being? We are witnessing a historic moment."

Maybe they got into a little too much fairy dust while we were away. "I have no idea what you are talking about."

Swift takes a deep breath, and then finally turns to face us. For a moment, he looks annoyed, and then his face softens. "You may be from the forest, but you still have much to learn." He rests a hand on my shoulder. "Close your eyes, all of you."

I do as he says, and my sense of hearing slowly expands, honing in on the chimes of fairies, the gentle bubbling of the lake, and the occasional crunch of the earth as a centaur repositions their hooves.

"Now focus within yourself." His voice is relaxed, soothing. "Life aura runs through the forest, and it beats within your heart. Just like the mana that powers your heroic abilities, life aura flows within your being. Focus on your center, on your own life aura."

It feels a bit silly, but I do it anyway. As I try to look inward, the world softens around me. The sounds of the village become distant. Like some hippie meditating in Central Park, I try to find my center, but all I hear is my own breathing.

"Limmy feels it!" the imp shouts excitedly. "Limmy feels its, Chods."

I try to dig deeper, searching for anything out of the ordinary, but nothing happens.

"I feel it, too," Taryn whispers. "Wow. You'd never notice otherwise, but it's like it's pulling a trickle of energy from me."

"Precisely." Swift's voice is calm. "The egg is growing, drawing life aura from its surroundings until it is ready to hatch. Over the past three days, a change has come upon the village. When the egg has gathered enough aura, it will begin to hatch."

I open my eyes to find Swift once again gazing upon the egg. "Are you telling me that you've all been out here for three days?"

He nods. "I agreed to help you hatch the egg. The more life aura it gathers, the quicker it will hatch. By gathering our herd around the lake, we are speeding up the process."

"I'm sure that's not necess—"

He turns on me in a flash, eyes flaring with intensity. "When the histories are written, it will not be said that the centaurs did not play a part."

I raise my hands defensively, startled by his outburst. "Sorry, I didn't mean to offend you. I just thought you might have better things you could be doing."

"Our forest is overrun with creatures we cannot fight, while darkness gathers in the shadowlands. Right now, there is nothing better for my people to be doing. A dragon has the power to balance the scales once again."

Taryn nudges me in the side. "You really have a way with authority."

I ignore his comment and try to ease the tension. "You're right, Swift. It's not my place to question you. We've cleared the forest of the mesmer wisps, and it's once again safe for the herd to move about the forest." Swift is clearly on edge, so I leave out the part about the giant crater for now.

"I had no doubts you would succeed. Once the dragon is hatched, we will return to our outposts once again."

"Since we're back, is there anything we can do to help?"

He shakes his head. "For now, we stand strong and we wait. You may come and go as you please. You are an honored guest while you are here, and the fairies will see to anything you need."

"That's very kind of you." I bow slightly. "Do you all not need to sleep?"

He laughs. "The herd can sleep while standing when needed."

I wave to get Taryn's attention and nod in the direction of the village buildings. We make our way through the herd to where we can speak freely.

I crouch near a tree once we are far enough away. "This is weird. Did you actually feel something back there?"

Taryn raises an eyebrow. "You didn't? I guess I shouldn't be surprised that someone whose first option is to punch things isn't in touch with the natural world. If you can't tell by looking, there's definitely something going on here."

I frown. That much is evident. "So what, we just wait? Our maid always said a watched pot never boils."

"Your maid..." He rolls his eyes. "You'll be right at home in your new castle." He mumbles the words, but I still manage to make them out. "After we eat, I'm going back down to the lake. They've piqued my curiosity, and I definitely want to be there when something happens."

I don't have anything better to do, so after eating, I join Taryn and the others at the lake. As much as I try, I can't seem to feel whatever is happening with the life aura. Maybe it has something to do with my rapid regeneration or high Constitution.

Over the next two days, the centaurs barely move or eat unless they're switching guard duty around the village. Two days of doing nothing, and I still haven't been able to talk with Swift or any of the others about how we cleared the forest.

The aura becomes denser by the day, and the egg continues to grow until it's as big as Limery, but nothing else happens. I have no idea how large the egg is supposed to get. Dragon's are huge, so if it hatches at the size of Jordy or Berry, we could be waiting a while. What I wouldn't give for a pair of headphones and some music as I sit around doing nothing.

I take a deep breath and lie on my back. As boring as this is, it could always be worse. At least I'm not in prison.

I close my eyes, once again trying to find my center so that I can feel this mysterious force supposedly draining my life. The world fades away, and my breathing takes center stage, in and out like a rising tide.

There's a dull rumble in my chest, and I think that maybe I'm close to breaking through. But then the rumble spreads, and I realize it's not coming from within, but from beneath.

My eyes snap open, and the ground continues to quake violently. The silent centaurs bump into one another as they search for balance. Voices suddenly fill the air. Next to me, Taryn attempts to calm his pets as they pace in alarm. Limery hovers in the air, searching for unseen threats.

Leaves fall from the trees, and waves crash along the shore. I crawl to my feet on wobbly legs, and as quickly as the earthquake came, it stops.

Murmured chatter stretches in every direction.

I push my way through the crowd until I find Swift, grabbing him on the shoulder. "What the hell was that?"

His eyes burn brighter than ever. "Verdaria is stirring."

Cold dread weighs on me like an avalanche, and I turn my eyes to the lake. I signed up to hatch a baby dragon, not wake a sleeping adult. "Stirring how?"

The last thing we need is an ancient dragon wreaking havoc through the village while the egg is still hatching.

A loud bang echoes from the middle of the lake, amplified by the turbulent waves. The aura around the altar blazes with power, flaring some twenty feet in the air. My heartbeat thunders in my ears and for the life of me, I can't look away.

The egg wobbles on the altar, and the shell cracks down the side.

15. HOW TO TRAIN YOUR DRAGON

The crack splinters along the egg like an arc of lightning. Pieces of jade eggshell flake off as it continues to shake against the altar. The ground quits quaking, and the green glow of the lake fades slightly. Turbulent waters continue to toss the raft, but the aura surrounding the items on the altar shrinks to its original size.

Minutes pass before the water stills, and the egg's movement ceases.

All eyes focus on the altar. The village sits in an eerie silence aside from the chiming of fairies overhead.

A low growl, almost like a puppy learning to bark for the first time, comes muffled from within the egg. It wobbles slightly, then a small green claw pokes through the crack, breaking off more of the shell. The claw wiggles before disappearing back inside.

The intake of breath around me is so pronounced that it could have come from the forest itself.

"Thannis, pull the altar to shore," orders Swift.

Thannis wades into the water and grabs the rope, pulling the altar toward the expectant crowd.

"Chod!" Swift shouts as if he's unaware that I'm right behind him. "Come down!"

"I'm right here." My chest is tight, and my hands tingle with excitement. Whatever is about to happen, this is the reason we came here.

Swift grips me firmly on the shoulder. "When the altar is ashore, take the egg and go deeper into the forest. Sit with the egg until it hatches. This will produce the strongest bond with the young dragon."

I have a million questions running through my mind, and Thannis has already pulled the raft halfway to the shore. "And then what? Should I try to help it free itself?"

His gaze is penetrating as he speaks calmly. "Wait for it to hatch. A dragon will bond strongly with the first being it sees. While it's not a permanent bond, this is your best chance of laying the groundwork for such a connection. Afterward, return to the village."

By the time he finishes, Thannis has lugged the altar onto dry land. Swift steps aside, gesturing for me to approach.

The crowd parts as I go to the altar. I hesitate for a moment, as muffled growls continue inside the egg and a tiny claw pokes in and out of the crack.

Alright, little dragon, come to papa.

Taking a deep breath, I pick up the egg. It's hot to the touch. If not for my tough troll skin, I'm certain it would be blistering right now. There's a hiss, and a second claw pokes through the crack, breaking off more of the shell.

"I'll be back soon," I tell Limery and Taryn as I walk carefully through the crowd. The last thing I want to do is trip and fall, crushing the poor creature before it's even hatched.

I walk deeper in the forest, away from the village and the hundreds of eyes following my every movement. The green aura of the forest has already faded dramatically by the time I reach a small clearing next to a towering tree.

Taking a seat on the ground in front of the tree, I cradle the egg in my palms. Three claws have managed to break through the shell. The talons grate against the exterior scales as it continues its struggle to break free.

The egg's warmth reminds me of the cold winters when I would sit on the balcony overlooking the city with a cup of hot chocolate. The toasty mug would keep the frigid cold at bay, steam trailing into the cool air of the bustling city.

A piece of shell breaks off, and the first full paw reaches through. The tiny leg is the color of freshly-mown grass, vibrant and untarnished by the world. It grasps at the air, and more cracks form along the egg as the dragon maneuvers inside.

Another large section breaks off and a snout presses through the opening. It sniffs at the air, and then a wisp of green smoke puffs out.

There's a tingle in my chest that I can't quite explain. Maybe it's the fact that I'm witnessing something that anyone back in the village would kill for. It's a once-in-a-lifetime—hell, once-in-several-lifetimes—event that could shake the world of Mythos as we know it. And I'm seeing it all by myself.

I shift the weight of the egg, cradling it in my left hand as I stroke the dragon's nose with my right index finger. The dragon lets out the most adorable snarl I've ever heard and snorts out another small plume of smoke.

"You can do it, little guy. You're almost there." I offer my best encouragement.

The egg shakes as the dragon applies pressure from within. For a moment, I consider whether or not I should help it, but then I remember Swift's directions to wait for it to hatch.

After about an hour of grumbling and growling, a piece of egg breaks off, leaving a hole big enough for the dragon's head to fit through. At this size, it looks more like a large lizard than a powerful dragon. Two nubby horns stick out from the top of its head like a young deer. Big, round, golden eyes blink rapidly as a milky fluid drips down its face.

I lift the egg to where our heads are at eye level. The dragon snaps at me, its jaws clacking from the powerful bite. Not even an hour old and it could probably draw blood.

"Easy there." I put my finger up, and the dragon quiets as its golden eyes follow my every movement.

"Trolls are friends, not food." I use the most soothing voice I can. "I'm gonna pet you. Do not bite me."

An inch at a time, I lower my finger until it rests on the dragon's head. The scales are smooth and covered in a layer of slime. Gently, I stroke the slick scales of its forehead, and the dragon closes its eyes. It growls, but this time, it sounds more like a purr than a warning.

I quit petting the dragon, and its eyes lock onto mine.

"Alright, you've got this. Show that egg what you're made of."

It struggles, writhing one shoulder through the opening and then creating another crack as it forces the other. Once its midsection is through, it uses its paws to slither the rest of its body out of the opening, plopping onto the ground with a thick, gelatinous sheen covering its body.

The hatchling shakes like a wet dog, flinging egg fluid in all directions, and a set of leathery wings unfurl from its back. The motion sends it tumbling to the ground, and with a grumble, it rises back up on unsteady feet. Standing at its full height, the dragon is about the size of a house cat.

Green Dragon. Unique Monster. Level 1. Green dragons rule with impunity over the forests they inhabit. They are the most territorial of all dragon species, and capable of spewing toxic gas in lieu of flames. Wherever a green dragon calls home, a dense fog is said to follow.

"Level one. We're going to need to change that pretty quick." I extend a hand, and the dragon walks awkwardly in my direction. It nuzzles against my palm, its cool scales a stark contrast to the earlier heat of the egg. "You're gonna need a name." I pick the creature up and it curls around my hand, sharp claws gripping me firmly. "Are you a boy or a girl?"

I look underneath its belly, but I have no idea how to distinguish a male from a female. Maybe Swift will have more answers.

"I guess we'll save the naming for later." I place him gently on the ground. "Just remind me not to ask Taryn for suggestions."

I take the time to enjoy the moment alone with the baby dragon. It's likely the only time we'll be truly alone for the foreseeable future.

Reaching into my satchel, I pull out a piece of jerky. The dragon immediately focuses on the strip of dried warthog.

"You must have a pretty good sense of smell."

It jumps into my lap, jaws snapping as it tries to bite the jerky from my hand. I grab the dragon by the midsection and place it on the ground.

"No," I scold. "We're going to need to teach you some manners. Now, sit." I hold the piece of meat over the dragon's head.

Its head tilts up as it eyes the jerky, forcing its hind legs to the ground. With the task completed, I drop the jerky into its mouth. It snatches the jerky out of the air, swallowing it after only a few bites.

"Are you hungry?" I ask, pulling out another piece of jerky.

The dragon jumps on its hind legs, trying once again to take the snack from me.

"No." I wag a finger. "Sit."

The dragon huffs and a trickle of green smoke erupts from its nostrils.

"Sit," I say more firmly.

It jumps in the air, nearly reaching the jerky, but I pull it away at the last second.

"No. Sit."

The dragon growls but then places its rear on the ground.

"Good job!" I excitedly drop the jerky into its mouth.

I've never had a pet before, but the pride from teaching it to sit has me understanding Taryn's bond with his own pets a little better than before.

"Alright, little dude. Time to show you off to the village and see if they have a copy of *Raising Dragons for Dummies* lying around anywhere."

When we return, the centaurs are no longer huddled around the lake, but it's clear that the majority of them are waiting around to see the dragon.

It walks by my side, easily distracted by the slightest movement or sound in the underbrush. Several times it pounces on a pile of leaves, growling and pawing at the earth.

"Chods!" Limery calls out as he zooms in our direction followed by a troop of fairies. "Did yous hatch the dragonses?"

He lets out a delighted squeal when he notices the small dragon catching up to me. Limery flies to the ground a couple of feet in front of the creature, and chimes fill the air as the fairies gossip and point. In the distance, the clop of hooves announces centaurs on the move.

The dragon backs away, its back arched as it stays close to my leg, unsure of Limery.

I kneel beside it, stroking between its wings. "It's okay. Limery is a friend."

Limery reaches his own tiny hand out. "It's okays. Limmy is yous friends."

"Here, give him this." I toss Limery my last piece of jerky.

Limery feeds the dragon, and its demeanor immediately changes. It nuzzles against the imp's belly, and Limery wraps his arms around it. Looks like the two of them have something in common already.

Swift and many centaurs trot over, followed by Taryn and his pets.

"I can already tell those two are going to be trouble." Taryn grins. "I can't believe it's moving around so well this quickly."

Swift watches the dragon and imp interact with wonder, as do the centaurs behind him. "If the tales hold true, young dragons are full of mischief. It will be your duty to raise it with honor, lest it becomes a terror in its own right."

They ogle over the newborn dragon, but Swift's words weigh heavily on me. The idea of having a pet dragon was so enticing that I never thought about the responsibility that would come with it.

Am I ready to take care of a pet this powerful? I probably should have considered that before going through all this trouble.

What if I can't control it and it grows into a monster capable of destroying villages and towns?

I'm so caught in my own thoughts that I don't even notice Taryn standing beside me until he taps me on the back.

"It's gonna be fine." Taryn offers me a kind smile. He must be able to tell I'm freaking out. "I say this from experience, but you figure it out as you go."

"I hope you're right." I don't point out the fact that all of his pets were full-grown when he bonded with them. Or that they have an actual bond due to his Tame ability.

For the next hour, we talk with Swift while the herd cycles through, giving each of the centaurs an opportunity to see the dragon. The solemn faces that greeted us upon our first arrival are filled with something else now. Hope, maybe? With the wisps gone and the forest free of threats, the centaurs can finally return to their way of life.

The fairies are particularly enamored with the dragon, filling him up with roasted meat. The little dragon turns out to be a quick learner and highly motivated by food. Limery and the fairies teach it several tricks using only hand motions, and pretty soon, it knows how to stay, lie down, and can do this weird little gliding hop by flapping its wings as it jumps.

"It is strong to be so small." Swift hardly ever takes his eyes off the dragon, even when he is talking to me directly. "I imagine it will be flying in no time."

"Will it learn on its own?" I rub my jaw as I think, unsure how I could possibly teach it to fly.

"It is said that the instincts of a dragon are superior to all creatures. It may need guidance, but you can see it is already learning the motions of flight."

"One more thing..." I hesitate before asking. "How am I supposed to know if it's a male or female?"

He laughs so loud, it takes me by surprise. "Dragons make their own destiny. You won't truly know until it is time for it to mature. Male green dragons will develop a scaled beard. The females do not. Though you may learn more from its nature as it continues to grow."

"Is one more powerful than the other?" Taryn runs his fingers through his beard.

He turns to Taryn, expression as placid as can be. "Is fire more powerful than water? Both have the power to preserve life. Both have the ability to wreak great havoc. A dragon is a dragon, no matter the sex."

Eventually, all the centaurs have their moment with the dragon and return to their duties. Swift invites us to join him for dinner so that we can finally discuss the quests with the wisps.

The fairies prepare us a table down by the water's edge. A platter of roasted vegetables sits in the center next to several pitchers of mead, and a warthog roasts over a spit to the side.

The village has finally returned to normal, with the lake a pristine blue and the green aura completely gone. Many centaurs remain, but a majority have returned to their normal duties, dispersed throughout the village and the forest of Wandermere.

Limery and the dragon play in the lush grass, wrestling and chasing each other. Occasionally, Limery flies into the air, and the dragon tries to follow. When its wings are unable to fully support it, the dragon roars and blows streams of smoke from its nostrils.

Swift carves a platter of sliced meat from the warthog and places it on the table before pouring us all a glass of mead. Limery abandons his playtime to join us at the table, leaving the dragon to play with Taryn's pets, who are not nearly as enthusiastic about the experience as it jumps and nips at them like a rowdy puppy.

Swift raises his mug. "A toast to Mythos's finest heroes, for saving the forest and hatching the first dragon in hundreds of years."

I tap my mug to his. "None of it would have been possible without your help."

"In the end, it's better to walk together than alone." He smiles. "Now, tell me. How did you manage to clear the wisps from the forest?"

The mead is a little too sweet for my taste, but it's plenty strong. Over several glasses, Taryn and I fill him in on our adventure in the forest, from our first encounter with the wisp to the grand finale.

He stares at us with wide eyes when I finish. "The lot of you are lucky to be alive. The forest will heal, but you—" He pauses, as if only just remembering we are heroes. "Well, maybe not you, but them—" He gestures toward Limery and then Taryn's pets. "—they are not so lucky. Not to mention the danger to an envoy from King Orso."

"Believe me, we know. The size of the explosion was a surprise to us as well." Taryn grimaces and runs a hand through his beard. "Pretty sure I singed a few hairs."

Swift sighs. "At least you survived. What is next for you all?"

I wipe mead from my chin before answering. "Emrak told us of a tournament in Pruxford. We plan to check it out before returning to Seascape."

A wide grin spreads across his face. "Draydon was fond of the tournaments. You must seek out his sculpture while you are there."

I lean forward. I completely forgot that Swift's brother used to compete. Maybe he will have insight into what awaits. "We definitely will. Do you happen to know what the tournaments are like?"

He shrugs. "Each tournament is different. I didn't make it to many, but Draydon loved to boast of his victories when he returned home. They were thrilling tales.

Some were battle royales, where they fought to the last man. Some were duels where the victor advanced. Some even pitted multiple warriors against monsters or other threats. There is no telling what awaits you, but I have faith you will make a name for yourselves."

By the time we are done with dinner, Limery is swaying back and forth as he stands on the table. The baby dragon is mesmerized by the fireballs Limery casts and tries to bite each one as the imp juggles them.

I'm feeling a little intoxicated myself as I wrap an arm around Swift. "I'm not sure when the tournament starts, but I don't want to miss it. We appreciate all of your hospitality, but I'm afraid tomorrow we must set out."

"I figured as much." He glances up to the village. "Come with me. I have a parting gift for the two of you."

Our drunken fellowship stumbles up to the main structures of the village, pets and dragon in tow, and we follow Swift through a maze of buildings until he leads us down a long corridor. At the end is a room filled with several chests. Its roof is open-air like the majority of the buildings, and a large tree towers over us from the middle of the room.

He turns around to face us. "Thanks to you all, the forest is free once more. We can finally return to our outposts across Wandermere."

He opens the chest in the far back, pulling out a dull gray shield and leaning it against the tree trunk. It's the same shield used to create the aura on the raft. Then, he removes the matching spear topped with an emerald spearhead, and finally, the stone etched with an ancient rune.

He extends the spear to me. "These items belonged to my brother. I hope that they will bring you the same fortune that they brought him."

"You don't have to do this." I try to hand the spear back to him, but he refuses, pressing it against my chest. "Hatching the dragon was more than enough payment."

He shakes his head. "This isn't about repayment. This is an investment in your future. In Mythos's future. Take it."

"Thank you." I take the items, and as soon as they are all equipped, I receive a notification.

Notice! Complete Set: Regeneration Triad. *While wearing all three pieces of the Regeneration Triad, user will be granted a ten-foot aura that provides 20% increased regeneration for companions within its radius.*

I look over the items one more time.

Item. Renewal Spear. *Capable of holding life aura equivalent to 500 HP. The Renewal Spear gathers aura passively while equipped and can steal health from enemies during* *battle. Life aura may be absorbed by the wielder at any time.* **Bonus:** *When paired with Regeneration Stone and Shield of Vigor, user will be granted a ten-foot aura that provides 20% increased regeneration for companions within its radius.*

    Item. Shield of Vigor. *Increases HP by 30%.* **Bonus:** *When paired with Regeneration Stone and Renewal Spear, user will be granted a ten-foot aura that provides 20% increased regeneration for companions within its radius.*

    Item. Regeneration Stone. *Increases health regeneration by 20%.* **Bonus:** *When paired with Shield of Vigor and Renewal Spear, user will be granted a ten-foot aura that provides 20% increased regeneration for companions within its radius.*

The fact that I get this bonus without needing to wear any additional armor makes it a perfect complement to my playstyle. The shield is a little heavier than I would like, but it opens a lot of possibilities for tanking the brunt of the damage.

    "And for you, master dwarf. This item has sat in our troves for far too long." Swift kneels, reaching deep within the chest and pulling out a leather thong with a brass key hanging from it. It's a slender skeleton key, but both the bow and the bit of the key have tiny gears and pistons. Even the shaft appears to be made of several rotating barrels. "Draydon won this item during one of his tournaments where each combatant wagered a powerful item as their buy-in to compete. After defeating a rather troublesome halfling rogue, he won the Nimble Key. Aside from these chests, there are no locks throughout the Hidden Village, so it has sat here unused.

    Item. Nimble Key. *When placed in a keyhole, the gears of the Nimble Key begin to turn, revolving and shifting to fit the dimensions of the lock. After one minute, even the toughest locks will open. Note: The Nimble Key is not effective against magical or enchanted locks.*

    Taryn takes the key and flicks the bow with his finger. The gears spin and the bit undulates as metal teeth rise and fall from the end of the key.

    "Now, that is cool." He flicks it again. "This can pick any lock?"

    "As long as it's not magically protected."

    "Nice." Taryn grins mischievously. "With my cloak and boots, I wouldn't be a half-bad rogue myself. And if I put my next ability point into Shadow Cloak, I'd be a ninja at night."

    Swift frowns. "I'm not sure what a ninja is, but if they are stealthy, then indeed you would be a ninja."

    I chuckle at that, but there is some truth to Taryn's words. With boots that leave no tracks and a cloak that conceals the sounds of his movement, he could definitely come in handy. Too bad dungeon doors are magically sealed, or we'd be speed-running through every one we could find.

    "What do yous haves for Limmy?" The imp clasps his hands together like a starving orphan begging for scraps of food.

    The dragon paws at Limery's leg, annoyed that his playmate has diverted his attention.

Swift grins. "For you, we have something extra special."

He whistles, and a moment later, several fairies fly in from the open roof. Two of them hold the ends of a silver necklace with a tiny vial of purple dust as the charm.

"They wanted you to have something to remember us by. Plus, if your antics in the forest are any indication, then it might come in handy if you're ever in a pinch."

The fairies chime as the two holding the necklace surround Limery on each side, draping the necklace around his neck.

The imp beams as they close the clasp and holds the vial in his hand like it is some precious jewel. "Limmy loves its."

The fairies giggle in response before disappearing back into the forest, leaving a glittery trail in their wake.

Swift closes the lid to the chest and faces us. "We are a simple people, but I hope these gifts will aid you in the future. We must first secure our borders, but I will send an envoy to King Orso in the coming days. If the centaurs are needed in battle, the herd will ride."

Taryn holds up the key, giving it a final spin before placing it in his satchel. "We're grateful for your generosity, and all of the help you've provided."

Likewise, I put my new items in my expandable satchel, even the mighty shield fits without much noticeable weight added. "I don't know that we would have had the patience to hatch the egg without your help. Thank you."

We take our leave, spending the night in one of the empty stables, where it turns out the dragon is a bit of a night owl. It runs around the room chasing its tail, growling, and pouncing on piles of hay while we all try to get some rest. Swift has the fairies bring it food almost hourly so that we can get a full night's sleep while we're still here.

At some point, I'm awakened as it climbs up next to Limery, curling in a ball on my chest.

16. ON THE ROAD AGAIN

I wake to the sound of the dragon wrestling with Berry against the far wall. The massive umber bear lies on his back, pawing at the young dragon as it tries to bite through Berry's thick fur. A powerful but playful paw sends the dragon tumbling into a pile of hay.

Above us, the forest is alive with chirping birds, rustling tree leaves, and the distant chiming of fairies. For a moment, I simply lay there, feeling Limery's warm body in the crook of my arm. I'm surprised he's not awake and part of the mischief.

My moment of peace quickly fades when I notice the message icon flashing in the corner of my vision. Since Taryn is still asleep next to me, that can only mean one thing.

I take a deep breath and focus on the icon. Two messages appear as a scroll across my vision. The first is from the admin, and the second is from Valery herself.

Incoming Message (Admin): Greetings, Heroes! The time has come for your regularly scheduled break. In three days' time, you will be logged out of Mythos while your avatar sleeps. Please make safe accommodations for yourself, preferably within a safehouse establishment such as an inn or castle. Failure to do so will result in automatic extraction and may result in loss of levels or items during your absence if your avatar is attacked while you are logged out.

Incoming Message (Admin): Chod, you continue to surprise us with the connections and the quest lines you have unlocked. The world is moving faster than we ever anticipated, and hatching a dragon will certainly have ramifications across Mythos going forward.

There have been some new developments regarding our understanding of the AI and the effect your presence has within the system. I would like to discuss further once you're out. -Valery

New developments? What could that possibly mean? Have they finally figured out why the system is only bugged when I log out?

Taryn stirs next to me, and Ruby yawns as she pokes her head out from beneath his cloak. She stretches her front legs out, hindquarters sticking proudly in the air before lying on her belly.

I poke Taryn in the shoulder, making sure he doesn't fall back asleep. "Check your messages."

Limery's bulbous yellow eyes flutter awake, and he grumbles something that sounds like jumbled words.

Taryn's eyes glaze over as he reads the message. I feed the dragon a few pieces of jerky, and it gobbles them up. Limery stares at me, drool dribbling down his chin, so I give him one as well.

"Three days, huh?" Taryn shakes the straw off his cloak and drapes it over his shoulders. "That's not a lot of time to get out of the forest. Guess we better get moving."

"No kidding. It'll take us close to two days just to get back to the portal with nothing slowing us down. Assuming there's an inn near the Pruxford portal, that's only a day of wiggle room."

We pack our things and find Swift with a handful of centaurs talking over breakfast. There's no sign of Thannis, Sylvie, or Daimun, so I assume they're back to patrolling the forest. I use the opportunity to ask Swift about the Pruxford portal.

He sets down a half-eaten roasted carrot and wipes his mouth with the back of his hand. "The portal empties into the heart of Pruxford. The main market will offer everything you could possibly need to resupply and prepare for the tournament. But don't fear, we will send you on your way with food and provisions."

The other centaurs abandon their breakfasts entirely to spend a few final moments with the young dragon, feeding it scraps and reinforcing the commands it already knows. The expression each of them share is so far removed from our first meeting.

The dragon eats the scraps from all of their plates and still begs for more. I'm not sure if my eyes are playing tricks on me or if it has already grown bigger in less than a day since hatching. Something tells me we're either going to be doing a lot of hunting or spending a fortune on food in the near future.

After a quick breakfast and a stop by the market to resupply with potions, fairy dust, and provisions for the road, we set out once again.

Swift walks us to the edge of the village, and the guards outside the wall of fog bid us farewell. While fog still heavily coats the forest floor, it has a different feel than previously. The forest feels more alive, more peaceful, and less ominous. I'm sure we could spend weeks exploring its vastness if we had time.

Travel is slow-going with a baby dragon, and it hates being carried unless by its own choice. Still, we make steady progress, and Limery enjoys putting his bird hunting skills to use to feed the small creature.

Pharos leads the way, using its passive ability to guide us back to the portal. Jordy walks beside my spirit guide, and the two frost goats hold their heads high as they parade through the forest. Next to me, Taryn rides Berry, with Ruby in her usual position curled between his legs.

I equip the Renewal Spear while we walk, using it as a walking staff. The end of the dull gray weapon sinks into the soft earth with each step. I can feel a change in the weapon as it fills its reserves with life aura. A faint glow surrounds the spear's emerald tip, rising as the weapon stores aura within. If I focus on it, I can see a gauge similar to a health bar that shows how much aura it has gathered.

While Limery is off hunting, I use the time to talk to Taryn about the messages we received. "Valery says she has an update about the system that she wants to talk about in person. I wonder if they've finally figured out what's causing the crash."

"Who knows?" Taryn shrugs. "She did say I'd be able to video chat with my family this time, so I'm looking forward to that."

"That's awesome! I'm sure that'll be nice. Make sure to tell them I said 'hello.'"

"Will do. It feels like it's been forever since we last logged out. It'll be nice to check in with everyone." His smile fades. "Think you'll hear from your parents?"

I scoff at the idea. "If so, that'll be the most surprising thing to happen since I've been in Mythos."

A solemn silence passes over us as we walk. I'm happy for Taryn. He misses his family, and they undoubtedly miss him too, but the only people waiting for me when I log out will be Valery and the technicians. Not that I'm complaining. I'll hear what she has to say, do my check-ups, and then gratefully log back in. One thing I've noticed is that the more time I spend here, the less I think about my problems in the real world.

Most of our day is spent traveling slowly and feeding the dragon. It eats almost hourly, and it never seems to be satiated. If I thought Limery was a bottomless pit, this dragon puts him to shame. I wonder if it will eat less frequently once it has matured.

We pass several centaur outposts on our journey. Once again, they are staffed and operating, usually with a single centaur. They're simple structures, with a stable and some supplies, mainly used for patrolling the forest and offering assistance to those who may need it. Though, hearing them tell it, the latter is much less frequent than it used to be. Given the appearance of the wisps, it's more important than ever to be vigilant.

We pass through a dense section of towering oaks when Pharos suddenly comes to a halt. Jordy bleats and lowers his horns at a boulder in the middle of the path.

The boulder is about the size of Jordy. I'm about to make a joke when I notice that the giant rock is actually a level-twelve golem. It looks like nothing more than a boulder surrounded by stacks of smaller rocks, but then the rocks shift as the golem moves.

The dragon runs up next to Jordy, growling at the monster and snapping its jaws.

I flash Taryn a devious smile. "Want to let the kids play?"

Normally, we wouldn't even bother fighting something so weak, but this could be a good opportunity to get the dragon some fighting experience. The golem out-levels it greatly, but Taryn's pets have enough of an advantage that they can protect the dragon.

He climbs down from Berry. "No reason we should have all the fun. Get him, squad!"

Jordy charges at the rock golem, horns smashing into the large boulder that forms its core and sending it into a nearby tree. Pieces of rock break off upon impact, scattering into the fog as the golem falls to the ground. The single attack took out a quarter of the golem's health.

The golem groans, and pieces of dirt and rubble roll across the forest floor toward the monster, replacing the damaged areas. At its full height, the golem isn't much taller than Taryn, but it's still a fearsome-looking opponent.

The dragon roars like a lion cub, gnashing its teeth and taking a step forward followed quickly by a step back.

"Try to pin it to the ground," Taryn calls to Berry.

The bear stands on its back feet, towering over the rock monster. The golem punches at Berry, but he absorbs the blow and lunges at the creature, tackling it to the ground.

The end of Taryn's staff glows as he casts Imbue on the dragon, doubling its size and giving us a preview of how big it will soon be.

Emboldened by its new size, the dragon pounces on the golem. Its sharp claws rake against the golem's body, leaving gashes in the stone. Even though it's only level one, the claws still manage to do slivers of damage.

The golem struggles against Berry's weight, but it's no match for the bear. The dragon continues its attack, learning with each strike until eventually, the golem crumbles to pieces as its HP reaches zero.

"Good job!" I reward the dragon with a treat. "You're going to be mighty strong one day."

"And it gained a level. Nice!" Taryn pumps his fist. "That's what I'm talking about."

There aren't a whole lot of low-level monsters in Wandermere, so Berry and Jordy do most of the work. Ruby isn't a fighter, so she sits around with Taryn watching the others battle it out. The dragon's instincts are excellent, especially on animals like warthogs and wolves. It's as if it knows it's the apex predator, and with each fight, we witness more of its potential.

"Gets its!" Limery shouts as he zooms through the air over the fight, offering encouragement as Berry and Jordy take turns assaulting a large warthog.

The imp is a great cheerleader, and nearly as entertaining as the action itself.

Jordy rams into the warthog, and it wobbles in place. The imbued dragon pounces on the stunned warthog's back, tearing through flesh and sinking its teeth into the beast's neck. By the time the stun wears off, it's too late.

Even with breaks for fighting and constantly feeding the dragon, we make good progress. By the end of the day, the dragon is already level four and nearly fifty percent bigger than it was this morning. Where it was the same size as Limery, it's now about as big as a medium-sized dog. Even the little nubs on its head have started to blossom into branchlike horns.

We sit around a campfire for dinner, roasting some of the meat from the animals we slaughtered. It smells delicious, and a little bit of Gherhardt's famous spice flavors the meat perfectly.

Taryn takes a bite of boar leg and juices explode into his beard. "All we need to do is find some super strong allies, and they can power-level us the same way. We'll be ready for the dark wizard in no time."

I laugh at the idea. "Good luck with that. I think they've all got better things to do than babysit heroes. Besides, I've already power-leveled you once. Can't have you going soft on us. Grinding builds character."

He throws a piece of meat over my head and the dragon pounces, snatching it out of the air. It can jump way higher than before, and the little flutter it used to do is now more of a glide.

After dinner, we spend the rest of the evening training the spunky creature. Once it's annoyed with the constant commands, it darts off and climbs up a tree like a cat, staring at us menacingly.

"Alright, fine." I shoo it away. "Go have some fun. Limery, keep an eye on him, please."

Taryn burst out laughing.

I frown. "What?"

"My mom used to tell me the same thing when I was watching my sisters. You're officially a parent."

I roll my eyes. "Oh, shut it."

I toss a bone in Taryn's direction, but he swats it away—to Berry's delight. The umber bear picks it off the ground and carries it away to munch on.

Taryn's joking, but that doesn't mean there's no truth to it. He's always had a great deal of responsibility. Growing up, his time with me was his escape. For me, this is the most responsibility I've ever had in my life, the first time I've really felt like what I did mattered.

It's a good feeling.

17. NAME DROPPING

The dragon's sharp claw rips open the chest of a large buck, advancing the dragon to level five and providing us with enough venison to feed the growing monster for most of the day.

It turns back to me and preens, proud of its accomplishment. A green aura flares from its body for a few seconds, and the young dragon begins hacking and coughing.

I rush to its side, patting it on the back to no avail. I'm not sure if it's choking on deer flesh or managed to eat something bad while I wasn't looking.

The dragon wheezes and a jet of dark green smoke pours from its mouth. The smoke flows into a nearby bush, withering the leaves and gnarling the branches before dissipating. There's a hiss as the bark constricts and splinters before the entire bush shrivels into wispy tendrils.

The hair on my arms stands on end. I forgot green dragons can shoot toxic gas instead of flames. If it can damage a plant like that, I can't imagine what it will do to an enemy.

After a few more hacking coughs, the dragon regains control of itself. Limery stands beside it, gently petting the creature and whispering, "It's okays. It's okays, little dragons."

Taryn gawks at the damage. "That's going to be dangerous."

"No shit." I scratch the dragon under the chin, and its eyes close to slits. "We're going to need to get that under control ASAP."

Not long after, we witness just how dangerous the toxic gas can be under the wrong circumstances.

While Taryn's passive, Nature's Bulwark, keeps him from being attacked unless provoked, it doesn't keep me from triggering a Wandering Creeper growing along the edge of the path.

The sentient bush has limbs covered in brambles capable of tearing flesh. It wraps one around my arm and cuts sting as it rips into my tough skin.

Jordy rams into the creeper, and it releases its grasp on my arm. I take a step back, and Berry pins it to the ground. The dragon pounces, ripping branches with its mouth and tearing through leaves with its claws. It roars before unleashing its new attack. Toxic gas pours from its mouth like a thick fog, covering both Berry and the tree.

Berry howls in pain from the burning gas, releasing the bush and running several yards to safety before licking his scorched paws.

The toxic gas finishes off the low-level bush, and Taryn casts Restoration on his injured pet.

I pull the dragon aside after the fight. "Look, you're going to have to be more careful. That's a powerful ability, and you can't go spewing toxic gas on your party members, got it?"

A dragon's intelligence is supposed to be incredibly high, so I speak to it like I would Limery. The dragon just stares at me, occasionally blinking.

"Got it?" I put my hand on my hips and ask again.

The dragon huffs, and a tiny puff of smoke plumes from its nostrils. Then it lowers its head and nuzzles my shins.

Taryn laughs. "I think he's got it."

I raise an eyebrow. "What makes you think it's a boy?"

He squints, looking over the dragon once more. "Maybe I'm wrong, but that's the feeling I get."

That's more of a feeling than I get, so I shrug. "You are a druid, so who am I to argue? I need to give it—or him—a name soon."

Taryn grins, and his eyes go wide. "Hear me out—"

I shake my head. "Nope. Absolutely not. Won't even consider it."

"Bro, come on." He puts his hands together like he's praying. "Just one suggestion."

I close my eyes, massaging my forehead in preparation for the headache I know is coming. "One suggestion. If it's shit, you're permanently banned from suggesting names ever again."

"Alright, hear me out. While Scaley would be the obvious choice—" He raises his hands in the air defensively before I have a chance to lose my cool. "—if he were mine, I think Caustic is a fitting name that inspires fear and terror in the hearts of enemies."

"Caustic. Huh?" I look at the dragon that's not so little anymore. Surprisingly, the name fits. Maybe not for a baby dragon, but he'll grow into it. The way his gas destroys anything it touches is the definition of the word. "Let's try it out."

I kneel in front of the dragon, scratching it on the head between its branchlike horns. "How do you feel about the name Caustic?"

He purrs, nuzzling his head against my hand to reach that perfect spot that makes his tail waggle.

"I knew it." Taryn smirks. "I am the king of names."

"You're a real wordsmith," I tease. "Let's get moving."

The trick to traveling fast with a baby dragon is to outsmart it. Luckily for us, Little Caustic's stomach far outweighs his stubbornness. We've taken to calling him Little Caustic while he's still small. Kind of like calling a baby Steve, it just doesn't sound right to call him Caustic until he grows a little bigger.

Judging by his current rate of growth, it won't be long before he earns his true name.

Limery flies in front of the dragon, dangling a piece of venison from a string while Taryn buffs us with Strong Wind. For minutes at a time, Little Caustic chases the meat at incredible speeds, teeth snapping as he avoids the temptation to pounce on monsters and follow every sound in the forest.

Taryn calls for us to halt as we come upon the massive crater left behind from our run-in with the wisps. This section of the forest already looks like a different place, and it's only been a week.

The life aura has healed the bark of damaged trees, those that weren't completely demolished in the explosion, and tiny limbs sprout from broken branches. New saplings grow from the deadfalls, and birds chirp in the treetops. The bottom of the crater has pooled with water from the thunderstorm we heard a few days prior. If the centaurs can manage to divert a creek or stream to this location, then maybe it could be a lake one day soon.

Out of the corner of my eye, I catch the glint of metal at the far end of the new pool. A massive boulder sits at the bottom of the crater, a sword halfway buried in the stone. Sunlight spills through the open canopy, hitting the protruding sword of the Wanderer and casting a kaleidoscope of colors from the jewel-encrusted hilt upon the nearby trees.

The sword-wielding stone has made a new home in the ruins of our battle. A deep rut runs along the embankment from where the enchanted creature slid down into the crater. Its massive boulder of a body stirs gently in the fading sun.

As the faceless golem stands, Little Caustic lets out a low growl, but the Wanderer is either oblivious or ambivalent to our presence. It takes a few steps into deeper water and sits again.

I crouch beside the dragon and take in the majesty of the Wanderer one last time. "That's not a fight even you want to take, little guy."

Defeating it would be an accomplishment, but I'm not sure we have the time to fight something forged from life aura and still make it to Pruxford in time to log out.

"Pretty swords." Limery eyes the shining weapon greedily.

I tap him on the back of the head. "Don't even think about it."

We leave the Wanderer in peace and set our sights on the portal once more. About an hour later, the sun dips below the treetops, casting the forest in the shade of twilight. Limery sits on Jordy's horns at the front of our party, and Pharos burns like a beacon against the darkness. As we come upon another centaur outpost, we're greeted by a familiar trio.

Sylvie absolutely beams when she sees the dragon, and Pharos's glow ignites her alabaster skin, setting her blue tattoos ablaze. She kneels, and Caustic totters toward her.

"Nice to see you again." Taryn blushes as he tries to make eye contact and avoid her bare chest.

She scratches Caustic behind the horns. "And you as well. The forest is better for your time in it."

Thannis strokes his forked beard, and even his stern demeanor is softened by the dragon's presence. "I agree. It is good to run free once again."

"We're glad. Have you seen the damage we left behind?" I gesture over my shoulder in the direction of the lake.

Daimun laughs. "Quite the destruction, I must say, but the forest will heal. With a little work, it will make a fine watering hole."

Taryn closes his eyes and shakes his head, as if clearing his mind, causing the clasps in his beard to jingle. "Just watch out for your friend, the Wanderer. It has made itself a home in the bottom of the pit."

"We are not so foolish to attack the Wanderer." Thannis smirks at Taryn. "Are you hoping to pass through the portal tonight?"

Taryn glances at me, and I pull up my map. We've still got a ways to go, but it would be nice to settle into an inn this evening.

"What do you think?" I ask Taryn.

"With Strong Wind buffing us, we could probably make it within a few hours."

Thannis nods. "Be careful. The wisps may be gone, but there are still dangers within the forest. Would you like an escort?"

I shake my head, summoning a Horror of Power as I do. "We appreciate the offer, but I think we'll be fine. If we don't get Taryn an ale soon, he'll turn into a real diva."

"Hey—" Taryn starts to argue, but Sylvie cuts him off.

"It is an attractive quality to know what one wants in life. I hope you find your ale." She winks at Taryn, and I'm surprised he doesn't fall from Berry's back.

He opens his mouth a few times, but all that comes out is a croak.

I pat Taryn on the back and bow my head to the others. "I think that's our cue to leave. I hope we meet again someday."

As we're leaving, I remember that I still have something that belongs to Thannis. I pull the Amulet of Sight from around my neck and hold it out to him. The stone in its center glows a dull yellow. "I almost forgot, but I believe this belongs to you. We never would have cleared the forest without it."

He takes it, rubbing his finger over the amulet. "I'm glad to have played a small part. Safe travels to you all."

Taryn waves at Sylvie as we leave, then mumbles, "She said I was attractive."

"Okay, playboy." I let Taryn have his moment and don't point out that she said it was an attractive quality.

When he finally returns to his senses, we're buffed with Strong Wind and follow Pharos as he prances through the forest. This is our first time actually traveling at night, and though the fog conceals most of what lies in the depths of the forest, green and red eyes stare down at us from the treetops.

Taking Thannis's warning to heart, I keep a steady supply of horrors just in case we come upon anything.

Much to his protest, I carry Caustic over my shoulder in order to make better time. For now, I'm much stronger than the dragon and he eventually tires of struggling against me. His scales feel cool against my skin as he holds on tight.

On my other shoulder, Limery perches quietly, his warm body a sharp contrast to the dragon's.

We travel quickly through the forest, and I almost feel bad that we're speeding through such picturesque scenery. Everything is so lush and full of life from the towering trees to the bats and nocturnal birds that swoop through the fog after some small creature on the ground.

Limery sighs. "Chods, is we's there yet? Limmy is ready to sees the cities."

"It shouldn't be too long, buddy. We'll be there before you know it."

Soon after, the glow of the portal shimmers in the distance. Something large rises from the fog, casting a silhouette in front of the silvery swirl of the arch.

Pharos halts, and we all gather behind the spirit guide. The shadow of a giant with harsh edges and jagged limbs blocks the portal. The shadow doesn't move, frozen like a statue.

I send my spirit guide closer, parting the fog until his light reveals the monster blocking our exit.

I let out a sigh of relief when it's nothing more than charred bark, moss, and lichen. "It's a dead tree. Any idea what it means?"

He shakes his head. "Never seen anything like it. I don't think it was here when we came through the portal, though. Let's approach with caution."

I set Caustic back on the ground and equip my warhammer just in case. This could be a trap, or it could be a dead tree that wasn't quite so spooky in the daylight.

Pharos and my horrors take the lead. With each step, the spirit guide pushes away more fog.

Taryn curses next to me, and a moment later, I understand why.

"What the shit is this?" I ask no one in particular.

A ring of giant mushrooms surrounds the portal on all sides, interspersed with three more creepy dead trees. These definitely weren't here when we came through the portal. I try to analyze them with my herbalism skill, but I get nothing. Large, bulbous mushrooms circle the platform to the portal, ranging in size from a small houseplant to some as big as Taryn. The three other trees are equally as unsettling as the first, but about three-fourths of the size.

I grip Destroyer tightly in my palm. This whole situation has my skin crawling. "Is this some weird forest magic to keep people out of Wandermere? Or is it meant to keep us from leaving?"

He frowns. "No idea. Whatever they are, I can't identify them."

At first, I thought it was my low-level herbalism skill, but if Taryn can't identify the creatures, something is definitely up.

I send my horrors closer to inspect, thirty of them bunched close together around Pharos while thirty more hang back with us.

I'm not sure what I expect to happen, but red eyes blazing to life behind a moss-covered face isn't it. A bone-chilling scream tears through the bark as it splinters into a monstrous mouth. In a quick and fluid motion, the tree steps forward, its trunk cracking as it splits into two legs. It swipes a massive limb through half of the horrors, exploding them and tossing others like bowling pins. The wooden fist passes through Pharos, dissipating the spirit guide for half a second before it reforms. The tree swings again and more horrors explode upon impact, and the rest are tossed back into the fog while the creature continues its assault, stomping and smashing in quick succession.

"Those aren't plants, they're monsters!" Taryn shouts.

"No shit, Sherlock." I take a step back and try to figure out how the hell we are going to deal with this monster when the surrounding mushrooms unroot themselves from the earth. Now that they're moving, I'm suddenly able to analyze them. I focus on the rampaging tree.

Woodland Horror. Level 20. *Born of the remains of once sentient trees, woodland horrors are bitter protectors of the forest. As life aura infuses the dead matter, they become watchful guardians, remembering the eons they lived before, but cut off from the web of roots that connects the forest and unable to communicate with the shared consciousness of the ancient trees.*

A fungi army surrounds the horror, composed of mushrooms in different shapes, sizes, and colors. One is purple and bulbous. Another is black with strings of black goo dripping from the edges of its cap. Some of them shriek at the night, while others emit poisonous gas. They walk on ghoulish feet of translucent roots, marching toward us.

In a matter of seconds, my horrors are obliterated. The monstrous plants seem unaffected by Pharos's presence, making it unlikely that they are from the shadow realms. They're still a threat, and unfortunately, they're standing in the way of us and a soft bed.

A bolt of lightning crashes into the charging mushrooms, ripping through the soft tissue of several and charring a few more. A squat green mushroom explodes, its innards raining down like jelly. Limery's claws dig into my shoulder as he takes flight and peppers the mob with fireballs. The skin of the mushrooms curls like wax paper against the heat of his attacks. Another fireball hits a woodland horror, setting its moss ablaze, and making the burning tree even more intimidating.

I kneel in front of Caustic, looking the dragon directly in the eyes. "Stay put. This is too dangerous for you."

I say it with as much authority as I can muster, but with the monsters approaching, there's no time to wait and see if he listens. I ready Destroyer and charge into the fray, summoning extra horrors as I do.

Ahead of me, Moonbeam streaks through the night in a silvery beam, way less effective than it had been on the wisps. Taryn stands back, Ruby hiding behind his legs as he casts spells as they become available. An imbued Jordy rams into a puff-ball mushroom, punting it into the fog like a soccer ball, and Berry's claws rip through mushrooms like butter. Poisonous gas and goo cover everything as the mushrooms explode, slowly ticking down the pets' health, but the real threats are the trees.

I smash Destroyer into one of their legs, and a shockwave of energy passes through, knocking down mushrooms in an arc behind the woodland horror. The splash damage from Ram's Rage doesn't disappoint. Red flares through my weapon as it gains a stack of inferno, and I swing again. This time, wood splinters, and the horror tumbles to the ground. My own horrors rush the downed monster, and Berry pries his claws between the scraps of wood that make up its shoulder, trying to rip it apart.

I flip the warhammer over, bringing the piercing end down on the tree's chest. There's a nasty crunch as wood splinters at the impact. Its jagged mouth opens, and a scream pours from the void, setting my hair on end. I press my foot against its midsection and pull Destroyer free before a well-placed fireball snuffs out the creature's remaining life.

The mushrooms fall quickly, leaving the three remaining trees in various stages of health. Two are half-dead, and one is nearly done for. A flame wall between two of them sets the monsters ablaze and their flailing arms light up the night. Taryn's lightning bolt hits the weakest of the three, stunning it in place while Destroyer finishes it off.

A flaming punch catches me unaware, hitting me in the jaw and knocking me to the ground. Stars dance in my vision as I try to sit up. There's a throaty growl as Caustic pounces on me, staring down the woodland horror that towers above us.

The scales on Caustic's neck stand on edge and he roars again, this time breathing toxic gas on the monster. The gas hits its flaming body like gasoline on a fire, erupting into a ten-foot blaze. The monster stumbles around for a few seconds before its charred flesh crashes to the ground.

Holy shit! His gas is flammable.

The flames on the final woodland horror are doused as it wrestles with Berry on the ground.

"Call him off!" I shout as I climb to my feet. "I want to try something."

Taryn calls for Berry, but the horror has no intention of giving up the fight. It lunges at the bear as he runs away.

I point at the woodland horror. "Caustic, hit it with your gas."

The young dragon obeys, snarling as it covers a small area in dense green smoke. The horror steps into the gas, which does very little damage by itself due to the gap in their levels.

"Limery, hit it with a fireball."

"Limmy's on it!"

He darts into position and a fireball erupts in his palm. He throws it, hitting the gas as the horror steps into the center of the cloud. An explosion engulfs the horror. Warm air assaults my face, and the monster falls to the ground, body sizzling and smoke rising from the corpse.

Taryn and I stare at each other for a moment in disbelief. The look on his face says he's just as surprised as I am. We've discovered a whole new level of devastation.

He casts Restoration on his pets while I survey the damage. Caustic gnaws on a piece of charred wood that used to belong to the woodland horror. The smell of burnt wood and dead fish linger in the air, and the ground is speckled with debris and fleshy pieces of mushroom. The scene looks like someone tossed colored chalk on the set of a horror movie.

Berry and Caustic gain a level from the fight, bringing the dragon up to level six.

When Taryn is done healing Jordy, he joins me among the wreckage. "That was weird. I guess the forest wasn't ready for us to leave." He chuckles.

"Maybe so. We should probably head through the portal before any other crazy monsters try to say good-bye."

He whistles, and his pets walk over. Even Caustic abandons his chew toy. "No shit. After that, I definitely need a beer."

With Caustic at my side and Limery on my shoulder, I focus on the rune for Pruxford and step through the swirling vortex.

18. PRUXFORD

Even at night, the city of Pruxford is one of the most beautiful places I've ever seen. As soon as we step through the portal, the glass palace shimmers at the far end of the city. It reminds me of the northern lights with the way streaks of emerald and amethyst fluctuate through the building.

Limery gasps. "Pretties."

While the palace is the focal point of the Pruxford, the rest of the city is just as beautiful. Glass sculptures are spread through the courtyard around the portal, reminding me that we need to go see Draydon's at some point.

A notification flashes in the corner of my vision, and I pull it up.

Regional Event Alert! *Welcome to Pruxford, the City of Glass! The Quincentennial Tournament of Champions is only a week away. The coming week will be filled with parties, parades, and celebrations honoring all of those who help make Pruxford the most amazing city in Mythos.*

Looks like we arrived just in time. A week of partying is exactly what the doctor ordered.

Behind us, thick glass walls wrap around the city. On the other side, sprawling fields of sunflowers take on the silver glow of moonlight. The walls must be enchanted to offer any sort of real protection, but their beauty is unmatched.

People traipse through the city. Gnomes, dwarves, humans, halflings, and beast-people in all shapes and colors. The only race I don't see are elves. Magical streetlights line the cobblestone streets, each one filled with dancing yellow lights. Aside from Sandholde, I don't know if I have ever seen such immaculate streets.

I can't quite explain it, but it feels like society has progressed quicker here than on Isle of Mythos while the portals were closed. The Pruxford gnomes are widely known as master tinkerers, but I didn't expect this. The contraptions and lights are far beyond anything I've seen so far. Signs on buildings rotate. Enchanted gemstones flash on each storefront, mimicking the effects of neon lights and igniting the window displays in an array of colors. The sign on a pub called The Brazen Swordsman has a wooden arm that slashes up and down. This is like being in a fantasy version of Times Square.

The city stretches out in all directions, with the Crystal Palace towering above it all. Seascape and Vanaria are massive cities, but Pruxford easily dwarfs them both by comparison. Most of the shops have shut down for the evening, but the inns, taverns, and restaurants bustle with activity. Minstrels play in the streets, and the porches are filled with laughter and conversation. A gnome wearing stilts clatters through the streets as he catches coins in a top hat.

Taryn takes a deep breath, breathing in the city. "This is what I'm talking about. Let's get the pets to a stable and find a place to stay for the evening."

"Good evening, sirs." An older gnome approaches us. He has shaggy blonde hair, a short blue beard, two golden hoops in each ear, and a rich purple tunic covered in a starburst of yellow and orange sequins. He eyes Caustic, licking his lips greedily, but shows no hesitation at the sight of the rest of our party.

He flashes us a brilliant white smile and bows. "Bildri Quilldrip, master travel guide, at your service. The city is a maze of fantastic shops and luxurious inns. It can be quite overwhelming to those unfamiliar. For a small fee, I will help you navigate the abundance of options before you." He holds a notepad in one hand and a feather quill hovers in the air next to him. "Oh, my, is that a dragon? And so young!"

Taryn urges Berry forward between the gnome and Caustic, forcing Bildri to step out of the way. "We appreciate the offer, but we'll be fine exploring on our own, thanks."

Bildri adjusts his robes and straightens his posture. "But, sirs, the city can be overwhelming for outsiders such as yourselves. Please allow me to—"

"I said we're fine," Taryn snaps, and Berry lets out a low growl.

"Very well." The gnome huffs before skittering to the next group that steps through the portal—a human couple wearing fine linens followed by a halfling in rags pulling a cart piled with luggage.

Taryn scratches Berry behind the ears. "Good boy."

I narrow my eyes at Taryn. "What was that all about? Don't you think it would be smart to have someone help us through the city? It's already late, and we don't know anything about this place."

Taryn laughs. "Rich people. That guy was going to hustle us. Did you see the way he was eyeing Caustic? He'd recommend us to places that are putting the most coin in his pocket and overcharge us for everything. If you want to find the best places in the city, you find a native, and one who isn't a salesman."

"I see. We're the prince and the pauper now." I laugh. "Alright, wow me with your street smarts."

"Hey, you!" Taryn waves down a young gnome in tattered clothing.

The kid reminds me of Brock, the orphan from the Underground Circus.

"Yes?" He eyes Taryn with suspicion.

Taryn pulls out a silver coin and flips it in the air. "Want to make a quick coin? Where's the best stable in the area?"

The kid grins. "That depends. The New Dawn has the nicer stables, but Farryn is an ass. The Rusty Bucket might not look like much, but Ms. Breebis has a way with the animals."

Taryn tosses the coin to the kid. "The Rusty Bucket it is. Which way?"

After a short trek, we arrive at the Rusty Bucket. True to the kid's word, it doesn't look like much. Compared to the fancy buildings with stained glass and elegant architecture on both sides, the stable looks like it belongs back in Lynchton. There's nothing off-putting about it, but it's rustic and out of place and I can see why people might pass it by.

The stables are quiet, minus the occasional bleat of sheep or grunt of some animal we can't see. A hammock gently swings across the pillars of the entry.

"Hello?" Taryn calls. "Anyone here?"

There's movement in the hammock, and then a mossy green head peeks over the edge. Deep red eyes look us over from beneath a large bun of dark green hair.

"Howdy," she says.

"Are you Ms. Breebis? We were hoping to house our pets for the night. You come highly recommended."

She swings her legs over the side of the hammock but doesn't climb down. "Is that so? We don't get many of your type around here."

"Dwarves?" Taryn asks.

I clench my fist. This was supposed to be a city where different races lived in peace, but here we are being judged by a three-foot-tall bean sprout.

"Foreigners." She slides off the hammock and lands softly on the ground.

She walks up to Caustic without fear, stroking him beneath the chin. To my surprise, he lets her, a soft purr rumbling within. She moves to each of the pets in turn, pulling a carrot from her pocket and feeding it to Jordy, and then scratching Berry behind the ear until he groans in pleasure. She even has a bite-sized treat for Ruby that she uses to make the jackal stand on its hind legs.

Taryn is enamored, and I must say, I'm impressed.

"Beautiful lot you have here. I'd be honored to watch over them for you. With me, you don't pay for the location, you pay for the service. They'll be fed. They'll be bathed and brushed. We have mind-building exercises in the morning and social time in the afternoon. Everyone gets a bedtime story at night, and my crew all sleep in hammocks from the rafters. There's no better place for your pets in all of Pruxford."

She's managed to put all of my concerns at ease. "I'm sold, but can I ask you something?"

She crosses her arms and leans against the wooden beam. "What is it, big guy?"

"If your place is so good, why are you hidden away like this?"

She scoffs, tossing her arms up. "Look around you. Pruxford is a city of glamor, but it's only skin deep. If you pull back the curtain, you'll see things aren't as great as they seem. The rich stick together, making each other richer, and the poor get swept under the rug. My family has owned this building for nine generations. Nine! We've always cared about quality over everything. We invest our gold in training, in quality food, and in workers with the right temperament to handle any creature. If anyone in the outer boroughs needs a stable, they come here."

"Then why aren't you more popular?" asks Taryn.

She laughs, but there's no mirth to it. "We're not a part of the 'in' crowd. The other stables can't compete with our quality, so they trash us with advertising and spread rumors. Farryn has friends on the advertising council, and they reject our requests and deny our appeals. Eventually, my father gave up the fight. You won't see our promotions in the market or plastered around town, but we don't lose customers. Their word of mouth keeps the torches burning."

"Damn, I'm sorry to hear that." Taryn hands her the reins to Berry. "I wish there was something we could do."

She smiles. "Your business is more than enough."

After we check in our pets, Breebis gives us directions to an inn she recommends. With only Limery joining us, our party feels unnaturally small.

Along the way, I take in the beautiful architecture and manicured streets of the city. There are specialized shops for just about everything, from toy stores to spice emporiums and several guild headquarters. Mixed in between them are houses and apartments.

A carriage passes us by, pulled by goats and loaded with boys about the same age as the one who gave us directions. The carriage stops next to an overturned trashcan, and the boys jump out, brooms in hand. They sweep up the trash in under a minute, and the carriage is clattering down the street once again.

I can't help thinking about what Breebis said. "You think it's true? About the city not being as great as it seems?"

Taryn nods. "Do you think your dad made all his money by treating his competitors nice? People are obviously doing well for themselves here, at least some of them. But I guarantee you there are more stories like Breebis's. There's no king here, so the power has to go somewhere."

I stare at my oversized feet, wondering how much truth there is to his statement. "Everyone has always said my dad was a shrewd businessman. I just assumed it was from making good decisions and not backing down, but I'm sure someone had to fail so that he could succeed."

"It's the American way. And maybe the gnomish way too." Taryn shrugs.

We stop in front of an inn called The Puzzling Peacock. There's a giant peacock sign above the porch. The peacock holds a magnifying glass over one of its eyes, making it much larger than the other. The tailfeathers of the sign glow with green and purple light. They must have a lot of enchanters in order to keep so many signs going all the time. Or maybe they're permanent or rechargeable enchantments. Either way, it has to be a lot of work for someone.

Limery claps his hands. "Pretties. Limmy likes the peacocks."

Inside, the inn is bustling. Only a few tables remain empty, and two bartenders work the bar, one gnome and one ivory dwarf, slinging frothy mugs of ale. A human woman rushes around, delivering giant mugs six at a time. There's a stage in the back, where a duo performs. A gnome with spiked blue hair plays a lute while one with pink pigtails sings a song of battle.

Taryn eyes the woman carrying beer greedily. "You see the size of those mugs? This is my type of place alright."

"Yeah, this is Limmy's types of place, too." He wipes a string of drool from his chin.

I squeeze in between a gnome and human at the bar, but it takes a minute for one of the bartenders to make their way over.

"What can I get fer ye?" The dwarven bartender places his palms down on the bar and leans forward like a bulldog.

"We need two rooms and three strong drinks."

"Aye, have a seat and I'll have Lissa bring 'em out for ye."

We claim one of the few open tables by a window. Here, no one seems to think we're out of place. No one stares at us. Even as a giant blue troll with horns sprouting from my head, people acknowledge me and look away.

This must really be a melting pot. About two-thirds of the patrons are gnomes, and they come in a wide array of skin tones and hair colors. The only thing they all have in common is their short stature and pointy ears. Scattered among them are a few dwarves, blue-skinned lizardfolk, a couple of catfolk, and a group of rowdy humans in the far back corner. In the midst of the humans, a tall, one-eyed giant holds a mug in each hand. His massive eye takes up most of his face, and when he laughs, it reveals a mouth full of sharp pointed teeth. I try to analyze him without staring.

Arty
> *Level 29*
> *Warrior*
> *Cyclops*

"Bro." I tap Taryn on the arm. "It's a cyclops. Look at the size of him."

Taryn looks over his shoulder and quickly turns around. "Whoa, that's a big mother—"

"Forgive me for the wait." Lissa places three frothing mugs of amber ale on the table. "The city is packed for the tournament, so consider yourselves lucky that you got our last two rooms." She reaches in her apron and hands Taryn and me each a key with a colorful rope lanyard. "The key matches the color of the door to your room. If you need anything else, wave me down."

We lift our mugs, Limery with two hands, and clink them together.

"To civilization." I tilt the mug up and let the malty goodness wash over me.

"That's the stuff." Taryn finishes his first mug in a matter of seconds and already has his hand waving after Lissa. He holds up two fingers when she acknowledges him.

Limery closes his eyes after the first sip, and he couldn't look more blissful if he tried. "Oh, yes! That's the stuffs, Taryns."

As soon as Lissa returns with our second round, Taryn orders a third. The drinks flow freely until the inn is roaring with laughter, conversation, and music. A queue forms in front of Arty as he arm-wrestles one challenger after another. One of the catfolk joins the two gnomes on the stage, and her powerful voice has the crowd going wild as she belts out some heroic fighter's victory over an orc chieftain.

Taryn slams an empty mug on the table and slurs his words as his head sways back and forth. "Lemme tell you, Limery and Caustic, those two're gonna be a scary combination when he gets older."

I turn back my mug and savor the last drops of my ale. I've paced myself better than Taryn, but my vision is still swimming. Limery, on the other hand, has his arms wrapped around the mug with his head resting on top. His eyes flutter as he fights sleep.

"I agree, bro. I can't wait to see what they're capable of."

A loud thud behind us startles Limery for a moment before he drifts back to sleep. I turn around to see the cyclops smirking as the human across from him rubs his arm. The cyclops puts his elbow on the table and clenches his fist.

"Will no one else challenge the mighty Arty?" He makes eye contact with me, holding my gaze for several seconds. "A hundred gold to anyone who can best me."

The music softens and murmurs snake around the inn. A hundred gold is a massive amount of money to wager on an arm-wrestling match.

I wave down Lissa. "Who is this guy?"

She smiles as she glances in his direction. "That's Arty, one of Pruxford's most famous adventurers. He might look mean, but he has a heart of gold."

"Really? He looks like he could rip someone's arm off without breaking a sweat."

She laughs. "And you don't, Mr. Troll? He's a good man. One of the best to come out of the outer borough. A human family found him crying and all alone while hunting in the dark forest. He was so small back then, now look at him. He's made us all proud. That's for sure."

I watch Arty for a moment as he waits for a challenger, laughing and joking with those at his table. He sits back and wraps his muscled arms around the two closest to him. The dude couldn't look any more monstrous, and yet he's earned the respect of not only his friends but the barmaid as well.

If he truly is as good as she says, then I want him on our side.

I equip Forlorn Scepter, holding it beneath the table. When I stand, the inn goes quiet, even the gnome playing the lute softens his music. My chair grates as it slides across the wooden floor, and I feel every eye lingering on me.

"A hundred gold? I'll take that challenge."

I point the scepter toward the floor, concealing the flash of green below the table as I summon a Horror of Power outside the window. The weapon's passive allows me to increase the range of summoned creatures by fifty percent. If this guy is competing in the tournament, then I want to keep as many surprises up my sleeve as possible. Not to mention the chaos summoning horrors in the middle of a crowd of drunks could cause. I quickly summon a Horror of Finesse and Vitality as well.

Arty stands, smiling dangerously. He's a few inches taller than me and every bit as muscled. I'm not sure about the perks that come with being a cyclops, but I have to imagine he has a pretty high Strength and Constitution build. Being a level twenty-nine warrior, he definitely has an advantage over me. Even if it's minor, he would win out in a test of pure strength.

He extends his hand. "You don't look anything like the troll paintings in the museums."

I grip his hand firmly in mine and squeeze. "I'm not your average troll."

"Hmm. It appears so." His massive eyelid blinks. "There have been stories of a troll hero making waves on the isle. Might there be some truth to those stories?"

I summon three more horrors outside as we continue our standoff. "There might be."

He sits down. "Then it will be an honor to test your strength."

Lissa was right. This guy looks like a one-eyed asshole, but he seems nice as can be. I take a seat across from him, draping my scepter across my knees.

I make small talk so that I can hopefully get in a few more horrors before the match begins. "So, you're planning on entering the tournament?"

He tilts back his head and laughs. "It wouldn't be a tournament without Arty. I've already won two tournaments this year, but this one is special. It's the quincentenary of Pruxford's first Battle of Champions. Five hundred years since heroes and powerful fighters fought one another for glory before a crowd. I expect a real challenge for this one." He places his elbow down on the table. "Are you ready?"

I plant my elbow and grip his hand. "Ready."

His fingers clench around mine and his strength clashes with my own. For a moment, we're in a stalemate, neither one of us giving way. His massive eye bores into me, but his face remains placid. My veins enlarge as I channel my strength against him with all my might, but damn, he's strong.

Slowly, he starts to gain leverage, pushing my arm toward the table a millimeter at a time. I cast another round of horrors, bringing my total to twelve, and use Sacrifice. They vanish outside the window, and four points flood into my Strength, Dexterity, and Constitution. My bicep bulges, and his arm starts to move in the other direction.

Arty's giant eye widens. "So, we're playing that way, eh?" He grins.

A red aura surrounds his arm, and he slams my wrist against the table with such force that the wood splinters. Pain flares from my wrist to my shoulder. I grimace as I clench my fist to make sure it still works.

Arty bursts out laughing and slaps the table. "That was good. For someone so big, you're a sneaky little goblin."

There's a brief round of applause before the music resumes and it's like the match never happened.

I shake out my sore arm. "What the hell was that?"

He leans forward. "I could ask you the same thing."

I laugh as the pain fades from my arm. "I can't reveal my cards before the hand is over." I glance over at the table, where both Taryn and Limery are dead to the world. "I should probably help get these two into bed. Thanks for the challenge."

He flashes a dangerously-toothy grin. "See you in the arena, Chod of the forest trolls."

I can't help but like this guy. "I'll be looking forward to it."

19. NO ONE SAID THERE WOULD BE A TEST

A knock outside my room wakes me from a blissful sleep. When I open the door, Taryn is bright-eyed and bushy-tailed, with no lingering effects from the exorbitant amount of alcohol he drank the previous night.

"Dude, have you heard of sleeping in? It's our first night back in a city." I stumble back to the bed and lie down, where Limery continues to snore.

"Exactly!" He rips the covers off the bed and tosses them to the floor. "All the more reason to get up. Pruxford is huge! We need to register for the tournament, and then I want to get some shopping in. Now, get up, you two."

"Limmy is sleepies." The imp tucks his head in the crook of my arm.

"Yeah, just give us a few more minutes." I place the pillow over my face to block out the light from the windows.

Taryn taps his foot against the floor, and I imagine him standing there with his hands on his hips. "There's breakfast downstairs."

The magic words.

Limery's head pops up like a meerkat. "Oh yes, Limmy is hungries." He pulls the pillow from my face and presses his bulbous eyes inches from my own. "Wakes up, Chods. Times to eats."

"Goddammit, Taryn." I throw the pillow across the room at him, but he just grins mischievously.

Once the food arrives, I'm glad that we didn't skip out on breakfast. A lilac-skinned gnome wearing a chef's hat sets a platter down in the center of the table. There's bread with an assortment of jams, crispy bacon and sausage links, and speckled baby blue eggs the size of a softball.

I bite into one of the sausages, and the juices explode in my mouth. Juicy, fatty, savory deliciousness. Limery holds a piece of thick-cut bacon in one hand and a sausage in the other, alternating between the two.

For the first few minutes, we devour the food in silence.

I wipe some of the grease from my chin with a napkin and fill in the others on what they missed the night before. "While you two were passed out at the table last night, I spent a little time with Arty. He's crazy strong, and I think he could be a good ally."

Taryn shoves a piece of bread slathered with butter into his mouth. "The scary-looking cyclops?"

Heavy footsteps clank down the stairs. "Master dwarf, I am wounded by your comments."

Arty smiles, revealing his sharp teeth, and it's difficult to judge the expression of his single large eye.

Taryn gulps. "Sorry, I just meant you're an intimidating presence. Kind of like Chod here."

Arty laughs. "I'm only kidding. I know what I am." He flexes his arms, posing like a bodybuilder. "A terrible, frightening warrior who abducts children and uses their bones as toothpicks after I'm done stripping the flesh from their bodies."

Limery's eyes go even wider than normal.

One of the barmaids pushes Arty in the side. "Oh, stop that. You're nothing of the sort." She turns to us. "Don't you listen to a word he says."

"If you say so." He shrugs. "Anyways, there's much to do. Have a good day, gentlemen."

I call out to the cyclops as he makes for the door. "Arty, hold up. Will you be staying here all week?"

"Until the tournament is over."

"I'd love to talk sometime. I've got a proposition for you."

His single eyebrow raises. "Consider me intrigued. I'll see you around, Chod."

Once Arty is out the door, Taryn massages his forehead. "If I mysteriously disappear, check his toothpick container for my bones."

After breakfast, we stop by the stables to check on our pets. Breebis is in the middle of training Ruby when we arrive. She taps her shoulder, and the jackal leaps high into the air, landing on the gnome with surprising finesse. The gnome feeds Ruby a small treat, and the jackal jumps back to the ground.

"She's a quick learner." Breebis grins. "They all are."

Taryn kneels, and Ruby rushes over to him. "Now I just need a mouse to climb on her shoulder and we can join the circus."

Breebis tucks a loose strand of green hair behind her ear. "How can I help you, gentlemen?"

Taryn scratches Ruby behind the ears and pulls her against his chest. "We just wanted to check in before we explore the city."

"Thanks for the recommendation for the inn, by the way. It was a great spot." I stand on my tip-toes to look deeper into the stable, where a pink elephant-type creature is munching on a pile of rainbow-colored hay. "I think I'm going to take Caustic with me today. We're still bonding, so I think it's good to spend as much time together as possible."

"Absolutely." She claps her hands together. "Let me grab him for you. Follow me."

She leads us through the maze of stables. There are traditional mounts like horses and oxen for pulling wagons, but also a camel and a large beetle with a metallic carapace. We pass Jordy's enclosure, where he practices his charging against a gnome covered in padding. The gnome holds a padded shield similar to the ones boxers practice with. Jordy slams into the gnome, rocketing it against the wall of the stable.

"That's my boy." Taryn puffs out his chest, preening like a dad whose kid just scored the winning goal.

Berry groans at us as we peek into his enclosure, where his fur is being brushed with a bone brush.

Taryn climbs on the railing. "Don't get too spoiled in there."

In the far back, we finally find Caustic. The trainer plays a game with him where she hides a treat under one of three metal cups. She then rearranges them all in a quick motion before Caustic chooses which one contains the treat. Three times in a row, he gets it on the first try.

Breebis turns to me. "I was surprised to learn that Caustic is a true green dragon. A lot of people try to pass off their winged lizards as dragons, but you can always tell by how stupid they are. Dragons are intelligent creatures, even lesser dragons like wyrms or wyverns. A true dragon is a rarity, but a young green dragon like this, I doubt even my father had the pleasure to see one in person. They must be challenged mentally or they'll grow restless, especially as they grow stronger. I'll give you a list of common training exercises before you all check out."

"Thanks, I appreciate it." I reach my arm over the railing, and Caustic licks my fingers. "Want to go explore the city, little guy?"

He leaps up to the wooden railing, his leathery wings now bigger than ever. His growth rate hasn't slowed, and he's easily the size of a large dog at this point. When he flutters down on the other side, Limery hops on the dragon's back and uses the growing antlers as handlebars.

"We'll have him back in time for dinner." I wink.

After a quick lecture on how to behave in a crowd and a stern warning that he'll never see the light of day if even a plume of toxic gas makes its way into the city, we step out into the street. Like any young child, Caustic is fascinated by all the people. He sniffs at stray dogs, pounces toward pigeons eating crumbs off the ground near a food cart, and continuously looks over his shoulder to make sure we're still following.

A wagon pulls to a stop beside us, and a group of hesitant young gnomes asks us to move out of the way so they can clean up a half-eaten sandwich off the ground.

After stopping for a few meat kabobs, we find a street vendor selling maps of the city for only five silver. Normally, I'd pass on the offer, but Pruxford is so big, we'd never explore the entire city on our own.

Once the map is in my inventory, it populates across my vision. Every shop in the city shows up with a directory separating them by the items they sell. There's a multitude of stores selling everything from armor to trinkets, clothing, and food. Every inn is listed, along with statues, public buildings, guilds, temples, and any public location someone would need. Personal quarters aren't listed, but everything else is. The only thing it doesn't have is a review system.

The sheer scope is overwhelming.

"Why doesn't every city have one of these?" Taryn holds the map spread out before him. "They could make a fortune."

I spread my arms, gesturing at how big the city is. "Most cities don't have this scale of commerce. They only need a public directory at the city or town hall. I'm glad we bought these, though. Best five silver I've ever spent."

I pull the map back up and find the closest notice board. Luckily, it's at the end of the street, and it'll be our best bet for finding info on the tournament without having to track down a city official.

Onlookers point at Caustic as we head down the street. For the first time since entering Mythos, I'm the least-interesting member of our party.

The notice board is filled with flyers and posters. There are non-guild quests, notices for clubs and guilds, concerts, events, and so much more. Underneath the new posters, there are faded pictures of missing children. Glenn crosses my mind, but there's no way he would risk being captured in a city like this. In the middle, there's a massive poster for the tournament. It has an image of the stadium and several silhouettes in the center with the slogan, "Who will reign supreme?" At the bottom, there's a row of fine print.

Notice: *Those who wish to compete in the Quincentennial Tournament of Champions must register with the Department of Entertainment and Events no less than three days prior to the tournament. Prospective combatants will be given a placement test prior to acceptance. Not everyone who enters will qualify. Adventurers and Heroes welcome.*

"Placement test? What do you think that is all about?" I ask.

Taryn shrugs, his eyes focused on another flyer. "They probably want to make sure no one gets accidentally killed."

I lean over his shoulder. "What has you so fascinated that you don't even care about the tournament?"

"Oh, I care. I just thought this was rather interesting." He rips the flyer off the board and hands it to me.

For One Week Only!
All The Way From The Isle Of Mythos

The Underground Circus!
Experience a Show Unlike Any Other!

I read over it several times to make sure there's not some mistake, but sure enough, the flyer is stamped with the black lion logo of the Underground Circus. They were in Sandholde last we saw, but I guess Hawkin set his eyes on more fruitful pastures. I'm glad he took my advice to heart. The circus has come a long way from performing in the streets of Vanaria and from the looks of it, they could be a hit all over Mythos.

"Good for them. We'll definitely have to stop by one night and say hello." I tack the flyer back on the board. "Let's get the boring part over with, shall we?"

We find the Department of Entertainment and Events located inside City Hall, along with dozens of other departments responsible for everything from cleaning the city streets to enforcing the amount of magical meat imported by local restaurants.

The foyer of the building has jaw-dropping architecture. Marble floors gleam from the light that passes through the crystal walls of the entryway. The entire front of the building is a mixture of crystal and stained glass. There's a central fountain with a gnome holding a staff overhead. Water shoots out from the staff, arcing across a glass bridge and splashing in a smaller pool some twenty yards away, where colorful fish dart through the water.

People hurry about like office workers in Manhattan, carrying scrolls from one department to another. This city feels more and more like New York every day.

We find the office we are looking for on the fourth floor. Caustic's claws clack against the marble with each step. We catch a lot of looks, but no one says anything. To the untrained eye, he looks no different than a large reptile someone might keep as a pet. Only a handful of people actually inspect him enough to recognize that he's a dragon.

The inside of the D.E.E. office reminds me of a whimsical clerk's office with colorfully-dressed gnomes sitting behind counters. Some wear monocles while others use magnifying glasses to examine documents. Feather quills hover in the air next to them, jotting down notes onto scrolls. Their conversations with those in line are somehow magically muted from the rest of us, because I can see their lips moving but no sound is coming out.

The walls are covered in giant paintings depicting the advertising campaigns of previous events.

"That looks like fun." I point to one showing a gnome riding some catlike creature as it races against a human on a horse. They race through the streets of Pruxford, the Crystal Palace towering in the background with *Pruxford Grand Prix* in giant red letters at the top.

"For sure. Imagine blazing through the city using Strong Wind with no pedestrians to slow us down. I bet Jordy could give any of those mounts a run for their money. Get a load of this one." He points to a painting of some gnome bard. Only instead of playing in a dimly-lit tavern, she's singing on a stage surrounded by thousands of people. Fireworks explode behind her underneath the words *Cecily Vanderpants* written in an elegant script.

"This city really does have everything."

After taking in our surroundings, my focus shifts to the others waiting in line. Some of these people look like average citizens, but many look like adventurers. I'm only now keenly aware of how few adventurers there were on Isle of Mythos. Here, it seems like there are enough that it must be a stable form of income. Either that or they've come from all over to enter the tournament.

A tall, female human wearing leather armor stands in front of us. She holds a spear in one hand that is a foot taller than she is. In front of her, a panda beast-person with broad shoulders blocks my view of whoever stands in front. The panda wears a wide-brimmed straw hat, silver bracers, and a loin cloth, but nothing else.

I catch a lizardfolk with golden scales watching us from the farthest line, his eyes fixated on Caustic. He wears finely-embroidered clothing with a well-tailored long coat in a regal plum color. Several golden amulets dangle from his neck. The gnome at the counter calls for the next-in-line and he heads over. Both the woman and the lizardfolk have their stats concealed, so I'm unable to gain much aside from their appearance. They both look like formidable opponents.

As we watch those go through the line before us, I get an idea of how the whole process works. Each gnome working the counter has an enchanted orb that scans each applicant. Some people are turned away on the spot. If they pass the scan, then the gnomes fill out a bunch of notes. I have no idea what the questions are, but the hovering pen writes rapidly. Once that portion is done, the applicant is either turned away or sent through another door to where I assume the next part of the test is administered.

After the female human goes through the mystery door, it's my turn. I step up to the counter with Limery on my shoulder and Caustic beside me.

A gnome with bright orange hair trimmed into a bob looks up from her stack of parchment. "One at a time, please."

I place a hand on the counter. "We're actually together."

She blinks a few times, staring at me like I'm some kind of idiot. "Are either of these beings a pet or summoned being?"

"Well, the dragon and I haven't permanently bonded yet. And Limery, the imp, he's—"

"Then one at a time, please." She stares at me blankly, waiting for one of us to leave the counter. When I don't immediately leave, she raises a hand. "Security!"

"Oh, for fuck's sake, lady! Give me a second." I turn to Limery, on the verge of losing my cool. "Hey, bud, I guess we have to do this one at a time. Will you wait with Caustic until I'm done?"

Limery frowns before hopping to the floor beside Caustic. "Okays. Caustics, come with Limmy."

I take a deep breath and return to the counter. "Happy?"

She doesn't say anything as she lifts a dark blue orb in front of me. Energy swirls within the orb and then there's a pulse as it scans me. A strange sensation passes through me, and just as quickly, it's gone.

The quill jots something down on the paper. The gnome reads it, and then looks up, no emotion on her face. "You are of satisfactory level to compete."

She then rattles off several questions in quick succession.

"Race?"

"Forest troll."

She raises an eyebrow. "Class?"

"I'm a dual-class barbarian summoner."

"Where are you from?"

"Isle of Mythos."

"Answer the next questions with your base stats only. Strength?"

"Forty-three."

"Dexterity?"

"Twenty-four."

"Constitution?"

"Forty-four."

"Intelligence."

"Ten."

She pauses for a second, coughing before asking for my Wisdom stat. I'm pretty sure this is her attempt to keep from laughing.

I give her my best fake smile. "Fifteen."

"Charisma?"

"Six."

"Any notable victories or accomplishments you would like the judges to be aware of?"

"Let's see. I completed a regional quest, defeating a mana-infused wyrm. I've cleared a faerie dungeon, a marsh dungeon, and a salt dungeon, defeated the leader of the mountain trolls in single combat, made peace with King Favian of Vanaria on behalf of the forest trolls, and fought the gladiators of Goldspire in order to deliver a message for King Orso of Seascape. I've fought a behemoth, cleared Wandermere of mesmer wisps, and hatched the first green dragon in hundreds of years. Oh, and I'm a hero."

Her expression never changes, as she's thoroughly unimpressed with my accolades. "That will be all. Please step through the door to your right and wait for your turn."

I take Caustic and wish Limery luck before heading to the other door.

I pass by Taryn, who's waving his arms animatedly as he tells a story to the clerk. The chubby gnome with purple curled hair tilts her head back, laughing at whatever he just said. Why couldn't I get the fun one?

A gnome wearing an orange sherbert-colored uniform waits by the door holding a notepad in her hand. "Name?"

"Chod."

"You'll have to leave the li—" She pauses, tilting her head as her eyes fix on Caustic. "Er, dragon, outside while you finish the test. I can arrange to have him delivered to you upon completion."

These guys are making this way too difficult.

I take a deep breath and sigh. "Fine."

Reaching inside my satchel, I pull out some rope and fashion it into a makeshift leash.

I place it around Caustic's neck and kneel beside him. "Please don't bite or burn anyone."

After handing the gnome the leash, she allows me to enter. I step into an empty room with three closed doors against the far wall. Each door has a different colored gemstone set in its center. Red, blue, and yellow. The door behind me shuts, leaving me in a dim room aside from the gentle glow of the three gems.

A soft voice speaks from all around me. "You have been judged worthy of competition. Ready your weapon and prepare to be tested. You may use any weapons in your inventory and all of your abilities, but the use of elixirs, potions, or other items will end the test."

The yellow gemstone in the door on the right lights up, and the door opens. I equip Destroyer and summon three horrors as I step into the next room.

The room is similar to the previous in its aesthetic but much bigger, about the size of a basketball court. In the center, rows of neatly-lined statues take up a quarter of the space. Warriors holding swords and spears make up the first two rows, each one kneeling with their weapon beside them. Behind them, there are two rows of mages wearing long, flowing robes that stand with outstretched hands. In the furthest two rows, archers point their bows toward the heavens. All in all, I count twenty-four statues.

Depending on how strong the statues are, I'm guessing the test is either how long I can survive before certain parameters are hit or how quickly I can defeat them all.

I eye them warily out of my peripheral as I take in the rest of my surroundings. Each wall has two torches, casting the room with a forest of shadows. The flickering flames give the statues a lifelike quality. The walls, ceiling, and floor are all a dull gray, which is a stark contrast to every other building in Pruxford—but it gives the statues an even more menacing presence. There are no other entrances and no obstacles to use for defensive positioning.

I keep my distance with the three horrors in front of me, summoning more and readying Destroyer for whatever comes next. I'm not practiced enough with my new weapons and there's no telling what these gnomes are going to throw at me.

The grumbling of my horrors is overshadowed by stone grating against stone as the first row of statues comes to life. Dust falls from their joints as they stand with clunky movements, reminding me of those humanoid robots that move in effective but unnatural motions. I try to analyze them, but their stats are concealed.

Gnomish Stoneguards. *Level ???*

Great. I guess I'll have to get punched before I know how strong they are.

With each step, their movements become more fluid until they swing swords and spin spears like seasoned warriors. I take a few steps forward, giving myself some space in case I need to retreat. The closest stone swordsman charges, weapon held over his shoulder. I order my horrors to the back wall and meet the attacker head-on. Destroyer clashes with his sword, shattering the stone weapon and sending broken shards clattering around the room.

A second swordsman slashes to my right, but I move quicker, spinning around and hitting him square in the chest. Energy from Ram's Rage ripples through the air in a cone, hitting the two spearmen behind him. Stone explodes in all directions, and a spear rips through my braid, narrowly avoiding my throat. All around the room, more statues begin to move. I dodge another spear jab and spot the glowing hands of the stone mages out of the corner of my eye.

I smash a stone spearman into oblivion, but an arrow catches me in the shoulder, sending white-hot pain flaring from the impact. With a grunt, I rip the arrow out and toss it to the ground. Then I equip the Halite Shield, using its translucent properties like a riot shield so I can formulate a plan while fending off two swordsmen and a barrage of arrows.

There's no way I'm taking down all of these guys, so I can only imagine this is a test to see how long I survive. Losing a level to qualify for this tournament is a shit gamble, but the payoff could open opportunities that are otherwise impossible.

A fireball explodes against the shield, and heat flows around all four edges. My eyes water, and the attack leaves a black residue on the outside of the shield, obscuring my vision as arrows continue to rain down around me. I push forward with all my might, but the stone warriors seem anchored to the floor.

I summon a horror in front of the soldier and cast Kamikaze, but the attack has little effect on the stone armor.

A second mage attack hits my shield, and this time, ice spreads around from the impact. I drop the shield just before frost creeps onto my hand. A second later, wind rips through the room, tossing shards of broken stone like shrapnel and peppering my body with damage.

Each of the mages must have a different elemental attack. If I keep playing this passively, I'm going to get backed into a corner. I'm so used to fighting alongside Taryn and Limery that I haven't had a need to go at it alone. The days of running headfirst into battle have been few and far between as of late.

I need to take this on the offensive if I'm going to have a chance.

The few Horrors of Vitality I have charge by my side, their passives slowing the stone warriors enough to give me a slight movement advantage. The pointed end of Destroyer shatters a swordsman. It flashes red from a stack of Inferno, and I spin, bringing the hammer in an upward swing that explodes the head of another statue. The other spearmen stab through my horrors in seconds, and a blast of water hits me like a firehose, knocking me off balance as three arrows tear into my chest.

I don't have time to pull them out before a spear jabs at my throat. I parry the attack, but a fireball catches me in the ribs. The smell of burning flesh is nothing compared to the searing pain that accompanies every movement.

A stone fist slams into my side, cracking ribs and bringing me to my knees.

"Fuck this!" I shout as I roll out of the way just as another fist crashes into the floor inches from my head.

I activate Berserker Rage and sacrifice all of my remaining horrors, boosting my stats by a few more points. My vision goes red, and the pain of my injuries becomes a distant memory as my muscles bulge with increased power and speed. Thanks to Ram's Rage, not only do I deal splash damage, but my barbarian rage now lasts twice as long. My wounds stitch themselves together thanks to my increased healing, and I jump to my feet.

Destroyer crushes the head of the closest swordsman, and I duck as an ice projectile soars by, smashing against the wall. Spells and arrows continue to assault me, but the stone warriors take some friendly fire from the attacks. If I can find a way to get past them then I can do some damage to those at the back.

I cast Champion and a mesmer wisp forms in the center of the room. Smoke pours from the creature, making for poor visibility, but the mages and archers immediately focus on the new target. Its tongue whips in and out of the smoke, and I use the momentary distraction to summon another Horror of Vitality. I make my move as the horror slows the spearman pursuing me.

I smash three archers with a fully-stacked Destroyer, the blazing heat from Inferno turning the stone black with each hit. The wisp shrieks as it dies, and the attention falls on me once again. A lightning bolt hits me, but thanks to my rage the stun is ineffective. I power through their attacks, my health dropping in chunks and climbing back as I smash through statue after statue. Nearly half of them are destroyed by the time my rage ends, leaving me a steaming pile of tattered blue meat.

Destroyer suddenly feels incredibly heavy, and as I raise it over my head, an arrow lodges in my throat. The warhammer falls from my hand, and the last thing I see is a fireball hurling at my head before everything goes black.

20. A DASH OF CHAOS

I come to inside of a plain room similar to the one I was just in, only this one is much smaller and there are no statues trying to kill me. A single door beckons from across the room, and a notification flashes in the corner of my vision.

Placement test complete. *Please await further instructions.*

I check over my stats, expecting to have lost a level, but whatever happened, I was brought here before I actually died. There must have been some kind of enchantment protecting me from death while inside the training room. Even Destroyer and the Halite Shield have returned to my inventory.

The door clicks, and Caustic runs into the room, tongue hanging from his open mouth while he pulls a worried-looking gnome by the leash.

"Here's your dr-dragon, s-sir," the gnome stammers as he hands me the leash. "You'll be notified of your placement when entries lock in two days."

I want to ask him more questions, but Caustic jumps on my leg like an excited puppy. With his sharp claws, we're going to need to nip that in the bud right away. I pull a piece of jerky from my satchel and hold it in front of the excited dragon.

"Sit," I say firmly. When he obeys, I toss him the treat. "Good boy! We can't have you crushing people when you become an excited thirty-foot-tall dragon, now can we?"

We exit the room into the same hallway where the D.E.E. is located. I send Taryn a quick message, telling him I'll be waiting downstairs for them when they are done. I wonder how Taryn will do without having his pets there. He's not exactly a master of hand-to-hand combat, and those statues sure pack a punch.

I sit next to the fountain in the foyer, watching the colorful fish dart underneath the bridge. Among the patter of feet and constant chatter, the bubble of the fountain is calming and the fish entrancing. Caustic chases the fish around the pond excitedly, and I have to scold him several times not to jump in as he paws at the water.

I'm not sure how much time passes before Limery perches on the ledge next to me.

"Ooh, pretties." He leans forward, dipping a finger into the water.

"How'd you guys do?" I fist-bump Limery before turning to Taryn. "Had to be pretty tough without your pets? Those stone warriors were pretty resistant to magical attacks, too."

Taryn frowns. "Stone warriors? I fought these demonic creatures. They popped in and out of shadows. What about you, Limery?"

The imp puffs out his chest proudly. "I fought scary plantses. The gnomes saids Limmy did goods."

"I bet you did." I hold up my hand, and he slaps his against mine. "There were three doors when I entered, so I guess they tested our strengths. How'd yours go, T?"

Taryn grins. "I think I did alright. I had to get creative, but I took out a few. Not bad considering my pets are my strongest advantage, and I didn't have any with me. Once I found out they liked to hide in the shadows, I cast Endless Night and went scorched earth on their asses. But I guess we'll know in two days. Want to get out of here and grab a bite to eat? The clerk at the D.E.E. was telling me about this great gnomish restaurant run by tinkerers where all of the food is served on little contraptions."

My stomach rumbles, and I realize just how hungry I am. Fighting always works up my appetite. "Yeah, that sounds go—"

"Well, I'll be damned," a familiar voice calls from over my shoulder. "Of all the town halls in all the cities..."

"You've got to be fucking kidding me," I mumble before I turn around.

The cleric standing before me has upgraded his robe since the last time we ran into him, but there's no mistaking the blue eyes, chiseled jawline, and blond hair of Richard Hummel—the cleric who serves the god of chaos. Everywhere he goes, trouble follows.

"Nice threads." I gesture at his chest, where his old robes had a hole from where Pressley stabbed him. His new ones are a dark gray, embroidered with silver. He still wears a thick, black chain around his neck. "Surprised no one has stabbed you again."

"Believe me, they've tried." He smirks. "I'm digging the new look, by the way. The horns are very menacing."

I sigh, massaging my temples just beneath my horns. He is one of the last people I wanted to see today. "Do I want to know what you're doing here?"

His smile broadens and he winks. "Just waiting on a friend to finish upstairs."

I cross my arms. "You're entering the tournament?"

"Me?" He laughs. "Gods no."

"Well, whatever it is you're doing, I want no part in it. Trouble follows you everywhere you go."

He shrugs. "I could say the same thing about you."

Taryn snickers beside me, and I scowl at him.

"What?" He throws his hands up. "It's true."

There's a splash as Caustic jumps into the pond. A moment later, he crawls out with a shiny purple fish in his jaws.

"Goddammit. Caustic, no!" I point my finger at Richard. "You're bad luck, dude."

He waves at us as a gnome security guard escorts us out of the building. "Good seeing you!"

Once we're out in the street, I clench my fists and fight the urge to punch something. "God, he's an asshole."

Taryn cackles beside me.

"What's so funny?" I snap.

He fights back a grin and his lip quivers. "Bro, you've got such a rage-boner for this guy, but what has he actually ever done to you?"

I'm keenly aware of Limery sitting quietly on my shoulder. Maybe I'm not being the best role model at the moment, so I take a deep breath and try to calmly explain my issues with the cleric.

"Look, he serves the god of chaos. So, if he's around, then shit is going to hit the fan. He tried to get me to trade him one of my gifts from Chief Rizza in exchange for information about Jude when I was in Vanaria. He got Pressley killed in Seascape. He's the reason Pressley is a death knight now instead of an actual knight."

Taryn stares at me blankly. "And?"

"What do you mean 'And'? Is that not enough?"

He purses his lips before speaking. "It sounds to me like he hasn't done anything to you directly. And if you recall, he paid a price for what happened to Pressley. So what if he serves the god of chaos? Whoever said chaos has to be a bad thing?"

"Whoever said chaos has to be a bad thing?" I mock him, rolling my eyes. "I just don't trust him, okay? If he'd ruin Pressley's life like that, then he's capable of anything."

Taryn shrugs. "Maybe. Maybe not."

"Whatever, let's just get some food."

The gnomish restaurant we stop at for lunch reminds me of one of those Japanese restaurants where you pick your food off little conveyor belts. Only this one has a tiny track that we all sit around, where little mana-powered contraptions deliver plates of food upon their backs.

We devour a plethora of meat-filled dumplings and drink exotic teas until our stomachs bulge.

On our way to the arena, we stop by a shop named Tinker Time. On the other side of the warped glass windows, gnomish apparatuses move of their own accord.

Limery presses his nose to the glass. "Cans we go looks, Chods?"

I'm sure everything in there is super expensive and easily breakable, but in the end, his excitement wins out over my hesitation. "Just promise not to break anything." I turn to Taryn. "Do you mind watching Caustic while we go in?"

He holds his hand out for the leash. "I'd be more worried about your big head knocking something over if I were you."

Inside, I feel like a bull in a china shop. Everything is packed so close together, I have to focus to not accidentally bump into a table. Spinning mobiles hang from the ceiling, and clockwork toys hop around the floor. After a close call nearly toppling a figurine that plays music as it spins, I decide to stand in a corner and take in the room from a distance.

Limery presses the button on a tiny red box. The box ticks rhythmically for about thirty seconds before a loud chime goes off.

He cackles at the noise before disappearing deeper into the store, where an older gnome with a long purple beard chats him up.

This place is full of interesting oddities and contraptions, most of which I'm not even sure what they do. The table in front of me has a flask that can purify water up to three times before it breaks. Next to it, there's a bowl of glittery ball bearings, but I'm unable to analyze them. There's also a pair of gloves with small hooks embedded in them that claim to make climbing easier. The whole place has the feel of one of those "As Seen On TV" stores at the mall. After a while, Limery returns carrying a small package.

"What'd you get?" I ask.

He grins mischievously. "Its is a surprise."

I narrow my eyes. "As long as you paid for it."

After the tinkerer shop, we walk over to the arena to get a lay of the land. Where the arena in Goldspire was rustic like the coliseum of Ancient Rome, the arena in Pruxford could be a modern attraction anywhere in the real world. If not for the imposing stature of the Crystal Palace next door, the arena would be the crown jewel of Pruxford in its own right.

A myriad of vibrant gemstones jut nearly a hundred feet into the air, giving the exterior of the arena the appearance of a crystalline bird nest. The towering prismatic structure sparkles in the sun with a variety of hues. The entry gates are closed for now, but a beautiful walkway wraps around the arena spotted with dozens of crystal statues of past champions. A towering centaur holds a spear tucked under one arm just outside the front entrance.

I grab Taryn by the arm and pull him over. "That must be Draydon."

The statue resembles Swift a great deal, minus the beard. A myriad of blue-shaded crystals make up the statue, from a sapphire lower half to an aquamarine upper body, indigo hooves, and intricate detailing of everything from the spear tip to the braids draping down his back.

"That's some amazing craftsmanship." Taryn traces his fingers along Draydon's hoof.

Limery flies over and perches on the spear, tugging at the spearhead.

"Don't even think about it unless you want to spend the night in jail," I warn, and he looks at me sheepishly. "Look at this." I point to a bronze plaque set a few feet in front of the statue.

Draydon Thundercrest

One of the greatest champions to ever come out of Wandermere, Draydon was a behemoth on the battlefield. Whether facing monsters or dueling against other adventurers, it was always said that the mighty centaur put on a show.

In an unfortunate accident, Draydon perished after an injury obtained during a duel where he was not given the customary protection spell. Through this statue, his legacy lives on.

"Protection spell? What do you think that is?" I wonder if that is what kept me from dying during the placement test.

Taryn strokes his beard. "No idea. Maybe it's something that keeps those competing from actually killing each other?"

We walk the perimeter of the arena, taking in the sculptures and the beauty of the architecture. Taryn and I sit on a bench while Limery and Caustic chase each other through the courtyard.

Something feels off as I watch the multitude of tourists admiring the Pruxford landmark. Then it hits me: there's not a single phone or camera in hand, just people enjoying life. They read the plaques and appreciate the statues, not for some meaningless internet points, but because they want to be here.

"What are you grinning about?" asks Taryn.

"Ha, is it that noticeable? I was just thinking about how no one has a phone or camera."

He frowns as he looks over the crowd. "Wow, it's a little unsettling, isn't it? Back home, there would be a handful of families and a dozen chicks posing in front of each statue."

"I think it's nice. The more I think about it, I don't know if I could ever go back to streaming after being here. It all just seems so pointless. I doubt another game could ever compare to this place."

Taryn nods. "You can say that again. Still, it has to end sometime, right?"

My focus wanes, and though I can still hear Taryn rambling in the background, my thoughts are on tonight. On logging out and discovering what updates Valery might have for me. Is it wrong for me to hope they don't have a solution? Rooting for the failure of the most immersive and advanced game there is just so it benefits me staying here?

Yeah, it's selfish, but aren't we all entitled to be a little selfish sometimes? It's not like I'm actively sabotaging their research.

The day passes quicker than expected, and after exploring some of the shops and boutiques, we drop off Caustic before heading back to The Puzzling Peacock.

We have time for a couple of drinks before bed, so we grab a table near the stairs. I scour the room for him, but Arty is nowhere to be seen. A band on the stage plays tranquil music.

"Much more calm than last night." Taryn takes a swig of his ale, and a thick layer of foam coats his mustache.

Limery laughs, not realizing he's sporting one of his own. When I point it out to him, he cackles even harder. "Limmy is an old mans."

Once we're on our second ale, I decide to broach the subject of Richard again. "So, who do you think the cleric was with? We should have stayed around to find out."

Taryn shakes his head. "Bro, you're starting to sound obsessed. I know he's sketchy, but that doesn't mean he's always plotting."

I cross my arms and sit back in my chair. "Honestly, I can't believe you aren't more concerned. It'd be one thing running into him in some small town like last time, but this is one of the biggest events on Mythos. If he's completing some quest for his mysterious god, then it's bad news for everyone here."

We go in circles for a while, with Taryn telling me I'm overreacting and me telling him he's not worried enough, until it's time for us to head upstairs.

I open the door to the room, and Limery stumbles inside.

Taryn stops me before I step through the doorway. "I appreciate that you're a little more concerned about this situation after everything that happened with Stompy, but you can't go searching for a boogieman around every corner or you'll live your whole life in fear." He taps me on the arm. "Something to think about."

Maybe he's right. It's possible I am just being overly paranoid after everything that has happened.

I squeeze him on the shoulder. "Say 'hey' to your folks for me."

21. FAMILY MATTERS

Taryn stared at his reflection on the tablet as he waited for it to connect for the video chat. The face that stared back at him was his, yet it wasn't. He'd grown accustomed to the round face, the larger nose, and the beard of his dwarven body. Still, this felt right too, like the opposite of a split personality.

He grabbed a few strands of hair from his afro and tugged. "I'd look good with dreads."

The dull melody of the tablet connecting ended, and then his family appeared on the screen. They sat on the sectional sofa and seeing their smiles instantly warmed his heart. Two of his sisters, Jada and Laila, sat sandwiched between his mother and father, but the oldest of the three wasn't there.

"Where's Dez?" Taryn asked.

"She's at a sleepover," Jada, the youngest, answered, crossing her arms. "When do I get to go stay the night with my friends?"

"How about when you learn to keep your room clean and do your chores?" Their father gave Jada a knowing look and she groaned, slamming her body back into the oversized pillow.

"You know how it is, Taryn. She's at that age." Taryn's mom leaned forward. "How's your testing going? Are they feeding you well?"

"Judging by the checks they're sending, I bet he's eating like a fat cat." Taryn's dad grinned.

"Oh, Peter. Don't be tacky." She gave her husband the side-eye Taryn had seen a million times.

"What?" Peter feigned innocence. His dad has always been one to speak exactly what was on his mind.

"I like the beard, dad." His father's normally clean-shaven face was now covered with a full beard. Streaks of gray ran throughout. "I didn't realize you were getting so old."

"I think it looks sophisticated." He carefully stroked the outer edges of the beard. "Your mother, however, said it made me look like a... What was it, dear?"

"A bum." She narrowed her eyes. "You have such a distinct jawline, and you want to cover it with that gutter trash."

"Trash? Woman, those are my follicles you're talking about." He mirrored his wife's expression. Their banter had been the highlight of many family dinners. "So, how is it? Still everything you hoped?"

Taryn grinned at his father. "You know I can't talk about the game. They made me sign an NDA, remember?"

"Right, right." He nodded. "So why are you here then?" His dad burst out laughing.

"Oh, you know, just wanted to see your ugly face and make sure you hadn't drowned Jada and Laila with attention since you don't have me to pick on." Taryn winked at his sisters. "Is he bugging you two to death yet?"

Both girls giggled, but Laila answered. "Daddy's been helping me with my homework since you've been gone." She looked at her father out of the corner of her eye, a spitting image of her mother's expression. "I'm not sure I trust him, though."

Peter laughed. "I'm not sure I trust me either. Who knew they could change how math works? I feel like I'm the one who needs a tutor for some of this fourth-grade math."

Taryn raised his eyebrows. "Maybe if you'd studied more in school instead of chasing mom around."

He tilted his head, sharing some secret look with his wife. "You ain't wrong there. How's Chad doing? He heard from his folks at all?"

Taryn shrugged. "I'm not sure. We won't see each other until we're back in the game. He said to tell you hi, though."

"You give him our best." His mother offered a sympathetic smile. "Tell him that we're praying for him."

Peter shook his head. "This is something else, I tell ya. The kid gets in trouble, and it turns out to be the best thing to ever happen to this family."

"Peter!" Taryn's mom scolded her husband. "Children."

"Sorry, what I mean is that the system is something else. You think Taryn would be in this situation if he'd been the one to get in trouble? Chad did his time, and I respect that, even if the charge was BS. My point is that I guess you never really know what connections you'll make in this life."

"Yeah, I think about that a lot." Taryn sighed. "We owe a lot to him. So, how's everything with you all?"

Peter tapped Jada on the leg. "Why don't you girls say good-bye to Taryn, and then head upstairs to get ready for bed. It's way past your bedtimes already."

"What time is it there?" asked Taryn.

"Here?" His dad laughed again. "We're in the same time zone, son."

"Yeah, there's just no clocks where I'm at."

"It's almost midnight." His mother tapped Laila's leg in a similar manner as her husband. "You heard your father. Go get yourselves cleaned up. We'll be up to tuck you in shortly."

The two girls said their good-byes, and then sulked their way up the stairs.

Peter watched them go before turning back to the camera. "They're going to be hell to get out of bed in the morning, but they'd be worse if they found out they'd missed seeing you."

"That's the truth," his mother echoed.

As much fun as he'd been having, Taryn had missed his sisters as well. They were growing up faster by the day, and he was sad to miss that.

His dad had a serious expression, and it put Taryn on edge. His father was normally a cheerful guy. He always had a smile on his face, but right now, he looked dead serious.

Taryn's chest tightened. "What's going on, Dad?"

His father took a deep breath. "Son, I owe you an apology. I know I always said that playing these games so much was a waste of time, that they'd never take you anywhere. But thanks to you, we finally feel like a family again. Thanks to the money from Mythos Gaming, I was able to quit the second shift at the factory. I can spend more time with the girls, and your mother isn't picking up extra shifts anymore. We missed a lot of moments just trying to keep a roof over our heads and food on the table. A lot of your special moments. And when it came to the girls, you picked up so much of the slack. Now, we can give your sisters more of what you deserved. I'm just sorry you aren't around here to experience it, too."

Taryn's eyes suddenly blurred, and his face flushed with heat.

"Oh, Taryn, don't cry." His mother's voice shook. "You're going to make me cry."

He wiped his eyes. "I'm just happy I can help. You guys always did everything you could to make sure that we had all of our needs met. We might not have had the newest shoes or cable TV, but every field trip, every extracurricular, everything we needed, you made it happen. You deserve a break."

Peter blinked rapidly, and Taryn could tell he was fighting back tears of his own. "You're a good son, Taryn. We're lucky you were the first born."

Valery stuck her head through the doorway and tapped her watch. Time was almost up.

"Alright, alright." Taryn wiped his eyes again. "Enough of the sappiness. I've got to get back in, but it was great seeing everyone. Tell Dez I miss her."

"We will." Taryn's mom blew a kiss at the camera. "We love you."

"Love you, too." Taryn tapped the end-call button and sat back against the chair. After a few sniffles, he took a deep breath and stood, clapping his hands together. "Let's go, baby. Time to shine!"

22. CHANGES

Beyond the haze of blue, two shadowy figures loom over me as I awake in the pod. I sit up, coughing as the nanites flow out of my lungs. It's a strange feeling, completely different from choking on water when it goes down the wrong pipe. No hacking, just a smooth stream as the nanites exit my body like a string of jelly being pulled from my throat.

Valery's eyes dart between me and the tablet she's holding while several technicians check readings on the display. Aside from them, the laboratory is pretty peaceful.

"Welcome back, Chad." Valery taps the tablet and then hands it to one of the technicians. "Or do you prefer Chod these days? How are you feeling?"

My gaze lingers on the technicians, waiting for any indications that the AI is acting up again. When one of them makes eye contact with me, I remember that Valery asked me a question.

"Uh, I'm good. Chad is fine." I'm not exactly in the mood for small talk at the moment. Too much is still up in the air.

"Good. Good." She smiles. "Hop on out. There are a few things we need to discuss, but first, let's get you out of the pod."

As I crawl out of the pod, I'm stunned by how defined my abs look. Valery said the nanites would be taking better care of me than I did myself, but I had no idea I was this muscular underneath my layer of skinny fat. Even my forearms look larger than I remember. And my quads, wow. Has being in Mythos for so long changed how I perceive myself or is this all thanks to a well-balanced and nutrient-rich diet?

I can feel Valery's gaze lingering on me, and I'm not sure if she is expecting me to say something or not. Once I'm out, she hands me a robe and leads me down the hallway to her office.

She gestures for me to sit and takes a seat across from me behind the desk.

"We'll do your physical and psychological evaluations shortly, but there's something I need to tell you."

My stomach tightens. Is this where she tells me they've fixed the bug and it's time for me to log out? My fingers dig into the hard plastic of the chair.

Something is definitely off. Valery's normal alluring confidence is gone, replaced by something else. Nervousness? What could she possibly have to be nervous about?

She takes a deep breath. "I'm going to be straight with you. We've isolated the incident that caused the AI to believe that you were part of the system. We still don't know how the error happened or if it can be replicated. To put it plainly, the AI for the system and the nanites are supposed to work separately from one another. The nanites keep the body in stasis, and the system interacts with the mind. In your case, when you jumped into that mana pit, somehow the AI and the nanites were able to communicate with one another. Our working hypothesis is that it was a perfect storm of your race, class, and current active abilities that kept the system from respawning you. Most other races would have died instantly, but you survived, and now the nanites in your pod interact with the system."

The lump in my throat makes it difficult to speak. "So, what does that mean exactly?"

"It means that the nanites are responding to the AI when it comes to your body. And that there have been... changes."

My heartbeat pounds in my chest as I wait for the hammer to drop. "Changes, what do you mean?"

She stands from the desk and walks over to the door, shutting it. A full-length mirror stretches the length of the door. "Come here."

I don't know why, but I touch my temples, half expecting to feel a pair of massive horns curling around my head. My fingertips graze my hair, and I laugh at my absurdity.

When I step next to Valery in front of the mirror, my jaw drops. She's a slender woman. Curvy, yes, but I don't think it would have been a stretch to say that she and I were a similar size when I first logged in. The person staring back at me is almost unrecognizable. After the nanites cleared up my acne and stripped some of my body fat after my first couple of weeks in the game, I thought it was pretty impressive.

This... This should be impossible.

I look like a fucking athlete. My hair is the same jet black, greasy-looking mess it has always been, and my eyes and nose are clearly mine, but the body, it could belong to a stranger. Even my jawline is more defined.

I open the robe, admiring my broad chest and defined midsection. Even my legs look bigger.

I stare at my reflection with wide eyes. "How is this possible?"

She sighs. "I wish I knew. But as your avatar grows stronger in the game, your body is responding to the same stimuli. This is the result."

I flex my arm, admiring the bulging muscles of my bicep that I've never seen before. "And this is only happening to me?"

"Correct. I understand that you may be a little freaked out right now, but I assure you, all of your vitals are completely normal. We aren't seeing any adverse effects, so there is no need to worry about—"

"Worry?" I look myself over in the mirror once again. "Why would I be worried? This is incredible."

Valery's shoulders relax and her frown fades. "Well, good. There's still a lot we don't know, but for now, we'd like to continue as usual. If there's any cause for concern, you will be informed immediately. Obviously, we would reward your efforts with a substantial pay increase."

"Give it to Taryn. As far as I'm concerned, he and I are in this together."

"I'm sure we can make that happen." All traces of her nerves have disappeared.

I get the feeling that she has been dreading this talk for a while. For me, I don't care about the money. I never have. I just want to continue playing Isle of Mythos, but I know that this kind of money could change Taryn's life.

Besides, I might not be able to get a phone call from the bastard, but I know that if anything bad happens to me, I can count on my father to sue this place into oblivion. I'm sure they know that, too.

In the mirror's reflection, Valery leans against the edge of her desk and crosses her arms. "We heard from your mother."

The words catch me off guard like a punch to the chest. I turn to face Valery, my furrowed brow narrowing my vision. "I'm sorry, what?"

"Your mother called last week." She purses her lips before continuing. "My father thought it would be a good idea to give your parents my direct number for some reason. She wanted to know when you would be able to talk."

I'm suddenly aware that my fingernails are digging into my palm. "And?"

She sits behind her desk once again. "I had to explain to her that you were no longer serving your sentence, but that you had volunteered to keep testing the program. I gave her the date and time of your next scheduled logout, but when we followed up earlier today, she apologized that they wouldn't be able to make it since they would be on a flight. I'm sorry."

I scoff. "Typical. At least I can count on dad to have the decency to be a shitty father from a distance. It was always mom who would get my hopes up. A day out together here, followed by twenty promises that got broken or canceled. Rinse and repeat. Somehow those always hurt worse." I fight the urge to slam my fist into the wall. "I'm sorry, I don't know why I'm telling you this."

"Hey, you have nothing to be sorry for." She gives me an apologetic smile. "If it's any consolation, I'm glad that you're here. It might have been under unfortunate circumstances, but this technology has the power to change the world. And thanks to you, maybe in ways we didn't even imagine."

After our talk, the doctor performs a physical, though I'm not sure why it's needed when the nanites monitor my every spec. When I point this out to him, he frowns, asking me how many years the nanites went to medical school.

The psychological assessment is more boring than the physical. I only half pay attention to the questions, constantly expecting a frantic technician to bust into the room and tell me that the system is crashing again. To my surprise, the system seems back to normal.

While they might not need me to keep the game running now, I'm essentially patient zero of the super-soldier program, so I think my time in Mythos is secured for now.

Before I climb back into the pod, I walk past some of the other players, wondering how many of them might be in Pruxford for the tournament. They're tucked away in various rooms across Mythos—all except for Jude and Glenn, who share a run-down shack with hobgoblins standing guard at the door.

Just looking at them sends my blood boiling. They'll get theirs in time.

Valery's heels clack against the floor as she returns to the lab, telling me my time is up.

I remove my robe, and with a final glance at my new body, I climb into the pod. "Game on."

23. THE CRYSTAL PALACE

Limery and I meet Taryn downstairs for breakfast. He already has a pile of food on the table and a mixture of eggs and syrup coating his beard. Limery flies over, taking a seat and sneaking a piece of sausage from Taryn's plate.

"Didn't want to beat down our door this morning?" I wink when he looks up from his food.

He returns my jibe with a grin. "You look chipper this morning. I'm guessing things went well?"

I sit across from him and lean in. "There's no way you're going to believe me. I'll fill you in later. How was yours?"

"Bro, it was just what I needed." He takes a bite out of a pink, hard-boiled egg. "I'm ready to grab this tournament by the balls!"

Limery takes an egg and tosses the whole thing in his mouth. "Yeah! Limmy is ready to grabs this tournaments by the ballses!"

I bury my head in my hands to keep from laughing.

After breakfast, we head out into the streets. The city is alive as the tournament festival begins in full force. There are street performers, minstrels, and many fanciful costumes of people dressed as monsters or fantastical heroes.

A young gnome races by in a red dragon costume, complete with a long tail that drags along the street as he chases behind a group of performers that hold up dancing fabric monsters on long poles. The monsters soar over the crowd, with glowing eyes and moving jaws, like something out of a Chinese parade.

We take in the excitement for a few minutes before heading to the stables to grab Caustic. In the end, Taryn decides to bring all of his pets into the city for the day. It turns out to be a good thing, because on Berry's back, Taryn can see over most of the crowd.

"If you asked nicely, I could have let you sit on my shoulder in your bird form," I tease.

"Hardy-har-har." Taryn rolls his eyes. "Maybe I'll perch on one of your horns and poop on your shoulder."

We take some of the outer streets that are less crowded as we make our way to the Crystal Palace. Since we still have two days before the tournament contestants are revealed, we decide to use today to try to speak with the gnomish council. If all goes well, we can make some headway with them before the tournament begins.

Jordy leads our little procession, followed by Caustic, who has put on a few more pounds since yesterday. Breebis must be feeding him well. The little nubby horns have started to split into full-blown antlers. Limery rides on the dragon's back, perched between the crest of his wings.

"So, how'd it go?" Taryn leans toward me so that he can speak over the crowd.

"You first. Mine is pretty big news. How's the family?"

He frowns for a second before his face lights up. "They're doing great, man. Mom and Dad have both cut back on their hours, and they're spending so much time with my sisters. Honestly, I'll never be able to repay you for this."

I slow my pace and look him in the eye. "You don't owe me anything. Mythos would not be the same without you in it. Oh, and you're getting a raise."

He jerks Berry to a halt, his face set in stone. "Dude, don't play with me like that. Are you serious?"

"Dead serious." I point toward Jordy and Caustic, who haven't slowed down. "Now, catch up with them, and I'll tell you all about it."

Berry grunts as he hurries to catch up with the others. We pass an interesting-looking building for the Cartographers Guild with a sign on the window stating 'Local Dungeon Maps for Sale.' I make a mental note to stop by if we have time to do any dungeon diving while we're in the city.

"If you drag this out any longer, I'll be old and gray," Taryn mumbles.

"Okay, okay." Even though I could send him a message, I feel like saying this out loud. It gives it more weight. I lean in close so that I can't be overheard. "They found out what was causing the system to crash when I logged out."

His eyes widen. "And?"

"Even though the nanites that keep us in stasis and the AI that is running the system are both groundbreaking technology, they're designed to work independently of one another. The nanites are a conduit for our brains to interact with the game world, but that's it. All of the bodily processes are independent of the AI. Somehow when I jumped into that mana pit, that changed, and my nanites have been responding to stimulus from the system."

His brow furrows as he processes the information. "What the hell does that even mean?"

"It means it's not just my mind being affected by the system. My body is growing outside of the game based on what I do in here. I've put on twenty pounds of muscle since I've been in here."

Taryn snorts, and then his face falls flat. "Oh, wait, you're serious? Is this happening to everyone?"

"No, just me." I shake my head. "Valery said it was the perfect storm of coincidences. I'm guessing that there's some connection between the AI and the ley lines. And when I didn't die in that mana pit, a switch that they didn't know could turn on got flipped. So they offered me a raise to keep playing—I guess kind of like hazard pay—but I told them to give it to you."

"You didn't have to do that." He looks at me with a worried expression. "Are you sure this is safe?"

"I jumped into that mana pit months ago. If something was wrong, I feel like they'd know by now. When I got out, I felt fine."

His frown deepens.

"What's up?" I give his shoulder a light squeeze. "Are you having second thoughts?"

He shakes his head. "Even if I were, it wouldn't matter. After seeing what this extra money has done for my family, there's no way I would back out even if it were a risk. You and I, we're in this together." He stares at me with a quizzical expression. "Twenty pounds, huh? What is that, like, half your body weight?"

"How the tables have turned." I shove him in the shoulder, laughing. "Seriously, though, I feel like this changes things big time. If they are able to replicate what is happening to me, imagine what kind of news that would be. You lay down in a pod for a few months and come out in peak physical health."

"Unfortunately, I agree. Nobody seems to care about mental health these days." Taryn sighs. "People sympathize with a broken body, but if you show an ounce of weakness when it comes to your mind then you're a pariah." His eyes narrow, and I see a glimpse of Taryn that very rarely comes out. "My dad, when he got hurt playing football, everyone showed up to support him. They brought balloons and flowers, celebrating the fact that he'd gotten hurt doing the thing he loved. As long as he pretended everything was fine, people wanted to be around him. But losing his passion took its toll, and when the rehab and the depression replaced his happy-go-lucky personality, people stopped coming. He was alone. It's fucked up, but that's how the world works."

"Damn, I'm sorry." Every time I was ever around Taryn's father, he was caring and funny. I can't even imagine him any other way.

"It all worked out." He winks, and his mustache twitches at the edges. "Eventually, he met my mother, and the rest is history."

The Crystal Palace has its own stable where we check our pets in while we visit. Each stall has translucent crystal walls, thick enough that I can't see through them, but I can still make out the silhouettes of the animals on the other side. We pay for a stall big enough to house all of our pets together. In spite of being twice the cost, it doesn't come with the amenities that Breebis offers, but we should only be gone for a couple of hours.

There must be a hundred stairs that make up the palace entrance, each one carved from dusty pink or lilac marble. Every third stair is made of clear crystal, allowing visitors to view a stream that flows beneath and runs through the city. Every so often, a bright-colored fish will flash by.

At the top of the stairs, several dozen guards, all wearing pearlescent armor that swirls with countless hues, stand sentry. The mixture of races has them all at varying heights from as short as three feet to a few that are taller than me. Each one holds a golden spear tipped with a sapphire.

Once inside the palace, it appears more like a tourist attraction than an actual government building. Statues line the outskirts of the hall, with one in central prominence of a gnome wearing a crown that towers above us all. The arched ceilings are painted with beautiful works of art, depicting great moments from Pruxford's history. There's a slew of gnomes scattered around, all wearing burgundy robes and black biretta hats, complete with fluffy poms similar to clergy.

One of them approaches us, bowing slightly before he speaks. "Greetings, gentlefolk, and welcome to the Crystal Palace, home to Pruxford's illustrious gnomish council. I am Pipten, one of the many palace guides. Tours are conducted every thirty minutes, and tickets can be purchased from the ticketmaster on the far left side. The gift shop is to the right, next to the famous Libation Station and Eatery that serves some of the most exquisite food and drinks in all of Mythos. What can I help you with today?"

I step forward, looming over the small gnome. "We'd actually like to speak with the council. We come on behalf of King Orso Brightgaze of Seascape."

"Oh, that is most unfortunate. The council does not take audiences without an appointment. I'd advise you to take your message to the borough office of your choice. However, if you are adamant about an audience with the council, you may accompany me to the administration corridor, where we can schedule you a meeting."

"Borough office." Taryn scoffs. "Why is it always the government that hires a dozen people to do the job of one?"

We make our way through the crowd, following Pipten across the entrance hall. Next to the ticketmaster, he brushes his hand beneath a painting of a hazy blue mountain range. Limery gasps as the painting elongates, stretching to the floor and opening into a secret entrance. We walk down a narrow hallway where my head nearly scrapes the ceiling. When the hallway forks, we go to the left and through an unmarked door so small that I have to crouch to enter, forcing Limery to abandon his perch on my shoulder. After going through the door, we descend a long spiral staircase that comes to an abrupt halt at an empty alcove.

Taryn and I cast each other uncertain glances as the gnome pulls the torch from the wall and uses it to light the shadowy area next to the stairwell. The word 'appointments' is engraved into one of the bricks. The gnome presses it, and a grating sound fills the alcove as bricks shift out of position to form a door.

This all seems a bit odd just to schedule a meeting, and I can't imagine it's very practical to make this journey several times a day, but maybe that's the point.

Inside, an old gray gnome wearing a teal outfit in the same style as Pipten sits at a table with a roll of parchment and vials of ink spread out in front of him. Behind purple spectacles, the gnome is fast asleep.

Pipten clears his throat. "Bertrand."

The old gnome stirs, mumbling something incomprehensible.

"Bertrand," our guide says more forcefully. "These fine guests would like to schedule an audience with the council."

Bertrand wipes his eyes and looks us over, frowning. "Yes, yes, let me see." He pushes around sheets of parchment, tracing their contents with a long finger. "Hmm. Let's see. Our next available appointment is on the fifth of Rineholm."

I'm suddenly aware I have no idea how days, weeks, or months function in this world. So far, I've never needed to know. My cheeks go hot. "Uh, when is that?"

"Nine months and two days."

"Are you fucking kidding me?" My voice echoes around the chamber. "What kind of racket is this? You hide away deep below the castle in an inaccessible room, making it nearly impossible to book an appointment, and then tell me the next one is in nine months. This is bullshit."

"Ah yes," the guide answers this time. "It is most unfortunate, but the council is busy with matters of the city. It is not prudent to waste their time with the day-to-day complaints of the realm. That is what the borough offices are for."

I clench my fist, ready to give these two an even bigger piece of my mind, when Taryn grabs me by the forearm.

"Hey, it's not worth it. There are other ways to get a meeting with the council. Let's just stick to the plan."

"Fine," I snarl, staring daggers at the two gnomes. "Let's get the hell out of here."

The long walk back is filled with silence, but by the time we reach the entrance hall again, I'm calm enough to have a conversation without yelling. "What is it with the government always giving you the runaround? It doesn't matter where you go."

"Some things are universal." Taryn gazes out across the crowd. "As long as we're here, we might as well take the tour. You never know what we might learn."

"Okay, but we're not going with that asshole." I point at Pipten, who just wasted a half-hour of our time.

After spending another half-hour in line to secure tickets, we have fifteen minutes to kill before the tour begins so we stop by the Libation Station for a quick drink. The pub is as eccentric as the rest of Pruxford, with crystal tables and chairs, and laughter ringing all around us. Their special for the day is called the Jester's Delight, so we order three.

The drinks arrive in prompt order, served in a chilled tulip-shaped glass. The cocktail is bright pink with baby blue fog that spills over the edges before dissipating.

"Pretties." Limery's bulbous eyes flash with greed as he lifts the drink.

Taryn holds up a hand between the glass and the imp's mouth. "Have you no manners?" He cocks his head and puffs out his chest as he mimics nobility before lifting his glass. "Cheers."

We clink our glasses, and I take a large sip. The drink is sweet and tangy, reminiscent of strawberry and cotton candy with just a hint of cream. As it works its way down my throat, a sense of elation passes through me.

Limery giggles and a moment later, Taryn joins in. My cheeks grow tight as an uncontrollable urge to smile comes over me. When I open my mouth, laughter pours out.

Taryn tilts his head back, his beard jingling as he unleashes a boisterous laugh.

Limery points at me, gasping for air as he fights through a fit himself.

Twenty seconds later, the urge fades but the sense of mirth remains.

"What the hell was that?" I ask, still unable to stop smiling.

"I think it was the drink." Taryn taps his finger against the glass, grinning.

Item. Jester's Delight. *This gnomish concoction is capable of bringing joy to even the most somber of occasions. One sip will ensure twenty seconds of uncontrollable delight and is a staple at comedy shows around Pruxford.*

We spend the rest of our time at the pub drinking and laughing until our cheeks hurt.

A loud gong signals the start of the next round of tours. Our tickets say to locate our tour guide next to the statue of King Prism, the last king of Pruxford. In the center of the entrance hall, an odd assortment of tourists stands before a gnome wearing the standard guide uniform.

She does a quick headcount before speaking. "Now that everyone is here, my name is Maripol, and I'll be your guide through the Crystal Palace today. Over the course of the tour, you will learn about the history and see the many wonders of the palace. As you can see, the other groups are gathering at various statues, each with its own piece of Pruxford's history, but none are more prominent than the statue before you. King Prism was the last king of Pruxford and the architect behind what this great city has become. Now, if you'll follow me, we'll begin our journey through the great hall."

Maripol leads us through a massive set of double-doors into a long room filled with magnificent tables, each one topped with the most elegant place settings I've ever seen. The tables shimmer and sparkle with a mixture of precious metals and gemstones. Along the walls hang elaborate tapestries and paintings that make the room even more imposing. At the front of the room, perpendicular to the other long tables, is the host table set a few feet off the ground so that they can look down on their guests.

My parents forced me to go to some amazing dinners in my day, but none of them compare to this. This is like something out of a fairytale, elegant and mesmerizing. I lose myself in the grandeur of it all, missing half of Maripol's speech.

"...and some of the greatest feasts in Mythos have been held in this room. After dinner, guests would then head over to the grand ballroom for a night of dancing and socializing. Follow me."

Taryn nudges me in the ribs. "So, you gonna have a fancy shindig like this when you get your castle set up?"

I laugh. "I doubt I could afford a place setting this nice for the three of us, let alone an entire keep. We'll have cheap drinks, and lots of it."

"Oh, yes!" Limery clasps his hands together, pulling them to his chin. "Limmy loves to parties."

Over the next hour, we tour what I imagine is only a small fraction of the actual palace. Maripol shows us an indoor pool with bubbling enchantments that make it a giant hot tub, an indoor garden full of glass flowers and mechanical birds, a library with thousands of books, scrolls, and artifacts, a picture gallery of famous Pruxfordians, and a music room with instruments that play themselves.

After ascending another staircase onto an open landing, Maripol comes to a stop, pointing at a closed door. The arched door is carved with intricate designs of birds and flowers, and the translucent crystal is set with hundreds of colorful gemstones. A beautiful mosaic covers the floor with a painting of the same mosaic along the vaulted ceilings.

"Once upon a time, this was the throne room for the royalty of Pruxford, until the day that King Prism turned over the governing of the city to the council. Since then, it has been known as the Grand Council Room. This historic date changed the fate of Pruxford from a fledgling kingdom into the most illustrious city in Mythos. The council room is not a part of the tour, but if you will follow me this way, we will take the Palace Chute down to the gardens. But first, we will stop at the viewing panel overlooking the city."

"Palace Chute, that sounds like fun." I get in line behind the others when Taryn grabs me by the arm.

He holds a finger over his lips, signaling me to be quiet.

I don't know what he's up to, but I follow him anyway as the group disappears around the corner.

Once they're out of sight, I break the silence. "What's going on?"

He grins mischievously, holding up the Nimble Key he got from Swift. "We're going to put this bad boy to use."

24. A LACK OF COUNCIL

Once the coast is clear and we're sure Maripol hasn't noticed our disappearance from the group, we head to the door of the council room with caution. Taryn's Cloak of Silence muffles his every step, and I do my best to walk gingerly behind him, but my claws tap against the marble floors with each step I take. My paranoia amplifies every clack like a gunshot even though there's no one around to hear. I'd take the soft muffle of earth over this any day of the week.

The door to the council room is a work of art, with the keyhole hidden within an elaborate display of gemstone flowers. I give the handle a tug, but it doesn't budge.

Every sound puts me on edge, so I turn to Limery. "Keep a lookout on the hallway while Taryn picks the lock."

The imp zooms away, hovering around the corner to watch the hallway.

Taryn grins as he raises the Nimble Key to the door. He flicks the bow, and the tiny pistons and gears on the skeleton key spin to life. The key bit resizes itself as he presses it into the keyhole.

"Open sesame," he whispers, releasing the key.

The key whirs as it works its magic, gears spinning, barrel rotating, and pistons undulating. After a minute, the gears stop spinning and an audible click comes from inside the lock as the door cracks open.

I pat Taryn on the back. "Well done."

He pulls the door open and gestures for me to enter. I snap my fingers, and Limery rejoins us. Inside, massive pillars run along both sides of the room. A set of rainbow-colored stairs ascend to a platform where I imagine a throne used to sit. Now, there's a jeweled cornucopia that must weigh several tons. At the bottom of the stairs, a single gnome sits at a hexagonal table with his head buried between hands covered with jeweled rings. Aside from him, the council room is empty. I focus on the lone gnome.

Felston Boonspan
   Level ???
   Gnome
   Pruxford Councilmember

The gnome looks up as we enter, eyes wide over his bulbous nose, and I recognize him as one of the envoys from King Orso's council meeting. "You can't be in here. Guar—"

I hold up a hand, cutting him off. "Please, we just need to talk. My name is Chod. I was at the council meeting in Seascape."

He sighs. "I know who you are, even with the new additions." He gestures to the sides of his head. "But breaking and entering is a crime, even for heroes."

"I'm sorry. It's just that we needed to speak to the council. There are urgent matters to discuss."

He sighs. "I'm sure I know why you are here, but trust me when I tell you that there is nothing you can say that hasn't already been said."

Taryn steps up beside me. "Where is the rest of the council?"

The gnome sits back against his chair, abandoning his protest over our entrance. "Out and about for the festival. It seems you have wasted whatever effort it took to unlock the council room door."

I step closer until I'm across from him at the table. "We need to speak to them. There have been more attacks. Wandermere was nearly overrun with mesmer wisps."

He scratches his chin contemplatively. "Your words will fall on deaf ears. Even with my report of the happenings at Seascape, the rest of the council are reluctant to believe it. 'The portals have been reopening for the last century,' they will say. 'It is not a cause for concern.'"

I slam my palms against the table. "Then how do you explain the monsters appearing from the shadowlands? You were there when the behemoth came through Seascape's portal. You promised that Pruxford would stand with us. Does your word mean nothing?"

The gnome's eyes narrow, and there is venom when he speaks. "My word is everything, but in case you haven't noticed, this is a council table and not a throne room. One person does not make decisions for the realm." He closes his eyes and just sits there for a moment. When he speaks again, it's calmer. "Pruxford will help if there is a direct attack on Seascape, but the council will not approve action based simply on roaming monsters, no matter their origin."

"Dammit!" My voice echoes around the room. "There has to be something we can do."

"I would advise against breaking into a government building. You will find that the other councilmembers are not so slow to serve justice as I am, and the dungeon of Pruxford goes very deep. If you want a chance to speak before the council, then win the tournament. In addition to the rewards, it will grant you an audience with the council."

My hand wraps around the back of the chair before me, and I'm sure I could crush it if I tried. "So, that's it? All our hope comes down to this tournament?"

He nods. "The wheels of government turn slowly, even for you. But if it means anything, I wish you luck."

"We'll take all the luck we can get."

By the time we drop the pets off at Breebis's stable and make it back to The Puzzling Peacock, it's nearly nightfall. We grab a quick dinner and some drinks before we head out to the Underground Circus for the night. After the disappointment at the palace, some entertainment sounds like exactly what we need.

I'm polishing off the last of my ale, belly full, when the door opens and Arty walks in with his adopted human brothers. They're all covered in dirt and blood, but they laugh and carouse as they stomp toward a table in the back.

Arty stops by our table, flashing us a smile that reveals his sharp teeth. "Getting a head start?" The cyclops's massive eye makes it hard to read his expression, but his tone is friendly.

"Grabbing a bite to eat before heading to the circus." I set the empty mug on the table. "You all look like you've been through hell."

He looks down at his filthy tunic, wiping away a patch of either dried mud or blood. "Me and the boys went dungeon diving. I was planning on going by myself tomorrow, but if you'd like to join, the dungeon is where bonds are built. You can tell me all about that proposition of yours."

I turn to Taryn. "What do you say? Up for a little action?"

Taryn nods, mouth full of bread.

I stand up and offer Arty my hand, only coming up to the cyclops's chin. "Sounds good to us."

His grip is firm. "Excellent, see you at sunrise."

Arty takes a seat among his brothers, and Taryn, Limery, and I leave the inn with a slight buzz.

Without Berry to carry him, Taryn walks speedily beside me. "You sure that's a good idea?"

"Sure, he's a giant teddy bear." I laugh.

He rolls his eyes. "Tell that to the remnants of whatever he killed on his tunic."

I poke him in the shoulder. "What, are you scared of dungeon diving all of a sudden?"

"No, it's just an awfully convenient way to eliminate a few competitors from the tournament." Taryn frowns, staring off into the distance as we walk. "He has to know you're one of his biggest threats."

"When did you become so cynical? I'd say there are very few people in Pruxford who even know I exist."

Taryn stops in the middle of the street, turning to face me. "I'm not being cynical. It's just that we have a lot riding on this tournament, assuming we even get to compete. I don't want to blow our shot."

I sigh as I struggle between my instincts and Taryn's concern. The last thing I want to do is dismiss him after everything that's happened. "I hear you, I really do, but that sounds like all the more reason why we should gain experience while we can. I trust him, and I hope you trust me."

He sighs. "You know I do."

"Good, now hurry up before all the good seats are gone."

25. THE WHOLE WORLD A CIRCUS

The cobbled streets are packed as we make our way toward the entertainment district. A steady stream of people travel alongside us in the same direction, and street performers line the alleyways, trying to make a few coins off those going out for the evening.

Once inside Millimoo Square, named after the gnomish actor, Taryn stops in front of the entrance to the Amazing Hydro Park. Streams of water form an arched entryway, and the nearby mist creates dozens of rainbows. The sign boasts that the venue is a water park run by one of Pruxford's famous water mages.

Taryn touches the stream of water and it splashes into a fine mist. Droplets cling to his beard. "This is cool. We could spend a week just visiting all of the attractions here."

He's not wrong. Some of the most popular attractions in all of Pruxford are located in this square. There are museums, theaters, a maze, menageries, and gardens—enough to keep anyone busy. In the heart of the square, there's a stage where a gnomish band is currently performing folksy music.

They sound pretty good, and I consider stopping for a song before I spot the black flag of the circus waving at the far end of the square. I suppress a laugh at the sight of the circus tent. It has changed shape and color once again, somehow able to morph to fit within the space provided. In Sandholde, the tent was wide and striped with an assortment of colors. Now, the pavilion can't be any wider than a small house, but it rises three or four stories into the air, towering above the other establishments. Red-and-white stripes run from top to bottom, further elongating its appearance. It looks like a strong gust of wind could topple it over, but the enchanted tent holds firm. People continue to funnel into the whimsical pavilion.

Atop the slender tent, the black flag emblazoned with the red lion logo of the Underground Circus whips in the wind. A line stretches from the entrance, hundreds deep even as they continue to disappear inside. The group in front of us talks in excited voices, and I overhear an older gnome telling a beastkin that he's been to the circus every evening since it arrived.

"They must be doing well for themselves." Taryn tilts his head back, looking up at the towering tent.

"Good news tends to travel fast. I wonder if they have any new acts since the last time we saw them." It feels like a lifetime ago that we saw the circus perform in Sandholde—back before Seascape, before the portals opened, before everything carried such weight.

"Limmy likes the bubble drinks." He grins with delight at the memory of the magical drinks that had everyone blowing bubbles from their mouths.

The line moves quickly, and soon we're inside where a large man stands sentry to the inner pavilion, taking coins from the circus goers. He wears a black tunic adorned with a red lion head, and I recognize his dual-colored eyes—one brown eye and one blue—from my very first encounter with the circus.

I pull out a gold coin and wait for him to let us enter.

He pushes my hand down. "A friend of the circus is always welcome." He winks and gestures us inside. "You're on the list."

I turn to Taryn, brow scrunched. "List?" I mouth. Did Hawkin somehow know that I would be here?

Taryn pushes me in the back. "We're VIP. Don't question it."

We step through the crease in the canvas into a world of the fantastic.

"Holy shit," I whisper, jaw hanging wide as I take it all in.

Taryn and Limery have the same reaction. Overhead, a night sky stretches on forever where the tent should be. Galaxies spin, distant planets twinkle, and stars shoot across the brilliant expanse. Gentle instrumental music plays in the background. It reminds me of the planetarium, only more detailed and majestic.

The smell of candied popcorn and exquisite delights assault us from every direction. Twinkling gemstones glow softly along the floor, marking aisles and seating, while glowbugs flicker through the air.

The inside of the tent is much bigger than it was in Sandholde. That one fit hundreds. This one looks like it can hold thousands. They must have some kind of enchantment that resizes it to each audience, making it always seem full.

Circusgoers fill the stands, and the magical concessions are showcased in all their glory. An elephant beastkin blows bubbles from its trunk while a young gnome pops them. Steam shoots from the ears of another gnome, while a dwarf blows smoke from her nostrils.

"This is amazing." Taryn walks past me. "Let's go find a seat."

"Mr. Troll! Mr. Troll!" an excited young voice calls from down below.

A kid with glowing face paint rushes up the aisle. He wears a red tunic with the circus emblem in black.

"Brock, is that you?" I recognize the black hair of the young boy who snuck into my room at the castle in Vanaria.

"Yes, sir, Mr. Troll. Me and Neville got us official circus uniforms and everything." He beams as he presses his palm against the tunic, which is a far cry from the tattered clothes he used to wear on the streets of Vanaria. "We saved you a special seat in the front row."

"How'd you know we were coming?"

He does an animated shrug, bringing his hands parallel with his shoulders. "I don't know, but Mr. Hawkin said he had a feeling you'd be stopping by."

Brock leads us to three seats in the front row. I offer him a coin for his trouble, but he declines.

"Can't take it, Mr. Troll. I'm official now." He puffs out his chest. "Have a seat and Neville will be by with some refreshments for ya." He tips an invisible cap and disappears back up the aisle.

A moment later, Neville shows up with a tray of concessions. With the circus uniform and face paint, he looks almost identical to Brock, except his fiery red hair. "I knew we'd see ya again, Mr. Troll. I tell ya, our lives certainly have changed since you came to town. Pick whatever you'd like, it's on the house."

There's popcorn and an assortment of candies on his concession tray, along with half a dozen drinks in the back row. Limery dives in, filling his hands with as many snacks as he can and stuffing them in his seat. Then he grabs a cup filled with a bright yellow liquid.

"Thankses!"

He takes a sip and immediately gasps as tiny bolts of electricity form along his fingertips. He stares at his hands with wonder, and when he moves them closer together, the bolts from each hand connect to one another with a crack. After about ten seconds, the energy fades, and Limery takes another drink.

"That's pretty cool." I lean forward, examining the other beverages. "What do these other ones do?"

Neville grins. "You'll have to find out for yourself, Mr. Troll."

I take a lavender drink with a thick fog floating on the top, and Taryn grabs a green one that fades from neon at the top to forest green at the bottom.

"I think Limery got enough snacks for all of us. Tell Hawkin I said thanks, Neville."

"Will do. Enjoy the show!"

I lift my drink and tap it against Taryn's. "Cheers!"

We both take a hearty swig as Limery continues to shoot lightning from one finger to the other, laughing maniacally as the electricity pops.

My drink is smooth and incredibly creamy. As it settles in my stomach, a feeling of calm washes over me and my arms feel almost weightless.

"Woah." The word warbles like a long piece of tin hit with a hammer, reverberating inside my mouth.

As my head swims without a care in the world, I analyze the drink.

Item. Tonic of Bliss. *This calming drink puts worries at ease and will have you feeling as if you were laying on a pillow of clouds. Spatial distortion may occur, but any effects are not permanent.*

"Dude, you've gotta try this." I offer my drink to Taryn and notice the effects of his own drink for the first time.

Vibrant flowers have bloomed along his dreadlocks and beard, with neon butterflies fluttering in the air around him.

A butterfly lands on his outstretched finger, and Taryn's eyes go wide. "Bro, I need more of this. It fits my aesthetic perfectly. I would honestly waste all my money just to walk around like Father Earth all day."

He takes a sip of my drink, but I decide to leave the bugs and foliage in the forest where they belong. Beside us, Limery pops candies and popcorn into his mouth like a crazed demon. I snatch a box filled with various colored candies from between our seats and toss a yellow one in my mouth. I bite into it, and a tiny jolt stuns my mouth shut. A red jelly causes smoke to plume from my nose, and the light blue candy sends chills down my body.

The candies are called Snickety Snelly's Mysterious Jellies, and there's a spinning wheel on the outside of the box in a rainbow of colors. Apparently, each of the jelly candies has a different flavor.

We continue sampling the snacks and drinks as more people flow into the pavilion. A gaudy-looking gnome couple wearing robes made of sequins sits beside us. The lady holds a pair of miniature binoculars with a long slender handle attached to one of the frames. She lifts the binoculars over her eyes and gazes at the night sky.

Soon after, the music swells and the universe overhead dims. The torches around the pavilion extinguish, and the bright stars and galaxies above fade to black until we're in complete darkness.

A single star flares overhead, a tiny dot in the blackness. Around it, several more flash to life, pulsing gently. Some burn brighter than others, and a constellation begins to form. Lines of light connect between the stars, painting the outline of a lion as the universe continues to reform itself in the background.

More lines connect, further detailing the lion until it looks almost realistic. The music dies, and the stars shift as the constellation roars so loud that a few children in the audience scream. The lion pounces from the stars and everyone gasps.

The lion plummets from the cosmos to the circus ring, galaxies swirling within its eyes. When it hits the ground, braziers roar to life around the ring, casting the circus in light as a warm breeze passes over us. Just as quickly, the fires fade, and a starry night reigns once more. The crowd applauds, and a spotlight falls in the center of the ring in a single beam, burning steadily. I look up but can't find its source.

A moment later, Hawkin steps into the spotlight. He wears his jester's clothing —a black-and-red-striped tunic, billowing pants, and fanciful red shoes that curl up at the end. His face is painted white, with a red clover painted over one eye and a black diamond over the other.

His voice is amplified when he speaks. "Tonight, you will enter a land of whimsy, where anything is possible if you only believe. You will see things that shouldn't be possible, things that are not possible, but for tonight, they will be. Welcome to the Underground Circus!"

The braziers erupt again, and the circus roars to life. The crowd applauds, and men on stilts emerge from the darkness, towering over us and juggling as they walk. Soon, there are fire breathers and sword swallowers. Glowing trapeze artists fly through the air while dancers contort themselves on the ground. There's so much action that it's impossible to follow it all at the same time.

Hours fly by and when the black lion returns to the stage, I know it's almost over. The lion jumps through a flaming hoop, and its red mane bursts into flame while extinguishing the fire of every torch and brazier around the stage. The lion leaps onto a platform at center stage, roaring at the crowd. When the fire fades from its mane, we're in darkness once again.

The blackness is impenetrable even to my night vision, and whispers murmur around us. The strum of a lute quiets the crowd, and glowing musical notes shoot across the ring from where the lion once stood. A silhouette begins to take shape in the darkness, outlined by the glowing melody. Hawkin's face appears, glowing with the same face paint as Brock and Neville—a heart and a diamond over his eyes. He strums again and musical notes shoot high in the air, exploding like fireworks and adding an echo to the song he plays.

The crowd oohs and ahhs at the spectacular display as the melody transforms into wispy animals that run overhead. A giant bird swoops over the audience, and a school of fish dart through the crowd, dissipating into our bodies.

The melody changes, and the glowing notes congregate over Hawkin's head. At first, they form a ball, but ever-so-slightly, it expands until a neon dragon flaps its massive wings. It circles around the circus, musical notes spewing from its mouth in lieu of fire.

Then the dragon dives for the crowd, exploding into a firework finale fit for the Fourth of July. Sparks rush into my body, and the circus goes dark for a final time. When the torches reignite, the stage is empty.

The crowd gives the performers a standing ovation, and a new notification flashes in the corner of my vision.

You have been targeted with Luck of the Dragon. The odds will move in your favor for the next twenty-four hours.

Wow! Hawkin has really stepped up his game since last time. Twenty-four hours of good fortune could change a lot.

"I can't believe he just gave us a luck buff." Taryn claps even harder. "No wonder people keep coming back."

"I know, right? And for a full day. That was a hell of a show."

Beside me, Limery lies passed out in his seat with empty candy wrappers all around him. His fingers are stained with chocolate, and drool runs down his chin.

I leave him be as the crowd funnels toward the exit, and we wait for Hawkin. After a few minutes, he pokes his head through the curtain.

"Enjoy the show?" He winks with his heart-painted eye.

I step down into the ring and shake his hand. "It was amazing. As hard as it is to believe, you outdid your last performance. How'd you know we'd be here, anyhow?"

He smiles mischievously. "I can't be giving away circus secrets, now can I?"

"I suppose not. We're grateful for the experience." I point over my shoulder to Limery. "He certainly enjoyed himself."

"The little ones do enjoy the treats." Hawkin's smile widens as he looks at Limery, and then it fades, suddenly serious. "We owe you a debt that a lifetime of shows could not repay, Chod."

"That's not—" I start to argue, but he holds up a hand, silencing me before continuing.

"No, it's true. Before you came to Vanaria, we simply survived. I guided the circus as best I could, and we held close to one another, outcasts of society. Many of us performed in the streets, making enough to get by and sharing what extra we may have among those less fortunate. We called ourselves the Underground Circus because that was the only place where we truly felt safe." He lifts his arms, gesturing to the pavilion around us. "It was your vision that inspired this. You believed there was a better life out there for us if we only believed in ourselves. Through all of that, the people of Mythos somehow came to believe in us. Our show has grown beyond my wildest dreams, and we are no longer simply surviving. We are living. And for that, I thank you. We all do."

"I—" My throat catches, and I take a moment to regain my composure, clearing my throat before continuing. "I'm glad for all your success, but I only gave you an idea. You made it happen. All of you."

He squeezes my arm, grinning again. "So modest for a troll."

"That was quite the buff you gave everyone." Taryn changes the subject, for which I'm grateful. "You better watch out or the gamblers will come hunting for you."

Hawkin laughs. "Fear not, that was a one-time buff for a friend. I hope it pays good dividends to your party."

The curtain at the back of the ring ripples, and a woman with flowing blonde hair pokes her head through. Leona. She and I shared a drink together at the Underground Circus in Vanaria.

She waves. "We're about to head to the Rocky Rooster for after-show drinks. You all are more than welcome to join us."

I return the gesture. "Any other night we would, but we've got a date with a dungeon bright and early tomorrow." I glance over my shoulder at Limery. "Plus, this guy is out like a candle."

"See you around then." She winks. "And good luck tomorrow."

As we say good-bye to Hawkin, I get the feeling we've already got all the luck we need.

26. THE ADVENTURERS' GUILD

Even though we wake early, Arty is already waiting for us downstairs the next morning. He sits alone at a table with enough food to feed half a dozen people.

"Dig in." He gestures at the massive spread before him. "Don't want to try and clear a dungeon on an empty stomach."

"You don't have to tell me twice." Taryn takes a seat and shovels bacon and sausage onto his plate.

Limery rubs his stomach. "Yums. Limmy is hungries."

"Eat your fill, little one." Arty stabs a massive sausage with his fork and rips into it with pointed teeth.

I take a seat next to him and pile a plate for myself. "Thanks for the food. So, what kind of dungeon are we headed to today?"

He talks with his mouth full, his massive eye focused on me. "There are plenty to choose from. Did you know that Pruxford has some of the most popular dungeons in all of Mythos? We're one of the few cities where one can make a living as a full-time adventurer."

I look at him quizzically. "I had no idea. How's that work?"

"Adventuring is practically an economy in itself. Some of the dungeons are ancient dungeons and some are mob dungeons. The ancient dungeons are filled with relics, but the mob dungeons are how most adventurers earn their living. In the same way that hunters keep the animal populations in check, the council offers rewards for killing dungeon mobs once they start spilling out of the dungeon. It keeps the monsters from attacking the unprotected towns and villages outside of the kingdom. Plus, we get to bring back any items or materials we find to sell or trade at the market."

"That's interesting." Taryn takes a swig of juice before continuing. "What's the difference between an ancient dungeon and a mob dungeon?"

He took the words right out of my mouth. We've explored our fair share of dungeons, but this is the first time I've heard these terms.

Arty's eye sparkles with excitement as he speaks. "Ancient dungeons are far more dangerous than mob dungeons. They're sapient, and they usually form around areas dense with magical energy, whether it be a ley line or something else. They offer better loot because their goal is to try and kill you, and they've built their troves by taking the items of failed adventurers. They also spawn items created from the remains of fallen monsters."

"Hold up." Taryn's brow furrows. "So, you're telling me that these dungeons are alive?"

"In a manner of speaking."

"And what about mob dungeons?"

Arty grins. "They're just areas where monsters naturally congregate. Sometimes they're the ruins of ancient dungeons."

I take the last bite of my food and push my plate forward. "It sounds like every dungeon we've explored has been an ancient dungeon."

Arty slides his chair back, signaling that it's time to go. "For a hero, I don't doubt it."

A blue rooster struts through the Rusty Bucket stable when we arrive, crowing loudly. The thing is twice the size of a normal rooster with a purple mohawk that flares with each crow. The stable-hands are already hard at work for the day.

Breebis approaches from the back, her dark green hair pulled up in a messy bun as she shoos the rooster out of the way. "Go on now, the whole neighborhood is up."

Caustic trails behind her, slightly bigger than the day before. He nips at the rooster, sending it fluttering to the rafters. When he notices me, he leaps toward me, his wings flapping like leathery sails a few times as he closes the distance.

I cup my hands around his head, and he licks me with a sandpapery tongue. "Did you miss me? We're going to have some fun today."

"By the gods, is that a dragon?" Arty sounds impressed as he moves closer, extending a hand. "May I?"

"Don't blame me if you lose a limb." I wink as I step out of the way.

He carefully inches closer until he places the back of his hand on Caustic's head. "So young. He can't be more than a few weeks old."

I laugh. "You're a good judge."

"Arty used to be obsessed with dragons as a kid." Breebis smiles and nudges the cyclops in the leg. "It was practically all he talked about."

He shows no shame in the comment, still focused on Caustic. "Part of the reason I became an adventurer, actually. They're such majestic creatures. I've only ever seen one in the wild, though."

Breebis scratches the dragon behind the horns, and he leans into her. "He's taken to following me around everywhere I go. Keeps the other animals in check." She laughs, turning to Taryn. "Taking the full squad out today?"

"Yes, ma'am." Taryn nods. "We're clearing a dungeon with Arty and need all paws and hooves on deck."

After Breebis brings us Taryn's pets, we're ready to hit the road. This early in the morning, the streets are as sparse as I've seen them, only filled with those preparing to take on their work for the day.

Taryn climbs atop Berry and sets off in the direction of the outer gate.

"It'd take us all day to reach the dungeons on foot," Arty calls from behind us, pointing the opposite way. "Follow me, and I'll show you how we adventurers do it."

Caustic catches a lot more curious looks this early in the morning, and I begin to understand why. During the day, he doesn't seem out of place among the costumes and celebrations of the festival. We've seen so many dragon costumes that I'm sure most people don't even think he's an actual dragon. But no one is partying this early in the morning, and people take notice, especially when he's traveling with a cyclops and a blue-skinned troll.

Limery rides Caustic as Arty leads us through a few alleys and across cobbled streets. Jordy's hooves clack against the stone as he keeps next to Arty, always wanting to lead the way.

The Adventurers' Guild is rather plain compared to some of the other buildings in the area. A shield crossed with a bow and a sword hangs over the porch, with "Adventurers' Guildhall" engraved in an elegant script. The double doors are wide enough that we can fit Berry through without issue.

Inside, a grizzled old man sits behind a counter with his feet propped up. His gray beard is dense like a lumberjack's, with a thick walrus mustache. He smokes a pipe, blowing smoke rings that slowly rise before dissipating against the ceiling.

There are a few chairs around the room, and a notice board pinned with quests.

He sits up when we enter, eyeing us all with intrigue. "Arty! You're in rare company. And a dragon! What are you up to, my boy? Are these new recruits?"

Arty leans against the counter. "Just taking a few new friends out for a little dungeon therapy."

"You put the rest of us to shame." He inhales from his pipe and blows another large smoke ring. "If you all have an interest in joining the guild, you look like you'd make a good fit."

"I bet the life of a hero is more exciting than anything we could throw their way." Arty gently taps his fist on the counter before heading deeper into the guild. "No rest for the wicked. See you around, old man."

The old man lets out a hearty laugh. "To be young and spry. Give the new recruits a little hell for me on your way out."

We follow Arty down the hall, and it turns out the guildhall is even bigger than I imagined. The building is a giant square, with an open area in the center for train-ing. We pass by a mess hall filled with long tables and a bar on the far end. On one side of the room, seasoned adventurers chat and laugh as they eat their breakfast. On the opposite side, the recruits eat in silence.

Arty stops by the recruits' table and narrows his lone eye at them. "Here I am about to hit the dungeons, and you lot haven't even finished your breakfast. Soft, I tell you. I used to be in the training pit at daybreak."

Laughter rings out from the adventurers at the far end as the recruits shovel their food faster.

Arty grins in our direction. "They'll be fine in time. It's the duty of us old-hands to give them a hard time. After a year of training, they'll be fit to test the world themselves."

Next, we pass the armory and the barracks before entering the open air of the training area. A veranda stretches around the perimeter. In the center, there's a sandpit and various stations dedicated to different styles of training. At the far back, there are five large boulders, each one painted a different color. A party of two gnomes, a human, and a lizardfolk stand around the purple boulder.

I stop in my tracks as the two gnomes touch the boulder and vanish into thin air.

"What the hell is that?" I ask as the lizardfolk disappears in the same manner.

"Portstones. They're very old magic used to travel short distances. They're not as powerful as a portal but accomplish the same goal on a shorter scale. Some of the guilds have one or two, but the Adventurers' Guild is the only place in Pruxford that has five. Their counterparts are scattered outside the city walls, allowing us to travel to the dungeons in a fraction of the time."

With a nod to Arty, the human touches the stone and vanishes.

Caustic jerks on his leash, pulling toward the stone, but I hold him firm. "How do they work?"

Arty laughs. "Don't worry. You won't accidentally port anywhere. They require a guildstone to activate, but if we're touching one another, we can port as a group."

We're a sight to behold as we gather around the yellow stone. Limery sits on my shoulder, and I hold Caustic by the tail. Beside me, Taryn and Ruby sit atop Berry. The bear has one paw on Jordy's back, and I grip Taryn on the leg. When we're ready, Arty grabs Taryn's forearm from the other side, and space distorts around me as the world goes black.

27. LUCK OF THE DRAGON

There's a slight pop, and we appear in a glade surrounded by trees on all sides. Limery's claws dig into my shoulder, and my stomach churns. I look to the trees overhead, taking steady breaths until the feeling passes.

"I think I'm gonna be sick." Taryn groans, followed by a splatter that I try not to picture.

Caustic seems unaffected as he jumps up and down excitedly. Apparently, he enjoyed the trip.

"The first time is always the worst." Arty grins as he pats Taryn on the back. "You'll get used to it."

Jordy prances around the lush meadow, and Caustic takes off in pursuit of the frost goat. A yellow boulder matching the one in the guildhall sits in the center of the clearing. Three well-trodden paths branch out from the portstone in different directions.

Arty points toward two of the trails. "Both of these lead to mob dungeons. Either one should do fine for us."

"What about the other one?" I nod toward the path leading in the opposite direction. After Hawkin's buff, I'd rather tackle a dungeon that provides some actual loot.

"That one is an ancient dungeon. We rarely tackle those, and the guild usually recommends a party of at least five. Even then it can be a struggle." He turns back to face the direction of the mob dungeons. "Not worth the risk."

Between Taryn's pets, my horrors, Caustic, and Limery, we're way stronger than the typical five-man party.

"I think we'll be alright." I summon a horror and smirk. "Taryn and I are feeling pretty lucky."

Arty reluctantly agrees to let us try the ancient dungeon on the condition that we retreat if things get too tough. The Pruxford countryside is as odd as the city itself, filled with rolling hills, giant mushrooms, and cartoonish trees with branches that curl and twist at odd angles. Some of them even grow hair instead of leaves. Massive gemstones sprout from the earth in clusters, making it evident how the city was able to build such lustrous crystal structures.

I summon horrors as we walk, and we fill Arty in on our playstyle and abilities. We keep a few of our abilities a secret, like my Champion summon and Taryn's Endless Night, just so he doesn't learn all of the tools in our toolbox. He shares his skills with us, but I'm sure he keeps a few hidden as well. As a warrior, Arty only has physical abilities, but they seem pretty formidable by his description.

While we follow the dirt path, I let Caustic roam without his leash. Breebis has definitely had a good effect on him, because he stays with us for the most part— only breaking off when he sees a creature or movement in the grass. I'm forced to give him a healing potion after he takes a bite out of a toxic ooze basking in the sun on the side of the trail.

Even with the portstone, we end up walking almost an hour to the ancient dungeon. For such a supposedly dangerous location, it doesn't look the part.

An arched cluster of gemstones forms the entrance, and an opalescent door with no handle blocks our entry. Speckled mushrooms line the path as we get closer, starting small and increasing in size until those by the entrance are several feet taller than me and Arty. As far as dungeons go, it seems pretty welcoming.

Arty stops at the entrance, his posture stiff. "Don't let the look of it fool you. She's out to kill you as much as the rest."

"She?" Taryn holds back a laugh from atop Berry.

The cyclops nods. "I always thought of dungeons as female. They're tough as nails and capable of ending you, but worth the effort if you treat them with respect and give them your all."

His answer takes me by surprise. It's a romantic thought for someone looking so brutish.

"I'll be honest, you act nothing like how I imagined you would based on your appearance." I pat Arty on the back and equip Destroyer. I'm not ready to reveal the weapons and armor I got from Wandermere quite yet, considering he could be an opponent if we qualify for the tournament. I do equip the Regeneration Stone in one of Destroyer's sockets, increasing my health regeneration by twenty percent. "Let's find out what Lady Luck has in store for us today."

Arty reaches into the satchel around his waist and pulls out a sword. The pommel is fitted with a polished emerald, with two more set at each end of the guard. The blade is beautiful, with dark gray swirls within the metal, and wider than anything I've ever seen, easily as wide as the cyclops's massive head. It seems never-ending as he pulls the weapon from the satchel.

I keep expecting to see the tip, but he continues to pull. When he finally frees it from his bag, the sword is nearly as tall as he is. He rests the flat of the blade against his broad shoulder, and it's almost comical.

"Damn! How do you fight with that thing?" I ask, still in awe.

He smirks, holding the sword in front of his body like it weighs nothing. "These muscles aren't for show."

"Sure you aren't overcompensating?" Taryn grins beneath his beard.

Arty laughs. "That's quite the insight from a dwarf who chooses to ride a bear. Were all the ponies taken by your kin?"

Taryn's cheeks flush with color. "Always with the short jokes."

I burst out laughing. "Let me get this straight. Everybody in Pruxford adores you. You're strong, perceptive, and quick-witted. How are you not married?"

Arty tosses the sword back over his shoulder and raises his lone eyebrow suggestively. "Why, are you interested?"

"Funny, too." Taryn joins in the laughter now that Arty's quick wit is at my expense. "This is going to be a fun day."

Arty digs a few more items from his satchel—a full set of studded leather armor and matching helm. We corral the animals and approach the dungeon entrance, where the door bars our entry. The opalescent door shimmers in the sun like oil on a water. Streaks of pastel blue and green seem like they are swirling within the stone. When I focus on it, a prompt appears.

Curio Dungeon. *Would you like to enter?*

I accept, and the door slides into the earth. The doorway expands, revealing a set of spiraling stairs that lead underground. Instead of torches, gemstones protrude from the wall, casting light in an array of colors. I send my horrors in first, all sixty of them. I might have overdone it, because it feels crowded as we make our way down. I follow the horrors, and Limery rides on Caustic's back behind me, holding onto the dragon's horns for balance. Taryn and his pets are next, and Arty brings up the rear.

Once we're all inside, the door rises and locks us inside.

"So you've really never beat this dungeon?" Taryn asks Arty as we follow the spiraling stairs.

Arty shakes his head. "No, I've only been to a few ancient dungeons, and it's always been a challenge just making it back out after our first few fights. It's like I said, as adventurers, we do the jobs no one else wants or can do. We track down bounties, return stolen property, things that would take the guards away from their duty to protect the city. When the mob dungeons start to overflow, we deal with that, but ancient dungeons are a different beast. They're old magic, back from the time of heroes. Or I guess I should say the old age of heroes. Occasionally, a young adventurer will enter one to try and prove his toughness. But the truth is that if we don't bother them, they don't bother us."

All that to say we have no idea what we're up against. Which is no different than any other dungeon we've faced, and we managed to squeak out a victory time and time again.

Out of my sight, some of my horrors begin to lose health faster than normal. I ready Destroyer, and the rest of the party follows my lead. The monsters' grumbles sound louder than normal in the stairwell.

The horrors charge forward, and Caustic follows them. The air crackles as Limery summons a fireball in one hand while hanging onto the dragon's horn like a cowboy with the other.

"Keep him to the outskirts of the fight, Limery! I'm counting on you," I shout over the chaos.

"Limmy's on it."

I turn the final curve of the stairwell and empty into a room shaped like a massive halfpipe. Across the way, there's a door. Clusters of gemstones hang from vaulted ceilings like stalactites, twenty to thirty feet off the ground.

A dozen furry balls about the size of a beachball roll from one side to the halfpipe to the other like bowling balls, crashing into and crushing my horrors, leaving a glittery trail in their wake. When they hit the other side, the balls rocket into the air, nearly touching the ceiling before gravity sends them plummeting back to the halfpipe to repeat the motion on the other side. Horrors that take a hit head-on explode on impact, and more lose their health in the dust that each ball leaves behind.

I focus on one of them to try and get an idea of what we're up against.

Floofer. Level 25. With bulbous blue eyes, and dainty paws as soft as silk, floofers may look cute and innocent, but these monsters have a vicious streak. Underneath their fluffy exterior sits an armored shell that can curl into a ball capable of wreaking immense havoc. While in ball form, their entire bodies remain protected, and they can generate enough force to self-propel, capable of escaping or wrecking anything unlucky enough to get caught in their path. Their fur contains a poisonous dust used in many death potions.

Shit, these things are going to be tough to stop.

Limery hits one of the floofers with a fireball. There's a small explosion as the fire interacts with the dust, burning away all of the hair but leaving the creature unaffected. Without the fur, it looks even more dangerous as it pummels through more horrors with its metallic shell.

One of the balls barrels toward Caustic out of the corner of my eye. I drop Destroyer without hesitating and pull him by the tail, saving him from death by only inches.

"Stay," I order, letting out a sigh of relief. "This is not your fight."

My horrors continue to drop left and right as they try to attack the floofers. Nearly a quarter of them are already gone, and the passive slow from the Horrors of Vitality is having no effect. "We've got to find a way to slow these things down. Taryn, can you summon a wall?"

He joins me at the edge of the stairwell, making it even more cramped as he lifts his staff. A twenty-foot-wide wall appears down the centerline of the room. There are several loud crashes in quick succession, and pieces of rubble rocket across the room.

A few of the floofers slow, only going a fraction of their normal height when they hit the ramp, but on the return, they self-propel, regaining their momentum in full. It only takes seconds for the wall to be reduced to rubble.

Taryn frowns as his wall comes crumbling down. "Dammit. The cooldown is too long for the walls to be useful."

"Any other ideas?" I look between Taryn and Arty.

Arty scratches his chin. "If we can get the floofers to open up, their underbelly is soft. We'll be able to kill them, no problem."

"I've got it!" Taryn shouts. "If we want to stop them, we just need to hit them with an equal force."

"And how do you plan on doing that?" I watch helplessly as more horrors vanish. I've pulled those I can onto the stairs, but more die by the minute as they try to play Frogger to return to the stairs.

"Not me, this is up to you two." He points at me and Arty. "Get out there and do what you do best. Smash."

"Say no more." I turn to Arty. "Ready to put those muscles to use?"

He stuffs the giant sword in his satchel and pulls out a dual-sided warhammer, slate gray with black runes etched along the handle. He snarls. "Let's do it!"

I sacrifice the remaining horrors that are stuck in the halfpipe of doom, flooding my body with increased Strength, Constitution, and Dexterity for the moment.

When the closest floofer comes rolling in my direction, I hit it with the flat end of Destroyer. The impact reverberates up my arm, shaking me to my core, but it works. The floofer unrolls, sitting dazed and confused in front of me. Bubbly blue eyes stare at nothing, and its dainty arms keep it from falling over. It's cute, I'll give it that, but it doesn't stop me from twisting the warhammer and bringing the pointed end down on the poor creature.

Behind me, Arty's arms take on a bluish aura as he swings his hammer. His arms don't so much as quiver from the impact.

"We're gonna hit them. The rest of you, finish them—" I jump over a speeding floofer that nearly takes out my legs, and the wrecking ball barrels toward the ramp on the other side. "—off."

The rest comes easy. Arty and I stun the creatures with our warhammers, and our party kills the floofers as they wobble with dazed expressions. Out of the corner of my eye, Caustic finishes off the last one, his muzzle covered in blood.

I kneel and he runs over to me, tail thrashing against rubble and dead floofers.

"What a good boy." I scratch him underneath the chin, and he groans with pleasure. He managed to gain two levels from the fight, bringing him up to eight.

Arty opens and closes his fist, his arm no longer glowing with the aura, reminding me of my own sore muscles.

I admire his weapon. "Those things sure packed a punch. You're pretty good with a warhammer."

He lifts it and gives the handle a spin against his palm. "There's not a weapon that exists that I can't wield."

"Ha! So much for being modest." Taryn strokes Ruby who sits on his lap.

The floor shakes, and a grating sound comes from behind us as one of the tiles in the center of the room sinks. A few seconds later, it emerges with a glowing chest.

"That's odd." Arty's lone brow furrows.

"What's odd?" I ask.

"Dungeons don't normally drop treasure in the first room."

Taryn hops down from Berry and runs over. "Must be our lucky day."

Thank you, Hawkin. The chest is smaller than most that we've found, but the magical aura is undeniable.

We gather around Taryn as he opens the lid, fighting against Jordy and Berry to see what's inside. Taryn pulls out a silver necklace with a black teardrop pendant. Gray smoke swirls within.

Item. Whispers of the Damned. +3 Constitution. *Infused with the last breaths of the dying, when this pendant is activated, the haunting voices of the dead will cast confusion upon their mark. For every kill accrued while wearing this necklace, Whispers of the Damned will gain a charge (Max. 3). Charges may be released to cast confusion on an enemy for up to five seconds. (Max. 3 charges per day)*

Taryn holds the necklace up. "How should we divvy this up?"

Arty holds up a hand. "That's a little too sinister for my taste."

"Yeah, it's pretty fucking creepy." I consider taking it, but before I do, Limery flies over, plucking the necklace from Taryn's hand and draping it around his neck.

"Limmy wants its!" The necklace automatically resizes to his tiny neck. He holds the pendant between his fingers, admiring it.

"That's settled." I walk across to the room to where the other door has opened. It leads to a similar stairwell as the one we entered through. "Who's ready to see what's next?"

28. LIGHTNING IN A BOTTLE

The stairwell spirals downward, nearly identical to the one we entered through. After a short descent, the floors and walls shake, and a loud grating noise comes from below. Jordy bleats at the sudden disturbance, and Caustic growls by my side. Ruby stands alert on Berry's back, staring intently down the stairs.

When the dungeon quits shaking, we all share a look of uncertainty.

"What the hell was that?" I pet Caustic reassuringly, his scales cool and smooth to the touch.

Taryn strokes Ruby, who hasn't looked away. "No idea, but something's up if Ruby is on alert. You know anything about this, Arty?"

"No idea." He shakes his head. "We can always turn back."

I squeeze his shoulder. "Come on, big guy. Where's the fun in that?"

He stares at me deadpan. "The fun is in the not dying. Lest you forget, I don't come back from death."

I give him my most heartfelt smile. "You're a world-class adventurer. I trust you can handle anything that comes at us. Plus, we're stocked on potions and elixirs. You'll be fine."

He grunts affirmation, and Taryn and his pets lead the way as we continue downward until the stairs empty into the next level. Even though the others block my view, I can see fresh grass growing along the floor beyond the bottom step.

"Bunnies!" Limery pulls his hands to his chest as he gushes.

Caustic, sensing prey, takes off running down the stairwell before I have a chance to inspect the room.

"Stop!" I yell, but he's already out of reach, claws clicking against each stair as he races downward.

A wall appears in front of the stairwell, and Caustic crashes into it.

"You're welcome." Taryn gives me a knowing look, his staff pointed in front of him.

Thank goodness for Stonewall. I let out a sigh of relief and grab Caustic, putting the leash on him.

"I hope that didn't use up all our luck." I kneel, looking into the dragon's golden eyes. "Do not go running off like that again."

He huffs and bites at the leash.

Tiny thuds sound against the other side of the wall, similar to darts hitting a board.

"Did anyone get a good look at what was in there? Everything happened so fast that I didn't see more than the grass."

"There was bunnies with hornses." Limery's bulbous eyes flash with excitement.

No one else got a good look aside from Limery. The thuds grow less and less until they stop altogether. The enemy aggro must have disappeared once they could no longer see us.

I summon a few more horrors while we try to come up with a game plan. "How many did you see?"

Limery hovers in the air, waving his arms wildly as he speaks. "Oh, theres was lots of bunnies. Lots and lots."

"Alright, once Taryn cancels his wall, we fan out into the room and try to get an idea of what we're dealing with. I think we've lost their aggro, but the ones at the entry point will lock onto us pretty fast. We take them out first. Taryn, do you think you can use Imbue on Caustic once we're inside? Whatever these things are might be a little more hesitant to attack him if he's bigger."

Taryn nods. "Not a problem."

Arty trades out his warhammer for the giant sword once again. I'm actually excited to see it in action.

After I summon another set of horrors, I face the others. "We ready?"

They all confirm, and Taryn cancels Stonewall.

Nearly a dozen bunnies fall to the ground as soon as the wall vanishes. They're all about the size of a large house cat, each one with speckled rainbow fur and a shimmering spiral horn that's about a foot long. The thuds must have been them lodging their horns in Taryn's wall.

My horrors swarm the bunnies, pinning them to the ground before they have a chance to attack. I cast Kamikaze, and the horrors explode, taking out nearly three-quarters of the bunnies' health.

"Caustic, gas them, then everyone get back," I order as I take cover up the stairwell.

He responds to my command, sending a stream of green gas that shrouds the bunnies.

Once we're out of range, Limery tosses a fireball and the gas ignites. Warm air rushes up the stairs, and we charge into the room.

I step over the charred remains and move to the left, quickly taking in our surroundings. This level is a similar size to the previous one but designed differently. It's all flat, with grass and boulders from end to end. The walls are made of polished stone and the ceiling glows with the light of gemstones. Close to two dozen more bunnies are scattered around the room, all standing on their hind legs, suddenly aware of our presence.

Bunnycorn. Level 25. *While they may look as cute as their non-horned counterparts, bunnycorns are deadly and tenacious. The vampiric bunnies travel in packs, hunting prey three to four times their size and using their horns to impale enemies before draining them of their blood.*

Vampiric bunnies? You have got to be shitting me.

Taryn casts Imbue on Caustic, just as a bunnycorn launches itself in my direction. Its powerful hind legs propel it like it was shot out of a cannon. I duck out of the way, and the creature snarls at me as it flies past until its horn clatters against the smooth stone of the wall. Whatever the dungeon walls are made of is a lot harder than Taryn's wall, because the horn just bounces off it.

Next to me, Caustic has doubled in size, taking on the appearance of a formidable dragon and giving me a glimpse into what the future holds. He breathes his toxic gas, and it spreads across the floor like fog. It doesn't do much damage, draining barely a sliver of HP at a time. But when Limery's fire hits it, bunnycorns explode across the room.

A sharp pain flares through my left shoulder, and I lose my grip on Destroyer, dropping it to the floor. I look down to see a bunnycorn horn buried in my chest all the way to the creature's head. The demonic bunny digs its claws into me as it tries to pry itself free. Every movement sends pain like hot iron through my chest and back, and I'm pretty sure it has pierced me all the way through.

I wrap my good hand around the bunny and squeeze until bones crack. In a quick and painful motion, I rip the horn free and throw the bunny against the wall with everything I can muster. It hits the wall and falls motionless to the ground. The wound suddenly feels icy, and I lose my breath for a moment.

"Fuck." I grunt as I pick up Destroyer. The pain starts to subside as my increased healing takes effect.

Fire and lightning rage around the room as Taryn and Limery wreak havoc. Taryn has used his Sapling Staff to form a protective cage out of vines on Berry's back, preventing the bunnycorns from attacking him. Two of them dangle from the cage with their horns stuck between the vines. Jordy prances around the room, ramming anything that gets too close to him.

At the far side, Arty's sword cuts through two bunnies with a powerful slash as they jump through the air, sending a stream of blood along the wall. He spins, moving the massive blade like a trained dancer, decapitating another.

Caustic rips a bunny to shreds with his claws, but he doesn't notice a second one running toward him from his side. The bunny sets its feet and launches at the dragon.

I call out to him, trying to get his attention to the blindside attack, but he doesn't hear me. There's no way he'll react in time, and I'm too far away to do anything helpful. I ready a health potion, cursing myself for bringing him here before he was ready and hoping that it will be enough to save him.

The bunnycorn horn aims for Caustic's throat, and my heart sinks. Then it bounces off of his body like it hit a metal wall and falls to the ground. Caustic turns, annoyed, and snatches the bunny in his teeth, tossing it in the air and swallowing it whole.

Tension releases from my entire body. Even a level-eight dragon is a dangerous enemy. I've been babying him for nothing.

"Good jo—"

Pain tears me from the moment as a second bunnycorn impales me, this time in the ribs. I pry it out, rage battling against the pain as I throw it to the ground and stomp its body with a sickening crunch.

"Fucking bunnies!" I shout as I activate Berserker Rage. "I've had enough of these motherfucking bunnies in this motherfucking dungeon!"

My vision goes red as I unleash a roar, and my healing kicks into overdrive. I swing my warhammer like a madman. It flares red with stacks of Inferno, splattering scorched bunnycorn corpses against the wall and floor. In this moment, I want nothing more than to kill every last one of these annoying little fuckers. Steam radiates from my skin as sweat mixes with bunny blood. Thanks to my Spirit of the Beast path, my rage lasts twice as long as it used to. When Berserker Rage finally wears off, I stand there heaving.

Arty and Taryn both look at me with a mixture of shock and amusement, while Limery tries to pry the horn off a dead bunnycorn.

Taryn stares, his mouth halfway open stuck between a smile and gaping wonder. "You alright, bro?"

"Did no one else get impaled?" I toss my hands up in frustration. "The little fuckers got me twice."

Arty bursts out laughing. "We've got lots of potions and elixirs. You'll be fine."

I just shake my head. "Famous last words, right?"

Taryn and Limery join in the laughter, and pretty soon, I do too.

"Your barbarian rage is impressive," Arty says as he stows his weapon.

Taryn climbs down from Berry. "Yeah, he's got anger issues. It's kind of his thing."

I roll my eyes. "It is not my *thing*. I don't have a thing."

The dungeon groans, interrupting our banter, and a chest appears in the center of the room, similar to the one before. We gather around it, and Taryn flips the latch. Inside, there's a steel blue helm with an open face and cheek guards. A crest of silver feathers with blue tips lines the top of the helm like a mohawk.

Item. Helm of Resolution. +3 Dexterity. *While equipped, consecutive attacks within two seconds of one another increase the user's attack speed by 1%, stackable up to 25%.*

"Nice," Arty whispers.

"That's a nice helm. A twenty-five percent bonus is pretty damn good." I grab it from the chest, admiring the craftsmanship, then I hand it to Arty. "Here, you deserve it."

He hesitates before taking it. "Are you sure?"

I point to my head. "I think I'm well beyond headgear at this point, and you more than earned it. I saw you slashing bunnycorns to pieces while I was becoming a Chod-kabab." I instinctively touch my shoulder where the first bunnycorn impaled me. "Besides, we wouldn't even be here without you. Put it to good use."

He removes his current helm and puts on the Helm of Resolution. It fits perfectly above his massive eye. "There is something strange going on with this dungeon. I can feel it."

"Maybe we're just lucky." I flash him a mischievous grin.

While we get ready for the next floor, Taryn heals a few minor wounds on Berry and Jordy, and I take a moment with Caustic while I summon more horrors.

With his imbued size, I'm able to look him in the eye while standing. "You did a good job during that last fight, and I think it's time I quit treating you like a baby. You're growing up fast. You're a strong and powerful dragon, and it's time I let you show it. You have my back and I'll have yours, got it?"

He licks me with his forked tongue, and I chuckle.

"Yeah, you've got it. And you gained another level, too, look at you." At level nine, he's catching up fast.

By the time we're ready to move on, Imbue has worn off, and Caustic has returned to his normal size.

Taryn approaches me and Caustic. "I'm gonna use Imbue on him again if you don't mind. It was pretty cool having a big-ass dragon fighting beside us."

"Go for it. He's an intimidating presence, that's for sure. And I think it's time to see what he's really capable of, because I had no idea his scales were that tough."

"I'm sure he's full of secrets." Taryn reaches out and pets Caustic. "We ready to get moving?"

Midway through our next descent, the dungeon shakes again, and I get the feeling that the rooms are somehow shifting into place. Maybe randomly, or possibly they are being influenced by our increased luck.

The next room is a plain slate gray on all sides, and the gemstones along the ceiling are dimmer than in the other rooms. Clusters of oddly-shaped mushrooms grow from cracks in the floor.

There are giant snails scattered around the room, along with slimy iridescent trails that follow them along the floor, walls, and ceiling. The snails' translucent shells reveal their colorful organs. Two long tentacles stretch from their pastel bodies, each one tipped with a giant bloodshot eyeball encased in a cluster of crystals.

Flail Snail. Level 25. Don't let their fragile appearance fool you. Though they move at a snail's pace on unslimed terrain, flail snails can travel with amazing speed along the slick paths they leave behind. Their tentacled eyestalks are capable of elongating, and when closed, they can be used as weapons. Once prey is subdued, the snail will devour it with the thousands of teeth hidden within its mouth flaps.

I shiver after reading the last line. Just what we wanted, snails with weapons for eyes, thousands of teeth, and probably a tough ass shell to go with it. This will be fun.

The snails move incredibly slow as they cling to the walls and ceiling, but as soon as we enter the room, their tentacles stiffen, and close to fifty eyes turn in our direction. Their sludgy mouths flap like a flag in the wind as they make a sound like blowing a raspberry. I'm guessing it's supposed to be a hiss or a growl of some kind, but it's not at all intimidating.

Until I see the vortex of teeth that looks like something from a horror movie.

The area around the entryway is clear of their slime trail, which doesn't start until about thirty feet from where we stand. There's no immediate danger of them speeding over, so we have a little time to formulate a plan.

"This'll be interesting." I ready Destroyer as the first snails start crawling over. "Limery, see if you can burn away the slime trail."

"Limmy's on it!" He flies over, summoning a firewall on a patch of slime. It sizzles beneath the flames, taking a good ten seconds to burn away.

It works, but not quick enough.

Caustic blows his toxic gas, and it settles around the snails in the center of the room. They immediately retract into their shells, taking no damage from the poisonous smoke once inside. Limery throws a fireball, and the explosion rockets them in all directions but they still don't take any damage while hidden within their shells.

When the snails hit the floor, their gelatinous bodies emerge, clinging to the stone and flipping the shells upright. One of them at the far back hits a slick of slime and zooms to the middle with blazing speed, coming to an abrupt halt once it reaches the unmarked flooring.

"Holy shit!" Taryn's eyes go wide. "Stay out of their slime trails. Those things travel faster than the floofers."

Several more connect to the slime trails, and pretty soon there are half a dozen looming ever closer. I summon more horrors and get ready to smash the snails across the room with Destroyer.

The closest group of snails all stop except for two that move in separate directions. One heads toward Arty on the far end, and the other toward me and Caustic. After a short distance, they quit advancing as well.

The snails close their eyes, turning their tentacles into crystal-tipped flails, and whip them in a circle like a cowboy readying a lasso. With each rotation, the tentacles grow longer, until they are spinning in a blur only a few feet from where Caustic and I are standing.

They suddenly seem a lot more menacing. The snail flails whir as they spin, and I prepare to take a swing.

I urge Caustic to back away and swing with all my might. Destroyer hits the flailing eyes with a clank. I expect the change in momentum to carry the snail to the back wall, but its body suctions to the floor and the flails circle back around, hitting me in the back. Jagged crystal rips into my spine with enough force that I drop to my knees.

All around the room, snails flap their gelatinous mouths at my pain. Somewhere nearby, Limery voices his concern.

The snail retracts its dangling eyes and whips them at me again. Caustic pounces on the snail, wrapping his mouth around its shell as he flutters by and causing the flails to smash against the wall. When his feet hit the ground, he slips in the slime trail, and his legs shoot out from under him. He falls on his back with a thud, and the snail retracts its eyes to a shorter length, pummeling the dragon with its flails.

There's a flash of red, and Limery is by my side. He activates Whispers of the Damned, and a silvery wisp shoots from the pendant. It hits the snail in the face, wispy tendrils dissipating into the creature's body, and the flails go limp as the snail wobbles in place.

The confusion won't last long, so I try to crawl to my feet. Out of the corner of my eye, Arty leaps across the room. His massive sword trails behind him like some badass action hero, and the plumage on his new helm ruffles as he covers nearly twenty feet in a single bound.

He lands inches from the slime trail, bringing his sword around in a blur and severing the snail's tentacles. The blade stops inches from slicing me in half in an amazing display of strength and control. The snail screeches as its eyes clatter to the floor, and Arty kicks the snail with enough force that it bounces off a mushroom near the back wall before crawling blindly away.

Arty offers me a hand. "New plan. Chod and I cut off their eyes, then they'll be easier to deal with. The rest of you try to find a way to kill the slimy bastards."

Limery, Taryn, and the others gather by the stairwell as more snails approach from across the room. I search through my inventory for anything sharp, but all I have are magical staffs, a spear, and a trident. Nothing with a sharp blade.

"You don't happen to have an extra sword, do you?"

"An adventurer is always prepared." Arty grins as he reaches in his satchel, pulling out a short sword. "You break it, you bought it."

Item. Brightblade. +2 Strength. *With every consecutive attack, the enchanted metal within Brightblade grows brighter. Once out of combat, the blade will dim 1% every minute.*

Sounds like a weird weapon, but it's better than nothing. I equip my Halite Shield in one hand and Brightblade in the other, avoiding the slime trail as Arty and I press the attack. The translucent shield allows me to see exactly where I'm going while using it as a riot shield to block their flails.

The closest snails whip their tentacles at our approach, and in seconds, the flails are whirring through the air.

I extend the shield and the flails bounce off, wiggling on the ground as the snail tries to retract them.

"Not so fast." I swing down with Brightblade and sever both tentacles.

The blade takes on a dull glow as the snail retracts into its shell. Arty has blinded his as well, so we press forward again.

Arty takes a more direct approach, using the length of his blade to his advantage and chopping the tentacles from a safe distance.

"Kick them back here," Taryn calls from behind. "I've got an idea."

As I pass the blinded snail retracted into its shell, I kick it backward to Taryn.

It rattles against the floor as the shell bumps along. Taryn climbs down from Berry and equips his Shadow Daggers. The shadowy blades pass through the shell without issue, capable of draining the life force from the snail without having to actually break through the tough exterior.

He says something to Limery, and the imp presses molten hands onto the next shell Arty kicks. His molten form is far hotter than his normal fire, causing steam to pour from the shell's opening as the snail shrivels at the intense heat.

Something splats beside me, and I turn to see a flail snail has fallen from the ceiling. It attacks me with its flails but only manages a few hits before I sever both spiked tentacles.

Arty and I stay close together, pressing forward and severing tentacles while kicking them back to Taryn and Limery to finish off. More snails fall from the ceiling, but now that we know to expect them, we respond quickly. By the time the room is clear, Brightblade shines so bright that it's almost blinding to look directly at it.

"That's some blade." I hand it back to Arty.

"That she is." He slides the blade into his satchel. "Not the most practical in many situations, but perfect for clearing mobs in a dark cave."

"I can imagine." I raise my arms overhead, stretching out the stiffness from the beating I just took. "That was great teamwork, everybody. The way everyone fell into position and adapted when things went south, I don't think we could have planned it any better."

When the room groans, we already know what to expect. We head to the center of the room, where a chest rises from the sunken tile.

Taryn opens it, pulling out a glass bottle topped with metal prongs.

"Hell yeah!" He looks at the bottle with admiration.

When I analyze it, I see why he's so excited.

Item. Lightning in a Bottle. *This one-time use item is capable of holding up to five charges of electricity. When the bottle is broken, charges will release, damaging up to five enemies within a 50-foot radius with a 50% chance to stun. To store a charge, simply leave the bottle outside during a lightning storm and the prongs will attract lightning bolts.*

Not bad at all. "Assuming you can use your spell to charge it, that has your name written all over it."

"Only one way to find out." Taryn places the bottle on the ground. "Everybody stand back."

He casts Lightning Bolt, and an arc of lightning shoots from above, striking the bottle. Once my ears quit ringing, I notice that there are bolts of electricity jumping throughout the bottle.

Taryn picks it up, admiring the miniature storm within. "With it being a one-time use, I'll need to make sure not to waste it, but it's essentially five Lightning Bolts at once without having to wait for the cooldown. A fifty-percent chance to stun isn't bad either."

We stay a little longer than normal before heading to the next level so that Taryn can fully charge the item, just in case we need it. I use the time to summon more horrors. Even though Caustic didn't play a major role on this floor, he still managed to gain another level, bringing him up to level ten.

In between our ability cooldowns, we ask Arty what he knows about the tournament.

He shrugs. "With this being the quincentennial tournament, it's hard to know what to expect. There are tournaments in most of the bigger cities, some big and some small, but Pruxford's is the most prestigious. Usually, the Pruxford tournament is invitation only, with the field consisting of either eight or twelve of the best fighters from across Mythos. This year, they added qualifiers, so there's a chance that a dark horse could make a name for themselves. I even saw a few farmhands entering," he says, grinning. "It was five hundred years ago that four heroes battled one another to be crowned the first champion. I think it's fitting that heroes might once again compete. But don't expect us to take it easy on you."

Limery perches on my shoulder, holding his pendant with one hand. "And we's won't takes it easy on yous, either." He crosses his arms, looking intimidating before ruining his bravado with laughter.

Arty grins. "That's the spirit, little one."

The dungeon shakes as we descend to the next level, where we fight a group of Rattling Ferretsnakes. The poisonous furry creatures have the head and tail of a rattlesnake with a six-legged body of a ferret. Taryn makes a point of letting us all know that a group of ferrets is called a business. I don't want to go anywhere near the rabbit hole of how he knows that information.

For the first time in this dungeon, we show them the business, destroying them with overwhelming force.

The chest on this level gives us a Nullification Bomb, which completely disables magical abilities for thirty minutes for anyone or anything caught within its blast radius. I put it in my inventory, but I have a feeling the best is yet to come.

On the next level, we face Armor Golems. The sentient plate armor is heavy and thick, but once I get full stacks of Inferno, the armor dents with every blow. Taryn uses Stonewall to separate one from the group, and the rest of our party focuses on distracting the others as I work my way through them one at a time, hammering away until the armor is nothing more than a pile of warped metal.

The dungeon drops a Vapor Elixir, which allows the user's body to take on a gaseous form for up to an hour. I hand it to Arty, and he tries to refuse.

He pushes the bottle of gray liquid back to me. "The helm was more than enough. I'm sure this will be more useful to you on one of your heroic adventures."

"Actually, that's what we were hoping to talk to you about." I hold out the elixir again. "Consider it a gift for listening to our proposition."

He reluctantly takes the bottle and stuffs it in his satchel. "Alright, let's hear it."

I sit on one of the crumpled pieces of armor, taking a drink of cool water from my Brimming Tankard before passing it around. "What do you know about Valmar Worren?"

"The elvish necromancer? Every child learns about the atrocities of the dark elves in school." He furrows his brow. "Why, what does that have to do with you?"

I look him straight in the eye, leaving no room for misinterpretation. "We believe he's still out there."

He starts to laugh, but then he frowns. "Oh, you're serious. What makes you think that?"

"King Orso believes he's still alive," Taryn answers. "He was never killed, and dark elves can live for centuries." Arty starts to argue, but Taryn holds up a hand, continuing. "It's not just that. A behemoth came through the Seascape Portal. Mesmer wisps threatened to overtake Wandermere. Another hero has made a pact with some dark god or being, with the goal of stopping us from gaining allies. There is movement from the shadowlands, and we don't know when or where, but an attack is imminent."

Arty stares at the ground. I can imagine it's a lot to take in.

After a long moment, he removes the helm and rubs his head. "Say I do believe you. Say there are forces gathering in the shadowlands. What does that have to do with me?"

I stand up, and there's a tightness in my chest that I can't shake. "If Valmar is out there, do you think he's waited hundreds of years to launch a half-assed attack? I don't. I think he's testing us slowly, sending monsters in a few at a time and sealing the portals until he's ready. If he brings an army through those portals, it will be with the intention of taking everything you and I and everyone else in this world holds dear. I don't—" My voice cracks, and I take a breath. "No, I can't lose that. Not any of it. So, when the time comes, we want you on our side."

"Shit." He sighs.

"Yeah, shit."

His eye narrows to a slit. "Why have we not heard about any of this?"

My grip tightens around Destroyer as our conversation with Felston replays in my mind. "Because only one of the councilmembers was in Seascape when the behemoth attacked, and even though he believes the threat is real, the rest of the council do not. They think King Orso is overreacting because Seascape is the newest portal to open."

Arty grunts. "Pruxford has one of the largest standing armies in Mythos. Without them..."

He leaves the rest unsaid. Without them, we are fucked.

Taryn pours water from the Brimming Tankard into a bowl for his pets, and they all flock around it. "This is the real reason why we entered the tournament. If we win, then we can speak to the council directly."

Arty's mouth tightens, and I can tell he's deep in thought. "If I win, I will let you speak to them in my place. And I will do all within my power to sway the Adventurers' Guild to your cause, with or without Pruxford." He extends a hand, and I grab it. "Though I may live to regret it."

I squeeze his hand firmly before letting go. "The barmaid was right about you. You are a good man."

He tosses his sword over his shoulder. "Enough of that. Let's go kill some shit."

My shoulders relax, and the tension fades from my chest as we prepare for the next level. If Arty can somehow convince the Adventurers' Guild to join the fight, they're the next best things to heroes.

"That went better than expected," Taryn whispers.

I nod. "Yeah, but I have a feeling he would have said yes even without the increased luck."

The extra time on this level allowed me to summon a full army of horrors, and sixty of them pack into the stairwell before us.

"Alright, everyone, ready up!" I call to the group and they all gather behind us.

Jordy lowers his head, forcing his way through my horrors until he's at the front. A Horror of Finesse climbs on the frost goat's back, holding on to his horns. We push forward, and a moment later, the dungeon shudders.

Lush green grass covers the floor of the next level. We fan out as we enter the room, with me and Caustic to the far right. Taryn and his pets are in the center, and Arty and Limery are to the left. On the far end, a group of small, blue-horned, pink minotaurs with big heads lie sleeping in the grass. They stir as we enter, standing and crossing their arms.

Mini Manataur. Level 26. *Small and mighty, until they're not. The manataur's name is derived from its ability to drain mana directly from opponents' bodies using its horns. The more mana a manataur consumes, the larger, more powerful, and more self-obsessed it becomes.*

Self-obsessed? I have no idea what that means. They're like cute little chibi versions of Dakota, the minotaur gladiator we fought to enter Goldspire.

Taryn snickers. "This has to be a joke, right?"

"Don't let their appearance fool you. If they're in this dungeon, then these are dangerous enemies." Arty readies his sword.

My horrors charge in, and the manataurs move in unison, planting one leg behind them and bending the other in front while they tilt their giant heads forward. Their horns point at the approaching wave of horrors.

This must be some kind of defensive stance, but my horrors should bowl them over with overwhelming numbers.

The Horrors of Finesse lead the way, sprinting through the grass on spindly legs slightly ahead of the others. As they're about to swarm the manataurs, I experience a strange sensation as my connection to their normally steady presence wavers. Usually, I can tell exactly where they are at all times, even if I can't see them. Their presence only vanishes when they die. This feels different. Something is definitely off.

And then I see why. The horrors grow wispy at the edges, their bodies turning to smoke that funnels into the tips of the manataurs' horns. As the smoke gets sucked into the horns, the manataurs grow, muscles bulging and limbs elongating. In a matter of seconds, the Horrors of Finesse are nothing more than a memory.

The Horrors of Power are not far behind, their powerful legs propelling them forward like a lion on the hunt.

I call them off, but it's too late. Their rear legs dig into the ground in an attempt to stop, but their momentum carries them sliding across the grass. Half of the horrors are already dissipating, their tusks and massive heads wisping away and funneling into the manataurs' horns like ships caught in a whirlpool. More horrors slam into one another and suffer the same fate.

Only a few manage to turn tail and retreat, along with the Horrors of Vitality.

"Chod, what the hell just happened?" Taryn watches with a confused expression.

"I guess my horrors are made of mana? I don't fucking know."

The manataurs continue to morph until they're nearly six feet tall and their bodies finally match their disproportionate heads.

"Jesus, man." Taryn grimaces. "You just gave them a fucking buffet."

I cast Sacrifice on the remaining horrors, boosting my Constitution and adding a few points to Strength. I'd rather use them now than lose more to the manataurs. "Any idea how we beat these guys when we can't get near them?"

The manataurs are easily twice as big as they were before. They stand across the room flexing their muscles and shooting steam out of their nostrils like furry body-builders. Maybe that's what the description meant by self-obsessed.

Arty growls as he reaches into his inventory, pulling out a glowing silver potion. "I didn't want to use this, but it might be our only option. Do you have any throwables?"

"Yes!" Taryn's eyes light up. "The Boom Dust!"

"Boom Dust?" Arty scrunches his brow. "Never heard of it, but if it does damage, we can make it work. This is a Frozen Earth potion. It will freeze the manataurs in place for ten seconds. If you can summon a wall and leave a little space at the top to throw your items, it should amplify the damage in an enclosed space."

"Dammit," Taryn says, frowning. "We don't have time to make a fuse, though."

"We don't need a fuse if we shatter the vials against the wall. Summon the wall after I toss the bomb, and Limery can hit it with a fireball." I pull out a vial of Boom Dust from my inventory. You'd never know the power of the pinkish-purple substance just by looking at it. I show the vial to Arty. "These are no joke. When they go off, we'll need to be in the stairwell."

"Alright, then let's hurry." Arty makes sure we're ready, and then he tosses the Frozen Earth potion.

A yellow aura surrounds Arty's body as he throws the potion, and it rockets across the room with the force of a major league pitcher. The bottle hits one of the manataurs and shatters, its contents exploding in all directions. Icy tendrils stretch out rapidly, covering the posing manataurs in a layer of frost and freezing them in place. The way they stand there posing reminds me of a renaissance painting.

I don't waste any time, equipping a half-dozen vials of Boom Dust and chucking them toward the far wall. They shatter upon impact, raining glitter on the frozen manataurs. I grab Caustic's attention, and we run for the stairs. Taryn's staff glows and Stonewall activates, summoning a wall with about a two-foot gap at the top.

"Now, Limery!" I shout.

The imp throws a fireball, then he zooms to the stairwell. Taryn and his pets are barely ahead of me, and Arty is already out of sight. A second later, there's a massive explosion.

The floor shakes, and a tidal wave of hot air rushes past us, followed by searing pain as flames kiss my back, peeling away layers of flesh.

I fall forward onto Caustic, and his scales sizzle against my skin like a hot iron as they scorch my frontside. The fire disappears as quickly as it came, but everything burns, even with my phoenix feather negating some of the damage. A notification flashes in the corner of my vision, but all I can focus on is the stinging sensation as my body begins to heal itself. I pop a health potion to speed up the process and check on the others.

Caustic nuzzles his head against me and licks at my peeling skin. His tongue is like sandpaper, but I appreciate the affection.

"Is yous okay, Chods?" Limery pats my head, his bulbous eyes full of concern.

"I'll be fine. How's everyone else?"

There's a loud groan, and I stand up to see Taryn with a golden aura as he hovers over Berry. His eyes are focused as he casts Restoration. The umber bear's backside is hairless and inflamed, but the others are fine. He must have shielded them with his massive frame. Berry whines as his flesh returns to its normal coloring and hair sprouts along his back.

Jordy licks Berry's forehead, matting the bear's fur while Ruby tries to tend to his wounds.

Arty peeks his head around the stairwell. "You weren't kidding, were you? That was something else."

By the time Taryn's finished healing Berry, my own skin is nearly back to normal.

Taryn pets Berry affectionately, and the bear nuzzles against his chest. "I think we might have overdone it a bit."

"Yeah, that was definitely overkill. One to two vials might have been enough."

When we return to the room, it's nothing more than scorched earth and charred remains. Every single manataur is burnt to a crisp.

The floor shakes, and a pristine chest rises to the surface. I'm the first one there, so I open the chest. At the bottom, there's a dark purple stone with a bright red center.

Item. *Effect Stone.* *Effect: Return to Sender. When activated, the item equipped with this effect stone will automatically return to user. Cooldown: 1 hour.*

This is an awesome stone, and I really want it, but I didn't clear this room by myself. I hold the stone between my thumb and index finger, showing it to the others.

"Do you have any weapons that hold enchanted stones?" I ask Arty.

He grins. "Those weapons are hard to come by, even for adventurers. It's all yours."

"Yeah, take it, bro," Taryn chimes in. "I can't count the number of times you lost your weapon during battle."

He has a point. I pull out Destroyer, and when I hold the stone to my weapon, a notification appears.

Effect Stone. Would you like to equip effect stone to Destroyer? 1/3 slots filled.

I accept, and the purple stone fits perfectly into the socket beneath the Mana Stone. Enchanted stones have been hard to come by, but I still have one slot left if I find another. They aren't permanently bonded to the weapon, but it takes time to unpair the stone and attach it to another weapon, so I'm not exactly switching them out mid-battle.

Having this new ability means I can use Destroyer in a variety of new ways, even throwing it. The effect might only work once per hour, but that doesn't mean it won't be invaluable.

Another notification flashes in the corner of my vision, and I remember that I never checked the ones from after the fight.

I hold up a finger. "Give me a second while I check my notifications."

Congratulations! You have reached level 27. +1 stat point to distribute. +1 Strength and Constitution racial bonus. +1 ability point to distribute.

Alert! *Luck of the Dragon has ended.*

When I focus on the others, both Taryn and Arty gained a level after the last fight. Those manataurs must have been packing a lot of experience.

Caustic is now up to level fourteen, and Limery is only one level behind me. Damn, we definitely put that buff to good use.

I have an ability point to use, and I can finally unlock the final stage of my Spirit Path. Even though I trust Arty, I don't want to give away any secrets before the tournament. I send Taryn a message.

Message (Chod): *Let's wait until we're back at the inn to allocate our stats. I'd like to keep any new abilities a secret for now.*

Incoming message (Taryn): *Lol. Why do you think I didn't say anything?*

Taryn looks at me and rolls his eyes. "I think we've grinded about as much as we can today. You gents ready to head back to town?"

"This was an experience, I'll tell you that." Arty takes a deep breath, exaggerating it as he exhales. "Arty is going to sleep like a log tonight."

"We couldn't have done it without you." I pat him on the back. "I'm sure the guild will want to hear all about it."

"Ha, they won't believe a word of it."

With that, we head back up the stairs toward the exit.

29. STATS ON STATS

When we make it out of the dungeon, it's nearly nightfall. Only a sliver of sunlight peeks over the mountains in the distance. My hands tingle with excitement at the prospect of unlocking a new ability, and I'm constantly pulling up my character sheet as we walk. I'm equally excited to see what Taryn picks.

I'm analyzing how best to allocate the eight stat points I have saved up when I bump into Berry's backside.

The bear grunts, and I close out the interface. "What's going on?"

Taryn shrugs. "Not sure. Something is in the path."

Both Caustic and Jordy are gathered around a small, translucent green blob in the middle of the trail. Caustic sniffs at the blob and a gooey appendage reaches out and smacks him before the entire thing goes bouncing down the road like a slinky.

"It's a slime!" Taryn claps his hands excitedly and urges Berry forward. "I've always wanted one. Don't let it escape."

Limery zooms ahead and casts a flame wall across the road. "Stop it, slimesies."

The slime stops in front of the flame wall and slinks to the right, where Caustic is waiting. It jumps back to the left, but Jordy has it pinned. The slime shrinks in on itself, trembling.

As it sits there, terrified to move, I notice there are small objects inside of the slime. Some pebbles and leaves that it must have absorbed while traveling. Two pebbles move to the top, and its body morphs into the shape of a miniature cartoon ghost. The pebbles form eyes, and the area just beneath shifts into what looks like a mouth, then a cartoonish scream pours out.

"I'm sorry, dude. This will only hurt for a minute." Taryn leaps off Berry with a Shadow Dagger in one hand, landing in front of the slime.

The ghastly slime vibrates in what I assume is sheer terror as Taryn plunges the dagger into its midsection. Its health drops quickly, and Taryn removes the shadowy blade once it hits five percent, picking up the gelatinous creature and cradling it in his arms.

When he activates Tame, a tendril of yellow energy flows from Taryn's hand to the critically-injured slime. Once the bond is complete, the slime's health starts to rise and it congeals back into a denser version.

Taryn looks down on the cradled slime like an adoring parent. "There we go. Nothing to worry about, little guy. Welcome to the family."

The slime gurgles, a much happier sound than before, and it slinks up Taryn's arm, settling on his shoulder. I've got no idea what Taryn plans to do with a slime that's smaller than his own head, but if it makes him happy, I'm all for it.

Taryn grins from ear to ear. "I've got the perfect thing for him."

He reaches in his satchel and pulls out a large potion bottle and some rope. He holds the bottle up to his shoulder, and the slime jumps in, morphing to fit the shape of the bottle. A small bit of slime peeks above the top, two pebbly eyes looking out.

Taryn takes the rope and ties each side beneath the lip of the bottle, making a sling that fits over his shoulder. "This will do until I have a chance to buy something better." He turns to the rest of us. "Isn't he cute?"

Limery hovers in the air, bulbous eyes watching the slime as it moves within the bottle. "The slimesies is so cutes."

The slime container rests against Taryn's side like a purse as he climbs onto Berry. Once he's situated, Ruby sniffs at the bottle and then taps the glass curiously. A slender slimy hand reaches from the bottle, tapping Ruby on the head.

Taryn chuckles. "Look, they're friends already."

"A slime?" Arty steps beside Berry, frowning as he inspects the creature. "Why in the world would you want a pet slime?"

"Hey, slimes need love, too." Taryn holds a finger above the bottle, and the slime surrounds the stumpy digit in a green casing.

Arty shrugs. "If you say so."

"Let me guess, you're gonna name him Slimey?" I ask.

"Actually, I was thinking of calling him Flubs."

"Of course you were."

Now that Flubs is bottled up, I take a second to analyze him.

Forest Slime. Level 9. Pet. *The forest slime is a subspecies of ooze. Though they do not possess a toxic exterior, forest slimes are still capable of trapping creatures and devouring them within their gelatinous bodies. It's not uncommon to see a forest slime with the skeleton of its victims still inside.*

That's both cool and creepy, but at level nine, I'm not sure how useful the creature will be in a fight. Then again, Ruby has made herself invaluable without needing to engage in actual combat. I trust Taryn to maximize the slime's capabilities, whatever they may be.

The rest of the journey to the portstone is uneventful. Porting through the stone is even a little easier the second time around.

We say our good-byes to Arty as he heads back to the inn, while we go to the stable to drop off the pets. Limery perches on my shoulder, somehow managing to stay upright as he drifts off to sleep.

I understand the feeling. It was a long day for all of us.

When we arrive at Breebis's, Taryn's pets head for the gate, but Caustic hangs back, sticking near my side as the other animals enter the stable.

Breebis closes the gate behind them and comes out into the street, where Caustic now stands a few heads taller than the gnome. I didn't notice at the time because of how frequently Taryn used Imbue on him, but gaining so many levels in one day has accelerated the dragon's growth. His antler-horns are more defined, with pointy tips instead of nubs. His wings have greater width, the small spikes along his spine and tail are longer and more rigid, and a scaly beard has started to come in around his jawline. He looks more fearsome than ever.

"You all must have been busy today." Breebis smiles as she looks up at the dragon. "And it seems your bond has grown stronger. Very good." She looks over to Taryn, who still has his slime in the bottle around his neck. "Will this one be joining me as well?"

Taryn shakes his head. "I think I'll keep him with me tonight. Have you ever kept a slime before?"

"We've seen all kinds of oddities in Pruxford over the years. Slimes are not common pets, but they aren't unheard of either." She turns back to Caustic. "You ready, big guy?"

Caustic looks at me, and his bright golden eyes are more intense than ever.

"Go on. You're gonna have to get used to stables, you're much too big to fit through the doors of an inn now. Don't worry, we'll be back around tomorrow." I scratch him under the chin, and when I stop, he follows Breebis into the stable.

Back at The Puzzling Peacock, a band plays in the tavern. Several of Arty's brothers sit at the back table, but the cyclops is nowhere to be found. If I had to put money on it, he's fast asleep already.

We already ate while on the road, so we head straight upstairs. I put Limery to bed, and then go to Taryn's room so we can allocate our stats.

He sets the sling on the bed, and the slime slithers out. It travels like a slinky, flipping end over end as it inspects the room, looking under the bed and pulling out dresser drawers.

"Alright, you ready to do this?" I ask.

Taryn nods. "You go first."

I have eight stat points to use, but the priority is the ability point, so I pull up my available abilities.

Available Abilities (*1 ability point to unlock*):

. . .

Massive Bite. *Deals double damage. Cost: 20 rage.*

Claws. Swipe at opponent with both hands, dealing extra damage. Cost: 10 rage.

Multi Attack. Bite and Claw at the same time. Cost: 20 rage.

Iron Will. Immune to slows and stuns for 30 seconds. Cost: 50 rage. 180 second cooldown.

Perception. For 10 minutes, gain increased awareness of your surroundings. Spot hidden objects, as well as unusual sounds, odors, and tastes. Cooldown: 6 hours.

Cleave. Your next attack causes bleed damage, dealing 1% of opponent's health per second for 5 seconds. Cost: 10 rage.

Battle Cry. You let out a ferocious roar, increasing rage by 20. No cost. 60 second cooldown.

Subclass:

Spirit of the Beast. *The Spirit of the Beast path is composed of five phases. (Phase 1-4 complete)*

Phase 5: Spirit Power. *The path of the beast is not for the faint of heart, and those who complete all five stages are blessed with a mighty power from their spirit beast. Gain a new active ability based on your spirit beast.*

Completion: Unlock using one ability point and the Spirit of the Beast path will be complete.

Class Advancements. *Upon reaching level twenty-five, you have unlocked a class advancement. You may only advance one class at a time. A second class may not be advanced until completion of primary advancement.*

Subclass:

Summoner Advancement.

Dreadbeasts. Unlock for further details.

Dual Subclass. Unlock for further details

Honestly, it's not that difficult of a decision. I can't wait to unlock Dreadbeasts and see what that is all about, but it's not even an option until I finish the Spirit of the Beast path. The older abilities just aren't as useful as they once would have been, especially since unlocking my summoner class. I use weapons so often that my rage abilities rarely come into play aside from Berserker Rage, so there's little reason to put a point into any of them when levels are so hard to come by now.

The only reason we're doing this at the inn now instead of the dungeon earlier is in case some kind of change comes over me like it did with the horns. I trust Arty, and I'm glad he'll give us his meeting with the council if he wins, but I still want to win on my own merit. Until the tournament is over, it's best to keep some things close to my chest.

I put my ability point into Spirit Power and receive another notification.

Alert! Spirit of the Beast Phase Five: Spirit Power complete. New ability available.

Ability: (New)

Concussive Force: *Physical attacks can be imbued with concussive force, knocking opponents back with a chance to stun them. Cost: 100 mana.*

Alert! Spirit of the Beast path complete.

That's awesome! There's no cooldown, and for only a hundred mana, I can knock opponents back no matter what weapon I'm using. A jab with Sea Scorpion would create even more distance. On top of that, the attack has a chance to stun.

I fill Taryn in on the details, and he nods approvingly.

"Nice!" Taryn pets Flubs, who has returned to his lap. The slime is somehow both firm and gelatinous at the same time, kind of like Jell-o. "We're starting to get a lot better crowd control abilities than we used to have. And you'll be able to use that a lot more often than my Lightning Bolt!"

"Now what about you? What are you going to spend your point on?"

Taryn's eyes glaze over as he pulls up his character sheet.

He talks me through his choices. "Let's see. I've got Barkskin and Stoneskin, but I'm not really feeling either one of those. Insect Plague is pretty cool, it lets me summon all of the insects within a fifty-yard radius to attack a target. That one could be OP in the right environment, but useless if there are no insects around.

"Then there's Conceal, but I've made it this far without hiding my level, so I don't see any point in starting now. I don't need Perception when I have Ruby. And then there's all of the newer abilities from my Shadow Druid class. Scry, which lets me locate a target on my map as long as I have one of their personal items." His fist clenches as he reads off the ability, and I know he's thinking about using it on Glenn and Jude. He still has the glove that he took during the fight where Stompy died.

"Mind Warp is cool. It makes an enemy attack their allies for thirty seconds, but it has a thirty-minute cooldown. That one could be pretty useful, though I'm not sure if it would be a great choice for the tournament. Tidal Wave lets me summon a wave from a nearby body of water, but it's just as limited as Insect Plague, maybe even more so. Shooting Stars is like Moonbeam, except it's a barrage instead of a single beam. Good if we want more burst damage. And then there's Shadow Cloak, which gives me increased stealth at night or in the shadows. With my cloak, boots, and daggers, I'd be as sneaky as a rogue."

The glazed look fades, and he looks me in the eye. "So, what do you think?"

I know this isn't going to be what he wants to hear, but I have to tell him the hard truth. Unlocking Scry right now would be wasting an ability point.

Taking a deep breath, I prepare to take whatever lashing he gives me and tell him what I think. "I know you want to unlock Scry and go after Glenn and Jude for what they did to Stompy, but I don't think it's the right move. Not right now. We have a chance to possibly make a difference with the fate of Mythos if we can win this tournament, and I don't see how Scry helps us win now."

I know I didn't answer his question, but it needed to be said before we even discuss the other options.

Taryn pulls down the collar of his tunic, revealing the carrot tattoo over his heart. His hand rests over it, and he closes his eyes for a moment.

God, I'm an asshole. If something had happened to Limery, I doubt there would be anything Taryn could say to keep me from moving heaven and earth to make those responsible pay. And here I am asking him to postpone his vengeance.

He opens his mossy green eyes, his hand still resting over the tattoo. "I've made my peace with losing Stompy. You best believe that those motherfuckers are going to get what's coming for them—I guarantee it—but I know that it's not today. We can't lose sight of what's in front of us, because if we do, then what did Stompy die for? So, I'll ask you again, what do you think I should spend my point on?"

His response is so stoic that I'm not sure how to respond. So, I don't. Instead, I answer his question. "You're right that Insect Plague and Tidal Wave are situational, but I think Insect Plague could be a good play. Maybe not for the tournament, but for our everyday lives—especially considering how much time we spend traveling. Having a swarm of high-level insect monsters suddenly on our side could be deadly, and at the very least, low-level insects would be annoying. But I also like Mind Warp considering how much people seem to want to gang up on us."

He nods. "I'd narrowed it down to those two as well. My gut is telling me to go with Mind Warp. The cooldown is longer, but it creates more chaos. It's like taking two enemies off the board at once. Because if their ally is attacking them, then they're going to have to defend and possibly injure whoever is under the spell."

"Sounds like a good plan then. I'm still not sure what to do with my stat points."

He shrugs. "I'm splitting mine between Intelligence and Wisdom."

I grimace as I think it over. "Part of me thinks I should get mine up as well. It could help with my Kamikaze ability."

"Bro, come on. You're not a mage. You're definitely not an Einstein. You have, what, one ability that does magical damage? Kamikaze. And half the time that you use it, most of your horrors are already dead." He narrows his eyes. "You are the bruiser. You deal damage and take a beating while doing it. Your horrors even build off of your Strength and Constitution. The only thing you're lacking is speed. Be the dumb strong brute you were always meant to be."

"Damn, T. Tell me how you really feel." I laugh at his brutal honesty. I can't believe I was the one worried about telling him the hard truth. "Sure you don't want to chop my balls off while you're at it?"

He grins. "You know I'm right."

My lip curls at the edge. "Maybe."

I put all eight points into Dexterity, bringing me up to thirty-two. Immediately, I feel more responsive to my body's movements, the same feeling that happens when I cast Sacrifice on my Horrors of Finesse.

Oh, yeah. This is gonna be good.

30. ROLL CALL

"Chods! Chods!" Limery shakes me awake. "We dids it! We dids it!"

He's so excited that tears well up in his giant yellow eyes. I groan as I sit up, and he releases me, hovering in the air.

"What are you talking about? What did we do?"

"We's gots in the tournament!" He does a backflip in the air and plops onto the bed. "We's dids it."

"We what?" But then I notice the notification in the corner of my vision.

I focus on it, and a wall of text fills my vision.

Alert! You have qualified for the Quincentennial Champion's Tournament!

Regional Alert! Over one thousand challengers took part in the qualification round of the Quincentennial Champion's Tournament. Hailing from all across Mythos, forty have been judged worthy to compete in this historic event. This is the most competitors appearing in one tournament since the three-hundred-and-twelfth tournament. With over a dozen heroes competing, this is destined to be one for the ages!

Beneath the regional alert is a list of all the challengers. The first thing I do is search for mine, Limery, and Taryn's names. Somehow, all three of us made it.

I scroll down the list, searching for the names of other heroes. They're easy to pick out, as every challenger has their home kingdom listed next to their name. I'm assuming that's so everyone who received the regional alert will know who they're up against.

Jason Montoya *(Vanaria)*
   Lester Hobbes *(Vanaria)*
   Randy Billson *(Vanaria)*
   Don Othello *(Vanaria)*
   Otis Wiggins *(Vanaria)*
   Ethan French *(Vanaria)*
   Kevin Harris *(Vanaria)*
   Michael Didato *(Vanaria)*
   Troy Malloy *(Vanaria)*
   Tommy Sullivan *(Vanaria)*
   Scotty Heyden *(Vanaria)*
   Sam Taylor *(Vanaria)*
   Bridger Phillips *(Vanaria)*
   Taryn Jones *(Seascape)*

I clench my fist as I read through some of the names. Out of the fourteen heroes, I've had a run-in with nearly half of them at some point.

I fought Jason Montoya and Lester Hobbes south of the troll forest. I can still remember the look on Lester's face when he ordered the hired soldier to slit Ismora's throat.

Randy Billson and Don Othello nearly found me and Limery on our way back from slaying the mana-infused wyrm. That was before the trolls had peace, and if not for my Camouflage ability, they probably would have killed me then and there.

None spark my ire greater than Otis, Ethan, and Kevin. Those three laid a trap for us after we left The Dancing Donkey. If not for the timely arrival of Limery and the trolls, they would have killed us and Taryn's pets. Those three are working for Valmar—if not directly, then on behalf of some being with the same goal. The fact that they didn't want us to ally with other heroes means their presence here may be more disturbing than the cleric's.

Michael Didato had the sense to abandon his partnership with Jude, but that doesn't mean he doesn't want to put a blade in my back, especially after our encounter outside the dungeon.

Of the remaining names, I recall seeing Troy Malloy and Tommy Sullivan's names when they killed a mana-infused wyrm. The other three, I've never heard of or met. Maybe I can use this as an opportunity to win them over if they aren't murderous assholes.

I guess Richard the cleric was telling the truth when he said he didn't enter. Either that or he didn't qualify, which wouldn't surprise me. His damage has always been done by utilizing others.

I'm a little surprised that Pressley isn't on the list, but the last time I saw the death knight, he was in Goldspire. If he's managed to clear any of those high-tiered dungeons, he could be stronger than all of us. I count it as a blessing that we won't be facing him.

Jon the enchanter is probably still training in Vanaria if I had to guess. Hopefully, his skills are leveled up when we need them most.

Aside from Jude and Glenn, who are probably still in Frostmoor, there's only one other hero that I know of that's not on the list—Percy Mcdonnell, who slew a mana-infused wyrm. Though I know nothing about him aside from his name.

When I count them all up, that's eighteen heroes I'm aware of. That means that somewhere out there, there are still six heroes I've never come across.

I scan through the list again finding one more name that I recognize. It seems Arty made the cut as well. The other challengers are all a mystery, though their location gives some clue to their race. Goldspire, Frostmoor, and Wandermere are not represented at all, and there are several kingdoms represented that we haven't visited. A few of the names stand out because of how different they sound, even by troll and gnomish standards.

Drizz'rt *(Ellynmylly)*
  Lanxkuri *(Antedale)*
  Tozzet Girok *(Mistville)*

I remember Jegaar telling us that Ellynmylly was the largest kingdom in Mythos, and so diverse that they called it the Melting Pot. There's no telling what race their challengers are. With six challengers, they're only outnumbered by Vanaria and Pruxford. There's no surprise that a kingdom so big would have such a large presence, even in a foreign tournament. Antedale has three challengers, and Mistville has two. Antedale is the home of the catfolk. If I remember correctly, they are known for their healers. I recall Mistville as the land of the merfolk.

With thirteen competitors from Pruxford, I have to think that there was some hometown favoritism involved in the selection process. Either that or not that many outsiders entered.

After I finish looking over the challengers, there's still one more notification.

Alert! *As a qualifier for the Quincentennial Challenger's Tournament, you have been invited to the Challenger's Ball. There is a strict "No Combat" policy at the Challenger's Ball. Anyone in violation of this policy will be removed from the tournament. Each challenger may bring one guest. Please arrive at the Crystal Palace tomorrow at sundown.*

. . .

I close out the notifications and just sit there for a moment. Limery continues to bounce around the room singing a song about how we're all going to the tournament.

There's so much to process. How in the hell am I going to make it through an evening with some of these assholes without fighting? Just the thought of Ethan and his goons sets my blood boiling.

Watching Limery, I wish I had his level of excitement, but all I see are threats and danger. I take a breath and try to steady myself. I can't concern myself with other heroes right now. This should be a moment of celebration. Because we did it. Out of all the people who entered, we made the cut. Along with Arty, we make up ten percent of the field. And now I have a dragon to go to battle with, a dragon that grows stronger by the day.

"We dids it! We dids it!" Limery sings as he zooms through the air.

"That we did." A smile finally overtakes me. "What do you say we go and tell Taryn the good news?"

We beat on Taryn's door for a solid minute before he opens it, dreadlocks askew and sporting a deep frown.

"I thought we were sleeping in?" he mumbles.

I push past him into the room. His slime sits perched on the windowsill over-looking the street. Limery sits on my shoulder, holding in the good news with both hands clasped over his mouth like he's about to explode.

"Limery has something he wants to tell you." I nod to Limery, and he erupts like a volcano.

"We dids it, Taryns!" He flutters through the air, alarming the slime, who slithers under the bed. "We dids it!"

Taryn raises an eyebrow. "What's he talking about?"

I grin, seeing the humor more now that Limery's antics aren't directed at me. "Check your notifications."

Taryn's eyes glaze over and after several minutes, he looks at me, wide awake. "We got in, but wow. That's a lot of heroes. Don't you have beef with some of them?"

I nod. "Want to talk through it all over breakfast?"

Downstairs, Arty is sitting at a table with his four brothers. He cheers when he sees us. "Fellow challengers! Congratulations."

Two of his brothers stand, both level twenty warriors with short brown hair and freckles. One wears a brown tunic, the other green. Honestly, all four of them look nearly identical.

The man in the green tunic extends a hand. "We haven't officially met. I'm Roddick, This is Reddick. We'll be seeing you in the tournament."

"I bet it was hell keeping the two of you straight growing up." I shake both of their hands in turn. "Three challengers from the same family, now that is impressive."

Reddick smiles. "Mom knows how to raise 'em, that's for sure. If not for all of the heroes, we might have gone four for four."

I share their laughter. "I don't doubt it. Good luck, and if we meet in the arena, I hope it's a hell of a fight."

"To hear Arty tell it, we're all competing for second place." Roddick shoves Arty in the shoulder, but the boulder of a man doesn't budge. "We were just about to head out to clear a mob dungeon today. You're more than welcome to come."

Taryn holds out his slime, who's nestled in his palm. "There are a few things I need to take care of around town for this guy. Some other time?"

The brothers scrunch their brows simultaneously at the appearance of the slime.

I hold back my laughter. "It's a no for me, too. I was planning to do some non-combat training with Caustic today. Thanks for the offer, though. But before you head out, I wanted to ask if you know anything about this Challenger's Ball?"

Arty pushes his plate forward, then stands. "It's just a little something they do before the tournament. The leaders of various kingdoms all gather to flaunt their wealth and feel important as they are surrounded by the best fighters across Mythos. For the challengers, it's an opportunity to get shitfaced on fine drinks for free and have two days to sober up before the fights."

That would be amazing any other time, talking about adventures and drinking. But now, with so many enemies that close together, it sounds like a recipe for disaster. "Isn't that a little dangerous considering the no-combat clause?"

He shrugs. "From what I hear, people usually find more creative ways of settling disagreements."

Somehow, I feel like attempted murder and the destruction of all that is good in the world aren't the type of disagreements settled over an arm-wrestling match. "Thanks for the info. Have fun at the dungeon."

After they leave, we take an open table and order our food. Taryn's slime slinks around the room, inspecting everything. It's a very curious creature. Maybe slimes are more intelligent than I thought.

Taryn leans forward. "Alright, I know about some of the heroes, but fill me in on the rest."

"Some of them we ran into very early on, so while I might know a little about them, they've probably progressed a lot since then. They might even have a second class or expanded their primary."

I pause my story when the barmaid comes over with a pitcher of milk, pouring us all a glass. Limery tilts his cup up, taking a massive drink, and when he's done, there's a thick milk mustache across his upper lip. He cackles when Taryn shows him his reflection in a knife.

"The first two I ran into were Randy Billson and Don Othello. Actually, we ran into them again at The Dancing Donkey. The rogue and the mage weren't half-bad the second time around. I almost forgot with everything that happened after leaving. I don't have a clue what type of mage he is, though."

Taryn nods along as I talk, only pausing when our food arrives.

"We saw Michael Didato, the paladin, in Seascape Square when he tried to unlock the portal, though I had a run-in with him long before that. Now that I think back on it, it was probably a shitty thing to do, but the trolls were on the cusp of extinction and my anger was running wild. We attacked him and Jude as they were leaving a dungeon south of the troll forest. I know he has a heal, some kind of buff that gives off a white aura, a holy light kind of similar to your Moonbeam, and then some other ability where light radiates from him, damaging everything nearby."

Taryn bites off a piece of sausage and points the rest of it at me. "So, you killed them for no reason? That explains a lot."

"Things were different then. The trolls didn't have peace with Vanaria. If they would have seen us first, they would have done the same thing."

He shrugs. "I guess we'll find out at the ball tomorrow night."

"On our way back to the forest after clearing a dungeon, we were ambushed by Jason Montoya and Lester Hobbes." As I tell this part, a scowl settles on Limery's face, and I'm sure the memory is still as vivid to him as it is to me. "Jason is a wizard, and he had these arcane chains that could hold an enemy in place. He also had this magical cube that he could hide inside and use as a shield. Lester is a ranger. He could shoot imbued arrows, but he also had an ability that allowed him to subdue other people's pets. He had to touch the pet to use the ability, but it could have evolved since then, so watch out for that if you're facing him. He's the one who ordered a soldier to kill Ismora. If not for Limery, she'd be dead now."

"That's good to know," he says with a full mouth. "I doubt he could subdue one of my pets without the others attacking, though."

"You already know about Otis the barbarian, Ethan the warlock, and Kevin the sorcerer. The other five, I don't have a clue."

Taryn sits back against his chair, his plate empty. "Sounds like we have our work cut out for us."

That's an understatement.

31. PECULIAR ITEMS

While Chod left for Breebis's stable to train Caustic, Taryn had a few errands to run. He'd stop to see his other pets once he was finished. For now, he was enjoying the alone time with Flubs.

The slime was a curious creature, somehow intelligent despite being an amorphous blob. It had taken to using pebbles to represent eyes but would shift them from one side of its body to the other in seconds. Its appearance could change at the drop of a hat, sometimes appearing gooey, at other times slick and gelatinous.

Flubs might be a nontraditional pet, but Taryn was certain he'd only scratched the surface of its capabilities.

Pulling up the detailed map he'd bought for only five silver, he searched through the list of shops for the ones he had mentally marked earlier.

Grimward's Collection of Oddities and Eccentricities
　　Titra's Formal Wear
　　The Crystal Ball: Precious Stones and Jewelry
　　Bottles Galore

The four shops were scattered around the city, so it would take a while to get everything he needed. He formulated the most expedient route to hit all the shops without having to backtrack and set off to Bottles Galore.

Flubs peeked above the lip of the bottle draped by Taryn's side, taking in the sights and sounds of the city.

"Compared to the quiet of the forest, I bet this is a lot for you to take in, isn't it?" Taryn gently stroked the slime, and it gurgled.

The closer they got to the city center, the more congested the streets became. The tournament celebrations were in full force. After getting recognized by a stranger, Taryn pulled his hood up, concealing his face as he hurried along.

The door to Bottles Galore had a large slab of glass set within the wooden frame. The glass twisted in a swirling pattern, changing from lighter to darker colors the closer the swirls got to the center. It was mesmerizing. Taryn couldn't tell if the glass was actually moving or if it was some kind of optical illusion.

A chime rang out as he pushed open the door, and an elderly gnome with purple spectacles poked her head above the counter. Dozens of small bottles and vials lined the counter, sitting on small racks and hanging from spindles. The gnome's faded purple hair was pulled up into a bun with two glass rods holding it in place.

She hobbled around the counter. "Welcome, welcome. Come on in." She stopped in front of the counter, gesturing to the many shelves lined with bottles in all shapes, sizes, and colors.

The store was like a library of peculiar glass containers. Some were big enough that Taryn swore he could climb inside them.

"We have bottles for every occasion. If you can't find what you need here, you can't find it anywhere." Though she moved slowly, the gnome's words were practiced and true, like any good salesperson's.

"Excellent." Taryn pulled back his robe, revealing Flubs and the potion bottle he nestled within. "I'm looking for something to hold my pet slime. As you can see, this one is rather cumbersome to be wearing around my neck. Do you happen to have anything that's enchanted so that he can fit inside, but that's small enough that I can also wear it around my neck?"

"Of course, master dwarf. As I said, if you can't find it here, you can't find it anywhere. Just give me a moment to go search. We keep the enchanted bottles in the back."

Taryn grinned as the woman disappeared down an aisle filled with colorful orb-shaped vases. He stood in place, keeping Flubs inside the container. The last thing he needed was to accidentally knock something over. There was no telling how much some of these bottles might cost.

She returned holding her hands behind her back. Grinning, she presented Taryn with a vial not much bigger than her outstretched hands. It was shaped like a swirling vortex, spiraling to a pointed end. A small lip jutted out from the top, stuffed with a cork, and a silver necklace attached at both sides.

"Wow. It's beautiful." Taryn's eyes widened as he analyzed the bottle.

Item. Small Abyssal Vial. *Although small, this enchanted vial can hold a great deal of material. Similar to an expandable item, the abyssal vial can hold what the satchel cannot—namely liquid, viscous, or granular substances.*

She held it up, letting the vial dangle on the chain. "The inside will expand to fit the vial's contents, up to the volume of a large barrel. I don't know how big your slime will grow, but this will accommodate you for a very long time."

"How much?" Taryn asked.

"For you?" She gave him a warm smile. "Three gold."

"I'll take it."

Her smile shifted to a smirk. "Three gold...on the condition that should you win the tournament, you will thank Bottles Galore for outfitting you with all your bottling needs."

She was good. Very good.

"Deal." Taryn shook her hand and paid for the vial.

He uncorked the stopper and placed it in his satchel. With Flubs inside of the vial, there was no need for the cork. As the slime slithered from the large bottle to the tiny vial, its body bulged at the lip. Even though it appeared that he wouldn't fit, Flubs slid inside no differently than he had in the larger bottle. Once inside, the vial changed to a forest green.

Flubs emerged partway from the bottle. As he did so, the slime expanded to its normal size, with a wispy tendril that connected to the vial like some kind of genie.

The next stop was The Crystal Ball: Precious Stones and Jewelry, where Taryn purchased two small amethysts. He traded Flubs for the pebbles, and now the slime's makeshift eyes sparkled from within.

After that was Grimward's Collection of Oddities and Eccentricities. The entrance to Twilight Avenue was nearly concealed between two buildings, so far down the depths of the dark alleyway that he'd almost missed it. The alley funneled into a dead-end street with four buildings on each side and a brick wall at the far end.

Compared to the elegance of most of Pruxford, calling this place sketchy would be an understatement. Taryn gulped as he stepped out of the alley, and Flubs gurgled from around his neck.

Somehow, the light was dimmer, despite being as open to the sky as any other street. A heaviness settled on the street that he couldn't quite explain. The cobblestones were stained and faded, littered with trash that blew around in the wind, occasionally clinging to the steps of one of the buildings.

All of the windows were a cloudy gray, hiding the contents within, and the signs offered little description of what awaited inside. If not for the map, he'd be lost.

He took a deep breath and opened the door to Grimward's. It creaked as it opened, and somewhere in the depths of the shop, a cat meowed, followed by heavy footsteps.

The smell of incense lingered above all else. The floorboards were dusty and warped, and cobwebs clung to most of the inventory. Taryn shivered, hoping that the spiders kept to themselves, while Flubs retreated to the safety of the vial.

The shelves lived up to the store's name, filled with an assortment of oddities that set Taryn's hair on end. Jars stuffed with eyes preserved in a yellowish liquid. Dolls with porcelain faces and way too lifelike eyes. Skulls of various shapes and sizes. Taxidermies that he was certain were created from parts of more than one animal. A necklace made of black pearls gave off a sinister red aura as it rested on a faceless mannequin, and candles burned with green and purple flames.

There was something off about a painting of what looked like a haunted castle. When a face suddenly appeared behind one of the castle windows, Taryn nearly screamed.

"Can I help you?" a raspy voice asked as a gaunt man stepped from behind a shelf filled with books covered with suspiciously human skin-like leather.

The man was halfway to becoming a skeleton, with sunken cheeks and milky eyes that only offered the faintest glimpse of pupils within their depths. The man's hair was gone, save for a few strands that hung across his face. Taryn could only imagine the frail body hidden beneath the black robes.

He had the urge to run out the door screaming, but he swallowed hard and pressed on with what he'd come for. "I was hoping to buy a skeleton of a small animal. Someone told me you might have one for sale."

"You came to the right place," the man croaked. "Do you need it for a potion or reanimation?"

The man's smile was unsettling as it stretched across the bony face.

"Uhm, neither." He tapped on the vial for Flubs to come out, and the slime slithered into his palm. "I was hoping to use it for my slime."

The man stared at Flubs with intrigue, before disappearing down the aisle. He returned carrying a small canvas bag. It rattled as he turned it upside down and bones clattered against the floor.

The skeleton was small. Judging by the skull, it was probably half the size of Ruby. Taryn wasn't sure he wanted to know what had happened to the poor creature.

He released Flubs, and the slime surrounded the bones, absorbing them into his body. It was like a science video as the bones moved within and slowly assembled into a skeleton. When Flubs was done, a layer of slime surrounded the bones of what had most assuredly been a cat at one point. The two amethysts Taryn had purchased sat in the eye sockets, and the tail swished back and forth as Flubs walked around the room. Whether it was from the slime's abilities or natural instinct, the movements were almost identical to a real cat.

"That's amazing." Taryn watched in awe.

He could store the bones in his inventory when Flubs was in the vial, but this would allow the slime to take a more solid form. And truth be told, it looked exceptionally badass.

Taryn paid for the bones and left the store in short order. Whether or not this purchase was entirely legal remained to be seen, and the less time spent in that shop the better.

With Flubs now walking alongside Taryn like a haughty housecat, the two made their way over to Titra's Formal Wear, where he purchased a set of emerald-green robes for the ball.

Chod might have no issue wearing a loincloth and flapping his junk in the wind for all the world to see, but this was Taryn's first time at a dignified event, and it warranted more than the clothing he wore in day in and day out.

The time had flown by exceptionally fast, and after picking up his formalwear, it was already early afternoon. He headed back to the stables. Flubs caught plenty of stares as they walked, and Taryn grinned underneath his hood.

When they arrived at Breebis's, Chod and Caustic were nowhere to be found.

Breebis stood on a stool, brushing Berry's dense coat in the outer pen. "Little Caustic—well, I guess he's not so little now—finally has the strength to keep himself aloft. Chod and Limery took him outside the city gates for some flight training. Less likely to cause a commotion that way." She frowned as she noticed Flubs arch his back and lean into Taryn. "Odd creatures, slimes."

Taryn gave her a devious smile. "Check this out. Flubs, release."

The skeleton within the slime detached, and the bones fell through Flub's body, clattering against the ground as he launched himself at Taryn's chest. He hit the vial, and in a flash, he was gone.

Breebis stared at Taryn with an open mouth, leaning from side to side to try and see where the slime had disappeared.

Taryn tapped the vial around his neck that was now a deep green, and Flubs peeked out. "Awesome, right? I could fit a dozen slimes inside this thing and still have room."

She nodded approvingly. "I must say, I've never seen that before."

They stood in silence for a moment. Breebis continued to brush the umber bear, and Taryn stared at the ground, gathering the courage to put himself out there.

A bead of sweat formed on his brow, and he cleared his throat. "Uh, there was actually something I was wanting to ask you."

Breebis looked up, one eyebrow raised. A strand of loose green hair fell across her forehead, and she blew it back in place. "What's up?"

"Well, uh..." Taryn's palms were suddenly so sweaty that he wiped them on his cloak. "Each of the challengers gets to bring a guest to the Challenger's Ball, and I was kind of hoping you'd want to go with me."

The tension was palpable as Breebis dropped the brush. It clanked against the stool, and Berry groaned, waggling his rear for more affection.

Taryn threw up his hands hurriedly. "But if you're busy, that's cool, too. I know you have a lot of animals to take care of."

"N-no." Breebis climbed down, picking up the brush with shaking hands and flushed cheeks. "It's not that. I was just surprised is all." She took a deep breath, and she seemed more herself. "I've never been to a ball, but I'd love to go with you."

Her cheeks grew even more rosy, and for a moment, they both just stood there awkwardly.

"I've never been to a ball either, so I guess we can figure it out together."

He smiled, and she did the same.

32. CHALLENGER'S BALL

After a long day of training with Caustic, Limery and I enter the Puzzling Peacock eager for a warm meal and strong drink. Taryn is already there, laughing with several gnomes while a bright-green-striped cat struts across the table.

"Don't tell me you've gotten another pet? Wait—" I do a double-take as I notice the gelatinous consistency of the cat's body and the skeleton that's clearly visible inside. "Is that Flubs?"

Taryn grins. "The one and only. What do you think?"

Limery flies over, poking the slime-cat with a pointy finger. It sinks into the slime's body up to his knuckle and the imp cackles.

How in the hell did it get bones? Honestly, I'm not sure if I want to know the answer to that.

I just shake my head. "Was this your special errand?"

"Part of it." His mustache twitches. "I hear Caustic can fly now."

Now, it's my turn to be proud. I can't help but stand a little taller as I brag about him. "He's getting stronger every day. Watching his wings flap, and the power it takes to lift himself off the ground... I can't explain it."

"I know the feeling." Taryn pulls a chair over from a nearby table and pats for me to sit. "Tell me all about it."

We spend the next few hours drinking, laughing, and boasting to our new gnome friends about how special our pets are. For a little while at least, I forget about what waits for us tomorrow.

The next day, I get in some more solid training with Caustic before we have to get ready for the ball. Taryn insists that he needs to go back to the inn beforehand. When he knocks on my door, I see why.

His cloak, tunic, and antlered helm are all gone. Instead, he wears a slick, emerald-green robe. Some of his dreads are pulled together in a tail and the rest drape over his shoulders. The clasps in his beard are extra polished.

"Alright, T. You really went all out, didn't you?"

He looks me up and down. "Some of us had to. Where's Limery? I got him a little something."

Limery is on my shoulder in a second, eyes bulging. "You's gots a present for Limmy?"

Taryn pulls a ruffled white collar from behind his back. "Sure did, buddy. Try it on."

Limery buttons the collar around his small neck and preens., then he flies down and wraps his arms around Taryn. "Oh, Taryns. Thank yous."

After getting a look at these two, I don't want to appear like a complete savage, so I change into the leather kilt and vest that King Favian gave me when I visited Vanaria. The deep brown leather looks great against my blue skin.

With the spooky slime-cat in tow, we set out for the ball, but Taryn heads in the opposite direction.

"Wrong way, dude," I call after him, gesturing over my shoulder with my thumb. "Palace is that way."

He stops and turns around. "We need to stop by the stable first."

"Bro, you spent all day with your pets. I think it'll be fine if we attend the ball without them."

He frowns. "We're not going for my pets. We're picking up my date."

"What!" My jaw nearly hits the floor. "Why didn't you tell me you were getting a date?"

He shrugs. "I didn't think you cared."

"I didn't, I mean, I don't." I groan. "I just wish I would have known so I would have had the option."

Limery pats me on the back of the neck. "It's okays, Chods. Limmy will be yous date."

Date? Five gold says I'll be babysitting his little imp butt after he's had too much to eat and drink.

* * *

The sun hovers above the horizon as we ride toward the Crystal Palace. After picking up Breebis, Taryn insisted we take a cart. A young gnome pedals up front as we bump along the stone streets. He occasionally groans, probably regretting accepting my enormous weight. I'll make sure to tip him extra for his trouble.

Breebis and Taryn sit awkwardly beside each other. In all the years I've known him, this is the first time I've actually seen him go on a date. Not that he didn't have opportunities. Unlike me, Taryn had no problem getting girls' attention. There's just something about being six-feet of caramel man muscle that would turn them into puddles any time he walked by. The fact that he didn't seem interested probably made him that much more desirable.

Seeing him nervously tapping his leg as he sits next to someone that wouldn't come up to his waist in real life is kind of heart-warming.

Breebis is almost unrecognizable from the gnome we first met. Her normally messy bun is neatly brushed and falls around her shoulders with an emerald luster. The dirty work clothes are gone, replaced with a black-and-silver ball gown that accentuates her pale green skin. I don't know if she and Taryn planned it, but their color choices complement each other very well.

I catch them stealing glances at one another, and it brings back memories of Senzala. Now that I have Caustic, the arctic troll and I have more in common than ever, though I don't know if her bond with Nesira is the same as the one I'm trying to form with Caustic. I imagine there's a big difference between having a dragon as a totem versus a pet.

I wonder how she and the other arctic trolls are managing in Seascape. Hopefully, Chief Rizza has made them feel like a part of the tribe.

"Oh, you've got to be fucking kidding me." Taryn's outburst pulls me from my reminiscing.

His eyes narrow as he looks past my shoulder. I turn around, wondering what has him so upset.

Several carriages wait in line before us, emptying as guests arrive for the ball. One is made of green crystal, with a stagecoach directing two ponies adorned with gaudy gold harnesses. The couple that exit the carriage are equally ostentatious. Where Breebis's outfit is refined and elegant, these gnomes look like they're wearing every piece of jewelry they own. At my dad's business dinners, there were always a few older women who dressed the same way. Hopefully, the perfume on this couple is more subdued.

My gaze shifts to the dusty pink and lilac stairs that catch the glow of the moon, every third stair reveals the trickling stream underneath. Even at night, it's a sight to behold. Dozens of extravagantly-dressed guests make their way up the hundred-plus stairs toward the Crystal Palace.

Midway up, a group has gathered in a circle, and they aren't moving. I finally understand what has Taryn out of sorts, and I let out a stream of curses myself.

It's impossible to miss the warlock's shadowy wings that spread a good six feet on each side of him—Ethan, the ringleader of the jerks who tried to ambush us. His party stands in front of him—Otis, the bald, bearded barbarian, and Kevin, the sorcerer—with a group of bystanders surrounding them on all sides.

"What's the matter?" asks Breebis.

"Trouble." Taryn scowls at the three assholes.

Ethan stands behind the other two with his phantom wings outstretched while Otis mimics slashing with an axe and Kevin extends his hands in a blasting motion. The warlock's wings fade away, and all three start laughing, followed by those around them. They're too far away for me to analyze them.

Limery hovers next to me, and the air around him distorts as he stares at the trio like a dog ready to pounce.

"Easy, buddy. Remember the rules. If we fight, we're out of the tournament."

The air returns to normal as the imp sighs. "Limmy hates thems. Theys tried to hurt Chods and Taryns."

"Don't worry about them," Taryn speaks to him softly. "Tonight is about us. Come on, let's go enjoy the ball."

Our driver pulls to a stop at the bottom of the stairs. Around us, people and carriages continue to arrive. I catch several looks as I climb down, first helping Breebis and then Taryn from the cart, before tossing a gold coin to the driver. His eyes go wide when he catches it.

"Thanks for the ride." I nod and turn toward the palace.

I set my face, showing no emotion, and Limery perches on my shoulder as we ascend the stairs. Taryn and Breebis take the lead, their short legs moving slowly toward the palace. Whoever designed the palace didn't want to make it easy for visitors, that's for sure, but as we pass each crystal stair, the view of fish swimming underneath makes it almost worth it.

Almost.

I can hear the loud voice of Otis as he tells the gathering crowd of some monster they killed, but I keep my eyes set in front of me. There's too much riding on this for me to get baited into a fight with these assholes.

"Would you look at that?" He abruptly changes the subject, and I can feel dozens of eyes staring in our direction. "Looks like Papa Smurf got a makeover."

I should have known they wouldn't let us pass without saying something. Limery's claws dig into my shoulder, and several people in the crowd laugh, but it's clear they're only mirroring the heroes' reactions.

"What's a smurf?" someone asks.

"Hey, blue balls! I'm talking to you."

I stop and look over to see Otis staring at us with a shit-eating grin. He's level twenty-nine now and has advanced his class to Berserker, but the other two both have their levels concealed. He wears a sleeveless black vest trimmed with white fur that cuts in a deep V over his hairy chest. The sorcerer mirrors his expression, wearing a long red cloak, absent the vials that he normally keeps strapped about his chest. The warlock watches us with a more intense gaze, his dreadlocks falling by his jawline and concealing some of the tattoos that cover his face. His only adornment is the purple amulet around his neck, hanging over a black robe with sleeves that cover more warlock tattoos.

Otis tucks his fingers in the V of his vest. "Ethan said if we waited long enough, you'd show your ugly face. You don't think you actually have a shot at this tournament, do you?" He smirks as he looks around the crowd for approval.

Some laugh, but more step away, putting plenty of space between us and the other heroes until there's an open line of sight between us.

"What's the matter, cat got your tongue?"

"Come on, Chod." Taryn grabs me by the arm, and I follow. "This clown isn't worth it."

"Yeah, that's right. Walk away, bitch."

I turn and roar. I can tell he wasn't expecting it because he flinches. Kevin jumps to his side, hand glowing with a toxic green aura. Ethan smirks, and several guests scream and more scatter up and down the stairs.

I smile, and it sets off a rage that burns behind the barbarian's eyes.

"When you tell your little stories, make sure you mention how you ambushed us and still managed to get yourselves killed. And don't forget the part where you squealed like a stuck pig."

Otis pulls an axe from his inventory and charges. He might be level twenty-nine, but he's still just a dumb brute. Fire crackles next to me as Limery summons a fireball.

"Enough!" Ethan's voice rings out, amplified by some dark power that reverberates within my chest.

Otis stops, letting his weapon fall to his side. It's no surprise who calls the shots in their crew.

"Now is not the time," Ethan says, his voice now normal. All amusement is gone from his face.

Limery puts away his fire, and I wink at Otis as we continue up the stairs.

Once we're far enough away, Taryn turns around, pointing a short stubby finger at me. "What the hell was that? What happened to playing it cool?" He's three stairs higher than me, so he pokes me in the chest. "New rule—we don't go anywhere near them for the rest of the night."

"Alright, alright. My bad." I force away my smile. "But you saw him jump, right?"

Taryn turns, but not before I can see the edge of his mouth curl up in a smile.

Breebis leans toward him. "Is there always this much drama among heroes?"

Taryn shakes his head. "Only when Chod's involved."

I roll my eyes. There's no way my reputation is that bad.

Several dozen guards wait at the top of the stairs, each one wearing gleaming armor with a rainbow of colors somehow infused within the metal. They stand sentry and don't so much as acknowledge us as we enter the palace.

In the lobby, the palace guides are here, but their burgundy robes are now a pale lilac. Lines form in front of each one. An orb hovers by their side, scanning people in a similar fashion to the qualifying line at the Department of Entertainment and Events.

"Guards!" one of the guides shouts at the far end before a gnomish couple are escorted down the steps.

The orb scans the three of us, and Taryn announces Breebis as his date, then we're allowed inside. Soon after, I receive a notification detailing the schedule of the night's events.

Welcome to the Challenger's Ball, a celebration of one of Pruxford's greatest traditions, the Champion's Tournament!

Schedule:
(To begin at dusk)

Social and Cocktail Hour
Opening Remarks
Dinner
Introduction of Regional Leaders
Introduction of Challengers
Dancing

"Well, that certainly saves a lot of paper." I close out the schedule and take in the ballroom.

Crystal chandeliers hang from the massive domed ceiling, which is painted with beautiful mosaic patterns. Bars are set up in at least eight different locations around the room serving vibrant cocktails, beer, and wine. There's a stage in the center, where minstrels play classical music as a distant backdrop to the chatter.

There have to be at least a few hundred people here. The majority of the attendees are gnomes, but I pick out an assortment of catfolk, merfolk, and humans. A giant of a woman towers above everyone, holding a mug of beer in each hand. She wears a tunic emblazoned with a silver teapot. I'm guessing she's from Ellynmylly.

Kazzandre Strongback
   Level 28
   Warrior
   Giant

Turns out she's a literal giant.

I nudge Taryn in the shoulder. "Looks like this is what we're up against."

His eyes widen when he sees her. "The bigger they are, the harder they fall, right?"

"That is a saying of small men so they can sleep at night." Deep laughter rings out as Arty steps beside us, his firm hand grabbing me on the shoulder. "She's a good fighter, strong as they come."

His brothers, Roddick and Reddick, stand behind him. All three wear a similar leather tunic with the sword and shield of the Adventurers' Guild embroidered over the heart.

"It's nice to see a friendly face." I shake his hand.

He grins, showing his daggers for teeth. "It seems you've already made your presence known."

Taryn scoffs. "I told you. We can't take him anywhere."

Arty notices Breebis for the first time. "By the gods, I didn't recognize you, Breebis. You clean up nice."

She laughs. "You don't do half bad yourself. We've come a long way from nicking apples off passing carts in the borough. Some things never change, though, I can still smell you before I see you."

"Hey now." Arty frowns. "You know I can't help that."

They both burst out laughing, and Arty kneels to accept her hug since she barely comes past the cyclops's knees.

Over the next hour, people continue to filter into the ballroom. I'm increasingly thankful for Arty as he points out some of the challengers. Some he knows personally, while others he's only heard of. The most curious is a gnomish monk with a class called Drunken Master. The gnome has a shaved head except for a single patch on his crown that grows a ponytail. He wears a tank top and harem pants, swaying as he walks, yet somehow never spills a drop of his drink. Being in the Adventurers' Guild, Arty's familiar with most of the action that happens in the region. He even introduces us to a few challengers.

In turn, we point out some of the other heroes. A group of them gather around Ethan and the others when they finally come inside. Jason Montoya and Lester Hobbes, the wizard and ranger I fought in the forest, cast menacing glances in our direction.

Michael Didato shows up in full-plate armor and has his own crowd of adoring fans gathered around him. Holy light follows him everywhere he goes, giving him his own personal spotlight. He seems in good spirits and even nods at me once. Maybe he's not so bad after all.

A few heroes either didn't show or are hidden among the crowd, but I do spot two new faces. Sam Taylor, another monk, walks barefoot among the elite, wearing simple green pants and a flowing shirt. Scotty Heyden, whose class is listed as sniper, stands beside the bar tossing back drinks left and right.

Before we've finished pointing out everyone, the music fades and the cocktail hour is over. We're ushered into the adjoining great hall, where the long tables have been replaced with a great number of smaller circular ones. Elegant crystal place settings sit on a silk tablecloth. A bouquet of glass flowers sparkles as the centerpiece, set in a vase where small brightly-colored fish dart within. A water mage walks from table to table, filling goblets with a wave of her hand.

At the far end of the hall, there's a raised platform with a long table that overlooks everything where the council will sit along with the leaders of the other kingdoms. Each challenger receives a notification with our table number among eight specially marked tables, each one seating five challengers and their guests. For the heroes who didn't bring guests, prominent citizens are offered the option to dine with the challengers.

Limery and I end up at a table with Randy Billson, Don Othello, and Drzz'rt, who, it turns out, is the golden lizardfolk that was in front of us at the D.E.E. He's the only one who brought a guest, another lizardfolk, so we're also sat with two wealthy catfolk from Antadale and two gnomes. I take a second to look over the other challengers' stats.

Randy Billson
> *Level 29*
> *Rogue*
> *Human*

The dark-haired rogue has gained a couple of levels since our last meeting in Lynchton. He still wears the boiled leather emblazoned with the silver wolf and his silver gauntlets, but the weapons he normally keeps strapped across his chest and legs must be stored in his inventory. All ten fingers glimmer with rings.

Don Othello
> *Level 30*
> *Void Mage*
> *Human*

The first thing I notice, aside from his new class, is the change in his eyes. The whites and pupils are gone and mesmerizing galaxies swirl within each eye. His robe is a fine purple, and a triangular amulet inset with a red and black eye hangs from his neck. His fingers are equally as adorned as his partner.

Drzz'rt
> *Level ???*
> *Assassin*
> *Lizardfolk*

An assassin? If I had to guess, that must be a class upgrade for rogue. If there's any truth to it, he'll be an especially dangerous opponent. He dresses similarly to our encounter in the D.E.E., wearing finely-embroidered clothing, a royal blue long coat that pops against his golden scales, and several amulets around his neck.

"We were—"

I start to make conversation, but one of the councilmembers clinks his glass and the great hall goes quiet.

For the first time, I notice the councilmembers together and can't help but smile. I'm not sure if this is their formal attire or what, but each one wears a long pointy hat similar to a garden gnome. Well, if that garden gnome was purchased at an upscale boutique in Manhattan. Each gnome has a hat in a different pastel color, as well as a complimentary robe. If someone took a picture, they'd make a killing around Easter. The gnomes make up for their simple clothing with a plethora of rings and necklaces.

The centermost councilmember stands. He wears a lavender hat with a lemon-colored robe. When he speaks, his voice carries across the room.

"Challengers and esteemed guests, for those who don't know me, I am Dezmin Dreamwader, Head of the Pruxford Council, and for tonight, your host for the Challenger's Ball. The Challenger's Ball is a tradition as enduring as the tournament itself, where the movers and shakers across Mythos gather to celebrate a test as old as time—combat. On the five-hundredth year since the tournament's inception, we have fielded one of the largest pools of challengers in nearly two hundred years. It has been longer than that since heroes have done battle in the Crystal Arena. We don't yet know the reason why the gods have blessed the Isle of Mythos with so many heroes, but in two days' time, we will all witness their power. But for now, we feast!"

Applause spreads across the room. I join in, but I can't help but notice the willful ignorance in his remarks. They don't know why we have spawned on the Isle of Mythos? I shake my head. Maybe it's because a dark wizard is coming. Did he ever think of that?

Food suddenly appears on the table, reminding me of Lord Kassidy. There must be another teleportation mage here somewhere.

The platters of food smell delicious. There are roasted meats, seasoned vegetables, bread, and some gelatinous things I'm not familiar with.

"What do you think of the city?" one of the catfolk asks us, her voice alluring. Her fur is gray and tinged with white. A hooped earring with a chain runs from her ear to her nose, and she wears a silky robe patterned with exotic flowers.

Limery answers with a mouth full of food. "Limmy likes it. Its is a very bigs city."

"The gnomes have a certain appreciation for their crystals," Don answers.

The two gnomes nod in agreement, and one responds. "It is said that the first gnome earth mage pulled crystals from the earth, forming a wall to protect his village. That wall now makes up the Crystal Arena."

"You don't say?" Randy stabs a piece of meat with his knife. "You learn some new shit every day."

Don casts him a sideways glance.

The second catfolk, a brilliant white with a large gray mustache, licks his paw and combs out a piece of food caught in his chin hair. "If you ever visit, you'll find Antadale much less of a spectacle. Our city is simple, elegant, refined."

The gnome's expression suddenly sours, and I cough to keep from laughing. While the two couples politely bicker with one another about which city has more to offer, I try to get to know the other challengers better, starting with the assassin.

"Are there many lizardfolk in Ellynmylly?" I attempt to break the ice before taking a sip of my gnomish wine. "I saw a few in Goldspire."

"You've been to Goldspire?" He hisses as he pronounces the S.

"Briefly. It's like a different world over there, that's for sure."

He nods. "It's said that all lizardfolk come from the same spawn, but it has been ages since we were one people. We scatter across the continents like leaves in the wind."

"Kind of like the trolls. Except now, there are three tribes gathered together."

"That is...most odd."

I want to break the news then and there, telling him about Valmar and everything we know, but I know it's too soon. If I can prove myself in the arena against so many challengers, they'll be more inclined to listen. One thing I know is that people respect power.

But the more challengers I see, it feels like our party has fallen behind. There are more level twenty-nines and thirties than I would have imagined.

"Hey, lizardman," Randy calls from across the table. "You mind switching seats with Don here, I'd love to talk to you about some rogue shit."

Drzz'rt whispers something to the other lizardfolk next to him, then nods.

Don sets his plate down next to me. "Randy might be crude, but he says what he means."

"I'll take earnest over pretentious any day." I shrug. "They invited a rogue to a ball, what'd they expect?"

He laughs. "Too true. It's a fitting class, that's for sure." He leans in a little closer, and I'm once again entranced by his eyes. "I heard about what happened after you left Lynchton. Damn shame, but I'm glad you made it out."

I find it hard to look away from the swirling galaxies. "How'd you find out?"

"After they respawned, Otis wouldn't shut up about how he was going to have his revenge. I've never seen Ethan so mad, I thought he was going to rip Otis's head off then and there. Practically all of us know. Well, maybe not Jude and Glenn. No one has seen them around in quite a while. What I don't get is why they attacked you? Seemed y'all were chatting it up the night before."

"You haven't heard about Valmar?"

He frowns. "That one of your troll buddies?"

While I fill in Don on the meeting at Seascape and King Orso's prediction, Randy and Drizz'rt talk shop. I'm not sure what they're going on about, but several times, one takes the other's hand and mimics a stabbing motion.

I debate whether or not to tell Don about what happened in Frostmoor with Jude and Glenn, but I elect to keep that part to myself. It sounds like news travels fast among heroes, and I don't want a super-villain team-up any time soon.

When I'm done, he sits back in his chair. "Damn, that's crazy. So, you think Ethan is in league with this Valmar guy?"

I nod.

"And you're wanting to do something about it?"

I nod again. "I'm not sure if he's in league with him directly, or his patron has something at play. Either way, he attacked us because he didn't want me uniting more heroes. So, I want to make sure that if we go to war, we're prepared."

He looks around the room before leaning in once again. "What's in it for us?"

His question takes me by surprise. "Saving the world not a good enough reason?"

"Some of you guys really embrace this, don't you?" He grins. "I'm all for fighting the good fight, but I worked too damn hard for these levels to throw them away on a lost cause. This place ain't no different than prison when you really look at it. People respect those with power. I've felt it myself. Anywhere I go, people look at me with respect—not for who I am, but for what I can do. I'm not a dirty player like some of these guys, but I'm not stupid either."

As much as I hate it, I can't argue with his logic. He sees this game for what it is. Maybe he hasn't had those special moments that make Mythos feel like more than a game. Even so, he's managed to play it well without being a giant asshole. If I can reason with him, I think he'll do the right thing.

"As heroes, we could be the presence that shifts the scales one way or the other. You've said it yourself, you're not a dirty player. When shit hits the fan, who do you want to have your back? Those that are fighting to keep their way of life, or those fighting to destroy it?"

"Look, I'll be real with you. This is the first time in years that I've had some actual freedom. Lord knows if I'll ever see it again once they pull us out for good." The galaxies within his eyes continue to swirl ever-so-slowly. "I'm as sentimental as the next guy, but not here. I like you, really, you've got bigger balls than most of these guys." He smirks. "If you want me to join you, then this is your chance to show everyone here why they can't afford to be on your bad side."

I force myself to look away, knowing that he's not talking about this dinner. He's right, though. In two days, for good or bad, they're all going to see what I'm made of.

Several people gasp as one of the gnomes at our table tosses his water in the catfolk's face. His fur drips with water, and his whiskers dip low. The cat blinks for a moment and then swipes, his claws extended. Inches before ripping off the gnome's face, a guard appears out of nowhere, lifting the catfolk in the air by the scruff of his neck.

"Both of you, out. Now." The guard grabs the gnome by the robe and drags them both toward the exit.

Each of their guests gathers their belongings, staring daggers at one another as they follow the guard. I'm guessing there's a bit of regional animosity between Pruxford and Antadale, which would explain why so few catfolk are here.

A glass chimes again, and Dezmin's voice carries over the crowd.

"And with that, here's another chance to remind you all that the no-combat policy goes for everyone, not just the challengers." A bit of laughter carries through the crowd. "Now that the main course is over—" Our plates suddenly vanish from the table, and Limery groans as his fork slams into the tablecloth. "—we'll begin the introduction of the challengers and their regional sponsors once dessert has been served."

Puddings and tarts appear on the table, and after Limery devours his, Drzz'rt passes several uneaten desserts from our departed tablemates to the imp.

"Thank yous, lizardmans!"

A shadow appears in front of me, and as I turn around, I realize it's my own. Michael the paladin stands behind me, beaming in all his holy glory.

He kneels between me and the void mage. "Don, if you don't mind, I would like a moment with the troll."

"By all means." Don moves back across the table, taking a seat next to Drzz'rt.

Michael moves into the empty seat. His hair gently waves, as if he's standing in front of a calm breeze. Whoever his patron god is, they really treat him right.

I cross my arms and lean back against my chair. "I'm guessing you're not planning to kill me in the middle of the ball."

"You're correct." He smiles, and I swear one of his teeth actually sparkles. "I carried that anger in me for a long time. You ambushed us, and though Jude might not be perfect, we had done nothing to wrong you that day. But as I have continued down my path and gained favor with my god, she has taught me forgiveness. In hindsight, I can see that had we happened upon you, the results would have been the same. It was you who braved the streets of Vanaria and brought peace between our people. For that, my god is thankful, and she has requested that I aid you going forward." He extends a glowing hand.

Alert! You have been offered Oath of Protection. Accept?

I'm speechless. I thought he might not be aiming for my head anymore, but I never would have expected this. Maybe this game can change people.

I shake his hand, and the oath activates. "I don't really know what to say, but thank you."

He winks as he lets go of my hand. "I will offer you my aid against the darkness, but shall we meet in the tournament, know that I will raze you to the ground with the cleansing light of Onera."

Wow, if he's this intense when he's trying to help me, I'm glad he's not still trying to kill me.

When I look over, Limery's face is covered in chocolate frosting, fruit filling, and crumbs.

He finally sits back in his chair, rubbing his bulging tummy. "Limmy is fulls."

I give him about two minutes before he passes out.

Soon after, crystal chimes again and Dezmin's voice carries across the great hall.

"And now, the moment you've all been waiting for. Everyone here tonight will get an exclusive first look at this year's challengers. We will begin with Mistville, represented by the Mistville Court."

Three merfolk at the raised table stand. Shimmering scales coat their bodies in shades of blue and green. Gills run along their necks and short tropical-colored fins streak along their heads and forearms. Their clothing is very simple, each one wearing only a sash that runs over one shoulder and wraps around their waists.

Among the crowd, two merfolk stand.

"And their challengers, Oruma Zenen and Tozzet Girok."

I analyze their stats.

Tozzet Girok
  Level ???
  Tidal Mage
  Merfolk

The tidal mage has deep-purple scales and bright-yellow fins. His chest and back are broad, like an Olympic swimmer, and he doesn't break eye contact with the merfolk standing at the council table. I'm guessing he's a pretty powerful water mage to be competing here.

Oruma Zenen
  Level ???
  Mesmer
  Merfolk

She's much slimmer than the mage, with turquoise scales and vibrant orange fins. A white sash covers her chest, and she also seems fixated on the other merfolk.

Next, they announce the representatives and the three challengers from Antadale. A fighter, a paladin, and most interesting of the three—a blood mage.

Lanxkuri
  Level 32
  Blood Mage
  Catfolk

Her fur is midnight black, but not nearly as void-like as Festa Forgetooth's, the Emperor of Goldspire. She stands tall, her golden eyes radiating with pride as her tail swishes behind her. She wears a black kimono patterned with blood-red flower petals. I know the catfolk are renowned for their healers, but I'm not sure if a blood mage powers their attacks with their own blood or uses the blood from their opponents. At level thirty-two, either one is a frightening proposition.

When the triumvirate of Ellynmylly is announced, there's actually applause from various tables. A halfling, a human, and a horned lizardfolk all wave from the council table. Both Drzz'rt and the giant stand when the challengers are introduced, along with two humans and two halflings, one of which has a super interesting class.

Erbin Longfoot
Level 29
Puppet Master
Halfling

No idea what that could be. Maybe some type of summoner?

Next up is Pruxford with thirteen challengers. Including Arty, Roddick, Reddick, and ten gnomes. The three adventurers and the drunken master monk make up the melee damage of the group. Of the rest, there are five mages, two tinkerers, a druid, and a cleric.

The gnomes in the crowd all stand, but I notice those from other regions do not.

Dezmin speaks again, this time announcing those of us from the Isle of Mythos.

"It is unfortunate that the leaders of Seascape and Vanaria were not able to make it this year in spite of having so many challengers, but we all look forward to seeing what their heroes are truly made of."

"And Limmy!" the imp shouts, still sprawled out in his chair.

There's some laughter, but Dezmin doesn't acknowledge Limery's outburst. One by one, we are introduced. When it's Taryn's turn, Breebis claps loudly, her face filled with pride. Limery raises a hand when his name is called, but he doesn't move from his slouched position in the chair. Three of the heroes aren't present—Troy Malloy, Tommy Sullivan, and Bridger Phillips.

We all take a seat again, and Dezmin delivers his final remarks.

"And there you have it, the challengers of the Quincentennial Champion's Tournament. Stop by the sporting district tomorrow to place your bets. It's sure to be a thrilling event this year, with some surprises no one will be expecting. The grand ballroom is now open. Enjoy the evening, and thank you all for attending the Challenger's Ball."

Chatter erupts as soon as he finishes, and our plates magically vanish. People begin moving toward the ballroom, but Limery has finally drifted off to sleep. I pick him up, cradling him in my arm as I go to find Taryn.

He's chatting with Breebis, a hand resting on her knee. I guess the liquid courage has put his nervousness at bay. They both smile and laugh.

I'm happy for him.

He stands up when he sees me. "Dude, some of these guys have crazy classes. I think we should hit the library tomorrow and see what we can find out."

"That's actually not a bad idea. You two gonna do some dancing?"

Taryn grins, turning to Breebis and extending his hand. "What do you think? You know us ebony dwarves have rhythm, right?"

She blushes but takes his hand. "I guess we're about to find out." She turns to me. "Are you coming as well?"

I shake my head. "As much as I would like to grace you with my moves, I think I'm going to call it a night. This one overdid it again." I gesture toward the sleeping imp in my arm. "You two have fun. We can talk strategy tomorrow."

Taryn pats me on the side and then heads to the ballroom with Breebis's arm interlocked with his. Limery snores gently, and I head for the exit. There's no telling what awaits us in the tournament, but it's never too early to start preparing.

33. THE CALM BEFORE THE STORM

Unlike Limery, whose snores could rival a freight train, I have a hard time finding peace once we're back at the inn.

Just a few days ago, hitting level twenty-seven felt like such an accomplishment. After the Challenger's Ball, though, I feel further behind than ever. The catfolk blood mage was a whole five levels ahead of us, and there's no telling if any of the challengers with concealed levels are even higher.

While we were spending days traveling through Goldspire, Frostmoor, and Wandermere, the rest of the heroes were killing monsters and exploring dungeons. With how long it takes to gain a level now, it feels almost impossible to catch up.

I try to tell myself that what we gained is far more valuable than levels, but Don was right about one thing: everyone respects power.

Eventually, I fall asleep, and far too soon it's morning. Only a day before it all comes to a head.

Downstairs, Arty and his brothers are already halfway through their breakfast.

He motions for us to join them. "You left the ball early last night."

"Yeah, Limery is a glutton with no self-control." I pull up a seat across from him. "Did we miss anything exciting?"

He shakes his head. "Not really. Though, Roddick caught the fancy of a halfling that wouldn't take no for an answer. He dances about as well as a fish on dry land."

I chuckle, watching Roddick's embarrassment. "Sad I had to miss that."

Roddick's ears flush a bright red, and he seems suddenly fixated on his plate. He doesn't look up until the barmaid comes over to take my order.

After Limery and I order, I rejoin the conversation. "So, what are you all up to on the final day before the tournament?"

Arty finishes the last bite of his food and lets his fork rattle against the plate.

"We're gonna hit up one of the dungeons. No better way to work out stress than stabbing things that want to kill you. How about you?"

"Taryn and I are planning to get in some research. Try to figure out what some of those classes are. You have any idea what a mesmer is?"

"Can't say I do." He frowns. "It's a shame they don't announce the brackets ahead of time. We'll take it as it comes."

The barmaid brings out our food while Reddick is still finishing up the last of his, so we've got a few minutes to talk before they head out.

"There's something that's been bugging me." I stab a piece of sausage and wave it around as I talk. "You said your parents live in Pruxford, but why are you always at the inn instead of with them or the guild?"

Arty lets out a loud laugh and exchanges knowing looks with his brothers. "Well, let's just say that at home, Mom runs the roost, so to speak. There's a little more peace and quiet, and a little more freedom, at The Puzzled Peacock."

Reddick nods in agreement. "You caught us at a strange time. We're actually on the road quite often with quests for the guild. We like a good drink or two when we visit home, and the ale doesn't flow quite as freely at our dear old mom's."

"Ain't that the truth," echoes Arty.

"Why not the guildhall then?"

Roddick pushes his plate forward. "If I have to listen to another fresh-faced recruit talking about what he's going to do, or an old-timer bragging about what he's done, I'll put a sword in my ear."

"Hear, hear!" Arty taps his fist on the table. "And it's always the same damn stories. At least we have new tales every time we return. Active adventurers stop by the guild, but we don't shit where we eat."

Light spills in from the doorway, and I turn around to see Taryn trying to sneak toward the stairs. He's still wearing his formal robes from the night before.

"Busted." He grins.

"Mornings, Taryns." Limery looks over from his plate of food, oblivious to the situation.

"I think the dwarf might have had more fun than all of us last night." Arty waggles his brow and then stands. "Save us the tale for another time. For now, the dungeon awaits. We'll see you all tomorrow."

Taryn takes a seat next to me as the others leave. "Dungeon?"

"Just some mobs." I raise my eyebrows. "So?"

He smiles mischievously. "What?"

"You clearly didn't come back last night. I need details."

"It's nothing like that." His cheeks go red. "For real. We were one of the last ones to leave the ball, but we were having such a good time, we didn't want it to end. We went back to the stable and were using Berry as a pillow to look up at the stars. I guess we fell asleep."

I shake my head. "Sounds like the plot of a YA novel."

"I'm sorry." He rolls his eyes. "Are you sad I didn't tuck you in?"

Taryn orders some food, and we sit around chatting while I wait for him to finish. Limery plays with Flubs as the catlike slime explores the room.

"So, I'm guessing you like her?" I ask.

Taryn narrows his eyes. "We doing this again?"

"I'm serious." I throw my hands up. "No judgment."

"I don't know. I mean, yes, but—" He pauses. "—it's weird, isn't it?"

I shrug. "Everything about this is weird." I hold out my arm. "This feels like my body. And when we 'go back,' that feels like my body, too. So, maybe it's only weird if you make it weird."

He laughs. "Bro, if anybody ever found out..."

"This is a top-secret government program. We all signed NDAs. I think you're fine."

"Maybe. But it's not like we're gonna be in Pruxford for long after the tournament. Still, it was nice to spend time together."

After breakfast, Taryn changes out of his formalwear, and we head to the library. It's a beautiful, cylindrical glass building that rises several stories. From the street, I can see shelves within filled with books and scrolls. If there's anywhere we can find out about some of these classes, it has to be here.

I pull the door handle, but it doesn't budge. I try again with more force, but there's no give, so I press my hands to the glass and peek inside.

"What's going on?" asks Taryn.

"Door's locked, and nobody's inside."

Limery floats down from my shoulder and places his feet against the door as he tugs.

"Library's closed today." An older gnome sits on the curb smoking a long pipe. "All government buildings are. For the tournament."

"You've got to be kidding me."

"Don't worry, I got this." Taryn crouches in front of the door and pulls out the Nimble Key. A moment later, he yelps and drops the key as a spark shoots out from the door. "Fuck." He shakes out his hand. "The door has a protection enchantment."

I lean against the wall. "Looks like we aren't getting any research done today. Might as well head to the stables and get in some training with Caustic."

"And Taryns can kiss his girlfriends." Limery returns to my shoulder, cackling.

"Hey! She's not my girlfriend. And besides, where did you hear that?"

Limery zooms overheard, laughing maniacally while repeating the same phrase. "Taryns has a girlfriends. Taryns has a girlfriends."

Taryn scowls at me, but I just laugh.

"Wasn't me," I say, grinning.

Taryn insists we practice outside of the city so that we can train without the risk of setting the borough on fire. I think it's actually to put as much distance between Limery's teasing and Breebis as possible.

Once we're out there, we take turns working on individual drills since Limery, Taryn, and I will each be on our own during the tournament.

We've gotten so used to working as a team that it feels like there are glaring holes in each of our styles when we're solo. Caustic and I lack any real burst magical damage. His poisonous gas is more lingering at his current level, and it's unlikely I'll have enough time to summon the number of horrors necessary to make Kamikaze effective. But with all my recent advancements, I'm a one-troll smash force.

Without me, both Taryn and Limery are severely lacking in crowd control abilities. The tournament will come down to the matchups we draw. Hopefully, they're random, and not designed to expose our weaknesses.

We spend hours correcting formations and picking apart tactics that we'll only ever use in this tournament. There are no breakthroughs, but by the end of the day, I've come up with some useful ways of deploying my horrors alongside Caustic, even having him drop them from the sky like bombs, and Taryn utilizes the full synergy of his pets and druid abilities.

We're stronger as a team, but hopefully, we don't get steamrolled.

After dropping the pets back off at the stables, Taryn decides to linger for a bit while Limery and I head back to the inn.

Not wanting to play over a hundred scenarios in my head that are likely to never happen, I take a small amount of sleep dust and am gone before my head even hits the pillow.

34. CHANGE OF PLANS

On the morning of the tournament, we receive special instructions detailing where the challengers should enter the arena. We eat breakfast alongside Arty and his brothers in near silence. For once, the brothers don't bicker or joke. Each one seems locked inside their own head, no different from us. I guess no matter our background, an event like this hits us all the same way.

I used to get the same way before an important stream. When I was goofing around for attention, it was more about the entertainment than my skill. When I was actually trying, that's when I would get inside my own head. That's when I'd snap if things went wrong. That's what got me here.

Arty and his brothers head to the arena after breakfast, but we stop by the stables for our pets. Caustic nuzzles me, nearly knocking me over, and Limery perches on the dragon's antler-like horns.

Breebis decides to accompany us to the arena early so she can get one of the better seats. She and Taryn talk as we walk, but I tune them out. My hands are jittery with nervous excitement. I have no idea what to expect, but this will be our chance to show everyone—heroes, challengers, and all of Pruxford—just what we're made of.

Even though we arrive several hours early, the streets are full and there's already a crowd gathering outside the arena. They gawk at Caustic, whose increased size is a lot harder to play off as some elaborate costume. Guards stand sentry at the gate, alongside a pair of palace guides. One of the guides holds a clipboard, and the other operates the scanning orb that hovers between the two. The orb scans a catfolk in a hooded blue robe, and then the guards allow her through the gate.

When it's our turn, Taryn hugs Breebis good-bye. The orb scans him and his pets in turn. As soon as he's through, Limery is right behind him.

I step forward, and the orb scans me and then Caustic. One of the gnomes raises his left hand, and the guards cross their spears, barring my entry.

The gnome adjusts her half-moon spectacles. "Unfortunately, sir, the dragon may not compete with you today."

"What do you mean he can't compete?" I frown. "He's my pet."

She purses her lips, and I get the feeling she wants to roll her eyes at me. "I do apologize, but the two of you are not properly bonded. Per tournament rules, only bonded pets and companions may compete alongside a challenger."

"What the fuck?" My chest tightens, and I clench my fist to keep from losing my temper. "Is there someone I can talk to? I just hatched him a few weeks ago. There has to be some kind of exception."

The gnome presses her fingertips together. "Unfortunately, sir, these rules have been in place for hundreds of years. You are not the first, nor will you be the last, to have an unbonded pet prohibited from the tournament."

Deep breaths. Now is not the time to lose my cool. I know this is nothing personal, but not having Caustic is going to be another blow against us.

I turn to Breebis. "They aren't letting me take him in because we haven't bonded yet. Would you mind taking him back to the stable for me?"

She takes the leash. "I can, but if you don't mind, I'd like to let him watch. It might be good for him to see you in action."

"Thanks, I appreciate it." I turn to Caustic, cupping his bearded jaw in my hand. "Sorry, boy. I wish you could come, but you're going to have to sit this one out."

Caustic huffs and a small puff of green smoke escapes his nostrils.

"Oh, calm down. It's not his fault you haven't bonded," Breebis reprimands Caustic before shouting behind me as I step through the gate. "Good luck!"

I throw up a peace sign and find Taryn and Limery waiting for me on the other side.

"What took you so long? And where's Caustic?" Taryn looks around me as if he's expecting the dragon to step through the gate any moment.

I shake my head in disappointment. "We haven't officially bonded yet, so they aren't letting him compete."

"Dude, that's wack." Taryn frowns.

"Yeah, dudes, that's wacks," Limery echoes, crossing his arms.

I sigh. "I mean, I get it. It keeps things fair, but it does suck to have wasted all that training time on things I can't even use."

"Hey." Taryn guides Berry closer to me. "It might not be something you use in this tournament, but it's far from wasted. Now, let's go see what's in store."

As we make our way through the arena, it appears that most of the palace guides are now stationed here. They stand everywhere we go, like guides at an amusement park, directing us to the Challenger's Pit located underneath the arena.

When we finally find the pit, it's like a cross between an underground bunker and a jewel mine. There are dozens of rooms carved within the stone tunnels. The walls are speckled with gemstones polished to a smooth finish. The gems within the walls produce their own light, casting each room in a different glow.

More than half of the challengers are already waiting throughout the tunnels. Some gather in the alcoves, while others stand or sit by themselves. They're all dressed in battle attire, but most of them have their weapons hidden—probably to keep the rest of us guessing as much as possible.

A gnome druid sits in a corner by himself, his mossy green skin almost identical to Breebis's. He wears a blue jewel-toned cloak, and a red falcon perches on one shoulder. Two wolves, one silver and one black, stand protectively in front of him.

In another area, a tinkerer fiddles with a contraption that scurries around on metal legs like some kind of steampunk spider.

Don's unsettling void-like eyes settle on me as we pass. He nods to me while Randy cleans his fingernails with a dagger.

Over a dozen guards are positioned along the corridors in addition to several more gnome guides. Though the guards' faces are concealed behind the shimmering helms, the size difference helps to identify those that are gnomes from the other races.

A gnome in a bright-yellow robe stands in the middle of the pit, waving her arms as she gives orders and directs people. "Welcome!" She locks eyes on us as soon as we enter, speaking a mile a minute. "Tatina Tinkerton at your service, Head of the Department of Events and Entertainment, and chair of the Challenger's Tournament. Most unfortunate news about your dragon, but rules are rules, and as cruel as it may seem, you are no exception to centuries of precedent. Please find a place to wait and one of our guides will be around to begin your preparations. Do try to savor the moment, for this will be a day unlike any other!"

As quickly as she came, she disappears, greeting one of the halflings from Ellynmylly as they waddle down the ramp.

"She seems excited." Taryn grins.

I laugh. "Who knows what kind of special dust the Pruxford fairies are cooking up."

Arty waves to us from an alcove at the far back. We pass the two merfolk and a group of three gnomes on the way to join him and his brothers. Before we have a chance to talk, a guide comes over pushing a cart filled with glowing potions. A guard stands on each side of him. The potions are white, with a yellow halo that extends beyond the glass. The bottles are nestled neatly in a container lined with felt, indented to the exact size and shape of each bottle. The guide hands out the potions one at a time, first to me, then Limery. He gives five to Taryn—one for him and each of his pets.

Legendary Item. Revive Potion. One of the most difficult and time-consuming potions to create, only one Revive Potion may be brewed by a grandmaster-level enchanter at a single time, and each potion takes one year to create. A revive potion grants one victory over death, portaling the user to a preset location with 1HP upon receiving fatal damage while simultaneously activating a full-heal and returning the body to its natural condition. A corporeal doppelgänger remains behind at the death site.

. . .

The gnome snaps his fingers, drawing my attention back to the present. "As I was saying, we are doing things a little different this year. Instead of the customary protection spell, each of the challengers and accompanying pets or familiars are given a Revive Potion for the tournament. So instead of fights stopping when the protective shield is broken, each fight will be to the death in order for each challenger to display the full-range of their abilities." He gestures toward the potions. "Each Revive Potion takes a year to brew under the strict supervision of our grandmaster enchanters. We have been preparing for the quincentennial tournament for many years now. Since this is a single-elimination tournament, the winner of the tournament will carry the effects of the Revive Potion as part of their prize. Drink your potion, and once we return to the arena, you will be given instructions on where to set your revive portal. You will also be able to set the portal of your pets or familiars at that time." He looks at us impatiently. "Go on, drink up."

I press the bottle to my lips, swallowing the syrupy, tart liquid. A warm buzz fills my stomach and a moment later, I receive a notification.

*Alert! You have ingested **Revive Potion**. Upon receiving fatal damage, your body will be transported to your revive location where you will be rebuilt anew. If you do not have a revive location selected, the potion will not activate. Would you like to set your revive location now?*

I close out the notification for now. Limery puckers his lips as he drinks his potion, and Taryn forces each of his pets to drink theirs. Jordy is so obsessed with his that his tongue writhes around inside the bottle as he tries to get more. When Flubs ingests the potion into his gelatinous body, a glob of yellow liquid sits in his core for a second before abruptly vanishing.

Once we've all drunk our potions, the gnome takes our empty bottles and pushes his cart along.

After drinking the potions, I can't help but think about Swift's brother Draydon. He died in a tournament just like this when his protection shield didn't activate. If he'd been given a revive potion instead of a protection shield, maybe he wouldn't have died.

I also can't shake the feeling that these potions would be better saved for the battlefield. The potions for Taryn alone have taken five years to brew. I've seen the kind of power King Orso and King Favian possess. Would it not be worth it to have those with that much power charge into battle again and again to inflict as much damage as possible? Or is there a limit to how far the portal can transport someone after dying? Years of work is about to be used up for a single day's entertainment. It doesn't feel right.

"So, where's the big scary dragon?" asks Arty.

"You're not going to believe this." I fill him in on everything that happened.

"Tough break. I guess your luck ran out in the dungeon." He grins. "Though I think it evens the playing field a bit."

I laugh. "You're worried about me when there are challengers five levels higher than me competing?"

He squints his single eye, not amused. "You'll find out soon enough that levels aren't everything."

More challengers continue to filter in, and the air is noticeably more tense compared to the ball. Even Otis keeps his big mouth shut as he walks by with Ethan and Kevin. The warlock has his dreadlocks pulled up in a bun and wears a sleeveless robe that reveals his many tattoos. The sorcerer wears a billowing cape over his robe, but I can see the straps across his chest loaded with an assortment of potions.

There are no groups bigger than three people, aside from ours, and most talk in hushed whispers. Once everyone has arrived, Tatina snaps her fingers, and her voice carries through the pit.

"Greetings, challengers. In just a moment, you'll be given the official seeding for the first round of the tournament. Please note that the seeding is final. But first, we will go over a couple of announcements. First, shield mages have been stationed around the arena. Shield mages are some of the most specialized mages across Mythos, and those in Pruxford have been honing their skills across the ages. After the opening ceremony, protective barriers will be erected to keep any potential projectiles or spells from hitting the crowd. You'll notice once the matches start that these barriers can also eliminate outside noise during the matches. There will be a special seating area for challengers still in the tournament and a secondary area to set your spawn point for those who are eliminated. Both areas will have protective barriers in place. Second, every challenger, pet, and familiar has consumed a Revive Potion for this year's tournament, therefore, you are encouraged to display your full potential on the battlefield. There is no need to fear for the well-being of your fellow challengers today. Give the crowd what they came for. As a final note, no legendary potions are allowed in today's tournament. Now, please stand by for the official seeding."

No legendary potions means I can't use my Angel of Death Brandy—not that I would want to waste it here. I wonder what other legendary potions might be out there.

A couple of minutes later, we receive a notification, and there's immediate grumbling. Cursing and complaints fill the challenger's pit. Instead of being separated into brackets, we're all divided into one of four groups. A quick scan shows Limery, Taryn, and I are all in separate groups. Before I even have time to process the names in each group, Tatina's voice carries above even the loudest voices.

"Hear, hear! As always, some of you are unhappy with your grouping. Well, let me tell you, you are not the first nor the last to be unhappy with your position in the tournament. Competing in the Champion's Tournament is an honor. Were this a normal tournament sent with only twelve or so challengers, most of you would not even be here. But with a field of forty, there's more opportunity than ever for a dark horse to rise through the tournament. Were it not a difficult task, then the Champion's Tournament would not be known across Mythos as one of the preeminent tests of combat skill. Nothing about this tournament is designed to be easy. Now, as you can see, you have all been separated into four groups. Further instructions will be provided shortly, but know for now that two challengers from each group will advance to the quarterfinals. After that point, it will be a single elimination bracket until a champion is crowned."

I try to piece together what I can from the limited information. Four groups, ten challengers each, only two advance. Will there be a point system for those who advance, or will the remaining brackets be randomized? More importantly, is there any method to the seeding of each group?

In only a few minutes, we'll be going aboveground for the opening ceremonies. While others bitch and moan, I take a moment to look over the groups, starting with my own. Luckily, Arty is also in group one, so we can watch each other's back. Otis is in our group as well, so I'm certain he'll be gunning for me after our run-in at the ball. The two I'm most worried about are Lanxkuri, the catfolk blood mage, and Erbin Longfoot, the halfling puppet master. We're also up against Scotty Heyden the sniper, a catfolk paladin, and three gnomes.

Group two feels like the group of death. Limery and Roddick are up against Ethan, Don the void mage, Michael the paladin, Oruma the mesmer merfolk, and Tozzet the tidal mage merfolk, Tommy Sullivan, who was one of the heroes that didn't show at the ball, a catfolk fighter, and a gnome mage.

Limery doesn't look the least bit intimidated as he high-fives Roddick, but there is a clear sense of concern on Arty's brother's face.

Reddick is in group three. Facing Drizz'rt and Kevin the sorcerer will be tough, but I'm not so sure about the rest. I haven't seen Jason and Lester since our first fight in the forest, but being in the same group means they can watch each other's backs. There's also Bridger, another hero I haven't met, and both a halfling and human from Ellynmylly, and two gnomes.

Taryn's group also looks pretty tough. There's the giant from Ellynmylly, Randy the rogue, both monks, in addition to three other gnomes, a human, and Troy Malloy, another hero who didn't show at the ball.

Gongs and cannons echo from above as the arena comes to life. In only a matter of minutes, we'll be introduced to Pruxford. I stand there frozen, eyes shifting between Taryn, who strokes Ruby's neck, and Limery. I wonder who I should talk strategy with first. Taryn has his pets, which is enough to give him an advantage over many of the challengers. But Limery, how is he supposed to compete against the likes of Ethan and Don, let alone a tidal mage who can likely douse any fire he summons?

Fuck. This is too much to process right now. Everything is happening so fast, and I'm not sure how I can worry about everyone's matchups, much less my own. It's easy when we're together, but how can I help them like this?

A firm hand grips my shoulder. "I can see the worry in your eyes. You fear for your friends." Arty moves in front of me, his massive eye staring into my own. "They are both strong. You must learn to let go and trust in their abilities. This is meant to be chaos. Every year, the matchups aren't announced until minutes before the tournament. No one is given time to prepare."

I take a deep breath and attempt to fight off the panic attack looming over my shoulders. I close my eyes and find my center. We can do this. It's just like with Caustic back in the dungeon. He surprised me. I'm sure Taryn and Limery will do the same. We've all gone through too much for me to worry if they are strong enough.

I walk over and wrap my arm around Taryn. "This is going to be a shitshow. Good luck."

"Just another day in paradise." He embraces me and squeezes. "Besides, this is the one time we can push our limits without the fear of losing a level. One way or another, I'm going to know what I'm capable of by the time this is over."

Limery flies over to my shoulder, grinning. "Limmy and Roddicks is togethers. We's goings to make a teams." He balls his small hands into fists. "Limmy is ready to fights!"

"Showtime, challengers! Group one, you're first out." Tatina's voice calls from every direction. "Line up. Group two, you're up next."

I fall in line behind Arty, and the guide leads us out of the pit and up a ramp that empties into the arena through a beautiful crystal archway.

"Watch your back, troll," Otis says from behind me, but all thoughts of him vanish as we step into the arena.

The design of this arena is on the opposite end of the spectrum from the one in Goldspire. We exit the archway onto a plain of crystal so smooth that it looks like a frozen lake. The stadium surrounding us is massive, with two levels of stands that wrap in a circle beneath the giant pillars of crystal. Thousands of fans fill the stadium, and their cheers roar like the tide.

This must be what it feels like to be a professional athlete in front of the home crowd. My skin tingles at the energy, and for a moment, I don't think about the stakes of the tournament. I simply appreciate being here.

The gnomish council sits in an illustrious booth on the lowest level, midway across the arena alongside the other heads of state. Guards stand at the edges of the booth, and it is already protected by a transparent barrier. It's almost imperceptible aside from the occasional flare of energy that ripples through the shield.

The booth next to theirs is empty. There's also a booth on the ground floor of the arena. I'm assuming one is for defeated challengers and one is for those still competing.

The announcer's voice carries as he introduces us one by one as we parade across the arena floor. We're escorted to an area near the center, where a large circle is etched into the crystal floor. Once we all step inside, the ground shakes briefly and we ascend on a cylindrical platform of raised crystal until we are twenty to thirty feet off the ground.

Once the platform stops moving, group two enters. This time, I'm able to watch as an earth mage raises their platform from the arena floor. Limery waves to me from his perch on Roddick's shoulder.

Groups three and four are announced in turn, and the crowd continues to applaud.

"There you have it—the field of the Quincentennial Champion's Tournament! Without further ado, transform the arena!"

The two earth mages stationed in the arena get to work. The arena shakes, and the crystal floor shatters into millions of pieces. It sounds like rain as crystal continues to disintegrate until the four pillars stand like tall islands among a sea of ice-blue sand.

Then, a silvery glow forms around the edge of the arena as eight silver bubbles begin to rise from the floor. The silvery shields continue to grow, and they connect like bubbles as they touch one another. As they morph into one another and grow bigger, the shields become more transparent until the last two barriers merge, creating a massive dome that arches over the arena like a snow globe. Four smaller barriers form around the tops of each pillar.

I'm trying to understand the need for the additional barriers over the platforms when something shifts in the sand beneath us. Out of the corner of my eye, I spot more movement across the arena floor as sand continues to shift.

The crowd's gasp is audible as a massive serpentine body launches from the sand, arcing over the shielded platform of group three. The silvery-gray creature has slick scales, miniature red eyes, and a massive cyclone of teeth beneath its hooked snout.

Sand Wyrm. *Level 40. These legless, wingless dragons burrow beneath the sands of sprawling deserts. Their slick scales allow them to travel through the sand unimpeded without the need for the toxic slime other wyrms require. With magic-resistant scales, serrated teeth, and powerful elemental magic, wyrms are some of the most dangerous creatures in all of Mythos.*

The mana-infused wyrm I fought in the forest is nothing compared to the size of this one. At level forty, I wouldn't be surprised if it could eat us in one bite.

"All right, folks, what do you think of our special guests?" The crowd erupts as a second sand wyrms reveals itself. *"The first round of the tournament will be a combination of a battle royale and king of the hill format. The final two challengers left standing in each group will advance to the second round. In this mode, there's nowhere to hide. You either fight on the pillar or take your chances with the wyrms down below. A word of advice to our challengers—the wyrms always win. Fight for your place in the next round. If you fall out of the platform's protective zone, you're wyrm food."*

The three other pillars shift their positioning as the earth mages move them around the arena, lowering and then sliding them through the sand until they surround the group one pillar in a triangle formation.

"Challengers, set your spawn points to the booth beneath the council and ready yourselves. The match will begin in thirty seconds."

After setting my spawn point, I immediately summon three horrors, making sure I summon Horror of Power last for the bonus damage on my next attack. Then I equip Destroyer. This is a bash-as-many-people-as-I-can situation, so I'll save the Regeneration Triad for when I know I can use it. Beside me, Arty equips his armor, helm, and insanely-large sword.

I lock eyes with the cyclops. "Watch each other's backs and try to take the center if we can."

Everyone on the pillar has put space between themselves and the others. A shirtless Otis wields a large double-edged axe with glowing runes. There's something different about his appearance that I struggle to name.

It takes me a few seconds, but once I spot the change, I can't unsee it. His neck is way thicker than it used to be, and a patch of bristly hair runs from the back of his head to his back like a wild boar. It was probably concealed beneath the heavy fur of his vest at the ball. I'm guessing he's unlocked a Spirit of the Beast or Totem Warrior path.

Next to Otis, Lanxkuri—the black catfolk blood mage—licks her paws. In lieu of her kimono, she wears a simple red robe that stops at her knees. Her tail flicks back and forth behind her. Next to the blood mage, a catfolk paladin with golden fur wears thick armor and holds a comically-large white warhammer over his shoulder. His fur shimmers with the same radiant energy as Michael.

Erbin Longfoot, the puppet master, watches my horrors like they are a delicious meal. Only the three gnomes still stand huddled together. I recognize one as the druid from before with the falcon perched on his shoulder. The two wolves stand in front of the group, teeth bared. There's also a cleric with a long gray beard. He wears a white robe with a golden symbol over his chest and holds a mace in his jewel-covered hands. At the back, a tinkerer kneels over several contraptions that I can't quite make out from where we stand.

To my other side, Scotty Heyden holds a slender bow that's nearly as tall as he is. An arrow with a spiraled tip is nocked and ready as he crouches to one knee.

"The archer is my first target," I whisper to Arty. "After him, I'm pushing the center."

Arty nods, and the crowd joins the announcer as he counts down.

"Five."

"Four."

"Three."

"Two."

"One."

35. MAKE THE CUT

I activate Berserker Rage as soon as the timer hits zero. The shield around our platform fades, and the cheers of the crowd abruptly cut off as the dampening effect of the outer barrier keeps the noise at bay.

Otis roars from across the platform as he activates his rage as well. My blood boils as increased stats flood through me, and thanks to my Spirit of the Beast path, it will last twice as long.

Next to me, Scotty draws the arrow back even further, and orange energy spirals around the arrow shaft. A hidden piece of the bow unfolds, revealing a glass contraption, almost like a sight. As he holds the arrow steady, the charge grows stronger, and the shaft elongates until it's almost the size of a spear.

This looks like a badass attack, but I'm not going to get skewered waiting around to see if he's aiming for me or someone else. Instead, I activate Concussive Force and swing for the fences with the increased damage buff from Horror of Power.

Scotty releases the arrow just as my hammer connects with his side. His neck and legs curl around the force of my attack, and he rockets off the side of the platform. It'd be comical if not for the searing pain around my midsection as the giant arrow flies past like it was launched from a cannon. Its dense energy peels skin and flesh from my ribs.

A sand wyrm arcs through the air beside the platform, devouring Scotty before he even hits the ground.

I touch my tender ribs, but thanks to my increased regeneration, the wound is already mending.

There's a scream behind me, and I turn just in time to witness the gnome cleric sliding off the end of Arty's sword into the arena below.

Two down, six to go.

The presence of my horrors suddenly goes dull. They aren't dead, but they're no longer responding to my commands. I find them stationed in front of the puppet master like guardians, along with the druid's silver wolf. When I try to regain control of my horrors, it's like the connection has been severed. So, I summon three more and keep them by my side.

Erbin's grin as he stares at the other gnomes makes my skin crawl.

Nearby, Otis battles with the catfolk paladin in the center of the platform. His axe moves with incredible speed and force, sparks flying as the paladin manages to deflect every blow.

Meanwhile, Arty's arms glow red as he slices at projectiles being shot from the tinkerer's contraption. Each of the mechanical orbs explodes upon impact, sending gears and springs bouncing across the platform.

With the cleric gone, the tinkerer and druid stand back-to-back. The tinkerer shouts for the druid to send out his remaining wolf against Arty, but the druid refuses. His eyes burn with hatred toward Erbin. The druid lifts his golden staff, and a gust of wind pushes the puppet master toward the edge of the platform.

Lanxkuri uses the distraction to attack, grunting as she activates her blood magic. Her eyes go red, and a stream of dark energy shoots from her palm, bringing the druid to his knees. The puppet master escapes the gust of wind just before blowing off the platform and sends his puppets at the downed druid.

"Not so fast." I cast Sacrifice on the three stolen horrors, and even though they aren't under my control, they vanish into the ether, giving me a point in Dexterity, Strength, and Constitution.

The silver puppet-wolf crashes into its black counterpart, and they go for one another. The falcon dives at the possessed wolf's eyes, meanwhile the druid slowly comes back to his senses.

I keep my eye on Lanxkuri as I wait for my moment to attack. She and I are the only ones not currently engaged in active combat.

Otis decapitates the paladin, and the head rolls off the edge of the platform as the body collapses. The barbarian hovers over the body, skin steaming as he beats his hairy chest with a fist.

Stupid oaf. I switch out Destroyer for the Renewal Spear and launch the weapon like a javelin. The emerald spearhead hits Otis in the shoulder, sinking in halfway up the shaft as blood splatters from the exit wound on his chest. I watch from behind as Otis pulls the spear through his chest with a rage-fueled scream.

He turns around, heaving as he tosses the spear to the ground.

"You're going to pay for that!" He charges across the platform with an insane burst of speed, the outline of a wild boar superimposed over his body.

His axe cuts through the air with enough power that it whistles. I dodge the attack, but not before it slices through the tip of my braid, unraveling the thick black hair. I summon a Horror of Vitality, but the passive slow doesn't affect him while he's raging. Both of our rages should be up soon.

He keeps pressing. The wound in his shoulder nearly healed when a giant glob of red liquid soars past me. It wraps around Otis's head and shoulders, forming a thick bubble. He drops his axe to tear at the liquid that clings to his face like cellophane. His fingers rip through it, but it's like clawing at water. The bubble reforms as fast as he tears it away, making it impossible for him to breathe.

I glance over my shoulder and see the shriveled, desiccated body of the paladin, all of the blood drained from the decapitated corpse. Behind it, the blood mage contorts her hands in the air, keeping the paladin's blood formed around Otis's head.

Otis drops to his knees, grabbing blindly for his axe. I want to kick it away, but I'm not getting anywhere near that blood. Finally, he grabs the weapon and swings. A stampede of wild boars similar to my spirit guide charge across the platform. One hits me in the leg, knocking me to the ground as my rage ends.

Otis swings again, his movements more erratic as the steam fades from his shoulders. With each swing, he moves slower and slower until the weapon drops from his grip. He falls to his knees, and a moment later, collapses on the platform.

I back away, keeping as much distance between me and the blood mage as possible. The puppet master must be dead because he's nowhere to be seen. Arty swings his sword wildly, fighting off the tinkerer's projectiles while keeping the two wolves at bay. Thanks to the Helm of Resolution, he's managed to gain a twenty-five percent Dexterity buff due to deflecting the rapid attacks. The massive sword moves faster than it has any right to.

The falcon screeches overhead, diving and clawing at the cyclops. The tinkerer now has five contraptions set up on the ground. They rattle and whir as they assault Arty like miniature cannons.

I smash one of the cannon's orbs out of the air and join the cyclops. "Sorry I left you hanging. Let's finish these two, but keep an eye out for the blood mage, she's opportunistic."

Arty grunts his affirmation as he splits another orb in two.

The projectiles continue to barrage us while the wolves snap at our feet. Out of the corner of my eye, Lanxkuri stands still, watching us and making this all the more difficult.

One crisis at a time.

Roots spring up from the ground, but Arty slices them before they can latch around us. The momentary lapse in concentration causes him to take several hits from the projectiles. One of the metallic orbs unfurls, and metal prongs extend from within, latching onto Arty's arm. He screams as he rips it off, pieces of flesh dangling from the prongs.

I smash another orb just before it hits him. "Fuck this, I say we charge them."

"Lead the way." He grunts.

My sudden surge catches the wolves off guard, and they retreat toward the gnomes, but not before I smash one of them in the rear with Destroyer. The splash damage from Ram's Rage carries forward, hitting the second wolf with a burst of magical damage and knocking two of the tinkerer's contraptions to their sides.

While the gnome crouches to reposition his devices, Arty leaps through the air, bringing the blade of his giant sword down like a sledgehammer between the two gnomes. Energy explodes from both sides of the weapon, tossing the tinkerer and one of the wolves over the edge.

The druid rolls across the platform toward the center. Lanxkuri groans as she activates an ability from across the platform. The gnome freezes in place, his fingers twitching like he's trying to move, but the rest of his body is stiff as a board. I don't care if it's the blood mage's doing, I bring Destroyer down on his head just the same, and then I kick the body off the edge just to be safe.

Arty gathers by my side, and we face off with Lanxkuri.

I lift Destroyer over my shoulder. "No matter how this ends, one of us advances."

He narrows his eye. "To hell with that. We finish this together."

I summon more horrors and immediately cast Sacrifice, boosting my stats. Arty and I spread out, making it difficult for Lanxkuri to focus on us both at the same time. I switch out Destroyer for Petrified Staff. The gnarled staff allows me to cast ranged physical attacks every ten seconds.

I use its ability, sending out a charge of energy that the blood mage dodges with ease from this distance. Arty attacks her from behind as she dodges, but she sidesteps the massive blade with practiced ease, raising her hand as a spear of blood shoots out, impaling the cyclops in the ribs. Her health drops by about five percent from using the attack, but Arty takes even more damage despite his high Constitution.

While she's facing away, I switch back to Destroyer and go for the kill shot. Somehow, she senses me coming, because she turns around and a beam of black energy hits me in the chest, knocking me on my back while simultaneously draining a chunk of my health.

A flash of blue trails back through the beam, and the blood mage's health returns to full.

She can attack with blood and replenish her own health the same way. This is going to be a pain in the ass.

I crawl to my feet, feeling slightly lethargic from the blood loss. Arty rushes toward me.

Destroyer feels heavy in my palm. "She's going to be—"

Arty swings his sword, and I barely manage to raise Destroyer so he doesn't take off my head. The force of the hit sends me sliding several inches toward the edge.

"Dude, what the hell?"

He attacks again, and I notice the blackness in his eyes. He's under some kind of confusion spell. I parry the first attack, then meet his sword with my full Strength. The clash echoes around us as our weapons collide.

I reposition to keep myself away from the edge when a bottle explodes between us. Hundreds of glass shards rip through my skin, speckling me with cuts like a bloody Easter egg.

The darkness from Arty's eyes fades, and he comes back to himself. "What happened?"

Before I have time to explain, the dozens of cuts burn like fire as blood explodes from the wounds in thick globules before transforming into bats that swarm us. More and more bats pour from our wounds, and my health continues to plummet. A shadowy aura spreads from each of the blood bats as they attack us.

The air teems with bats, and their aura begins to block out the sun. Wings flap and bats screech as my world descends into darkness. I swing Destroyer, but there are too many bats. With each new bite, they spawn quicker than I can kill them.

Before I know it, my health is more than halfway gone, and I'm nowhere near ready for another rage. I summon horrors, casting Kamikaze as soon as they spawn, but it's no use. Dozens of bats assault me at a time, their bites like pinpricks. The blood loss continues to mount, and it will eventually kill me or Arty. At least one of us will advance.

Then it hits me. I summon Pharos and blinding light spills out in front of me. The bats squeal as the spirit beast charges at the shadowy monsters. Some of them combust into globs of blood that fall to the floor, while others fly high into the air to escape the frost goat's light.

Next to us, Lanxkuri stands with both arms curled up by her side. Black energy radiates from her palms as her index finger and thumb form a circle. Her eyes go wide when she notices my spirit beast, but before she has time to react, Arty and I attack.

From opposite sides, his sword goes low and Destroyer goes high, connecting at the same time. His blade severs her legs, and the hit from the warhammer sends her body windmilling over the edge of the platform. She extends a glowing red palm, and a black aura surrounds her just as the sand wyrm snatches her from the air.

With her gone, I drop Destroyer to the floor, suddenly drained beyond belief.

Without warning, the noise of the outside arena returns. Cannons erupt from all sides, and the crowd cheers louder than ever.

The announcer's voice echoes around us mid-sentence. *"—and there you have it. Chod and Arty survive group one, securing their place in the quarterfinals! What a start to the first round of the Champion's Tournament!"*

I tune out the rest of what he says and go to Arty. He heaves as he leans on the guard of his sword.

I grip his shoulder and lean next to him. "I can't believe we pulled that off."

"Me neither. That attack..." He shakes his head in disbelief. "I've never experienced anything like it. If not for your goat, one of us would certainly be dead."

The platform shrinks, lowering and contracting as one of the earth mages maneuvers us around the arena. Group two's pillar rises above the others and takes center stage.

As our platform glides through the sand like a hockey puck, I spot the seating area for those who were defeated. There's a tunnel at the back of the booth that goes into the outer arena, and some of the challengers have already left. Others sit idly by while the gnome tinkerer and druid appear to be arguing.

Our pillar comes to a stop, docking against the booth next to the council. Several of the council members stand and clap as we step off the pillar. There are a half-dozen guards stationed in their booth, as well as two in ours. Once we're inside, a barrier forms around the booth.

"Let's give it up one more time for the champions of group one, Chod the forest troll and Arty the cyclops!" The crowd roars, and the announcer continues. *"Group two is sure to be just as exciting, so join me as we count down to the next battle."*

36. GROUP OF DEATH

From where we sit, it's hard to see Limery in much detail. I can make out Ethan's shadow wings and Michael's gleaming armor. There's a small red dot that I assume is Limery.

Arty pokes my forearm. "Check this out."

He holds a metal tube up to his eye. At the end of the tube, there are several rows of rotatable glass lenses.

He taps one of the lenses into place with his finger. "It's a magnifying lens. You can adjust them, and they make it easier to see things far away."

I find a similar item next to my seat and hold it up to my right eye. It works like a scope, allowing me to zoom in with amazing detail based on which lens I choose. It wouldn't be a bad idea to have one of these for personal use, especially while traveling.

With the magnifying lens, I spot Limery hovering over Roddick right as the countdown hits zero and the protective barrier fades from their pillar.

Come on, Limery. Just stay out of the action for as long as possible.

Limery flies higher, and the announcer does a play-by-play of the action. I do my best to tune him out, focusing on what is actually happening, but it's hard to keep out the amplified voice entirely.

"And we're off! That's a mighty strike from the paladin, but victory won't be that easy..."

My claws dig into my palms. Come on, little guy, you've got this.

The beginning of the fight is complete chaos. Beams of energy explode, fire erupts, and metal clashes. Don summons a void portal behind the gnome mage that looks like a black mirror floating in the air. The mage's robe flutters behind her before she's violently sucked in.

A second portal spits her out off the edge of the platform. She raises her staff as she falls, and a beam of light gathers at the end, but a sand wyrm swallows the diminutive mage before the spell fully activates.

"Wow, folks! What a tactical display of void magic. One challenger down, and now the warlock is making his presence known."

Ethan takes to the air on his shadowy wings, shooting bolts of dark energy from his palms. The black lightning bolts crack with thunder as they crash into opponents.

Oruma, the merfolk mesmer, and Tozzet, the tidal mage, stay near one another. Beams of water pour from the tidal mage like a firehose, blasting against Michael's giant shield and pushing the paladin toward the edge before he's able to dash out of the way. A miniature waterfall shifts around the merfolk duo at shoulder height, forming a shield and mitigating many of the attacks thrown their way.

The mesmer's hands flash silver as she creates a clone of both her and Tozzet while Ethan targets the two merfolk with his bolts. Black lightning rips into one of the tidal mages, and his body shatters like a broken mirror.

"You can always count on a good mesmer to bring chaos to the battlefield. Let's see if the challengers can locate the real Oruma. But wait, we've got a clash on our hands center stage. Listen to that metal sing!"

Roddick and the speckled catfolk fighter go at it. Roddick wields a shortsword and buckler while the nimble catfolk uses two shortswords. Sparks fly as the two clash repeatedly. They seem evenly matched in technique, but it's clear that the catfolk has the speed advantage. Limery summons a flame wall between the two to give Roddick a moment of respite, but the tidal mage extinguishes the fire with a whirlpool that sucks in the catfolk.

While the soaked cat fights to free himself, Michael seizes the opportunity to attack. His sword glows with radiant energy and lightning explodes into the sky as he brings down his sword on the fighter, killing him instantly.

"The paladin delivers the judgment of Onera, and the god of light has found the catfolk fighter unworthy!"

Roddick stands there with his mouth agape, but the momentary lapse proves his downfall. Arty curses next to me as Ethan flies behind the cyclops's brother. A chain of dark energy forms between the two, and the color quickly drains from Roddick's face. He tries to run, but the link between them doesn't fade. His body shrivels until he collapses to the floor.

"An essence drain from the warlock has removed another challenger from the competition. Watch out, though, now we've got an angry imp on our hands."

A streak of bright orange darts through the air as Limery goes molten, barreling into the warlock with ridiculous speed. There's a flurry of activity as the imp attacks the warlock like an angry wasp, avoiding Ethan's attacks and countering again and again.

"Goddammit, Limery! Leave him be!" I shout, knowing he can't hear me.

A shroud of darkness surrounds Ethan and a dark, clawed hand the size of his body reaches out from the void, smacking Limery to the ground like a fly. My heart drops as the imp bounces off the ground like a ragdoll.

I can't tell how low his health is, but he's not built to take hits like that.

Next to me, Arty clicks another lens into place and leans forward.

Behind Limery, one of the mesmers morphs to look like the dead catfolk and pounces, weapons drawn, toward Limery who's curled up on the platform. The catfolk has Limery in his sights when Michael appears out of nowhere, using his massive shield to protect the imp. A white glow explodes from the paladin and Limery, and the next moment, Limery is flying again.

"Would you look at that? Saved by the paladin! Who saw that coming?"

Tommy Sullivan stabs the catfolk in the back, and the clone shatters into mirrored pieces just like the tidal mage. The real mesmer teleports from across the platform, reappearing behind the hero and pressing her hands to both sides of the hero's head. When she releases, Tommy drops to his knees, screaming as he tears at his hair.

"Tommy looks to be suffering from Torment. Oruma is not holding anything back today."

Don blasts the downed hero with a bolt of dark energy. At the same time, Tozzet hits him with a water whip. The human fighter's hands drop to his sides, and he collapses to the ground.

"And another one bites the dust! Wait, look at that. The warlock is calling for backup from his patron!"

A tear rips through the air around Ethan, revealing a backdrop of lava and darkness as two demons crawl through the rift. The purple-skinned demons have horns that swirl upward like an antelope, and they crawl on spindly arms like a monkey with long, clawed hands and feet. A barbed forked tail whips behind them and they snarl, each one revealing a dangerous set of teeth. They're too far away for me to identify them, but these are definitely different from the flying demons we faced outside Lynchton.

Tozzet summons two water elementals to fight the demons, each one nearly six feet tall. They tower over the demons like a raging ocean in physical form. I expect a good fight, but the demons tear through the elementals and swarm the tidal mage, raking their claws across him and stabbing with their barbed tales until the mage stops moving.

Michael raises his sword overhead, and it glows yellow before twin beams of holy light shoot from the sky, vaporizing the two demons in puffs of smoke.

"The demons might not fear elementals, but they are no match for the Smite of a god."

Limery goes after the mesmer now that the tidal mage is gone, but she teleports away. Don follows behind her with his own teleport, somehow getting to her destination faster and summoning an orb of darkness that swallows the mesmer whole as soon as she reappears.

"Wow! There's your overwhelming proof that in short distances, Blink is faster than Teleport. And now we're down to the final four!"

Arty and I are both on the edge of our seats. Somehow, Limery is still in the thick of it. I just hope he stays out of the action long enough to secure a spot in the next round. There's no need for him to be a hero.

Ethan presses his hands together. His tattoos glow, and the air crackles as two massive balls of shadow form beside him, each one pulsing with dark energy. The shadows are so dark that they seem to swallow the light around them. A black-clawed hand breaks through the darkness. Then another, gripping at the edge of the shadow until a demonic skull resembling a horse's pokes through. The demon emerges from the darkness, unfurling the same shadowy wings that keep Ethan aloft, its hoofed feet hovering above the platform. It looks up, and blue fire blazes within its eye sockets.

Shadow demons. Fuck.

Nebulous blades form in each of the demon's hands. Just like Taryn's Shadow Daggers, they are capable of bypassing weapons and armor to inflict damage. The last time we faced these demons, a single hit from one of their blades took out half of my health. The only reason we defeated them was because of the phoenix's sacrifice. This isn't good.

"The warlock has certainly evened the odds. It appears the paladin, imp, and void mage have formed a temporary truce. This is going to be good."

Don and Michael gather side by side with Limery hovering between them as they face off against Ethan and his demons for a spot in the quarterfinals.

I hope the three of them can band together to take him out, because I don't know if any of us can defeat Ethan one-on-one with a patron as powerful as his.

Ethan unleashes a black bolt at Limery, and it crashes between the two heroes as Limery dodges the attack. One of the demons dives for Michael, swinging its shadow sword as the paladin raises his own.

I curse Michael's stupidity. As a paladin, he should know better! The demon's sword can bypass metal, and there's no telling how much damage it's about to inflict.

Somehow, the paladin's sword blocks the shadow blade, and molten energy burns where the two weapons touch. Hot sparks erupt between the blades. The demon grows darker and Michael glows brighter until an explosion blows them apart.

Damn, I was wrong. I guess holy magic can stop a shadow attack after all. That will be useful information going forward.

Limery throws a barrage of fireballs, and Don opens a void portal in front of them. The fireballs disappear inside the void, reappearing behind Ethan and exploding against his back. The demon that had been guarding Ethan dives for Don, but the void mage blinks to the other side of the platform. Limery chases the demon, hurling fireballs but careful to stay out of the reach of the shadow blade.

Michael returns to the center of the platform, all visible remnants of the explosion gone as his armor once again shines bright. Ethan's tattoos glow a platinum blue as he fires a barrage of dark energy at the paladin. Michael crouches, raising his shield as the dark bolts fizzle out upon impact.

Meanwhile, Don continues to Blink in rapid succession like a laggy video game as both demons pursue him around the platform.

"I don't know how much longer the void mage can keep this up. That much spatial

travel in such a short time has to be taking its toll." The announcer has everyone on edge as the battle continues to unfold.

I flip one of the lenses and zoom in further. Sweat beads from the void mage's brow as he continues to Blink around the platform. I don't think he can keep it up much longer.

One of the demons transforms the blade of its sword into an infernal whip. As Don Blinks, the demon flicks the weapon and it whips across the platform, wrapping around the void mage's ankle as he reappears.

Don Blinks again, but this time, the demon travels with him as he teleports away. Ethan abandons his fight with the paladin as if he knows exactly where Don will emerge and hits the void mage with a spell the moment he reappears, shrouding Don and the demon in a dense fog.

Michael doesn't move as both demons plunge their swords into the void mage. Instead, he targets Limery with a buff.

The imp goes molten once again, only this time he blazes with a bright light similar to the paladin's as he dives at the demons. Their swords are still buried in the void mage when Limery melts through the chest of one demon. Light explodes at the point of impact, and the shadow demon bursts into millions of particles of black ash.

The light around Limery fades, and the second demon takes to the air, rejoining Ethan.

Ethan nods toward Limery, and the demon flies after the imp. Limery zooms around the platform, weaving like a fighter jet as the winged demon pursues.

"Demon versus imp. Paladin versus warlock. Who will survive and secure their place in the quarterfinals?"

While Limery and the demon play their game of cat and mouse, Michael and Ethan showcase the power of light and darkness. Bolts of sinister energy crash against the paladin's holy weapons and armor. Every time holy and infernal attacks touch, they explode with violent power. Michael casts buff after buff, avoiding the damaging effects of Ethan's attacks. As the paladin's aura continues to change time and again, I realize I never knew there were so many shades of white.

In the battle of speed, Limery proves faster and more agile than the demon. As they fly by the warlock and paladin, Ethan calls the demon off. Limery doesn't notice, leaving Michael two against one.

The demon dives for Michael from behind to attack the paladin unaware. It swings the shadow blade for Michael's head, but the blade crumbles to ash inches from the paladin's neck as if blocked by some unseen force. In an impressive display of finesse, Michael blocks Ethan's corrupted bolts with his shield and spins around, slicing the demon in two from groin to head.

The entire stadium gasps at the heroic display.

There's little time to appreciate the effort as Ethan puts his hands together overhead and a bolt of lightning so dark it shrouds the arena shoots from above. It hits the paladin with a thunderous crash, and Michael vanishes.

Cannon blasts and cheers echo around the arena.

"Oh my gods, folks! That's what this tournament is all about. It's not every day you witness a patron banishing a paladin from existence. A stunning display of power. Give it up for the winners of round two, Ethan and Limery!"

Arty and I share the same shocked expression. Limery did it! Holy shit, he did it! I jump to my feet, clapping with the rest of the arena.

After a long bout of applause, platform two descends and slides across the arena with Ethan and Limery standing at opposite sides. Limery scowls at the warlock as our barrier disappears and they dock with our booth.

Limery flies over and wraps his arms around my neck. "Limmy dids its! Limmy wons!"

"You did a great job." I pat him on the back. "I'm proud of you."

"Who knew imps were so powerful?" Ethan leans against a column and stares out at the crowd. "To hear others talk of them, you'd think they were nothing more than glorified messengers."

Limery grows hot as he sits on my shoulder. "Limmy doesn't like yous. Yous is a bad mans."

The warlock grins but doesn't look our way. "Don't you forget it."

The entire time we wait for the next match, Ethan never looks in our direction. He keeps his gaze focused on the inner arena. Maybe it's his attempt to further get into our heads. Not that he needs any help with that. He might have scrapped his way into the quarterfinals, but he did it going one against three and prevailing.

Do any of us really have a shot at beating him when he can summon demons to fight on his behalf? I honestly have no idea the scope of his power when his patron is involved.

"Look, Chods. It's Caustics." Limery grabs my horn and pushes my head to the left, pointing into the stands.

Sure enough, Caustic's large frame sticks out like a sore thumb against the sea of gnomes. I really wish he'd been allowed to fight with me. We're doing better than I could have hoped, already clinching three of the final eight spots, but a dragon is a dragon.

Putting on a good show might gain us a few new allies, but nothing beats winning. As Don said, everybody respects power.

The impossibly-hard-to-tune-out announcer's voice begins the countdown for group three. There are some dangerous opponents in this group that I know of, including Drizz'rt, Kevin the sorcerer, and Jason the mage.

I grab a magnifying lens from a nearby seat and hand it to the imp. When he holds it up to his bulbous eye, it's nearly as big as he is.

I focus mine on the platform. Everyone is scattered around the perimeter except for Jason, who stands right in the middle. A bold strategy. He doesn't wear the traditional wizard robes of most mages and sorcerers. Instead, he wears a slim-fitting black tunic and a red shawl draped around his shoulders and head like a hood. The center seems like an awfully dangerous spot for the mage to start, leaving his unprotected back exposed to an attack.

The countdown ends, and the barrier fades. Drizz'rt is the first to move, leaping toward Jason's backside with daggers clutched in both hands. A blindside attack from an assassin is going to be gruesome.

Jason kneels, and a cube of energy forms around him, blocking Drizz'rt's attack as the rogue lizardfolk stabs into the barrier with his daggers.

Energy flares along the cube and it expands, rapidly swelling beyond the edge of the platform and pushing every challenger off the ledge into the sand below. Two of the challengers die to the sand wyrms before ever hitting the ground.

Reddick survives the fall, but he only lasts a moment before a wyrm gets him too.

A moment later, cannons fire to announce the end of the match, but I can't tell who the other survivor was.

Ethan curses, shaking his head as he stares into the arena.

"Would you look at that! Our quickest round yet. Jason puts his arcane Cube of Protection to great use, but Drizz'rt, the infamous assassin, has managed to cling to the cube's exterior with his sharp claws, securing his place in the next round!"

Sure enough, Drizz'rt is latched onto the far side of the cube, claws digging into the shield's surface. Jason cancels the spell, and Drizz'rt plummets into the sand below. One of the earth mages quickly forms a one-person platform to save the lizardfolk from the wyrms, raising him back to the main platform.

The assassin and the mage exchange heated words while the crowd continues to applaud.

I send Taryn a quick message, wishing him luck. Not that I imagine he's checking his notifications right now. I'm sure he's feeling the pressure, especially after Arty, Limery, and I all advanced.

I know I would be.

When the platform docks, Drizz'rt is still glaring at Jason. The mage nods to Ethan and takes a seat in the back corner of the booth. The assassin offers Limery and me congratulations before taking a seat behind us.

Before I have a chance to ask him why he's so upset, the announcer begins counting down for the next match.

I turn my attention to Taryn. Come on, bro. You've got this.

37. RAM, BAM, THANK YOU, MA'AM

The platform was like the eye of a hurricane, an eerie quiet amidst the roar of the crowd.

Taryn sat on Berry's back with Ruby between his legs. Instead of curling up, she stood on all fours as Berry shifted his feet, groaning and huffing at the other challengers.

Jordy stood in front of them, head lowered and ready to attack. Flubs tried to peek above the lip of the vial around Taryn's neck, but he ordered the slime back inside. No one knew about Flubs aside from his friends, and he wanted to keep it that way.

He gently stroked the soft fur of the jackal's ears. She was on high alert, just like Taryn. The texture of her fur was calming, and Taryn needed it now more than ever. Chod and Limery had both made it to the next round. No one would ever call him a failure if he didn't make it, but he wanted to push himself. He was a good support, but now was the time to see what he was truly capable of when his back was against the wall. He couldn't compete with many of the challengers when it came to burst damage or raw power, but if he played it right, he had a chance to outsmart them. And for once, he could do that without fear of losing one of his pets.

His hand instinctively moved over his heart, over the carrot tattoo that rested there.

Taryn's pulse thundered in his ears as he watched the nine other challengers. To his left, there was Sam the monk. He knew precious little about him aside from the fact that he was another hero that had managed to keep a low profile. Then there was Kazzandre the giant and a gnome mage.

Kazzandre towered over everyone else, wearing studded leather armor while wielding twin warhammers that would be full-sized weapons for anyone else. He'd heard some of her adventures at the ball, and when it came to raw strength, she might give Chod a run for his money. She spun the weapons against her palms. Taryn wondered if it was out of excitement or nervousness? Perhaps both.

The gnome wore a sky-blue robe embroidered with silver snowflakes along the arms. The end of his staff looked like it was carved from ice. He'd need to be extra cautious of abilities that could freeze or slow.

To Taryn's right, Randy the rogue sported a full arsenal of knives and daggers strapped about his body. The silver thread of the wolf on his chest sparkled as it caught the light of the sun. Their eyes met, and the rogue winked before returning his gaze to the giant.

Next to Randy stood Troy Malloy, a fire mage, and a little further down was the drunken master gnome. Even just standing there, the monk wobbled like he could topple at any moment.

Taryn grinned, wondering if it was a requirement to be drunk for the class to work or if the class made the gnome appear drunk.

On the far side of the platform, a human adventurer from Ellynmylly looked about uncertainly. Two gnomish tinkerers sandwiched him from both sides, already setting up their gear.

The countdown hit zero and Taryn summoned a ring of poisonous mushrooms around himself and his pets. His goal was to lay low for as long as possible. Berry looked threatening in his own right but the less attention they garnered, the better.

Next to him, Sam the monk narrowed his eyes at Taryn. He drew his fist back and a watercolor outline of a tiger formed over the monk's arm. As his torso twisted to unleash the attack on Taryn, a warhammer hit the monk in the side. Ribs audibly cracked, and the tiger attack wisped away as he flew off the edge.

The giant smirked at Taryn, stomping in his direction, but Taryn cast Stonewall between him and the giant, keeping her at bay for now.

"Why the hell are they targeting me? Maybe we need to look more intimidating."

Berry groaned in response as Taryn summoned more mushrooms, creating land mines of poisonous fungi between him and the others. For now, he had a narrow strip of safety protected by Stonewall and mushrooms with the platform's edge at his back.

At the other end of the platform, the gnome tinkerers joined forces, setting up a fortress of metal plates complete with mounted turrets. The contraptions fired on the drunken master, who somehow dodged every projectile shot his way.

Closer, Troy battled the gnome mage in a dazzling display of fire and ice. The occasional errant spell flew past Taryn as fireballs collided with ice daggers, creating a fine mist that streaked with rainbow in the sunlight.

The human from Ellynmylly ran toward the center of the platform as Randy chased him, his head on a swivel as chaos raged all around him. Taryn saw the patch of ice before the adventurer hit it, slipping and sliding off the edge of the platform without ever being touched.

Taryn turned his attention back to the rogue, but it was already too late. A dagger was coming at his neck too fast for him to react or dodge.

His neck stung like a pinprick, and Taryn reached for the wound, wondering how long he could survive with a dagger in the neck. His blood was surprisingly cool to the touch as he searched for the wound, but then it gurgled. Taryn realized it wasn't blood at all. The tip of the dagger had barely grazed his skin thanks to Flubs.

Taryn removed the dagger that was encased within the slime's body. In the blade's reflection, his neck barely had a scratch. Flubs had been on alert even when Taryn's attention was elsewhere.

"Thanks, buddy." Taryn stuffed the dagger into his satchel.

Randy frowned, saw the many mushrooms in front of Taryn, and then set off for less defensive prey.

Meanwhile, Troy and the ice mage's battle crept ever closer to Taryn. The ice mage had his back turned as he formed ice shields to block a barrage of fireballs.

Taryn couldn't pass up the opportunity for an easy kill. Mushrooms exploded as Jordy ran across the platform, ramming the unsuspecting mage off the side. The poor gnome flew like a soccer ball, and a sand wyrm snatched him out of the air.

"Ram, bam, thank you, Jordy."

On the other side of Stonewall, Taryn could hear the giant fighting someone. She groaned and grunted as metal clinked.

Taryn needed to get a better view of the battlefield, so he summoned more mushrooms to protect his pets and transformed into his bird form.

He flew up and perched on the stone wall, where Randy and the giant danced in a circle on the other side. Taryn then flew higher, taking in all the action at once. Since his pets couldn't advance to the next round without him, no one was paying them much attention for now as long as they kept out of the way.

The fire mage lurked at the edge of the platform now that the ice mage was gone, just out of the action as the two tinkerers continued to assault the monk.

Might as well sow a little chaos. Taryn flew low, casting Mind Warp on one of the tinkerers before returning to his pets.

One of the tinkerers suddenly turned on the other. There were loud crashes as their contraptions and turrets fired at each other from close range, destroying the fortress they'd created. While the one tried to calm the mind-warped gnome from attacking him, the drunken monk leapt with a flying kick that sent the first tinkerer off the edge. The monk landed in the middle of the wreckage, spinning around and connecting an elbow that launched the second tinkerer off the platform to be devoured by a sand wyrm.

And then there were five.

A section of Taryn's wall crumbled as one of Kazzandre's warhammers smashed into it, giving Taryn line of sight on the raging battle between her and the rogue. The quick-footed rogue appeared to be too nimble for the giant, dodging her attacks with ease. She swung for him again, but he evaded, somehow sliding between her legs and stabbing her in the groin along the way.

The giant roared in pain as her hammer eviscerated another section of the wall. She winced as she brought the second warhammer down on the rogue that had repositioned behind her. He dodged again, this time rolling to the side and slicing behind her knee as her warhammer crashed into the platform. With each new wound, the giant moved slower, making it easier for Randy to tear her down.

Eventually, she could barely stand, wobbling like a newborn fawn as Randy circled her like the wolf on his chest. Then a fireball exploded against Kazzandre, sending the giant toppling over the edge.

Randy turned on the fire mage, snarling. "She was mine!"

Troy shrugged. "If she was yours, I wouldn't have killed her."

While the two argued, the gnome monk attacked Troy from behind, kicking the mage in the back and knocking him to his knees.

The mage stood, fists covered in flames. "You're going to pay for that!"

Randy readied his daggers as the three challengers squared off, oblivious to Taryn standing idly by. Shit was about to hit the fan.

This time, Taryn was ready for it. Troy punched and a stream of fire shot at the monk, while at the same time, Randy sprinted for the mage with his daggers tucked by his side.

"Good night, boys," Taryn whispered as he cast Endless Night.

A veil of impenetrable darkness settled over the center of the platform, preventing those inside from seeing or smelling anything. He had thirty seconds before the ability ended, and he planned to use every second of it.

Taryn pulled Lightning in a Bottle from his satchel and tossed it into the darkness. It was a one-time use item, but now seemed like the perfect opportunity. Glass shattered and thunder cracked from within as the stored lightning exploded from the bottle. With five charges inside, there was a good chance someone was taking multiple strikes, along with a fifty percent chance of being stunned.

Next, Taryn cast Lightning Bolt in the center of the dark cloud. With its ten-second cooldown, he'd be able to use it once more before the cloud dispersed. He picked a spot at random and cast Moonbeam. A stream of silver light disappeared within the cloud.

He summoned poisonous mushrooms along the cloud's edge to prevent anyone from fleeing the carnage in his direction, and when Lightning Bolt came off cooldown, he cast it again. Taryn commanded his pets to retreat to his crumbling wall and summoned a second wall for their protection before taking to his bird form. He flew high above. Hopefully, when the spell faded, no one would notice him.

The spell ended, and the three challengers picked up where they left off. Troy cast a massive fireball at the drunken master that swirled in a vortex toward the gnome. As soon as he unleashed it, Randy stabbed the mage in the back with a dagger.

The monk swayed drunkenly as the fireball approached, but his hands moved in a practiced formation. Wisps of orange energy trailed his fingertips, and he took a step back, extending his hands as the fireball hit him, then he was somehow cradling the blast. The flames rolled across his chest with the finesse of a Harlem Globetrotter and as he redirected the fireball with his off-hand, the outline of a fiery eagle soared alongside the attack.

Randy dove out of the way as the blast engulfed the fire mage.

The monk raised his hands in the air like he'd just won, but Randy looked over his shoulder, scanning the perimeter of the platform.

His eyes lingered on Taryn's walls before he looked overhead. "Son of a bitch."

The drunken master grinned as he walked across the platform, swaying as he extended a hand to the rogue. "Congrats on making it to the next round."

Randy laughed. "You are a dumb motherfucker."

The rogue extended his hand. The moment he was about to shake, Randy's entire body shimmered. Shadow copies of himself spread out to both sides, and the real Randy appeared behind the monk. He buried his dagger in the gnome's neck, and the cannons echoed from around the arena.

"Wow, folks! With a bag of tricks like that, who would have thought it would be the druid pulling the wool over everyone's eyes? Congrats to Randy and Taryn for securing the final two spots in the quarterfinals."

The crowd cheered as Taryn returned to his dwarven form. He canceled Stonewall, and his pets came running over, Berry nearly knocking the druid to the ground as he nuzzled him.

Berry growled as Randy approached.

The rogue threw up his hands. "Don't worry about me. Just paying my respects. That guy might have been an idiot, but you played your cards to perfection." He grinned. "You won't fly under the radar in the next round."

Taryn smiled. Somehow, he and his friends made up half of the final eight spots.

38. FIGHTING, FRIENDS, AND FOES

Between rounds, the earth mages return the sandy floor to gleaming crystal, and the platforms disappear. The sand wyrms are once again returned to wherever they dwell somewhere deep underground. A band plays in the stands, their music amplified across the arena while giant kites shaped like dragons, phoenixes, and other winged creatures soar above the crowd.

Taryn gestures wildly as he recounts his fight for us. He hasn't stopped grinning since he joined us in the booth. "I wish I could have saved Lightning in a Bottle for a later round, but I don't know if I would have survived without throwing everything I had at them." A green string of slime reaches out from the vial and taps Taryn on the cheek. "Or without Flubs. He saved me big-time."

"You put on a show. People will be talking about that fight for years to come. I still can't believe the monk thought the match was over." Arty's eye widens slightly as he shakes his head. "Crazy. Maybe he was drunk."

The four of us laugh, but no one else in the booth seems to be paying much attention to our conversation. Drizz'rt and Randy have become fast friends, once again talking shop and breaking down their moves for one another a couple of rows behind us.

Jason and Ethan stand in opposite corners on the other side of the booth. Ethan continually stares out into the arena, while Jason sits alone in the back corner.

"Any idea what we'll be up against next?" I ask.

Arty shrugs. "I don't think any of us were expecting four battle royales to start off with, so there's no telling what they have planned. She did mention that the next round will be single elimination."

Down below, the earth mages begin redesigning the arena, this time pulling crystal from beneath the floor to form obstacles, ravines, cliffs, and rock formations across the battlefield. A water mage fills a dip in the ground with water, forming a large pond, and then an earth mage creates a bridge and several steppingstones across it.

When they're finished, the entire arena is the battlefield, opening up a slew of possibilities for the next round.

The music stops, and the announcer's voice carries above everything. *"As our mages prepare the arena for the quarterfinals, the moment has finally come to announce the seeding for the rest of the tournament."*

Massive slabs of glass rise from the arena floor on opposite sides of the stadium like giant scoreboards. One of the mages waves his hand, and an eight-person bracket carves into the glass. As each of our names are announced, they fill in on the display.

"On the left side, we have Chod versus Arty for match one, a true battle of the brawlers, and then it's rogue versus rogue in match two as Drizz'rt takes on Randy. On the right side, Ethan the warlock will face the deceptive druid, Taryn, for match three. And for the final match of the quarterfinals, Limery the imp is up against Jason the mage."

"The deceptive druid." Taryn puffs out his chest. "That has a nice ring to it."

Randy bursts out laughing behind us. "This is really going to be a strain on our friendship, Drizz'rt."

The lizardfolk laughs for the first time since I've known him. It's unnerving the way he chirps like a dolphin as his jaws widen, revealing a set of dangerously-sharp teeth. "The deepest bonds are forged on the battlefield. I look forward to testing your skills."

"Please never make him laugh again," Taryn mumbles.

Arty grins as he cracks his knuckles. "This is a fight I look forward to."

Having all four of us in a separate bracket was wishful thinking. I doubt even Hawkin's buff would prove to be that lucky.

I wink at the cyclops. "Well, then I guess we better put on a show."

With all three pieces of the Regeneration Triad equipped, I have an additional thirty percent HP, bringing me to over nine thousand without any of my horrors. For every horror I summon, I'll gain an additional ninety health as long as they remain alive.

If I were able to summon the full sixty horrors before they started to decay, I'd more than double my resting HP. There's no way I'll have the time to pull off something like that in this tournament, but the twenty percent regeneration buff and the bonus healing from both the Renewal Spear and Horrors of Finesse make me pretty damned hard to kill.

Arty's giant eye threatens to pop out of his head when I equip the new weapons. I almost feel bad for keeping them a secret.

He laughs. "I should have known you had something up your sleeve."

"Sorry, friend, but I came to win."

The countdown ends, and I summon my horrors. There's a good fifty feet between me and Arty, and I aim to keep my distance while I continue to build up my horrors.

Arty must know my motive, because he moves in, intent on engaging me early.

As much time as we've spent alongside one another the past week, this is the first time I've tested Arty's strength directly aside from our arm-wrestling match.

He's every bit as strong as me, maybe even more so.

I parry his sword attack with my spear, and it takes everything I have not to lose my grip on the weapon. He swings again and this time, I take the hit full on against my shield. The force from the attack sends my feet sliding several inches.

For now, I play on the defensive, using the terrain to my advantage to slow the pace of the fight and let the cyclops continue to press me as I summon more horrors. I send them running off to the bridge over the pond at the opposite end of the arena, careful to keep Arty far away from them. With his Helm of Resolution, each attack he lands within a certain time frame increases his attack speed. So many horrors would be a feast for him.

After five minutes of letting Arty pressure me around the arena, absorbing hit after hit, I dash back and shake out my aching hands. "Tired yet?"

"Hardly." A red aura surrounds his legs as he closes the distance in a single jump, bringing his massive sword down on my shield once again.

Pinned underneath the shield, I summon a Horror of Vitality. The horror's passive slows Arty, and I sacrifice my horrors all at once.

With an influx of stat points, I roll out from under the shield and activate Concussive Force as I stab at Arty's ribs. He dodges, spinning and countering with an overhead strike. Thanks to my bonus stats, I'm now faster and stronger than the cyclops. I pull my weapon back and parry with the butt of the spear, but I still can't land a hit. Sparks fly as the weapons grate against one another.

I rotate the spear, parrying his attack and using the momentum to slam his blade into the ground. Arty drops the sword and pulls out a warhammer. The hammer's weight is much harder to deflect with the spear, but it gives me the longer reach. I jab it at him and when he swings, I let him knock the spear from my hand. It spins like a helicopter blade out of my palm.

As his momentum carries him forward, I roll to his blindside and activate Return to Sender from the new effect stone. The spear abruptly shifts course like it's pulled by a powerful magnet.

When it returns to my hand, I jab the spear underneath the back of Arty's helm until the spearhead pokes through his eye socket, skewering his eye like a martini olive.

The announcer's voice returns alongside the celebratory cannons. Even though he's not truly dead, I try not to look at the body of my friend. It's a sight I hope to never see.

Instead, I raise my arms and bask in the glory of the crowd. One step closer to the finals.

"For our second match of the quarterfinals, it's a battle of blades as Randy the rogue and Drizz'rt the assassin vie for a place in the semis."

The fight between Randy and Drizz'rt is like watching a dance of shadow and misdirection. The action is so fast that the announcer can barely keep up. The two rogues move with amazing finesse and speed, steel clashing in a spray of sparks as they dash around the battlefield.

From up in our booth, it's almost impossible to tell who is winning. One minute, they move in a blur, and the next their blades are ripping through shadowy silhouettes and doppelgängers.

Watching them, I realize just how valuable a good rogue can be.

Randy and Drizz'rt clash, and their blades sing. Randy activates Shadowstep and Doppelgänger, and two versions of himself split in opposite directions while the real Randy blinks behind Drizz'rt.

The lizardfolk buries his blade in one of the doppelgängers and it turns to dust just as Randy appears behind Drizz'rt, plunging his blade into the assassin's neck. The golden lizard turns to dust, with the real Drizz'rt already behind Randy. He slams both of his daggers into the rogue's shoulders.

With arms immobilized, Randy's weapons fall to the floor. Drizz'rt pulls a vial from across his chest and smashes it against the ground, where a plume of gray smoke explodes, concealing both rogues.

When the smoke clears, Randy lays on the ground with a half-dozen blades sticking out of him while Drizz'rt leans against a nearby boulder, sharpening his dagger.

"What a display of speed and deception! This fight looked to be over a half-dozen times, with each challenger two steps ahead of the other, but there you have it, a remarkable finish. Round one of the semifinals will feature Chod vs Drizz'rt. Now stand by for the second half of the bracket featuring Ethan and Taryn."

Taryn huddles in the corner of the booth with his pets, giving them a pep talk. Berry, Jordy, Ruby, and skele-cat Flubs nod along as Taryn pumps his fist and points at each of them in turn.

Right now, he's in the zone, and I don't want to interrupt his focus. Ethan, on the other hand, has barely moved from his position leaning against the column, still staring intently into the arena.

Limery scowls at him from atop my shoulder. "Limmy hopes Taryns beats the bad mans."

Ethan glances at us out of the corner of his eye. "It's important to have dreams."

Jason snickers in the back corner, but I pay him no mind.

The platform returns, and the shield fades as Drizz'rt steps into the booth. He nods at me as he takes a seat in the back row.

Taryn climbs onto Berry, and both Ruby and Flubs leap into his lap.

"Good luck!" I call out as Jordy leads their troop onto the platform.

"Good lucks, Taryns!" Limery waves.

"See you soon." He winks as he turns to the crowd.

Ethan casually joins Taryn on the platform, and it descends into the arena. The earth mages showcase some of their skill as the base of the platform widens and shrinks as it moves around the terrain. It stops in the center, and a ramp descends on each side as the challengers take their positions.

The announcer blathers on about each of them, recounting their progress in the tournament as if we all haven't been watching it unfold over the course of the day.

I lift my magnifying lens as Taryn dismounts from Berry. He sends the bear to the right and Jordy to the left while Ruby and Flubs stay behind Taryn.

I understand what he's doing, but I don't like it. Freeing up Berry to attack for when the warlock inevitably summons demons makes sense, but it puts Taryn on the ground. If he can stand back and use his spells from a distance, he might have a shot.

When the countdown ends, Taryn summons a ring of poisonous mushrooms between him and Ethan. The warlock unfurls his shadow wings and takes flight. Reality tears and portals appear beneath both of his feet. Crab-like demons the size of a small dog crawl through the dark portal, each one has six barbed legs, pincers, and a flattened midsection covered in eyes. The dark red eyes on their shells are unsettling even from this far away.

The demon crabs fall to the ground and scatter. Jordy rams into one and launches it across the arena. It lands with a splash in the pond. Berry crushes a demon with his paw while ripping off a pincer with his teeth. Green ichor trails from the appendage, and Berry spits it out.

Lightning crashes from the sky, arcing toward the warlock. A quick flap of his wings avoids the strike, and he counters with a demon bolt of his own. The black lightning explodes against a boulder a few feet away from Taryn.

Demons continue to funnel out of the portal like ants until dozens of them swarm the battlefield. Berry and Jordy destroy as many as they can, but they aren't quick enough. Taryn casts Strong Wind, increasing their movement speed and allowing his pets to evade the swarms more easily when they need to. Moonbeam is especially effective on the demons, but the cooldown is too long. The mushrooms deal lingering damage when they burst, enough that Taryn can finish the crab-demons off with a stab from his Shadow Dagger.

"It looks like the warlock has taken a page from the druid's playbook. He seems content to stand back for now, watching and waiting for Taryn to make a mistake."

There's no way Taryn can fight off the demons and Ethan at the same time—and Ethan knows it. He hovers with a bemused expression, occasionally firing a demon bolt but otherwise watching the chaos unfold.

Taryn casts another Moonbeam, and it hits one of the portals directly, incinerating the demons crawling through. Smoke billows up from their dried corpses, and when the smoke clears, the portal is gone.

Ethan frowns, swooping across the chaos and hitting Berry with a purple beam of energy. A purple haze forms around Berry, and his health begins to drop. Taryn reacts fast, casting Imbue and doubling the bear's size while summoning more mushrooms.

"That got his attention! Ethan is on the attack, hitting the bear with Corruption."

Unfortunately, Imbue doesn't raise Berry's health or Constitution, so it continues to trickle down. There's no way Taryn will have the time or space to cast Restoration on him.

Demons continue to crawl through the open portal faster than they are being destroyed. Jordy leaps around the rocky terrain, launching himself from a boulder headfirst and stomping crab-demons before climbing back to the high ground.

Berry is having a tougher time. Even though he's larger, the demons cling to his backside and pinch at any area not covered by his golden armor. Blood mattes the rusty fur along his legs.

Taryn casts Lightning Bolt around the second portal, and demons explode across the arena. The attack does nothing to the portal itself, though.

Ethan shoots another demon bolt at Taryn, and he dives out of the way, but it was only a distraction. While Berry fights with the swarm of demons, crushing them and tearing them apart, Ethan casts Essence Drain and a channel of purple-and-black energy forms between the bear and the warlock.

Taryn's head swivels between Berry and the portal, and I know exactly what he's thinking. He can either use Moonbeam to buy Berry some time or he can use it to close the portal, not both.

Berry's health continues to drop rapidly when a silver streak shoots from the sky.

Moonbeam hits the portal, killing demons and sending up more smoke. At the same time as the attack hits, Taryn's remaining pets charge for the warlock.

He's going all in.

Ruby leaps toward Ethan, launching herself high enough to sink her teeth into his boot. She dangles there, refusing to let go.

Ethan blasts her at point-blank range with his free hand, and her body collapses to the ground.

"Oh noes," Limery gasps beside me.

I place a hand on his feet, feeling the same dread.

Flubs abandons his skeleton and shoots through the air like a spitball. The slime wraps around Ethan's hand but immediately turns solid. The warlock shakes his wrist and Flubs slides off, hitting a boulder and shattering into hundreds of pieces.

"Ethan refuses to abandon Essence Drain, using his off-hand to cast Frozen Touch on the slime. Is there anything Taryn can do to stop him?"

Taryn transforms into his bird form and dodges a blast as he goes for the warlock's eyes. Ethan swats at the bird with his free hand but still doesn't release his hold on Berry.

Taryn swarms Ethan again and again like an angry mockingbird. While we're all focused on Taryn, Jordy launches himself off a boulder, hitting the warlock in the back and breaking the spell.

Berry shambles a few steps before collapsing under the attacks of the demons. Ethan searches for Taryn, but he hovers high overheard still in bird form. The crowd gasps as he changes back into a dwarf some hundred feet off the ground and falls with both daggers equipped.

He lands on Ethan's back, both blades plunging into the warlock. With both weapons embedded, Ethan's health is actually dropping. He reaches for Taryn, but he can't seem to get a hold of the dwarf. Instead, he dives toward the ground as his health plummets, crashing into a cluster of crab-demons. They swarm Taryn, forcing him to let go.

Ethan unleashes a slew of attacks on Taryn while he's pinned beneath the demons. When his HP reaches zero, I avert my gaze as Ethan turns his eyes on Jordy.

A few moments later, the cannons fire.

When Ethan returns, I have to physically restrain Limery to keep him from attacking the warlock.

"It's okay, buddy. Taryn is fine. He'll be waiting for us when this is over."

Limery snarls at Ethan. "Limmy doesn't like hims."

I pull Limery aside. "Look, it's okay to be mad, but you have a fight coming up. You can either channel that anger and use it to power you, or you need to let it go so that you can focus." I pat him on the shoulder. "I'm not going to tell you what to do, just don't let it make you sloppy. Got it?"

He nods, but I can see the rage burning within his bulbous eyes. He sits on my shoulder and stews as the announcer prepares everyone for the next fight.

When it's time for them to go, he hugs me and flies over to the platform. Jason mumbles something to Ethan as he walks past, but the warlock rolls his eyes.

Me, Drizz'rt, and Ethan are now alone in the booth that once felt crowded. Soon, we'll be down to the final four.

Limery flies around the battlefield, darting back and forth before the match starts. I don't know if I have ever seen him this worked up. Maybe when he showed up with Chief Rizza and the others as we were being ambushed by Ethan and his crew, but this feels different.

I glance into the stands to check on Caustic. He's still sitting with Breebis, so I guess he's behaving himself.

Drizz'rt climbs over the seat and sits next to me. "You have fought well today. You bring honor to the trolls." He hisses as he pronounces the last word.

I acknowledge his presence before returning my gaze to Limery. "Thanks. You were pretty impressive yourself—especially against Randy. That was amazing to watch."

He ignores my compliment, turning his attention to Limery. "The little one, he is strong."

"He is. Passionate, too."

"I wish him well."

The countdown ends, and the fight begins. Jason's hands glow and arcane chains appear out of nowhere, wrapping around Limery's body and tethering the imp to the ground. He struggles against their hold, but the chains don't budge.

Limery goes molten, his entire body burning like flaming lava until the chains vanish into the ether. Before he flies away, an octahedron prism forms around the imp, locking him in place and quenching his fire.

For a moment, he seems suspended in time. Rainbows ripple through the prism as it catches the light, and then Limery's body begins to glow, at first in his chest, and then spreading out along his belly and arms until his entire body pulses with orange and yellow. Flames lick at his body and he ignites, going full molten.

Still, the prism doesn't give. Jason's hands glow, fingers outstretched as they point at one another like he's trying to contain the imp. His brow furrows, and a bead of sweat trails down his nose.

Come on, Limery. Keep pushing.

Fire bursts to life around the imp, not the flames of his molten form but something more intense. The mage falters, nearly falling to his knees, but he catches his balance. The fire burns within the entirety of the prism, concealing Limery as the flames swirl. The air around the prism shimmers from the intense heat.

A crack forms, and then the entire thing shatters. Limery hovers in the air, and fire continues to blaze around him, spinning in a circle like a miniature sun and hiding the imp from view.

"Oh gods, I can't believe this, folks! The imp just broke through an Arcane Prison using Fire Shield! That's not an ability you see every day. What more does this miniature hellraiser have in store for us today?"

Fire Shield? When the hell did he learn that? I bet the little bugger has been hiding his new ability since he hit level twenty-five!

A barrage of spells hit Limery's fire shield, but they all fizzle out on impact. Jason casts more and more, hitting him from all sides, but Limery's shield holds.

Then it expands. As it does, some of the rocky terrain gleams as it turns to glass from the heat. Once the fiery shield doubles in size, flares pop along the outer surface, licking at the air. Jason takes a few steps back, and the heat increases again, so much so that a gust of warm air hits us in the stands.

"Wow, did you feel that, folks? He's turning up the heat. Let me remind you that the shield mages have invoked every precaution to keep our wonderful guests safe from the conflict. Nothing capable of damage will pass through the barrier. And speaking of shields, Jason has just cast Cube of Protection."

I remember that spell. It was the one he hid inside back in the forest when he nearly killed Ismora. Apparently, Limery remembers it, too because as soon as it's cast, he goes on the attack. The fire shield fades, and he moves like a fireball toward the mage, summoning a flame wall on all four sides of the cube. Landing on the top of the cube, he presses his hands to the glass. His body goes molten and the entire scene is nothing but hazy, distorted heat.

Only a few seconds pass before the cube shatters, and a flame-covered Jason runs through the fire wall. He stumbles across the battlefield, searching for the pond, but Limery pursues like an arrow, latching his burning body onto Jason until the mage falls to the ground, and the cannons boom.

The crowd erupts, and I release the breath I was holding. Drizz'rt is on his feet, but Ethan shows no emotion as he stares down into the arena.

Limery doesn't wait for the platform to carry him back, choosing to fly over instead. One of the mages cancels the barrier, and Limery flies into my arms.

"Limmy dids it. Limmy is tireds." His eyes flutter, and then he's asleep in my arms.

I sit down, cradling him as he snores. You did it, Limery. You certainly did.

39. CHALLENGER OR CHAMPION

The break between the quarterfinals and the semis is longer than the others. The gnomes put on some kind of show, but I pay it no attention. Limery snores in my arms while my mind runs through tactics for dealing with an assassin who can probably run circles around me.

We're so close to pulling this off. Two more wins and it could be me and Limery in the finals proving to everyone that they don't want to cross us.

I catch the end of the intermission as a group of gnomes hang-glide across the arena. Streams of brightly-colored smoke trail behind them as they make designs in the sky. The gliders barrel-roll, spin, and do loops to the delight of the crowd.

Drizz'rt shakes his head, muttering "gnomes" as if that explains everything.

The announcer goes through his usual pre-fight buildup, and I wake Limery. After the last match, he's gassed. Even though he could use the rest, I don't trust Ethan not to pull some shady shit, so I give Limery a stamina potion that will hopefully help rejuvenate him a little. He extends his small hand for a fist-bump, and then I step onto the platform across from Drizz'rt.

Regardless of what happens, there's no animosity between the lizardfolk and me. I fully expect him to test my limits, but I can't lose. I just can't. There's too much on the line.

As the platform descends, I search for the booth with the eliminated challengers. About a third of them have already bailed. Who knows, maybe they didn't want their failure on display, or maybe they've joined up with friends and family in the crowd.

Taryn sits in the front row, giving me a thumbs up with Berry and Jordy sitting to each side of him, and Flubs and Ruby each occupying one of his legs.

For some reason, the gesture takes me back to the trial, back before I knew this place existed. I had just been sentenced, and I was terrified at not knowing what awaited me. Taryn shouted his encouragement from the back of the courtroom. When I turned around, there he was, thumbs up as he towered over everyone around him, his giant afro making his presence even more imposing.

He's the only person in my life that I can say has always been there for me, even when I haven't always been the most pleasant to be around. He lifts Ruby's paw, making her wave, and I throw up a peace sign.

Behind Taryn, Arty, Reddick, and Roddick sit next to Randy, Don, and Michael. The rogue laughs and nudges Roddick in the shoulder. If nothing else happens, we've made at least a few allies from being here.

The platform stops moving near ground level and ramps descend from each side. Drizz'rt and I take our position opposite one another and wait for the fight to begin.

"Chod has made a name for himself across Mythos, but it pales in comparison to the legend of Drizz'rt. There's a saying amongst the rogues of Pruxford that if Drizz'rt has marked you, you're already dead. Let's see how well brute strength matches up against the skills of a trained killer, shall we?"

The crowd cheers, and the countdown begins. Drizz'rt stares at me from across the arena. He wears a leather vest that reveals his slender but muscled golden arms. Half a dozen daggers are strapped to each side, and several amulets are tucked inside the vest. A shortsword hangs from his hip and more daggers are strapped along his form-fitting pants. His tail flicks back and forth like he's ready to pounce.

The countdown hits zero, and I summon three horrors in quick succession. Almost as soon as they appear, they vanish in a puff of smoke as Drizz'rt hits each one with a well-placed dagger. He's seen the buffs my horrors give me and he's not going to let me take advantage of them.

I've still got a nice health buff from the Regeneration Triad, and I keep the massive shield out in front of me as I try to close the gap. When I'm within spitting distance, Drizz'rt makes his move.

He charges straight at me, catching me off guard. I position myself behind the shield and ready my spear. He continues his push, and I jab once he's in range. The assassin spins out of the attack and runs up my shield, launching himself from the top and hitting me in the shoulder with two daggers as he backflips away.

I grimace as I pull the daggers out and the wounds continue to burn. The distraction leaves me open to two more attacks in my bicep and chest. I duck behind the shield, using it as cover as I remove the weapons buried in my body. With the twenty-percent regeneration buff, my wounds should heal without issue, but once the blades are out, nothing happens. Instead, the wounds continue to sting, and my health actually trickles down.

Dammit! I've been poisoned.

I could use my Tiger's Eye Pendant to clear the poison, but I'm sure he has plenty more coated with poison so I can't waste it. Going into a rage will cancel the poison as well, but I'm holding on to that card for now. I've got enough health that I can spare to lose a little.

For now.

Standing up, I keep as much of my body behind the shield as possible. I summon more horrors behind me, using Sacrifice before Drizz'rt has a chance to kill them.

He circles around me, keeping his distance from my spear. I'm twice his size, but somehow, it feels like I'm the prey.

Drizz'rt uses his doppelgänger ability, forming two clones to each side of him. I've seen this attack before against Randy, so I turn around, ready for the assassin's sneak attack.

Pain flares along my back as several blades stab into me. I turn around, unable to tell which of the doppelgängers is the real Drizz'rt when fresh pain flares through my back again.

I roar, swinging wildly with my spear to clear some space. My health drops faster than ever with a half-dozen daggers buried in my back. Drizz'rt explodes a vial at my feet, and smoke fills the area as all four assassins swarm me.

I can't see anything as the wounds in my back surge with pain and then relief as the blades are pried from my flesh, followed by more burning and a fresh wave of cuts along my arms and legs. I try to run from the smoke, but it follows me as the assassin continues to pick me apart. There's no way I can beat him on speed alone, so I need to show him something he's not prepared for.

I summon three horrors and cast Kamikaze while they surround me. The damage pushes my health into the red, but I hit Drizz'rt as well. He grunts, revealing his position, and I swing the spear until I hit something firm. I summon Pharos as soon as I do.

The spirit guide pushes back the smoke, revealing the assassin as he moves out of range. The brief encounter with the Horror of Vitality, before I exploded it, has slowed him for a few seconds. He's probably still faster than me even with a twenty-percent slow, but this is my chance. I activate Berserker Rage and go on the attack.

The poison vanishes from my body and my healing kicks into overdrive. I chase after Drizz'rt, but he uses the terrain to his advantage, jumping from boulder to boulder like Jordy. When the slow wears off, he stops on top of a giant emerald and pulls out his sword, gesturing for me to attack.

I swipe at his legs with the spear and he jumps, flipping through the air and landing behind me.

This time, I'm ready, letting the momentum of my attack carry me around just in time for my shield to block his swing. The sword grates against the metal shield, and I counter with a spear jab loaded with Concussive Force. He sidesteps it again and again as I press the attack.

Even with the added stats from my rage, at best this is a draw. As soon as it ends, he'll pick me apart again. I toss the shield aside and put everything I have into attacking, jabbing, and swinging with two hands, but I still can't manage to land a hit.

When my rage ends, I stand there heaving.

Drizz'rt sheaths his sword and takes out two daggers, spinning them against his palm. He grins. "Good effort, but it's over. There's nothing left to save you."

I stab the spear into the sand and take a few steps back, equipping Destroyer. The weight of the warhammer feels more natural than anything else I own.

I ready my next ability. "Why don't you come and find out?"

His tail flicks, and he takes a few steps in my direction—slowly this time, like he's savoring the moment. "Do you want this to end quick, or should I drag it—"

The spear jabs through his throat from behind, and blood pours down his neck. His eyes are full of surprise as his jaw opens and closes, blood gurgling in his throat as he tries to speak.

I take a step closer, dusting sand off his shoulder. "Quick works for me."

Behind him, Arty releases the spear, and Drizz'rt topples on his face as the cannons boom.

"Would you look at that, folks! And here I thought rogues were sneaky. It looked like Drizz'rt was about to have this one in the bag, and then Chod uses Champion to summon a copy of the challenger he defeated in the previous round."

The crowd's roar is deafening. For a moment, I close my eyes and listen. There's electricity in the air, and it dwarfs anything I've ever experienced streaming or at an in-person tournament. This is special.

I open my eyes and pump my fist in the air. I'm in the finals, baby!

When I arrive back at the booth, Limery and Ethan stand on opposite sides. Limery scowls at the warlock, but when he sees me, his expression changes into a giant smile. Ethan purses his lips but says nothing.

"Chods! Yous dids it!" He shakes his small body in the air as he dances and sings. "Chods is going to the finals. Chods is going to the finals."

I take a seat once he finishes. "How are you feeling?"

"Limmy was tireds, but Limmy feels better nows."

"Good." I lean in close. "To beat him, you can't afford any mistakes. I'm sure he has some moves that we haven't seen, so keep your guard up. You're stronger than I realized, but he's cunning."

He nods, then his eyes narrow as he glances at Ethan. "Limmy is going to hurts the bad mans."

I hope he does.

Once their introductions are over, the two step onto the platform. After witnessing Limery's last match, I wonder if Ethan is nervous at all. If he is, he doesn't show it. He's as composed as ever, arms tucked behind his back as the platform slowly descends.

For the first time today, I'm completely alone in the booth. As they take their positions, my pulse races. Sitting back and watching as Limery takes on a warlock backed by some powerful being, I'm more nervous than I have been for my own fights.

I just hope Limery has enough left in the tank.

Not that long ago, I woke up to Limery's bulbous eyes inches from my own as he tried to steal my necklace. But ever since that funny, caring, annoying, mischievous, greedy little imp has come into my life, everything has changed. If only the other heroes had that same kind of experience, then maybe they wouldn't hesitate giving everything they have to keep from losing it.

The fight begins, and Limery is instantly on the attack, hurling fireball after fireball at Ethan as the warlock moves through the air on shadowy wings. His tattoos glow as he tries to counter the imp's aggression by casting spells of his own. Limery flies through the air like a hummingbird, zigging and zagging. Fireballs and dark lightning shoot across the arena as the two dance high above the ground.

Fighting solely in the air forces both to switch up their usual style. Ethan can't exactly summon demons to fight on his behalf unless they have wings, and I'm beginning to think there's a long cooldown on the flying shadow demons since we haven't seen them since the first round. Limery is without his Fire Wall that high up, but it doesn't seem like much of a hindrance so far.

Ethan is nowhere near as fast as the imp, taking several hits without landing any of his own. Limery sticks to what's working, flying circles around the warlock and attacking from all angles. He does it for so long that the announcer runs out of commentary.

The entire arena is quiet except for the whir of magical attacks. Their fight slowly rises higher and higher until they are fighting above the lower-level stands.

Limery manages to whittle the warlock down to half of his HP with no signs of slowing down.

Then forty percent.

Thirty.

Twenty.

"This matchup is unfolding in a way none of us expected. Is there anything Ethan can do or are we watching his slow but inevitable demise?"

I can't help but wonder the same thing. Did Ethan blow his most powerful abilities in the earlier rounds? My Champion ability has a six-hour cooldown, and I'm sure that some of his are much longer.

"What's this? Is Limery finally going for the kill shot?"

My chest tightens as Limery goes molten in front of Ethan.

No, no, no, no, no. Dammit! Stick to what's working. I don't like this one bit.

Limery darts at Ethan, smashing into the warlock's shoulder before zooming off. Ethan tumbles through the air before regaining his bearings, just in time for Limery to smash into him from the backside, sending him spinning once again.

Three more times, Limery hits him like a flaming fastball until the warlock is at ten percent health.

"Now finish him off."

Limery dives again, just as a shroud of black energy surrounds Ethan and a dark, clawed hand the size of the warlock's body reaches out from the void. It plucks Limery from the air, holding his flaming body still as Ethan casts Essence Drain.

A line of black-and-purple energy forms between the imp and the warlock.

Limery burns brighter, but the hand doesn't release. When the warlock's spell activates, Limery's health plummets far quicker than Berry's did.

Ethan's health creeps up to twenty and then thirty percent as Limery's continues to fade.

Helpless, I clench my fists until my claws dig into my palms and blood trickles into a pool around my feet.

Limery's fire dims as his health drops into the red, and his bulbous eyes grow heavy. His body goes limp against the giant hand, and then it releases him.

I can't pull my eyes away as he falls lifelessly to the ground.

And then the cannons fire.

40. THE STORM

Ethan and I sit at opposite ends of the booth waiting for the intermission before the final match to end. A tinkerer has a contraption set up in the stands that shoots out bubbles two to three feet in diameter. An orchestra plays calming music as a wind mage sends the bubbles floating across the arena.

When they pop, the bubbles explode into a kaleidoscope of butterflies that flutter among the crowd.

The sun dips near the horizon, and the sky streaks with lilac and magenta, the perfect backdrop to the jeweled outline of the Crystal Arena. By the time our fight starts, I expect it will be almost nightfall.

The music fades, and the announcer begins our introductions.

"What a day! What a day. This has truly been one of the most exciting Champion's Tournaments in recent memory. We've seen some impressive displays of both might and magic, none greater than the two finalists about to take the stage.

"When rumors first began spreading that heroes had returned to the Isle of Mythos, I think most of us were skeptical, to say the least. After all, it had been ages since the last hero was recorded. Many wondered if this new breed of hero could measure up to the legends that came before them. Could they right the wrongs of Mythos and tackle the challenges no one else could? After today, I think we can agree that these heroes are the real deal. So, let's all cheer for the new age of heroes, and enjoy the match between Chod and Ethan!"

We step onto the platform outside our booth, and the crowd cheers even louder. I wave to them, but Ethan keeps his eyes focused on the battlefield. Caustic leaps onto his hind legs when I wave at him, and Breebis wrestles him back to his seat. I take a quick glance at those who have been eliminated and spot Limery sitting on Arty's shoulder. The imp waves with one hand while he devours a meat skewer with the other.

After a few moments in the spotlight, I tune out the distractions. I have a fight to win, and I need everything I have focused on taking out Ethan.

We take our positions on the battlefield, and the announcer keeps going, recounting our fights in vivid detail. The sky has now faded to a deep purple, and the gemstones around the arena flicker to life like old lampposts, each one producing a dull glow.

Time seems to grind to a halt as we wait for the announcer to finish, but then the barrier surrounding the battlefield shimmers slightly as the roar of the crowd abruptly cuts off, leaving us in an uneasy silence.

There's a slight pop as I summon my horrors, followed by their grumbling.

Ethan and I stare at each other from across the platform. This is it. My chance to show everyone why they should be on our side. After watching him dismantle Taryn and then Limery, though, I doubt anyone has their bets on me.

A dark aura surrounds the warlock as he hovers several feet off the ground. His shadowy wings extend behind him, flapping gently as they hold him aloft. I wish I had a better idea of his cooldowns, so I could know what to expect. As it is, I'll have to play this like all his cards are on the table.

I hold the Shield of Vigor in front with one hand, and the Renewal Spear in the other. I'm much more comfortable with my warhammer, but with the full set active, I can drag this battle out forever as long as I can hit something to replenish my health. I'm going to need to close the gap to do so, which won't be easy considering Ethan can fly. Not to mention figuring out how to deal with any new demons he may introduce.

He hasn't summoned any of the flying shadow demons since the first round—maybe they're still on cooldown or limited to once per day. I doubt that he's shown us all his tricks, though, and I can't help but feel like there's something big he's been holding on to.

Ethan smirks. "You really think you have a shot? The druid is gone. The imp is gone. There's no one here to save you this time."

I summon more horrors as I slowly approach. "I'll take my chances."

"I admire your spirit, but this isn't a fight you can win." He laughs. "The game's over."

He moves his hands in front of him, drawing symbols in the air that leave a trail of glowing energy. When he finishes, two rifts form in the air behind him, each one about six feet tall. They pulse with an energy much more vibrant than any of the previous portals he's opened.

I grab a Horror of Finesse and toss it by the horns at the warlock. With a flick of his wrist, a beam of dark energy explodes the horror mid-air.

There's a ripping sound, like tearing fabric, as the rift grows larger. Blinding white energy spills from within, similar to the portals that connect the kingdoms. Water gushes through as the tear widens. The smell of saltwater fills the air, then the rift splits further until the portal is several stories high and thousands of gallons of water rush into the arena like a dam just broke.

I jab my spear into the ground to hold my position as water pounds me, but my horrors wash away to the back of the arena. Water splashes all around me, and I inhale the salty mist.

What the hell is he doing, summoning some kind of sea monster?

Thunder roars from the other side of the portal as it expands a final time. Two large pirate ships break through, crashing against the arena floor and dislodging some of the gemstone boulders. Massive black sails adorn each ship, emblazoned with the symbol of the Blacktide portal—two curved horizontal lines with a vertical slash going through each.

Shit, did he really just open a portal from Pruxford to Blacktide?

Each ship is full of creatures that look like trolls but with more slender frames, smaller ears, and less defined jawlines. Sea orcs. They're almost like a cross between a forest troll and a seaside troll, but with more goblin-like features. Their skin is sea-foam green with streaks or patches of black that give them a sinister appearance. Each one has a weathered look about them, and they sport a variety of facial piercings. Their noses are hooked, and their lips turn up in a permanent snarl. Short tusks help to frame their pointy jaws. Each orc wears tattered black clothing, and almost every one of them has a cutlass at their waist.

They hang over the edges of the ships, snarling and yelling, waving weapons in the air. More hang from the masts and crow's nests. These ships are massive, so it's impossible to tell how many are aboard.

Water continues to pour through the portals like a geyser. Pretty soon, I'll be swimming around the arena.

What the hell is he trying to do?

A cannon blast erupts, only this time it's from within the battlefield. A flaming projectile shoots from one of the ships and explodes against the barrier meant to protect the crowd.

On the other side, the crowd panics. Gnomes climb over one another as they race for the exits, and the guards in the council booth draw their weapons.

This is definitely not part of the tournament.

"What are you playing at, Ethan?" I shout over the boom of more cannons as streaks blast through the night.

The barrier ripples against the impact, but it holds for now.

Ethan unleashes a demon bolt, and it explodes against my shield. "You think I care about some tournament? This is only the beginning—just a taste of the terror coming your way if you continue to meddle. A storm is coming, and there's nothing that you or anyone else can do to stop it." He grins and it fades to a scowl as he flies between the masts of the two ships and points at me. "Finish him!"

Sea orcs growl as they leap over the ship's railing.

"Oh, fuck."

Nearly two dozen orcs land in the water before I have the sense to get moving. I stow my weapons and run, summoning horrors and sending them on the attack behind me.

As I look over my shoulder, there are at least fifty sea orcs on the ground, all ranging between level fifteen and twenty. They continue to spill out, and for every one that jumps into the arena, another replaces it aboard the ship's deck.

The orcs cut through my horrors almost instantly, but the passive slow manages to hinder a few of them. As they are trampled, I put a little more distance between me and the horde. There's no way I can fight this many on my own.

Cannons continue to fire, shooting some sort of magical projectiles at the barrier. For now, it continues to hold strong with all but one of the shield mages positioned outside of the arena.

What I don't understand is that if this is an attack, why is no one helping? The guards are on alert and there's commotion in the council booth, but they aren't doing anything.

So far, I don't have a plan, so I continue running, trying to put as much distance between me and the orcs as possible.

Then I see the booth with the defeated challengers. If they join in, maybe we can push the orcs back through the portal before anyone gets hurt.

The shield mage responsible for their protection stands at attention, not a care in the world as invaders launch an attack on Pruxford.

Something large moves in my peripheral, and I look up to see Caustic clawing at the barrier. He flaps his wings, biting and clawing at the invisible shield. Breebis holds the leash, trying to pull him back, but he attacks like a rabid animal. He must know this isn't like the other fights. The barrier ripples around his attacks, and I wish he was with me right now.

Once I'm close enough, I shout at the shield mage protecting the challenger's booth. "Let them out! We're under attack."

"I have orders." He frowns, his voice stern. "No one is allowed on the battlefield until the match is over."

"Are you stupid? Does this look like part of the match to you?" I point at the hoard of approaching orcs. "What do you think happens to you once they kill me?"

He glances between the orcs and the challengers, where Taryn and Arty beat against the shield surrounding their booth, yelling for their release. I wonder if they could break it if they tried.

"Goddammit." I can hear the grunt of the sea orcs as they get close. "I'm screwed, and then you're fucked."

I reequip the Regeneration Triad and try not to think about the impending pain. I bang the spear against the shield as I backpedal around the edge of the battlefield, trying to gain their attention so that none of them go after the idiotic mage.

They follow, and I greet the first sea orc with a spear to the throat. Ram Rage sends out a ripple of splash damage into the orcs behind him, lowering their health by a fraction. A second orc slices at me with its cutlass, but I block it with my shield and follow up with Concussive Force. The hit knocks the orc back, stunning it and sending splash damage to those behind. More try to swarm me, but I kick, jab, and deflect their attacks as best I can. Though I manage to keep them from surrounding me, cuts well up all over my body.

My health drops with each wound I take. Once the Renewal Spear has a full charge, I activate it and gain a burst of health. Every time I summon a Horror of Finesse, my next attack heals me again. Combined with Concussive Force's knockback, I'm a pain in the ass, but even with nine-thousand HP, I'm losing more than I'm gaining.

I continue maneuvering around the arena to keep the horde in front of me, but I know that I can't do this forever. Not against this many enemies.

As I run to my next position, Caustic is still going crazy against the barrier. His section of the stands has completely vacated except for Breebis. I'm thankful she's not leaving him alone, but Caustic can protect himself. I'm not so sure about Breebis.

A blade rips into my calf from behind and I stumble to one knee. If I don't use Berserker Rage now, I'm done for.

I activate the ability and the wound stitches itself together in seconds. My muscles bulge, and my health immediately begins to replenish. I swing the shield in an arc, dislocating one orc's jaw and clearing space. Once I'm on my feet, I use the shield like a battering ram, shattering bones and sending orcs flying until I have enough room to fight.

My attacks are faster, and I skewer several orcs until a pile of bodies lies around me. But not enough. It's never enough.

Once my rage is nearly over, I reposition, letting the orcs come to me. I back into a boulder I didn't see and the orcs press in on me. Curved blades tear into my skin until even my increased healing can't keep up.

My health drops, and just as my rage ends, I receive a notification.

Alert! *Caustic has initiated Draconic Convergence. Accepting Draconic Convergence will create a permanent bond between the dragon and its chosen counterpart. Do you accept?*

I accept, and a wave of anger and panic unlike anything I have ever experienced flares through me. More notifications come through, but I can't focus on anything other than the crippling pain and overwhelming emotions.

In the distance, cannons continue to fire. And then a mighty roar cuts above it all.

An anger that isn't mine continues to rage inside of me, like it's superimposed over my own thoughts. There's a heavy pressure against my body, and then orcs are ripped away. Caustic's neck whips as he tosses them aside. When he sees me alive, I feel his panic turn to relief, but the rage burns even hotter. Orcs run from the intimidating monster. He unleashes a stream of toxic gas to both sides and steps in front of me like a lioness protecting her cubs. The orcs retreat, but Caustic arches his back and spews green gas that shrouds them as they run back to the ship.

The air crackles as a fireball flies past us. Time seems to slow as the fireball hits the gas and orc body parts explode across the arena. Chunks of flesh splash into the water all around us.

I search for the source of the fireball and see Limery speeding toward me while the challengers continue to climb through one of Don's portals from the booth to the battlefield. The shield mage argues with them but doesn't try to stop it otherwise. Don allows everyone through but Otis and Kevin, closing the portal before they can step through.

"Fuck you, buddy." Randy flashes the shield mage a crude gesture as he runs toward the chaos, Drizz'rt by his side. He raises his sword. "Let's fuck up some orcs!"

"Is yous okays, Chods?" Limery presses his small hands to my face.

Before I have a chance to respond, Taryn hands me a potion. "Drink this." He looks out at the chaos. "What the hell is happening?"

Berry and Jordy stand protectively behind him.

I take a gulp of the sweet red liquid, and the pain ebbs as my health recovers even faster than normal. "This is Valmar using Ethan to make his presence known. We need to stop them before they break the barrier and get into the city."

Taryn looks out at the chaos. "I think we've got a few people down for the cause."

A massive wave carries Tozzet across the watery battlefield like he's some godly merfolk surfer. His hands glow and a larger wave swells behind him. He rides the pipeline as waves curl around him, avoiding the tidal wave as it surges past, completely obliterating the remaining orcs as they retreat. But there's still a multitude waiting for us aboard the ship.

I crawl to my feet, pointing my spear toward the ship. "Let's go!"

We come upon Scotty, the sniper, as he kneels in the water charging the same attack that he tried on me in the first round. Only this time, he succeeds. The arrow elongates and tendrils of energy curl around the shaft as he releases it. The spear-sized arrow flies like a javelin, skewering three orcs on the bow of one ship.

There's a loud explosion as part of the barrier protecting the crowd shatters. Screams and blaring alarms from outside suddenly fill the battlefield, along with the announcer's voice as he tries to maintain order among the chaos. Ballistae clank as they fire giant grappling hooks into the stands, and the orcs begin crossing using a pulley system.

"We are under attack. I repeat, Pruxford is under attack. Please remain calm and exit the arena in a safe and orderly fashion. Shield mages are attempting to contain the threat within the arena, and city guards are mobilizing around the Pruxford portal. Whatever you do, stay out of the streets. I repeat, the city is under attack. Find a safe space and remain calm until the threat is under control."

Sea orcs zip across the ropes like they've practiced this a million times. Once in the stands, they kill indiscriminately. One of the shield mages dies while trying to maintain her shield, causing another piece of the barrier to fall.

More grappling hooks land among the stands. Magic explodes as the guards, councilmembers, and heads of state join the fight.

Good. We've got enough problems down here.

Ethan hovers above the two ships, casting spells at the challengers who have decided to fight back. Some of the sea orcs have crossbows, and there appears to be at least one mage or cleric on each of the ships casting buffs on the others.

"Limery, I want you to stick with Caustic. Everywhere he blows gas, hit it with a fireball. Burn those ships to the ground."

Limery flies over to Caustic and perches behind the dragon's antlers. "Come on, Caustics! Let's burn those shipses to the grounds!"

Caustic looks at me, and I can feel his affirmation as he takes flight. I can already tell this bond is going to make everything smoother between us. It's like I can feel what he's thinking without the need for words.

The announcer addresses us directly. *"Challengers, if you can hear this, hit those ships with everything you have. Destroy their weapons and do not let any more orcs breach the barrier. The council and guards are mounting an offensive to take back the upper arena. Gods be with you."*

Caustic swoops over the ship, releasing a dense green stream of gas. A second later, Limery sets it aflame. The explosion rocks the arena and topples one of the masts, but the water pouring through the portals quickly extinguishes it.

"I got this!" Don forms a void portal in front of one of Ethan's portal with its counterpoint near Tozzet to funnel the rushing water directly to the tidal mage.

"Hit the ship again!" the void mage shouts, and Caustic and Limery take another pass. This time, they set the ship ablaze.

Taryn casts Lightning and Moonbeam, and orcs leap from the burning ships where Randy, Drizz'rt, Arty, Roddick, Reddick, and the drunken master all wait to dish out some physical punishment. I continuously summon horrors and send them on the attack.

"That's it, the barrier is almost re—" the announcer's voice cuts off mid-sentence as the shield mages manage to repair the barrier.

A few dozen orcs remain trapped on the other side against city guards and the council. Even from down here, I can see the orc bodies speckling the stands. One of the earth mages topples a giant emerald pillar, and it crushes a handful of orcs.

Kazzandre chops at the hull with her axe, wood crunching beneath each blow. She lets out a groan as one of the orcs leans over the edge of the ship with a crossbow, hitting her in the shoulder.

I'm about to toss my spear at the orc when Sam the monk runs past. The watercolor outline of a tiger forms over his arm, and the air ripples beneath his bare feet as he wind-walks up to the ship's deck like he's climbing stairs two at a time. The tiger superimposed over his arm roars as he punches the crossbow-wielding orc with enough force that it flies across the ship, cracking one of the masts.

I run to Kazzandre, joining her attack and smashing the hull with Destroyer. Together, we break through the wood, forming a hole big enough for several gnome challengers to enter. I send in a few horrors alongside them for the surprise attack.

On the opposite ship, Lanxkuri wreaks havoc with her blood magic, using the fiery corpses against those that still survive.

Jason sneaks around the edge of the arena, forming steps with his Cube of Protection as he and Tommy scale the ship. For a moment, I think they're about to attack the orcs, but then they both disappear through Ethan's portal back to Blacktide.

Ethan dodges a blast of holy light from Michael the paladin, and it sizzles against the deck of the ship. The warlock hovers in front of the portal over the ship on the right.

"This isn't over!" he shouts, as he casts a demon bolt at the paladin. Then he flies through the portal and it blips closed.

With Ethan gone, the sea orcs are no match for the challengers that remain. The smell of burned corpses and saltwater is overwhelming. We manage to take one of the captains alive, but he refuses to talk, so Taryn binds him with the vines of his Sapling Staff until one of the guards can escort him to the palace dungeon for more thorough questioning.

Once the fight in the upper arena is over, the shield mages cancel the barrier and the heads of state make their way down to the arena floor with the council to inspect the damage.

Oruma, the mesmer, points out where the portals were to the bureaucrats as Taryn and I join them.

Dezmin, the head of the gnomish council, barks out orders to a handful of palace guides that follow him around. His normally-friendly face is contorted in a mixture of despair and anger. "I want Ethan marked as a wanted man across all of Mythos. I want the Pruxford portal guarded by no less than a hundred soldiers at all times. For this to happen in Pruxford, of all places... Gods help us."

The horned lizardfolk from Ellynmylly kicks a piece of wreckage, shaking his head. "How is this possible? There's not a mage alive capable of opening a portal from Blacktide to Pruxford. There hasn't been a new portal constructed since the Age of Mages, and to open them on a whim..."

I push my way to the front of the group. With the devastation surrounding us, my word will never have this much weight again. "This is what we have been trying to tell you. Valmar is still alive. He's growing stronger. He's testing you. King Orso believes a war is coming, and he wants to be prepared when it does."

"Now is not the time," Dezmin snaps. "Can't you see we have a crisis to deal with? If you hadn't let the warlock escape, then maybe we would have answers right now."

"Me?" I clench my fists, but it's not me who shouts back.

"Enough!" Felston's voice booms over his superior, and his eyes narrow above his bulbous nose. "I've had enough of your arrogance, Dezmin. You were warned of this threat, and yet you did nothing. I told you of the behemoth in Seascape, and you chose to brush it off. You can no longer afford to bury your head in the sand. How many lives were lost today because you chose to do nothing? How much blood is on my hands because I let you? You're angry and full of hate for those that attacked our city? Good! It's about time you took this seriously. But don't you dare take it out on those who risked their own lives to stop this atrocity. If not for Chod and his dragon, and everyone else still here that fought for our entertainment today, our losses would have been much greater."

The arena is so quiet that the crackling, burning embers of the wreckage are the loudest sound.

"You're right." Dezmin sighs. "I am sorry. I failed spectacularly, and it will forever stain my legacy. I should have listened to you, Felston. Your council has always been wise beyond measure. I just hope it is not too late to right the wrongs I have made."

"What do we do now?" asks one of the catfolk from Antadale.

"We act." Dezmin snaps his fingers, and palace guides scurry in front of him. "Send a message to every kingdom informing them of what has happened. Send special instructions to Seascape, Vanaria, and any kingdom not present today that there will be a meeting in Pruxford and many heads of state are already here. Tell them we request their attendance. If a war is coming, then it is time we prepare."

Taryn and I exchange glances. War. Somehow that three-letter word fills me simultaneously with hope and dread.

EPILOGUE

The aftermath of the attack is more bureaucracy than anything, and most of the challengers leave to get some much-needed rest. Even though the other leaders aren't here yet, the heads of state have been meeting with the gnomish council since we left the arena.

Those of us that remain sit on the steps of the Crystal Palace, looking out over the city. The streets are empty except for the city watch patrolling. You'd never know the chaos from earlier just by looking.

This wasn't an invasion. It was a terror attack, and it worked. You can see it on the face of every leader, like the boogeyman they heard about for so long turned out to be real. Maybe now we can all take this seriously.

Two shield mages and an earth mage died in the attack on the arena, along with nearly fifty attendees. A second attack inside the city left hundreds more dead. The sea orcs blindsided the citizens as they funneled through the city portal. With most of the guards stationed at the arena, it was a bloodbath. No one was prepared for the attack.

Otis and Kevin disappeared, along with the shield mage responsible for the booth they were in. Nobody seems to know if he went willingly or not. No one has seen Richard the cleric since then either.

"I don't know if anyone else could have held off the orcs long enough for us to get in the fight." Arty pats me on the shoulder. "Congrats on bonding with Caustic, by the way. It couldn't have come a moment too soon."

"Thanks, I just wish we were never in this position to begin with." I laugh dryly. "All of this just to get a meeting with the council."

"We did it, though. Everyone is finally on the same page." Taryn stands in front of us a few steps down, Flubs arching from one hand to another like a slinky. "Nothing we can do now but wait for the others to arrive. Maybe explore a few dungeons in the meantime. Speaking of which, that was crazy with Caustic. One minute, he's clawing at the barrier; the next, he's flying straight through it. What kind of new abilities does bonding with a dragon unlock?"

Caustic lays on the marble platform next to me, his giant head resting in my lap. His thoughts are calm and content. It's going to be strange getting used to having his feelings merged with my own.

I smile as I stroke his snout. "I was pinned beneath a mountain of orcs, and I got a notification saying that Caustic was initiating Draconic Convergence. I guess bonding was his choice all along. The next thing I know, he was saving me, and I could kind of feel what he was feeling, if that makes sense. Like if someone could accurately explain what they were thinking, but without words, just feelings. Honestly, I haven't checked any of the other notifications with everything that has happened."

Taryn raises an eyebrow. "Well, what are you waiting for?"

I pull up my notifications, and the first thing I notice is that I have a new message. Who in the world would be sending me a message at a time like this? I focus on the icon, and the message appears across my vision.

Incoming Message (Admin): *Chad, I apologize but believe me when I tell you that this was out of my control. -Valery*

I stare at the message, wondering what she could possibly mean. Did Valery have something to do with the attack today? How is that even possible? And why? I close out the message and notice there's a tab I haven't seen before. It pulses slowly.

Message Requests.

That's odd. Let me guess, it's probably Ethan or Otis trying to get in a few last words. I focus on the tab, and it expands. When I see the name of the sender, my heart skips a beat and I find it hard to breathe. The world goes quiet, and a dull ringing fills the silence.

Message Request: Dorothy Jordan

The woman I raged at to get me sent here? What? This doesn't make any sense. How is she able to send messages to me in-game? Is this what Valery meant when she said something was out of her control?

I focus on the message, and a wall of text appears across my vision.

Incoming Message (Dorothy Jordan): *Chad, Chad, Chad. I wondered what had happened to you. Your sentence passed and I kept wondering if I'd see you streaming again. When I didn't, I thought that maybe your little stint in rehab had finally put you in your place. Maybe you'd given up being a jackass for entertainment for good. Truth be told, that thought brought me solace.*

Imagine my surprise when I get a call from someone claiming to be the head of Mythos Gaming telling me he has a once-in-a-lifetime opportunity for me.

Funny how the world works, isn't it?

Now, I know the truth as to why no one has heard from you. Looks like little ol' daddy saved your ass again, didn't he? Not that I should be surprised. There's no such thing as justice in this world. You got to run away to this game, while I continued to deal with the fallout of your actions.

After you humiliated me on the stream, my crying face became a meme. After the trial, it went viral. Imagine that—your lowest moment posted across the internet for laughs, haunting you everywhere you go.

And when your little band of troll followers no longer had you to entertain them, they joined my stream, harassing me to the point that I had to shut it down.

But now, here I am, and I finally see what the fuss is all about. You got lucky being sent here. But I wouldn't get too comfortable, Chad. Payback's a bitch.

My entire being feels like I'm encased in ice. Caustic stirs, now able to sense my unrest.

I don't understand how any of this is possible. How is she here? And more importantly, why? What possible reason could Mythos Gaming have for bringing her into this world?

SENTENCED TO TROLL 6

NOTABLE CHARACTERS AND LOCATIONS

Main Party:
Chad Johnson (AKA Chod)- Forest Troll. Barbarian/Summoner. Hero of the forest, mountain, and arctic trolls.

Limery- Imp. Everyone's favorite character. Talks like he lived in a cave for hundreds of years guarding his "Precious."

Caustic- Juvenile green dragon. Bonded with Chod via Draconic Convergence.

Pharos- Chod's Spirit Guide (frost goat).

Taryn Jones- Ebony dwarf. Shadow druid. Chod's best friend.

Berry (pet)- Umber bear.

Ruby (pet)- Jackal.

Jordy (pet)- Frost goat.

Flubs (pet)- Forest slime. Sometimes absorbs a cat skeleton and takes on the appearance of a spooky gelatinous feline.

Notable Heroes:
Pressley Allen- Death knight
Randy Billson- Rogue
Michael Didato- Paladin
Don Othello- Void mage
Scotty Heyden- Sniper
Sam Taylor- Monk
Jon Bailey- Enchanter
Richard Hummel- Cleric
Otis Wiggins- Barbarian
Ethan French- Warlock

Kevin Harris- Sorcerer
Jude Duggan- Warrior
Glenn Orickson- Warrior
Dorothy Jordan- ???

Isle of Mythos:
    King Orso Brightgaze- Blood dwarf. King of Seascape.
    King Favian- Human. King of Vanaria
    Kurzol- Blood dwarf. Cleric. King Orso's advisor.
    Warwick- Human. Captain of King Favian's kingsguard.
    Lord Kassidy- Human. Teleportation mage.
    Lady Brollen- Ebony dwarf. Ice mage. Leader of Sandholde.
    Hawkin- Human. Bard. Ringmaster of the Underground Circus.
    Lillith- Imp. Limery's mother.
    Bazel- Imp. Limery's father.
    Leo- Imp. Limery's brother.

Forest Trolls:
    Chief Rizza- Chieftain of the forest trolls. Wyrm rider.
    Yashi- Potions master/archer. Wyrm rider. Smallest of the forest trolls.
    Ismora- Weapons master.
    Tormara- Councilmember. Wyrm rider.
    Gord- Councilmember. Guardian troll.
    Jira- Shaman. (Phoenix totem)
    Malak- Guardian troll.
    Jojin- Guardian troll.
    Watu- Guardian troll.

Mountain Trolls:
    Kronan- Former chieftain of the mountain trolls.
    Brutus- Kronan's second-in-command.
    Cheevus- Goblin. Leader of the goblins that formerly served the mountain trolls. They now follow Chief Rizza and the wyrms. Rides a mangy wolf.

Seaside Trolls:
    Chief Lida- Chieftain of the Seaside trolls.
    Imoko- Seaside troll who captured Chod when they stumbled upon the seaside troll village.

. . .

Arctic Trolls:
   Chief Laojin- Chieftain of the arctic trolls.
   Senzala- Shaman. (White dragon totem)
   Nesira- White dragon that roams the mountains of Frostmoor. Senzala's totem.

Goldspire:
   Jegaar- Wolfkin. Battle scholar.
   Portia Swiftwill- Foxkin.
   Dakota- Minotaur. Gladiator.
   Festa Forgetooth- Tiger beastkin. Emperor of Goldspire.

Wandermere:
   Swift Thundercrest- Centaur. Leader of the Wandermere Herd.
   Daimun Stonewhisper- Centaur. Wandermere scout.
   Sylvie Redmane- Centaur. Wandermere scout.
   Thannis Smokehoof- Centaur. Wandermere scout.

Pruxford:
   Dezmin Dreamwader- Gnome. Head of the Pruxford Council.
   Felston Boonspan- Gnome. Pruxford Councilmember.
   Breebis- Gnome. Owner of the Rusty Bucket Stable.

Tournament Challengers:
   Arty- Cyclops. Warrior.
   Roddick- Human. Arty's adopted brother.
   Reddick- Human. Arty's adopted brother.
   Drizz'rt- Lizardfolk. Assassin.
   Tozzet Girok- Merfolk. Tidal mage.
   Kazzandre Strongback- Giant. Warrior.
   Lanxkuri- Catfolk. Blood mage.

Shadowlands:
   Valmar Worren- Elf. Wizard/necromancer. Ruler of Mosstar. BBEG (Big Bad
Evil Guy).

Kingdoms:
   Seascape- Home of the Dwarves
   Vanaria- Home of the Humans

Goldspire- Home of Beastkin

Frostmoor- Home of the Mountain Tribes

Wandermere- Home of the Centaurs, known for its ancient forest

Pruxford- Home of the Gnomes, known as the City of Glass

Antadale- Home of the Catfolk

Mistville- Home of the Merfolk

Ellynmylly- Home of Elves, Halflings, Giants, and many others. Known as the Melting Pot of Mythos

Shadowlands- An area shrouded in perpetual darkness. Home to creatures of shadow. Over the ages, its darkness has spread to surrounding lands, enveloping Mosstar, Blacktide, and others.

Mosstar- Home of the Elves

Blacktide- Home of the Seafaring Orcs

Characters from Outside Mythos:

Valery Barrett- Head of the Mythos Rehabilitation Project.

John Barrett- Valery's Father. Head of Mythos Games.

CURRENT STATS

Chod, Level 29 Barbarian/Summoner Forest Troll
HP: 7755/7755
Mana: 5000/5000
Rage: 0/1000
XP: 1,031,344/1,095,000

Strength: 46
Dexterity: 32
Constitution: 47
Intelligence: 10
Wisdom: 15
Charisma: 6

+1 Strength and Constitution racial bonus per level.
+1 Ability point per odd level.

2 stat points available.
1 ability points available.

Abilities:

. . .

Bite. *Using your massive tusks and powerful jaw, you take a bite out of an opponent, dealing immense damage. Cost: 10 rage. Level 2.*

Claw. *You attack with sharp claws, swiping at an opponent and dealing extra damage. Cost: 5 rage. Level 2.*

Intimidation. *You stare down your opponent, confusing them so that they are unable to attack for two seconds. Cost: 10 rage.*

Berserker Rage. *(Ultimate) Attacks and physical damage build your rage meter. 5 rage per attack. Rage meter deteriorates over time when out of combat at a rate of 5 rage per second. Activating Berserker Rage fills rage meter. For 30 seconds, rage meter does not decrease, deal increased damage, health regenerates at 5x the normal rate, cannot be stunned, slowed, or otherwise affected. Cooldown: 10 minutes.*

Increased Regeneration. *(Passive) Regenerate health at a faster rate. Level 2.*

Rapid Regeneration. *(Passive) When below 10% health, regeneration is doubled.*

Nightvision. *(Passive) Increased vision in darkness and low light.*

Thick Skin. *(Passive) Take 10% less damage from physical attacks.*

Savage. *(Passive) Ability to eat uncooked meat without consequences.*

Camouflage. *(Passive) When out of combat and not moving for 20 seconds, trolls blend in with their surroundings.*

Sweeping Slash. *Form a sweeping arc in front of you, dealing damage and knocking your opponent off balance. Cost: 5 rage.*

Conceal (Passive). *Hides level from anyone who is not a guard on city grounds.*

Summon Horror (Passive). *Ability to summon a horror. Each horror grants a unique ability. For every horror active, gain 1% increased damage and health points. Horrors decay 10% for every minute outside of combat.*

Horror of Power. *Summon a horror with 20% of your Strength. Cost: 100 mana. Cooldown: 30 seconds. Bonus: Your next attack deals double damage.*

Horror of Vitality. *Summon a horror with 20% of your health points. Cost: 100 mana. Cooldown: 30 seconds. Bonus: Opponents near Horror of Vitality are slowed by 20%.*

Horror of Finesse. *Summon a horror with 20% of your attack speed. Cost: 100 mana. Cooldown: 30 seconds. Bonus: Your next attack heals you for damage dealt.*

Sacrifice. *Sacrifice X amount of horrors to receive a temporary buff. Horror of Power: +1 Strength. Horror of Vitality: +1 Constitution. Horror of Finesse: +1 Dexterity*

Kamikaze. *Sacrifice a horror to deal a burst of damage.*

Champion. *Summon a copy of the most recent enemy you have defeated. Decays 10% every minute out of combat. Cost: 50% of mana pool. Cooldown: 6 hours.*

Spirit of the Beast. *The Spirit of the Beast path is composed of five phases.*

. . .

Phase 1: Spirit Inquiry. *A spirit animal is a guide from the spirit world, possessing traits similar to those of the individual. Unlocking one's spirit animal leads to a better understanding of the self and one's place within the world.*

> ***Spirit Animal:*** *Frost Goat*

Phase 2: Spirit Embodiment. *Bonding with a spirit beast is only the beginning of the Spirit of the Beast path. By finding an amulet that connects you to your beast, the bond between the two will grow stronger, unlocking further advancements.*

> ***Spirit Embodiment****: Ram Horns*

Phase 3: Spirit Enhancement. *Just as your body has undergone a change reflective of your spirit beast, your spirit may be enhanced in the same manner. Gain a new passive ability based on your spirit beast.*

> ***Spirit Enhancement:*** *Ram Rage: Barbarian rage now lasts twice as long. Physical attacks deal splash damage.*

Phase 4: Spirit Guide. *Your body and spirit have undergone great changes, but your bond with the spirit world is only beginning. Summon a spirit guide of your spirit beast.*

> ***Spirit Guide:*** *Summon a frost goat spirit guide. The spirit guides may lead you through darkness and guide you to locations you have previously visited, even if you do not know the way. Spirit guides may be consumed for a 50% increase to Wisdom for 10 minutes. Cooldown: 24 hours.*

Phase 5: Spirit Power. *The path of the beast is not for the faint of heart, and those who complete all five stages are blessed with a mighty power from their spirit beast.*

> ***Spirit Power:*** *Concussive Force: Physical attacks can be imbued with concussive force, knocking opponents back with a chance to stun them. Cost: 100 mana.*

Spirit of the Beast path complete.

Draconic Convergence: *The convergence fuses an unbreakable bond that grows stronger over time. No two convergences are the same, each one evolves based on the relationship between the dragon and their chosen counterpart.*

Name: *Caustic*

> ***Species:*** *Green Dragon*
> ***Level:*** *15*

Convergence Level:

1. *Draconic Bond- You have made an unbreakable bond with a dragon and forged a telepathic link that may expand in the future. In its current state, intense spikes in emotion may blend between psyches.*

Available Abilities *(1 ability point to unlock):*

Massive Bite. *Deals double damage. Cost: 20 rage.*

    Claws. *Swipe at opponent with both hands, dealing extra damage. Cost: 10 rage.*

    Multi Attack. *Bite and Claw at the same time. Cost: 20 rage.*

    Iron Will. *Immune to slows and stuns for 30 seconds. Cost: 50 rage. 180 second cooldown.*

    I'm Always Angry *(Passive. Available at level 10). Once rage meter is at 50%, it will not deteriorate below 50% when out of combat.*

    Perception. *For 10 minutes, gain increased awareness of your surroundings. Spot hidden objects, as well as unusual sounds, odors, and tastes. Cooldown: 6 hours.*

    Cleave. *Your next attack causes bleed damage, dealing 1% of opponent's health per second for 5 seconds. Cost: 10 rage.*

    Battle Cry. *You let out a ferocious roar, increasing rage by 20. No cost. 60 second cooldown.*

Class Advancements. *Upon reaching level 25, you have unlocked a class advancement. You may only advance one class at a time. A second class may not be advanced until completion of primary advancement.*

Summoner Advancement.

    Dreadbeasts. Unlock for further details.

    Dual Subclass. Unlock for further details.

Current Items:

Item. Phoenix Feather. 10% resistance to fire-based attacks. *A very rare item, phoenix feathers can only be gathered if they are willingly given by the host. Feathers plucked from unwilling birds turn to ash.*

    Item. Tiger's Eye Pendant. Removes one debuff. Cooldown: 10 minutes. *A rare stone believed to ward off evil and bring balance to life.*

Item. Aquatic Boots. *Allows user to walk on water.*

Item. Petrified Staff. An enchanted staff capable of taking on the properties of up to 3 attached stones. +3 Intelligence. +3 Wisdom. Bonus: *While holding Petrified Staff, the user can cast ranged physical attacks once every 10 seconds.*

Item. Forlorn Scepter. +5 Intelligence. *Increases the range of summoned creatures by 50%.*

Item. Glouwseeker Venom. *When injected into the bloodstream, glouwseeker venom immobilizes target. Length of stun dependent on size of target, resistances, and amount injected.*

Item. Sea Scorpion. +3 Strength. *An enchanted trident capable of taking on the property of 1 enchanted stone. Bonus: deals splash damage.*

Legendary Item. Angel of Death Brandy. *When drinker falls below 1HP, a metaphysical event will occur, rewinding time for the user to two seconds prior to death.*

Item. Brimming Tankard. *A magical tankard that, once filled, will never go empty. Warning: Once filled, contents cannot be changed. Only works on beverages.*

Item. Expandable Satchel. *A bag capable of holding enormous content and only burdening the wearer with ten percent of its weight. Simply focus on the item inside and it will appear in your hand.*

Item. Destroyer. An enchanted warhammer capable of taking on the properties of up to three stones. +2 Strength, +3 Constitution. *This ancient warhammer was forged in the heart of a volcano.* **Bonus Ability: Inferno.** *With each consecutive hit, Destroyer grows hotter, allowing it to warp or pierce through even the hardest metals. Multiplier works when hits are less than five seconds apart. Cost: 10 mana per attack. Cooldown: 10 sec.*

Item. Spaulder of Swiftness. +1 Constitution, +1 Dexterity. *Lightweight, durable leather mail designed to protect the off-hand shoulder during battle.*

Item. Halite Shield. *A lightweight translucent shield capable of taking damage without reducing visibility.*

Item. Frosted Buckler. +2 Constitution. *A lightweight and small shield capable of deflecting blows as well as being used offensively.* **Bonus Ability:** *Physical attacks blocked with Frosted Buckler cut attacker's Dexterity in half for ten seconds.*

Item. Dream Dust. *A powerful and potent substance capable of unlocking hidden realms of the mind. Effects are dependent upon amount ingested.*

Item. Sleep Dust. *Often mixed with liquid and drank as a tonic, sleep dust offers effects ranging from drowsiness to instant deep slumber.*

Item. Renewal Spear. *Capable of holding life aura equivalent to 500 HP. The Renewal Spear gathers aura passively while equipped and can steal health from enemies during battle. Life aura may be absorbed by the wielder at any time.* **Bonus:** *When paired with Regeneration Stone and Shield of Vigor, user will be granted a ten-foot aura that provides 20% increased regeneration for companions within its radius.*

Item. Shield of Vigor. *Increases HP by 30%.* **Bonus:** *When paired with Regeneration Stone and Renewal Spear, user will be granted a ten-foot aura that provides 20% increased regeneration for companions within its radius.*

Item. Regeneration Stone. *Increases health regeneration by 20%.* **Bonus:** *When* *paired with Shield of Vigor and Renewal Spear, user will be granted a ten-foot aura that provides 20% increased regeneration for companions within its radius.*

__Notice! Complete Set: Regeneration Triad.__ While wearing all three pieces of the Regeneration Triad, user will be granted a ten-foot aura that provides 20% increased regeneration for companions within its radius.

__Item. Nullification Bomb.__ Disable magical abilities of those within the blast radius for 30 minutes.

__Item. Effect Stone.__ Effect: Return to Sender. When activated, the item equipped with this effect stone will automatically return to user. Cooldown: 1 hour.

__Active Buffs:__

__Oath of Protection:__ The goddess Onera's champion (Michael/Paladin) has sworn to offer you aid against the forces of darkness.

__Revive Potion:__ Upon receiving fatal damage, user will portal to a preset location with 1HP while simultaneously activating a full-heal and returning the body to its natural condition. A corporeal doppelgänger remains behind at the death site.

PROLOGUE

Valery stood overlooking the two newest pods at the far end of the laboratory. Several technicians worked behind her, taking readings and analyzing data for the other twenty-five pods.

Things had finally been running smoothly. At least until her father had started his meddling.

She crossed her arms and sighed, wondering just what he was playing at. Taryn Jones's participation, she could explain. The program had been on the verge of collapse and introducing him to the game was enough to keep Chad content while they searched for a solution. But Dorothy Jordan... She was a wrinkle no one had expected.

The young woman had a history with Chad, and it seemed the months since the trial had done nothing more than stoke her anger.

Chad was widely known as a rager in online games. His outbursts had landed him here in the first place. But looking at Dorothy's avatar as she wreaked havoc across Mythos, Valery couldn't help but wonder if all gamers were a dormant volcano just waiting to erupt. Dorothy had only been in the game a few days, but she'd left a trail of destruction in her wake.

Valery rubbed her temples, pushing back the inevitable headache. Her father loved to stir the pot, introducing chaotic factors just to see what would happen. It was part of the reason her mother had left him. It was also the mindset that had made him one of the greatest innovators in gaming. Valery respected her father as a businessman and visionary, but this wasn't his pet project. It wasn't a test for an expansion or new mechanics for one of his games. This was Valery's passion. This world, the AI, it had all become something more, something special. Not only was rehabilitation happening before her eyes, but they'd only begun to scratch the surface of how the AI and nanites could work together. If Chad's situation could be replicated...

She'd started this program with a desire to help people. She'd wanted to help those that society said were irredeemable through methods no one else had attempted. She'd given them a chance to become heroes.

Some had taken it. For others, time would tell. She'd always known it would take time to see progress. If half of the test subjects showed improvement, she'd count that as a success.

Her father was risking everything she'd built when they were already balanced on a razor's edge.

Valery straightened her back. The next time she saw him, she'd tell him to stop meddling.

The elevator beeped just before the door whooshed open and a man wearing a black suit stepped into the laboratory. His face was set in a straight line as he tapped at his tablet. The technicians froze at the appearance of an interloper, and the man's shoes clicked as he walked across the pristine floor.

Valery forced a smile. "Can I help you?"

"Jim Cradle, Federal Bureau of Prisons. I'm here for an inspection." He swiped through his tablet without meeting her eyes.

"Inspection?" She frowned, stepping away from the pods.

"Yes." He looked up, taking in her appearance before finally meeting her eyes. "I assume you're Valery Barrett. I've been looking through your files. It seems you're overdue."

A knot twisted in her stomach. "Is that so?"

He nodded.

She regained her composure and turned on the allure that had opened countless doors for her. "Would you like the tour?" She smiled. "I'd be happy to show you around."

"He'll do fine." Jim pointed at Thompson, and the technician gulped, his eyes darting between Valery and the inspector. "Now, if you please. Give us some privacy, and I'll find you when the inspection is complete."

Valery's heart pulsed, and she fought to steady her trembling hands. "Certainly. I'll be in my office."

The minutes ticked by while Valery paced next to her desk, unable to quiet her nerves. The psychologists and doctors responsible for inmate safety were all appointed by the Bureau of Prisons, but this was the first time an inspector had returned to the lab since the project began. Her mind raced. Had someone filed a complaint or was this merely a coincidence?

The knock on the door startled her.

Valery took a deep breath before opening the door. She gestured for Jim to enter, but he stood there, face as stoic as ever.

"I've seen enough." The man's tone was so sharp it cut through the air like a knife. "There's no point in beating around the bush. I will be recommending that the Mythos Rehabilitative Project be shut down immediately."

"Shut down?" Valery stepped toward Jim as he tapped his tablet. "Inspector, you can't be serious."

He met her eyes. "Do I look like a man who plays games, Miss Barrett?"

"But, sir, we're only scratching the surface of what this technology is capable of. Look what we've accomplished already. This could change the way we look at rehabilitative therapy going forward."

"Accomplished?" The man looked over his shoulder at the laboratory, shaking his head. "The only thing you've accomplished is a blatant disrespect for operating procedure. Not only are you allowing those under your care to run through this world unchecked, you've allowed civilians into the game. Not one but two now. You breach protocol at every corner. Honestly, I'm surprised you've stayed in operation this long."

"It's a process. We've seen improvement in a majority of the inmates, and the AI has made great strides in—"

"You had a strict set of guidelines, Miss Barrett, and you didn't follow them, regardless of what you may think you have accomplished." He shook his head. "This may be hard for you to comprehend, but this isn't corporate America where you can do as you wish and ask for forgiveness later. You signed a contract with the Federal Bureau of Prisons and the State of New York. I mean, really, you bring civilians into this? What did you think would happen? I suggest you begin making arrangements because we *will* be shutting this project down."

Valery blinked rapidly, fighting back tears that threatened to pour out like a waterfall. She'd spent years laying the groundwork for this project, and it was on the verge of collapse after only a few months.

She took a shaky breath. "How long do I have?"

1. KILLING TIME

Dust covers my feet as I descend deeper into the cavernous dungeon alongside Caustic, my bonded dragon, and Limery. The area has been overtaken by tunnel drakes, and their claws scrape against stone as they scurry about, agitated by our appearance. The monsters are great at burrowing, constructing dozens of tunnels through the various levels of the dungeon.

Caustic sniffs at one of the empty tunnels and huffs while Limery sits on my shoulder playing with a shiny pebble he found in the last room.

The dragon has been growing at a rapid rate, and he's nearly twice my height now. His green coloring has darkened, and the golden scales of his beard grow denser by the day. The little branch-like horns atop his head resemble full-blow antlers.

Breebis has warned me that she won't be able to feed a creature of his size for much longer, and he'll need to start hunting exclusively for himself soon. Dragons grow up quickly, but they require a massive amount of sustenance to do so.

Compared to some of the other dungeons we've cleared, this one is pretty monotonous work. Pruxford has enough dungeons that adventuring is a full-blown industry, but ancient dungeons are in short supply. Adventurers like Arty and his brothers make a living clearing mob dungeons like this one to keep the local monster population in check.

With so many heroes still in Pruxford in the wake of the tournament, we've agreed to take turns with the ancient dungeons since there are so few of them. While we might not have any epic loot in store for us today, it still beats sitting around and twiddling our thumbs. For the past three days, there's been little else to do until the leaders of Mythos all convene, so we've been grinding.

This particular dungeon is home to a hive of tunnel drakes. They're a subspecies of dragon, kind of like wyrms with legs, and the thick-scaled, armored bastards are pretty pissed we've encroached on their nest. They were living here happily, filling the caverns with thousands of eggs. I don't blame them for being upset, but it's our job to put a dent in their numbers before the eggs hatch and they start invading neighboring towns and villages.

While Limery, Caustic, and I work our way through the dungeon, Taryn is enjoying a night away from the grind. We had tickets to revisit the Underground Circus, but I gave him mine so that he could take Breebis. He's grown rather attached to the gnomish stablemaster, and the circus will be a lot more fun than hanging around the stables all evening. Not that Taryn would complain. Between Breebis and the animals, he'd be happy to be there.

He deserves some time to unwind, though, and I know I've been a pain to be around. Between the attack at the tournament and the letter from Dorothy, there's a lot on my mind.

The dungeon offers me an outlet for my frustrations, and I unleash them with every hit of Destroyer. Drakes scurry across the muddy floor, hissing and biting, each one the size of a crocodile but with longer legs and a hooked snout for burrowing. I lose myself in the primal power of Berserker Rage, and it flows through the warhammer as I cave in the armored hides of the countless tunnel drakes as they crawl down the cavern in a steady stream. As the cooldowns allow, I summon horrors, casting Sacrifice and buffing my stats until I'm a hulking brute of a troll.

Steam wafts from my shoulders as I rage. The end of Destroyer sizzles as it gains stacks of Inferno, and with each consecutive hit, the tip glows like molten lava.

I try to focus on the fight, on the monotony of ruthless smashing, but thoughts cloud my mind. Things were finally looking up when I made it to the final match of the tournament. We had allies and new friends.

And then it all went to shit. Anger surges as I recall the attack on the arena, where countless gnomes died.

That's what it took for the council to finally understand the severity of the situation—a warlock opening a portal to Blacktide and killing hundreds of innocents. War is brewing, and Valmar is testing us. I'm certain of it. His tendrils snake out from the shadows with an attack here, a roaming monster from the shadowlands there. and a growing list of heroes under his command.

Ethan, Otis, and Kevin have admitted to joining the dark wizard. At the Challenger's Ball, they were awfully friendly with some of the other heroes, and no one has seen Richard the cleric since the tournament.

Jude and Glenn will take any chance they can to gain the upper hand over me. It's only a matter of time before they join as well.

All the more reason to act before it's too late. But the wheels of politics move slowly.

With each swing, sludge flies in an arc, painting the walls and ceiling with the viscous goop secreted beneath the drake's armored scales.

And then there's Dorothy. She warned me to watch my back, but I haven't heard from her since. I think it's best to ignore her. At least until I have more information on what she's doing here.

I'm more concerned by what Valery meant when she said things were out of her control. I've sent her countless messages, but she still hasn't responded.

More tunnel drakes crawl into the cavern, and I redirect my frustration. I smash as many of the monsters as I can, but there's enough that they swarm past me toward Limery and Caustic. Each one is nearly six feet long with a flat tail meant for swiping. Their sharp claws are dangerous, but it's their hardened snouts that are capable of tearing through flesh and bone. One rears onto its back legs and roars, flashing dangerous teeth before it charges.

Destroyer smashes into the side of its head, sending the drake spinning into the wall. Behind me, Caustic unleashes a roar of his own as he and Limery take on the drakes that get by me. Their synergy of toxic gas and fire has become extremely effective, and when Berserker Rage finally times out, I fall back and let the duo mop up the rest.

Steam fades from my body, leaving mud and gore caked upon my shoulders like hardened clay.

I watch Caustic unleash his fury on the poor creatures, and when the last drake falls, notifications flash in the corner of my vision.

Congratulations! You have reached level 30. +1 stat point to distribute. +1 Strength and Constitution racial bonus.

I stare at the notification. Level thirty! It's about damn time.

This means I can finally track down Jegaar about unlocking the legendary Warforged class in Goldspire. If we didn't have the council waiting, I'd already be on my way.

I dismiss the notification and move on to the next one.

Congratulations! Draconic Convergence has reached level 2.

Draconic Convergence: *The convergence fuses an unbreakable bond that grows stronger over time. No two convergences are the same. Each one evolves based on the relationship between the dragon and their chosen counterpart.*

Name: *Caustic*
    Species: *Green Dragon*
    Level: *15*

Convergence Level:

1. Draconic Bond- You have made an unbreakable bond with a dragon and forged a telepathic link that may expand in the future. In its current state, intense spikes in emotion may blend between psyches.

2. Spatial Bond- You are now able to mark the location of the dragon no matter how far apart you are.

. . .

Caustic's approval radiates through me as he gnaws on the remains of one of the drakes. With each passing day, our telepathic bond has grown stronger, allowing me to better understand the dragon's emotions. It's been weird, having another's feelings intrude into my mind at times, especially the overwhelming hunger that envelops me each morning before Caustic has eaten. But I believe that with practice, our bond will be another valuable skill in our arsenal. Now that we have Spatial Bond, it'll be easier to keep tabs on him as he hunts.

"Limmy is hungries." The imp lands on my muck-covered shoulder and rubs his belly. "We's been in the dungeonses all days. Limmy wants to eat and sees Taryns."

I can't blame him. It's almost nightfall, and this is the third mob dungeon we've cleared today. At least we got what we came for.

"Alright." I close out my notifications and gently poke his belly. "I guess that's enough for one day. Let's head back to the city."

Enchanted signs and lampposts cast the streets in a neon glow by the time we arrive at the Puzzling Peacock. The tail feathers on the sign flick back and forth above the rowdy inn. The tavern downstairs has somehow become the watering hole for many of the heroes and contenders from the tournament. Even though the inn has been at full capacity since we first arrived in Pruxford, it doesn't stop others from swinging by for an evening of drinks before stumbling back to their rooms down the street.

At the far wall, several tables are pushed together and littered with empty plates and mugs. Arty lets out a boisterous laugh that carries across the room. The muscled cyclops sits between two of his adopted human brothers. Next to them, Randy the rogue and Drizz'rt the golden-scaled assassin huddle over the table, pointing at a map and talking in hushed voices. Randy laughs and squeezes the lizardfolk's arm excitedly. Those two have become fast friends, tackling dungeons with their speed and deceptive tactics. Michael the paladin has an arm draped around Don the void mage, the two deep in conversation. Don strokes his long gray beard as galaxies of the void swirl within the mage's eyes.

I spot a few others I recognize as I search the room for Taryn, but he's nowhere to be found. He must still be at the circus.

"There he is!" Arty yells across the room as he points at me, his large eye bloodshot from drinking.

Limery flies over, stealing a piece of sausage from Arty's plate before perching on the cyclops's shoulder.

"Here I am." I smile, walking over. As shitty as things might seem, there's still hope. Looking at the eclectic group before me, there's a small comfort in knowing my attempt to find allies hasn't been in vain.

The barmaid brings Limery and me each a drink, and I take a seat across from the cyclops.

Arty leans forward, both elbows shaking the table with his weight. "I thought I was a hard worker, but you've put me to shame. First one out the door and last one in." He raises his mug. "Cheers."

"It keeps me grounded." I clink my mug to his and take a big gulp of the malty ale. After a long day in the dungeons, it hits the spot. "I'm trying to make the most of our time here."

"You're c-certainly doing that," Drizz'rt hisses his words.

"Someone has to keep up with you two scoundrels." I grin.

"Hey now." Randy wags a finger and flashes me a smile. "All rogues aren't scoundrels. Drizz'rt here is halfway decent."

The lizardfolk cackles in a way that's part screech, part growl, and completely unsettling.

"Any word on the council?" I ask.

Michael the paladin answers. Even in the dimly lit tavern, divine radiance casts him in a soft glow. "The centaurs arrived this afternoon. Those from the Isle of Mythos should be here tomorrow. Apparently, there was another attack on Seascape."

My hair stands on end. "What happened?"

"More monsters from the shadowlands. The kingsguard dealt with them swiftly enough, but King Orso has chosen to wait until the last moment to leave the city."

"He's a good leader."

There are several nods of agreement. Without the support and initiative of the dwarven king, I doubt we would have made any progress in uniting the other kingdoms.

We share a few more drinks, detailing the day's exploits from the many dungeons around the city. Taryn must be enjoying his day off because he's still not back by the time Limery and I head up for the night.

"Good nights, Chods." Limery plops in the bed and begins snoring before I have a chance to respond.

I lay down beside him, and the imp nestles instinctively in the crook of my arm. His naturally warm body is like a heating pack against my ribs.

Even with a buzz from the many ales, my mind still comes back to the situation at hand. There are only two more days until the council meeting, where leaders from across Mythos will once again gather to discuss Valmar Worren.

Last time, King Orso's goal was to warn them of the dark wizard's return. Now, his resurgence is all but certain. This will be a council for war.

I push the thoughts aside and pull up my stats. With nothing to do but grind dungeons, I've managed to level twice in the past week. Fighting sea orcs during the attack put me on the edge of leveling. I hit level twenty-eight on the first day back in the dungeons. Three days of constant grinding and now I'm level thirty.

Just as I have for the past two nights, I pull up my available abilities and consider what I should use the ability point on.

. . .

Available Abilities *(1 ability point to unlock):*

Massive Bite. *Deals double damage. Cost: 20 rage.*
 Claws. *Swipe at opponent with both hands, dealing extra damage. Cost: 10 rage.*
 Multi Attack. *Bite and Claw at the same time. Cost: 20 rage.*
 Iron Will. *Immune to slows and stuns for 30 seconds. Cost: 50 rage. 180 second cooldown.*
 I'm Always Angry *(Passive. Available at level 10). Once rage meter is at 50%, it will not deteriorate below 50% when out of combat.*
 Perception. *For 10 minutes, gain increased awareness of your surroundings. Spot hidden objects, as well as unusual sounds, odors, and tastes. Cooldown: 6 hours.*
 Cleave. *Your next attack causes bleed damage, dealing 1% of opponent's health per second for 5 seconds. Cost: 10 rage.*
 Battle Cry. *You let out a ferocious roar, increasing rage by 20. No cost. 60 second cooldown.*

Class Advancements. *Upon reaching level 25, you have unlocked a class advancement. You may only advance one class at a time. A second class may not be advanced until completion of primary advancement.*

Summoner Advancement.
 Dreadbeasts. Unlock for further details.
 Dual Subclass. Unlock for further details.

If I were strictly a barbarian, the Massive Bite, Claws, or Multi Attack would be fine. They would imbue each attack with bonus damage powered by my rage. Between my horrors, weapons, and other abilities, my barbarian attacks are severely lacking compared to what I'm capable of with my summoner class. Every time I cast a Horror of Power, my next attack hits for double. While new barbarian abilities might stack, making the attacks even more powerful, I know it's not the right choice for now.

There's really only one ability I'm interested in. Dreadbeasts. It's an advancement of my horror summoning, and I'd unlock it right now if I wasn't worried that I might need an ability point for the Warforged class.

As it is, I don't know if the class requires an ability point or if it's something that unlocks automatically upon completion. Until I meet with Jegaar, I can't risk using this point.

According to the battle scholar, the Warforged were a subclass of barbarians, and the most dangerous fighters in Goldspire long ago. The process of becoming a Warforged was said to kill more than half of those who attempted it. Those who survived were granted abilities that turned their skin to fluid steel when they raged. On the battlefield, they were unmatched, and when we face down Valmar, that's the exact kind of advantage we're going to need.

No one has attained the class in many generations, but Jegaar said that once I hit level thirty, I should return to Goldspire and find him. That's exactly what I intend to do once the council is over.

Unlocking the dreadbeast path would help me survive whatever challenges may be waiting, but until I know more, I'm not ready to risk it.

Even though Taryn's not here, I already know what he would say. He'd tell me to go to the library and do some research. Maybe he's right. Tomorrow, I'll stop by the Pruxford Library and see what they know.

2. PRECIOUS KNOWLEDGE

Taryn is already downstairs when we arrive for breakfast. Platters of sausage, bacon, and biscuits fill the table. Flubs sits on the windowsill in the form of a cat. Morning light shines through the window, giving a glow to the slime's gelatinous body and setting its jeweled eyes ablaze. The skeleton that floats inside the creature only adds to the hypnotic effect. I don't even want to imagine what kind of shady back-alley establishment Taryn purchased that from.

The barmaid places a bowl of brown gravy in the center of the table. "I hope you're hungry, big fella."

My stomach rumbles as I inhale the savory aroma. "That's my secret. I'm always hungry."

She taps me playfully on the arm. "You and the little one both, enjoy."

"Morning!" Taryn says with a full mouth. Biscuit crumbs speckle his beard and tunic.

"Mornings, Taryns!" Limery flies over, taking a sausage in one hand and several pieces of bacon in the other.

Ruby places her paws on Taryn's leg, begging until he gives her a piece of meat. She takes it and prances toward the corner with her prize.

"You were out late." I raise a brow suggestively. "Must have been a good night."

"It was a great night." Taryn grins. "The circus was amazing as always, and then afterward, Breebis and I went out drinking with Hawkin and some of the other performers. Let me tell you, those guys know how to party. They said to give you their best." He picks up a sausage and bites it in half. "How were the dungeons?"

I fill a plate of my own until it's overflowing. Caustic must sense my hunger because I'm suddenly overcome with a ravenous desire to eat even stronger than my own. I'm not sure if I'll ever get used to having another's emotions inside my head.

"Not as fun as a night at the circus, but we managed to clear three mob dungeons. And I finally hit level thirty." I stuff more bacon in my mouth and savor the smokey flavor. "Saving an ability point for this long seems wrong, but it'll take at least a couple of days of constant grinding to gain another. I wish I had Jegaar on speed dial right about now."

"Well—"

I hold up a finger, and he pauses. "You'll be proud of me. I've decided to stop by the library and see if they have any information about the Warforged."

"Warforged?" a deep voice calls as heavy boots thunk down the stairs. "I thought that was the stuff of legend. Goldspire propaganda used to make them seem even more fearsome than they already are." Arty takes a seat at the table. "Is there actually truth to it?"

"You know it's rude to eavesdrop." I narrow my eyes at the cyclops until his cheeks flush, then I grin. "There's truth to it, alright. I saw one with my own two eyes. He was a watered-down version from where the trait had passed through generations, but even so, he was a force to be reckoned with. If there's a chance to unlock that kind of power, I have to take it."

Arty sits back and crosses his arms. "Dark wizards. Warforged. This world grows more ludicrous by the day."

Limery lets out a loud belch that carries across the tavern. Several guests glance at him, but he rubs his belly. A look of contentment spreads across his demonic features as he fills his plate with more food.

"What are the lot of you up to today?" I ask Arty.

"Michael and Don have asked me and my brothers to join them with clearing one of the ancient dungeons. Roddick wasn't interested at first, but Michael promised a blessing from Onera if we helped. It's not often one has the opportunity to receive a divine blessing."

I recall the Oath of Protection that the paladin swore to me at the Challenger's Ball. The description was kind of nebulous, but I get the feeling it prevents him from stabbing me in the back. I still don't know much about deities and their role in this world, but being in one's good graces can't be a bad thing.

We finish the rest of our meal with small talk before heading to the library.

Compared to the hustle and bustle during the Quincentennial Tournament, the streets are a vestige of the excitement and grandeur that waited on every corner a week ago. Gnomes come and go with their business, but the street performers and mirth are gone. It's as if a cloud has descended over Pruxford.

Limery perches on my shoulder as we pass through various neighborhoods on our way to the library. Taryn walks to my right, Ruby darting between his legs with every step while Flubs leads the way. The slime's skill for mimicry is unmatched, and if not for its slimy appearance, I'd never be able to tell it wasn't a real cat. Flubs has the feline movements and mannerisms perfected, complete with flippant attitude as it struts through the city. The gelatinous cat garners more attention than the rest of us combined.

The last time we attempted to visit the library, it was closed in celebration of the tournament. With the festivities canceled in the wake of the attack, I'm hopeful we'll have better luck this time.

While we walk, I focus on my bond with Caustic. The young dragon is much too big for casual walks through the city now, so I use our time apart to strengthen the link that tethers us. The description for Draconic Bond says that it should grow stronger over time, and I've found that I can always sense his presence if I try hard enough. It's similar to my horrors, but where my connection to them is more of a generalized feeling of their location, with Caustic, it's almost like I'm sensing his mood.

Right now, he feels unfettered and free. He must be exploring somewhere across the countryside for his morning hunt. Now that he's capable of flying, Breebis says he should spend as much time in the air as possible to build his endurance.

The Pruxford Library towers over the surrounding buildings. Much like the arena and Crystal Palace, it's a work of art. The beautiful, cylindrical building is several stories tall with an exterior of sea-green glass. Its many shelves are visible through the translucent windows, each one filled with books and scrolls.

A ravenous and primal hunger overtakes me, and I relax my connection to Caustic while he hunts. It wouldn't be a bad idea to also research our bond while we're here.

Taryn stops to admire the building. "You know, the color reminds me of this antique glassware my mom keeps in the dining cabinet. The glass is supposedly mixed with uranium and somewhat radioactive. It looks cool, but we never got to eat off it. Sometimes, I would see its faint green glow when I was sneaking into the kitchen for a late-night snack."

"So, every night?" I grin.

Taryn shoves me in the side. "How do you think I got so big and strong?"

I look him up and down. "Big, you say?"

He rolls his eyes, and we enter the library. Inside, the scent of parchment welcomes us, along with a gnomish clerk wearing a seafoam green robe. He stands behind the desk, organizing a cart of books. His half-moon spectacles with amber-colored lenses nearly fall from the tip of his nose.

The gnome has a light blue tint to his skin and thick curly, sapphire hair that's cropped close at the sides. "Welcome to the Pruxford Library, the crown jewel of our fair city."

Taryn tilts his head. "I thought that was the Crystal Palace?"

The gnome scoffs. "So they would have you believe, but tell me, master dwarf, what is more precious than knowledge?"

"You've got me there."

The gnome clasps his hands behind his back. "Calfin Dazzledust, at your service. How may I assist you today?"

I step forward, and his eyes widen slightly. "We're here to do a little research."

"Most excellent! Just let me send this on its way and I'll be right with you." Calfin picks a book from the cart, and it flies from his hand, floating through the air toward the shelves. That's when I notice several more books flying of their own accord throughout the library.

Limery grows warm against my shoulder. "Spooky bookses."

"Levitation magic?" I ask, watching the book as it soars across the library before finding its place among the shelves.

"Gods, wouldn't that be something." Calfin chuckles. "No, I wasn't blessed in such a way. The book fairies are the ones that keep the shelves in working order."

"Book fairies?" I look around, but I don't see any signs of fairies. Is this what counts as a joke among librarians?

"Well, technically, they're called bibliophilic fairies, but that's a mouthful. We call them book fairies around here." He removes the glasses and hands them to me. "Here, take a look."

The frames are much too small to fit my head, so I hold them in front of my eyes, looking through the crescent-shaped lenses.

"Shit..." I move the lenses up and down several times, amazed at what I'm seeing. There are at least a dozen fairies flying about the library.

Each fairy is about the size of Limery, with small gray bodies and wings so dark that they scream of nothingness. Short, pearlescent horns jut upward from just above their brow line. Unlike the celestial fairies in Wandermere that leave a sparkling trail of glitter in their wake, these leave a trail of shadow that dissipates as they fly.

I focus on one as it returns to the desk to retrieve another book.

Bibliophilic Fairy. Level 22. Book fairies, as they are commonly known among scholars and academics, are a rare breed of fairy only found within the halls of the Prux-ford Library. The first book fairy was bred by happenstance ages ago when two scholars found themselves trapped among the snowy peaks of Frostmoor during a research mission. Their fae companions—a void fairy and a light fairy—mated, producing offspring with the more temperate demeanor of the light fairies and the ability to vanish without need of the void. Since then, book fairies have been the primary assistants to the librarians at the Pruxford Library.

I hand the glasses to Taryn and return my attention to the gnome. "So they just work here?"

He nods. "Indeed. Before they were discovered, we used a variety of fairies. Celestial fairies are great workers, but they leave a dust trail everywhere they go. Void fairies would occasionally lose a book while traveling through the void. Don't even get me started on the various elemental fairies. Book fairies have the best qualities for our particular field. They can stay within our realm while still hiding from sight so as to avoid disrupting our patrons. We have these special lenses for tracking them down if we need to."

"That's wild." Taryn makes to hand the glasses back, but Limery flies from my shoulder and grabs them.

"Limmy wants to sees." He uses both hands to hold the frames to his head so they don't fall off. When he sees the fairy, Limery gasps in delight before zooming away.

"He'll bring them back." I apologize before he gets us kicked out.

"Do not worry. I always bring an extra pair." Calfin winks as he pulls another pair of spectacles from his robe. "Now, what is it that I can help you with today?"

I close another ancient tome and slide it across the table next to a dozen other books and scrolls.

"Nothing?" Taryn lifts his gaze from a massive book bound in green leather.

"More of the same." I press my knuckles to my eyes and take a deep breath. "They have the entire lineage of Goldspire's emperors, tables of various sub-races of beastkin, lists of gladiators and their victories, but when it comes to the Warforged, it's like they never existed. Do you think Jegaar was messing with us?"

Taryn shakes his head. "No, I don't."

"Then what gives?" I gesture at the stack of books we've already pored through.

Taryn strokes his beard, and the chime of the metal clasps carries across the empty library. "Jegaar is a member of the Scholars Guild. He said their job is to maintain the histories of Goldspire and to search out rare items and artifacts. He also said they do foreign reconnaissance. So maybe the reason you can't find information on the Warforged is because they don't want you to."

"You might be right." I sigh. "I guess I won't be spending that ability point any time soon then."

"Maybe not, but there's still plenty we can learn while we're here." Taryn taps the book he's holding. "There's a wealth of information on the various druid classes. I bet you can at least learn something about dreadbeasts and your bond with Caustic."

"You're right. I'll go see if the clerk can help point me in the right direction." I look around, suddenly aware that Limery has disappeared again. "Where is the little guy, anyhow?"

Taryn grins. "He saw a book floating by and went to investigate."

I laugh. Of course he did.

In the center of the library, there's a resource desk located next to a spiral staircase that goes all the way to the top floor. I find Limery zipping through the air and waving his arms as he talks to Calfin.

The gnome smiles when he sees me. "Were the materials helpful in your research?"

I push the cart loaded with books on Goldspire to the desk. "Unfortunately not. Do you have anything on dreadbeasts or dragon bonding, specifically, a Draconic Convergence?"

He taps his chin and flips through a massive book that I assume is an index.

"Hmm, let me see what I can find. I'll bring them to you when I'm done." He turns to Limery and grins. "Would you like to see how we request books from the fairies?"

"Oh yes! Limmy would loves to sees." The imp clasps his hands together excitedly. "And then we's can sends thems back to the shelveses."

I meander through the library while Calfin and Limery work with the fairies to locate more books. As frustrating as it is to come up emptyhanded regarding the Warforged, I can't help but be impressed by the depth of this world once again. We're in a library filled with thousands of books that detail the history and lore of Mythos long before anyone logged in. Each piece of info has been created by the AI in vivid detail, existing whether we discover it or not. No wonder Valery would try anything not to lose this place. If a reset means starting from scratch, there's no promise that they could recreate any of this.

Taryn has his face buried in a book when I return.

"Find anything good?" I ask.

"Tons." He taps the page. "I'm reading about Rane Darkbrow. She was a shadow druid who tamed some of the most dangerous creatures from the shadowlands. Pretty fascinating stuff."

I sit in silence while Taryn reads, ruminating and brooding until Limery flies over carrying a stack of books nearly as tall as he is.

"Calfins saids these should helps." He drops the books to the table with a thud. "Limmy has to goes now."

He disappears down the aisle of books before I have a chance to respond.

"Maybe he's making a career change." Taryn grins, but he doesn't look up from his book.

I sort through the material Limery brought and a few of the titles catch my eye. These might be exactly what I'm looking for.

Beasts of Shadow
    Dragons: A History
    The Untamable
    Summoners Through the Ages

Over the next few hours, I manage to gain some useful information. *Summoners Through the Ages* has detailed accounts of various summoners and sheds light on some of the paths I could have taken. If I had a higher Intelligence, the elemental class would have been pretty destructive. The brood summoner also has some pretty nasty abilities. There's only one mention of horrors, though.

Elwin Iceheart. *Horror Summoner. Known in her time as the Wayward Summoner, Elwin toed the line between decency and devilry. While she fought for the forces of good, she would use any tactic at her disposal to achieve victory.*

Her summons were dark and foreboding, some referred to them as nightmare beings, capable of casting fear into the hearts of her opponents before the battle started. Where most summons are formed from the world around them, horrors come from another plane altogether and are considered a true rarity among summoners. Little is known about the origin of horrors, save that they reside somewhere between the mortal and shadow realms. Some believe that they thrive in the darkness of the shadowlands, but there is little evidence to support this theory.

She sounds like a badass to me.

Beasts of Shadow mostly focuses on monsters found in haunted forests and dungeons, but there are a few references to the shadowlands and dreadbeasts.

This tome would not be complete if I did not at least touch on the beasts of the shadowlands. Those unforgiving lands remain a large mystery to academics and scholars, for far too many who have ventured into the darkness in search of enlightenment have become victims of its gloom. I have no understanding of why a portal was erected into those lands in the first place. If I had the authority to close it, I would.

The Scholars Guild no longer sanctions research missions into the shadowlands. For those who would seek out its secrets, know that its reputation has been paid for in blood. The horrors, demons, dreadbeasts, behemoths, terrors, and monstrosities within these lands were born in suffering. If they do not kill you, they will lure you to join their ranks, for the call of darkness is sickly sweet while on shadowed ground. The search for knowledge is a noble pursuit, but some secrets should remain hidden.

A chill passes through me as I recall the mesmer wisps in Wandermere. Their whispers were all-consuming, drawing me toward them. Valmar was born in the elven lands of Mosstar but according to King Orso, the dark wizard's journey into the shadowlands is what gave him the strength to invade the other portals.

I close the book when I realize my claws are starting to dig into the binding. Reading about dreadbeasts and the shadowlands is only adding to my already high anxiety, so I decide to focus on one of the bright spots from the past few weeks—my bond with Caustic.

Dragons: A History is so fascinating that I could read it all day. Its pages are filled with tales of the dragons of Mythos. From the legend of the first dragon all the way to Verdaria's appearance in Wandermere. There's even a section on Senzala's totem, Nesira.

I wonder if the powerful white dragon joined the arctic trolls when they traveled to Seascape, or if like Jirra, Senzala can still tap into her totemic bond when they are far apart. Now that I think of it, I wonder if something as large as a dragon can enter a portal, and what I'll do with Caustic once he's full-grown if he can't fit.

The pages are full of illustrations as well. There are at least a dozen species of dragons across Mythos, each one as interesting as the last. The black dragon looks like a terror to behold with its obsidian scales and wings made of darkness. While the gold dragons are one of the smallest species, they are said to hoard the biggest treasures.

According to the book, most prefer to stay far away from civilization, and anyone who would disturb their peace must be prepared to face judgment. It makes me feel even luckier to have bonded with Caustic.

While *Dragons: A History* focuses on dragons as a species, *The Untamable* is exactly what I'm looking for, a plethora of information on dragons and their interactions with people.

A dragon does not heel like a pet, nor does it follow orders like a work animal. A dragon cannot be tamed. They are proud creatures and bond with those they choose. A dragon would rather die than bond with someone it believes unworthy.

Throughout history, several types of bonds have been recorded. Totemic bonds are the most common, where a dragon bestows favor upon someone, granting a sliver of their power to mages or shamans. The bond remains until it is severed by the dragon.

Some dragons have been known to grant pacts, where there is no tether between the two, but a commitment to work together until a goal is achieved. The most famous is the case of Lady Stonearm of Pruxford, when the gnomish princess partnered with a blue dragon to force her father from the throne. Lady Stonearm never revealed the details of her agreement with the dragon, but mining in the Sapphire Mountains was abandoned soon after she took the throne.

The most prized and rarest bond is that of the Draconic Convergence. A convergence only happens when a dragon has determined someone worthy of binding their spirits. The two spirits converge, granting a familiar link between a dragon and its partner. Senses and emotional pathways become one in this unbreakable bond, and as it develops, both are able to see through the other's eyes. This has granted tactical advantages to mages as their dragons survey the battlefield from above, but none more so than the illustrious dragon riders.

The book goes on to detail examples of the various bonds throughout history, but all of the accounts are several hundred years old. There is one part that I find particularly interesting.

Dragons are solitary creatures by nature, though they do convene with one another on occasion. Once a century, dragons from around Mythos gather in secret for a draconic conclave. Even those who have bonded with a dragon are forbidden from attending the assemblage.

· · ·

I wonder when the last conclave was, and if there are enough dragons across Mythos to hold one again.

"Chod. Earth to Chod" Taryn waves a hand in my face, pulling my attention from the book.

"Sorry, I got sucked into this one."

"No kidding. I've never seen you so enthralled." Taryn laughs. "Are you ready to head out? It's almost nightfall, and I'm sure Calfin could use a break from Limery. Plus, I want to stop by the stable to check on Berry."

"Check on Breebis, you mean?" I pucker my lips and mimic a kiss several times. Too bad Limery isn't here to chant a chorus of 'Taryns has a girlfriends.'

Taryn narrows his eyes. "You're just jealous."

We gather Limery, and I give my thanks to Calfin as we depart. Once we're outside, I realize just how dangerous the green-tinted windows are for losing track of time. Across the city, enchanted lights flicker to life in the twilight.

I didn't learn as much as I would have liked, but it was far from a wasted day. While I have no better understanding of the Warforged class, I deepened my knowledge of dragons. When it comes down to it, my bond with Caustic might be the greatest advantage I'll have going forward.

3. REUNIONS

"Limmy loves the libraries!" The imp zooms through the air, telling us all about his adventures with the book fairies. "Calfins says Limmy can comes back anytimes."

As we make our way down the sparsely populated streets toward the Rusty Bucket stable, I lean into my bond with Caustic to let him know we're coming. I get nothing, so he must be taking an evening nap after a long day of hunting. Either that or he's ignoring me.

There's a faint crackle as an enchanted streetlamp flickers to life, giving the cobblestones a warm glow.

Up ahead, there's a crowd gathered around the square of the Pruxford portal. It's strange considering how empty most of the streets are. My heart races as I recall the attack on the square, and my hands buzz with mana. The moment passes as I realize there's no fighting and no terrified gnomes trying to escape. Whatever it is, though, it has them intrigued.

"What's going on up there?" I squint to try and get a better view.

"Oh, nice! They're finally here." Taryn points. His causal tone confirms that there's not a threat.

"Who's here? I can't see that far away." He must have better eyesight than me because I can't make out much more than a mass of people from so far away.

"Limmy sees! It's Daddies!" He darts toward the portal faster than I've ever seen him move.

My chest flutters, and the blue sheen of a mana-infused wyrm shimmers in the glow of enchanted lights as it rises like a cobra. Chief Rizza sits upon the wyrm's back, waving to the crowd while they gawk and point.

Now, that's badass.

I take off running, and my excitement stirs Caustic, piquing his curiosity. Behind me, Taryn curses as he tries to keep up. I catch several puzzled looks as I sprint down the street, but I don't care. After the past week, it'll be nice to see some familiar faces.

Guards have been stationed around the portal since the attack, and they clear a path as the large group exits. Several dozen people spill into the square. In the center, Limery hugs his father. Tears well in Bazel's bulbous yellow eyes as he has a long overdue reunion with his son.

This is the first time I've seen the two together, and Limery is the spitting image of his father, though about half the size. Both have the same shade of reddish skin, spindly limbs, and forked tails.

Limery's mother, Lillith, and brother, Leo, hover next to them. Leo looks like a little punk rock imp with his black mohawk but once Limery releases his father, the brothers embrace as well.

I wave to Lillith and return my attention to the rest of the group.

To the left, there's a mixture of ivory, ebony, and blood dwarfs that make up King Orso's personal guard. The dwarven king stands out among his kingsguard, nearly a foot taller than the rest. His bushy black hair falls to his shoulders and his dark beard is braided and oiled, a shadow against skin the color of cooling magma. Silver clasps catch the light and glimmer. Power radiates from his crimson armor and glowing red crown. The king's senior advisor, Kurzol, stands by his side.

To the right, a group of humans wear the silver-and-blue armor of Vanaria's kingsguard, led by Warwick. The man's youthful eyes scan the crowd for threats. Next to him, Lord Kassidy the teleportation mage, holds a pastry in one hand as he whispers something into King Favian's ear.

Closest to the portal, Chief Rizza towers above them all upon her massive wyrm. It's nearly full-grown now, and almost the size of the one I fought in the forest so long ago. I search for Gord's massive frame among the crowd, but the only other troll I see is Jira. The wizened shaman stays close to Chief Rizza's wyrm as it slithers across the square.

"Chod, is that you?" King Favian raises a hand, and the escort stops. "By the gods, what have you done to your head?" He pushes his way through and extends a hand, gripping me around the forearm.

Warwick stays at Favian's side, his dark eyes always alert. His state of alarm makes me wonder what all I've missed on the Isle while we've been traveling. Kassidy gives me a nod as he stuffs the last remnants of the pastry into his mouth.

The King of Vanaria is the picture of royalty as he stands before me. He's put aside his boiled leather armor and riding gear in favor of polished plate mail. Adorning his breastplate is detailed metalwork in the shape of a griffin with a sapphire for the eye. A flowing blue cape hangs from the king's shoulders, and a sword with a jewel-encrusted pommel rests at his side. King Favian's brown hair is as windswept as ever, but it only adds to his aesthetic. He knows just how important this meeting is.

I squeeze his arm. "A lot has changed since we last saw one another."

"Too much, I fear." His tone is somber.

Leathery wings flap over my shoulder, and Favian's eyes go wide as Caustic descends, landing beside me with a huff. The dragon sniffs at the air, like a dog picking up a scent. The king takes a step back, and both kingsguards draw their weapons.

King Orso calls them off. "Lower your weapons." His deep voice booms as he joins King Favian, patting him on the back. Orso raises a brow as his gaze shifts between me and Caustic. "So this is where my dragon egg went."

Caustic sniffs at the air as if sizing up the group before him. He clicks his snout, and Chief Rizza's wyrm responds in kind.

I rest a hand on the dragon. "I hope you aren't angry. You said we had full access to your troves."

"That I did." King Orso laughs and casts a glance at Kurzol. The cleric was with us when I snuck the egg into my satchel. "When I was a young dwarf, I won the egg in a game of gloomkeeper with my father's advisor, Durkis. He was a renowned tactician and said to be the best in the kingdom. It was that day that I won not only the respect of my father but his council as well. Alas, there's nowhere on Isle of Mythos with the life aura needed to hatch a dragon, so the egg has sat among the treasures of Seascape ever since. Truth be told, I hadn't thought about it in years. But if you've found yourself worthy of a dragon's companionship, then who am I to argue? We will undoubtedly need you both in the days to come."

Taryn finally catches up with Ruby and Flubs in tow. He bends over, bowing as he gasps for breath. "Your Highness."

"Master Taryn." King Orso grins. "A shadow druid? You make our kingdom proud."

I lean in and whisper to Taryn, "Why didn't you just fly?"

He rolls his eyes. "And leave my pets to walk by themselves? Now, that's just cruel."

I chuckle at his theatrics. "Whatever you say, T."

Chief Rizza's wyrm lowers its body, and she slides from its back. Her golden eyes lock onto mine, and she rushes forward, embracing me with her lithe but powerful arms. "It is good to see you, Chod."

I return the embrace. So much has happened since the days when my biggest challenge was restoring the ley lines to the troll forest. "Where are the others?"

She releases me, smiling as she touches the tip of my horn with her finger. "We all have our parts to play. Gord, Laojin, and Kronan are attempting to unite the seaside and desert trolls."

"Wow. Do you think they can do it?" Chief Lida had made it very clear that the seaside trolls would take no sides in the issues outside of their village, but perhaps a visit from the chiefs of the arctic and mountain trolls might be a little more convincing.

"I believe that they must." She holds out a hand to Caustic, and he nuzzles against it. "Who do we have here?"

"This is Caustic. He's a juvenile green dragon."

She caresses the dragon's jawline. "A worthy member of our tribe."

Caustic's chest rumbles like the purr of a monstrous cat. He must sense my attachment to Rizza and the rest of the tribe.

"How is everything on the Isle? We heard there have been more attacks in Seascape."

Before she can answer, a horn blares just before wheels clatter down the street behind us. A crystal carriage, pulled by the whitest ponies I've ever seen, comes to a stop at the edge of the square. Guards from the Crystal Palace march beside the carriage, their rainbow armor gleaming like the iridescent shell of a beetle.

The carriage door opens and Dezmin, the head of the gnomish council, steps down. His matching yellow robes and pointed hat remind me of a garden gnome, but there is nothing humorous about his grave expression.

He nods slightly. "Your graces, chieftain, we are glad for your safe arrival. Normally, we would welcome you to settle in first, but time is not on our side of late. We have elected to convene a midnight council."

4. MIDNIGHT COUNCIL

By the time we arrive at the Crystal Palace, night has fully descended upon the city. Somehow, it makes Pruxford even more beautiful. The glass palace shimmers in the light of the moon with streaks of emerald and amethyst that remind me of the Northern Lights.

Chief Rizza and Jira are amazed by the enchanted lights and signs that give the city a life unlike any other I've traveled to.

Taryn converses with Kassidy and Kurzol, and Limery has been talking nonstop, giving Leo and Bazel an account of our adventures together since we first set out to clear the obstruction of the ley line so long ago.

Lillith sits on my shoulder while her boys talk. "You know, Chod, before you came into our life, Limery and Leo bickered all the time. I was hesitant to let them out into the world, but it seems they've finally found a common interest."

"It's our experiences that make us who we are." I smile at Limery and Leo laughing together. "The more we have, the more we become."

Once Limery and I left their little burrow, Leo set out on his own adventure, and he's been busy exploring dungeons on the Isle with some of his friends ever since. He's managed to reach level nineteen during the past few months. If he's anything like Limery, then his level is only a glimpse into the imp's true power.

Chief Rizza walks beside me, her wyrm lying low to the ground as it slithers beside us. She stops for a moment, letting several guards pass us as she admires the palace. "I never left the confines of the forest before you showed up, Chod. Not in all my years. Now, in a matter of months, I've traded with the humans in Lynchton. I've traveled to Seascape and Vanaria, where they have buildings that stretch taller than our mightiest trees. I've held council with kings, and now here I am about to sit among the great leaders and discuss the future of Mythos." She intertwines her arm with mine. "When you left us to continue your adventures, you said it was time for the trolls to find our place in this world once again. Thanks to you, we've unlocked a world beyond even our wildest dreams."

My cheeks burn under her intense gaze. "It wasn't all me. I had a lot of help along the way."

We stop to let King Favian and King Orso pass before continuing. They are more subtle in their admiration of the illustrious city than the trolls, but I catch them gawking as we arrive at the palace. There's a moment where everyone just stands at the foot of the magnificent structure, taking in the spectacle before climbing the hundreds of stairs.

It's easy to lose focus as we climb. Every third stair is transparent, granting a view of a stream that runs down from the palace. Colorful fish dart through the water beneath our feet.

King Orso leans toward Favian, but his deep voice still carries. "I can admire gnomish craftsmanship. Their ability to bend glass and gemstones to their will would impress even our foremost jewelers. But to me, there is nothing greater than stone. It has a presence that is powerful and unforgiving. When you touch it, you can feel a connection to the earth from which we sprang."

Dezmin turns around from the front of the procession. "I assure you, Your Highness, that these walls could withstand the attack of a dragon and neither melt nor shatter. We don't just craft, we enchant."

King Favian coughs to cover his laughter.

At the top of the stairs, guards stand sentry. Their iridescent armor fits perfectly among the palace's exterior. Since the attack, the palace has been closed to tourists and only open to those there on official business.

The palace has its own stables, but Chief Rizza and I elect to have Caustic and her wyrm wait outside the entrance to avoid the detour. One guard shifts uncomfortably when the dragon and wyrm begin clicking their snouts at one another. Maybe Caustic has finally found a playmate he doesn't have to hold back with.

I give Chief Rizza a reassuring smile as we enter. As great as it is to have found a place in the world, there may come a time when the trolls wish they were still forgotten within the forest. The stakes of this council are far greater than the last.

Valmar's presence is no longer just a worry.

Limery rejoins us, taking a seat on my shoulder opposite his mother.

He wraps his small arms around my neck and squeezes. "Limmy wants to thank Chods for bringing Daddy backs."

"You're welcome, buddy." I reach up, caressing him gently on the back. "I'm sure he's glad to see you."

"Oh, yes." He clasps his hands together and grins devilishly. "And one days, Limmy and Leos is going to goes into the dungeonses."

Footsteps echo through the cavernous building as we ascend the stairwell toward the council chambers. At the top of the stairs, we return to a familiar landing with its elaborate mosaic mirrored on the floor and ceiling. Guards and escorts of various kingdoms fill the landing. There are several merfolk, lizardfolk, and catfolk mixed with a spattering of humans, halflings, and gnomes that obscure the council room entrance. Some talk in hushed voices, but more stand silently.

The clack of hooves against the marble floor draws my attention to two centaurs from Wandermere. I acknowledge Daimun Stonewhisper and Sylvie Redmane with a nod. That must mean that their leader, Swift Thundercrest, is already inside.

"Make way," Dezmin orders. The crowd parts, revealing an arched door carved with intricate designs of birds and flowers and fitted with hundreds of colorful gemstones. It wasn't that long ago that Taryn used his Nimble Key to pick the lock.

Back then, Councilgnome Felston Boonspan said there was nothing he could do for us. Aside from him, the rest of the council refused to believe the threat was real.

This time, we are welcomed inside. Massive pillars run along both sides of the room, and a set of rainbow-colored stairs lead to a platform where a throne once stood. Now, there's a massive sculpture of a cornucopia and giant gemstone fruits spill out from the crystal horn. There are lemons carved from topaz, emerald limes, sapphire and ruby berries, amethyst grapes, and more I couldn't begin to identify. According to Felston, it is a reminder to the council that the citizens are the bounty of Pruxford.

The smaller hexagonal table where the council meets has been replaced with a circular table that fills the majority of the room. More chairs have been placed around the perimeter. Even with the guards waiting outside, the room doesn't feel quite as big as it did on our first visit.

The doors shut behind us, and there are a few minutes of chaos as old friends and acquaintances reconnect. I recognize many of them from the Challenger's Ball, and several more from the original council in Seascape. King Orso greets Councilgnome Felston, and I make my way over to the centaurs Swift Thundercrest and Thannis Smokehoof, his most trusted advisor. Swift is as stout as ever with his silver lower half and matching gray beard trimmed to a point. His beard ends just above a large chest tattoo that depicts a dragon curled around the base of a towering tree.

"It is good to see you again, Chod." Swift squeezes my shoulder. "Though I wish it were under better circumstances."

"Better than pretending there's no need for this meeting." King Orso joins us, grasping Swift firmly around the forearm.

"Don't hold it against them." Swift looks around the room. "Better late than never."

At the last council, most of the attendants were advisors from other kingdoms. This time, everyone with a position of power is here.

"You'd have better luck uprooting a mountain than softening the edge of a dwarven grudge." King Favian grins. "Dwarven anger cuts deeper than enchanted steel."

"Too true." Swift laughs and turns to me. "How are you faring with the young dragon?"

Before I can answer, Dezmin clears his throat and it carries above the chatter, magically amplified. "As much as I wish this were a festive occasion, there are grave matters to discuss. Please, take a seat so that we may begin with the business at hand."

Everyone takes their seats, with kings, queens, councilors, and heads of state sitting at the main table and advisors and other attendants sitting in the chairs around the room. I sit between Jira and Taryn. Limery and his family claim the top step near the cornucopia.

"I didn't realize there would be so many people here," Taryn whispers.

He means it as a compliment, but as I look around, I realize that this is it—the totality of kingdoms not allied with Valmar. Somehow, it doesn't feel like enough. How many of these leaders will rally to the cause? Or will some be content to hide away until the darkness inevitably swallows them?

Dezmin stands and bangs a crystal gavel until the room falls silent. If not for the severity of the situation, I would laugh at how he and the council look like a set of garden gnomes dipped in watercolor with their matching clothing in an array of pastel shades.

Instead, I hang onto every word the gnome says, sunshine yellow outfit and all.

"Several days ago, Pruxford fell victim to a senseless attack. Many of you were here that day. When we should have been celebrating the quincentennial and the achievements of hard-fought battles in the arena, we were instead forced to bury hundreds of innocents who lost their lives. A warlock sworn to Valmar Worren opened a portal inside the Crystal Arena, allowing two ships filled with sea orcs from Blacktide to lay siege to one of our most timeless traditions. At the same time, there was a secondary attack outside of our primary portal, where hundreds of innocent civilians were killed in cold blood. The arena can be repaired, but those lives will forever be a grim reminder of the evils of this world."

Dezmin pauses, taking the time to make eye contact with many of the leaders. "The worst part is that it could have been prevented. We should have listened when King Orso first called a council in Seascape. We should have listened when rumors began to swell of monsters appearing from the shadowlands. I chose to ignore it because it was far easier than admitting what might actually be happening—that Valmar Worren is still out there. Still plotting. This is the reason why the Pruxford Council has called you all here today." Dezmin leans forward, resting his hands on the table and sighing. "There are those of you who still doubt if the threat is real. You believe King Orso too cautious or too worried because of Seascape portal's recent awakening. Pruxford and Seascape are not the only ones to face attacks, and I encourage others to share their accounts now."

The first to speak is Swift. He tells the room of the mesmer wisp invasion of Wandermere and how if not for Taryn, Limery, and myself, the herd would have eventually been cut off from the portal and the other kingdoms.

Next, a member of the Mistville Court stands. I recognize the merfolk from the Challenger's Ball. He has slick green skin and a set of gills along each side of his neck. Sunset-colored fins streak from his head to neck, fading from orange to yellow. He clenches his webbed hand into a fist when he speaks, slow and deliberate.

"After the attack on Pruxford, we returned home with our challengers while we waited for the council to gather. No more than a day passed before a dark fog began to encroach upon Mistville from the south. Shrieks howled through the night, and tumultuous waves crashed into our cove. The next morning, bodies of our sea guardians washed upon the shores. We gathered all of our fighters and searched the waters until we found a kraken lurking within its depths. We lost two of our own in the battle, but we forced the beast to retreat with grievous injuries. It had already laid dozens of eggs, but we dispatched those easily enough. Had we not acted swiftly, we would have found ourselves in a similar state to Wandermere."

I'm surprised it's King Favian who stands to speak next. His armor gleams beneath the enchanted chandelier, and the griffin on his breastplate seems almost alive as its eye catches the light.

"Many of you are familiar with the hesitancy of my forbearers, and how hiding behind the safety of our ivory tower almost ensured the defeat of those who stood against Valmar in ages past. That is precisely why I am here today. To make sure those mistakes are not repeated."

I'm always amazed when Favian puts on his kingly persona. It's so different from the carefree spirit who would prefer to spend his days flying among the clouds on the back of a griffin. When it's time to rally the troops, I don't know if there is anyone better.

"For those of you who might not recall, Vanaria is home to perhaps the greatest threat to the undead in all of Mythos. Our tower was constructed during the Age of Heroes and consecrated by the most powerful cleric this world has ever known. The tower still blesses the lands that fall beneath its shadow. Recently, Valmar has chosen to test the tower's constitution. For a full day, undead poured from the portal." He pauses, letting the words build in the silence. "Their bodies vaporized as they entered. The stench of sulfur swelled within the city walls, but the blessing held. There is no doubt of what we are up against. Valmar tests us one at a time. He is searching for weakness. To what end, I'm not sure, but now is the time for us to present a united front and to finally admit that the threat is real."

"How are you so certain?" A silver-haired catfolk stands at the opposite side of the table. She's from Antadale, but she wasn't at the last council. "How are you so certain that this wasn't the result of a hero gone rogue, the work of someone without the fear of true death meddling with powers beyond their control? I have heard the stories. Tales of heroes appearing upon the Isle of Mythos, and somehow, only the Isle. Tales of humans, and dwarves, and..." The catfolk looks at me and her whiskers twitch. "Trolls. Why is it that they appear and now we find ourselves in danger? Why is it that none of this began happening until Seascape and Vanaria opened their portals?"

Swift huffs before Favian can respond, and his tail flicks in agitation. "You've always been a sourpuss, Ofelia. Many owe their lives to these heroes. If not for this troll, then those from the Isle of Mythos would not be here today. If not for this dwarf—" Swift gestures to Taryn. "—then the centaurs of Wandermere would not be here. If not for the many human heroes from Vanaria, then who knows where the death count of Pruxford would have ended. They fought among your challengers hand-in-hand. Forget your grievances with the heroes, or the lack of them, in Antadale, and look at the evidence before you. There have been attacks all over Mythos. If we stand idly by, there will be more."

"Call me names if you wish, Swift, but I will not spread panic and fear among my people when there is nothing to be done." She crosses her arms. "Even if there is a threat out there, the portals to Mosstar and the shadowlands are still closed. Yet you call us here as if an attack is on our doorsteps. To hear my kin tell it, the warlock was engaged in battle with another hero when he summoned the orcs. Many died, yes. A tragedy, certainly. But squabbles among heroes are hardly a call for war."

I know it's not my place to speak, but I can't help myself. "A war is coming whether you choose to acknowledge it or not." Several heads turn in my direction, but I continue. "You have the luxury to dismiss it now, while Antadale and Ellynmylly remain untouched, but eventually, you won't."

There's a murmur around the room, and Taryn pokes me in the side. "Chod, what the hell are you doing?" he whispers.

Ofelia's claws emerge from her paws as she presses them to the table. "Is that a threat, troll?"

"That's enough." Dezmin's voice booms as he tries to regain order.

I stand, staring down the elder catfolk. "I have no grievance with you or your people. Since coming to Mythos, I've found a tribe, I've found friends, and more than that, I've found a purpose. Death might not mean the same thing to heroes as it does to you, but I will die a thousand times if that is what it takes to protect this place."

Every part of me wants to scream and yell and pound the table until I can make everyone here understand. Not that long ago, I might have done just that. It's taken me a while to realize it, but I know that's not the way. At least not every time.

I rest my hands on the table, feeling the cool marble against my palm before continuing. "I know that I can't do this alone. I don't know how we can defeat Valmar. I don't know how we can open the portals. There's so much that I don't know, but I do know that we have to try. There has to be a way. Where I come from, there's a saying, and I've never paid it much attention until now. United we stand. Divided we fall."

Ofelia and I lock eyes for a long moment, neither one of us wanting to be the first to break eye contact.

Eventually, her claws retract. "I admire your commitment. If you and the other heroes fight for Antadale with the same fervor, then perhaps there is hope."

Dezmin lets out a sigh of relief. "So we are all in agreement then."

Ofelia nods. "We will listen to your proposals, but I don't see how this changes anything. Valmar has the advantage because he has the ability to open and close his portals at will. We have all found ways to open our own portals, but there is no way to open those still closed from the other side."

"Actually, I might be able to help with that." A hooded figure wearing a dark gray robe emerges from between two lizardfolk on the far side of the room. I recognize the black chain around his neck immediately.

Taryn grips my forearm. "Stay calm."

"And who are you?" asks Dezmin.

"Me? I'm just the messenger." He removes the hood, revealing the blonde hair and chiseled jawline of Richard Hummel, the cleric who serves the god of chaos. "But I'm here to help."

5. MARK OF THE DAMNED

Some time ago.

Dorothy crept silently through the forest. On the outside, she was calm and collected, a hunter on the prowl, but inside, a maelstrom of emotions swirled. A child-like wonder fought against the grudge that weighed heavily on her slender shoulders. High above the obsidian trees, lightning cracked, igniting their skeletal branches, and strands of Dorothy's silver hair fluttered in the electric air as the thunder rumbled.

Not far ahead, the blaze of a low fire flickered where several hobgoblins sat around the camp muttering to one another.

Dorothy stalked her prey, a shadow among the darkness. She was on top of the group before the first hob noticed her, its orange, cat-like eyes wide as she plunged her dagger into the skull of the hobgoblin across from it. Bone shattered beneath the ancient blade as the hob collapsed to the ground. With the finesse of her elven body, she spun, stabbing the next hob in the throat and pulling the blade until a streak of crimson arced through the air. She moved like a huntress, sharpening her skills with each kill until only one remained.

The lone hobgoblin ran through the woods in an attempt to escape. Dorothy activated True Strike and threw the dagger. When the weapon released, it flew like an arrow, lodging in the back of the creature with a thunk.

Over a dozen hobgoblins lay scattered throughout their primitive outpost, the unfortunate victims of her destruction. This was the third camp she had destroyed this evening, and it wouldn't be the last. Notifications flashed in her vision, but she pushed them away.

Dorothy should be having fun. On some level, she was. She was experiencing the best gameplay of her life, and full-immersion was better than she could have ever dreamed. The sights. The smells. The feel of the leather-wrapped hilt of a dagger against her skin, and the tactile feedback of bone crunching beneath the blade. It was amazing, and yet all she could think about was how Chad Johnson had gotten to enjoy this at her expense. In a land of darkness, he still managed to cast a shadow.

They could call it punishment all they wanted, but the truth was that he'd been rewarded for making her a laughingstock.

Dorothy pressed her foot on the hobgoblin and pulled out the dagger lodged in its ribs, imagining the creature as a monstrous blue troll. She wiped the blood from the blade on her pant leg and sheathed the weapon. When she focused on her map, it appeared across her vision. The location of her mark pulsed slowly.

That brought a smile to her face.

He was still in Pruxford, and the word *Mark of the Damned* hovered over Chad Johnson's icon. No, not Chad Johnson. Here, he was Chod, and he had the nerve to call himself a hero.

The guy was anything but. He was a bully, a rager, an asshole, and he was a middling gamer at best; otherwise, he would have gone pro. Instead, he hurled insults at teammates who were trying their best and belittled people for comedy.

Thanks to John Barrett, Dorothy would have the last laugh.

The man had been right. His daughter was on to something special with this game. Valery wanted to use it to help people. To try and rewire neural pathways and reform criminals. John believed it could be more than that.

Judging by the few days Dorothy had spent in Isle of Mythos, Valery had her father's knack for innovative gameplay.

John had hand-picked Dorothy, pulling the one card he had over his daughter. Finance.

He was fascinated by his daughter's work. Not just the technology of the pods, but the AI and how it allowed for world-building that constantly evolved.

Dorothy had encountered more depth during her first day in this world than she had in years playing other games. Part of her wondered if John was jealous of his daughter's creation. Not that it mattered. Dorothy had her own reasons for agreeing.

As the head of Mythos Games, John Barrett was a gamer to his core. He studied lore like some studied business and finance. It was the reason he ran the best gaming company on the planet. Profit was a byproduct of his success, not the reason for it.

Thanks to him, Dorothy had entered Valery's trial with knowledge the other testers didn't have. She picked her race and class with one goal in mind—revenge. Soon enough, she was going to destroy everything Chod loved about this world. But first, she might as well enjoy herself a little.

Playing as an elf was the only way for her to choose a class that would spawn her in Mosstar. The kingdom's portal was closed to the rest of Mythos, but John assured her that wouldn't matter for much longer. If she allied herself with Valmar, it would put her on a collision course with Chod.

For her class, she'd chosen revenant. It allowed her to keep some of the traits of her original race but altered her appearance, giving her elven body ashen gray skin and eyes that burnt like embers. As an undead, she wouldn't need to sleep or eat, and poison had no effect. But that wasn't the best part.

The biggest advantage of being a revenant was that, unlike the other heroes of Mythos, she had no reason to fear death. When a revenant died, they didn't lose a level. She'd used this to her advantage several times already and was already at level fourteen.

Dorothy took a final look at Chod's icon before dismissing the map. Finding an item to use to bind him as her mark had been difficult, but Valmar had his ways. In exchange for her loyalty, the dark wizard had had one of his minions secure what she'd needed. She had a long way to go before she would be ready to fight the troll, but unlike him, she had plenty of time to prepare.

She glanced at the bar filling the corner of her vision. *Rage of the Damned* was nearly replenished.

The scouting outposts were all gone, leaving the hobgoblin encampment free for the taking. Clearing it out would be a nice chunk of experience. Once Dorothy hit level twenty, she'd return to the necropolis for her next mission. Until then, she could hone her skills.

6. NO MORE HEROES

Valery's eyes burned, and she fought the urge to cry. Her father had instilled in her early on that in a world where the strong survived, crying was a sign of weakness. Those words had hurt, and yet controlling her emotions in the corporate world had been a blessing to a young woman climbing the ladder.

For the first time in a long time, she felt helpless, like everything she'd worked for was collapsing all around her. What did it matter if she shed a tear? The inmate rehabilitation program was going to be shut down soon. There was no getting around that. Not even her father could stop that train now that it was moving. His little stunt with Dorothy Jordan was going to ensure there were no pieces left to pick up.

Valery never should have allowed him to get anywhere near this project. When the game first started crashing and the only option to stabilize the AI was to keep Chad Johnson immersed, she'd asked for her father's advice. A one-time favor to see if he could find the problem. If there was a way to exploit a game, John Barrett could find it. In the end, asking for his help had been her undoing.

She stood over Dorothy's pod as the woman massacred another encampment. It was unsettling how often she chose violence.

A revenant? Valery cursed her lack of foresight. She'd unlocked the advanced races for Taryn when he'd logged in, but she'd never turned them back off. Why would she? There weren't supposed to be any more testers, much less someone who would want to spawn in Mosstar while Mythos was on the brink of war.

Now, Dorothy was advancing her character at a rapid rate. Not even Chad had leveled up this quickly. It was only a matter of time before the two met, and their personal rivalry would leave a lasting change on the course of Mythos.

The AI wouldn't favor the heroes, especially when a handful of them had already joined forces with Valmar. It would let the chaos play out, and if the forces of darkness won, the game would continue to evolve. In a few months, the entire world could shift.

Part of Valery wanted to force Dorothy to log out, but that would only make things worse. Her father had financed this venture, and he hated when he didn't get his way, especially now that she'd given him a peek behind the curtain. Crossing him would mean a freeze on her funding and the certain demise of this project instead of what she was facing now.

She should have known better than to trust him when he said this was her show and he wouldn't get involved.

He'd never believed she would be able to succeed in using artificial intelligence to mimic therapy in a fantasy video game. Now that she had, of course, he was interested.

Removing his little pet from the game might be worse than what was coming from the Bureau of Prisons. He'd destroyed upstart companies for less.

Valery turned to one of the bright spots of this whole endeavor—Chad Johnson. His bravado and interaction with the ley lines had provided hope for advancements beyond mental rehabilitation. Like some of the greatest inventions, the connection had been discovered by accident. If she had more time to study the effects on his body, they could be in store for something truly groundbreaking.

She had more of her father in her than she'd like to admit. She'd grown attached to this world. It evolved by the day. Every choice the players made reverberated across the continents. Starting from scratch would be like losing a child. It would be the end of the AI as she knew it. There was no telling what the next iteration would be like. They'd gone through half a dozen before this one.

If the inmates were all going to be pulled, then they needed to leave Mythos in a state where it could survive with no heroes.

Valery wiped her eyes. The clock hadn't run out yet. She still had work to do.

7. BEYOND THE VEIL

My claws dig into the chair as Richard weasels his way toward the table. He stands next to Councilgnome Dezmin, so close that he practically hovers over the gnome. The cleric's blue eyes scan the room, and when he finds me, a wry smile spreads across his stupid face. It takes everything I have not to explode a horror on top of him.

Taryn has told me countless times that I'm overreacting when it comes to Richard, but the man is responsible for turning Pressley into a death knight. Who knows what other calamities he's caused in the name of chaos.

Whatever he has planned, it can't be good. There's too much on the line to trust the word of someone who causes chaos for fun. Or his god.

Richard runs his fingers over the black chain around his neck and it jingles softly. The full attention of the room is on the cleric.

"You say you can help us." Dezmin shifts uncomfortably at the cleric's proximity before taking a step to the side. "What exactly is it you're offering?"

"I can get you to Mosstar." He says it so nonchalantly, like it's the easiest task in the world and not something that has plagued Mythos for hundreds of years.

"Impossible." Ofelia laughs and sits back against her chair. The silver-haired catfolk crosses her arms. "Everyone knows it's impossible to open a portal from a foreign side. Otherwise, it would not have taken our kingdoms so long to regain contact."

Richard's grin grows more mischievous. "Impossible for you, maybe."

"Tell me, who are you?" The merfolk with the sunset-colored fins glares at the interloper.

"Like I said, I am but the messenger. My god has taken an exceptional interest in the predicament you find yourselves in. They have asked me to lend my services to the cause."

"And what cause might that be?" King Orso's voice booms. "Don't think I have forgotten your actions in Seascape."

I turn to Taryn, giving him a knowing look. I'm glad to see I'm not the only one who distrusts this guy.

Richard throws up both hands. "Once again, Your Grace, I am only the messenger. Would you punish your guard for following orders?"

"Carry on with it, then," Orso growls. "What is it that your god can help us with?"

Richard grabs his chain and squeezes, almost like a priest clutching a rosary. "When the time comes, I will be granted the authority to open portals for your forces. When this happens, you must be prepared to enter immediately. The gateway will be open to both sides, putting all of Mythos at risk the longer it remains open. The most prudent course would be to route the portals outside of the city to allow you time to mobilize your forces before storming the city."

"Is this possible?" someone asks, followed by a roar of chatter around the room.

Dezmin bangs his crystal gavel to gather everyone's attention. While he's regaining order, a message notification flashes in the corner of my vision. My chest tightens at the thought of another message from Dorothy. What else could she possibly have to say? More threats, perhaps. There's too much going on right now for me to deal with her revenge quest, but I am curious. I pull up the message while Dezmin attempts to quiet the room.

I frown when I notice the message is from Valery. That's some relief, but she's picked a terrible time if this is about scheduling the next logout.

Incoming Message (Admin): *Chod, I realize this is not the best timing, but what I'm about to share with you cannot wait. There may not be another opportunity for you to be in a room with this much influence, and time is of the essence. For both of us.*

I'm not sure where to begin or how much to say, but the short of it is that the rehabilitation program is being forced to shut down. That means all of the inmates and testers will be pulled from the program, and the lab will be shuttered while the bureau conducts an investigation. I don't know how much time we have before that happens. Maybe a few days. A few weeks if we are lucky. The wheels of government turn slowly, so I'm praying for the latter.

You're probably wondering why I am telling you this. That's one of the few answers I do have. You've grown attached to this game and this world as much as I have. It's easy to see. Like me, you view Mythos as more than lines of code. That's not the case for most of the inmates. I trust that you will only divulge the state of the program to those you can trust with such information.

Even with the program's impending demise, not all hope is lost. The system will still run, and the AI will allow the world to propel down whatever path it is taking. I never imagined the scope of these quests would move beyond the Isle of Mythos during the first phase of trials. Thanks to you, all of Mythos has been unlocked. With the portals opened, we have seen the true breadth of this world, but that has also left it in a precarious position at the most inopportune time.

Which is why I'm reaching out to you directly. We've worked so hard to build this world, and I don't want to see it crumble. So, I have a quest for you, Chod. With however much time we have left, I need you to leave Mythos in a state so that it can survive without heroes.

If you can do that, I'll do everything within my power to make sure there's something to come back to. -Valery

My ears ring, blocking out all sound aside from my thunderous heartbeat. For the longest time, I just stare at the message. Why would they just shut down the program? How could they do that?

I close the message, and the conversation with Richard continues around me. I can't hear anything over the ringing in my ears.

My gaze lands at the top of the stairs where Limery sits next to his brother, an arm wrapped around Leo's shoulders. His bulbous yellow eyes lock with mine, and he grins his devilish smile.

The pit in my stomach widens to the point that I think it may swallow me from the inside. What would happen to Limery if the program ends? What would happen to all of this? As absurd as it is, my mind goes back to grade school on the day that Ms. Harris asked us what we'd do if we knew the world was ending. How would we want to spend our final days? Kind of morbid when you think about it, especially for children, but it was supposed to remind us of our priorities in life. Some kids said they would spend time with their families. Others wanted to go on a trip or play their favorite games. I don't remember what my answer was, but here I am, presented with the same question all these years later.

Whether it's three days or three weeks, this world is ending. My friends. My tribe. Everything I've grown to care about. All gone.

My world is ending.

Unless I save it.

I read the message again, trying to parse out any information I can from Valery's words. She wants to save this world as much as I do, and we don't have a lot of time. She's right, though. There may not be another chance where I'm in a position with this much influence.

The phrase cycles on repeat in my mind—what would I do if the world was ending?

I'd save it. I have to save it. For Limery and Chief Rizza, for the trolls, and for everyone who lives a life as real as my own even when I'm not around.

The ringing fades and chaos resumes as leaders argue over whether or not Richard's offer is real.

I move toward the table. Taryn reaches for my arm, but I shrug him off. I make my way between King Orso and King Favian and slam my fist down with enough force that the table splinters.

Several people jump at the sound, and one of the halflings squeaks with surprise.

My chest heaves with each breath as I fight the panic rising inside. I meet Richard's eyes. "Tell us, after all you've done, why should we trust you?"

Richard meets my gaze, and the smile he's been wearing all night finally fades. "There it is."

I'm not sure what he means, but something changes in his demeanor. He closes his eyes and clenches both hands around the obsidian chain. Power radiates from the man. The air in front of him crackles, and dark energy sparks above the table.

Chairs screech against the marble floor as people move back. I don't flinch an inch even as my braid rises from my shoulder from the electricity in the air.

The darkness flares until it is about the size of a doorframe. There's a ripping sound as a gash forms in the void, as if the fabric of reality is tearing in front of us. The rift widens, giving us a bird's-eye view of a city at night. The buildings are outlined in an eerie green glow. The view shifts, as if we're flying over the city. We pass a castle, where four massive green flames burn on the tops of towers surrounding an obsidian keep. A spire sprouts from the center of the castle, even taller than the flames, and the walls gleam with their reflection. The perspective shifts again and we're soaring over the city. Far below, the buildings are speckled with the dull light from thousands of windows. We move higher until clouds conceal our view. For a long moment, all we see is gray mist. The silence of the room is palpable as we pass through the clouds until suddenly, they are gone.

An expanse of darkness stretches forever across the horizon. Then, the view shifts again. Patchy snow covers the ground outside the city walls. We zoom closer, and my blood runs cold when I realize it's not snow.

An army of skeletons stands outside the city, unmoving. The view zooms in on the bone-white warriors with their rusted weapons and shields. They stand, lifeless, like a group of mannequins. There's no telling how long they've been stationed there. The view widens, revealing more and more skeletons that stretch around the perimeter of the city. Thousands of them. Tens of thousands.

The portal closes, and the entire room sits in shocked silence.

Richard clears his throat. "Why should you trust me?" His gaze is still fixed where the portal was moments before. "Because I'm your only hope."

8. PARTS TO PLAY

The air above the table crackles one final time as the portal vanishes. We all stand in shocked silence. Any doubts about Valmar's resurgence have been demolished. Not only is he out there, he has an army.

A fucking big one.

My hands twitch with nervous energy. I knew Valmar was the big baddie ever since I saw the paintings and tapestries in Vanaria that depicted the battle against his forces I knew, but I wasn't prepared for this. Thousands of undead warriors wait outside the gates to Mosstar, and that's not even counting whatever monsters and other kingdoms he's rallied to his cause. Inside the city, there are elves that haven't had contact with the outside world for hundreds of years.

According to Valery's message, we have weeks, maybe days, to deal with this threat. Without heroes, what chance does the rest of Mythos have against an undead army?

It almost feels hopeless, but I refuse to wallow in self-pity. In a world where anything is possible, there has to be a way out of this. There aren't that many heroes, but together, we have the power to turn battles. We don't die like everyone else. And when we do die, we only lose a fraction of our power each time we return. If I have to, I'll charge the gates of Mosstar until there's nothing left of me.

Somehow, I'll need to convince the rest of the heroes to do the same.

"Can any of our clericss confirm that what we ssaw is real?" one of the lizard-folk hisses.

"It is," Kurzol answers, his face grim. "I could sense a divine radiance surrounding the portal. Ithus may be a trickster, but the portal was true."

Ithus. That's the first time I've heard the God of Chaos's name said aloud.

"What now?" Ofelia's gaze darts around the room, the hair on her neck more bristled than usual. "Much to my dismay, the threat is real. Valmar has an army in waiting. How do you propose we prepare?"

"I take no pleasure in this confirmation." King Orso's face is set in stone. "But we must mobilize our forces, empty our troves, and end this threat once and for all." He speaks with authority, but not everyone is convinced.

"We must not rush into battle." A shaggy-haired halfling shakes his head. "We don't know the full extent of Valmar's resources. It would be more prudent to take our time and prepare."

"Take our time?" King Favian scoffs. "That must be easy for Ellynmylly to say when the dead are not spilling into your streets. Every minute we delay is another moment for the dark wizard to grow stronger."

"Now, now." Dezmin raises his hands in an attempt to calm the room. "We are all on the same side here. We must fight, but Milbun is right. We cannot be quick to dismiss caution out of fear. We must be prudent, and we must choose our course of action wisely."

"How long would it take?" I speak calmly despite the worry that continues to build inside of me. Monsters, the undead, and even Valmar himself don't scare me, but the possibility of losing all of this does. "How long would it take to mobilize your forces if you had to?"

There's a moment of chatter as the leaders speak with their advisors.

"Fighting with only what we have at the ready, a week," Dezmin answers. "But we have precious few Revive Potions. Not enough for even a quarter of our greatest warriors. Too many were used during the tournament."

I recall the description of the Revive Potion I was given before the tournament started. The one that still buffs me and Ethan the warlock even now with an extra life since neither of us died in the final match. Each potion takes a year to brew. Forty years' worth of work was wasted during a single day of entertainment. If only they'd listened...

Richard taps his fingers on the table. He's the only one still standing close to it. "As thrilling as it would be to watch these negotiations play out, I do have other matters to attend to. If you decide to partake in the service my god has to offer, you can find me at the Dragon's Rest Inn." He looks in my direction. "Chod, would you do me the honor of escorting me out of the palace?"

I'd like to give him the honor of a swift kick in the nuts, but he may have a part to play in all of this.

"Give me a moment." I sigh before turning to King Orso and whispering in his ear. "I don't know what he's up to, but we must convince the council to attack Mosstar within a week. There's not enough time for me to explain right now, but I will."

Orso's eyes widen slightly and I wonder what must be going through his mind. He nods solemnly, and I'm grateful to have earned his trust.

Next, I move to King Favian and then to Chief Rizza, telling them the same thing. I've earned their trust through my actions. Convincing everyone here to go against the greatest threat this world has ever seen on a week's notice will take a skillset that I don't have—diplomacy. The three of them will have more influence over the other leaders than I possibly could.

Finally, I kneel next to Taryn. "When this is over, there's something I need to tell you. Don't let them leave this council unless they are ready to fight."

His brow arches. "Should I be worried?"

I nod grimly. "We all should."

"We'll handle them." He pats me on the arm. "Just keep your claws to yourself."

That may be easier said than done.

Richard and I pass the guards and envoys outside the council chambers and descend the stairwell into the vacant palace. Without the throngs of crowds waiting for tours, it seems even larger. Our footsteps carry across the emptiness.

"What is it you want?" I ask once we are out of earshot.

"If only it were that simple." He gestures down an empty hallway, and we walk. "You know, when I was a child, my mother took me to mass every Sunday. I was always enthralled by the priests. They wore these vibrant vestments, each piece with its own special meaning. Fragile clothing, but somehow, it was the armor of God. They looked divine, almost magical, standing on the pulpit with the crucifix behind them and the statues, tapestries, and morning light shining through the stained glass. I always thought it must be pretty special to hear the voice of God." He chuckles. "Turns out it is."

For a long moment, he doesn't speak. I stare at him, unwilling to play whatever game he has planned.

"I know you don't like me." He turns, tilting his head until he's looking up at me. "Trying to take a meaningful item from you when we'd just met. I'll admit my first impression was a bit heavy-handed. But as I've explained before, the rules are different when you don't have the brute strength to clear a dungeon by yourself."

I scowl at the man. "What are you getting at, Richard?"

"Fair enough. I suppose time is of the essence. There's a difference between causing pain and causing chaos. Despite what you may think, Jude, Glenn, and I are not the same." He resumes his stroll down the corridor, not waiting for me to catch up. "For what it's worth, I hope you're able to figure this out. Everyone loves a good underdog story."

Richard disappears around the corner, and when I arrive, he's nowhere to be found.

There might be some truth to his words. They aren't the same. Glenn is a legit psychopath, and Jude has anger issues that trump my worst days. Richard, I'm not sure. There's something about him that doesn't sit right with me, but maybe Taryn is right. It could be that I've never given him a real chance because of our first meeting. Or maybe this is just another thread of chaos. Either way, while the council decides the fate of Mythos, I have work to do.

Outside the palace, Caustic and Rizza's wyrm peck at one another with their hardened snouts, almost like birds grooming one another. I give them both a firm pat, but they pay me no mind. The palace guards on each side keep a safe distance from the two young dragons.

I elect to leave Caustic at the palace while I handle business. Once the council is over, he'll fly back to the stables, but for now, it'll be good for him to spend some time bonding with a similar beast.

Knowing how stubborn some of the leaders are, I wouldn't be surprised if they are arguing about the best course of action through the night. There's no point waiting around for the council to finish their discussion, so I head back to the Puzzling Peacock.

As I walk through the barren streets, I send a message to Michael the paladin. One of the benefits of his Oath of Protection is that we have access to message one another without being in a party.

Message (Chod): *Are you at the inn by chance? The leaders are having a council right now and things are about to hit the fan. If you're able, I need you to gather as many heroes as you can. I'll be there shortly to explain.*

After a few minutes, he responds.

Incoming Message (Michael): *You're going to make me regret this oath, aren't you? There's a few of us here already. I'll see who else I can track down.*

I run through various scenarios while I walk, trying to decide the best way to deliver the information. If I tell the other heroes that they're soon going to be pulled from the game permanently, I doubt any of them would agree to go to battle. They'd likely party away their final days in inns and taverns across Mythos.

I'll need to be creative, and I'll need to convince them to grind harder than ever over the next week.

By the time I arrive at the inn, the ground level is filled. There are the usual heroes and champions from the tournament that have made the Puzzling Peacock a bustling tavern the past few days, but there are some new faces.

"A few of you." I laugh as I join Michael by the bar. "Right."

Michael grabs a half-dozen mugs from the barkeep. The paladin's hair shimmers with divine radiance even in the dull light of the tavern. "Lucky for you, it was two-for-one night at the Brown Boar Tavern a few blocks over. It only took a promise of a round on me and some news from you to get them over here." He nods toward the barkeep as he fills more mugs. "Help me pass these out."

I grab as many drinks as I can carry and begin disseminating them among the crowd. Arty and his brothers are here, and the cyclops chats with a half-dozen others who I can only assume are adventurers. Randy the rogue and his newfound friend, the golden-scaled assassin Drizz'rt, claim a table in the center. Don the void mage sits with them, galaxies swirling within the depths of his eyes. Next to them, Sam the barefoot monk, and Scotty the sniper accept their mugs with a smile. I'd never spoken to them before the attack on the arena, but they both joined the fight just the same.

Lanxkuri, the catfolk blood mage, and a couple of her companions sit together at the far wall with the giant Kazzandre Strongback. She's by far the largest person in the room, making the halfling next to her look comically small. Across from them, another halfling and a lizardfolk I don't recognize sit with a pair of gnomes.

This isn't everyone, but it's a damn good start.

Once we've passed out the drinks, Michael clears his throat, and the beam of light that falls upon him intensifies. "Thank you all for gathering tonight, even if I had to bribe some of you. Leaders from across Mythos are currently holding council at the Crystal Palace, and Chod assures me he has some big news."

The tavern is quiet aside from the slurping of drinks and the noises of people shifting in their seats. Even the bartender leans against the counter in rapt attention.

For a moment, I just stand there, stomach in knots and unsure of the best way to proceed. I have to persuade them to fight, convince them that the possibility of dying on a battlefield is a better cause than what they're doing right now.

My mind wanders to the Christmas parties and business functions I was forced to attend with my parents as a child. There were always speeches. I never really thought about it, but it takes a special skill to convince those with everything that you have something they want. Or if you're real good, something they need.

My father was always great at that part of the job. Mom said he could sell water to a drowning man and leave him thirsty for more. Right now, I wish I had some of that confidence.

How can I possibly convey the gravity of the situation to people who weren't there to witness the portal? I don't know, but I have to try.

"What Michael says is true. Right now, leaders from all over are currently meeting to discuss the fate of Mythos. Ithus granted one of his clerics the power to open a portal above Mosstar, allowing us to view the city for the first time in centuries." Michael frowns at the mention of the trickster god, but I continue. "It's worse than we feared. Valmar has an undead army surrounding the city. Thousands of skeleton warriors that are waiting for his command. Not to mention the other kingdoms and alliances he has under his thumb."

"What's that have to do with us?" asks Randy.

My grip clenches around the mug. This is the reaction I was worried about.

"By the end of the night, I expect the council to give the order to prepare for war. We've found a way to bypass the locked portals, and if we can rally together in time, there may be a chance to attack Valmar before he suspects anything."

Randy takes a long swig of his ale. "Let me guess, you want us to come fight the undead army?"

"That's the gist of it."

Now comes the part where they argue that this isn't their fight and that none of this really matters.

Randy drains the rest of his mug and slams it to the table. "Alright, tell me when and where."

I cross my arms, staring at the troublesome, dark-haired rogue and wondering what I actually heard him say. Because there is no way he agreed that easily.

"What?" Randy frowns.

"You'll fight?" I can't keep the incredulous tone from my voice.

"That's what we're here for, right? To be heroes?" He grins.

"I'll be honest, I thought you would take more convincing."

"What? You think we were all just hanging out in Pruxford after the attack for our health?" He laughs. "We made our choice when we decided to fight back in the arena. We could have tucked tail then. For me at least, competing in the tournament made me realize something. That I can actually leave my mark on this place. And how better than cutting my way through the biggest bad this world has ever seen." He stands up and looks around the room. "Who's with me?"

Heavy mugs thud against the tables in response.

I turn to the bartender and raise my glass. "Keep 'em coming. We've got a lot to discuss."

We stay downstairs until the wee hours of the morning discussing the best ways to level and grind over the coming week. There's still no word from Taryn on the council's decision, but we're moving forward with our plans all the same.

As stressful as it may be, my heart is full by the time we say good night. Tomorrow, we'll go our separate ways and reconvene in a week.

Michael the paladin is the last one to leave. He puts a firm hand on my shoulder, and his deep blue eyes stare into my own. "The goddess approves of our work here today, though she is wary of the promises of Ithus. They are a trickster by nature, but chaos itself is not inherently bad, just unexpected."

I take a deep breath and pat him on the back. "I hope you're right."

I'm walking upstairs when several notifications flash in the corner of my vision. I hurry to my room and open them.

Regional Alert! *The Pruxford Council has declared war upon Mosstar. Able-bodied citizens must report to the Crystal Arena at first light for conscription.*

Regional Alert! *Mistville has declared war upon Mosstar.*

Regional Alert! *Antadale has declared war upon Mosstar.*
Regional Alert! *Ellynmylly has declared war upon Mosstar.*
Regional Alert! *Vanaria has declared war upon Mosstar.*
Regional Alert! *Wandermere has declared war upon Mosstar.*
Regional Alert! *Seascape has declared war upon Mosstar.*

Holy shit! They did it! I can feel the knots in my shoulders release as I read through the alerts from each kingdom.

Below the regional alerts, there is one more.

Alert! *The Forest Troll Tribe has declared war upon Mosstar. Gather at the troll castle in Tawdrybluff for further instructions from Chief Rizza.*

I imagine every citizen from each kingdom received a similar alert with instructions on what to do next. My plans lie far from Tawdrybluff, but I'll convene with Chief Rizza in the morning before leaving.

We've crossed the first hurdle, but we are far from the finish line. Now, we're in a race against the clock.

9. SOMETHING WORTH FIGHTING FOR

The next morning, Taryn and I sit down for a final breakfast at the Puzzling Peacock before heading to the palace to meet with Chief Rizza and pick up Limery. After that, we'll be off to our next adventure.

We grab a table in the far corner, out of earshot of the other patrons. None of the other heroes are here, so they're either already on the road or still sleeping. Considering I was the final person to turn in last night, my money is on the former.

I still need to tell Taryn about the message from Valery, but I haven't found the right opening. Flubs perches on the windowsill, pawing at the glass as the streets come to life. Ruby curls between Taryn's feet underneath the table. It's strange not having Limery here, but he's long overdue for some family time.

The barmaid quickly brings a steaming platter of food, and we fill our plates. The smell of savory sausage and bacon has my mouth watering.

"Remind me to never go into politics." Taryn talks with a full mouth as he holds a piece of buttered bread as if deciding whether or not to stuff it in as well. "What did Richard want with you, anyway?"

"More of the same." I roll my eyes. "But he says we can trust him. Not that we have much of a choice." I take a bite of warm sausage, letting the sweet and spicy juices explode in my mouth before changing the subject. "Was the rest of the council that bad?"

Taryn leans his head back, and his dreadlocks fall down the back of the chair. He stares at the ceiling a moment before answering. "Worse."

"For what it's worth, I never doubted you for a second."

He chuckles. "It wasn't me. It was all Orso, Favian, and Rizza. Between the three of them, they weren't letting anyone leave that council room without getting what they wanted. Some of the others though, ugh. They were so stubborn."

I take a bite of egg and let my fork rest on the plate. "They're scared. Worried for their people, too."

"Yeah, I know. But we're here to help." Taryn sighs. "We won't be here forever."

My posture stiffens, and he immediately notices.

"What?" His brow arches as he gives me a questioning look.

"There's something I need to tell you." I nervously run a claw through the tip of my braid. "I received a message from Valery while we were at the council."

I do my best to keep my voice down as I read him the message in full.

Taryn's eyes go wide, and he forgets all about the plate of food in front of him. "Why do you think they're shutting it down? You think it's unsafe?"

"I don't know. She didn't make it seem like we were in danger. Maybe it has something to do with letting me stay in here after my sentence. Or you and Dorothy joining. Somehow, I get the feeling that mixing a program designed for prisoners with the general public might be frowned upon." I shrug. "Whatever it is, she thinks there's hope to keep the program running even if we're forced out. You're the only one I've told, and I think we should keep it that way. The other heroes are going to help us fight. But we need to level up as much as we can between now and then, starting with Goldspire."

Ruby places her paws on Taryn's leg and nuzzles against his arm, begging for food.

Taryn scratches her behind the ears. "I know, girl. I won't let anything happen to you."

We finish our meal in silence, each of us left to our own thoughts. Taryn cares for his pets just as much as I care for Limery and the trolls. I know he'd do anything to save them.

Our first stop before heading to the palace is the Rusty Bucket so we can gather Jordy, Berry, and Caustic. Berry stands on his hind legs, looking over the enclosure, and nearly tackles Taryn to the ground when Breebis opens the gate. Jordy is more reserved, lowering his head and gently ramming Taryn in the leg until he gets his attention.

Caustic's wingspan is now wide enough that he's forced to tuck his wings and waddle down the corridor as he exits. He's almost unrecognizable from the dragon that was smaller than Jordy when we first arrived in Pruxford. He huffs and lowers his head until it's inches from mine.

I lean forward and touch my horns to the top of his head. "I hope you had fun last night, because we've got some tough times ahead of us."

His chest purrs in affirmation, and I stroke the firm, cool scales of his jaw.

After we pay for the pets's stay, there's an awkward moment where Taryn and Breebis are staring at each other. I get the sense that they're wanting a chance for a more intimate good-bye.

A grin tugs at my mouth, and I clear my throat to try and conceal it. "Thanks for taking such good care of Caustic. I'll be outside whenever you all are done."

Breebis offers me a warm smile. "Stay safe out there. Caustic is powerful, but he's still young."

I raise my brows suggestively at Taryn, as I leave and his cheeks flush with color. I'm glad he's found someone he enjoys spending time with. It's just one of the many reasons why we have to leave this world better than we found it.

A few minutes later, he rejoins us outside the entrance.

"Not a word." He narrows his eyes at me.

Luckily for him, Limery isn't around to sing "Taryns has a girlfriends" on repeat.

***

We make our way through crowded streets toward the palace. This is the busiest the city has been since the tournament as all of the able-bodied citizens in Pruxford report to the Crystal Arena to begin the war effort. Taryn rides atop Berry with Ruby curled in his lap and Flubs tucked somewhere within his cloak. Jordy brings up the rear, following close behind the umber bear and occasionally ramming Berry in the backside when traffic slows. We tower over the diminutive gnomes all around us, surrounded by a sea of jeweled-toned skin and hair.

I can sense the tension in the air as gnomes talk in hushed voices about the threat beyond—and within—their borders. There's mention of the sea orcs from Blacktide and the elves of Mosstar, but no one speaks of the undead army lying in wait. They have no idea what's coming. Everyone knows of the attack on the arena, but the regional alert didn't explain what we are up against. Most of them don't even know that Valmar still exists, let alone what he's been up to.

They will soon enough.

The flow of traffic shifts when we pass the arena and continue toward the palace. We push our way through the steady current of gnomes, and a gnawing thought tugs at me as we pass by. How many of them won't return from Mosstar? How many families will be forever changed by what happens in the next week?

I wish there was another way, but there isn't. There's a time for diplomacy and there's a time for action. After seeing the undead army, I know we're going to need every able body we can find to put an end to it.

Caustic roars overhead, pulling me from my morose thoughts. There's no doubt that he senses my unease.

Up ahead, carriages are parked outside the steps to the palace as the leaders depart. I catch a glimpse of sunset-colored fins through a carriage window as the Mistville Court passes by. At the bottom of the stairs, the gleam of the mana-infused wyrm's scales shimmers in the morning light. Caustic dives from the sky, landing with a thud beside the wyrm.

The two dragons click their snouts and peck at one another in greeting, and the guards surrounding the palace entryway take a couple of steps back.

Chief Rizza, King Favian, and King Orso stand together, their conversation interrupted by the raucous dragons. Jira and the other advisors are nearby. Lord Kassidy waves his hand, and a fruit tart teleports in front of him. Limery and Leo sit on the stairs, watching the bright-colored fish as they dart beneath the translucent glass while Lillith and Bazel sit a few steps higher, holding hands and watching their children.

"Chods!" Limery flies over once he notices me, wrapping his warm, spindly arms around my neck. "We dids it! Now we's can fights the bad mans."

"You did good." I pat him on the back. "We're going to have to leave soon to go train. Spend some more time with Leo and I'll come get you when it's time to go."

"Okies." He squeezes me one more time before returning to his brother.

"There's the troll of the hour." King Favian offers me his arm, and we shake. His smile is friendly, but his gaze is penetrating as he squeezes my forearm. "We held up our end of the bargain, but we'd all like to know what is so urgent that we're rushing the attack?"

I look around at the crowd of soldiers, advisors, and leaders. "Is there somewhere we can talk in private?"

Between the crowded streets and departing council, there's not a lot to choose from. We cross the street and enter an alley between two shops that are currently closed. Taryn and Berry guard the entrance to make sure no one overhears.

The three leaders of the Isle of Mythos watch me expectantly.

I meet each of their eyes before speaking. "I need your word that what I'm about to share with you will remain between us. Not even the other heroes can know."

They each share a questioning glance before voicing their agreement.

"There's no easy way to put this." I rub the back of my neck as I try to find the best way to deliver the news. "The reason we need to rush the attack is because the heroes won't be here for much longer. Taryn and I are the only ones who know this, but we'll be returning to the world from which we came soon. There are powers beyond our control. I'm not sure how much time we have, but I believe it's at least a week. Possibly longer, but there's a chance we have even less time. That's why we must act now, while we have the opportunity." I pause to let the words sink in, and though each of the leaders holds their stoic expressions, I'm certain this is alarming news for them.

"I'm not sure if or when we'll be coming back to Mythos, but I want to end this threat before we're forced to leave. The good news is that most of the heroes have agreed to fight Valmar. They'll be training and preparing as much as possible between now and then. As much as I'm grateful for their participation, I don't know if they would have the same fervor if they knew their days here were numbered."

"I see." Chief Rizza nods solemnly. "Mythos will be forever grateful that a troll such as yourself showed up in the forest when you did, Chod. If this is the time we are given, then the trolls will be ready."

"Vanaria as well." King Favian echoes. "We face the challenge of our lifetime.

It's a chance to leave the world better for our sons and daughters, and for those who come after."

King Orso strokes his beard. "You were wise to press the matter as you did. Seascape will be ready when the time comes. What are your plans in the meantime?"

"We'll be returning to Goldspire. There's a final task I must complete."

King Orso glances at Taryn before extending a hand. "If you require anything of us, you need only ask."

"Thank you."

We say our farewells, and then Taryn guides Berry into the street so that we can exit the alley.

I stop beside him as the leaders return to the carriages. "What was that all about?"

"What?" He shifts uncomfortably in the saddle.

"That look between you and Orso."

"I'm..." His brow furrows, and he wears a pained expression. "I'm not going with you to Goldspire."

I take a step back, surprised at his words. "What do you mean you're not going?"

"I mean I'm not going." He sets his jaw with determination. "I love you, Chod. And I love the adventures we've experienced together in this world, but right now, we need to do what is right for all of Mythos. Your path is in Goldspire. You need your warforged class for what's coming. Limery and Caustic will be there to help you but for me, I feel like I need to be in Seascape with my people. I can help the dwarves. Maybe Chief Laojin can guide me further down my druid path. There's a lot I can do that doesn't involve waiting around while you get your ass kicked." He offers me a weak smile. "I hope you understand."

As much as I don't want to see him go, I do.

"You're right. Now is the time to push ourselves, and you should do that in the way that's best for you. Once I become Warforged, we'll find you. And then we can kick some undead ass together."

Taryn laughs. "Try not to die too much without me watching your back."

I give him a hug. "I'll do my best."

We return to the others as they are saying their final good-byes. Lillith and Bazel's bulging eyes glisten with tears as they embrace Limery.

"Don't cries, Mommy and Daddies. Limmy will be back soons."

Lillith locks her bulbous yellow eyes with mine. "You take care of my boy, Chod."

"Most of the time, he's the one taking care of me." I wink. "We'll see you soon enough."

Once his parents release him, Limery turns to his brother. "When we's gets back, maybe Limmy and Leos can goes on adventures together?"

Leo runs his spindly red fingers through his mohawk and grins. "Sounds good, little brother."

Limery extends his hand like I taught him, forming a fist, and the two brothers fist-bump, mimicking an explosion as they pull apart.

The imps join Chief Rizza atop her wyrm, and Taryn follows behind King Orso and King Favian's carriage on Berry as they clatter down the road. My best friend gives me a salute and turns away.

Limery perches on my shoulder, and Caustic grunts his displeasure as his new friend slithers toward the portal. For a moment, I stand there, watching them go. These are the people I'm fighting to protect. They might not be living, but they're real, and they've changed my life for the better because I met them.

If some dark wizard thinks he can take that away from me, then I'll raze his entire kingdom to the ground.

10. GOLDSPIRE

Limery, Caustic, and I arrive at the Pruxford portal ready for our next adventure. While there are more guards stationed around the square than when we first arrived in the city, it feels strangely empty with most of the citizens at the arena.

White energy swirls within the portal as I search the gateway for the rune to Goldspire. I find the one resembling a house with two vertical lines and a caret symbol over the top. The land of beastkin is the only portal I know of that has two separate entrances—one for newcomers that exits into a gladiatorial arena and a second one for those who have already proven themselves worthy.

Despite having open borders, Goldspire is a tough place to enter. Anyone who wishes to visit the kingdom must defeat one of the gladiators in combat. The first time we tried to enter, I got my head stomped in by a minotaur, losing all of my items in the process. According to Portia Swiftwill, the foxkin bartender, those who have passed the test enter through a separate portal on subsequent visits. This will be the first time I put it to the test. Just in case, I summon horrors and equip the Renewal Spear before we enter.

While I wait for the cooldowns on my horrors to reset, I talk to Limery. "I'm not sure where the portal will send us since Caustic has never been to Goldspire. We'll need to be prepared for a fight either way."

If we're forced to fight again, we're going in guns blazing.

We go over a few tactics as my horrors slowly build up. Aside from the dungeon with the tunnel drakes, this will be the first time the three of us have fought together without Taryn, so we need to be on the same page. We'll have less support than usual, but I'm confident in the synergy of our abilities.

Once I have sixty horrors summoned, I turn to Limery, who still sits perched on my shoulder. "You ready?"

He flashes me a demonic grin. "Limmy is readies."

Caustic growls his affirmation. We're ready.

The rune for Goldspire flares red when I focus on it, and white energy surrounds us as we enter the portal enveloped by a soundless vacuum. A weight settles on my shoulders in that brief moment. I might have the benefit of the Revive Potion but failure is not an option. Not anymore. Bright light greets us as we enter an arena, along with the chaos of battle.

Of course. I should have known this wouldn't come easy.

We're surrounded by a rustic stone coliseum with high walls that block the view of the city beyond. The air is hot and dry from the morning sun that beams across a clear blue sky, casting much of the arena in shadow and showcasing the gladiators as violent silhouettes across the sandy expanse. Several battles rage around us, and the clink of clashing metal sings a harmony with roars, screams, and blaring trumpets that echo across the pit. In the center, Mordrir—the spear-wielding satyr—fights a lion beastkin. They trade blows in a flurry until the spear pierces the lion's chest to the delight of the crowd.

Caustic's chest rumbles in challenge.

As I take in the gladiators, I notice something that I missed during my first two times here. Most of the fights are actually gladiators fighting one another to entertain the crowd. Since the arena is enchanted, whenever a gladiator dies, they respawn a little while later.

Challengers are not so lucky.

My grip tightens on the Renewal Spear, and mana surges to my fingertips, tingling with the excitement of battle. "I guess we're going to have to do this again."

When we first entered Goldspire, I was only level twenty-one. With Taryn and Limery, it had proven too much of a challenge. On our second attempt, I was level twenty-four and aided by Pressley, Limery, and Taryn.

This time, I'm level thirty with a dragon.

"Nice horns." Dakota's deep voice carries over the other fights. The level-thirty-three minotaur cracks his knuckles as he approaches, every bit as intimidating as I remember. "Seems you've been busy." His mouth curls into a smile.

I return his smile with a grin of my own. "I'm just getting started."

The minotaur is as tall as I am and a bit wider, with broad shoulders covered in radiant golden fur. His muscles ripple and sand stirs with each step, leaving a plume of dust in his wake. Two massive obsidian horns stretch the width of his body, and a silver nose-ring gleams in the morning sun. He wears a black leather loincloth, and two vambraces cover his powerful forearms. His weapon is unique, a thick chain weighted on one end with a metal ball and tipped on the other with a sickle. When out of combat, he wears the weapon wrapped around his waist like a belt.

He stops a few dozen paces from the portal and steam shoots from his nostrils. "You know the rules. If you wish to enter the lands of Goldspire with your new companion, step forward. Otherwise, be gone."

Limery grows warm against my shoulder before taking to the air, and Caustic huffs as he moves to my side.

I step into the arena, and my hands tingle with excitement. "Unfortunately for you, we're in a bit of a hurry, and you're standing between me and something I desperately want." I grin again, showcasing my tusks in all their glory. "Limery, use Whispers."

Limery pulls the stopper from the Whispers of the Damned pendant around his neck, and the screams of sea orcs flow out in silver wisps. The dying breaths of the last three enemies he killed charge toward Dakota, penetrating his fur and confusing him for the next five seconds.

The giant minotaur sways back and forth as the sounds of anguish surround him. I almost feel bad for the guy as we go on the attack.

Almost.

Caustic's wings flap like sails as he flies, and he unleashes a stream of toxic gas that shrouds the gladiator in a green cloud. As soon as the torrent of gas halts, there's a crackle as Limery summons a fireball, tossing it at the gas and setting off a thunderous explosion.

Warm air whooshes past, stirring up sand as the smell of toxic gas and singed fur fills the area. I cast Sacrifice on all of my horrors and wait for the smoke to clear. My muscles bulge from the influx of stats to Strength, Dexterity, and Constitution. As soon as I see the tips of Dakota's horns appear, I take a step and throw the Renewal Spear like a javelin with every bit of power I can muster. The bonus Dexterity keeps my aim true. There's a half-second where the minotaur regains his senses and his eyes go wide in surprise before the tip of the spear plunges into his skull.

Dakota collapses to the ground, a pile of smoking meat, and the crowd erupts. I wave to them, savoring the moment because I know things will only get tougher from here.

Congratulations! *You have defeated a gladiator in the Goldspire Arena. You now have access to the continent.*

Caustic lands next to the downed gladiator and sniffs at the burned corpse. I activate Return to Sender, and the spear dislodges from Dakota's skull with a sickening crunch before flying back to my palm. In a few minutes, he'll respawn to battle once again.

"Easies peezies." Limery returns to his perch on my shoulder, his body still warm from the fight.

I chuckle at another of the phrases Taryn has taught him. "Good job, both of you. Now, let's get the hell out of here."

Once outside the arena, Goldspire is just as I remember it. The city moves around us without a care in the world. Beastkin of all shapes and sizes stroll leisurely down the stone streets, as if time doesn't exist. There are temples with colorful mosaics, and olive trees sway gently in the breeze on every corner. Many of the businesses are open-air, with beautiful arches and elaborate columns, and verandas with expansive views line the top floors of buildings along the streets.

Caustic catches the eye of many beastkin as we make our way to the Wilty Rose Inn. Even in a land of beasts, dragons are still revered. And unlike the last time I was here, I can finally hold my own against the threats of this continent.

We pass several gardens with lush vegetation, and Caustic stops for a drink by a gurgling canal that carries water to the many bathhouses. In the forum, there are musicians and poetry readings around the towering golden spire for which the city is named.

From the open courtyard, we can see the far side of the city where the royal palace looms from the hilltop. As much as I disagree with Emperor Festa Forge-tooth's decision to keep her lands free from foreign conflicts, I do understand it. They have a thriving, peaceful way of life here.

Compared to the tension in Pruxford, this is like a different world. But even if Goldspire doesn't join the fight, this is what we are fighting for, to ensure that every kingdom has the opportunity for this kind of peace.

First, we must find Jegaar. Portia will be our best hope of tracking down the battle scholar since I don't have the faintest idea of where the Scholars Guild is located or where her childhood friend may be. Luckily, I still have the Wilty Rose Inn marked on my map.

When we arrive, I order Caustic to wait outside now that he's much too big to enter most buildings. The days of him snuggling on my chest as I fall asleep are long gone. Now, I'm the one to rest against his massive body.

Inside the inn, a black-feathered falcon beastkin works the bar. The downstairs tavern is empty except for a minotauress and a panther beastkin sharing a bottle of rose-colored wine. They play a game with different colored stones on a checkered board.

"How may I help you today?" the falcon asks.

"We're looking for Portia. Any idea where she is?"

He shakes his head. "Currently, no, but she should be in for her shift in a couple of hours. You're welcome to have a drink and wait."

Limery's eyes bulge as he leans against the counter. "Oh, yes. Limmy would loves a drinks."

"Excellent. It's a warm day out. Might I suggest an ice wine? The rosé we just got in is especially nice."

"Limmy loves the ice wines!" The imp clasps his hands together and grins. "Its makes hims feels tinglies."

I hold up two fingers. "Make it two."

The bartender pours us both a glass and slides them across the bar. The wine has a faint pink color and the bubbles that rise from the bottom of the glass have a calming effect.

Item. Ice Wine. *-2 Intelligence for one hour. Bonus Effect: Grants a cooling chill all over the body.*

I take a sip, and it's like I've stepped into a freezer on a hot day as chills erupt along my body. The sweat on the back of my neck crystalizes, a welcome feeling, and next to me, Limery sighs contentedly. The feeling must be euphoric to his naturally hot body.

I raise my glass to the bartender. "Good choice."

He raises an eyebrow as he examines me. "You know, you look familiar. Unless I'm mistaken, you were here with a dwarf some time ago." He leans in closer, squinting. "Something's different about you, though."

I laugh, tapping a claw against my horn. "These are a new addition."

"That's it." He snaps a feather-covered finger. "You wear them well."

We make small talk over the next half-hour, which eventually turns to talk of our travels and the world outside of Goldspire. I tell him about the attack on Pruxford and the other kingdoms.

"I had no idea." He leans back against the wall, crossing his wing-like arms. They're covered with feathers, but strangely humanlike at the same time. "Though we're free to come and go as we please, Goldspire doesn't interact much with the outside world. Why would we?" He shrugs. "Life is good here. The loss of life is a travesty nonetheless, but I trust that Emperor Festa keeps us isolated for good reason."

That's easy for him to say when orcs and the undead aren't spilling into his backyard.

Even though I know it's not his fault, I finish off my glass of wine to keep from biting his head off. "I'm going to step outside for some fresh air."

Limery leans against the bar, softly snoring with his head on his hands.

Outside, a crowd has gathered around Caustic. The dragon preens himself, and I can tell he's putting on a show for the onlookers.

The beastkin admiring him are all leveled into their twenties. The strongest of the bunch is a small, cream-colored ratkin that's level twenty-nine.

Another reminder that there's so much power here. Most of Goldspire's civilians are on par with the other kingdoms' soldiers, and yet we can't convince them to lift a paw or a finger.

Caustic senses my frustration and nuzzles his head against my chest.

"A magnificent creature." The ratkin places a hand on its chest. "It has been far too long since I've last seen a dragon. And a green one at that, magnificent."

"Thank you." I scratch Caustic underneath the chin. "He's still young, but he's growing fast."

They stand around for a few more minutes, ogling and asking questions before heading on their way. Once they're gone, I take a seat on the steps, stewing in silence. Caustic rests his head on my lap with a huff.

"Is that you, Big Blue?" I recognize Portia's vulpine voice before I see her.

The foxkin is a sight for sore eyes, and I forget about my frustrations for a moment as I take in her striking figure. Her orange fur is vibrant in the midday sun, and she wears a teal sash around her head, just below her pointy ears, that perfectly complements her coloring. Several small golden hoops dangle from her left ear. She wears a yellow tunic embroidered with a wilted red rose and silky pants that match her teal headband, almost mesmerizing the way they flow with her every movement. On her right hip rests an ornate dagger.

Portia stops next to me, fluttering her lashes and smiling. "You know, just the other day, I was wondering what you all had gotten yourselves into. Last we talked, you were heading to Frostmoor, was it?"

"We've been busy, alright."

"You'll have to tell me all about it." She reaches out a hand, hovering it a few inches from my horn. "May I?"

I nod, and she caresses her finger around the icy blue tip of the horn.

"A ram?" Portia laughs. "You did strike me as the stubborn type. I've heard of the Spirit of the Beast path, though not many beastkin have taken it. What brings you back to Goldspire?"

"I need to find Jegaar. Any chance you can point me in the right direction?"

She smiles. "Of course, but why don't we step inside first?"

I stand, crossing my arms. "I'll be honest with you, we're on a bit of a time-sensitive mission. I'd love to sit and talk about all we've been through since leaving Goldspire, but it's imperative that I meet with Jegaar as soon as possible."

Her brow furrows. "I see."

She steps past me and enters the inn. Limery is still passed out and has a giant snot bubble expanding with each breath.

"Falc, can you cover my shift tonight?" Portia gives him a pleading look. "I'll owe you one."

The falcon beastkin narrows his eyes at the foxkin and sighs. "I was supposed to go see Uncaged Minotaurs perform tonight. You owe me more than one."

"Deal." Portia smiles as she turns to me. "Find the dwarf, grab the imp, and let's get moving."

I can't help laughing at her enthusiasm. "It's actually just us this time. I guess you'll get to hear the whole story soon enough."

"Alright, big guy, try to keep up. The Scholars Guild is on the far side of the city."

"Of course it is." I scoop Limery off the bar and follow Portia out the door.

11. SCHOLARS GUILD

Portia takes our urgency to heart, moving swiftly through the streets. Caustic flies overhead, his shadow occasionally crossing our path. The foxkin is quick on her feet, like a breeze flowing through the city. In contrast, I lumber behind her carrying Limery, the imp's head bobbling in my arms as I hurry to keep up.

"Wake up, you little drunk." I jostle Limery enough to stir him awake.

He grumbles something unintelligible and buries his head against my chest.

"Wake up." I prod him again. "We're going to see Jegaar."

Limery lifts an arm, attempting to block the sun with his spindly fingers. "Okays, okays. Limmy will gets up."

He crawls from my arm, hovering in the air for a moment before fire flashes across his entire body and the effects of his day drinking vanish in an instant.

"That's betters." He grins as he darts upward to join Caustic.

Portia looks over her shoulder and laughs. "He's a funny little guy."

"He's something, alright." I smile at Limery and Caustic overhead as the duo perform a series of synchronized barrel-rolls. It must be amazing to see the city from that high up.

Portia leads us through a maze of streets and alleys as we journey across the city. I'm sure she's taking the most expedient route, but Goldspire is a sprawling city, and I don't recognize any of the structures from our last time here. At one point, we cut through a butterfly garden full of fragrant flowers. A pleasant aroma envelops me, and I stop, admiring the beauty of the butterflies as one lands upon my arm. I suddenly have the urge to lay down for a nap. The butterfly flaps its wings, and a prismatic dust sprinkles upon my blue skin.

"Oh no you don't." Portia wipes away the dust and grabs me by the arm, pulling me across the garden until the urge passes.

Soon after, we enter an imposing section of tall buildings and temples near the outer wall. Part of me wonders what threats wait beyond the borders of a city this powerful to warrant such defenses. Several guards patrol the parapet as the sun begins to set, and their shadows streak across the city like giants.

Portia stops in front of a building with colossal columns running along its facade. A multitude of stairs lead up to the building, and a statue of a lion beastkin stands out front, nearly as tall as the structure itself. The lion holds a book in one hand and a torch raised in the other. I stop for a moment to take in the beauty of the figure.

"Is this it?" I ask Portia.

"Close, but no." She grins. "This is the Goldspire Library. It pays for the Scholars Guild to be nearby in case they need reference materials. Follow me, though you'll probably want your dragon to wait outside."

Caustic lands at the foot of the statue, and I scratch him underneath the wing. "Wait here until we return."

He replies with a low growl and curls up in front of the lion's feet.

Portia leads us around the side of the library to a topiary garden filled with half a dozen fountains. Bushes are shaped into tigers, elephants, giraffes, and a host of other creatures, and calming water trickles all around. I could imagine losing hours to this place with a good book under the bright Goldspire sun.

Limery sits on my shoulder as I follow her further into the garden to a pergola covered in gorgeous pale-purple flowers. They dangle from the posts like curtains, rustling gently in the breeze. Inside the pergola, there's a raised pool on one end with four small tiger statues on each corner gazing into the water.

Portia rests her hand on one of the statues and pushes. The stone clicks as a mechanism activates, followed by the gurgle of water as it's displaced. The bottom of the pool lowers, forming stairs that lead underground.

I peer over the edge of the pool. "You guys really love your hidden entrances, huh?"

Portia smirks. "The surface of Goldspire may glitter, but the heart of this city is buried beneath."

I'm reminded of the underground fight club from our last visit, and how different it felt from the relaxed and peaceful atmosphere aboveground.

In one graceful movement, Portia leaps over the edge. "Watch your step. It can be a bit slippery."

I step into the pool and descend the stairwell into a surprisingly pristine corridor. The walls are polished marble, with elaborate sconces lighting the way.

Portia waits for us a short way into the tunnel.

"How do you know about the secret entrance?" I ask.

"Jegaar showed it to me many years ago when he was just a pup filing papers for the guild, long before he was a revered fighter and battle scholar. Sometimes he needed a break from the monotony. I would meet him by the pool, and we'd go for a little adventure around the city." Her green eyes sparkle at the memory. "There are a few more entrances I know of—one within the library, and the official entrance near the city offices, and probably a few more known only to the guild."

We follow Portia down the corridor, taking a sharp left and then a right before coming to a stop in front of a secure bronze door. Its massive hinges and sleek face remind me of a bunker entrance. There's no handle or knob, only a series of runes running along the outside.

"How are we supposed to get inside?" I ask.

Portia bursts out laughing. Then she raps her knuckles against the door.

The runes around the edge flash turquoise, and an orange circle forms in the center of the door at about eye level. The circle grows brighter, almost as if the metal is melting, and an eyehole forms through the thick slab.

A moment later, a bright blue eye peers through the peephole, and I swear someone laughs on the other side. As quickly as it appeared, the eyehole vanishes and the runes fade. Metal clicks, clanks, and grinds as hinges and latches unlock.

When the door opens, Jegaar wears a look of amusement. Gone are the gladiator skirt, buckler shield, and morning star he wielded at our first meeting at the underground fight club. Instead, he looks every bit the scholar in a neatly buttoned shirt and khaki pants. Some kind of magnifying contraption covers one eye, and he holds a massive bone nearly the size of a club. His fur is the arid tan of desert sand, so thick and shaggy that I'm still not sure how he's native to a climate as warm as Goldspire and not the frigid lands of Frostmoor. His bright blue eyes are piercing as he takes us in, his gaze lingering on my horns for a moment before moving to Limery and Portia. His husky tail swishes behind him, tipped black at the end to match his pointed ears and paws.

"You're not at all who I was expecting but a pleasant surprise nonetheless." He laughs as he removes the spectacled contraption and steps aside, gesturing with the bone for us to enter. "Come in. I'm in the process of cataloging some rare bones for the library."

Inside, the room is even more bunker-like. There are no windows, but plenty of lamps cast the room in a warm glow. All four walls, the ceiling, and floor are constructed from the same bronze metal as the door. There are two other exits, each one as impenetrable as the door we entered.

For all of its imperviousness, the room still resembles the haphazard office of a professor. Shelves line the perimeter, filled with books, scrolls, and manuscripts. There are locked boxes, precious stones, and artifacts scattered everywhere, along with a litany of notes and scribblings I can't decipher. In the center, one table is covered with the bones of partial skeletons. There's a skull of a ram with horns nearly as big as my own, and what I think to be the vertebrae of a snake mixed among the scatterings. The table next to it is littered with journals and textbooks, and a ring is clamped beneath a magnifying glass. It shimmers in the light of a white-flamed candle.

Item. Mysterious ring. *???*

That's odd. The description reminds me of the Mysterious Green Egg I hatched Caustic from. The description didn't change to Green Dragon Egg until I discovered what it was. Whatever this ring is, it's either very rare or very powerful.

Jegaar steps beside me when he notices me staring at the ring. "This one has baffled the entire guild. It was recovered from the tomb of an infamous rogue. Supposedly, the ring grants the wearer invisibility when activated." He tilts the magnifying glass until it settles on cursive script barely readable within the metal. "This inscription is a language I haven't been able to decipher. The ring was found in Ellynmylly, but the text doesn't match any of their native tongues. I've been sorting through dead languages but so far, no luck." He shakes his head. "But never mind that. To what do I owe the pleasure?"

"Chod is in need of your help..." Portia's attention falters, and she turns to the opposite table, examining the collection of bones. "Jegaar, is that one creature or three?" There's a reverence to her voice that I don't understand.

The wolfkin grins, revealing his sharp canines. "That is what I intend to find out. Either these are the remains of a chimera, or I have the useless bones of a lion, a goat, and a snake that happened to be buried in the same location."

Chimera? I remember the name from our days studying Greek mythology in school. As far as monsters go, they're pretty badass. I recall the creature having the body of a lion, with the head of a fire-breathing goat, and the tail of a venomous snake. This one seems different somehow, though I can't place what exactly is throwing me off.

Portia moves closer and runs her fingers over some of the bones. "How? I thought it was a myth."

"So did I, and yet..." He chuckles.

"What exactly is the chimera?" I ask.

Jegaar leans against the table. "There are some who believe that the chimera was the first beastkin. They believe that after the gods forged our lands and populated them with flora and fauna, they created the chimera as a guardian. The chimera was a mighty beastkin said to have two heads. One head was pure chaos— a goat capable of breathing fire that rivaled a dragon's. The other head was cunning and intelligent—the lion. Upon its rear, it had a tail tipped with the head of a venomous viper. Long before Goldspire had a name, it roamed the lands, guardian of everything within its domain."

That's what makes the bones look so different. It has the humanoid body of a beastkin and not the four-legged skeleton of a goat or lion.

He continues, "As time passed, the natures of the three beasts conjoined into one body began to darken. Its hunger grew, and it hunted the lands until no creatures remained. The gods looked down upon it with disdain, for they hadn't created a guardian but a creature with nothing more than an appetite for destruction. Even dragons take time to savor their kill and guard their hoard, but the chimera hunted day and night until the lands were barren. With the animals gone, chaos reigned, and the natural world fell out of balance. But still, the chimera's hunger grew, and with nothing to hunt, its powerful muscles shriveled away. When it was nothing more than skin and bones, the chimera turned to the gods. 'Save me,' it screamed. The gods were merciful, but they knew there was no place for this creature. They offered the chimera a choice. They could strike it down and end its suffering, or they could sate its hunger and allow it to make use of the time remaining.

"For the first time in its life, the chimera found peace. Its hunger abated, and it set about the task at hand. While it could not live on, it could leave a legacy. The gods granted the chimera the ability to infuse its remaining life force into the remains of whatever beings it chose. So, the chimera traveled through the graveyard of its destruction, giving life to bear and bird and all manner of animal it had once hunted. And that is the origin of the beastkin." Jegaar shrugs. "Or so they say."

"Do you believe it?" asks Portia.

"I'm a scholar. What I believe doesn't matter." He circles the table, eyes fixed on the scattered bones. "It's only what I can prove. Right now, I have someone searching the area where these were found for a split vertebrae. If it's located, then there may be some truth to the legends after all." He looks up, as if suddenly remembering we had a reason for being here. "You said Chod is in need of help?"

I nod. While the mythology of the beastkin is something I would love to dive into any other time, there are more pressing matters, so I elect to get straight to the point. "You told me to come find you when I reached level thirty. I'm ready to attempt the trials of the Warforged."

"So I did." He taps his chin with a dark claw. "I can sense a fire burning within you. I'm guessing this has something to do with the other kingdoms declaring war on Mosstar?"

"War?" Portia gasps, clearly unaware of the chaos happening beyond her borders.

"Yes, war." He shuffles a few papers and sets them aside. "There are few in Goldspire outside of the emperor's inner circle who are privy to the regional notices of other kingdoms. The Scholars Guild is an exception."

"Should I be concerned?" Portia's normally alluring tone is full of worry. Between learning of the chimera and Mosstar, her head must be spinning right now.

I look them both in the eye, answering before Jegaar has a chance to. "Kingdoms across Mythos have been attacked by creatures from the shadowlands. Pruxford suffered an attack from the sea orcs of Blacktide. And I've seen what waits for us in Mosstar. It's surrounded by an army of undead capable of razing cities to the ground. In a week, we plan to attack with everything we have. We'll gather with other heroes, adventurers, kings, and their armies in an attempt to end this threat once and for all. So, yes, you should be concerned. We know that Goldspire will not intervene, but know that if we fail, you will stand alone."

"As we always have." Jegaar's tone is gruff, but I can't tell if it's at me or the situation. He pauses for a moment, staring at his paws. "Though I may not agree with her decisions, our emperor has spoken, and our borders remain secure."

"Then I hope for your sake, we are successful." I take a breath to try and push the thought from my mind. For now, I need to focus on the present, on the reason I'm here. "So, can you guide me on the path to become Warforged?"

He looks me up and down. "We have a week?"

"Less. I will need time to return and prepare for the attack."

"I see." Jegaar strokes the fur on his chin. "I cannot promise you anything. I don't know what awaits within the trials, however, I do know the location for the trials' entrance. Once inside, there is no escape save death or victory. The challenge will be difficult, and more likely than not, you will fail, but if you have the mettle to endure, then you have the opportunity to reforge yourself into something greater."

"That's all I ask." My mouth curls into a devious snarl, and Limery's warm body matches my energy. "When can we start?"

Jegaar reaches for a notebook across the table. "I just need a minute to—" A knock at the door causes him to abandon the task. "Pardon me. As I said, I was expecting someone else when you arrived. This is probably them."

He traces a pattern on the door and runes blaze once again, mirroring the other side as a peephole forms. After Jegaar confirms the visitor, the latches and plates rearrange themselves, and the heavy door silently opens.

Armor clanks, and heavy boots thud against the floor as a tall figure steps inside covered in dark plate mail. Portia takes a step back at the stranger's appearance. A black aura seeps between the armored plates, and a dull buzz rattles within. A massive sword hangs from the visitor's waist.

"Chod." The stranger's voice is deep and distorted, like they're calling from the end of a cave. The warrior lifts his visor, revealing the blackness of death. "I like the new look."

"Thanks." As shocked as I am to see Pressley the death knight here, I'm even more surprised by his level.

Pressley Allen
   Level 40
   Death Knight
   Human

Whatever he's been up to since we left, he's been busy.

12. A BAG OF BONES

Pressley's appearance is more sinister than ever as he stands in the doorframe. He's upgraded some of his gear since we last saw one another, and it has only added to his intimidating presence.

He's replaced the traditional knight's headgear with a black helm that has two horns jutting forward like a charging bull. The metal has red flecks that catch the lamplight, reminding me of Destroyer. Perhaps it too was forged in the heart of a volcano. A black iridescent cloak hangs from his shoulders, making him appear even larger, with a red skull that latches the cloak at the front. The dark metal of his breastplate is molded into a skull and crossbones, with a similar design on both kneecaps. The armor covering his boots curls up into a pointed spike at the ends.

"Presslies!" Limery flies over, grabbing hold of one of the horns and tapping the death knight's helm with his claws. A dull ring echoes from the opening, where his face is concealed behind a shroud of darkness.

Pressley grunts in response, and he hands a large satchel to Jegaar as he steps into the room. The way the bag rattles when it changes hands, I can tell that it's filled with bones.

My gaze shifts from the death knight to the battle scholar and back again. "How the hell do you two know each other?"

Pressley went his own way once we entered the city, so it's a crazy coincidence that we're all here now.

"We're working together, in a manner of speaking." Jegaar sets the bag on the table. "You could say we each have something the other wants."

I look the death knight up and down. He must have been grinding nonstop since we parted. "How are you level forty? We weren't that far apart when I last saw you."

"I stay busy, and these lands are ripe with opportunity if you know where to look." He turns to face me, and I can feel his gaze even though his eyes are hidden behind darkness. "You seem to have done alright for yourself."

"I've been busy, too." I tap one of my horns and smile. "Though, it seems half my time is spent politicking lately. You're really leaning into the whole prince of darkness vibe, aren't you?"

"If people are going to fear me, I might as well act the part." He laughs, and the hollowness of it is a bit unsettling. "It's funny, though. The beastkin don't seem bothered by me nearly as much as the dwarves."

"We do not fear death." Jegaar peeks into the bag he's holding. "We welcome it with open arms when it arrives."

"Yeah, well, when it comes to those I care about, I want to fight it off for as long as possible." I turn back to Pressley. "What are you searching for, anyhow?"

"There's a creature called a manticore that resides in one of the dungeons outside of Goldspire. Apparently, only the Scholars Guild knows the exact location." He lets out a noise somewhere between a grunt and a sigh. "To save myself some time, I've been enlisted as an errand boy in exchange for the knowledge."

Jegaar scoffs. "I'd hardly call you an errand boy. You've gained a great deal of experience and levels in the name of academic research."

"Funny how this research consists of me fighting my way through a graveyard of dying beasts while you sit here playing with bones."

I can't help but laugh.

"What's so funny?" Pressley's armor clanks as he crosses his arms.

"It's not you. It's just that everything's a mystery here—hidden dungeons, hidden trials, hidden entrances to underground offices. The beastkin sure have a flare for the dramatic."

"What's life without a little mystery?" Jegaar turns to Pressley and gestures at the satchel. "May I?"

"Help yourself," Pressley's voice rumbles.

Jegaar empties the satchel onto an open section of the table, and bones spill from the bag. "To answer your question, Chod, Pressley is helping me with the chimera project. Being a death knight, he can sense bones in an area, locating them better than I could ever dream of. He can find corpses and remains, no matter how old or how deep they're buried. It would be a shame to waste an opportunity to use his skills. The chimera was long rumored to have been the first body to pass on in what is now known as the Valley of Death. So, I sent him there in search of the missing pieces."

The beastkin takes a bone and fits it in an open space along the lower spine of the chimera skeleton. His tail swishes as he searches the pile for another. I imagine fitting all of the pieces together is part of the joy of being a scholar.

"That's interesting. And in exchange, you show him how to find a manticore? Which is what, exactly?" I ask.

"It's a unique monster, and very powerful," Pressley answers. "They have the body of a lion, the wings of a dragon, and the tail of a scorpion. If I can defeat one, then I have an ability that allows me to enlist the reanimated corpse of a single unique monster to fight for me. I plan to use it as a mount."

The last time we fought together, his army of skeleton minions rivaled my horrors. At level forty, I can't even imagine what he's capable of summoning.

"Wouldn't the chimera be a better prize?" I ask.

"If it were a corpse, maybe, but the bones are so old that it could only be reanimated as a skeleton warrior. It would likely lose the perks of breathing fire and the venomous bite of its tail."

"Considering the chimera's history, that's probably for the best." Jegaar chuckles as he takes another bone and rearranges it several times in an attempt to fit it into place.

Pressley sighs, and it reminds me of a death rattle. "We'll be here all day waiting for you. Allow me to help."

Jegaar steps back, throwing his hands up. "By all means."

A deep purple aura swirls around Pressley's armored hand as he lifts his arm. The bones that were emptied from the bag all rise, glowing a vibrant white as they hover in the air. Limery's eyes bulge with anticipation when an outline forms over each bone, almost like a scientific diagram. I'm equally intrigued. With a flick of Pressley's wrist, the bones dart across the table, finding their proper position and forming the skeleton of the chimera in a matter of seconds. Midway up the spine, the vertebrae split into two separate columns, one for each head. Where a tailbone would be on a human skeleton, the end of the spinal column extends into a tail-like set of vertebrae ending with the head of a snake. It's both grotesque and strangely intriguing to look upon.

Portia covers her mouth as the pieces fall into place. Jegaar claps his hands and shakes his head in wonder.

"It's true," he whispers. "The legends were true."

"I can't believe it." Portia's eyes are as wide as saucers. "We've just witnessed history."

"You can write your histories later." Pressley flicks his hand, and the bones move from the air to the table, arranging themselves in perfect order. "I held up my end of the bargain, now it's your turn. Where can I find the manticore?"

"Heroes." Jegaar shakes his head. "Always in a hurry."

"My haste is none of your concern." There's an edge to his hollow voice that presses the issue. If there's anything I've learned about Pressley, it's that he doesn't stop when he's on a mission for something.

"No need to scuff your armor. I'm an honorable wolf, and you'll have your directions." Jegaar approaches the death knight and lifts a hand until it rests on the outside of Pressley's helm. There's a tiny spark just like when Chief Rizza gave me the knowledge of the ley lines on Isle of Mythos. "You're a powerful warrior, but the manticore will be a challenge even at your level."

Pressley grunts. "I will take my chances."

He turns to leave, but I call out after him.

"Wait." I rush across the room, blocking his exit. "You made a promise to me in the Glossop Forest. After we defeated the covey of hags you said, '*I will be there for you when the time comes for us to band together.*' Those were your words. And that time has come. In a week, all of the heroes and kingdoms I've been able to recruit will go to war with the dark wizard. We need you there."

The buzzing within his helm grows more intense and for a moment, I think he's going to push past me. But then he nods. "Then I will be there, but for now, I have business to attend to."

I press my hand against his breastplate as he tries to walk by. "Just wait a moment. There might be a way for us to help one another." I turn to Jegaar. "These trials, will I be forced to enter alone?"

He looks at Limery and nods. "Unfortunately, yes."

Limery frowns. "Limmy can't goes?"

"Don't worry, buddy. It'll all work out." I pat him on the leg before returning my attention to Jegaar. "And what about a pet or a bonded creature? Can they enter?"

He shakes his head. "No. Your horrors will be available to you once inside, but no living creatures may pass into the trials or they will not begin."

"Not even a bonded dragon?" I ask, just to confirm.

"A dragon?" Jegaar's brow scrunches. "You have a dragon?" There's surprise in his voice, but he shakes his head. "Even still, no living creatures may accompany you."

I return my attention to Pressley. "It sounds like you're going to need help with this dungeon, and we're going to need everyone as strong as possible when the final battle comes. Take Limery and Caustic with you and they can help you with the manticore."

Limery flies across the room and perches on Pressley's shoulder. "Oh yes, Limmy and Caustics loves to fights."

There's a deep rumble within the death knight's armor. "Fine, but let's be on with it."

Jegaar looks pleadingly at the chimera skeleton. "One of the greatest mysteries of Goldspire's history unlocked, and I can't even savor the discovery before being whisked away." He sighs. "Come on, then. We're going to need a carriage."

He activates the runes on one of the interior doors and leads us down a pristine hallway. We pass at least a dozen other heavily armored bronze doors as we follow Jegaar through the maze of the Scholars Guild. Eventually, we come upon an opening where a wide stairwell leads to a massive arched doorway nearly two stories tall and embellished with elaborate knotwork.

"If you ever find yourself here again, those doors lead to the library." He points down another hallway. "This way leads to the stables, but we'll have to pass through Kolak's workroom to get there."

The second corridor has just as many closed doors as the first. I wonder how many scholars are a part of the guild. When we're almost at the end of the tunnel, Jegaar stops in front of a door and traces his fingers across the outside. Runes flash in a pattern different from the first, and then the mechanisms activate on the other side.

Inside, an elephant beastkin leans over a table examining a large shield covered with colorful gemstones. Dozens of golden earrings run along the edges of her massive ears, and she wears a magnifying contraption similar to Jegaar's over one eye. I take a moment to analyze the beastkin.

Kolak

Level ???
Scholar
Beastkin

She's not a battle scholar like Jegaar.

Kolak's trunk twitches as she makes eye contact with the wolfkin. "Do you ever knock?"

"We're just passing through." He holds up a hand in defense. "We'll only be a moment."

The room is similar to Jegaar's but with fewer bones, and two entrances instead of three. She has shelves filled with collections of precious stones and jewels. Many more sit on the table where she's working, and it appears she's trying to fill the empty sockets on the shield where some of the jewels have been removed.

Kolak lets out an agitated trumpet that reminds me of Stompy. "Just don't touch anything."

"I wouldn't dream of it." Jegaar smirks as we walk past. "I have something to show you when I return. It will blow even your giant mind, Kolak."

The elephant sits up, raising her magnifying contraption before her gaze pierces into the wolfkin. "Don't tease me, Jegaar. You know I hate being teased."

His lip curls from a smirk into a devious snarl. "I wouldn't dream of it." He runs his fingers across the outer door, and the runes flash. "See you later."

We exit into another marble corridor.

"She seems feisty." Portia laughs to herself. "There aren't many who will stand up to the mighty Jegaar."

"Oh, she is." Jegaar looks over his shoulder at the closed door. "And one of the best scholars in the guild. She has a knack for decoding, but she hates being disturbed."

"You all have access to one another's workspaces?" I ask.

"Not exactly. There are only two battle scholars in the guild, and we have the same access to guild workrooms and archives as the guild master. The scholars don't appreciate it when we barge in, but we're in a bit of a hurry at the moment."

Judging by Kolak's reaction, I get the feeling he's in a hurry more often than necessary.

As we near the end of the tunnel, the scent of hay and barn animals fills the narrow passage. The exit is less glamorous than the gardens by the library. There's no switch to activate, and instead, Jegaar pushes open a wooden door like one might find above an underground cellar. We step into an empty stall within the stables, and the neighs of horses and shouts of workers welcome us aboveground.

No one bats an eye as the four of us exit the stall into the main corridor.

"The manticore dungeon lies along the same route as the trials. We will travel together for part of the journey," Jegaar tells us before requesting a carriage from one of the stable-hands.

We wait out front as they prepare our ride, and I call to Caustic through our bond. A few minutes later, the flap of leathery wings announces his arrival. Jegaar watches him land with appreciation, and I'm not quite sure what Pressley is thinking.

"Is it friendly?" the death knight asks.

"Depends on who's asking." I grin as I call Caustic over and introduce the two. "This is Pressley. He's an old friend. While I'm completing the trials, you and Limery will be training with him, helping to clear a dungeon." I scratch him under the chin. "I need you to watch his back."

Caustic's chest rumbles, and he lowers his head until it's inches from Pressley's helm and sniffs. For a moment, I wonder if the aura around the death knight might be unsettling, but then Caustic extends his forked tongue and licks Pressley's helm, leaving a thick layer of slobber on the outside.

I laugh at the death knight as he tries to clean his helm. "I think you guys will be just fine."

13. COUNTRY ROADS

After a quick good-bye, Portia leaves us to return to the inn, and we find a carriage ready for us in front of the stables. It's pulled by two giant oxen, each one with a set of small wings just above the hooves on each leg. The two animals are both gray around the snout and not nearly as muscled as some of the others inside the stable. One of them has the milky eyes I've seen in older dogs.

Did we get the leftovers because of such short notice?

Pressley crosses his arms and huffs. "Do you expect me to reanimate them once we're on the road?"

Jegaar scratches one of the oxen behind the ears and smiles. "Winghoof oxen age like a fine wine, and these are two of the oldest in the kingdom. We use them for guild business whenever time is of the essence. I promise you, they are faster than they appear."

I take a moment to analyze the animals.

Winghoof Ox. *Level 28. Contrary to their appearance, winghoof oxen are not flying creatures. They are, however, fleet of hoof while still managing to pull heavy loads. Unlike most working cattle, elder oxen grow faster with age. They are most commonly used by farmers outside the city walls of Goldspire for transporting produce and grains to the market.*

Strange creatures, but if they get us to our objectives quicker, then I'm all for it.

We load up and leave the safety of Goldspire's high walls pulled by the two geriatric oxen. They move faster than I would have expected, leaving a trail of dust in our wake as we journey from the city, almost as if the animals are buffed by Strong Wind. My horrors quickly fall behind, but Jegaar assures me we have a ways to travel before I'll need them so I let them expire.

We pass by olive groves, golden meadows, and the occasional roadside tree ripe with oranges or figs. Farms speckle the landscape and far ahead, there are low-lying dark mountains on the hazy horizon.

Every so often, I spot a marker made of blue stone on the side of the road.

"What are those?" I ask Jegaar after we pass the fifth one.

"Wards. They're designed to keep some of the more dangerous beasts from the main roads so that the farmers can transport crops to the city."

"Do they work?"

He nods. "They do, but they only extend for a dozen or so miles around the perimeter of the city. There aren't any farms beyond their range. If certain beasts get too close, the runes will activate, emitting an unpleasant energy to drive them back."

That's interesting. I haven't had many interactions with wards in Mythos, at least not that I'm aware of. The tower in Vanaria serves as a sort of ward against the undead. I wonder if it might be possible to construct smaller versions for the impending battle, using them to disorient the masses of undead at Valmar's disposal.

We pass the farms, and the land quickly becomes untamed, hilly terrain spotted with shrubs and bushes. The countryside is much dryer than Wandermere and Isle of Mythos, but underneath the desolate facade, it's teeming with life. A deer with glowing antlers grazes atop one of the hills, and giant birds circle overhead. Just like the beastkin themselves, the animals beyond Goldspire are large and intimidating. There's a scent to the air that's clean and crisp, almost calming in its simplicity.

Limery points at the birds, licking his lips. "Looks, Chods, big birdies."

"I'd be careful with those." Jegaar laughs. "My mother used to tell me stories of how the shadow vultures would snatch up the pups who didn't finish their meals and take them to their nests in the Black Mountains."

Limery's eyes widen slightly. "What do the birdses do with the pups?"

"To hear my mother tell it, they eat them in one bite." Jegaar chomps his teeth, and Limery lets out a squeak.

A herd of fiery-maned bison stampede through the hills, diverting our attention from the vultures overhead. Caustic's shadow stretches across the landscape as he soars above the herd. Maybe the bison sense the presence of the apex predator.

Not far ahead, a fluffle of bunnycorns lies on the road, bathing in the sun. Their pearlescent horns shimmer in the sunlight. When they notice the sound of our carriage, they dart into the underbrush in a blur.

I chuckle to myself that I actually remembered what a fluffle is, and I recall Taryn promising that he wasn't messing with me. He would love it here, far from the city and surrounded by nature. I wonder what he's up to right now, and how the preparation is going elsewhere.

Limery flies forward and perches on one of the oxen's horns, tapping it with his claws. "Look, Presslies, it's yous." He cackles as he points at the death knight's new helm.

"Humph," Pressley grunts.

"Get used to it." I laugh. "He's a real comedian."

Pressley leans forward, burying the front of his helm in the palm of his hand. "I'm going to regret this, aren't I?"

"Don't worry." I put a hand on his armored shoulder. "Once he's fighting beside you, you'll be thankful for the little guy. He's even stronger than last time, and the synergy between him and Caustic is pretty amazing."

"Speaking of Caustic..." Jegaar snaps the reins, but his eyes follow Caustic as he soars across the road. "I still can't believe you have a dragon. How'd that happen?"

I chuckle. "How much time do we have?"

As we travel through the countryside, I fill Pressley and Jegaar in on everything that has happened since leaving Goldspire. The beastkin is attentive, but it's impossible to read Pressley's emotions aside from the occasional grunt. The mountain range draws steadily closer as I tell them of the Mysterious Green Egg I found in Seascape, Stompy's death, the monsters from the shadowlands, our time in Wandermere, and the attack on Pruxford.

When I'm finished describing the council of leaders, there's silence aside from the crunch of earth beneath the wagon wheels and the breathing of the oxen. It's a lot to take in, I'm sure.

"I think you're right to mount an attack." Jegaar turns to me, his face stern. "If Valmar is testing the other kingdoms' defenses, then it means he's nearly ready himself. He wouldn't risk it otherwise."

"Have you noticed anything out of the ordinary in Goldspire?" I ask.

He shakes his head. "Valmar wouldn't be so foolish. Not again."

I hope he's right. The emperor turned Valmar back once, but if his goal is to spread his empire, then I can't imagine he would stop after conquering the rest of Mythos. If we fail, their paths will eventually cross again.

We come upon a fork in the road, and Jegaar pulls the wagon to a stop. "The path to the right leads to the Valley of Death and the Bleak Canyon beyond, the center will take us to the Narrow Pass within the Black Mountains, and the left leads to the abandoned city of Sungrove."

"Abandoned?" I raise a brow.

Jegaar turns to Pressley. "That's where you'll find the manticore. Her dungeon is located near the city. Long ago, Sungrove was the second-most populous city on the continent. Before we closed our borders, it was the trade hub of the region and populated by races from far and wide. When the manticore first laid claim to the dungeon, she began her stay by looting ships as they arrived at the port. After our borders closed and there were no more ships, she began abducting citizens under the cloak of darkness. Many ventured into the dungeon to try and stop her, but none returned. Eventually, more and more beastkin left the city for the safety of Goldspire, and Sungrove faded from relevance."

"What happened to the other races that were living in Sungrove when the borders closed?" I ask.

Jegaar furrows his brow. "They were banished from our lands, only allowed to return if they could defeat our gladiators in the arena."

I turn my gaze in the direction of Sungrove, wondering what awaits Limery and Caustic. "And the manticore has been living there ever since?"

"So the legends say."

I turn to Pressley. "You sure you want to go through with this?"

Darkness swirls beneath his helm as he nods. "I've made my choice."

Jegaar flicks the reins, and we veer to the left in the direction of Sungrove. "I'll leave you outside of the city gates, then Chod and I will make for the Narrow Pass so that he may complete the trials."

"This is kind of far from the city. How are they supposed to get back?"

Jegaar laughs. "On the back of the manticore, if they are lucky. And if they are not, the walk back should offer enough time to think about the foolishness of this endeavor."

My stomach tightens. For Pressley, failing the dungeon is merely a setback. He'll respawn wherever he last set his spawn point with the inconvenience of a lost level and his items. For Limery and Caustic, failure is death. They're strong, but I worry about what may happen when I'm not around to protect them.

Limery sits perched on one of the oxen's horns, bobbling along with each step, unaware of the apprehension brewing within me.

I gaze into the darkness of Pressley's helm in an attempt to see the man beneath. "Promise me that you'll play this smart. If it feels like you're out of your league, wait for me, and I'll help you once I'm done with the trials." I place a hand on his armor. "Please."

He takes a deep breath that sounds like the rattle of a hundred flies. "Fine."

"Thank you." I know it goes against everything he is to wait or ask for help. He's been going nonstop since he logged into Mythos on a quest to be the most powerful one here. We'll need that spirit for the battle ahead, but I need Caustic and Limery by my side when it happens. They're the reason I'm doing all of this.

True to Jegaar's words, Sungrove is nothing more than a ruined city when we arrive outside the gates. I inhale the salty breeze as we come to a stop. The buildings are worn and eroded by time and the coastal weather. Several tall arches have crumbled at their peak, leaving slanting columns that frame the overgrown entry into the city. The walls that once protected it from the dangers outside are covered in moss and vines. Large black birds caw at us from the parapet, as if informing us that they're now the city's watchful protectors.

Pressley's armor clanks as he climbs down from the carriage.

Jegaar stands, stretching his arms overhead. "Say your good-byes quickly. We still have a ways to go, and we don't want to be caught on the roads after nightfall if it can be avoided."

Judging by his ominous warning, there may be more than bison and bunny-corns lurking within the countryside.

Caustic lands beside me with a thunk as his massive frame touches down. Limery tries to take his usual spot on my shoulder, but I cradle the imp in my palm so I can look him in the eye.

"I need you to watch out for one another, and Pressley, too. But if you get the feeling that this dungeon is too strong, you leave. We'll tackle it again another day."

Caustic huffs and his meaning is clear. *A dragon does not run.*

I look into his golden eyes. "It's not running; it's living to fight another day. Beside me, together, when it really matters. I wish I could take you into the trials, but I can't. This is a way for us to help Pressley and grow stronger at the same time, but we have to remember that there is something bigger at stake. A lot of people are counting on us to make it back."

"Don't worries, Chods." Limery grins. "Limmy will take cares of Caustics."

"I know you will, buddy." I run a finger down his spine and then turn to Pressley. "Good luck. I'll see you back in Goldspire when this is all over."

He extends a hand, and when I grasp it, he pulls me close. "I may not understand the bond you have with the imp, but I know what it's like to care for someone. You have my word that we'll all make it out of here." Pressley releases his grip, nods to Jegaar, and turns toward the city. "Let's go."

Limery wraps his arms around my neck, giving me a final hug before perching on Pressley's helm. Caustic lowers his head, nuzzling against my chest and growling. Then he takes to the air, sending the birds along the wall flying.

I watch them go as they enter the open gates before joining Jegaar in the carriage.

He pats me on the knee. "Best to let the worry leave your mind. When you enter the trials, you must be focused."

Jegaar does his best to prepare me for what's to come as we travel back. According to him, the warforged trials are less about what I face and more about how I face them. For most races, and even most modern beastkin, completing the trials would be an impossible feat. Even in ancient times, the trials killed more than half of those who attempted them. If not for the combination of my race and barbarian class, I'd have no shot at completing them.

We reach the fork in the road once again and take the middle path toward the Black Mountains. As we journey closer, I realize that the mountains get their name because they appear to be made of solid black rock. There are no trees, just dark shards jutting from the earth.

By the time we arrive, the sun is setting behind their peaks. A gorge passes through the mountains, revealing a sliver of orange and purple sky on the far side that stands out in stark contrast to the obsidian stone. When we set out from Goldspire, the mountains were nothing more than dark shapes on the horizon, but the oxen are true to their description. Thanks to them, we made great time. There's no telling how long this trek might have taken on foot.

Jegaar tugs on the reins, and the carriage comes to a stop. "The Narrow Pass is barely wide enough to fit the carriage through. It's best if we go on foot. You may begin summoning your horrors now."

I do as he says, and three of the demonic creatures burst to life before me. "What's on the other side of the pass?"

"The Burning Desert that separates Goldspire from the rest of Mythos. In its center, the Lonely Volcano looms over its surroundings, scorching the earth for leagues in every direction. It makes the land so hot that wheels catch fire and hooves melt when they touch down. It's the reason our city is only accessible through the portals. With the monsters of the sea to three sides and the Burning Desert to our backs, there is no kingdom more defensible than Goldspire. The beasts capable of surviving in the desert are practically unkillable and too wild to be tamed. Those foolish enough to test them earn a quick death."

"There's always a bigger fish."

"True words, but I pray I never see them." Jegaar chuckles. "Now follow me."

The Narrow Pass is true to its name. The gorge is barely ten feet wide, and it keeps the same width from bottom to top, as if the gods had cleaved the mountain in two. The walls are jagged and dangerous, still sharp after who knows how long. The more I look at them, it appears like the two sides could fit perfectly if they were pressed together. I'm sure there's a history lesson Jegaar would love to share about this place, but right now, he's focused on finding the entrance.

My hands twitch with nervous energy. I continue summoning horrors and try not to think about failure and what that might mean.

I attempt to distract myself while Jegaar examines the rock face for some unseen sign. "Portia mentioned that there were trials you completed when you were children. Are they located here as well?"

He shakes his head. "No, those are beyond the other side of the city. Compared to what awaits you, they're quite literally child's play." He runs his claws along the walls, occasionally gripping rocky formations and pushing. "Just give me a moment. It's been a few years since I've ventured here."

He stops and presses an ear against the canyon wall while tapping his finger on its surface. Then he moves down and does the same thing several more times before stopping.

"Ah, there we go." He grabs a protruding shard of rock and pushes. The stone grinds as it moves, and a chasm forms along the left side of the wall.

He motions me forward. Heat radiates from within the cavern beyond, similar to when we found Limery's father trapped in the Greystone Mountains.

"This is where I leave you. When you enter, you'll receive a prompt from the trials. Please give me time to exit the pass before you accept." He places a hand on my shoulder and squeezes. "Good luck, Chod. I hope to see you later rather than sooner."

I take a deep breath and nod. If he sees me sooner, it's because I failed.

"Thank you." I extend a hand, and he shakes it. "For everything."

"Good luck."

I summon another round of horrors and step inside.

14. DUNGEONS & DEATH KNIGHTS

Creatures scurried in the maze of ruins as Pressley, Limery, and Caustic entered Sungrove. The coastal breeze rustled vines and overgrown foliage that had claimed the city, while the vultures perched atop the walls watched them with intrigue. The birds kept a safe distance from Caustic as he stalked behind Pressley, only occasionally squawking. With his wings tucked, the dragon was like a beast on the prowl, his tail dragging behind him on the ground.

Pressley's daughter had loved dragons. When Eva was young, she'd had a pink plushie of the one she watched on TV. Pressley couldn't remember the dragon's name, but he'd tucked it in bed alongside her at night, even going so far as to kiss it on the forehead. Eva took the toy everywhere she went, but that was years ago. Back before he'd gotten tangled up with the wrong people. He wondered if she still did.

The memories caused something within him to pulse at the emotion. Whatever energy powered his new form seemed to thrive whenever he thought about his daughter. He'd often used her as a catalyst when a fight was falling out of his favor. At level forty, that didn't happen often, but it gave him joy to know she could help him get through the tough times. He only wished he could do the same for her.

One day, he thought. *One day, I'll tell you all about my adventures in Mythos. About how Daddy rose to power and became a hero.*

He pushed the thoughts aside and returned to his new companions.

Pressley wasn't sure what to make of Caustic. Chod said the dragon was a juvenile, but he was already an intimidating presence, larger than any horse or oxen, and that wasn't accounting for his massive wingspan. The dragon had daggers for teeth, capable of ripping off Pressley's arm with ease, and his massive talons dug into the earth with each step. Pressley pitied whoever ended up on the business end of those monstrosities.

Once inside the gates, Pressley activated his Bone Detector ability. Glowing white outlines appeared across the city, but there wasn't much of note—dead rats, birds, the body of a long-dead beastkin buried beneath a stone building. That one had to be an interesting story.

Far off to his right, a white haze caught his attention. There were so many bones that their outlines merged together from so far away. Not as bad as the Valley of Death, but it was close for such a small area.

Pressley focused on the map Jegaar had given him, and it populated across his vision. The entrance to the dungeon was marked with an orange dot in the same location as the bones.

He chuckled to himself, the sound reminiscent of a hornet's nest. The manticore would be a worthy challenge, but Pressley had a dragon by his side. He glanced over his shoulder at the creature to analyze it again.

Green Dragon. *Unique Monster. Level 17. Green dragons rule with impunity over the forests they inhabit. They are the most territorial of all dragon species, and capable of spewing toxic gas in lieu of flames. Wherever a green dragon calls home, a dense fog is said to follow.*

The dragon's power was nice, but Pressley found himself in awe of the creature's beauty. The emerald scales that always seemed to shimmer. The antler-like horns that sprouted from his head. Not to mention the golden beard coming in around his chin. And when Caustic's golden eyes fell upon Pressley, there was an intelligence there that he hadn't seen in any other beast or monster. If this was what Caustic looked like as a juvenile, he could only imagine what the dragon would become.

Chod might have a target on his head more times than not, but he was a lucky son of a bitch. Stealing a mysterious item that ends up being a dragon egg? Pressley would kill for a dragon, but the manticore wouldn't be a bad consolation prize.

And then there was the imp. Limery hadn't been with Chod when he and Pressley fought side by side in the Glossop Forest, but he'd witnessed the imp's raw power when they faced the gladiators in the arena. He was fire made flesh, and he'd leveled up quite a bit since then as well.

Imp. *Level 27. Small, angsty creatures, imps often align themselves with beings on the more chaotic side of nature.*

Pressley laughed at the description. Chod seemed like a good dude, but chaotic was a fitting descriptor. Wherever the troll went, chaos followed.

They had that much in common.

"Where's the dungeonses?" Limery tapped Pressley's helm with a claw, and a hollow ring echoed from within.

The imp had taken to riding on the death knight's shoulder the same as he did with Chod. His natural body heat radiated through the metal of Pressley's armor, warming his core. The sensation was captivating. So much so that it took all his willpower to fight against lying down and basking in the warmth.

His appearance wasn't the only thing that changed when he'd become a death knight. When he first went through the transformation, there was a hollowness that pervaded his very being. His mental faculties hadn't changed, but anger and sadness had settled on his soul like an anvil. It had eased with time, but his body still felt like a cold echo of itself. The imp's heat was a reminder of what he'd lost.

And what he'd gained.

The power was worth the trade-off. He never would have accomplished some of his feats had he still been human. Technically, he was still human, just undead. Flesh and blood might be a more appropriate term. He still had the same bones, only now they weren't held together by ligaments and muscle but by some infernal energy.

"Presslies..." Limery tapped the helm again. "Helloes!"

"It's nearby." Pressley lifted an armored hand and pointed. "Over there."

"Limmy and Caustics loves to fights." The imp squeezed his small hands into fists. "We likes to make big booms."

"So I've heard. You'll need to show me what you're capable of before we enter."

"Okies." Limery flashed him a demonic grin.

They headed in the direction of the dungeon. The vultures followed at a distance, hopping from building to building and occasionally squawking at them. The same thing had happened to Pressley at the Valley of Death. He wondered if they could sense the death radiating from within him.

The entrance to the manticore's dungeon was barely more than a collapsing tunnel. It looked like the entrance to an old mining shaft. For a creature so feared and respected, Pressley had expected something more resplendent.

Manticore Dungeon. *Would you like to enter?*

He dismissed the notification and turned to face Limery and Caustic. "Chod was right when he told you this is a dangerous dungeon. I'm glad to have you by my side because this would be a challenge for me alone. He tells me you are both very powerful." At that, Caustic huffed. "Since we haven't fought as a team before, we should familiarize ourselves with one another's abilities. Limery, tell me what you can do."

"Oh, yes. Limmy can do lots." The imp took to the air, hovering a few feet in front of Pressley. "Limmy is very fasts."

He darted through the air, zigzagging several times before stopping to conjure a fireball in his palm. The flames licked at and distorted the air, but the imp remained unaffected. Pressley longed for the fire's warm embrace.

"Limmy can throws fireballs and make fire walls." With a flick of his wrist, the fireball soared toward a ruined building, hitting a vulture. Limery cackled as feathers exploded, and the bird took to the sky with an angry caw.

When the imp recovered from laughing, he conjured a flaming wall nearly six feet high and two feet wide.

"Very good." Pressley nodded his approval.

"Limmy can also dos mega-fireballs." He summoned a fireball and spread his hands wide. Each second, the flames grew until the fiery ball was larger than the imp itself.

The heat radiated like a furnace, and Pressley grinned beneath his helm.

Limery let the fireball dwindle into nothing before continuing. "Limmy can also turn to fires." In the blink of an eye, his entire body was engulfed in flame. He burned like a little impish torch, his eyes molten lava. "And now, Limmy can makes a shields."

Flame expanded from his body in a sphere, forming a fiery barrier around the imp. If Pressley had to guess, it would burn anything that tried to pass through.

The flames faded, and then Limery reached into a small satchel hanging from his waist. "Limmy also has somes of the fairies dust. It makes yous sleepies."

The imp had more abilities than Pressley had anticipated, and even though he was only level twenty-seven, he was raw power. A wrecking ball of fire. "Anything else?"

Limery tapped his chin as if considering before his eyes lit up. "Limmy has the necklace." He raised a silver necklace with a black teardrop pendant from his neck. Gray smoke swirled within. "It makes peoples confuseds. Limmy cans use it three times every days."

"Very good. I'm lucky you're on my side." Pressley turned to Caustic. "And what about the dragon?"

In answer, Caustic reared back and unleashed a stream of toxic gas that poured down the alley to their left. The gas was heavy, sinking to the ground and lingering like a dense fog. Being a death knight, Pressley was immune to most toxins and poisons, but the gas had the appearance of something especially potent.

"Chod says you two can use your abilities together. How does that work?"

Without responding, Limery tossed a fireball at the thick green gas. The gas ignited, and the world seemed to slow down for Pressley as chaos blossomed. There was a flash of green light, and then the alley exploded. Rubble flew across the city, and the force of the explosion knocked Pressley against the wall. The world sat in silence for a moment, and then a thunderous clap echoed, followed by another wave of energy. If he still had ears, he was certain they'd be bleeding.

"Damn." Pressley's voice was barely a whisper. Those two were dangerous.

The smoke cleared, and Limery grinned at the death knight. "What can Presslies do?"

"I'm similar to Chod in a way. I summon things to fight for me." He removed the satchel from his side and turned it upside-down. Bones and rusty weapons fell out, rattling against the dusty street. They poured out until the pile was waist-high, and then he stepped aside, shaking the bag again. Bones flowed from the satchel like a waterfall.

One thing he'd discovered since entering Goldspire was that he could store the bones of his minions in an expandable satchel when they weren't in use. It allowed him to keep a bigger army in reserve, and it accrued a lot less stares and panic in populated areas.

Limery grabbed a bone and tossed it to Caustic. The dragon snatched it out of the air with a crunch.

"Please, don't do that." Pressley sighed.

"Sorries." Limery gave him a sorrowful look.

Pressley activated his ability to summon skeleton warriors, and the bones rattled and clacked as they assembled themselves with dark energy holding them together at the joints. The warriors ranged in size from the thick, short bones of dwarfs to those with more human proportions. There were even a few beastkin and animal skeletons mixed in.

As the warriors animated, they grabbed weapons from the pile and formed into lines five wide. There were forty warriors holding swords, spears, and axes, and another twenty archers in the rear.

Pressley gestured at the group. "This is my skeleton army. They'll fight beside us until their bones shatter. As we make our way through the dungeon, I'll be able to reanimate some of the monsters we defeat to fight alongside us temporarily. All of my abilities are powered by my health, so the weaker I become, the more difficult it will be to use some of my abilities. I have ranged attacks that can replenish my health, as well as some area-of-effect abilities for tackling groups."

Limery flew over to one of the skeleton warriors and tapped it on the skull. The skeleton stood at attention, unflinching.

The imp frowned. "Theys is not very funs."

"No, but they are persistent." Pressley had witnessed his summons continue to fight after losing an arm or leg. Even without a skull, they would swing blindly. It wasn't until their HP depleted completely that they would turn to dust. They might not be semi-intelligent like Chod's horrors, but they could fight. And that was all he needed. Pressley turned to his two new companions. "Are we ready?"

Caustic growled and pawed against the earth with his massive talons.

Limery flashed a mischievous grin. "We readies."

The army of skeletons marched into the dungeon, their footsteps perfectly synchronized as they descended underground. At first, Pressley had been unnerved by his minions' lack of sound. There were no groaning or hellish grunts like in the movies, just silent motion as the bones moved, propelled by infernal energy. The corpses he reanimated were a different story. Much like the imp, those things never seemed to shut up.

Pressley followed with his sword at the ready and Limery perched upon his shoulder. Caustic brought up the rear, head raised as he sniffed at the surroundings.

The air changed as soon as they stepped out of the corridor and into an enormous cavern. There was a heaviness about the place that he hadn't felt on the surface. Pressley felt it, and judging by the rumble in Caustic's chest, no doubt the dragon did too. Somewhere nearby, they could hear the sound of running water, and straight ahead, a platform barely wide enough for the skeletons to stand five abreast led across a nebulous chasm that seemed to descend forever.

On the other side of the platform, stairs led up to an expansive hall that stretched deeper into the earth, supported by colossal columns. Massive gargoyles of watchful lions loomed from above the stairs, water spouting from their roaring mouths into the chasm below. Mist hung in the air in a prism of colors, rainbows ignited by torches that lined the walls. Shadows danced from their flames, giving the gargoyles a lifelike appearance.

"Who dares enter my domain?" an amplified voice sounded all around them. It was feminine and somehow simultaneously alluring and threatening. "Who is foolish enough to challenge my might?" Laughter rang out. "It matters not, for I shall clean my teeth with your bones. Welcome to my dungeon."

A chill ran along Pressley's already frigid spine.

"Scaries." Limery's head swiveled as he inspected their surroundings.

Behind them, Caustic's chest rumbled as he surveyed the area.

"Are you familiar with the manticore?" Pressley asked.

The imp shook his head. "Limmy doesn't knows."

"I read of her exploits in the Goldspire Library, though I found no mention of what we should expect within the dungeon. But I know she will be a challenge. In most sources, she's described the same—the body of the lion with a woman's face and sprawling wings. She has the tail of a scorpion, though there were multiple accounts of its capabilities. Some say it has a single stinger. Others say it is barbed from base to tip and capable of shooting projectiles. She has an appetite for beastkin flesh and other humanoids, and she's said to have the ability to mimic their speech. Some reports say she can cast illusions, too, so be wary." The warmth radiating through Pressley's armor increased slightly, and he basked in the sensation. "Once we cross this bridge, be prepared for anything."

Limery's brow furrowed, and he nodded.

Pressley ordered his minions across the narrow platform. Their bony footsteps clacked along the smooth stone along with Caustic's talons and Pressley's boots. They wouldn't be winning any awards for stealth. Wind swirled underneath, and he wondered if the chasm led to a waterway that filtered into the sea. However deep it went, it was far enough to where the splash of water couldn't reach them.

They crossed the bridge and ascended the stairwell into the grand hall. It seemed to stretch for eternity with torches and columns as far as they could see. Up close, the gargoyles were made of white marble laced with red veins. It gave the lion's stone eyes an almost humanlike appearance.

Caustic's chest rumbled, and Pressley scanned the area for threats. With the columns, it would be easy for enemies to lurk out of sight.

"Do you see anything?" he asked Limery.

"Noes." The imp gulped.

The heat radiating through Pressley's armor intensified, making it harder for him to concentrate. "Let's move forward. Stay alert."

Pressley noticed the gargoyle's tail move a moment before a stone paw swiped for him. Limery flew from his shoulder, and Pressley raised his sword just in time for it to rain sparks through the eye-slit of his helm, briefly igniting the skull beneath.

A second paw knocked him to the ground from behind, and all around, the lion gargoyles leapt from their pedestals, leaving a fountain of water gushing in their wake.

Fire crackled as Limery summoned fireballs and began pelting the lions. Skeleton warriors charged the beasts, and their weapons clanked against the creatures' stone hides.

Pressley barely had enough time to analyze the monsters as he crawled to his feet.

Gargoyle. *Level 34. Made of enchanted stone, gargoyles serve as excellent guardians with their ability to conceal their true nature until they move. While gargoyles have no magical abilities, they are extremely tough and can only be killed by shattering their core.*

A lion pounced on Pressley as he gained his footing, but the death knight was ready. He side-stepped the lunging beast and brought his sword down on its side. Sparks erupted from the hit, leaving a small crack in the stone.

Pressley grunted. The sword wasn't the weapon for this fight, and while Limery's fire was scorching the lions and coating them with soot, it didn't seem to be having much effect otherwise.

Stone paws padded against the floor behind him, and Pressley raised his sword just in time to block a set of claws from removing his head from his shoulders. He counted nine lions, their eyes now blazing with golden fury. Roars echoed down the hall, and Caustic answered the challenge.

The dragon's talons scraped against one of the beasts, leaving a deep gash in the stone, far more effective than Pressley's weapon. All around, the skeletons were scattered and shattered from the gargoyle's attacks. While his minions didn't expire, they could be disassembled. Once their HP depleted, the bones would turn to dust.

Pressley quickly summoned more warriors from the scattered bones and reached into his satchel for a weapon better suited to the challenge at hand.

An explosion rocked the cavern, and skeletons tumbled through the air like ragdolls along with giant chunks of stone that had been at least two gargoyles moments ago. A large lion head rolled to a stop at Pressley's feet.

"Sorries." Limery grimaced as a crack splintered up the column where the explosion had occurred.

That was two down, and a few lost skeletons was a small price to pay. If they defeated the manticore, it wouldn't matter if they destroyed the entrance.

Pressley gave the imp a thumbs-up. "Good job. Keep it up."

Limery grinned and returned to the fight.

Pressley cast Reanimate over the destroyed gargoyles but received a notification that it was unsuccessful. Cursing his luck, he pondered a new strategy for dealing with them. Nearly half of his abilities only worked on living creatures, and just as many only worked on the dead. The gargoyles existed somewhere else entirely.

He stored his sword and pulled a warhammer from his satchel. The silver head gleamed in the firelight. One end was a large hammer, and the other had a spike tipped with diamonds. He preferred the precision and weight of the sword, but he'd have better luck smashing the lions to bits with this.

His first victim sat in waiting, preparing to pounce from behind the nearby column.

"Here, kitty, kitty," Pressley's hollow voice called.

The stone cat leapt through the air, claws extended, and Pressley planted his foot. He swung upward with the spiked end and connected with the lion's jaw. Stone shattered against the diamond-tipped spike, and the gargoyle spun mid-air, somehow managing to land on its feet. It attempted to roar, but its lower jaw had been obliterated, so a pitiful groan was all that escaped.

Giant wings flapped like sails as Caustic flew by with a gargoyle gripped in his talons. He soared over the chasm, dropping the lion into the depths below.

Pressley pushed the attack on his own opponent, but the gargoyle still had cat-like reflexes. It swatted away swing after swing.

Another explosion rocked the hall, giving Pressley an opening as one of the pillars collapsed. He caught the lion in the side of the head, turning it to rubble just as dust filled the area and obscured Pressley's vision. He stepped back, waiting for the dust to clear, when something knocked his chest like a sledgehammer and pinned him to the ground. Hot breath filled his helm as the lion roared, and his armor creaked beneath the weight of the stone monster as claws attempted to pull his chest plate away. Had he been human, they'd likely be ripping into his flesh.

But he wasn't human. He cast Lifesteal, and purple energy shot from his hands. At such close range, the effect was instantaneous. The damage he'd taken from the previous attacks healed instantly.

The lion gnawed at the horns protruding from Pressley's helm, wrenching the death knight under powerful thrusts as it attempted to pry the helm away. Pressley's health trickled down with every thrust as his bones creaked beneath the weight. Several skeletons had gathered around, hacking and slashing at the gargoyle to no avail.

Eva's face flashed across his vision, and power pulsed within his core. Energy built within him, just as a flaming outline blazed through the smoke. "Let go of Presslies!" Limery shouted as he landed on the lion's back, molten hands pressed against the gargoyle's head.

The lion yowled in pain, and Pressley activated Lifesteal again. Health surged into his body as the lion released the death knight, its jaws snapping over its shoulder at the imp.

"Gets it, Caustics!" Limery ordered, and the dragon descended, grasping the thrashing lion in his powerful claws.

The pressure released from Pressley's chest, and Caustic flew over the chasm to drop another victim into the depths below.

Pressley grabbed his warhammer, ready to fight, but the hall was quiet aside from the debris crunching beneath his boots. The skeletons that remained stood motionless with no threat left to fight.

Out of the nine gargoyles, he'd killed one. He was a higher level than both the dragon and imp by a wide margin, and yet they'd dispatched eight of the lions with ease.

Pressley needed to up his game going forward, or Chod was never going to let him hear the end of this.

15. TRIALS AND TRIBULATIONS

Horrors grumble all around me as I wait for Jegaar to exit the Narrow Pass. We stand outside the entrance to the trials, and one of the Horrors of Finesse puts its long, spindly blue finger into a Horror of Power's ear. The stout warthog-like horror snaps its head around, snarling, and a scuffle breaks out. Dust flies as they tussle in the dirt before several of the furry, rotund Horrors of Vitality step in to separate them, grumbling something in their language my communication stone can't translate.

I've noticed recently that my horrors will sometimes mimic my emotions. When I'm more on edge, they seem to be as well.

"Calm down, everyone. We're all in this together." I equip Destroyer and let the comforting weight of the warhammer rest against my palm.

Jegaar looks over his shoulder a final time and then disappears from view. I summon Pharos, and my spirit guide appears. The frost goat blazes with white-orange ethereal energy that ignites the dark cavern. I follow Pharos inside, trailed by a platoon of horrors, and soon I'm greeted with a prompt.

Trials of the Warforged: *Would you like to enter?*

Once all of the horrors are crammed inside the cavern, I accept. The ground rumbles, and dust and debris fall from the walls and ceiling as the mountain outside shifts. The grind of a mountain moving reverberates in my chest and assaults my ears until both sides of the Narrow Pass fit seamlessly together. A solid wall of stone blocks the exit.

There's no going back. If I want to get out of here, I have two options: complete the trials or die trying.

The cavern empties into a room with enchanted pyres burning in the corners with a ghastly flames. In contrast to the rugged entrance that blends in with the outside pass, this room is polished obsidian that has been meticulously carved from the mountain. The white flames of the pyres reflect off the eyes of my horrors.

I step forward, and a molten orange outline forms in the center of the far wall. There's a hiss before a section of wall grates against the floor as it disappears, revealing the next room.

Please remove all items before entering the trials.

That's unfortunate, but I understand. If the goal is to forge me anew, then I can't complete the trials with outside help, even in the form of items. I'm not sure what would happen if I tried to sneak something in, but that's not a risk I'm willing to take.

I set my expandable satchel on the floor and place Destroyer beside it. With the pass closed, at least I don't have to worry about having my gear stolen. The first item I remove is the spaulder that has protected my shoulder on many occasions. With so many horrors active, I barely notice the loss of stat bonuses as I set the armor aside. Next, I untie the Tiger's Eye Pendant from around my neck. That little necklace has saved my hide more times than I can count with its ability to remove one debuff every ten minutes. It has been a constant reminder of how generous the forest trolls were when they had so little to give. After I remove the phoenix feather from my braid, I place the items inside the satchel. The last item to go in is Destroyer.

For as long as I've been in Mythos, I've had a weapon. From the gnarled branch I found on day one to Peacemaker and half-dozen others, I've always chosen to wield a weapon first and use my claws second. I guess I'm about to find out how big of a crutch that has been.

With nothing but a loincloth covering my trollberries, I follow Pharos into the first room of the trials.

The room is a long rectangle, crafted from the same gleaming obsidian, with an empty trough that runs around the edge of a raised platform. Numerous tunnels slightly wider than my head disappear into the walls. My heart races, and I try to find comfort in the mana that rushes to my fingertips, calling another round of horrors to replace the ones that expire.

I have zero doubts that something I'm going to hate is coming out of those tunnels sooner or later, so I position myself in the center of the platform, surrounded by horrors on all sides. The width of the platform is just big enough for them to surround me without falling into the trough.

A notification flashes across my vision.

Trials of the Warforged: *Commencing*

Stage One: *Heat*

There's a loud clank and steam shoots from the tunnels around the room. Horrors grumble at the disturbance. There's a sizzling sound and a faint glow comes from deep within the tunnels. Molten metal pours from within, slow and steady, filling the bottom of the trough that runs the perimeter of the room. With nowhere for the heat to disperse, the temperature surges immediately, and sweat erupts across my brow. The Horrors of Vitality pant with their tongues drooping from their mouths, sweltering beneath their thick fur.

I stand on guard, pulse thundering in my ears, ready for whatever monster I'm about to face. Sweat drips from my nose, and my eyes burn from the heat, but nothing appears.

Molten metal continues to fill the trough, and the temperature steadily rises. My body shimmers from the perspiration beading down my chest and arms. One of my horrors groans, and I notice their health is depleting more rapidly than normal.

My vision blacks at the edge and for a moment, I think I'm going to pass out. I concentrate on my breathing and focus my gaze on the steady stream of liquid metal pouring from one of the tunnels. One breath at a time, I wait for my head to clear.

Once I regain my composure, I scan the room, searching for a way out—a crack in the wall, a hidden tile on the floor, anything that might make this end.

There's nothing.

I think back to Jegaar's words. *The trials are not about what you face but how you face them.* He told me I would need to endure. I thought he meant in battle, but it seems not. The heat dries the moisture from my eyes until every blink feels like a scrape of sandpaper. Sweat sizzles against my skin, and my health finally begins to drain.

The other horrors now have their tongues out, and their panting rivals the slosh of molten metal that surrounds us. There's nothing they can do to help me here, so I cast Sacrifice to save them from this misery. At least I can relish the influx of bonus stats for the next few minutes.

Pharos paces back and forth across the platform, his spirit hooves silent against the stone. I could sacrifice him for a boost to Wisdom, but then I wouldn't be able to call upon him again for twenty-four hours. Right now, his company is more valuable.

As tough as things seem right now, I try to think about all of the Warforged that came before me. They are legendary for a reason—because they completed the trials. If they can do it, so can I. I just need to take stock of the situation and see what my options are.

I have over seven thousand HP but at the rate it's draining, I don't know how long it will last. The floor grows hotter, and even my tough troll hide begins to blister, adding to my health decay. Every movement stings like the worst sunburn I've ever had. Eventually, I stand still.

Berserker Rage will boost my healing for a short time, but without anything to fight, I'll be unable to increase my rage meter. It's full now, but that means I'll only have one opportunity to use it unless lava monsters start climbing out of those holes.

On second thought, please don't let lava monsters crawl out of those holes.

Unable to move without pain, I'm left to my own thoughts as my body slowly roasts. I close my eyes and do my best to block out my discomfort. I'm not sure how much time passes, but eventually, my health drops to less than half.

I try to send Taryn a message, but the magic powering the trials must be blocking outside communication between him or any of the other heroes I have in my contact list. Valery is still an option, and for a moment, I consider messaging her to say just how fucked up all of this is. I think better of it. This was my choice to enter the trials, and the tone of her last message makes me think she has a lot going on outside the game, especially with the Dorothy situation.

I open my eyes, and fresh tears sizzle against my cheeks. Pharos stands before me, his head tilted up, and his fiery eyes gazing intensely at me. I lean into them, pushing away everything but the swirl of energy within his pupils.

I've never been one for meditation, but I lose myself in his spirit, blocking out the world around me as if nothing else matters. My health continues to trickle down like a leaky faucet. When it hits ten percent, I ready the only card up my sleeve—using Berserker Rage to amplify the increased regeneration that occurs when my health goes into the red.

Before I do so, something surprising happens. My health hovers at around ten percent. My HP drops, then the increased regeneration kicks in and brings it out of the red. Once above ten percent, the increased regeneration cancels, and my HP drops again. The cycle repeats over and over, with the increased regen enough to stay the damage as long as I remain below ten percent health. The relief is enough to make me laugh, sending a wave of pain through my searing flesh.

I take a breath of hot air and lock eyes with Pharos again. I can survive this. I just need to endure.

16. DISGUISES

Dorothy glanced at Valmar in the mirror's reflection as she adjusted her features. He stared ahead, the green light from the throne room's many torches reflecting off the necromancer's chiseled jawline. His deep red eyes burned intently, beacons upon his pallid gray skin, as he stared into oblivion. He wore his thick raven hair slicked back, and it fell just above his shoulders. For being nearly a thousand years old, he looked good. Not everyone could pull off the sexy Dracula vibe.

Valmar's fingernails tapped against the obsidian throne. "Are you nearly finished?" His tone was exasperated. "I have a council to attend."

Dorothy finished adjusting her eye color and met his gaze in the mirror. "With the warlock? That guy is such a tool."

Valmar nodded. "He has been a useful tool, and the reason you have been able to track your prey."

Dorothy smiled. She found it humorous when he took her words literally. "Yeah, well, he gives me the creeps. I'm sure he'd lick your boots if you let him."

Valmar's brow narrowed, and his glare pierced through Dorothy before he stood to join her by the mirror. He hovered behind her, resting a hand on her shoulder. The touch sent a chill down her spine, and she fought the urge to shiver. "You could learn from his devotion."

She met his gaze in the mirror as she changed her skin color from gray to ivory. "Have I not proved my worth?"

His mouth curled into a sinister smile. It reminded Dorothy of a predator, always a heartbeat away from attacking.

"You show great promise for an outworlder. It is the reason I have granted you so many boons. I would hate to see my investment wasted."

Dorothy scoffed. "I'll do what the warlock couldn't. The troll won't be a problem for you much longer." She altered her hair from silver to blonde and then dismissed the Disguise template from her vision. To anyone looking, she no longer appeared as an undead elf with the blazing eyes of a revenant, but a golden-haired, blue-eyed elf from the lands of Ellynmylly. "I'm ready."

Valmar's eyes took on the same eerie green as the flames, and a giant shadow appeared in the center of the room. A demonic finger the size of a man extended from the void, and its pointed nail ripped through reality, revealing a swirling white portal.

"You remind me a great deal of my sister." He removed his hands from Dorothy's shoulder and gestured toward the portal. "She had your spirit."

Dorothy wore a curious expression. "What happened to her?"

"It does not matter." For a flicker, his eyes lost focus as if Valmar was transported to some far-off memory. "She serves me now."

Dorothy glanced around the perimeter of the room, where several dozen armored skeletons stood sentry in deathly silence. Was his sister one of them, or was she elsewhere? Dorothy had seen the army of the dead beyond the city walls. Thousands of skeletons and undead. When they attacked, they would raze Mythos to the ground. She didn't care what happened to the rest of this world. She'd come here with one purpose—vengeance. If she had to ally with the villain to get it, then so be it.

Valmar squeezed her shoulder, and a revolting darkness seeped out from his touch. Thankfully, Dorothy's disguise concealed her grimace.

"Do not fail me." There was no room for argument in his words.

"Yes, master." She nodded, thankful to free herself from his grasp as she stepped into the portal.

At level thirty-three, Dorothy finally felt comfortable entering the broader world. She'd been in Mythos for two weeks—plotting, planning, and grinding—but when she'd learned from Ethan the warlock that Chod was only level twenty-eight during their fight in Pruxford, she made the decision to finally reach out to her old friend.

What she would have done to see the look on his face as he read that message.

Since then, she'd grinded a few more levels just to be safe. To hear the others tell it, Chod always had something up his sleeve. And if not, he seemed to have friends everywhere who would swoop in at the last minute to save the day.

That part bothered her the most. He'd seemed like a nice enough guy when they'd first met, but once they started gaming, he became a complete asshole. He snapped at her for every little thing, even though he was doing no better. Games were supposed to be fun. For her, they had been. Streaming had been fun.

Chod had taken that away from her.

Now, he was about to find out just how unfun games could be.

Dorothy exited the portal into Goldspire, and she felt the sun's warm embrace for the first time. In Mosstar, it was always cloudy. Perfect for Valmar's little act, but it was a real drag.

She grinned as she looked across the sweeping coliseum. It was an imposing presence, and the stands were filled with beastkin that cheered as gladiators clashed in the arena. No one talked about it, at least not openly, but this was the first place Valmar had ever been turned back. She'd been warned that mentioning Goldspire's emperor around her master would result in a fate worse than death.

Dorothy rolled her eyes. For all his villainous tendencies, and Valmar had plenty, he was just as sensitive as the next man.

He'd sent her to Goldspire for two reasons—to gather intel and to eliminate the troll problem. With her Disguise ability, even if she were apprehended, no one would know her true origins.

"Having second thoughts, girly?" A lion beastkin grinned in her direction from the sandy arena. Two massive gauntlets with spikes on the knuckles covered each hand. A matching set of spiked armor protected his knees and elbows. Aside from that, he wore nothing but a loincloth.

Easy pickings.

She returned his smile. "No, just monologuing."

He frowned in confusion. "If you wish to enter Goldspire, then you must defeat a gladiator in the arena."

She curled both hands into fists and placed them under her chin, speaking in a high-pitched voice. "Let me guess, I'm the lucky gal who gets to dance with you?"

The beastkin huffed. "You talk a lot."

She scoffed. "Yeah, and you breathe through your mouth."

He clinked his gauntlets together and growled. "Enough of this. Show me what you've got."

Her smile shifted from playful taunting to something more dangerous. "Oh, baby, I thought you'd never ask."

Dorothy activated One with the Shadows and darkness cloaked her, unyielding to the bright sun. She jumped from the platform, and two shadow copies sprang from her, surrounding the beastkin with a triangular formation. Until she attacked, she would remain cloaked, indistinguishable from the two clones. While her shadow copies couldn't fight, they offered something more valuable—she could switch places with them at will, almost like teleportation.

The beastkin held his gauntlets in front of him like a boxer, shifting his weight from one foot to the other. His head turned on a swivel, waiting for the attack.

Dorothy equipped one of her many daggers and waited until the beastkin's back was facing her. She activated True Strike and tossed the weapon. The poisoned blade lodged in his beefy neck just above the shoulder. The beastkin groaned as he spun around, and she ported to the shadow across from her, throwing another poisoned dagger at his backside. Without the aid of True Strike, it stuck in the beastkin's mid-back.

He growled, turning around and swinging wildly. An outline of an eagle covered his arm as he punched, and it ripped through the shadow, dissipating it as Dorothy ported away. She threw another dagger, sticking him in the ribs. With wild eyes, he attacked again. This time, a streak of orange energy blasted from the gauntlet and destroyed the second shadow.

The beastkin wobbled as the poison began to take effect. He reached for the tainted blade in his beefy neck, and Dorothy used the opportunity to push the attack. She activated Sleight of Hand, feigning an attack with her left hand. When the beastkin raised his gauntlets to block, she went low with a blade in her right, slicing him across the thigh.

Blood streaked his fur, and his health dropped rapidly as the poison stacked with each subsequent hit. His movements grew sluggish, and he no longer shifted from foot to foot.

Dorothy held up her middle finger. "How many do you see?"

He stumbled back and forth before falling face-first to the ground.

"Attaboy." She straddled his back and slid a dagger across his throat.

The crowd erupted, and Dorothy waved to them as they tossed flowers into the arena. She picked up a rose and sniffed it, surprised at how fragrant it smelled.

"I could get used to this." She tossed the rose aside and pulled up her map, locating Chod's position. "But first, I've got a troll to hunt."

17. MOONLIT FLIGHTS

Taryn's first day in Seascape was full of councils and strategy meetings. Now that war had been declared, there were a great deal of preparations to make, first among the individual kingdoms and then for the war effort as a whole.

A bevy of familiar faces sat around the council room—the two kings, Orso and Favian, Kurzol the cleric, Kassidy the teleportation mage, Chief Rizza and Jira of the forest trolls, Chief Laojin and Senzala of the arctic trolls, Lady Brollen the ice mage from Sandholde, and nearly a dozen other advisors. The most powerful and influential people on the Isle were in this room. They had days to gather their armies and prepare for an invasion that would determine all of their fates long after the heroes were gone.

They each took turns reporting on the current status of the guards, soldiers, and mages. Compared to the other kingdoms, the Isle of Mythos had fewer mages, but their heroes would more than make up for the deficiency. They did have something the others didn't, though—trolls. When it came to raw strength and power, only the beastkin of Goldspire rivaled the trolls.

Able-bodied men and dwarves would need to be recruited from across Seascape and Vanaria to serve as a last line of defense. While the two kingdoms both had a city watch, their militias had shrunk in the years after the portals closed, and neither kept a large standing army in waiting. Soldiers and guards would be part of the initial attack, but there was no room for failure. Farmers, miners, and everyday citizens would be forced to answer the call and fight if necessary.

Taryn prayed they never had to lift a weapon in battle.

He rubbed his eyes with both palms while King Favian continued his report on the state of Vanaria. The king had removed the stately armor he wore to Pruxford and now sported a simple blue tunic with a griffin crest. He looked tired. They all did. Taryn imagined Chod was having a much more exciting time in Goldspire. At least he wasn't cooped up in a castle every hour of the day.

But this was what Taryn had chosen, to aid his king in whatever manner His Highness deemed fit. He should be honored that King Orso valued his opinion so highly to allow him a seat on the council, and he was. He just wished he could be of more use.

With the portals opened, travel between Vanaria to Seascape was easier than ever. They could coordinate their efforts without delay, and messengers carried intel between the two kingdoms at all hours of the day.

If they were lucky, they might just be ready in time.

Taryn tried to send Chod a message, but it wouldn't deliver. The trials must have been blocking outside communication.

Flubs slinked out of the vial around Taryn's neck and poked the druid with a slimy appendage.

"Taryn..." King Favian raised a brow. "Do you think they will agree?"

"Come again?" Taryn sat up, completely oblivious to the question he'd just been asked.

"I said we should have the heroes lead the charge into battle. They'll be able to cause the most destruction. Do you think the others will agree to this?"

"I believe so." Taryn stroked his beard. "They're all training in Pruxford currently and making the most of the kingdom's many dungeons."

"Good." King Favian nodded. "I don't yet know what the other kingdoms will provide, but you will have air support from Chod's dragon and my griffin. The front lines will also have ground support from the forest trolls' three mana-infused wyrms." He gestured to Chief Rizza. "The troll tribes have requested to follow Chod into battle, assuming he doesn't have other plans once he returns. If so, then they will join our vanguard.

"Our plan, for now, is for King Orso to flank the heroes with both of our kings-guards. The city watches will follow, and I'll be able to offer tactical advice from above. We will continue to update our tactics as more information becomes available, as fluid as a slime." He winked at Taryn. "When we reconvene in Pruxford, we'll compare our plans with the others. Our citizens who take up arms will form a militia to serve as the last line of defense. We want to attack swiftly with the full force of a dwarven hammer." King Favian turned to Chief Rizza. "What news of the other tribes?"

Chief Rizza frowned. "The envoy has not yet returned, but I have confidence in Gord and the others. Lillith and Bazel have been sent to inform them of the Pruxford council and to return with an update as quickly as possible. We should have word soon."

"Keep us informed." King Favian leaned forward, resting his hands on the table. Dark circles underscored his bright blue eyes. Like many here, he had slept little in the past two days. "We never thought we would be in this position again—the fate of our world hanging on the outcome of a battle between the living and the dead—but here we are. We have overcome this challenge before. Search your records and your histories, empty your troves. Any weapons that offer an advantage against the undead must be equipped. Our enchanters in Vanaria are hard at work as we speak." He nodded to the dwarven king.

King Orso stood. "I think that is enough for today. I must address my people, and there is still much to do. Shall we reconvene tomorrow evening?"

After several nods of agreement, he banged his gavel, and the table dispersed.

A large, charcoal-colored hand gripped Taryn on the shoulder as he was leaving, and Taryn turned to see Chief Laojin towering above him. The arctic troll's shaggy white fur looked out of place among the harsh lines of dwarven architecture. It covered the majority of his massive frame aside from his face, hands, and a patch on his stomach.

"I tire of these meetings." The troll chief smiled beneath his thick white beard. "Would you care to join me for a moonlit flight?"

Taryn laughed. "There is nothing in the world I would love more right now."

Moonlight cast the towers and spires of the castle in a silver glow. The gargoyles that sat upon the buildings looked as if they might spring to life and defend the city if necessary. Perhaps they would. Taryn still knew very little of Seascape's history.

He stood in the king's courtyard overlooking the turbulent waters of the sea below. How different the world might be if sea travel had been possible when the portals closed.

"Heavy thoughts weigh on you, young druid." Chief Laojin's icy blue eyes offered sympathy.

Taryn watched the waves crash against the rocks below. He wondered if he was the rock or the wave. Was he set to try again and again only to be faced with the inevitable? Or was he the rock that endured the never-ending barrage? Images of his pets crossed his mind—Berry, Ruby, Jordy, Flubs. He rested his hand against his heart where Stompy's memory was tattooed on his chest. And then there was Breebis. He smiled at the memory of sitting with her in the hammock, dark green hair cloaking her shoulders as she looked at him with those warm red eyes. They'd rocked together underneath starry skies as she told him of her dreams and passions.

Bits of data or not, when he looked into the eyes of Breebis or his pets, he knew they were looking back at him. Taryn wouldn't be here forever, that much was certain. He needed to make sure they would be okay.

His fingertips pressed into the stone barrier, and he fought back tears. "We only get one shot at this, you know." He sighed. "One shot to save it all."

"You cannot dwell on the future, young druid. Be thankful for what you have accomplished already." Laojin squeezed Taryn's bicep. "When we last met, you and Chod were on a mission to unite Mythos against this threat. By my estimations, you've done a job to be proud of. If you can convince a tribe of trolls to fight alongside dwarves and men, then I believe you can do anything."

"It wasn't all me."

"You give yourself too little credit. Come, let's take to the air and ease your mind." Without waiting for a response, Laojin climbed on the wall and jumped.

Taryn leaned over the barrier, watching the chief fall as air fluttered through the thick fur covering the troll's body. Halfway down, there was an explosion of silver feathers as the chief transformed into his falcon form. The falcon dove deeper before extending his wings and catching the swirling air and soaring high. With a few flaps of his navy-tipped wings, he coasted high above the sea, a beacon under the light of the moon. It was like watching a shooting star as Laojin screeched and dove through the clouds.

A smile crept over Taryn's face. He hadn't flown for pleasure since that day high in the Frostmoor mountains when Laojin had tossed him from the cliffside. He still remembered Laojin's words from that day. *This is how I take care of myself and clear my mind. Plummeting through the clouds has a way of putting things in perspective.*

If Taryn wanted to help those he cared about, he needed to clear his mind. He needed to be focused and determined, sure of his actions. Letting the heaviness of the future hang around his neck would only pull him into depths where he could help no one.

He tied the necklace containing Flubs around Ruby's neck, then hefted himself onto the wall and jumped. His cloak flapped like a sail and the clasps in his beard jingled as he fell. For a moment, he embraced the thrill of falling and the wind against his face. Then he used Transform. There was an eruption of red feathers as his body shifted, and his short red wings fluttered against the strong oceanic winds. He didn't have the same powerful wings as Laojin, but he soon found balance and flew upward.

Taryn embraced the cool air against his beak and soon Laojin joined him, the falcon's eyes alert with black slits that cut through their icy blue.

Together, they soared above the city. From a bird's-eye view, Seascape was gorgeous. Its gothic architecture shimmered in the moonlight, more beautiful than anything he'd ever seen in New York. The mosaic of hammers and axes across Seascape Square glowed from the torches. Taryn recalled when they'd fought Glenn and Jude, and how Stompy had broken free from the stables to protect him.

Across the city, thousands of windows flickered with firelight, and forges burned as blacksmiths worked tirelessly into the night. He would fight to protect these people with everything he had.

But for now, he soared.

18. UNDER PRESSURE

I have no idea how much time passes as I stare into Pharos's ethereal eyes. My vision blurs at the edges against the relentless heat, but I stand strong, my body statuesque even as my feet burn and sweat sizzles against my skin.

My health continues to rise and dip at ten percent, caught in a perfect equilibrium as my increased regeneration activates and cancels in perpetuity. At some point, I enter a trancelike state, mesmerized by the swirl of energy that makes up my spirit guide. Without him, I would have succumbed long ago.

A loud clank pulls me from the trance, and the last of the molten iron drips into the trough. The tunnels along the walls close, followed by a patter of clacking noises as new tunnels open above. It sounds like a pack of dogs with untrimmed nails running across a wooden floor.

Orange bulbs of freshly blown glass fill the openings overhead, and the chittering sound that follows sets my hair on end. I barely have a moment to process what's happening before the bulbs descend, legs protruding from them as glasslike threads lower arachnids into the room.

I'm much too weak to fight anything in my current state, leaving me with no other option than to activate Berserker Rage. As soon as I do, my health rises rapidly, and bonus stats flood my system. Wounds stitch themselves together, burns mend, and for the first time in who knows how long, I don't notice the pain of the scorching temperature.

I take a step back and analyze the creature.

Molten Spider. Level 30. Forged in the fiery tunnels beneath the Burning Desert, molten spiders can withstand intense heat. While their bodies are fragile, their legs are covered in glass barbs capable of ravaging enemies, and their venom causes temporary paralysis. Their unfortunate victims often find themselves immobilized in glass cocoons where they slowly roast alive.

Thanks for the offer, but I'm gonna have to pass. I've had enough roasting for one day.

I count a dozen spiders lowering themselves into the room. I summon three horrors, and they stand by my side. Not wanting to wait for the spiders to turn me into minced meat, I punch the closest one and my fist shatters its glassy abdomen. The hit deals double damage thanks to Horror of Power, and the passive from Ram Rage activates, unleashing a wave of splash damage that sends several spiders spinning as they descend. A lava-like substance pours from the spider's broken abdomen like hot jelly, and the jagged carapace rips into my arm as I pull my hand free. Blue blood trickles down my arm, steaming as it hits the floor.

The creature hangs limp from its webbing, and another carves into my shoulder from behind with its barbed legs. I grab the spider, smashing its abdomen against one of my horns before tossing it into the molten iron surrounding the platform.

Another spider lunges at me, jabbing its pincers into my arm. Thanks to Berserker Rage, the venom has no effect as it's injected into my bloodstream. I rip the spider free and crush it against my horns like a frat-boy chugging beer on game day.

Two more spiders dangle in the air beside me, grasping for me with their barbed legs. I grab one with each hand and smash them together. They break like glass bottles, leaking orange fluid all around.

Even without my weapons, I'm a force of nature as I rage against the creatures. Every punch leaves me with dozens of cuts that my increased regeneration fights to heal. I'm a bloody mess as I stomp and smash.

Pharos charges around the platform with his horns lowered, but his ethereal form passes through them like a ghost. His presence only ever seems to effect shadowy beings.

I kill the last spider with a punch powered by Concussive Force, and it rockets into the far wall, shattering its fragile body just as my rage ends. The full force of the high temperature hits me like a hammer, and I wobble before gaining my bearings. Luckily for me, the fight was enough to build my rage meter back up, so I'll have at least one more opportunity to use it going forward.

As the last of the spiders sinks into the molten iron, I receive another notification.

Trials of the Warforged: *Stage one complete. Stage two commencing.*

Stage Two: *Pressure*

Awesome. Not even a chance to rest before I have to tackle the next phase. With the spiders gone, my horrors' health once again begins to deteriorate. Pharos stops his pacing and looks up at me.

I take a deep breath of hot air and sigh. "I'm gonna need you, boy."

The walls to my left and right shift, and the sound of grating stone echoes around me. Slowly, the walls close in, passing over the molten trough and then grinding across the platform.

I pace back and forth, searching for a way out, but once again, there's nothing.

Scaling the wall crosses my mind, but the obsidian walls are slick, and the spider tunnels are much too small even if I were able to climb to them.

If I was Taryn, I could fly out of here. But I'm not. I'm not here to escape. I'm here to survive. To forge myself anew. Stage one was called heat, and I had to endure it. If stage two is pressure, then I think I know what I need to do.

I turn sideways, take a wide-legged stance, and extend my arms. I wait for the walls to come to me, knowing that if I'm wrong then I'm about to be a Chod patty, extra well-done.

The walls touch my fingertips, and the hot stone burns against my skin. A moment later, the pressure locks me in place as I set my frame and brace myself against the massive walls with both arms and feet. Tension builds against my muscles, and they burn with the effort as I attempt to become an immovable object. It only takes a few seconds for my joints to ache as the force pushing against me threatens to dislocate my bones.

Sweat beads down my face, this time from effort as much as heat. Pharos moves before me, and I once again lean into his gaze.

This is going to be a long night.

19. THE BONDS OF BATTLE

Pressley and company pressed onward. Traps lay in wait down the grand hallway, but one of the best perks of having a skeleton army meant his minions could set them off without dying. They passed through tripwires, spiked pits, and poisonous darts with ease. As long as his minions had HP remaining, Pressley could reconfigure them even after disaster.

"Ouchies." Limery grimaced as a spear shot from the wall and impaled a skeleton between the ribs, pinning it to the wall.

Minions swarmed their compatriot, prying the spear loose in quick order, and they continued down the passage. Over the course of the day, they'd fought cobras with broad hoods that swirled with mesmerizing patterns, black ooze that seeped between tiles on the floor and ceiling, and giant hammerhorn beetles with metallic exoskeletons.

So far, nothing had given them as much trouble as the gargoyles. Throughout the dungeon, there were faces carved into the walls and columns depicting various forms of beastkin. Sometimes, Pressley swore that he saw blue eyes following him out of the corner of his vision. Whenever he focused on one, though, it was nothing more than stone. Probably just a trick of the light.

He'd managed to add several cobras and beetles to his undead army, but thanks to Limery and Caustic's explosive combination, all of the oozes had been obliterated into gelatinous mist. They decided it would be wise to use the dragon's toxic gas in planned situations going forward.

Caustic walked on all fours, munching on the remains of a cobra. Soon, they arrived at a narrow bridge crossing a pit of sapphire blue water. Shadows moved beneath the water's surface.

Pressley crossed his arms as he took stock of the situation. "You two fly across. I'll take the bridge."

"Is yous sure?" Limery asked.

Pressley grunted his affirmation at the imp. He was beginning to understand why Chod was so fond of him. For all his antics, Limery was caring and protective, always watching out for others despite his small stature and chaotic nature. Pressley hated to admit it, but the imp was growing on him.

Once Limery and Caustic were on the other side, Pressley ordered his skeleton warriors to cross the bridge. They made it halfway before the waters stirred, and winged crocodiles jumped from below, gliding through the air on tiny wings as they arced over the bridge and knocked many of his minions into the pit. The wings were more suited for a bird than a large reptile, making it impossible for the creatures to actually fly, but they were enough to keep the crocodiles airborne for a brief period of time.

Fire crackled in Limery's palms, and Caustic roared his challenge, but Pressley held up a hand.

"Leave it to me."

He counted at least eight of the monsters, but it was possible there were more in the water. He didn't want to risk losing his newly reanimated undead, especially the hammerhorn beetles, so he kept them on solid ground. Unlike the gargoyles, the crocodiles were living beings that allowed the death knight to use most of his abilities.

Pressley cast Pestilence in the pit, and darkness permeated the water. It would drain the health and lower the Constitution of whatever lurked beneath, giving his skeletons an advantage. From the tumultuous water, he assumed the pit couldn't be that deep, so he sent more skeletons into its depths. They fought as disease ravaged the winged crocodiles and blood swirled in dark tendrils.

He unsheathed his sword and marched onto the bridge. Midway across, a croc launched itself at the death knight. He activated Defile, and corrosive energy coated his blade as he sliced the monster along its side. The attack wasn't fatal, but it wasn't meant to be. The crocodile dove back into the water as the wound festered and after a few moments, the crocodile floated to the surface belly-up.

Caustic stood at the edge of the pit, chomping at the bit to join the action. His feet shuffled with excitement and his chest rumbled.

Pressley shook his head. "Don't worry. I've got this."

He cast Reanimate on the dead crocodile, and the death knight's health dropped as a tendril of purple energy slithered from his palm, encircling the dead monster. The beast twitched, and then its body thrashed as it came to life under Pressley's control. More crocodile bodies floated to the surface from a combination of Pestilence and skeletal fortitude. He cast Reanimate again and again, draining half of his health but adding five more undead minions to his cause.

The last few crocodiles were easy work after that.

Limery grinned devilishly when Pressley made it to the other side. "Presslies is strongs."

The death knight leaned over the edge, chugging a health potion and watching as skeletons climbed atop one another, making a bony ladder against the wall for the rest to climb out. A few had missing arms or legs from the crocodiles' rampage, and one had a tooth lodged in its skull, but most had survived the encounter. His undead crocs swam above the surface, their hides punctured in dozens of places, and all but one had damaged wings. The biggest downside of casting Reanimate was that the undead were summoned in whatever condition they were killed in. With broken wings, his new pets weren't flying out of the pit.

Pressley turned to Caustic. "Any chance you can help me get them out of the water?"

The dragon huffed.

"Please," he added.

With a grunt, Caustic took to the air. The flap of his wings sent waves splashing as he hovered above the water. He lowered, clenching one of the monsters in his talons. One by one, he gathered the undead reptiles and placed them safely on land until six of them groaned and snarled as they roamed the expansive hallway.

The rest of Pressley's undead crossed the bridge unimpeded, and the skeletons once again led the way, disarming more traps until the wide corridor emptied into an even larger atrium. Colossal pillars ran the perimeter of the large concourse, and massive doors lined the room on each side. They probably led to more monsters and hidden treasure, but straight ahead was the prize—a wide set of stairs leading to a massive golden door that could only be a throne room.

"That's where we need to go. But I don't think we'll make it across without trouble." He pointed to the doors on opposite sides of the atrium. "You can never trust a room that has closed doors before the big boss."

Caustic growled his challenge. It was clear that the dragon wasn't scared of anything. He'd managed to gain two levels over the course of the day, but they had to be in the late hours of the night at this point.

"We should go back and get a few hours of rest before we press on."

Limery yawned, stretching his thin arms overhead. "Oh, yes. Limmy is sleepies."

"Let's go, then." Pressley sent his minions ahead of them. "I'll keep the first watch."

He was sure that he didn't actually need sleep to survive as a death knight. Before his transformation, he'd received debuffs and notifications when he'd push too hard. But now, nothing. He wasn't sure how a lack of sleep in-game would affect his body in the real world, however, so he always made time to rest just to be safe. He had a daughter waiting for him outside, and there was nothing he would do to jeopardize that.

They returned to the pit where they'd fought the winged crocodiles, using it as a natural barrier while Pressley ordered his minions to guard the tunnel in the direction of the throne room. He positioned a handful of skeletons on the other side of the bridge to guard their rear just in case there were monsters they'd missed. During his grind to power, he'd spent a lot of time in dungeons and had become familiar with how most of them operated. They could only be entered by one party at a time, and the monsters within wouldn't respawn until the dungeon was cleared or the party was defeated. Compared to most dungeons, this one was enormous, and there was no telling if they'd bypassed hidden doors or passageways.

Pressley's armor clanked as he rested against the stone wall. Caustic curled at his feet like a giant cat, tucking his massive tail and burying his head beneath a wing.

Limery stood before the death knight, arms clasped behind his back as he gave Pressley a pleading expression.

Pressley recognized that look. "What is it now?"

Limery's bulbous yellow eyes fluttered. "Can Limmy sleeps with yous?"

Pressley grunted. The little guy was probably used to sleeping next to Chod during their travels. Limery was cute in his own way, so Pressley relented, holding out his hand. "Fine. Come on over."

The imp nestled within the crook of the death knight's arm, and his body heat radiated through the armor. The sensation was like being covered with a warm blanket on a cold day. Pressley let out a pleasant sight as he embraced the warmth.

The ground vibrated as Caustic snored, and Limery soon joined him, a giant snot bubble inflating from his nose with each breath. Beneath his helm, hidden by darkness, Pressley smiled. He recalled rocking Eva to sleep when she was a baby, his daughter's gentle snores, and the connection of her warm skin against his own.

He sat there in blissful peace for hours until Caustic woke. The dragon yawned, stretching his front legs while his tail swished from his raised hindquarters, knocking an unlucky skeleton into the wall. He huffed, then took a watchful position behind the undead army.

With a dragon watching over him, Pressley drifted off, experiencing the best sleep he'd had since entering Mythos.

A hollow ring woke Pressley from dreams of a life he'd lost. Bulbous yellow eyes blinked inches from his helm before a second gong reverberated through his skull.

"Wake ups." Limery tapped the helm again. "Limmy is hungries."

"I'm up." Pressley groaned, and another gong rang out. "Dammit, stop that. I'm awake." He gently swatted the imp's hand away as he came to his senses. The pervading cold cradled him in its frigid embrace, amplified by Limery's absence. An uncontrollable shiver passed through Pressley as he stood, but after a few moments, he grew accustomed to the chill within his armor once again.

Since becoming a death knight, Pressley no longer had a need to eat in-game and thanks to the nanites, his body was nourished within the pod. He still had rations of cheese, hard bread, and cured meats from before his transformation, so he shared them between Limery and Caustic.

He watched as the dragon ate, swearing that the creature had grown overnight. Caustic's paws seemed bigger and the bearded scales around his chin denser. After they finished the meager breakfast, the group set off toward the atrium.

"Stay close to me," Pressley ordered. "Things will only get more dangerous from here."

Limery perched on the death knight's shoulder, calm as ever, while Caustic scanned the room with the same intensity as Pressley.

The minion army passed the closest columns that ran the perimeter of the domed ceiling. Pressley gripped his sword, ready for whatever awaited. Once the last of their party exited the hallway, a giant slab of stone fell from the ceiling and blocked their exit.

He'd expected as much. With the boss room so close, they would be tested.

The towering doors to each side of the atrium groaned as they opened, and an unsettling clacking stirred within their depths. Ghastly shapes moved in the dim torchlight as nearly a dozen bone-white scorpions, each one the size of a small car, spilled into the room. Red eyes blazed as pincers snapped, and their dangerous stingers pulsed with venom.

Bonecrusher Scorpion. *Level 35. The aptly named bonecrusher scorpion is not only capable of breaking bone with its serrated pincers, but it can also grind bones to dust within the vortex of crystalline teeth located behind its chelicerae. Ingesting the bone dust replenishes weakened or damaged areas of the scorpion's exoskeleton. The venom secreted from the stinger has paralytic properties, making it even easier to separate its prey limb from limb.*

Pressley gulped. Bone-eating scorpions, and he'd just brought them a buffet.

While Caustic and Limery shifted the odds in their favor, his skeletal minions had a tendency to lose limbs during battle, and he couldn't afford to offer up free health potions to his enemies. He needed the skeletons off the playing field ASAP.

"Don't let the scorpions anywhere close until my skeletons are gone." He opened his satchel and tossed it on the ground. "Inside."

The closest skeleton jumped into the bag, disappearing as if it were the hatch to a submarine.

Caustic roared and unfurled his wings, ready to fight, while Limery took to the air. Fire crackled in the imp's palm as he summoned fire walls around the perimeter. Pressley spread out the rest of his undead in a defensive formation, protecting the skeleton warriors as they filed into the expandable satchel. One by one, they jumped inside, their entire bodies disappearing into the bag no bigger than their rib cages.

All the while, scorpions scattered, skittering around the room. Some climbed columns and a few more scaled the walls as the sound of snapping pincers filled the area. One of the scorpions passed through Limery's flame wall, and Pressley's undead cobra rose in challenge. It spread its mesmerizing hood only for the scorpion to sever the snake's head with one quick snip of its pincers.

Caustic dove at the scorpion, smashing it against the marble floor with his full weight and sinking his teeth into the arachnid's tail. With a sickening crunch, the tail ripped free, leaving a trail of fluid and sinew as the dragon flew away with it in his mouth.

Maybe this would be easier than Pressley had thought.

A terrifying shriek drew his gaze back to the dying scorpion. Its mouth opened, revealing a swirling pattern of teeth that spun like a buzzsaw. Using its pincer, the scorpion stuffed the cobra's limp body into its vortex, and Pressley fought the urge to gag as churning teeth ripped the snake apart like a meat grinder.

Almost instantly, the scorpion stopped bleeding and a new, shimmering tail sprouted from the wound.

"Shit." Pressley unsheathed his sword, urging his skeletons to climb in the bag faster.

He grimaced as a hammerhorn beetle charged the scorpion, expecting the worst. The scorpion opened its pincer, clasping it around the metallic, hammer-shaped horn on the beetle's head. Pressley expected the horn to shatter but somehow, it held. The beetle thrashed until the pincer slid free. The scorpion countered with its giant stinger, but the barbed tip clacked against the beetle's hardened shell as it bounced off and lodged in the marble floor. The scorpion jerked its tail, but the barbed tip didn't budge. While its opponent was stuck, the beetle swung its horn, hitting the scorpion with enough force that it unfurled like a whip, falling belly-up with its stinger still trapped. Caustic seized the opening, descending on the arachnid and ripping through the monster's underbelly with his claws.

"The bellies are their weakest part," Pressley shouted as the last skeleton disappeared within his bag. Now, he could focus his attention on the fight.

Nearby, another cobra fell, severed in half, and a winged crocodile took a stinger to its undead brain. The death knight cursed under his breath. It had been a while since a dungeon challenged him this much. His minions were fodder, but at least the beetles were a formidable force.

Pressley joined the fight, and dark energy coated his sword as he activated Defile. A scorpion set its eyes on the death knight, its stinger striking with impressive speed. Pressley parried one attack, and then another, before a pincer clamped around his midsection. His armor groaned as pressure mounted and his health trickled down.

He cast Unhallowed Ground while he parried another barrage of strikes. The ground took on a deathly hue, and the scorpion's health began to drop alongside his own. Pressley hacked at the scorpion's backside, but its exoskeleton was too dense for his cursed blade to penetrate. The stinger lashed at him again and again. A few times, it pierced the crease in his armor, but the venom had no effect against the death knight. The two were in a stalemate, slowly draining one another while chaos reigned all around.

A second pincer grasped Pressley above the first, pinning his arms to his side. The scorpion's red eyes blazed, and the death knight's health dropped faster. If he could find a way to free his arms, then he could use Lifesteal, but he needed a plan. Brute force wasn't getting him out of this. He needed to be smarter.

Pressley quit fighting, and the claws pressed against him with their full force. Bones creaked within his armor as they threatened to pulverize.

He closed his eyes, embracing the pain until a high-pitched ringing filled his helm. His daughter's face appeared in the void, and Pressley let Eva fuel him as he cast Forlorn Wail.

An unholy scream tore from the death knight's visage, stunning enemies directly in front of him. The grip relented just enough for him to free his arms, and he removed the gauntlet from his left hand, dropping it to the ground. The stun faded, and the scorpion's chelicerae clicked at the sight of the death knight's bony arm inches from its face. Its mouth opened, ready to turn bone to dust. With his other hand, Pressley shoved his Defiled sword into the arachnid's mouth. Disease spread from the wound, turning the exoskeleton black as the monster rotted from the inside out.

The death knight pried himself free and re-equipped his gauntlet. Nearby, Limery zoomed through the air, dodging stingers and peppering fireballs on their enemies. The scorpions were quick for their size, but the imp was faster. He summoned a firewall beneath a scorpion trapped between two hammerhorn beetles, charring and weakening its exoskeleton. A hit from the beetle's horn shattered the scorpion's carapace, leaking a creamy fluid onto the floor.

Caustic roared above the carnage, plucking a scorpion from a pillar by its tail. He landed, shaking his head like a dog with a toy, and smashing the scorpion against the column.

Over half of the scorpions were now dead. Pressley had lost all of his cobras and all but one crocodile, but the beetles were holding their own. Their metallic shells were a formidable armor capable of withstanding pincer and stinger. Pressley wanted to add a scorpion to his army but using Reanimate now would put his health dangerously low. Instead, he sheathed his sword and prepared to cast Lifesteal. Purple energy swirled within his palms and spread up his forearms as the magic built. He held the attack as long as he could, charging its power, and then released.

Energy shot across the room in a long tendril, hitting a scorpion. The arachnid flashed purple and then a bulb of life force channeled back toward Pressley. The increased health hit him like a shot of adrenaline, raising his HP to forty percent and weakening the scorpion enough for Limery to finish it off.

Pressley burned through his newly replenished HP as he cast Reanimate on the monster. Its body twitched back to life, and he commanded it to fight. It charged into battle, severing the tail of a surprised scorpion with its pincer. Pressley downed a health potion and activated Blight of the Undead. The death knight's armor rattled as a swarm of insects poured from within, surrounding him with a dense shroud that functioned as a shield.

The buzz was deafening as Pressley followed on the heels of his new pet. He cast Defile and stabbed the open wound of the tailless scorpion. His swarming armor blocked a vicious stinger strike as he moved onto a second scorpion whose severed pincer lay harmlessly on the floor. The death knight slashed at the twitching nub, infecting it with disease.

The plague spread through the open wounds, and the creatures quickly fell to

Caustic and the hammerhorn beetles. When the last one died, Pressley canceled Blight of the Undead, and the remaining bugs dissipated into the ether.

An eerie quiet lingered over the carnage. His cobras and winged crocodiles were gone. All that was left of his undead minions were a singular scorpion and three beetles. The latter had turned out to be stronger than he'd imagined.

Pressley chugged several more health potions. He offered some to Limery and Caustic, but the imp had taken no damage while fighting from the air and Caustic's tough scales seemed to have gone unscathed.

Once his health was replenished, Pressley reanimated three more scorpions that hadn't been ripped apart in the carnage. He emptied his satchel of bones and resummoned his skeleton warriors. Between the skeletons, scorpions, and beetles, his army was still looking pretty good.

He faced Limery and Caustic. "Good job today. One more baddie and we can get out of here. You two ready for the boss?"

Caustic growled, and Limery perched on Pressley's shoulder, clenching his fist in determination. "We's readies."

"Good." The death knight's gaze settled on the golden door, wondering what might wait inside. "Let's go over some tactics."

───────

Pressley stood in front of the throne room with Limery and Caustic at his side. An army of skeletons lined the steps beneath them. There were precious few undead left, but they were as prepared as they could be in the current situation.

The enormous door was nearly twenty feet tall. Pressley ran an armored finger across the metal, and it scratched beneath his touch. Solid gold. From the far side of the room where they'd entered, he'd thought the door was engraved with an ornate pattern of flowers that resembled fleur-de-lis. He'd seen the golden lilies every-where the few times he'd visited New Orleans.

Up close, he realized that each engraving was a unique face recessed into the gold, similar to those that were scattered throughout the dungeon. Hundreds of them covered the massive door from floor to ceiling, and the eyes seemed to follow Pressley no matter where he stood.

"Creepies." Limery tapped one of the eyes with a claw.

"You can say that again." Pressley pushed the door, and it slid open without any effort.

The way the hinges silently opened was unsettling. They'd fought tooth and nail to get here, and now it was as if they were being welcomed into the final battle.

Although the rest of the dungeon was grand with its marble floors and elaborate pillars, it did nothing to prepare Pressley for what awaited inside the throne room.

"Pretties." Limery's eyes were full of greed as he took in the scene.

There was so much opulence that it was almost overwhelming. White marble speckled with gold flakes coated the floor, and golden walls lined the room engraved with detailed landscapes of mountains and cliffs overlooking the sea. The arched ceiling was decorated with beautiful, jeweled mosaics separated by ornately carved gilded ribs. Sconces burned along the walls, setting the entire room ablaze in all its shimmering glory.

The door closed with a click as the last of the minions entered the room.

"You made it further than most," a voice called out. It was the same one from when they first entered, simultaneously alluring and threatening.

Pressley's gaze followed the voice's origin, up a set of golden stairs to a platform where the manticore sat perched like a cat. She was everything he'd imagined and more.

A lion with crimson fur loomed above all, her large leathery wings tucked at her sides. A black, scorpion-like tail curved upward from behind, hovering above the manticore's head like a hellish crown. The tail was tipped with a thick stinger surrounded by several long barbs that stuck out like spikes on a morning star.

She wore a golden mask surrounded by a mane of luscious black fur. If not for her icy blue eyes, she'd be indistinguishable from the many faces that lined the door. Pressley stared at the manticore, unable to decipher if it was an incredibly detailed mask or if her face was truly golden.

"A dragon, too." She looked down upon them with an unforgiving leer. "You'll all make wonderful additions to my collection."

A chill ran up Pressley's already frigid spine. He wasn't sure what she meant by collection, but it undoubtedly had something to do with all of the bones he'd seen earlier. He activated Bone Detector, and thousands of white outlines filled the perimeter of his vision. Directly beneath the throne room, bones were piled several stories high. The way they sat in a perfect rectangle, he assumed there was some sort of pit. As the ability cataloged and organized each bone, the list grew so long that Pressley had to scroll through it. There were bones from elves, dwarves, monsters, and beastkin. So many beastkin. How many had she plucked from Sungrove in its prime?

Pressley analyzed the monster before him.

Manticore. *Unique Monster. Level 42. Man-eater, Beast-killer, Winged Fright, The Golden Devourer—the manticore has earned many names during her time in Mythos. While her origins are murky at best, some say she was sent as the gods' judgment, and her reputation had been paid for with blood all across the continent. From EllynMylly to Goldspire, she has left terror in her wake, along with legends and stories used to frighten unruly children—tales of winged monsters with stolen faces and purloined voices who dine on the bones of their victims. Though she has many names, they all come with the same warning. Beware.*

Pressley had read many monster descriptions during his journeys, but none were this intense. The manticore was a higher level and a force to be reckoned with, but he didn't come here to be anyone's plaything.

The death knight stood straight, locking eyes with the manticore's withering gaze. "Actually, you'll make a nice addition to mine."

She leaned forward, arching her back as she stretched her forelegs. Caustic growled as her obsidian claws curled around the edge of the platform, digging into the gold. She stepped forward, descending the stairs like a lion on the prowl.

With each step, her gilded features shifted, as if her face was made of fluid gold. Her guise morphed into a wolf beastkin, and she spoke with Jegaar's voice. "Is that so?"

She transformed again, this time taking on the wrinkles and raspy voice of an elderly man. "You have courage. I like that."

She licked her lips, and her face rearranged into a golden troll with horns that curled around her mane.

"Chods?" Limery squeaked, his face radiating concern.

Caustic unleashed a roar that shook the cavern, and the manticore grinned. Pressley had never seen such malevolence on the real Chod's face.

"Fear has a way of contaminating everything it touches." Her voice matched the troll's in every aspect. "It infects the flesh, seeps into the marrow of bones. I welcome a worthy challenger, anyone who can oppose my dread. To taste the bones of the brave and fearless is a delicacy—" Her eyes narrowed. "—but they are always tainted in the end."

Her visage shifted into a dwarf with dreadlocks and a thick beard, then to an imp.

"Taryns... Mommies..." Limery turned to Pressley, his bulbous eyes glistening. "Limmy doesn't likes this."

Pressley touched the imp's feet, the only comfort he could offer.

The manticore laughed, the impish cackle reminiscent of Limery's. In rapid succession, the mask transformed into the faces of other heroes and people Pressley had interacted with during his travels. Some he didn't recognize, centaurs and gnomes, likely memories from Limery or Caustic. The face morphed again and again, like a slot machine cycling through images.

The manticore descended the final step onto the marble floor and the mask settled on the face of a young girl with curly hair.

"Daddy, come home," an innocent voice begged.

Eva's voice hit Pressley like a sledgehammer, and he dropped to his knees. "No," he whispered as the golden visage of his daughter stared at him with a pleading expression. "How..."

She had never been anywhere near this game. How was her face here now? And her voice, it was just as he'd remembered.

Pressley covered the eye-slit of his helm, blocking his vision. The AI was inside his mind, using his memories in the same way that made all of this seem like reality. Eva wasn't here. He repeated the phrase. *Eva isn't here.*

No, that was a lie. His armored hands dug into the floor. She'd been with him every day since he'd entered. She'd pushed him to go harder, to be stronger, to fight. He saw her face when he needed strength, when he needed to be better. Eva was his motivation, and he'd be damned if he let a monster use her against him.

Anger burned within the death knight, so pure that it pushed the cold at bay.

"How dare you!" Pressley roared as he stood and pulled an enchanted spear from his satchel.

He stepped forward, activating Defile as he launched Shadowweaver with all of his might at the monstrosity before him. Tendrils of dark energy coated the weapon, and the torchlight dimmed as it whistled through the air directly at the manticore's head.

Her tail twitched at the last moment, hitting the spear with enough force that it lodged in the wall, humming as energy reverberated down the staff. The manticore's face returned to its original form. Golden brows narrowed above her blue eyes, and she pounced.

"Supernova!" Pressley shouted, activating Blight of the Undead as he turned his back to the manticore.

Toxic gas poured from Caustic like a fog machine as insects swarmed around Pressley. There was a risk with using his gas in enclosed spaces with Limery around, but they'd prepared a few contingency plans. Flames crackled in the imp's palm as he tossed a fireball over Pressley's shoulder. The death knight tucked the imp against his chest as the gas ignited with violent thunder and a fiery shockwave slammed him into the wall.

His insect shield disintegrated from the blast, and a ringing echoed inside Pressley's helm as he stood. His vision blurred at the edges from the impact. Ten percent of his health was gone even with the shield, which was better than he'd hoped for. Smoke drifted through the air, obscuring sight of the manticore.

"You okay?" He still held Limery cradled in his arms.

The imp shook dust from his head and then took to the air. "Limmy is okays."

There was a dragon-sized indentation in the wall behind Caustic. He'd lost a quarter of his health from the backdraft of the attack.

Bones lay scattered across the floor from unlucky skeletons that had taken the blast head-on, and the gilded walls were warped from the heat. Pressley repaired his minions as quickly as possible while he searched for the manticore. His scorpions and beetles were still alive, but they'd lost a chunk of health from the blast.

Leathery wings flapped in the dust, and a mixture of gold rubble and jewels clinked across the floor as the air cleared.

"You hurt me, Daddy." The manticore wore Eva's face once again, mangling it into a sinister sneer. She'd lost nearly the same amount of health as Pressley from the direct attack, but her HP was already replenishing at a rapid rate.

Pressley growled as he equipped his sword and ordered his minions to attack.

The manticore took to the air as the undead swarmed her, black wings flapping like sails to keep her aloft. Her tail swung like a wrecking ball beneath her, tossing skeletons like bowling pins. Their bodies broke apart as they collided with the walls. Scorpions snapped their pincers and struck with their stingers, but the manticore evaded them with ease. Skeleton archers fired arrows that fell from her hide like they were nothing more than toothpicks.

They needed something stronger.

Pressley turned to Caustic and Limery. "I need a distraction. As much time as you can buy me."

Caustic took to the air, gathering the manticore's attention while Pressley readied Blood Strike. It was one of his most powerful abilities since it dealt damage equal to the amount of HP he channeled into it. If they wanted to win, then he needed to go big.

Limery darted through the air behind the dragon, peppering the monster with fireballs. Caustic chomped at the manticore, but she was quick to evade and left him snapping at air. He roared his disapproval, lunging at the beast with his talons outstretched.

The manticore spun mid-air, hitting the dragon in the side with her barbed stinger. Caustic cried out in pain as he launched into the wall. Blood trickled from between his armored scales where the spikes had pierced him.

Limery pressed the attack while Pressley continued to charge his ability. An orb of crimson energy pulsed in front of him, powered by nearly a quarter of his health. The imp zoomed through the air, dodging the mace-like stinger and dangerous claws.

The manticore shot spikes from her tail, narrowly missing Limery and turning the far wall into a dartboard as they buried in the metal.

Almost ready, Pressley thought as his health dipped below half.

"Yous can't hits Limmy!" the imp cackled as he dodged another set of spikes.

"Are you sure about that?" Chod's voice boomed as the manticore's face transformed into the forest troll.

Limery's eyes widened, and the momentary hesitation was all the manticore needed. A spike hit the imp in the wing, pinning him to the wall.

Pressley unleashed Blood Strike just as the manticore lunged toward Limery. The death knight's health plummeted as his life force imbued the attack. Crimson energy exploded across the room, blasting the manticore in the side and knocking her from the air inches from tearing the imp in two.

She landed on her feet, snarling as she steadied herself.

The death knight had channeled three-quarters of his health into the attack, but the manticore had only dropped to half. His minions charged, but she swiped them away with her tail. A gong-like sound reverberated as a hammerhorn beetle's shell was dented from a hit.

Pressley cast Pestilence and Unhallowed Ground on the area where the manticore stood, and her health once again started to dip.

Limery struggled against the spike pinning him to the wall, grimacing as he tried to pry himself free. He was too high for Pressley to reach, and the spikes were too thin for Caustic to remove. The golden walls around the imp shimmered as they softened against his warm skin.

"Limery, go molten," Pressley shouted.

Flames engulfed the imp, and gold trickled around him like hot wax as the wall melted. The spike fell, clinking against the floor.

"You okay?" he asked the imp as he returned to his side.

Limery nodded, his eyes focused on the manticore. There was a hole in his wing, but it didn't seem to be hindering him. Caustic wobbled to join them, and the death knight patted the dragon on the side.

"I've got a plan, but I'm going to need some time." He pulled two vials from his satchel. "Stay safe until I get back."

The first vial was filled with a deep purple liquid. He'd found it clearing the bogs in the Marshlands long ago.

Item. Infernal Darkness Potion. *Covers opponent in a veil of darkness, making them unable to see or smell their surroundings for one minute.*

Pressley tossed the Infernal Darkness Potion at the manticore, and the vial shattered against the floor. Dense black smoke spread from the bottle, surrounding the dungeon boss. She roared, and spikes shot out blindly from the darkness, clinking as they stuck in the walls around the throne. Pressley had one minute before the effects faded and they'd be facing one pissed-off manticore.

He cast Blight of the Undead, and a swarm of insects poured from his armor. It might be overkill with the potion, but while active, the ability not only functioned as a shield, but his location also couldn't be tracked.

He held the second vial in front of him. A cream-colored liquid sparkled within. It was one of the three legendary potions he'd attained.

Legendary Item. Sub-dimensional Serum. *User gains access to the sub-dimensional plane, allowing them to phase between objects for up to one minute.*

Pressley had envisioned big plans for this item, but right now it might be the only hope for all three of them to make it out alive. He downed the sweet, frothy serum, and the world shifted from color to black and gray. Everything became translucent, allowing the death knight to see the thickness of walls and what lay beyond. He could see through everything except for the veil currently surrounding the manticore.

A timer ticked down across his vision as he searched for the bone pit. At the foot of the throne, there was a trapdoor hidden within the floor. Pressley descended through the door, almost like he was flying, and lowered himself down onto the mountain of bones.

Using his Bone Detector ability, he started filling his satchel. He needed to be out before the potion ended or he'd be trapped, and Limery and Caustic would be consigned to death. Chod would never forgive him if something happened to either of them.

He floated back to the surface just as the Infernal Darkness Potion ended. With Blight of the Undead still active, Pressley hid behind the throne, undetected by the manticore.

He emptied his satchel, summoning the bones of beastkin, monsters, and the many warriors who had attempted the dungeon over the years. Their bones clattered to life, and they charged the manticore.

She swiped at them with her tail, but the minions kept coming as bones poured from the bag. Pressley's health drained rapidly from the effort as dozens and then hundreds of skeletons enclosed upon the manticore, pinning her beneath a mountain of bones.

"Gas her up," Pressley ordered Caustic.

He unleashed a stream of green gas that seeped between the bones of Pressley's minions.

"Behind the throne." He waved them over, and once they were shielded, he turned to Limery. "Boom time."

The fireball hit the gas and exploded like a skeleton grenade. The throne room shook, followed by an overwhelming heat as bone shrapnel bounced off the walls and ceiling. White dust filled the area, and notifications flashed across Pressley's vision.

As the dust settled, Pressley stepped out from the cover of the throne. Half of it had been melted by the blast, and chunks of bone were lodged in the gold. His entire minion army was destroyed, but he could repurpose many of the bones.

In the center of the room, the manticore lay on her side. Caustic sniffed at the body.

Limery frowned at the dead monster. "Limmy didn't likes this monsties."

"I hate to break it to you, but she's going to be sticking around for a while." Pressley removed two Hag's Eyes from his satchel, and the purple gemstones glittered in his palm. He'd taken them from the covey he'd fought in Glossop Forest and had been saving them for just the right moment.

Item. Hag's Eye. *The jewel from the eye of a hag. This enchanted jewel is created when a hag joins a covey. It replaces one of their eyeballs. The original eyeball is then worn by a minion, sealing the pact between them. The minion then functions as a summon, controllable by the hag.*

Pressley could reanimate lesser monsters to join his army without issue, but he couldn't reanimate unique monsters like the manticore. Thanks to the Hag's Eye, he could change that. While a hag used the eye to bring a living being under her control, two Hag's Eyes could be used to link the death knight with a unique monster that he could summon to fight for him.

"Look away if you're squeamish." Pressley took a dagger and removed the manticore's left eye, replacing it with one of the jewels.

Limery picked the manticore's eye off the ground, scrunched his nose, and then fed it to Caustic.

"That's disgusting." Pressley placed the second jewel in his own eye socket.

The purple stone glowed within his helm, and he cast Reanimate on the manticore. Her eye flickered to life but she lay there, unmoving.

Pressley wondered if he'd made a mistake, then her paw twitched, and he felt the connection establish. As an undead, the manticore could no longer speak or use her magical abilities to shift faces and mimic voices. However, she kept her incredible stats and fighting prowess.

The manticore stood. Although she was shorter than a horse, her powerful muscles were capable of carrying the death knight without issue. He mounted the manticore and trotted her around the throne room. Once they returned to Gold-spire, he could purchase a proper saddle but for now, he could hold onto her mane for stability.

Limery watched the manticore uncertainly. "Presslies can flies now?"

Pressley tested his mental connection with the undead mount, and she extended her wings, jostling the death knight as she took to the air and glided across the throne room. When they landed, he pulled several health potions from his satchel and shared them with his companions. They were all worse for wear after the boss fight.

While Pressley waited for the potion to work its magic, he looked through some of his notifications.

You have defeated Manticore Dungeon. *Claim dungeon prize.*

Congratulations! You have reached level 41. +1 stat point to distribute. +1 Strength and Intelligence class bonus. +1 ability point to distribute.

He'd managed to gain the last bit of experience he needed to hit level forty-one, and he already knew what he wanted to unlock with the new ability point.

Frost Reaper. *A layer of frost coats your body, slowing the movement speed and dexterity of enemies within your immediate vicinity. Can be channeled into ranged physical attacks. Melee attacks double the debuff.*

Since he was already cold all the time, what would a little frost hurt? With his new mount, he could put his crossbow to use, firing bolts that would slow enemies on the ground for his minions to overtake.

Pressley dismounted. Caustic sat on the floor nearby, munching on a large femur that had once been a minion. Something seemed different about the dragon. He was bigger from the levels gained during the fight, that much was certain, but there was something else that Pressley couldn't quite put his finger on. Maybe Chod would be able to tell. Fighting such a high-level opponent had given Caustic two more levels, pushing him to level twenty-four. Limery was now level twenty-nine.

"Looks!" Limery dug through the rubble at the base of the throne, tugging on the handle of a large chest. "Limmy founds the treasures!"

Pressley joined the imp just as his little hands pried open the lid. Golden light emanated from inside.

"Golds!" Limery cupped a handful of gold coins and let them fall through his fingers.

Pressley dug through the coins searching for items, but there was nothing else there. Not that he was complaining. With this much gold, they could buy their own rewards.

He patted the imp on the back. "According to Jegaar, Chod is going to be in the trials for a while. What do you say we get back to the city and spend some of this hard-earned gold?"

Limery flashed a devilish grin.

Pressley activated the exit prompt, and they were portaled to the dungeon entrance, where the late afternoon sun beamed down. He mounted the manticore and took flight, her massive wings carrying the death knight above the clouds.

He'd never been a fan of heights, but the view was magical. One day, he'd tell Eva all about it.

20. A TEST OF METTLE

My joints throb and muscles ache from the constant pressure as I keep the two enclosing walls from crushing me into pulp. Sweat steams from my body amidst the unrelenting heat, and the smell of charred meat fills my nostrils with every breath of hot air. I'm pretty sure the skin of my palms has melted to the obsidian, but that's the least of my problems as my bones threaten to snap from their sockets.

All I can do is grimace and bear it as time loses all meaning aside from the debuffs I receive due to lack of sleep and nutrition. In my early days in Mythos, they would have incapacitated me, but sheer determination and troll fortitude keeps me going.

According to the debuff notifications, I've been at the first two phases for at least twenty-four hours, probably a lot longer. These have been the most grueling hours of my life but right now, enduring these trials is the best thing I can do to keep those that I care about safe. If I falter in the slightest, I'll be crushed to death and all of this suffering will have been in vain.

Pharos stares up at me, a calming presence amid the heat and pressure that promises to forge me into something stronger if I can just hold on. Whenever I feel myself giving in, I look into his swirling eyes.

As my spirit beast, he and I are connected in a way I can't fully explain. While he's a representation of the stubbornness and determination of my spirit, part of me resides in him as well. Maybe it's the heat or dehydration, but I can see myself in the depths of his eyes if I look hard enough. It's almost as if his spirit is composed of the memories that have made me who I am—the accomplishments but also the failures and struggles.

I lose myself in his eyes as visions of my past play out in shimmering hues of orange and white. I watch myself in some of my proudest moments as I win my first gaming tournament at school, when I gain my first followers on my stream, and then again when Taryn and I set a new record for active viewers during a dungeon raid. I see my struggles as well. Nights alone in an empty penthouse as I stare over a bustling city. Dad leaving a meeting and walking past me like I don't exist as I wait in reception.

And then there are my failures. The first time I was denied a spot on a pro team. The second. The third. Those failures shaped me, pushed me toward streaming as an alternative to still do what I loved. Taryn was right when he said I lost myself somewhere along the way. At some point, streaming became less about entertainment and having fun and more about proving everyone wrong. With so many people watching, I needed to be the best. I needed to show the world that those pro teams had made a mistake when they passed on me. To do that, I couldn't be the problem. If there was a mistake, I blamed it on my teammates. If things went south, then they were the reason.

The charity match—the one that got me here—appears in ethereal detail. I was at the Mythos Gaming headquarters with more eyes watching me than ever before. The event was supposed to be a fun time bringing streamers together from across the country to play before a live audience. For me, it was more than that. I wanted to show everyone once and for all that I deserved to be pro.

But I didn't. I was playing sloppy, and I knew it. It was my fault that Dorothy got ganked by the enemy. I'd pushed too far in my lane and then had to retreat to heal, leaving my opponent free to wander. I called out that they were MIA too late, and Dorothy paid for it. Our team started snowballing after that, and what did I do?

I raged.

I close my eyes when that portion plays out, but I still see it crystal clear in my mind. Ruthless, that's what I was. I was embarrassed, and I wanted to make someone else hurt the same way I did. Shame sinks into the pit of my stomach. Dorothy has every right to hate me for what I did. I deserved to be punished for my actions, and yet somehow, I got sent here.

I blink away the tears that burn my eyes and sting my skin. Dorothy will come for me. She deserves her vengeance for what I said and for everything that came after. This isn't a fight I can win, no matter the outcome. Still, I can't afford to let her kill me. Not when we're this close to the end.

The pressure against my palms relents, and I collapse to the floor. Heaving breaths wrack my body, and my muscles tremble uncontrollably.

The walls only retreat about a foot to each side, and I barely have time to savor the release before molten spiders descend from the ceiling again. With the limited entry points, fewer spiders enter at once, but I'm forced to fight them off in a narrow corridor.

I activate Berserker Rage, and all of my aches and pains alleviate as I smash through the crystalline arachnids. Their bodies and barbed legs tear into me with every punch, and shattered glass litters the floor. I leave smoldering blue footprints in my wake as I take out every frustration from the last few days on the fragile creatures until none remain.

Once my rage ends, the debuffs return in full force. I steady myself against the blistering wall and notice the vital fluids seeping from the broken legs and cracked abdomens that line the floor. I gather what I can salvage, tilting a leg until the hot, mucous-like liquid drips into my mouth. My passive Savage ability allows me to drink the fluids without getting sick. I fight the urge to gag as the unpleasant taste trails down my throat. While I can't do anything about the sleep debuffs, this should put the hunger debuff to rest for now.

The next phase of the trials will be starting soon, but I check the notification that I received from killing the spiders.

Congratulations! You have reached level 31. +1 stat point to distribute. +1 Strength and Constitution racial bonus. +1 ability point to distribute.

Hell yes! I saved the last ability point I received in case I needed it for the Warforged class after the trials, but now that I have two, I can finally unlock a summoner advancement.

Summoner Advancement.
   Dreadbeasts. Unlock for further details.
   Dual Subclass. Unlock for further details.

There's no point in unlocking a dual subclass when my horrors already synergize perfectly with my troll stats. I unlock Dreadbeasts, and a new set of abilities appear.

Summon Dreadbeast. (Passive). *Ability to summon a dreadbeast (limit 10 per subspecies). Each dreadbeast grants a unique ability. For every dreadbeast active, gain 1% increased damage and health points. Unlike horrors, dreadbeasts do not decay outside of combat. While a dreadbeast is active, horror decay is reduced by 50%.*

   Dreadbeast of Torment. *Summon a dreadbeast with 20% of your Strength. Cost: 500 mana. Cooldown: 30 seconds. Bonus: While Dreadbeast of Torment is active, your attacks have a 20% chance to induce fear.*

   Dreadbeast of Despair. *Summon a dreadbeast with 20% of your health points. Cost: 500 mana. Cooldown: 30 seconds. Bonus: Opponents near Dreadbeast of Despair lose 1% health per second. (Maximum 10%)*

   Dreadbeast of Agony. *Summon a dreadbeast with 20% of your attack speed. Cost: 500 mana. Cooldown: 30 seconds. Bonus: Attacks from Dreadbeast of Agony reduce healing and health regeneration by 50%.*

Holy shit. I read over the descriptions several times, and my mind envisions numerous possibilities for each dreadbeast. I can only summon ten of each, and with my mana pool still at five thousand, that means I can only summon ten at a time before it needs to replenish. But since they don't decay over time, I can wait for my mana to refill and summon a full army. With only one dreadbeast active, my horrors will last twice as long. A grin plasters my face. These are going to be awesome!

Just like when I unlocked my horror summoning path, I still have the ability point to use on one of the dreadbeasts. As much as I would love to use both ability points and unlock two dreadbeasts, there's no way I'm risking not being able to unlock the Warforged class when I've come this far.

Each dreadbeast is similar to one of the horrors, basing their attributes off my Strength, Constitution, and Dexterity but their bonus abilities are completely different. Ten Dreadbeasts of Torment with a twenty percent chance each to cause fear could turn a battle. The Dreadbeasts of Despair can kill weak enemies just by being in their presence. And then the Dreadbeasts of Agony will make it difficult for opponents to heal during a fight.

While I'm thinking it over, I receive a new notification.

Trials of the Warforged: *Stage two complete. Stage three commencing.*

Stage Three: *Forge*

The walls start closing in again, and I unlock Dreadbeast of Torment while I get into position. If I can only summon one dreadbeast, then having the strongest seems like the best option.

I extend my hands and only have a few moments before the walls lock me into place once again. Heat swells in the narrow corridor, and I try to piece together what the third stage will entail in an effort to take my mind off the discomfort.

Stage one was Heat and to complete it, I had to endure the high temperatures. Stage two was Pressure, forcing me to keep the walls from crushing me. Stage three is Forge.

Pharos stands in front of me, and I look into his eyes.

"What do you think stage three will be, bo—"

A piece of the ceiling dislodges, and a hammer-shaped slab of obsidian swings on a pendulum, passing through Pharos's head and hitting me in the chest at the same time as an equal force smashes me in the back. The hit knocks the air from my lungs, and I gasp for breath while I try to hold my position between the walls.

An unseen force pulls the slab through the air until it rests against the ceiling, and then it drops again. I tense my muscles as the hammer falls, unable to protect myself from the impending blow. The two hammers crush me, and I scream as the pain radiates across my midsection. I'm thankful that I at least have air in my lungs.

Pharos paces in front of me as the hammers rise.

"It's okay, boy." I grimace as the agony from the blow fades. "There's nothing you can do."

He takes his customary position in front of me, and I brace for impact. The hammers fall again and again, each time threatening to unravel me. Even with my high Constitution, my health chips away with each hit, falling in slivers like in the first trial. Eventually, my increased regeneration will kick in. I just hope it will be enough.

The hits are rhythmic, like a metronome of abuse that I must endure. Unlike the first two trials, the pain isn't constant; it ebbs and flows, forcing me to acknowledge it each time.

I close my eyes and tense my muscles. All I can do is wait for it to end.

21. FATHER KNOWS BEST

Valery glared at her father as he hovered in the doorway to her office.

"Don't look at me like that. It reminds me of your mother." He scrunched his brow, squeezing the bridge of his nose between his fingers. "May I come in? We need to talk."

She ignored the jab, leaning back in her chair and crossing her arms. This was the first time she'd seen him since the inspector for the Federal Bureau of Prisons had announced he was recommending her program be shut down. "What do you want?"

"Come on, Val." Her father let out an exasperated sigh, as if she was the one inconveniencing him. "Can't you see I did this for you? You'll soon realize that this is for the best."

"Shutting down my program and causing trouble with the federal government is helping me?" Valery's lip curled in disgust. "If this is you helping, then please continue. Maybe I'll be an inmate for the next round of testing."

"Always so dramatic." He laughed, entering the room and sitting across from her. "Do I need to spell it out for you?"

Valery narrowed her eyes. She couldn't believe the gall of her father, not only showing up after wrecking the program she'd spent years working on but then acting like he was doing her a favor. "Please do."

"I owe you an apology."

Her frown faltered. An apology was unexpected. He was a man who never apologized to anyone. It was one of the many reasons her mother had left him.

When Valery didn't respond, he continued. "I'm sorry that I didn't believe in your program from the start. It seemed too unrealistic, too unachievable, and the practical applications never made the investment worth it from a business perspective." He leaned forward. "I was wrong. It has potential, real potential, but you're wasting it on a government program. I'm sorry I blew the whistle, but it's for the best. Once the program is shut down, it will allow us to develop the technology however we want."

"Us? This is not an 'us' program. This was my idea, my brainchild. I spent years in the research phase. Years failing. And when I finally start to see real progress, you decide to meddle around and fuck it all up." Valery stood, her finger striking like a viper as she pointed at the door. "Get out of my office."

Her father looked shocked. His expression was almost enough to make her smile. She'd never spoken to him like this before, but she was at her wit's end.

"Fine." He stood, pausing for a moment as if gathering his thoughts. "If you don't want me involved, then that's fine, but you'll still be better off doing things without government oversight."

"You still don't see it." She clenched her fist, and the nails dug into her skin. "That wasn't your decision to make. You could have talked to me. You could have told me what you were thinking. Maybe I would have agreed, maybe not, but goddammit, Dad, you're not the only person with a brain in this family."

"I know that, Val." He looked at his feet, and for what might have been the first time in Valery's life, she saw the man beneath the mythos. "You're right. I should have talked with you. You've built something truly amazing, and I want to see you make the most of it."

"You sure have a funny way of showing it." She sighed and leaned against her desk. "We built this amazing world, but that was only part of the goal. Using the nanotech, I thought we could actually use it to help people in a way that had never been done before. We could heal trauma and provide therapy, all while the user becomes a hero in their own story. And believe it or not, it's actually working. I've witnessed some of these men changing right before my eyes." She met her father's gaze. "Now, I'm afraid we're going to lose it all."

"They aren't going to take what you built. You know that, right? They'll pull the prisoners, but the game will go on."

"That's what I'm worried about. The game is constantly evolving, reacting to the world as the users influence it. Right now, they are on the precipice of a war that could completely shift the nature of the world, and you may have shifted the odds just because you wanted to watch a little drama." Her hands shook as a fresh surge of anger coursed through her. She took a deep breath to steady herself. "You've seen the data. You've seen how many instances of the AI we tested before we got to this one. It doesn't matter how many opportunities there are if we can't recreate this again. Most of all, there's no guarantee we can recreate what happened to Chad Johnson." Valery turned to face the wall. Everything had been going so well, and now there was nothing left to do but let the chips fall and see if there were any pieces to pick up. "Now, please leave."

22. FORGED

I'm not going to make it. That's the only thing I can think as the obsidian hammers fall from the ceiling and slam into my stomach and back. Pain erupts from the hit, jolting through my nervous system all the way to my toes and fingers. Heat and pressure were one thing, but getting my ass beaten for hours on end is going to break me.

The blue skin around my midsection glows orange from the repeated hits I've taken. Luminous veins branch out from those spots, arcing down my thighs and across my chest. I'm not sure what's happening, but it feels like I'm about to combust. My head throbs with every beat of my racing heart.

Each time the hammers crash into me, my body grows hotter and my health drops into the red. Increased Regeneration takes effect as the hammers rise to the ceiling, and I replenish just enough HP to survive the cycle again.

The hammers fall, battering against my midsection. Every breath of hot air sends a wave of pain through my ribs and abdominals. I roar from the misery, my screams echoing through the narrow corridor. My eyes burn, my head throbs, and my muscles spasm as if they are about to give out. I've pushed myself to the brink, but I honestly don't know how much more I can endure.

Another blow, and my knee buckles for a moment. Cold sweat erupts across my body, quickly turning to steam as I force myself back into position.

My head tilts back, and I squeeze my eyes shut until stars dance in the blackness.

"I'm sorry," I whisper to no one.

As much as I want to succeed, my body is failing me. I should have been stronger before I attempted the trials. Now, I understand why the process killed most who attempted it.

"Do not give in," a husky and somewhat youthful voice calls to me.

"Who said that?" I look over my shoulder, but the corridor is empty. The tunnels above as well. "Pharos?" I scrunch my eyes at the spirit guide just as the hammer passes through his face, colliding with my body. A loud groan escapes as my chin falls to my chest.

"*Do not give in,*" the voice says again.

This is it. My head bobbles as I force a laugh. I've finally lost my mind and now I'm hearing voices from a goat.

"*I would be insulted that you confuse me with a goat were it not for your situation.*"

There's an edge of pride to the snarky voice. Is this some kind of bonus from my dreadbeast class? I haven't summoned one yet, so maybe it's talking to me from the shadowlands or wherever it is the creatures spawn from.

"Dreadbeast?" The hammers slam into me, and red veins spread from my chest to my shoulders.

"*The dwarf is right. You can be very dense.*" The voice scoffs. "*Perhaps I should have bonded with him instead.*"

Bonded? "Caustic? Is that you?"

"*It is good to see the trials have not turned your brains to mush.*" Another wave of pain passes through me as the hammers collide. "*You have the heart of a dragon. I know because I chose you. You will not give in to this torment.*"

I gasp for breath and hot air fills my lungs, igniting my throbbing ribs. "Where are you? How is this possible?"

"*I have grown stronger during my time in the dungeon, and thus, our bond has strengthened. You are no longer alone.*"

This is crazy. Or maybe I've lost my mind to the trials. I wait for the next hit to pass and then speak. "I have so many questions."

"*They will be answered in time. For now, you must endure.*"

"I don't know how much more I can take." My voice shakes along with my muscles.

"*You will not give in.*" Caustic is still only a juvenile dragon, but there is no room for debate in his tone. "*You have been through much already. This is but another challenge to overcome.*" His growl rumbles in my mind. "*You will not break.*"

Against all odds, I believe him. *I will not break.* I repeat the mantra in my mind with every hit I take. *I will not break.* When the hammers crash into me, and molten veins branch down my arms and legs, I stand strong. *I will not break.* When my fingers and toes turn orange, like the blazing coals of a fire, I stay standing. *I. Will. Not. Break.*

When my vision blurs from the heat and all I can see is orange, I scream the words with primal ferocity. "I will not break!"

Something shifts within me, and Berserker Rage activates of its own accord. My muscles bulge, and stats flood my system. There's a gurgle overhead just before rushing water pours from the tunnels, hissing against the hot surface as a waterfall cascades over me. It does nothing to cool my molten body, and steam fills the corridor, thick and muggy as it obscures everything, even Pharos's glowing form.

When the obsidian slabs fall, they clank against me like a hammer striking the anvil. To my surprise, it doesn't hurt. Powered by unbridled rage, I extend my arms, and the walls grind against the floor, moving back several inches. The hammers fall again, and I push against the walls with everything I have. They grind several inches across the floor, allowing me to move as the stone slabs collide. I wrap my arms around one of the hammers, ripping it from the ceiling and turning it sideways to wedge between the collapsing walls as a brace. I wait for the second hammer to fall and catch it mid-swing, tearing it down.

Eventually, the steam fades, and I look down at the corded muscle of my troll body, no longer green or blue but the shimmering silver of fluid steel.

Metal as fuck. I did it!

A notification flashes across my vision.

Congratulations! You have unlocked the Warforged class. Through willpower and determination, your body has been honed and reforged into a weapon of war. This is a specialized barbarian sub-class.

New Abilities:

Warforged *(Passive): When entering a rage, your body transforms into fluid steel, increasing your Constitution tenfold. You cannot be stunned, slowed, poisoned, or otherwise affected.*

Cold Rage: *The Warforged are weapons, always prepared for a fight. Unlike Berserker Rage, which requires a full rage meter to activate, Cold Rage is always at your disposal, granting the same perks whenever they are needed.* ***Bonus:*** *Rage meter increased to 1000.*

This is too good to be true. I read over the ability descriptions several times to make sure I understand. If my interpretation is correct, I'm now able to activate my rage any time I want, and when I do, my Constitution is multiplied by ten. That would increase my already high Constitution from around fifty to almost five hundred. That's god-tier tanking ability. Not only that, my rage meter has grown from one hundred to a thousand, and I can use the rage I build up at any point without needing a full rage meter.

I just became a huge pain in the ass for someone.

As if to test my hypothesis, I hear the clatter of molten spiders just before they descend from the ceiling. My metal fist shatters the first, and shards of glass clink against my silver skin. A spider lands on my shoulder, and its barbed legs screech across my metallic body, leaving me unharmed. I crush its abdomen with my fist, grinding its glass body into dust.

What may prove to be the biggest advantage of Cold Rage is that my attacks still build my rage meter, even when I'm in my Warforged form. Berserker Rage has a time limit that counts down from activation, but I can use Cold Rage continuously as long as I'm building up my rage meter while I fight. This is a game-changer.

One by one, I destroy the spiders with ease. When there's nothing left but me and Pharos, I cancel Cold Rage. My body returns to its natural blue state, along with the sleep debuffs. I wobble under the stress of that before activating Cold Rage again. With a half-full rage meter, I can keep the debuffs at bay for a little while longer.

"You must rest," Caustic warns me. *"Even dragons need sleep."*

Before I have time to respond, another notification flashes across my vision.

Trials of the Warforged: *Complete*

Stone grinds as the walls retract across the platform, over the now empty trough and back to their original position. A glowing outline forms in the wall behind me, and I see a door leading back into the cavern I entered from.

As soon as I leave the trial room, I'm inundated with several notifications. My ability to send messages also returns and I reach out to Taryn, letting him know that I completed the trials.

I'm not sure what time it is, but Caustic is right. I need to rest. Once I check these notifications, I'll be out like a light.

The first one is no surprise.

Congratulations! Draconic Convergence has reached level 3.

This place must have blocked out any updates that weren't happening within the trials. I pull up the stats for our bond to see exactly what we unlocked.

Draconic Convergence: *The convergence fuses an unbreakable bond that grows stronger over time. No two convergences are the same. Each one evolves based on the relationship between the dragon and their chosen counterpart.*

Name: *Caustic*
   Species: *Green Dragon*
   Level: *24*

Convergence Level:

1. Draconic Bond- You have made an unbreakable bond with a dragon and forged a telepathic link that may expand in the future. In its current state, intense spikes in emotion may blend between psyches.

2. Spatial Bond- You are now able to mark the location of the dragon no matter how far apart you are.

3. Communication Bond- You are now able to speak to one another through your telepathic bond.

. . .

Damn, Caustic wasn't lying. He gained seven levels clearing the dungeon with Pressley. I can't wait to hear all about that.

The second notification is a message from Valery. My stomach sinks as I open it.

Incoming Message (Admin): *I don't have any updates for you on the state of the program, but I just wanted to say that I'm proud of you. You've come a long way from the kid I first met.*

I barely know the woman but for some reason, my eyes are misty. Valery is definitely not the person I envisioned that first day I walked into the lab. She's proud of me. How long have I waited to hear those words? I close the message and blink back the surge of emotion that those two sentences evoke. It's suddenly hard to swallow.

I don't know if she's watching me right now, but I look to the ceiling.

"Thank you," I whisper.

Pharos stands by the cavern that leads to the Narrow Pass. The exit is still closed, sandwiched between two sides of the mountain until I decide to leave.

I gather my weapons from the center of the room and reequip my satchel, eating some of the rations before finding a corner to sleep in. As I settle down, I realize that I didn't have to use an ability point to unlock the Warforged class. That means I can unlock another dreadbeast!

Sleep can wait. I pull up my stats to refresh my memory on the two remaining options.

Dreadbeast of Despair. *Summon a dreadbeast with 20% of your health points. Cost: 500 mana. Cooldown: 30 seconds. Bonus: Opponents near Dreadbeast of Despair lose 1% health per second. (Maximum 10%)*

    Dreadbeast of Agony. *Summon a dreadbeast with 20% of your attack speed. Cost: 500 mana. Cooldown: 30 seconds. Bonus: Attacks from Dreadbeast of Agony reduce healing and health regeneration by 50%.*

The likelihood that I'll gain two more levels between now and the invasion is slim, so whichever one I pick will be joining the Dreadbeast of Torment in Mosstar. A monster that inflicts reduced healing seems great for battle, but then I recall the thousands of undead outside the city gates. We're going to be surrounded by enemies and having a constant health drain will likely be even more valuable.

I select Dreadbeasts of Despair, and then I put my new stat point into Dexterity.

"*Sleep,*" Caustic growls at me.

"Soon." He's the juvenile and yet it's me who feels like a kid being bossed around. "I just want to see one thing."

I summon a Dreadbeast of Torment, and the air in front of me cracks as reality tears and a demonic canine steps through the rift. Where my horrors only come up to my knees, this one is nearly waist high and the size of a massive wolf. The dreadbeast has black fur aside from a silver mane that runs the length of its spine. Its orange eyes stare at me, and two short horns jut upward from its head, arcing backward between its pointed ears. A set of dangerous fangs descend several inches past its snout.

The dreadbeast's massive paws pad against the floor as it approaches Pharos. Its hackles raise, and it snarls at the spirit guide. Pharos lowers his head, scraping his hooves against the floor.

"Easy now. We're all on the same side."

Shadow and light—the two animals are about as opposite as possible, but I'll need them both in the battle to come.

The dreadbeast continues to snarl even as it joins my side. Next, I summon a Dreadbeast of Despair. It appears in a similar fashion, stepping through a rift. The creature that emerges is both majestic and terrifying.

A giant black bison stands nearly chest high with thick, ebony fur so dark it's almost a void. Shadowy tendrils flicker and flare from its body, and two blood-red horns curve upward from its mighty head.

"Well, you guys are fucking scary." I pat the bison on its broad side, and it huffs, smoke shooting from its nostrils. "Now, that's badass. I need the three of you to keep an eye on me while I sleep."

The wolf-like dreadbeast settles at my feet, its gaze focused on the exit. Pharos stands by my shoulder, and the demonic bison doesn't move as tendrils of dark energy flicker along its body.

"Good night, Caustic." I reach out to the dragon through our bond. "I think I'm in good hands."

I cancel Cold Rage, and I'm asleep before my head hits the floor.

23. STONES

High in the clouds, Pressley watched the sun set beyond the Black Mountains. Streaks of pink and orange framed their dark silhouettes. The sight was beautiful, peaceful even.

This sure beat the dull monotony of a prison cell.

He held onto the manticore's dark mane as she shifted course, jostling the death knight with a flap of her black wings. Her normally curled tail lay flat like a rudder, helping to guide her path. They were almost back to Goldspire and had made the flight from the dungeon in a fraction of the time it had taken the wing-hoof oxen.

To his right, Caustic soared, his outstretched wings shimmering emerald in the fading daylight. The dragon's movement was smooth and graceful as his wings rode the current, as if he weighed nothing.

Limery darted through the air like a hummingbird, joining Pressley atop the manticore's back. He was an antsy little imp. The entire journey, he'd been zipping from the death knight to Caustic, or yapping about some adventure he and Chod had gotten into. Pressley had no idea how Chod put up with it, but he was stuck with the little guy until the troll returned. And probably after.

Pressley took one last look over his shoulder at the hazy mountains as they began their descent.

Chod had held up his end of the bargain. Pressley fully recognized he wouldn't have bonded the manticore without Caustic and Limery's help. Now, he had to fulfill his part. If war awaited, he could put the full extent of his abilities to use. For most of his time in Mythos, the death knight had sought gold and power. It had been the driving force behind his every action. Now, he felt his priorities shifting. Gold and power were nice, but he wanted to make his daughter proud. He wanted glory.

The manticore landed outside of the city gates as surreptitiously as a cat. For all of Caustic's grace in the air, the dragon thudded to the ground, stirring a cloud of dust.

"We's backs." Limery somersaulted in the air a few feet ahead.

Pressley dismounted the manticore. "Let me check her into the stables, and then what do you say we go grab a drink? We can spend some of this hard-earned gold."

"Oh, yes!" The imp clasped his hands together. "Limmy likes thats."

Pressley turned to Caustic. "Want me to book you a room, too?"

The dragon huffed before turning his back on the death knight and launching himself into the twilight sky. Pressley looked at Limery and shrugged. Maybe the dragon wanted to hunt something more challenging. Regardless, it wasn't as if Pressley could do anything about it.

The city guards were hesitant to let the manticore through the gates, but Pressley still had the parchment signed by the Scholars Guild for his last venture. When he showed them Jegaar's signature, they reluctantly allowed them to enter.

Beastkin stared at the manticore as she strutted through the streets. There was a terror to her beauty, or more likely a beauty to her terror. In a place where Pressley had walked unmolested, she captivated every eye they passed. She held her head high, the gilded visage reflecting every face that looked upon her. The purple Hag's Eye glowed in one eye, matching Pressley's, and her barbed tail swayed with her movements. With wings tucked at her side, she followed the death knight to the stables, where a minotaur was sweeping the entrance as they arrived.

"I need a stable for the night. The best that you have." Pressley jingled his coin purse.

The minotaur's gaze shifted from the coins to the manticore, and his eyes widened. "Is that..." His words trailed off as he stared at the manticore.

"A manticore." Pressley patted her shoulder. "She's my mount."

"Is it safe?" The minotaur was still transfixed by the manticore, unable to look away.

Pressley cleared his throat, and the sinister sound was enough to draw the beastkin's attention. "*She* is under my control. That is all you need to know."

The minotaur gulped. "Very well. If you'll follow me right this way."

Pressley sighed. It was customary for the stable-hands to take the animals back themselves, but he couldn't blame the minotaur's reticence. Unlike a dragon, who claimed respect, the manticore was feared. She'd earned her reputation through her reign of terror. In that way, at least, she and the death knight were the perfect pairing.

After leading the manticore into a large stable, Pressley faced the wide-eyed, hulking minotaur. "See that she's fed and groomed. I'll return tomorrow."

Outside the stables, he searched for the nearest tavern and spotted a building with a sign depicting a silver falcon wearing an eye patch and holding a glass of wine. "That should work."

"Presslies." Limery stood in the street, his arms clasped behind his back.

"I know that look." He'd seen it from his daughter when she wanted ice cream before bed. "What do you want now?"

The imp fluttered his eyes. "You's saids that Limmy can spends some of the golds."

The death knight grunted. "I did."

"Limmy wants to buys something before we drinks."

"Of course you do." Pressley pushed thoughts of a relaxing ale aside. "What is it?"

Limery grinned, taking to the air. "Follow Limmy!"

He followed the imp down several streets, passing through alleys and over a bridge where gurgling water fed the bathhouses. Limery finally slowed down in front of a basilica, where the vendors of the open-air market were packing up for the day.

"This ways." Limery pointed, leading Pressley into a long, open hall. The interior was lined with ornately carved columns and a vaulted ceiling painted with colorful landscapes and floral designs.

Pressley grunted, not sure why this couldn't wait until the morning, but he followed nonetheless, reminding himself that Limery was a key piece of their success. There would be no gold without the imp.

The death knight had passed by the basilica on occasion during his time in Goldspire. It reminded him of a flea market with the variety of items for sale. Everything from spices to wool, clothing, and ancient books.

An owl beastkin leaned over a crate, packing away vials of pink perfume. Its gaze followed the death knight as he passed, its head twisting to the point that it looked like it would snap.

Pressley kept the owl's gaze as he walked by, and his helm twisted backward, his skeleton body no longer restricted by ligaments and muscle. The death knight's jeweled eye glowed menacingly, and the owl hooted in surprise, packing faster.

He found Limery talking to an elephant beastkin. The imp stood atop a table filled with dozens of flat, circular stones, each one with a hole in its center.

Pressley held one and examined it. They were communication stones, exactly like the one he'd been given in Vanaria. He couldn't recall the exact history of the items, but he knew they had something to do with the imps. They had been messengers once upon a time.

"What do you need a communication stone for?" Pressley set the stone back on the table. "Don't you already have one?"

Limery nods. "Yes, Limmy has ones. But these isn't for Limmy. If Presslies is sharing the golds with Limmy, then Limmy wants to takes thems homes."

"Don't you want to spend the gold on weapons and items for the battle? Things you can actually use."

Limery's eyes glistened, and he shook his head. The elephant behind the table wore a sad expression.

Pressley looked from the imp to her giant blue eyes. "There's something I'm missing here."

The beastkin nodded. "I've seen this imp before. Not long ago, he stopped by my table with a troll and a dwarf. I told them of the history of these items, and it seems they have become personal to him."

Pressley frowned, and then he scooped Limery off the table, stepping a few feet away to talk in private. "Tell me what's going on."

The imp's lip trembled. He was on the verge of tears, but Pressley had no idea why.

Limery's voice shook as he spoke. "Limmy doesn't want to leaves thems."

"I can see that." Pressley patted him on the back. "Why are these so important to you?"

A tear ran down Limery's cheek and fell against the death knight's armor with a tink. "Because theys belonged to the impses. The impses that was tricksed by the bad wizard. He tricksed thems and nows theys is all dead." He glanced over his shoulder to the table. "These is alls that's left of thems."

The floodgates opened and tears streamed down Limery's cheeks. Pressley cradled him against his chest as he sobbed, warm tears spilling through his armor. It all finally made sense. Every communication stone on that table belonged to an imp who had been tricked into joining Valmar's army. For all the power flowing through Limery's tiny body, he was scared. Scared of suffering the same fate. Afraid of dying and having no one left to remember him, his legacy nothing more than an untraceable piece of stone.

Pressley placed a finger under the imp's chin and lifted until the imp looked him in the eye. "This is not your fate. Chod will tear this world to the ground before he lets anything happen to you. You understand?"

Limery whimpered and gave a slight nod.

"No one will forget you. I might be scary and ugly, but I carry you with me here." Pressley pointed to his own chest. "You will be remembered for all you've done. When my time here is finished and I return home, I'm going to tell my daughter all about you. How does that sound?"

Limery sniffled and then wiped away a string of snot running down his chin. "Limmy likes thats."

"Alright, good." Pressley sat Limery down and returned to the table. "We'll take them."

The elephant grabbed a small bag. "How many would you like?"

Pressley dropped his coin pouch on the table. "All of them."

A wide grin swept over Taryn's face as he dismissed the message, and the interface vanished from his vision. "He did it. He actually did it."

"Who did what now?" Jon tilted his head in confusion, shaggy brown hair falling across his forehead. He looked over his shoulder as if Taryn might be talking to someone else. "I was saying that my enchanter class has turned out to be a real blessing. I've gained over ten levels just from crafting and enchanting objects for King Favian."

Taryn and Jon sat alone in one of the castle's many meeting halls. King Favian had brought Jon from Vanaria to Seascape to showcase for King Orso some of the items he'd been working on. The meeting was scheduled to begin after the two kings spoke in private, so Taryn had invited Jon to catch up while they waited. The message from Chod had caught the druid off guard.

"Sorry. Not you." Taryn returned his attention to the enchanter. "I hadn't heard from Chod in three days and he finally checked in. He's unlocked the Warforged class."

"Warforged? Never heard of it." Jon adjusted his dual-colored glasses and brushed a strand of hair behind his ear. The red and blue lenses were supposedly helpful with carving runes for enchantments. "Sounds dangerous."

Taryn nodded. "Supposedly, the class will turn his skin into fluid metal when he rages."

"Yep, that sounds dangerous alright."

"He's been looking forward to it for a while now. Since our first visit to Gold-spire. I was getting a little worried because I hadn't heard from him and none of my messages were delivering." He sat back against the chair, stroking his beard until the metal clasps clinked. "So, what was it you were saying about your levels?"

Jon removed a gold ring inlaid with rubies from his finger, turning it over as he talked. "I was doing it all wrong from the start. Not that I need to tell you. You and Chod saw the trouble I was in the first time we met."

Taryn chuckled at the memory. Jon had been under-leveled and alone. Things had gotten so bad that he'd taken to bribing kobolds with enchanted Charisma rings so they would rob local farmers. "You seem to be doing better now."

The enchanter wore a finely tailored blue robe embroidered with yellow stars and moons. Rings adorned every finger, and the chains of several necklaces disappeared beneath his collar. Somehow, the man had made it to level twenty-five since they'd last seen one another. No small achievement, considering where he'd started.

"Aside from you and Chod, and, well, I can't forget the graciousness of King Favian either, Sirina is the best thing to happen to me since I've been here. She's the head enchanter in Vanaria, and she's taught me how to expand my abilities better than I could have ever imagined. I've gained ten levels without having to kill a single thing. It's great!" He leaned in close, lowering his voice. "Don't tell anyone, but she's a fox. I think I've got a bit of a crush on her."

Taryn fought the urge to laugh. Not because it was funny but because of how secretive Jon was being. After spending time with Breebis, he couldn't fault anyone for growing attached to an NPC. From the outside looking in, it might seem weird, but anyone on the outside had no idea what it was like to talk to these people and live in this world.

"I'm happy for you. Truly." Taryn gave him a reassuring smile. Jon had been afraid of his own shadow when they'd first met, but now he was thriving. "What is it you've been working on?"

"To tell you the truth, I was a little worried about working in the castle. I'm not exactly the finest ilk back in the real world, you know. King Favian offered me this great opportunity, but it felt like a lot of pressure working among mages and royalty. But they treated me like I belonged, and I finally understood what Chod meant about finding his tribe. From day one, I had tutoring with Sirina and council meetings with King Favian and Lord Kassidy. They took heed of King Orso's warning with the belief that Valmar would return, and so I've been specializing in enchantments against the undead from the start. When they started spilling through the portal, I was glad that I did." Jon grimaced. "I went down there once just to see what it was all about. They vaporized as soon as they entered the city, but the smell..." Jon gagged at the memory. "God, it was so bad."

"I bet." Taryn grimaced. "We've seen our fair share of creatures from the Shadowlands. I wouldn't—"

There was a knock on the door, and Kurzol entered. The blood dwarf cleric motioned toward the hall. "The king is ready for you now."

Jon rubbed his hands together. "Showtime, baby."

Kurzol led them to King Orso's council room. Outside the entrance, the blood dwarves of King Orso's personal guard stood to one side, and the human guards of King Favian stood to the other. Inside, the two kings sat side by side at a round stone table in the center of the room. They couldn't be more different in appearance. Orso's thick black hair rested on his shoulders, neatly combed and contrasting against his dull-red skin. His beard was braided to perfection. Favian, on the other hand, sported three-day-old scruff he hadn't shaved since the council in Pruxford and tousled hair that looked like he'd just come in from a griffin flight. Dark circles rested beneath his eyes.

Next to King Favian, Kassidy waved his finger and a bowl of grapes teleported onto the table. He winked at Jon before tossing a grape into his mouth.

The massive table was carved from a single piece of stone and was big enough to seat at least twenty people. Similar pieces of furniture were located throughout the castle—all of them cumbersome items that weighed thousands of pounds. Taryn wondered if they'd been moved into the castle using teleportation magic or if someone actually had to carry them inside.

Compared to many of the meetings Taryn had attended the past few days, this one was small. Chief Rizza and Chief Laojin were training with the trolls that were already in the city, and more were scheduled to arrive any day now.

"Here's the man of the hour." King Favian winked at Jon as they entered. "I didn't want to steal your thunder, so please do the honors and show King Orso what you've been working on."

"Your Highness, er, Highnesses." Jon bowed slightly and then removed the satchel from his shoulder, setting it on the table.

Taryn took a seat next to Orso and waited for the big reveal.

Jon fumbled through his bag. "I, uh, thank you for allowing me to, uh. Shit." A white gemstone the size of a fist slipped from his fingers, clattering across the stone table. Jon scrambled after the object, cursing all the while. "Shit. Sorry. Shit."

"Take a breath." King Orso grinned beneath his beard. "You're among friends here."

"Right." Jon gulped, clenching the gemstone between both hands. He took a deep breath before continuing. "What I mean to say is thank you for the opportunity to showcase what I've been working on. Thanks to King Favian's support, and Sirina's training, I've been able to unlock a new specialty for my class." He held up the gemstone for everyone to see. It was transparent, and a silver substance swirled within. "Along with my normal enchanting abilities, I've also become a wardmaster. Due to your warning—" He nodded to King Orso. "—I chose to specialize in, uh, I wouldn't exactly call them holy wards, but they do affect the undead. While clerics and paladins have abilities that are extra powerful against the undead, I wanted to help the rest of us. These items aren't anywhere near as powerful as the protections in Vanaria, but they are portable and to hear King Favian tell it, we're going to need all the help we can get."

"Your king speaks the truth." King Orso leaned forward, examining the ward. "Tell me what they do."

"Yes, Your Highness." Jon pointed to the gem. "This one is capable of mimicking the effects of Divine Radiance. When it's activated—" Jon traced a pattern over the stone and a silver light erupted across the room. "—the ward weakens the Constitution of any undead or shadow creatures within thirty feet." He canceled the ward and light faded. "These take a while to enchant, but we hope to have a hundred ready. If you spread them across our forces, they should prove valuable, especially to those on foot."

Jon placed the ward on the table and removed a small pouch from his bag. "I've also been able to make these rings." He smiled at Taryn as he jingled the bag. "Each ring is capable of holding a single charge of Divine Blessing. We'll need clerics to bless the ring but once it is charged, whoever is wearing it can cast the ability once, either to bless someone nearby or to use it as an attack on the undead. They can be recharged, but I'm not sure how practical that will be on the battlefield. We'll have close to a thousand of these in a few days."

He reached into his bag, pulling out a silver chain that held an amulet set with an iridescent stone. "This one is a unique item. I'll leave its potential usage to brighter minds than myself, but I believe it's my greatest achievement as an enchanter. I call it the Amulet of Undetection. While wearing this, the wearer can pass undetected by undead unless they are physically engaged with them."

Taryn's mouth dropped. Jon had been busy, alright. Every item would prove valuable in the battle to come, but the amulet was a game-changer. Whoever wore it would be undetectable by Valmar's forces.

King Orso nodded approvingly. "You have done well. Thank you for your service, not only to Vanaria and Seascape but to the war effort as a whole."

Jon's cheeks flushed. "Thank you."

The door opened, and Kurzol stepped into the room.

"Kurzol, this is a closed-door meeting." King Orso narrowed his eyes. "I thought I told you we were not to be disturbed."

"Apologies, Your Highness, but you also instructed me to alert you once the imps returned."

"Ah, yes. I did. Bring them in." He turned his attention back to Jon. "Thank you again. Pardon my brevity, but there are many moving parts at play."

Jon bowed before gathering his items and moving against the wall.

Kurzol stepped aside, and Lillith and Bazel flew into the room. The two imps had been flying around the Isle for the past three days, but they looked no worse for the wear. Both had the same bat-like wings and dull-red skin as Limery, only Lillith had a patch of dark hair in the shape of a heart on her chest. Bazel was nearly twice Limery's size, but there was no denying their relation. Taryn imagined that Limery would look almost the same when he was older.

"What news do you bring?" asked King Orso.

"Gord and Kronan shall return tomorrow," Lillith answered. "They are a half-day's journey from Vanaria."

King Favian rubbed his tired eyes. "And what news of the other troll tribes?"

Lillith smiled. "The seaside trolls march with them."

"That is excellent news, indeed." King Orso patted Favian on the back. "And the desert trolls?"

Bazel moved forward slightly. "Gord says that they are with the forest and mountain trolls in Tawdrybluff, though there are not many of them. According to Chief Rizza, they shall arrive tomorrow or the next day."

"The five troll tribes reunited at last." King Favian turned to King Orso. "This must be a good omen."

King Orso's brow furrowed, and his gaze seemed to look beyond the room. "I pray you are right and we are not sending an entire race to their doom." The room sat in an awkward silence before the king shook his head, as if clearing his mind. "Apologies. That is enough for today. Let's reconvene tomorrow and continue our preparations."

King Orso's momentary lapse sent chills up Taryn's spine. The king had been a pillar of strength in these tough times, but it was clear that even he had his doubts. They were preparing to attack Mosstar with everything they had, and there would only be one chance for success. Even though they weren't his people, King Orso felt a responsibility for the trolls' well-being. They had precious little and yet were risking it all for the fate of the realm.

Taryn shared his king's worry. There was still so much to do, and the days seemed to grow shorter. He said farewell to Jon and set off in search of Chief Laojin.

24. OUT OF THE PAN AND INTO THE FRYER

When I wake up, it's like a weight has been lifted from my shoulders. The sleep debuff is gone and I feel like myself again, even after sleeping on the hard surface all night. At my feet, the wolfish Dreadbeast of Torment sits on its haunches, standing guard. The Dreadbeast of Despair lurks by my shoulder, and shadowy tendrils flick and flare from the massive bison. Standing between the two, Pharos glows like a beacon.

His light reflects off the obsidian stone around the room, but it does nothing against the darkness of the two dreadbeasts. It's like their bodies pull the light into the void, never to release it. I bet they're hard as hell to see at night.

"Good morning," I say to my companions as I push myself up, and they all look in my direction. "Glad to see the three of you are tolerating each other."

Pharos turns around, lowering his head to me. The Dreadbeast of Torment snarls when the spirit guide moves too close to him, but the spirit guide ignores it.

"For the most part." I chuckle. "I think it's time for us to head back to the city."

"I am glad to see you're well-rested," Caustic speaks to me telepathically.

"You can tell when I'm awake?" I ask him.

"Our tether strengthens when you are conscious. I have guarded over the mountain while you've slept."

I smile to myself. With a dragon, two dreadbeasts, and a spirit guide watching over me, I really am in good hands. *"How long was I out?"*

"It is nearly midday."

Wow, that sleep debuff was no joke. The last time I pressed too hard, I spent several days recovering. *"Where's Limery?"*

"He is with the dead one. I trust him."

"Good. Me too." I gather my satchel. *"I'll be out in a moment, and we can head back to the city. I've got some new friends for you to meet."*

"Be warned, there is an elf pacing in front of the mountain, and I do not trust their intentions. I believe you were tracked." There's an edge to his husky voice. *"Shall I eat them?"*

"An elf?" Odd, considering I haven't seen any elves in Goldspire. *"That's strange. And no, do not eat the elf,"* I add before Caustic decides to have a quick lunch. *"Let me handle it."*

Caustic growls his disapproval, but I have a strong suspicion that I know who it is.

Three days in the trials gave me plenty of time for self-reflection. Maybe I can set things right before anyone gets hurt.

The prompt appears across my vision, and I confirm that I'm ready to exit the trials. The ground rumbles and the walls shake as the mountain splits, revealing the rugged pass that runs between the boundary of the Burning Desert and the lands of Goldspire.

The midday sun shines down the Narrow Pass, casting shadows along the jagged rocks. In the daylight, my dreadbeasts are just as intimidating as they were in the cave. Their dark fur blends in with the obsidian stone of the mountain. The Dreadbeast of Torment and Pharos lead the way with the bison following on my heels.

"Stay where you are," I order Caustic.

If Dorothy is here, I want to appear as non-threatening as possible. Aside from the three summons I have with me, I'm not bringing anything else. No weapons. No horrors. No more dreadbeasts. And definitely not a dragon.

"That is unwise," Caustic growls.

"Trust me, please. I have my respawn point set outside of the city gates. If anything happens to me, go there."

I'm sure he could have kept it to himself, but his huff of irritation passes through our bond.

With each step, I'm aware of the crunch of earth beneath my feet. My pulse thunders in my ears as my heart races, not out of fear but apprehension. My fingers ache for the comforting grip of Destroyer, but I keep it stowed in my satchel.

I've made enough enemies in this world already. With Glenn and Jude, there's no coming back, but maybe I can make things right with Dorothy for what I did.

Either way, it's time for me to face the music. If I die, then the Revive Potion from the Quincentennial Tournament will keep me from losing the Warforged class I just worked so hard for. I pray that doesn't happen.

I take a deep breath to steady my shaking hands and exit the pass. A lone figure stands against the arid landscape, a tan shawl draped over her head and shoulders to protect her from the sun. She wears a form-fitting brown vest strapped with daggers and vials over a blue tunic and tan pants with calf-length brown boots. Several pouches hang from her belt and more daggers line her thighs. Aside from the pointy ears, she looks just like I remember her. Strands of golden hair whip in the breeze, and blue eyes stare at me with murderous intent.

. . .

Dorothy Jordan
> _Level 33_
> _Marauder_
> _Elf_

Level thirty-three. How the fuck is that possible? Has she been in here for months just biding her time until she was strong enough to make a move?

And what the hell is a marauder? I hold up my hands in a gesture of peace. "Dorothy, I—"

The words barely leave my mouth before a dagger whistles in my direction. I activate Cold Rage, and my body turns to fluid metal as I jump out of the way. The dagger's path shifts mid-flight, tracking me like a homing missile. I throw up my arms to block the blade, and it darts between my forearms, clanking against my neck before falling to the ground.

That would have been fatal if not for my godlike Constitution from being Warforged. Shit. She's really going to try and kill me.

The Dreadbeast of Torment takes off after Dorothy, but I call it back before it has a chance to attack. Thankfully, it responds to my internal commands as easily as my horrors, but that doesn't hinder the menacing growl rumbling in its chest. Shadows flare from the bison, and smoke pours from its nostrils as it unleashes a deep bellow.

Her gaze flickers to the dreadbeasts, but her focus is on me. I've made some enemies, but I don't know if I've ever seen such a hateful glare.

I don't want to hurt Dorothy if I can help it, but she's making it hard as she slings another dagger toward me. Whatever ability she used on the first one must have a cooldown because I knock this one aside at the last second.

"Dorothy, please, listen. Just give me a chance to explain." I hold up my palms.

"Explain?" She scoffs. "What is there to explain? You ruined my life, you piece of shit, and now I'm going to make you pay for it."

Dorothy has the draw of a gunslinger as she pulls a vial of purple liquid from her vest and slings it in my direction. The vial smashes against the rocky terrain, and a cloud of black smoke spreads around me. I recognize the effects of the Infernal Darkness Potion from previous battles. The cloud blinds those within and follows them around while also obscuring their sense of smell.

Thanks to my rage, I can't be blinded by the potion, but I'm still unable to see through the dense smoke while I'm inside, like I'm stuck in a heavy fog. I step backward until my head breaks through and I see sunlight, just in time for an explosion to knock me into the mountain.

With my increased Constitution, I barely feel the impact of my body slamming into the mountainside. There's a loud crackling noise within the fog, and my Dreadbeast of Torment's presence vanishes. Soot covers my metallic skin as I crawl to my feet. Dorothy doesn't hesitate, unloading a half-dozen more vials in a matter of seconds. Lightning and fire flare within the darkness like the heart of a raging volcano and soon, the Dreadbeast of Despair and Pharos vanish as well. If she killed the bison, then she's not pulling her punches at all. *Dorothy wants me dead by any means necessary.*

A maelstrom of smells spread out from the fog, sulfuric and sickly sweet, as my rage ticks down by the second. The meter sits at two hundred thanks to my battle with the molten spiders, but unless I start hitting back, I've only got a few minutes of continuous rage left before it hits zero.

"Can I eat her now?" asks Caustic.

"No!" I shout, but it only draws Dorothy's attention to me.

"I heard you were hard to kill." Her lip curls in a snarl. "Just like the cockroach you are."

"Please, just listen. I don't have a problem with you."

She laughs, but there's no mirth in it. "In that case, I guess I can pack my bags and go home."

Her movement blurs as she reaches down her side and pulls back with a set of knives clutched between her knuckles like claws. She slashes through the air, releasing the knives and pirouetting before unleashing a second barrage with her opposite hand. The six blades fly like a volley of arrows, clanking against me with enough force to knock me back a step. She might not be big, but damn if she isn't strong.

Dorothy uses Shadow Step and appears in front of me while leaving a shadow doppelgänger in her original position. She slashes with incredible speed. I manage to block the first attack, but the next screeches as the blade grates against my metallic skin. For every attack I block, she lands three more.

Caustic's frustration seethes through our bond, and I try to block it out as I stay on the defensive. With every scrape of metal on metal, Dorothy's anger builds, and orange rings form around the blue of her eyes. She refuses to let up, and my rage continues to dwindle.

I've never seen this side of her. From what I remember, she was witty and a bit crass but never angry. She was known as a tactician, someone who planned several moves ahead. Right now, she's a rabid dog.

"Die already!" Dorothy screams as her blade grates across my chest in a burst of sparks. The orange outlines completely consume her eyes, and they burn with a molten ferocity.

A wave of energy surrounds her. Her moves quicken, so fast that I can't block anything as she picks me apart. Sparks fly with every hit as metal clashes.

"Enough!" I roar as I extend my arms and hit Dorothy square in the chest. Her health dips by a fraction from the blow, and she flips over backward. Just before she hits the ground, she activates Shadow Step and switches places with the doppelgänger. The shadow copy bursts into dark mist upon hitting the ground, and whatever rage is powering Dorothy heals her damage almost instantly. Her eyes smolder like embers as she charges again.

I block the first stab with my forearm, but the next scrapes against my ribs, and the lack of damage only fuels her anger. I can't fight her off forever, and soon, I'll be forced to either fight back or die. The look in her eyes tells me she won't be happy killing me once.

"Do you really think hurting me is going to make you feel better?" I ask as I stay on the defensive, backpedaling as she carves me up.

"Only one way to find out." Dorothy goes for my neck, but I swat her hand away with enough force that the dagger flies from her grip.

She reaches behind her back, cursing when she comes up empty. At least a dozen of her weapons litter the mountainside, so the one she's holding must be her last. I have maybe thirty seconds before her attacks start spilling blood.

I take another step back, keeping her at a distance. She circles me like a predator, spinning the dagger across her palm without taking her eyes off me.

"I'm sorry." My shoulders slump forward, and I stop retreating.

Dorothy's eyes flare, and her jaw stiffens.

"I know it doesn't do much good now, but I'm so fucking sorry, Dorothy. I was an asshole, and you didn't deserve what happened to you."

Her lip twitches and her grip tightens around the dagger. "You're damn right, I didn't."

She activates Shadow Step again, appearing behind me and plunging the blade between my shoulder blades. Metal screeches, and I turn to face a shadow with Dorothy already returned to her previous location.

I cancel Cold Rage before it completely runs out, leaving me with a few seconds of protection if I need it. Whatever rage is empowering her fades as well, and her eyes return from orange to deep blue.

"I wish I could change what happened, but I can't. I was a stupid kid, and you were the unfortunate victim of my anger. Believe it or not, this place has changed me. I found something I never had in the real world—a sense of purpose." I spread my arms wide and take a step forward. "So if you need to kill me, if that is what will make you feel better, then go ahead. You deserve it."

She buries the dagger in my chest, just beneath the shoulder, and white-hot pain flares from the impact. My jaw clenches, and it takes everything I have not to fight back.

Dorothy looks me in the eye as blue blood trickles down my chest, and her lips curl into a smile. She twists the blade, and pain surges across my chest.

"*I'm coming,*" Caustic growls.

"*Do not move.*" My order is firm, and I pray that he listens. "*I can handle this.*"

Dorothy kicks at the dirt, and a dagger flies into her free hand. She stabs it into my ribs. Warm blood runs down my midsection.

"Tell me," she leans in and whispers, setting my hair on edge. "What purpose could be so important that anyone would believe you're not an asshole?"

I grimace at the burning sensation spreading from both wounds. "They know I'm an asshole." My health goes down with every word, and I'm certain the blades are coated in poison. "I'm just *their* asshole."

She pulls the blade from my ribs and slices it across my stomach.

"You're really not going to fight back, are you?" She watches me with a curious expression.

"You deserve your vengeance." My breaths grow labored as the knife in my chest twists under her pressure. "If you want to kill me, go ahead. Make it quick or bleed me out. It doesn't matter to me." I wrap my hand around hers, and her eyes widen as I pull the blade deeper into my chest. "The first one's free, but this is it. This is your chance to kill me, to torture me, to do whatever you need to make me pay for my actions. Right here, right now—I deserve it. But if you come for me again, I won't hesitate to kill you. Our beef can wait, but I can't let your actions hurt those that I care about. There are a lot of people counting on me right now."

Dorothy pulls the dagger from my chest and steps back, her brow furrowed. "Shit. You really believe that, don't you?"

I nod. Blood pours from my open wounds, and the poison burns as it spreads through my shoulder and down my thigh. I never re-equipped any of my items in the cave, so I can't use the Tiger's Eye Pendant to clear the effect.

Dorothy wipes the blood from the dagger on her pant leg and sheathes it. "So the rehabilitation, it really works?"

"That depends on who you ask." I shrug. "Maybe I'm just growing as a person."

She scoffs. "Playing the hero in a game doesn't make you a hero."

"It doesn't make me a villain, either."

"No, I suppose not. You look like one, though, especially with those monsters you had." Dorothy crosses her arms. "What were those things?"

"Dreadbeasts. I'm a barbarian summoner."

"Dreadbeasts? That definitely doesn't sound villainous." She arches a brow. "So, Chod, you pick that name out yourself?"

I'm not sure what's going through her mind right now, but something has shifted between us. I elect to run with it. "No, I think it was the game's way of trolling me when I first logged in. Everyone else got to use their real name."

She chuckles, and for the first time, there's no hatred in it. "This place is something else, isn't it? When John told me what it was that you were up to here, I was pissed. And then once I logged in, I was even more pissed." She looks around as if she can't believe the world we're in. "This is the future of gaming, and you got sent here as a punishment." She shakes her head. "Such a lucky son of a bitch."

"It hasn't all been roses." I wince as a fresh wave of pain passes through my chest. "Trolls were attacked on sight when I first logged in. I put in a lot of work to earn respect from the other kingdoms."

"So I hear." Dorothy reaches into one of the pouches on her waist and pulls out a vial of yellow liquid. "Here, take this." She tosses the potion to me. "It's the antidote for the poison."

As soon as I down the antidote, my health stops depleting. I let out a sigh of relief. We may be on shaky ground, but she's offered me an olive branch, so I press onward. "How long have you been here? You're a higher level than some of the heroes who've been here since day one."

"Heroes. That still gets me." She laughs, taking a seat on one of the boulders and brushing a strand of golden hair behind her pointed ear. "I've been here a while. I chose to spawn in Ellynmylly so that I wouldn't accidentally run into you before I was ready. I didn't have any world-spanning quests, so I was able to grind through the dungeons and loot. It would have been a lot more fun if I weren't so pissed at you."

"That's fair." I sit on the ground and try to keep the conversation going. "It says your class is marauder. This is the first time I've seen one of those."

"It's pretty nice." She leans back, letting the afternoon sun warm her pale cheeks. "I get bonus loot and can sense where the most valuable items are in a dungeon."

"Is that how you got all of those potions you nearly killed me with?"

"Something like that." She grins. "Though you're not exactly easy to kill."

I return her smile. "I just spent the past three days going through hell to unlock that ability."

"I guess it was worth it, then." Dorothy leans forward, looking at me with a serious expression. "You said there are people counting on you. What did you mean by that?"

Her gaze is intense, so I look away, focusing on a flock of vultures circling in the distance. "There's a battle coming, one I'm not sure we can win."

I go on to tell Dorothy about Valmar, and most of what has happened in the past few weeks. She hangs on to every word, genuinely interested in what I have to say. Just another reminder of how fucked up my actions were. When I finish my story, she stares at me incredulously.

"That's crazy. And this Valmar guy, he has no idea you're about to attack him?"

"How could he?" I pick up a pebble and toss it. "He's the only one with the power to open the Mosstar portal. After the attack in Pruxford, he must assume we'll be preparing for war. He has to think the odds are in his favor, though, that we can't all unify because we need to be prepared for him to invade any of the portals. My guess is that he's gathering his forces as we speak, and he thinks he'll attack us before we're ready. But there's no way he could know that we're going to open our own portal outside of the city."

Dorothy walks over to me and offers me her hand. "I want to help."

"Why?" I'm unable to conceal the surprise in my voice.

Thirty minutes ago, she wanted to kill me, and now she wants to help. Putting our beef aside so that she can enjoy her time in Mythos is one thing, trusting her to watch my back and protect the ones I care about is quite another.

Dorothy keeps her arm extended. "You say you're not the same asshole that made me cry on a televised stream. I hope that's true, but I want to see it. I might have come here for the wrong reasons, but I've grown attached to this world. It'd be a shame to see it crumble."

I meet her eyes, and the friendliness in them is so far removed from the murderous rage I saw not long ago.

She has a point, though. Saying that I've changed is not the same as showing it. It was my actions that proved to the trolls I was one of them. My actions convinced

King Favian and King Orso to put their faith in me. My entire time here, it's been my actions that have gained trust and helped me to unite Mythos. Why should it be any different with Dorothy?

Letting her in might be what she needs to put this mess behind us, but is that a risk I'm willing to take?

Can I trust her to have my back when the lives of Limery and the trolls are on the line? When the fate of Mythos hangs in the balance?

In my heart, I know the answer. As uncomfortable as it might be, trust is a two-way street.

"Alright." I take her hand, and she helps me to my feet. "If I'm being honest, we can use all the help we can get. Best to get moving, though. It's a long way back to the city."

I reach out to Caustic through our bond, and a moment later, he soars down from the mountain. His shadow stretches across the landscape. He's grown a considerable amount over the past three days. His beard is a deep gold, and his wings are as wide as a small plane.

Dorothy equips her daggers, ready for a fight.

I hold up a hand to stop her. "Don't worry. He's with me."

Her mouth drops open. "You had a dragon this whole time, and you still let me stab you?"

"I do not trust her." Caustic's throat rumbles. *"She reeks of ill intent."*

"She thought the same thing about me not too long ago. Be nice." I pet Caustic on the belly once he lands, and then turn back to Dorothy. "Like I said, I'm trying to be better."

"I will not fly her." Caustic may not eat her, but there's no room for argument in his tone.

"Wait, you can bear a rider now?" Now, I'm the one who's shocked as I look into his golden eyes.

He huffs and raises his head to its full height, striking an imposing figure. After gaining so many levels, he must be at least twenty feet tall. *"I can bear you."*

Caustic takes some convincing, but he eventually agrees to carry Dorothy in his talons. Against his protests, I made him promise that he wouldn't drop her once we're hundreds of feet in the air. Dorothy isn't too happy with the situation, but she understands that time is of the essence.

I understand Caustic's hesitance to trust her. Dragons are not ones to easily forget, and he just watched her try to kill me. If not for my newly Warforged body, she might have succeeded. He'll come around in time.

My braid whips in the wind as we soar above the countryside. I welcome the cool air and bask in the moment since this might be the last bit of peace I have for a while. Caustic's scales are smooth and cool against my thighs, his muscles powerful as he flaps his massive wings occasionally.

After the past few days, it's nice to sit here and appreciate the beauty of this world and everything I have accomplished. I mean, I'm riding on a fucking dragon!

Still, I can't believe Dorothy found me. She's still angry, of that much I'm certain, but I have hope that I may be able to mend that fence with time. There's nothing better to forge a bond than fighting side by side. As strong as she is, she'll be a valuable asset in the battle to come.

As we approach the city, the golden spire gleams in the fading sun. From this high up, it's magnificent. Once we're back, I'll track down Limery and Pressley, and we can head to Seascape first thing in the morning.

25. A TROLL AND AN ELF WALK INTO A BAR

Caustic is officially so big that booking him a stable has become an effort in futility. The first stable doesn't have an enclosure large enough for a dragon his size, and when we finally find one that can house him for the night, he holds his head high and refuses to look at me.

"A dragon should not be caged."

I roll my eyes at the stubborn ass. *"You didn't have a problem with it before."*

"Before, I was a hatchling." His head tilts and his golden eye meets mine. *"Do I look like I need protection?"*

"Fine." I let out a sigh. Caustic may still be young, but he has a point. He's not a pet that I have to look after. We're bonded, so more than anything, we're partners. "Come find us in the morning, then."

"Trouble in paradise?" Dorothy arches her brow.

Caustic growls, and she takes a step back.

"Something like that." I narrow my eyes at the unruly dragon. "He's in his rebellious phase."

"I wonder where he learned that." A smile tugs at the edge of her mouth.

I laugh, but Caustic lowers his head, blowing hot air that unravels the shawl covering Dorothy's head and shoulders. Her smile twists into a frown.

"I still do not trust her."

"I'm well aware." I pat him on the chest. *"Go have some fun doing whatever it is that dragons do."*

His body rocks back and forth before he launches himself skyward.

Dorothy is transfixed as she watches Caustic fly away. "I've always loved dragons. In books, games, films, you name it, they're always so majestic, you know? Beauty and power all rolled into one." She turns back to me once he disappears into the night. "None of it compares to actually seeing one."

"Yeah, it's pretty amazing." I smile at the thought of Dorothy finally experiencing this world as it should be, without the burden of revenge weighing her down. "If you think Caustic is cool, just wait until you meet Limery."

Using my map, I track Limery's location until we come to a tavern called South of the Spire. It's a bustling business near the city's center, and beastkin of all shapes and sizes drink wine as they chat and listen to music. A couple of ratkin weasel through the crowd, delivering drinks and food. At the far wall, a goat-like beastkin with the long horns of an antelope plays a lute. She's tall and wiry, with a wispy goatee, and her hoof taps against the floor like a woodblock, keeping time with the music.

I spot Pressley sitting at a table in the corner, his dark and sinister appearance out of place in such a lively establishment. Limery stands in his chair across from the death knight, holding a wine glass as he sways to the music. A wide grin spreads across my face. Pressley raises an armored hand at me, and Limery turns around.

"Chods!" His bulbous eyes nearly pop from his head when he notices me, and he darts across the room, jostling a ratkin who miraculously avoids spilling the bottle of wine he's pouring. Limery wraps his arms around my neck and squeezes. "Limmy missed yous!"

I hug him back. "I missed you too, buddy. You having fun?"

"Oh, yes! Limmy loves the musics and the drinks."

"Why don't we have a seat, then." I turn to Dorothy and nod toward the corner table. "There's someone I want you to meet."

We follow Limery to the table, where Pressley sips on a glass of rosé. A purple gemstone pulses within the death knight's dark visage. Looks like he finally put the Hag's Eye to use. He lifts the glass to his visor, and the pinkish wine disappears into the void beneath his helm. Considering he's nothing more than bones and energy, I'm not exactly sure where it all ends up. I glance beneath the table just to check if there's a puddle underneath, but it's as clean as the rest of the tavern.

"You didn't strike me as the rosé type." I give him a friendly smirk as I take a seat.

His breath rattles within his helm. "Wasn't it you who said not to judge people based on their appearances?"

"Fair enough." I laugh and gesture to Dorothy. "This is Dorothy. She wants to join the fight. Dorothy, this is Limery, my partner in crime, and Pressley. He might be the strongest hero we've got."

Limery climbs on the table to shake Dorothy's hand. "Nice to meets yous." He burps and then cackles. "Excuse Limmy."

Dorothy smiles as she holds his tiny hand. "Nice to meet you, Limmy."

Pressley offers her his armored hand and nods. "How'd he convince you to join us?"

She looks from Pressley to me and shakes her head. "Despite my best intentions, somehow, I managed not to kill him."

Pressley laughs, and it sounds like bugs flying into a wood chipper. "He certainly has a way with people." He waves the ratkin over and asks for two more glasses. Once we have them, he pours Dorothy and me a generous amount of rosé, finishing off the bottle. "We might as well celebrate our last night in the city."

"Cheers to that." I raise my glass in a toast. "How long have you all been here?"

"Not too long." He swirls the wine and then takes a sip. "We spent most of the day running errands. I had to restock potions and supplies after the dungeon, and then Limery wanted to watch the performers in the square. I figured we deserved a little downtime after the past few days."

Limery grabs my arm excitedly. "We's saws the fire-breathers, and the dancers, and the buffaloes that plays musics with they's horns."

"Sounds like a blast." I'm not quite as elegant with my wine, taking a healthy gulp. It's crisp and refreshing and goes down way too easily. "I hear the dungeon was a success. Tell me all about it."

We go through two more bottles of wine as Pressley recounts their time in the dungeon, explaining the various monsters and the strategies they used to defeat them. A drunken Limery offers his input when he feels the death knight isn't doing the story justice, acting out several fights and giving his best imitation of the various monsters.

After detailing the boss fight with the manticore, Pressley's jeweled eye lingers on me. "Fighting alongside Caustic and Limery, I took to heart what you've been saying all along. There are some things that can't be done alone. I wouldn't have been able to bond the manticore without your help."

"I'm glad it worked out for you." I smile at the fact that even he has managed to open himself up a little, a far cry from the surly knight I met in Lynchton. "To be honest, I don't think I could have completed the trials if Caustic and Limery hadn't joined you."

"What do you mean?" asks Pressley.

Limery grumbles as he leans back against his chair, eyes heavy now that the story is over. I give him two minutes before he's snoring like a freight train.

I take another sip of the refreshing, tart rosé, letting the flavors linger on my tongue before swallowing. "I almost didn't make it. There was a moment when I felt like giving in, but then I heard Caustic's voice in my head, encouraging me to keep going. He'd gained enough levels during the dungeon that our bond strengthened and now we can communicate telepathically. So I think we can call it even on who owes who for our adventures outside of Goldspire."

"One less debt for me to repay." Pressley flags down the ratkin for another bottle of wine then returns his attention to me. "I've done enough talking for one night. What were the trials like?"

My story doesn't take nearly as long as I describe my experiences in the trials. It's hard to really do justice to just how grueling the first two phases were. Saying that I stood in a hot box and held some walls apart doesn't sound as cool as fighting bone-crushing scorpions and flying crocodiles but when I get to the third trial, where my body was pulverized like raw meat, Dorothy grimaces as I describe the searing pain and constant torment. Pressley makes a noise that I'm pretty sure is a groan.

"That sounds like torture." Dorothy shivers as if she's imagining what the experience was like.

I shrug. "It was rough, but I was warned that it would be challenging plenty of times. It had a level cap just to be able to enter."

"And yet you still did it." The look she gives me is, I'm not sure, respect, maybe.

My gaze drops to Limery, who snores softly in the seat next to me. "I didn't really have a choice."

"There's always a choice." Pressley sets his glass on the table, and it clinks against his armored hand. "We make them every day. Some choose the easy road or the road without conflict. Others choose to wander through life without ever finding a sense of purpose. And then there are those who choose to take their lumps in the name of what they believe is right or noble. I wish I'd chosen differently at times."

"We all make mistakes." I reach across the table and tap his armored hand. "The real choice is in how we respond to them."

He nods silently, and the swell of music fills the void before he takes a deep breath and stands. "I've had enough socializing for one evening. I'll see you in the morning for Seascape. Limery and I have a room booked at The Merry Minotaur a block over."

"See you in the morning." I wave to him as he leaves.

Dorothy shifts her chair so that she's sitting across from me. "He looks scary, but he seems like a nice guy."

"He is." I laugh. "He was actually a human knight when I first met him, but then there was this whole thing with a cleric and the god of chaos. He's definitely a force to be reckoned with."

"You both are." She pours the last of the bottle between our glasses. "With a death knight riding a manticore and a troll on a dragon, you two are gonna be pretty damn fearsome on the battlefield."

"And what about you?" I tilt my glass in her direction. "You're pretty formidable yourself."

"Not my style." She smirks. "I prefer to go unnoticed and strike when they least expect it."

As we finish the last of the wine, I do my best to prepare Dorothy for what's coming tomorrow. I'm sure it'll be pandemonium in Seascape, so I try to give her a rundown of all the major players.

The past few days may have felt like an eternity, but I have a feeling that once we're back, time will be the one thing there's not enough of.

26. GOOD-BYE GOLDSPIRE

"Ungh." Limery stirs next to me, his miserable grunts pulling me from sleep.

I open my eyes just as he turns over and his hand swats me on the side of the head. He sits up, groggy-eyed as he looks around the room uncertain of where he is or how he got here.

"You really need to learn some moderation, you know that?" I fold the pillow over my ears to drown out his groaning.

He grumbles something unintelligible and then hovers in the air. There's a sizzling sound, and the room's temperature rises by several degrees as he burns through the toxins of the previous night.

"That's betters." He grins as he lands beside me on the bed. "Time to goes sees Taryns!"

I prop myself on my elbows. Compared to some of our rowdier nights, I didn't drink that much. For my part, I'm feeling fine, and I'm sure Dorothy is, too. Pressley, on the other hand... I wonder if death knights can even get hangovers.

After gathering our things, we find him downstairs a short while later, but his demeanor gives nothing away. He's as dour-looking as ever as the morning sun spills through the open window. Dorothy sits across from him, sipping on a mug of steaming tea.

The bottom floor of the inn has a cozy feel to it, with warm light shining on the pristine tile. The entire room is decorated in shades of yellow and green, reminding me of spring flowers. The smell of fresh bread wafts in from the kitchen, mixing with the smoky aroma from the platter of bacon a wolfkin picks at while reading her scroll.

My stomach growls, and I wipe away a bit of drool forming on my lip. For the past three days, all I've had to eat was the blood from the molten spiders and the rations I had stored in my satchel. They satiated my hunger, but it was hardly a meal.

"Good mornings!" Limery beams as he joins Pressley and Dorothy at the table.

"Good morning to you." Dorothy smiles in response, pulling out a seat for the imp.

I order some food for Limery and myself from the barkeep and then take the chair next to Pressley. A few minutes later, a platter of assorted meats and wheat pancakes drizzled with honey arrives along with a carafe of juice. I don't waste a moment before digging in. Limery's appetite matches my own, and we devour the deliciously fluffy pancakes and savory strips of bacon like we may never eat again.

My mouth is stuffed when I notice Pressley and Dorothy watching us.

"What?" The words come out muffled, but the meaning is clear enough.

Dorothy's lip curls in disgust. "It's like watching pigs eat from a trough."

"Hey, I didn't eat for three days, and then all I had was days-old bread and cheese." I stuff another sausage into my already-full mouth. "Forgive me for enjoying myself."

"There's a fine line between enjoyment and gluttony." She scrunches her nose. "I have a cat that used to do that. He'd eat his food like I was going to steal it, and then five minutes later, I'd have to clean it off the floor." She shakes her head in disappointment. "That's the bar you're failing to meet, Chod."

Pressley lets out a raspy laugh, and I narrow my eyes at him.

"She's not wrong." He scoots back from the table and stands. "I need to go pick up the manticore from the stables and make sure she hasn't seriously injured anyone. She's on the other side of the city. Want to meet at the portal in an hour?"

I wash down the food with a giant swig of juice. "Sounds good. I was planning to see Jegaar before we left anyway."

After I settle the tab, we leave The Merry Minotaur. Outside, a large, green tail dangles from above the porch. I step out into the street and look up to find Caustic sprawled out on the roof of the inn. Many of the clay tiles are cracked and disheveled, and the edge of the roof is clearly sagging from his weight. Tiles crunch as he sits up, and broken pieces fall onto the street.

"Did you sleep there all night?" I ask.

Caustic hops down from the roof, landing on the cobblestone with a thud. He breathes hot air at Dorothy, tousling her hair, before turning his gaze to me.

"I did many things during the night." He lowers his head until it's level with my own.

"Of course you did." I scratch him on the chin.

Dorothy takes a few steps back. "I don't think he likes me."

I shrug. "Well, you did try to kill me."

"Fair enough, I suppose."

Limery flies to Caustic's head and wraps his fingers around the golden antlers like they're handlebars. "Limmy wants to flies with Caustics."

"Alright then, meet us at the library." I pet Caustic on the chest. "Dorothy and I will go on foot."

The dragon launches himself into the air, and Limery laughs maniacally as the duo takes flight. Every beastkin on the block stops what they're doing to watch them soar across the sky.

Dorothy and I enjoy a peaceful stroll on the way to the library. Long fronds rustle in the gentle breeze, and the aqueducts gurgle as they carry water across the city. Judging by the calm streets, you'd never know the majority of Mythos was on the brink of war. Several beastkin walk by at a leisurely pace as if they don't have a care in the world.

"You're really attached to him, aren't you?" Dorothy finally breaks the silence.

"Who do you mean?" I ask.

"Limery." She glances at me, then fixes her gaze straight ahead. "I could tell by the way you carried him to bed last night. You cradled him like he was made of glass. I do the same thing with my cats."

"As powerful as he is, he's still childlike in so many ways. I worry about him, probably more than I should, but he's been by my side pretty much since the beginning. I don't know how deeply you've interacted with the NPCs, but it's like he's real. He has his own personality. His own dreams and fears."

"A weird little accent." She chuckles.

"That, too." I laugh. "I'd do anything for him."

Caustic and Limery sit by the fountain outside of the library when we arrive, both of them basking in the sun. I have Caustic wait outside while we head through the front of the library this time, using the special entrance to the Scholars Guild that Jegaar showed us. We catch a couple of skeptical looks, but no one stops us as we make our way to the wolfkin's office in his underground bunker.

I knock on the blank metal door and a moment later, the runes flash bright orange before a peephole appears. A bright blue eye peers through and then the door opens. Jegaar welcomes us inside.

He places a hand on my shoulder and gives me a wolfish grin. "Good news, I assume?"

I activate Cold Rage for a few seconds, and my skin turns to metal. "Good news," I echo. "We're in a hurry, but I wanted to stop by to say thanks for all of your help."

The battle scholar leans in close, looking at his reflection on my chest. "May I?" He gestures toward my arm.

I lift my hand, and he wraps his paws around my wrist and forearm, examining my skin and testing the metal with his claw.

He nods approvingly. "Well done, Chod. I knew you had it in you."

"We'll be heading to Seascape shortly." I cancel Cold Rage to save the precious few moments I have left. "Pressley is gathering his manticore from the stables."

"Sounds like a productive outing all around. Too bad you're in a hurry or I would love to study the Golden Devourer." He turns to Dorothy. "And who do we have here?"

"I'm Dorothy." She extends her hand. "Here to lend my talents in the upcoming battle."

He grasps both hands around hers. "Dark tidings, but you'll be in good company. I wish you all the best."

I pace across the room, wishing I had the magic words to bring Goldspire into the fray. "Is there nothing we can do to convince you to join us? There has to be some of you willing to fight."

"There are many of us who would welcome the glory of a battlefield." He clenches his fist, and his eyes burn with passion as he stares into mine. "But the emperor's word is law. We will not be joining this fight, as much as I may wish otherwise."

I nod solemnly. "This is it, then."

"No." He places a paw on each of my shoulders and shakes his head. "This is not the end. This is just the beginning."

I force a smile. "Take care of yourself, Jegaar."

Pressley waits for us by the portal next to one of the most badass monsters I've ever seen. Limery flies over and perches on the death knight's shoulder, laughing as he taps his claw on Pressley's helm. A hollow gong reverberates within the void but to Pressley's credit, he joins in the laughter. A couple of days together in the dungeon has brought out a side of the death knight I've never seen.

Looking at the monster before me, I understand why he was so keen on finding the manticore. She's a massive beast, not nearly as big as Caustic, but her frame rivals a draft horse. Plenty large enough to make Pressley an even more imposing figure when mounted.

Her golden face is strangely human as she watches us approach. Beneath the gilded mask, her one blue eye tracks each of us in turn, while the Hag's Eye glows eerily in the other socket, matching the death knight's. Her luscious black hair gives way to the crimson fur of a lion's body, and large, leathery wings are tucked at her sides. A dangerous scorpion tail curls up from behind, the end tipped with a thick stinger and several barbs.

The manticore approaches Dorothy, scrunching her nose when she sniffs at the elf's hair. Dorothy wears a nervous expression as the manticore breathes in her scent. The undead monster attempts to speak, but the words are an incomprehensible mess.

"She lost her ability to speak when I reanimated her." Pressley pets the manticore on the shoulder, and she loses interest in Dorothy. "She can still fight, though."

"She's badass." I examine the manticore from several angles, and when I step too close, she hisses at me, earning a reproachful growl from Caustic.

"Be careful." Pressley tugs on the reins. "She's not the friendliest."

Dorothy scoffs as she looks at Caustic. "Seems to be a lot of that going around."

The dragon curls his lip and unleashes a menacing rumble, making Dorothy take a few steps back.

Pressley laughs. "When we're on the battlefield, friendly won't matter." He tugs on the manticore's reins, repositioning her toward the portal. "We ready?"

I take one last look at the beautiful city and try not to think about how many of its citizens would fight by our side if given the opportunity. Wondering about the what-ifs will get me nowhere. What matters are the ones we have, and they're waiting on the other side of the portal.

"Let's go."

27. HOMECOMING

We exit the portal into Seascape Square, where tall buildings and gothic architecture surround us. The dwarven capital might not be made of crystal but its craftsmanship is a work of art, and unlike most kingdoms who have their portals set at the edge of the city, Seascape's is at its heart.

Behind us, King Orso's castle looms from the city's highest point. I take a moment to admire the beauty of fine lines and details on the behemoth of a structure. Somehow, it manages to appear both fragile and imposing. Dozens of towers, spires, and flying buttresses claw at the heavens, and hundreds of stained-glass windows reflect the midday sun, depicting scenes and imagery from Seascape's long history.

Proud and menacing gargoyles watch over the city below, which is equally magnificent. Every building is built from brick or stone and so tightly packed that it reminds me of New York.

Living there day to day, it was easy to lose sight of the magnificence of the city when it became a background to the chaos of life. But whenever I'd return from a trip and see the towering skyline, I was always reminded that it was like no place on earth.

This is no different. So much has happened since I was last here, but it still feels like a homecoming. I've traveled from Goldspire to Frostmoor and then to Wandermere and Pruxford, but Isle of Mythos is where it all began. From the troll forest to Vanaria and Seascape, this is my home. These are the lands that made me, and this is what I'm fighting for.

Ivory, ebony, and even a few blood dwarves bustle about as the kingdom prepares for the upcoming battle. Carts of weapons and armor line the edge of the square as soldiers pass out gear to citizens. More dwarves carry crates filled with vials of colorful liquids down from the castle, where a lava-skinned blood dwarf marks inventory as each box is loaded into a wagon.

There's a shout as someone notices us exiting the portal, and the square goes silent. In the lower city, the rhythmic clank of the blacksmith carries on as every eye falls on the dragon and manticore. The legendary monsters are so enthralling that no one seems bothered by Pressley's presence.

Caustic raises his head high, and several of the commoners drop to one knee.

"Don't let this go to your head," I tease.

Caustic huffs. *"A dragon commands respect by simply existing."*

If this is his attitude now, I can only imagine what it's going to be like when he's fully grown.

"Chod!" a deep voice calls to me from the crowd.

I do a double-take when I see a massive forest troll making his way through the crowded dwarves that are half his height. Malak grins, and I return his smile. He's one of the guardians that protects the borders of the village, a beast of a troll but innocent and friendly in a way Gord could never be. The last time I saw him, he was nearly swindled by a human trader selling a knife for ten times its value.

Beyond him, a large group of forest, mountain, and arctic trolls stand together. Brutus is a head taller than the rest, a mountain of lean muscle with a hawk nose, braided mohawk, and an unmistakable scar that runs across his lilac chest. He and I nearly came to blows when I first encountered the mountain tribe.

"Damn, that's a lot of trolls," Dorothy mutters under her breath.

Limery is unusually quiet as he takes in the scene. Pressley sits stoically atop the manticore, and his mount's one good eye scans the crowd as if she's deciding which one she wants to devour.

Malak extends his arm, and I clasp it in mine as we embrace.

"Good to see you." I grin, patting him on the back.

He looks at me with wonder in his green eyes as he takes in my appearance. "You have horns."

"That I do." I laugh. "There's a lot to catch you up on."

The other trolls follow Malak's lead, Brutus leading the throng of green, purple, and white bodies through the sea of dwarves. More trolls than I imagined spill into the square from the side street, all of them eager to see the two mighty beasts. The dwarves that aren't focused on Caustic and the manticore ogle at the massive trolls nearly double their height. For those traveling from the countryside, I'm sure this is their first time seeing a troll in person.

"Chod." Brutus nods, which is a friendlier greeting than many of our encounters have been. We stare at one another for a moment before his mouth twists into a grin and he extends his hand. "It has been too long since I've cracked heads. I look forward to fighting by your side for the fate of Mythos."

I chuckle as I grip him around the forearm. "Likewise. It is good to see you. Where's Chief Rizza and the others?"

Brutus gestures toward the castle. "Chief Rizza and Laojin are meeting with the king. The forest and mountain trolls only just arrived this morning. A messenger from Vanaria has sent word that Gord and Kronan should arrive with the others by nightfall."

"Chod!" I recognize her feminine voice, but I can't find Yashi among the crowd. The trolls part until the diminutive troll steps into view. She's a good two feet shorter than the others and wears her hair in two long braids that reach her waist. What she lacks in size, she more than makes up for in skill and knowledge. I doubt there's a better archer or potion-maker among all of the trolls. Plus she has a mana-infused wyrm now. "You big oaf. I was worried I'd never see you again." She wraps her arms around my midsection.

"It's good to see you too." I return her embrace and glance through the crowd, searching for the other two members of our original party. "Where's Ismora and Tormara?"

"Ismora is meeting with the blacksmith about weapons more suited for trolls. Tormara is still in Vanaria. She'll be arriving with Gord and the others."

I lose focus of what Yashi is saying when I see Senzala watching me from across the square, her blue eyes locked on mine. The shaman is just as tall as the other arctic trolls, but about half their width. She has the same white fur across most of her body, except where the males have an exposed patch of black skin on their chest, hers is covered in fur. Her white hair is pulled into a bun that rests atop her head. She raises a hand in acknowledgment and smiles, and I can't fight the grin that consumes me. Her tusks are much smaller than most trolls, barely rising above her lips. They only add to her beauty, which is both reserved and ferocious at the same time.

Our time together in Frostmoor was too short, and things have gotten so crazy that I haven't even thought about what I might say if I saw her again. All I know is that I enjoyed being in her presence.

Yashi and Brutus both follow my gaze and then share a mischievous look.

Brutus claps me on the back. "I hope your luck is better than mine."

"I don't think your luck was the problem." Yashi laughs. "You're about as smooth as a splinter. Judging by the way she's looking at Chod, he's clear blue water, and she's ready for a drink."

My cheeks burn at her comments, which only makes Yashi laugh harder. Dorothy snickers behind me, and Limery questions what's so funny.

In an attempt to change the subject before the imp starts singing "Chods has a girlfriends," I introduce my new companions to those still watching us. Both the trolls and dwarves are mesmerized by Caustic and the manticore. Eventually, the fascination dies down, and the dwarves return to their business of handing out armor and weapons.

Pressley dismounts from the manticore and joins my side. "Sounds like we're still waiting for some of the major players to arrive, so I'm going to check into the stables and find a room for the evening. Send me a message if you need anything."

"Will do." I shake his hand. "Thanks again for everything."

"Mind if I join you?" Dorothy places a hand on Pressley's shoulder and smirks at me. "I don't want to get in the way of Chod and the lady trolls."

"It's not like that." I try to sound cool, but my cheeks flush uncontrollably.

She blows me a kiss as she walks away. "See you later, lover boy."

Limery waves to Pressley and Dorothy from between Caustic's horns as they leave. "See you laters, lover boys!"

I bury my head in my palm and hope he forgets that phrase as quickly as he learned it.

With the manticore gone, Caustic basks in all of the attention, preening himself as the trolls gather around. The dwarves carry on with their duties, but they're constantly glancing in the dragon's direction.

Senzala makes her way over, and Yashi wraps her arms around Malak and Brutus's backsides, ushering them away.

"What was that all about?" Senzala smirks.

"Beats me." I shrug and attempt to regulate my breathing so that my cheeks don't burst into flames. "How have you been?"

"Good." She nods. "It has been good for all of us to be around our kin."

"I understand that feeling. I thought the desert trolls were here as well?" I frown as I search the crowd. They're the biggest of all the troll races, and I don't see one anywhere.

"They are with the chiefs. There are so few of them left, and King Orso wanted to meet them personally." She looks toward the castle. "He is a good king. I see why you support him."

"He's a good dwarf. That has made him a good king."

Caustic yawns, and Limery dangles from the dragon's horns like a monkey in a tree. There's an audible gasp from those around us as Caustic's deadly teeth show in all their glory.

"Taryn told us some of the story, but I really want to hear all about how you hatched a dragon." Senzala shifts her gaze from Caustic to me. "I'm sure Oyana would like to record the tale for our histories when there is time."

"I'd love to tell you about it sometime. Where are you all headed now?"

"Nowhere at the moment. We've been training since dawn, and preparations are being made to acquire more weapons but for now, we're waiting for the rest of our people to arrive from Vanaria." Her blue eyes lock onto mine. "Until then, I'm all yours, if you'll have me."

I choke on my saliva at her words and cough as I try to regain my composure. Senzala pats me on the back, laughing softly.

Once I'm back to normal, she and I find a less crowded area in front of an apothecary. A sign on the door reads, '*Closed to help with the war effort.*'

All hands are on deck.

As I look over the crowded square, I realize it's true for the trolls as well. There are so many faces I recognize. Jojin and Watu, both guardians of the forest. Ahso, the leatherworker, and Kina, the council member with some of the most gorgeous hair I've ever seen. She's one of the few forest trolls that doesn't wear her hair in a braid. There are a dozen others that I've interacted with during my time in the forest, and many more I never had the chance to. Aside from those still in Vanaria, the only forest trolls who aren't here are the elderly and the children. This is true of the mountain and arctic trolls as well.

Many trolls are gathered around Limery as he sits on top of Caustic's head with his legs crossed, recounting their adventures in the Goldspire dungeon. For now, at least, they can enjoy a distraction. Soon, every troll hand will hold a weapon as we march.

"You sure you don't want to hear his story?" I gesture at Limery as he summons a fireball in his palms. "He has a way with words and he's quite the performer."

Senzala laughs and places her hand on my arm. "I'm more interested in what you have to say."

"Okay, then." I gulp. "When we left Frostmoor, we went straight to Wandermere. It was unlike any of the other kingdoms I'd traveled to. The portal emptied into a sprawling forest with trees so tall that they blotted out the sun. There was fog everywhere, and all we had was the egg and no sense of direction."

She hangs on my every word as I recount our adventure through the forest, meeting the centaurs, and our agreement to clear the forest of wisps in exchange for help with the egg.

"There's a green dragon that sleeps underneath the lake?" She wears a shocked expression when I tell her about Verdaria sleeping within the Hidden Lake.

"Yep." I grin. "That's where all of the fog comes from that protects the village. She's been there for over a hundred years, I think. Speaking of dragons, will Nesira be joining us?"

Senzala places a hand over her chest. "Her place is in Frostmoor, but our bond is still strong."

I still remember the dragon's power from the first time I saw her. A blizzard followed the white dragon everywhere she went. It makes me wonder what other abilities Caustic might unlock as he continues to grow. Nesira and Senzala aren't bonded in the same way as he and I are, but as a totem, Nesira grants the shaman powerful abilities just as the phoenix does Jira.

"So then what happened?" She nudges me in the side. "After you put the regeneration items on the raft?"

"We waited as the life force gathered. Taryn, Limery, and I went to fight the shadow wisps, and when we returned to the village, it was almost time. The entire herd had gathered around the lake, and it was like I could see the life aura flowing through the forest." I close my eyes, remembering the scene in vivid detail. "And then I took the egg into the forest to hatch."

"To witness a dragon hatch..." She squeezes my arm, and goosebumps sprout along my body. "It must have been amazing."

"It was." I tell her about our first moments together, our training in Pruxford, and the final fight of the tournament, when Caustic chose me as his bond. I'm in the middle of explaining our bond when the portal flares and a mass of bodies enter into the square.

Gord stands at the front, the broad-shouldered troll as fearsome as ever. He wears the bone armor that we looted in Paltras Ruins, and the massive battle axe—

Peacemaker—is strapped across his back. One of his yellowed tusks is snapped in half, and a large metal ring dangles from his nose. His black eyes scan the crowd.

To his side stands Kronan, who rivals him in size. The chief of the mountain trolls has skin the deep purple of a plum, and one of his tusks is splintered at the tip. He wears his hair in a braided mohawk that hangs over one shoulder, and the shaft of a silver warhammer rests on the other. Two giant scars cross his chest in an X, and several more cover his arms and shoulders. He's a fighter first and foremost.

Kronan lifts the warhammer in the air. "The trolls are united at last."

A booming roar sweeps over the square, startling many of the dwarves going about their duties. Kronan steps aside, revealing a short blue troll no bigger than Yashi.

Chief Lida raises a staff tipped with a white shell into the air, and the roar intensifies. The seaside trolls are the smallest race of trolls, their small stature and webbed fingers and toes making them perfect for semi-aquatic life. She wears loose fabrics adorned with shells that sway with her movement and a shell necklace. Her eyes are as blue as the sea as she looks out at the trolls before her, and the water mage's navy dreadlocks stand out against her baby-blue skin. Despite her fragile appearance, she commands powerful magic.

The crowd parts as the group exits the portal, followed by more seaside trolls. Each one is the same light blue as the chief.

Behind them, Tormara rides her wyrm. Her braids are as fiery as her personality, and they sway from the movement. I nearly burst out laughing when I see the goblin Cheevus following her on his mangy wolf. Several dozen of his kin trail close behind him. The goblins all have the same dull-green skin, lanky arms, and pointed ears. Their eyes are a dark shade of orange, and tiny noses hook over wide mouths full of sharp, triangular teeth.

Altogether, the four tribes take up the majority of the square. We might not be an army, but we're a force to be reckoned with.

Caustic moves to greet the newcomers, Limery still sitting on his head. The seaside trolls take a defensive stance at his approach, raising their spears at the dragon's sudden appearance. Both Gord and Kronan have their weapons at the ready.

The dragon huffs, and his breath rattles the many seashells adorning their clothing and hair. There's no malice in his temperament, but I rush over in case the trolls do something stupid.

"I hope you're a better judge of friend or foe on the battlefield," I shout as I arrive at Caustic's side.

"Chod?" Gord lowers his weapon when he finds me among the crowd, and his eyes go wide. "Just when I thought you couldn't get any uglier." He booms with laughter as he strolls over and wraps his arms around me, his bone armor rattling as he lifts me off the ground. "Good to see you brother!"

I laugh when he lets me go. The two of us have come so far from wanting to kill one another. "Good to see you too." I nod toward the seaside trolls. "Looks like you finally did something I couldn't."

"A dragon?" Kronan steps up behind him, extending his arm as his gaze shifts from Caustic to me. "You're always full of surprises."

"What can I say?" I grip Kronan around the forearm with one hand and pat Caustic on the chest with the other. "This is Caustic. He'll be watching your backs."

Chief Lida makes her way between the two massive trolls and kneels before the dragon. "I was wrong to have ever doubted you."

Caustic lowers his head, sniffing her head. *"She smells of fish."*

I try not to laugh as I extend a hand and help Chief Lida to her feet. "You're here now. That's all that matters."

"You have done the impossible." She shakes her head in disbelief as she takes in the mob of trolls. "I didn't believe it could be done, but you've united the trolls."

"I didn't do it alone. Gord, Chief Rizza, Kronan—none of this would be possible without them." I turn to the many trolls watching our greeting unfold and raise my voice so it carries across the square. "We may be from different tribes but when the time comes to raise our weapons, we'll fight as one horde."

I reach out to Caustic through our bond, and he unleashes a powerful roar. It echoes off the buildings, and I feel an energy building among the tribes. Several trolls beat their chests in response, and Caustic roars again. This time, I join in, beating my chest and roaring as power pulses through my veins. These are my people. Every troll present answers the call, and their roars echo in my bones.

The dwarves within earshot stand frozen, mesmerized by the display of unity.

Cheevus weasels his way through the trolls, followed by the goblins until they are at Caustic's feet. He looks from the dragon to me and then grins. "Dragon strong. We follow."

28. UNITED WE STAND

Limery stands on Caustic's head, using the dragon's horns as a podium. He's been entertaining the trolls and goblins with stories while we wait for Chief Rizza and the others to finish their meeting. He's a natural storyteller, acting out many of the scenes in detail. At one point, he slides down the dragon's snout with fireballs blazing in each hand as he recounts one of their battles in the dungeon with Pressley. When that story ends, he jumps into the next, narrating our experiences in the Pruxford tournament.

To Caustic's credit, he's been exceptionally patient with Limery. I'm pretty sure he's basking in the attention just as much as the imp.

"Your kin approach," Caustic speaks to me through our bond, and his head shifts slightly as he looks toward the top of the enormous set of steps that lead to the castle.

I follow Caustic's gaze and find Chief Rizza standing on the terrace overlooking the square. She looks mighty in her leather vest that showcases her lithe and defined arms. Her dark hair is braided perfectly and rests on her shoulder. She's the personification of what it means to be a strong leader. She's made the tough decisions, and the unpopular ones, all in the name of preserving the tribe. I can only imagine what she must be feeling seeing so many trolls gathered together.

She's brought them so far. When I first came to Mythos, the ley lines were blocked, cutting off the mana that kept the trolls hidden within the forest. The tribe was hunted and faced death just for existing. Now, here they are, about to go to war for the fate of not just the trolls but for all of Mythos.

Chief Laojin steps by her side, his thick white beard blowing in the breeze, followed by Jira. The forest troll shaman has a bird perched on his shoulder with fiery feathers in shades of reds and oranges. The phoenix picks at the white tips of his dreadlocks with her beak. After the fight with Ethan and his goons outside of

Lynchton, the powerful bird was reborn as a chick. She's a far cry from the magnificent creature we found chained in a cave, but she's about the size of a parrot now.

A moment later, five massive desert trolls join them, each one at least a foot taller than the arctic chief. I recognize the centermost troll from our run-in in the desert outside of Sandholde. Back then, he wanted nothing to do with me but somehow, they convinced him to come. His skin is a dull tan with patches of toffee-colored skin on his shoulders and neck from the harsh desert sun. His hair is the deep burgundy of dried blood, pulled into a ponytail, and his thick, short tusks frame his stumpy, bulbous nose. The desert trolls carry a thick layer of fat over their muscles, much like a camel, but I have no doubt he's a formidable force. He wears armor made from bone and pieces of a scorpion carapace lashed together with strips of leather.

Two female desert trolls stand to his right. Their bodies are not that different from his own except for their wider hips. One has hair that's a deep brown, pulled into a bun. The other sports an orange, braided mohawk. Two males stand to the left, only a fraction smaller than the one I met in the desert. One leans against the stone balustrade, his brown hair braided to drape across his left shoulder. He's missing his right ear, and a nasty scar runs from the crown of his head to his jaw. He's definitely seen better days. The last troll has a bald head, and though he's still stout, his body is marked by age. Dense wrinkles frame his eyes, and sunspots speckle his skin. He reminds me of an old wrestler, where the muscles are still there but the skin hangs just a tad too loose.

Five desert trolls. Is that all that remains of their race?

There's movement at the bottom of the steps as a green figure maneuvers against the tide of dwarves bringing supplies from the castle. I recognize Ismora's striped skin marked with the hard-earned lessons of combat as she takes the steps three at a time. Lines of faded green and white run along her powerful arms like a tiger. The weaponsmaster is the only troll capable of rivaling Kronan for sheer number of battle scars.

She climbs the steps that wind up the landing until she finds the chief. The two have a brief conversation, and then Chief Rizza returns her attention to the square and raises her arm. The square goes quiet aside from the distant sounds of the city. Even the dwarves pause to hear what she has to say. Outside the square, carts clatter along the streets carrying supplies, hammers beat in rhythm as the smiths prepare weapons of war, and coastal birds caw from their perches upon the buildings.

The chief's golden eyes fall upon Caustic, and then me. She nods, and I return the gesture. Anticipation builds as the silence lingers, and she scans the crowd, taking in the many faces that have chosen to join her in battle.

"I wish this were a time to celebrate." A sad smile forms across her narrow face. "For the first time since the mother birthed five troll sisters and sent them out into the world, all five tribes have gathered together under one banner. Despite our differences, we share a common ancestry. We are bonded by the blood of the earth.

For too long, our numbers have dwindled, and we've hidden away in fear and isolation while the world passed us by.

"And now we face an enemy that threatens to destroy not only the great kingdoms of Mythos but what little we have—" She pauses, and her fists clench. "—what little we've gained. We face an enemy with an army that doesn't tire, and soldiers that do not feel pain. They will attack, never slowing, until their bones turn to dust. I have witnessed its scope with my own eyes, and I assure you, they will not show us mercy until we vow to give up everything that makes us who we are."

She shakes her head, and her hands grip the stone railing. "But we are trolls, and we do not yield. We do not bend. We do not break. Our young ones are safe in the castle at Tawdrybluff, cared for by the elders. It is our job to ensure that they grow up in a world where trolls are free, where the legends of our might upon the battlefield are sung in every tavern and told by every campfire across Mythos." She takes a deep breath and leans over the balustrade. "We come from the earth, and when the time comes, we will return to it again. For we are the bedrock of Mythos, and we will not fade silently into the night. Together, we will fight because even if we fall, this will not be our end!"

A fire burns in my bones, and goosebumps cover my body by the time she finishes. There's an energy among the trolls that tells me every one of them feels the same way.

The largest of the desert trolls beats his chest and unleashes a deep roar. His cheeks flap and spittle spews from his mouth as the baritone cry echoes off the walls of the square. His fellow trolls join in, amplifying the thunderous howl like a crashing wave.

Caustic answers with a roar that rumbles in my chest and an intensity that rages through our bond. For the second time today, the square thunders with the raucous clamor of the trolls as we all unite. The cries of the desert trolls fade, and their bodies heave with deep breaths, but the storm of the tribe swells. For several minutes, we unleash our frustrations in the most primal way we know how.

There's no doubt about it. The trolls are ready for war.

Chief Rizza looks over her shoulder, and a moment later, King Orso joins her side followed by several members of his council and Taryn. The kingsguard stands sentry at the rear.

The crown atop King Orso's bushy black, hair glows red like hot lava, its tines shaped into alternating battle-axes and warhammers. He wears a black cloak and tunic, each one embroidered with silver thread, and a red breastplate engraved with a warhammer that matches the dull-red tint of his skin. Even though Orso is tall for a dwarf, he only comes up to the chief's elbow.

He waits for the commotion to die down before speaking. "It is an honor to have the trolls gathered in Seascape, and it will be an honor to fight by your side. For my kingdom's part, I am sorry that it took such circumstances for the trolls to be treated with the respect they deserve. Know that from this day forward, you will always be welcome within our borders, and the castle in Tawdrybluff will be given all the privileges of a sovereign nation."

King Orso looks to Chief Rizza before continuing. "This is a momentous occasion for your tribes, and I do not want to detract from that. Once you've had the opportunity to acquaint yourself with one another, I will be opening the troves of Seascape to the trolls. When we march into battle, I do not want a single piece of armor or weaponry left in the castle that can be used."

Wow. My jaw drops. Opening the treasures of Seascape to me and Taryn was one thing, but offering its contents to all of the trolls is something else. There are treasures and items beyond measure within the vault, and the gesture will not be forgotten.

Chief Rizza and King Orso embrace one another around the forearm. As the king turns to leave, Limery shouts over the crowd.

"Waits!" He hovers in the air above Caustic's head. "Waits! Limmy has somethings to say!"

King Orso turns around, a smile forming beneath his twitching beard. "Yes?"

Limery flies up to the terrace, settling on the stone railing in front of Chief Rizza. "Limmy has somethings for the trollses."

Chief Rizza finds me among the crowd and raises her brows. I shrug. For once, I have no idea what the little guy is up to.

"What is it you have for us?" Her voice is full of kindness.

Limery reaches into the tiny pouch tied to his waist and pulls out a small object. Chief Rizza's eyes soften when he hands it to her.

"A long times agos, there's was many impses. The bad wizard tricks thems to fight for hims, and theys all dies. Limmy wants to gives these to the trollses so that theys can talk with the others. And so that theys can remembers the impses. Theys wasn't bad. Theys was just tricked."

Limery reaches into the pouch and pulls out another, handing it to Chief Laojin. Then one by one, he gives a communication stone to each of the desert trolls. "Limmy has hundreds of thems. Enough for all the trollses."

So, that's what he spent his gold from the dungeon on. He could have used that gold for anything and yet he chose to honor those that history had forgotten. A lump forms in my throat, and I blink back the tears forming at the edge of my eyes. I don't know if I'll ever know how truly lucky I am that he came into my life.

While King Orso and the other leaders have been able to communicate with the trolls through their own communication stones, this will be a monumental advantage on the battlefield. Most of the other kingdoms speak the common tongue, but now the trolls will be able to converse with them without the need for a translator.

"Thank you." Chief Rizza bows slightly to Limery. "You are a truly special imp. Would you be so kind as to hand them out?"

"Limmy can doos its!" He smiles devilishly as he flies down over the crowd, tossing out communication stones like they're candy at a parade.

King Orso and his council return to the castle while Chief Rizza and the other trolls descend the steps. Taryn follows, trailed by Ruby and Flubs. The slime is in its natural form and springs down the steps like a gelatinous Slinky. Jordy and Berry are nowhere to be seen, so they must be in the royal stables.

The chief heads for the newly arrived seaside trolls, and I take a moment to catch up with Taryn, though there's not nearly enough time to fill him in on everything that's happened the past few days.

He grins when we're face to face. "That was some speech."

"Yeah. It gave me goosebumps." I lift my arm to see if the hairs are still raised.

Taryn steps back, taking in Caustic's appearance. "How is it you were gone for a handful of days and he's nearly doubled in size again?"

I pat the dragon on the leg. "He and Limery cleared a dungeon with Pressley while I was doing the trials. He gained seven levels, and now we can communicate telepathically."

"You're kidding me?" He shakes his head and the clasps in his beard jingle. "I want to be able to talk to my pets telepathically."

"*I am no pet.*" Caustic huffs, and Taryn's dreadlocks fall across his face.

"Don't call him a pet. He's a little sensitive about that." I smirk at the irritation I feel seeping through our bond. "How are things coming along here?"

"We're almost ready. Or as ready as we can be on such short notice. The imps have been invaluable. Lillith had the idea to station those who wanted to help in Pruxford since that's where we'll be launching the attack from. They've been delivering messages between all of the other kingdoms faster than we could have ever hoped. There's a lot to catch you up on, and I didn't want to send it all through message."

"You have no idea. There's so much I need to tell you." I chuckle. "You're never going to guess who I ran into in Goldspire."

Taryn raises his brow. "Who?"

"Dorothy."

"Shit. How the hell did she find you?" His eyes are wide as he looks me over for signs of injury. "I'm guessing you survived the encounter."

"It's a long story, but the short version is that I was going to let her kill me to try to make things right. She didn't, and instead, she wants to fight alongside us. I think I convinced her that I'm not the same asshole I was a few months ago."

"And she believed you? Just like that?" Taryn gives me a questioning look.

I shrug. "I'm not dead. And she's here in Seascape."

"Wait, what?" Taryn's head swivels like a sprinkler as he searches the crowd. "She's here?"

"Relax." I laugh as I clasp him on the shoulder. "She's with Pressley at the moment. I'll give you the full story when we have time to talk. Right now, I need to talk to Chief Rizza, and then I need to find King Orso."

Taryn grips me on the arm, his brown eyes locking with my own. "I'm glad you're back."

"Me, too, buddy." I wrap my arm around his shoulder and squeeze.

We search for Chief Rizza among the crowd. Ruby and Flubs are both naturally evasive, weaseling through the throng of bodies like water, somehow evading danger at the last second. Caustic waits by the portal, surrounded by plenty of admirers.

Many of the trolls are examining their communication stones. Malak, bold as ever, has already put his to use and is engaged in conversation with the dwarves handing out weaponry.

I find Chief Rizza standing in a circle with the desert and seaside trolls. Gord, Kronan, Jira, Chief Laojin, Senzala, Yashi, and Ismora are there as well.

Jira's phoenix chirps when it sees us, and Taryn hurries over excitedly to scratch its head.

Chief Rizza gives me a warm smile when I arrive. "For those of you who have yet to meet him, this is Chod. He's the hero of the forest trolls, and we would not be where we are without his aid."

"He's also the hero of the mountain trolls," adds Kronan.

"The arctic trolls stake claim as well." Chief Laojin smirks.

"How about we just say 'Hero of the Trolls'?" I laugh.

Chief Lida nods. "I have heard tales of your bravery since you left our beaches. Long have the days been since the trolls have left such a mark on the world. It will be an honor to fight by such a hero."

The biggest of the desert trolls steps in front of me. His heavy breaths rattle the bone armor on his chest as he looks down at me. "I am called Abo. You tried to help me once," his voice booms a deep baritone, "but I was too blind to see it." He extends his arm. "If you fight for the trolls, then we will fight for you."

"No." I shake my head, and a deep frown sets on Abo's face. "You will not fight for me. If you fight, then you fight *with* me, because we're in this together."

I clasp his forearm and squeeze.

His scowl shifts into something resembling a smile, and he clamps a vice-like grip around my arm. "It has been spoken."

"It has been spoken," the four desert trolls echo, and Abo returns to his position among them.

Gord crosses his arms and leans closer to Kronan. "If they blow any more smoke up his loincloth, he may get lost in the clouds." His attempt at a whisper is loud enough that everyone in the circle hears it.

Taryn and Kronan snicker.

Chief Rizza narrows her eyes at Gord and clears her throat. "There is still much to do as we prepare for the impending battle. The dwarven blacksmiths will be forging as many weapons fit for a troll as they can in the time we have, and we now have access to the items stored within Seascape's vaults. I suggest we send a small party from each tribe to sort through the items and decide what will be most fitting. We must not be swayed by the glamour of wondrous artifacts but choose the items that will aid our cause. Once you've decided on who will go, meet me atop the terrace."

The trolls split up into their respective tribes, and Chief Rizza finally has a moment to talk to me in private. "It is good to have you back among your people."

"It's good to be back." I place a hand on her shoulder. "Good call about the vaults. There are way too many trolls to fit inside."

She smiles. "I trust your time in Goldspire was fruitful?"

I give her a mischievous grin. "It was. I've got a few new tricks up my sleeve."

"I look forward to seeing them." She lets her arm fall to her side. "King Orso has permitted us to use the royal training grounds this evening. I'm sure there's much for a hero to do, but we would be honored to have your company."

"I wouldn't miss it."

"Good. I will see you then."

Chief Rizza rejoins the forest trolls, where Taryn is still playing with the young phoenix, feeding her something from his pocket. Rizza gathers Gord and Ismora and heads for the steps. Kronan and Brutus follow, representing the mountain trolls. For the arctic trolls, Chief Laojin and Senzala go. The seaside trolls send Chief Lida and Imoko, the little turd who captured me at spearpoint when I was swimming outside their tribal grounds. Abo is the sole representative of his small tribe.

After giving the phoenix a final pet, Taryn returns. "Bro, I can't wait to see the trolls decked out in magical gear."

"We'll take every advantage we can get." I gaze up at the castle where the midday sun is starting its descent. The closer we get the faster time seems to move. "Let's go find King Orso."

29. SHADOWS

I fill Taryn in on as much as I can while we go in search of King Orso. Limery and Caustic stay in the square with the trolls, which is probably a lot more fun for both of them. I tell Taryn about Pressley and the manticore first, and then move to my own adventure. When I get to the trials, I gloss over the challenges and focus on my new abilities instead.

"Bro." He looks at me with disbelief. "So, you're telling me that you can rage indefinitely as long as you're hitting shit and that you basically have an unkillable Constitution while you're doing it? That's so OP. And now you've got dreadbeasts and a dragon to go along with it. Why don't we just send you in alone to bash your way to the gates and then join you after?"

"If it were only that easy." I rub my forehead.

"You are the main character, after all." He grins. "Just think of the stories they'd tell about you."

"Oh, shut up." I shove him in the shoulder. "I never would have gotten this far without you. Without everyone who has helped me along this path."

"I'm just messing with you." He pushes me playfully. "I have a feeling we're going to need every trick you've got when the time comes. It's a shame that we couldn't convince the beastkin to join us."

"Yeah, none of them were willing to go against the emperor's will. It speaks a lot to how much they respect her, but it's a fucking shame." I kick a loose pebble from the courtyard, and it hits a dwarf carrying a crate of potions.

"Hey, I'm walking here!" The potions rattle as he adjusts his grip.

"Sorry!" I throw my hands up in apology and try not to laugh at how much he reminds me of a New Yorker before I return my attention to Taryn. "Still, if you would've told me a month ago that we'd have seven kingdoms and all of the trolls on our side when it finally came time to fight, I never would have believed you."

Taryn laughs. "What if I told you that Richard was the one responsible for getting us there?"

"Ugh." I let out a long sigh. "I still don't trust him, but it is what it is at this point."

We arrive at the castle entrance, and the guards step aside for us to pass.

"Follow me." Taryn motions toward one of the stairwells. "He should be in his chambers drafting letters to send abroad."

"We've been talking a lot about me. What have you been up to this whole time? More than just sitting in meetings, I hope."

"So many meetings." Taryn rubs his eyes and then pinches the bridge of his nose. "But there have been some benefits to being here. Analyzing plants in the royal gardens gained me enough experience for another level. Check this out." He stops in front of a dark corridor and waggles his brows. "Hey, what's that?" He points over my shoulder.

I follow the direction of his finger, searching the ancient stone of the circular stairwell for anything out of the ordinary, but there's nothing there. "Very funny, Tar—" I turn back around but he's gone, and Ruby and Flubs are standing at my feet.

The slime gurgles as it clings to my feet, its cool body tickling the space between my toes. I fight the urge to kick it away.

I turn back toward the dark corridor we just passed. "I'm sure you're real sneaky, but you know I have nightvision." I look down the empty hall, and my nightvision cuts through the shadows. It's just a storage alcove, and there's not even a door at the end.

"Where the hell did he go?" I ask Ruby, but she just stares at me.

Did he just sneak off and leave me with his pets? He has the Cloak of Silence that allows him to move silently but if this is his idea of a joke, he's definitely been sitting in too many meetings.

I kneel and stroke Ruby behind the ears. "Not his best work."

Something grabs me around the midsection, followed by a shrill scream that echoes through the stairwell. A shiver runs up my spine as I turn to see two arms reaching out from the darkness. Taryn pounces from the corridor, screaming like a banshee, and I roar in alarm, falling on my back and tumbling down several stairs. Taryn watches me fall, cackling like it's the funniest thing he's ever seen.

"What the hell was that?" I rub my backside as I climb to my feet.

"Shadow Cloak." He grins. "That's what I used my ability point on. I figured it would be pretty useful in the shadowlands."

"And they say I'm the asshole." I chuckle. "How's it work exactly? I have nightvision and couldn't see you at all."

He gives me a mischievous grin. "It's a shadow druid ability that gives us increased stealth at night or in the shadows. As long as I don't attack, I'm pretty damn sneaky. Not even nightvision can see me when I'm hidden. It doesn't even need to be full darkness; I can blend in with twilight."

"No shit? That's badass. Kind of like the trolls' Camouflage ability, except you can actually move around." My brow furrows when I realize what using his ability point on Shadow Cloak means. He was supposed to be saving it for something else. "Why didn't you use your ability point on Scry? Don't get me wrong, I think you made a great decision, but I thought you wanted to track down Jude and Glenn."

"I did. I mean, I do." He sighs. "This is bigger than me now and having Shadow Cloak is going to make me a lot more useful than being able to track down those two assholes. Besides, if they're in Mosstar, I have zero doubt that they'll make their presence known."

I wrap an arm around his shoulder. The fuckers do always show up when we least expect it. "If they do, we'll make them pay."

He nods solemnly. "That's enough of that, though. You want to hear something cool? King Orso told me there's an active dungeon located in the volcano underneath Seascape. I knew the city was built on a dormant volcano, but I had no idea that there was a dungeon down there. I wish we had more time to explore it."

"After the trials, the thought of a volcanic dungeon makes my stomach turn." I grimace. "How about we add it to our bucket list for when all of the fighting is done."

"Deal."

The kingsguard allows us entry into King Orso's office, and we find him leaning over a sheet of parchment with a black feather quill in his hand. The king's lips move silently as he formulates his thoughts, the quill hovering an inch off the parchment.

Limery's parents flutter in the air to each side of the king. Bazel holds a letter sealed with wax clenched in his spindly fingers. Lillith smiles as we enter, pressing a finger to her lips for us to remain quiet.

King Orso's desk is a thick slab of black stone flecked with red. It reminds me of Destroyer the way the red catches the light of the sconces. Large jewels serve as paperweights, pinning down a plethora of letters and scrolls. Shelves line the walls behind him, each one filled with leather-bound books, ancient tomes, scrolls, and stacks of parchment.

The king's face is set in deep contemplation as he writes the letter. He pauses, mumbling something to himself, and then scribbles another line before finally setting down the quill. After blowing the ink dry, he folds the letter and stamps the wax seal with his royal crest, never once acknowledging our presence.

"Please deliver this one to the Pruxford Council." He hands the letter to Lillith and then turns to Bazel. "Yours will be going to the Mistville Court."

"It will be done, Your Majesty." Bazel bows, and both imps head for the exit.

They stop for a moment in front of Taryn and I.

"I trust Limery is well." Lillith gives me a motherly look that says he better be.

"Never better." I grin. "He's down in the square with Caustic. You should see him on your way out."

"Good. We'll see you soon, Chod." She winks, and they disappear out the door.

Traveling by portal, I'm sure she'll be back within the hour. For Bazel, though, I have no idea what the journey to Mistville entails.

"Chod, I'm glad to see you return. Forgive me for not greeting you upon arrival, but there is so much to do." King Orso stands from his desk. "Who would have thought a day would come where the trolls are the second-most populous race in Seascape?"

"It was kind of you to offer your vaults to arm them."

"It was the least I could do. What good is it to sit on our treasures when we are fighting for our right to live?" He gestures for us to sit. "We'll need to keep this brief, but tell me, how was your travel abroad?"

"Eventful," I say as I take a seat in the plush leather chair. Somehow, it manages to comfortably fit my large troll body. Taryn takes the chair to the right, and Ruby curls between his legs. Flubs gurgles as he crawls into the vial around Taryn's neck. "I attained the Warforged class, Caustic is now strong enough for me to ride him, Pressley the death knight acquired a manticore as his mount, and I found another hero who wants to help us fight."

"Good news all around. A manticore, you say?" He strokes his beard. "A fearsome beast of legend from what I recall."

"She'll be dangerous on the battlefield, and we now have two more options for aerial support."

He nods. "Good, good. Have you learned any more details regarding when you and the other heroes may be forced to return?"

I shake my head. I haven't heard anything else from Valery since the trials, and judging by her tone, she has her own problems to deal with. "Unfortunately, no. When are we planning to attack?"

King Orso sighs. "You said that we may have as little as a week. If that's our timeline, then we need to be ready in two days' time. That means we need to gather our forces in Pruxford tomorrow. It will give us a day to finalize our plans with the other kingdoms before we attack. Our soldiers and mages have all gathered in the city. They will be the frontlines of the assault, and citizens are still traipsing in from across the kingdom. Those that are unable to reach the city in time will stay behind to guard the portal in the event of an attack." He massages his temple. "There is very little room for error."

"I understand." It's honestly amazing how they've been able to rally so much in such a short amount of time. Then again, Seascape has been on high alert since the behemoth came through the portal. "Do we have a plan of attack yet?"

"Not as firm as I would like. The imps have been instrumental in transporting information between kingdoms in record time. I have an idea of each kingdom's forces, and the heroes, but it will be hard to know for sure until we are all gathered."

"You want me on the frontlines?" I ask.

He leans forward, and his forehead scrunches. "I want you to do what you think is best. You know the heroes and what they are capable of better than I, and I know the trolls would follow you to the ends of Mythos if you asked. Our objective is to end Valmar once and for all. The undead outside the city and the elves within are merely obstacles in our way."

"Your Highness, if I may." Taryn, who has been unusually quiet, raises his hand.

"Go on." King Orso sits back in his chair.

"I think I might have a solution for defeating Valmar, or at least how to get to him."

King Orso and I both perk up. Taryn has always been a great tactician, so I'm intrigued by what he's come up with.

"I want to use the Amulet of Undetection that Jon crafted." When he sees the look of confusion on my face, he elaborates. "It's an item that allows the wearer to pass by undead without detection unless they are actively engaged with them. I already have my Cloak of Silence and the Smuggler's Boots that allow me to walk without making noise or leaving tracks. And now that I've unlocked Shadow Cloak, I can hide among the shadows. With the amulet, I could walk right into the city without being spotted."

"And then what?" I raise my hands, palms up. "What's your plan to kill Valmar when you find him? It's not a bad idea, but you're not exactly an offensive juggernaut. We don't even know how strong Valmar actually is. What are you going to do if it's just you and him all alone?"

"That's the part I'm still working out. I was hoping that between seven kingdoms, someone might have a weapon capable of killing him. And if not..." He reaches into his cloak and pulls out the Shadow Daggers. The twin daggers have broken blades but when he holds them, shadowy blades form that can bypass armor and drain an enemy's health directly. "I was thinking a surprise attack with these." He looks to King Orso expectantly.

King Orso strokes his beard as he ponders the situation. "I fear Chod is right. It's an intriguing prospect, but Valmar will most certainly have his castle warded for intruders. Bypassing the undead might get you into the city ahead of us, but it does not guarantee you entry into the castle. As far as weapons go, it's not so simple. Valmar walks hand-in-hand with death. Save the death knight, necromancy is not practiced within our kingdoms, and we don't know the true breadth of his power. While we have strategies to deal with the undead, Valmar is a different matter, and I fear a single strike will not slay him, no matter the weapon. However, I will present the idea to the council and perhaps they will have a better idea of how to utilize your skillset."

Taryn nods, sitting back in his chair. I can tell he's disappointed, but I agree with King Orso. The likelihood that this war could be won so easily is almost zero.

I tap Taryn on the hand. "Don't worry. We're going to figure this out."

Before he can respond, there's a knock on the door, and an imp I don't recognize enters the room.

She dips her head slightly. "I have word from Wandermere, Your Majesty."

"Give me a moment." King Orso says to the imp as he stands, his gaze shifting from me to Taryn. "We leave for Pruxford tomorrow. Make the most of what time you have."

Taryn and I take our leave, and the door closes behind us.

I squeeze him on the shoulder. "Ready to meet Dorothy?"

30. TROLLBREAKER

Taryn and I stop by the portal to find Limery before we go in search of Dorothy. She and Pressley were headed to find a tavern, and the little guy would never forgive me if I went without him. The trolls are disappointed to see their entertainment go, but it's the goblins who are inconsolable after Caustic flies off to hunt.

A tear runs down Cheevus's cheek as he watches Caustic disappear among the clouds.

The goblin leader looks up at me with determination in his orange eyes. "Cheevus serve many masters in his life. He never dreams to serve a dragon."

"Don't worry, Cheevus." I kneel beside him and pat the wiry fellow on his bony back. "He'll be back."

The mangy wolf nuzzles against Cheevus, and he climbs on its back. The goblin leader turns to his kin who still stare longingly after Caustic. "We go. Find food."

The troupe of goblins disappears into one of the side streets amidst a patter of bare feet.

"Strange little dudes." Taryn chuckles as we head further into the city.

"See yous laters!" Limery shouts from my shoulder, waving to the trolls. He turns back around and sighs contentedly. "Limmy likes the trollses. They's fun."

I pull up my map as we move against the flow of dwarven citizens retrieving weapons and armor from the square.

Since Pressley agreed to join our party after he acquired the manticore, I can finally track his location on my map. I find his marker located at The Gargoyle Inn, an elaborate stone building with intimidating gargoyles perched on every corner of the roof. The stonework is so detailed that it includes indentations around the gargoyle's feet as if their claws are actually digging into the stone.

Inside, the tavern on the ground floor is rowdy with flowing ale and chatter. Ebony and ivory dwarves from across the kingdom intermingle, and their newly acquired weapons and armor are spread about the tables among even more empty mugs.

"Me grandpappy was a great warrior." A drunken ivory dwarf wearing a helm sways like a flower in the breeze. The helm is well-made, with a warhammer-shaped noseguard that comes down to his salt-and-pepper mustache. "This helm belonged to him." He knocks the helm with his fist and nearly falls from his chair before I catch him.

"Easy there." I lift him beneath the armpits and position him back on the chair.

Taryn covers his mouth and leans in. "These guys are sloshed."

"Can you blame them?" Tomorrow, they'll be going to war. These precious moments of camaraderie could be their last.

I search the room for Pressley, but his massive frame is nowhere to be seen. After scouring the room, I finally spot Dorothy in the corner, hiding in the shadows. Her brow is knitted, and she wears a murderous frown as she stares into a half-empty mug of ale. I wonder what has her so sour.

"There she is." I point. "I'll introduce you, and then we can order a drink." When we arrive at the table, I rest my hands on the chair across from Dorothy. "Having second thoughts?"

She looks at me with a scowl for a fraction of a second before it shifts into a bright smile.

"No, just thinking." She laughs. "You get the trolls all settled in?"

"Something like that. They're gearing up right now." I step aside and usher Taryn in. "This is Taryn. I don't think you two have ever formally met."

Dorothy extends a hand, and they shake. "Not officially, but I saw you on a few streams together. It's easy to see who the brains of the operation is."

"Game recognizes game." Taryn grins, elbowing me in the side. "I caught a few of yours as well. You're a hell of a jungler."

"Depends on who you ask, I guess." She gives me a knowing look that tells me even though we're cool, I'll never be able to live that moment down. "Well, are you going to stand there all day or are you going to have a seat?"

Limery hops from my shoulder to the closest chair and leans against the table. "Limmy wants a drinks."

"I'll grab a round for everyone." Judging by how crowded the place is, I'll have better luck at the bar than flagging someone down, but even the bar is packed three to four dwarves deep.

I tower over everyone around me, making it hard to ignore all the staring. Most of these dwarves come from the smaller towns and villages outside the capital, where troll appearances are all but unheard of. At least they're staring out of curiosity and not malice.

While I'm waiting in line, I glance over my shoulder and notice Limery has stolen Dorothy's mug. He tilts it back, and amber liquid trickles down his chin.

Taryn and Dorothy are both laughing as they chat it up. For being so skeptical of her, he seems to be getting very chummy. Or maybe it's just the effect of being around someone from our world with similar interests.

"Oy!" The bartender shouts, and I turn to see he's looking at me. "Friends of the king don't wait. What'll it be?"

"A pitcher of your best ale, please." I hold up three fingers. "And some mugs."

He nods and fills the pitcher to the brim, placing three mugs on the bar beside it. I reach over the dwarves in front of me, pay for the ale, and grab the pitcher.

When I return to the table, Limery lets out a loud belch and smacks his lips. "Yummies."

I narrow my eyes at the imp. "What did I tell you about stealing?"

"Limmy didn't steals." He shakes his head rapidly.

"I gave it to him." Dorothy meets my eye. "I'm not much of a drinker."

"More for us, then." Taryn takes the pitcher from me and fills our mugs, pouring a splash into Dorothy's. He raises his tankard. "To fighting the good fight."

We clink our mugs, and I let the cool amber ale wash away my troubles if only for a moment.

"Where's Pressley?" I set my drink on the table. "I figured he'd be with you."

"He's in his room. He said something about wanting some alone time." She arches her brow. "Not sure how to take that."

Taryn laughs. "He's a bit of a loner. Probably wants a chance to gather his thoughts before the shit hits the fan."

"It's still crazy to me that this program was developed to help prisoners." She sits back, gesturing at the tavern. "I mean, look at this. There's not a gamer in the world who wouldn't do anything to experience this, and Mythos isn't even talking about it."

The dwarves at one of the nearby tables bust out a chorus of some drinking song about axes stuck in the wall, and Limery flies over to join them.

"It's something else, that's for sure." Taryn takes another swig of his ale. "Chod tells me you want to join the fight. If your streams are anything to go by, we'll be lucky to have you."

"You flatter him this much, too?" Dorothy smirks. "If so, I see why he keeps you around."

Taryn rolls his eyes. "I'm just a nice guy."

"Sure you are." Dorothy laughs. "So, what's the plan? I'm itching for a fight."

"You won't be waiting long. We leave for Pruxford tomorrow." I take a swig of my ale. "Once all of the forces are gathered, the leaders will finalize battle plans and then we attack the next morning. I expect the heroes will lead the charge, so you'll have plenty of opportunity to scratch that itch." When I finish my ale, I stretch my arms overhead. "We're gonna head back up to the castle soon. King Orso opened his vault to the trolls, and they're going to be training with their new weapons. You want to come?"

"Do I want to watch some trolls smash about with their shiny new weapons?" She shrugs. "Sure. Not like I have much better to do."

We climb the steps to the royal courtyards just as the sun dips beneath the flying buttresses of the magnificent castle. The setting sun paints the sky with shades of vermillion and coral, igniting the clouds with a purple sheen and casting the castle's many spires as silhouettes. From our vantage point, it's like we're walking into a work of art.

Dorothy stops at the top of the steps, taking in the view. "This never gets old."

"I'm gonna miss it. That's for sure." Taryn kneels to scratch Ruby behind the ears, and the jackal grunts in pleasure. "Back home, you'd be lucky to catch a sliver of sunset passing through the buildings."

For the past few days, I've tried to keep my mind on the task at hand—saving everyone I care about. Taryn's comment is a reminder of what comes after. My days in Mythos are numbered, and this time when I log out, there's no coming back.

I give Limery's leg a gentle squeeze as he sits on my shoulder. Everything I do over the next few days is so that he can live a happy life long after I'm gone. For now, though, I push those thoughts to the back of my mind. Right now, I need to focus on preparation.

In the rear of the castle, there's a sprawling courtyard that ends at a rocky cliffside overlooking the turbulent waters of the sea. The center of the courtyard has stone tiles depicting the warhammer of the Brightgaze crest. To one side, there's a fountain with a statue of a dragon that shoots water from its open maw. To the other, a dwarf holds a warhammer overhead, and water spouts from each face of the weapon. Topiaries shaped like animals are speckled throughout.

Aside from the handful of blood dwarves that guard the entrance to the castle, the courtyard is occupied by nothing but trolls. They're split into five groups, with each tribe gathered around its leaders as they pull a seemingly endless supply of items from satchels no bigger than a backpack. A few trolls have already equipped armor, and the polished metal gleams in the fading sun. Fortunately for them, enchanted armor resizes itself to fit the wearer.

Limery zooms across the courtyard to see the action up close, but Taryn, Dorothy, and I stand back to watch. Among the forest trolls, Gord holds a bag while Chief Rizza removes its contents. By the looks of it, each item was selected based on the individual skillsets of each troll. She hands Yashi a pearlescent bow that's intricately carved. It has an obsidian grip and a golden string that gives off an aura as she holds it. Ismora is gifted a set of daggers as well as a sword unlike any other that I've seen in Mythos. It has a curved blade that is only sharpened on one side, and a red ribbon wraps the grip. Tormara still has her enchanted daggers from our venture into Paltras Ruins, but she's given a pair of vambraces with hooked spikes, turning her forearms into deadly weapons.

For the guardian trolls, the chief hands out an assortment of maces, axes, and warhammers. One thing that trolls and dwarves have in common is our desire to smash things. A few of the guardians select shields, but the troll way is to dish out pain. With only a few days to prepare for this battle, I doubt any of them were comfortable learning a completely new fighting style. For herself, the chief takes a shortsword that has a red hue to the blade. While the majority of trolls prefer the freedom of movement over wearing armor, I see many wearing spaulders and vambraces, and a few who have donned helmets.

I'm reminded of when Taryn and I were lucky enough to search through the vault. It's where I found Destroyer, thanks to Kurzol's guidance, as well as my expandable satchel and the Mysterious Green Egg that would one day become Caustic.

King Orso's generosity has been the difference between life and death on countless occasions, and it still proves so. He could have had armor or weapons forged, but instead, he's given away the treasures of the Brightgaze lineage. The weapons and armor the trolls wear are priceless, many of them gifts from foreign kingdoms given long before the portals closed.

As I look around the courtyard, I recognize a few of the weapons Kurzol showed me before I settled on Destroyer. A seaside troll wields the long pike capable of dealing air damage, and a female mountain troll has the slightly smaller twin warhammers that are meant for speed bludgeoning. Brutus holds a massive axe forged from the same metal as Destroyer. Both weapons were forged in the heart of a volcano, and I had wavered between the axe and the warhammer, but Destroyer seemed more practical at the time. Seeing Brutus's corded muscles flex as the axe cuts through the air, it's undeniably badass, and it'slarge enough to rival Peacemaker in size.

I leave Dorothy and Taryn to join Brutus, equipping Destroyer for him to see. "You have good taste. That weapon will serve you well."

He raises the axe and nods. "For the tribe."

I raise my warhammer, in a kind of cheers of weapons. "For the tribe."

Maybe he's not such an asshole after all.

Nearby, Chief Lida is nearly finished outfitting the seaside trolls. She had her people's best interest in mind as she chose her weapons, bringing enough spears and pikes for the tribe to replace their wooden weapons with metal.

The desert trolls all wield massive morning stars, and the spiked maces look terrifying in their hands. Abo pulls a silvery-green helm etched with leaf patterns from his bag, handing it to the troll missing an ear. The disfigured troll shoves Abo in the chest and then lets out a deep laugh that carries over the courtyard. When other tribes turn to look at the disturbance, laughter rings out. The one-eared troll slides the helm over his head and then equips the full set of armor. It's some of the most beautiful plate mail I've ever seen, almost like a layer of metallic vines have covered the troll's sun-worn skin.

Once all of the items have been doled out, the trolls show off their new weapons and armor to the other tribes. It's like watching kids show their new outfits on the first day of school. Malak is particularly proud of his golden warhammer as he swings it through the air.

While trolls are natural warriors, these weapons will raise their destructive capabilities to new heights. Unfortunately for the trolls, most of them have no mana, so they can't activate any special abilities. Any passive abilities will still work as intended, though. These are powerful weapons, each one buffed with stats and more deadly than anything the blacksmiths could craft on such short notice.

I clap Gord on the shoulder when I see him. He already has Peacemaker and the bone armor, so he was the only troll not to receive anything. "Was someone a bad troll this year? I hope you're not feeling left out."

He lifts Peacemaker, and his mouth curls upward around his broken tusk. "I have all I need right here."

Chief Rizza stands off to the side, admiring her new weapon. Up close, I notice a flame pattern etched into the metal.

"That's a nice sword," I say.

"Its name was Trollbreaker. A gift from Vanaria to Seascape during a time when the trolls were feared for their might, not just as monsters." She holds it up, and the metal seems to flicker under the last rays of sunlight. "If I had mana, every strike would deal burn damage. I'm sure you can see why it was named."

"I do." A weight settles in my chest as I imagine how it earned its name. "Why would you take it?"

"Who am I to let the past define my future?" The flames of the sword reflect in her golden eyes. "You're the one who opened my eyes. We're here to blaze a new future. How fitting would it be for a weapon meant to break trolls to be their savior?"

She grins as she places it in the scabbard.

"How fitting, indeed." I return her smile. "I spoke to King Orso earlier. Tomorrow, we leave for Pruxford."

She nods. "So I heard. Are you ready?"

I look over the hundreds of trolls gathered in the courtyard, each one armed with some of the best weapons in the kingdom. Am I ready to go to battle knowing that it'll be the last time I'll ever see some of them? Because no matter how strong we are or what weapons we have, I don't see a future where every troll makes it back. The true cost of war is paid in lives lost, and there's nothing I can do to change that.

"No, I'm not ready, but *we* will be."

31. ANCIENT PROTECTIONS

Thanks to Taryn's connections, Limery and I have a room in the castle for the evening. With how crowded the city is, I'm not sure how Pressley and Dorothy were able to find a room at the Gargoyle Inn. I imagine the death knight's intimidating presence was enough to convince some of the villagers that they'd be better off sharing a room for one evening.

If the amount of ale they drank was any indication, they wouldn't be remembering most of their stay anyway.

The guest quarters in the castle are remarkable, not that I expected anything less. The only other time I've stayed somewhere this opulent was when I visited Vanaria. If I had to compare, I think Seascape takes the cake. Our room has a four-poster bed resting against the far wall, its frame carved from dark gray marble with veins of gold. The four posts are more like columns of elaborate dwarven knotwork. Lace curtains adorned with seafoam-green pearls drape from the frame. As beautiful as it is, the mattress is even more comfortable and covered with the finest silk sheets and soft pillows. Not that I need it with my troll body, but it's still nice.

Limery sighs as he falls onto his back, sinking into the lush fabrics. He digs his fingers into the blankets. "Oh, yes. Limmy likes."

The rest of the room has an air of sophistication. There's a desk, shelves filled with books, and figurines carved from precious stones placed all around the room. A long leather couch and reading chair make up the lounge area in front of the hearth. The fire within radiates a gentle warmth. There's a tapestry of an erupting volcano on one wall and a large painting of a female blood dwarf on the other. Her vibrant red sideburns are braided and hang across her shoulders. *Queen Lumona Brightgaze* is inscribed on the metal plaque at the bottom.

I crawl into bed and sink into the mattress. After a long day of socializing, I welcome the gentle embrace. Tomorrow will be a busy day.

The next morning, there's a regional notification waiting for us when we wake up.

Regional Alert! *The time has come to join King Orso as he fights against the darkness. All able-bodied dwarves are to report to Seascape Square this morning to travel to Pruxford. Those who have not yet gathered weapons and armor must report to one of the mobile armories located throughout the city. Stay alert for further updates from your king.*

I send a message to Pressley telling him we'll meet him in the square after breakfast. Then, I find Taryn and we head to the great hall, where royal banners hang from the rafters and jeweled chandeliers paint a kaleidoscope of colors on the ceiling. Before us, several rows of long tables are filled with platters of food.

We're some of the last to arrive, and for the first time, I see the scope of King Orso's inner circle. The king sits at the royal table with Kurzol and Lady Brollen, the ice mage from Sandholde, as well as two generals who will be in charge of the infantry. Their table is located at the far end of the hall, sitting perpendicular to two rows of tables that stretch the length of the hall.

Taryn informs me of who the rest of the dwarves are as we find a place to sit.

The various tables are filled with kingsguard, clerics, and mages, along with some of the nobility and higher-ranking officials in the city. Together, these are the king's most trusted advisors and most powerful magic wielders—the dwarves he trusts with his life and the fate of his people. It's an honor to be counted among them.

Everyone talks in hushed voices as if speaking at full volume might erupt the dormant volcano slumbering beneath the city. I can't even imagine how much there is to coordinate, not just from Seascape but across all of the kingdoms. Imps come and go by the minute, delivering scrolls, letters, and sometimes verbal messages.

Once we take our seats, Limery dives into his food like he hasn't eaten in days, but I can't seem to focus on the plate before me. My mind is elsewhere, consumed by my own obligations. I need to get to Pruxford and reconvene with the heroes. As much as I want to be in the know about the war plan as a whole, I know it's not my place. I have to trust that King Orso, King Favian, Chief Rizza, and the other leaders can handle their own forces. Not only that but that they can coordinate together. I may be a strong fighter, but I know next to nothing about controlling an army, let alone multiple. Even with my horrors, we're more like a stampede than a tactically trained unit. My job is to take the most powerful fighters in Mythos and wreak havoc on the battlefield. We're the hammer of Mythos, and the leaders are the hands that guide us.

I pull up my message interface so that I can send Michael the paladin a message. Thanks to the Oath of Protection, I'm able to contact him even though we're not in a party.

·   ·   ·

Message (Chod): *We'll be returning to Pruxford in a few hours. Can you gather all of the heroes together by then?*

I expect to wait a while for him to respond, but he answers almost immediately.

Incoming Message (Michael): *Already done. This place is pure chaos right now, but we've been keeping close and training together. We've all gained at least a couple of levels since you left. I hope your travels were as beneficial.*

"You good over there?" Taryn looks at me with concern, the honey from the biscuit he's holding dripping onto the plate. "You've barely said anything since we sat down."

"Sorry, I was just thinking." I massage my eyes with my palms. "I sent Michael a message. He says the heroes are all together and that Pruxford is chaos."

"I bet." He takes a bite of the biscuit, and crumbs fall into his beard. "I'm sure some of the kingdoms are already arriving."

Limery burps and covers his mouth with spindly fingers. "Oopsies."

I can't help but laugh at how nothing fazes him. We're in a room surrounded by royalty, mages, and nobility, and he acts the same as he does around the trolls.

When I finally take a moment to focus on my food, to no surprise, it's delicious. I indulge in crisp bacon, savory sausages stuffed with spices, and a purple egg that's so spicy it leaves my tongue tingling. The food takes my mind off everything if only for a moment.

When we finally leave the castle, there's already a crowd formed in the square. We wait atop the terrace, looking down upon hundreds of soldiers in plate armor that await King Orso's command to enter the portal. A train of wagons loaded with supplies spills down the streets and deeper into the city.

From our vantage point, there's not a section of street that isn't occupied. Though I can't see them, I'm sure the trolls are down there somewhere.

The only place where there's any breathing room is the circle of space about three feet wide surrounding Pressley and the manticore. Dorothy is the only one brave enough to stand beside the death knight. I wave to them, and Pressley lifts his gauntlet in acknowledgment.

"This is crazy." Taryn leans on the balustrade. "Reminds me of the city on New Year's Eve."

A shadow moves across the crowd, eliciting gasps as Caustic's billowing wings announce his arrival. He lands next to us with a thud, his green scales shimmering in the morning sun.

I reach out to him through our bond. *"How was your night?"*

"The sheep in the countryside are more flavorful than those in Goldspire."

"I hope you weren't a glutton." Looking at the crowd below us, a few missing sheep are the least of their worries.

Caustic blows warm air against my shoulder. *"They should be honored that I desired their flock."*

Before I have the chance to explain property ownership to him, I hear the clank of plate mail as the guards escort King Orso from the castle. We step to the side, joining the rest of his entourage as the king takes his place overlooking his people.

He wears his battle armor, all black except for the red breastplate engraved with a silver warhammer. An obsidian horn covered in gilded runes hangs by his side. In his hand, he grips the shaft of a mighty warhammer. The head of the weapon is black and flecked with red, the same as Destroyer and the axe that Brutus now carries. The sides of the hammer are engraved with gilded knotwork, each pattern centered with a rune. Three sockets run along the upper half of the shaft, each one fitted with an enchanted stone. I watched the king wield it only once when the behemoth attacked Seascape, but I saw enough of its power in that moment.

King Orso clears his throat. When he speaks, his voice is magically amplified and carries across the city. "Seascape, I address you today not only as your king but as a citizen of Mythos. Generations past, before any of us had taken our first breaths, the portals far and wide were locked, and Seascape was cut off from the world at large. In these times, our ancestors did what we as dwarves always do. They persevered. Our kingdom flourished in isolation even as a great darkness lurked beyond the portal languishing in our city's heart. We thrived, and in doing so, many forgot about the atrocities that our forebears faced in the greatest war Mythos has ever known."

King Orso lets the heavy words settle on the crowd. "I was not afforded that luxury. As a prince, I was raised to remember the battles my ancestors fought, the lives that were lost, and the darkness that would one day return. I prayed that I would not be the one forced to answer that call, for I wanted what all leaders should want for their people. Peace and prosperity. Unfortunately, the gods have other plans—for me and for you. We've been preparing for this moment since the portal first stirred back to life. When the shackles broke and fast-travel once again became possible, we compounded our efforts even more."

He takes the obsidian horn from his side. "Not many know that there are ancient protections built into our city. Defenses that a king may call upon if his lands are ever under siege. I will not sit idly by and wait for war to come to us. In order to protect our home, we must take the offensive. Therefore today, I call forth a garrison to aid us on the battlefield as we defend our way of life."

King Orso lifts the horn to his lips and blows, his red cheeks puffing as a cavernous note echoes all around. The buildings shake as the reverberations wrack the city. I feel the thrum through my bones, and a piece of stone crashes against the courtyard.

There are shouts of surprise from below, and I look up to see the gargoyles sculpted upon the castle moving. Red fissures sprout upon their stone bodies like molten lava as all across the city, the stone guardians spring to life.

My hair stands on end, and even the kingsguard are awestruck as the gargoyles pry themselves from their posts. The sound of flapping wings fills the air as hundreds of guardians find a place to perch around the square. Heads twist on a swivel, and so many whispers pass through the crowd that even this high up it sounds like a den of snakes.

King Orso lets the horn fall to his side once again. "There is a darkness out there that wishes to subjugate us all, to grind us to dust beneath a boot of disorder and chaos. I do not intend to let that happen. When we march on Mosstar, your king will not sit in a tower watching the battle unfold. I will be by your side, ready to bleed and die for you and yours. So I ask you this, who will fight side-by-side with your king?"

The words boom through the city as King Orso lifts his hammer overhead. His entire body takes on a golden aura, and when the resounding call of the dwarves thunders in response, a shimmer sweeps across the city, buffing every dwarf with some unknown power.

King Orso lowers the warhammer, and his face is carved from stone as he passes by. Passion burns in the depths of his eyes like a volcano ready to erupt. If I were one of his subjects, I'd follow him into the depths of hell and back again.

That time may come but first, we go to Pruxford.

32. ALL QUIET ON THE PRUXFORD FRONT

I stand behind Caustic as he steps into the whirl of white energy. While his body is still capable of fitting through the portal, his wings protrude beyond the arch, even when tucked. Lucky for us, the magic powering fast-travel doesn't seem to mind, and he vanishes in the ethereal swirl.

Our group exits into the square, which is just as crowded as Seascape's, if not more so. The first time I visited, this area was full of merchants, peddlers, tourists, and travelers all coming and going. Now, it's a one-way route as guards and city officials direct traffic from the platform toward the outer gate.

Even though Pruxford is a gnomish kingdom, a large percentage of their city guard is composed of different races. Though they come in many shapes and sizes, the pearlescent armor is their defining characteristic. The city officials are mostly gnomes, easily recognizable in their matching robes and biretta hats topped with fuzzy little balls.

"Wow, that's beautiful." Dorothy stops and grabs my arm, pointing toward the Crystal Palace on the far side of the city.

The building is like something out of a fairy tale with its translucent crystal in hues of green, pink, and violet. Emerald and amethyst spires catch the light of the morning sun and glow like beacons. I remember the first time I set eyes on the shimmering palace. At night, the view was awe-inspiring as the moonlight reflected off the palace's exterior like the Northern Lights.

"Keep it moving!" a guard yells, waving his arms like a traffic cop. He's taller than most, so definitely not a gnome. His pearlescent armor shifts through a rainbow of colors as we pass him. "All foreign kingdoms are assembling outside of the city gates. Keep it moving, people!"

"Alright, alright." Dorothy rolls her eyes. "We're moving."

Our small group looks like a circus of misfits surrounded by dwarves on all sides as we follow the never-ending line toward the outer gate. Taryn leads the way, riding Berry, with Ruby curled in his lap and Flubs peeking from the vial around Taryn's neck. Jordy flanks their right side, the frost goat lowering his horns whenever someone gets too close.

I walk next to Dorothy, sandwiched between Pressley and his manticore on one side and Caustic on the other. Limery stands on the dragon's head, holding onto Caustic's horns like he's a captain at sea. I'm almost certain Caustic has grown a bit more since his feast throughout the Seascape countryside. He's a towering presence, and if his growth continues at this rate, I'm not sure how much longer the portal will make an exception for his size.

Dorothy gawks at the Crystal Palace as the foot traffic slows before we're ushered along again. Even though the guards give Caustic and the manticore a wide berth, they keep us moving.

"This is too many people," Pressley's hollow voice rumbles. "I'll find you once you're settled in."

He grips the reins of his manticore, and she extends her wings, nearly knocking a dwarf over as they take to the air. Caustic has no such qualms as he lumbers beside me, basking in the reverent looks of everyone he passes.

"Not much of a people person, is he?" Dorothy grins as the death knight soars away.

"He's a nice guy." My gaze follows Pressley until he disappears beyond the wall. "Probably just tired of all the sour looks."

She shrugs. "What do you expect? He's a walking bag of bones."

Taryn looks over his shoulder, a few paces in front of us, and smirks. "A can of bones would be a more fitting term."

Dorothy scrunches her brow. "You really have a way with words, you know that?"

"What can I say, I'm a—" Taryn's eyes go wide as saucers as he passes through the gate. He gestures for us to hurry up. "Damn. Bro, you've got to see this."

Caustic's chest rumbles, buying us some space as we push our way through the gate. I don't know what I expect to find on the other side, but this isn't it.

Tents, pavilions, and caravans stretch for as far as I can see around the city's perimeter. It's like we've arrived at an outdoor festival. I spot the blue-and-silver banner of Vanaria, followed by the white and gold of Antadale's catfolk. Further down, there are even more banners that blend together in a multi-colored mosaic.

Chills run up my arm. "This is unbelievable." I can't fight the sense of amazement at seeing so many people banded together under a common cause. When we were traveling from kingdom to kingdom, it always felt like the odds were stacked against us. Even in the council room, surrounded by the leaders of Mythos, it felt like we were outnumbered as we gazed through the portal into Mosstar.

Spending most of my time on the Isle of Mythos, it's easy to forget that Seascape and Vanaria are relatively small kingdoms compared to the vastness of greater Mythos. There are thousands gathered here, maybe tens of thousands, and this isn't even everyone.

"Keep it moving!" a guard shouts from behind, and I realize I'm holding up the procession once again.

"I'll catch up with you all shortly. I want to get a look at our forces." I pat Caustic on the chest, and he lowers his body. "Let's fly."

"First Pressley, now you." Taryn lifts his arm and sniffs under his pit. "Do I smell or something?"

"That's a conversation for another time." I use Caustic's wing to pull myself up, straddling just below the base of his neck. "Hold on, Limery, we're going for a ride."

Caustic shuffles back and forth, and dwarves scatter just before he extends his wings and launches skyward. It's impressive how something his size is able to fly, but the boisterous sound of his wings flapping is proof that it's no easy task.

People rush out from their tents to catch a glimpse of the dragon as we pass over the Vanarian camp. We fly higher until their bodies are like ants as they scurry around. From this height, I can see the far side of the city past the Crystal Palace and the gemstone arena where we fought the sea orcs. To my other side, beyond the camps, there are rolling hills filled with dungeons and the occasional farm or village strewn across the countryside.

Limery laughs like a madman as Caustic dives. My braid whips behind me, and cool wind assaults my face as we plummet toward the earth. I clench my thighs and wedge my claws between Caustic's thick scales to keep from sliding.

At the last moment, Caustic pulls back, sending ripples through the white-and-gold circular tents and pavilions of Antadale. Armored elephants trumpet as we pass, jostling the catfolk sitting in the covered saddles on their backs.

We soar over the colorful array of tents that make up the Ellynmylly camp, and their rainbow banners blow in the breeze of Caustic's wake. At the back of their camp, the eclectic nation has a row of catapults and wagons filled with boulders. Several dozen giants roam through their campgrounds, nearly twice as large as the other races that make up Mythos's Melting Pot.

We reach the final camp, where banners of green and purple make up the Mistville forces. They have the largest caravan of wagons. Some of them are massive, as big as a bus, and resemble giant casks on wheels. Something slithers across the ground near one, and a merfolk activates a massive spigot at the back of the cask-like wagon. Water flows out, and a giant sea snake nearly as long as the mana-infused wyrms rises, basking in the water. Several more slither out from beneath the nearby wagons to enjoy a drink. I'm sure it's a challenge being away from the waters of Mistville, but they came prepared, which is good considering I doubt there will be much water where we're going.

Caustic ascends, flying over the city walls, where guards are stationed around the battlements, before turning to soar over the camp once again. This time, the camps are full of people eager to catch a glimpse of the dragon. Caustic is more than just a powerful weapon to everyone below, he's a symbol, something for them to believe in.

Looking at the kingdoms gathered, we're still waiting for Wandermere to arrive. All of Pruxford's forces are within the city. Even so, we have a more formidable force than I could have ever hoped for.

As we near the Seascape camp, I search for Taryn and Dorothy and find them outside of the largest pavilion, which I assume belongs to King Orso. With its red and silver stripes, it looks almost like a circus tent.

Caustic hovers above the campsite, making it increasingly difficult for the dwarves attempting to stake the tents, and I slide down his backside before he takes off into the hills to go hunting.

"Where's King Orso?" I ask. There are plenty of mages and nobles in the area, but the king and his guards are nowhere to be seen.

"He went straight to the palace." Taryn scratches Berry behind the ears, and the umber bear groans. He looks past me into the endless sea of tents. "I can't believe how many of us there are."

I laugh at Limery as he plays a game with Flubs where the two toss a pebble back and forth. Every time the slime shoots the pebble from his gelatinous body, there's a loud slurping sound that sends Limery cackling.

"Yeah, it's crazy. You're not gonna believe some of the things I saw. The catfolk have elephants, and Mistville have an army of sea snakes nearly as big as wyrms." I turn to Dorothy and gesture over my shoulder. "Ellynmylly is just past the catfolk, if you wanted to say hi to anyone."

"I'm gonna pass." Dorothy shakes her head. "I'm not quite as beloved as you are. I kept a pretty low profile because I had other priorities than being a hero."

Right. Making me pay was all she thought about for the longest time. Even if things are better now, she missed out on a lot because of me. An awkward silence lingers in our little bubble as tents go up all around us. The billowing flap of wings saves me from crawling into a hole as Pressley finally rejoins us.

"You weren't lying. Mythos is going to war." He dismounts from the manticore and removes a handful of bones from his satchel, tossing them on the ground along with some folded canvas. While he's pulling out rods and rope, the bones assemble themselves into skeletons and immediately get to work erecting a tent. "I haven't needed a tent since my transformation, but we should stake our claim to an area before we lose it."

"That's generous of you. And to think, someone called you a bag of bones." Taryn nods in the direction of Dorothy and then settles his gaze on the skeletons as they work. "How many of these guys do you have?"

"Lots and lots." Limery abandons his game with Flubs and perches on Pressley's shoulder. "Limmy seens thems."

Pressley grunts, but there's no telling what it means or who it's intended for.

Eventually, the trolls make their way through the gate. Chief Rizza, Yashi, and Tormara lead the way on the backs of the three mana-infused wyrms. Behind them, Chief Laojin rides a mammoth that made the trip from Frostmoor. He's flanked by Cheevus and the goblins. The rest of the trolls follow, the tribes intermingled. It turns out Ellynmylly isn't the only melting pot. Ours is just a blend of Mythos's so-called monsters.

The trolls lay claim to a field with a copse of trees not far away. While I may have managed to get some of them into a castle, I doubt I'll ever see a troll use a tent.

More dwarves pull up the rear, followed by the troop of gargoyles. The stone guardians position themselves around the perimeter of Seascape's camp before settling into sculpturesque sentries. Each one must weigh a ton, because they leave craters for footprints.

Pressley's skeletons finish setting up the tent, and it's much bigger than I expected. More like a canvas room than a camping tent, and it manages to fit all four of us comfortably with room for Taryn's pets. He and I are used to sleeping under the stars when we're on the road, but it's nice to know we have this as an option since I'm sure there won't be an empty room in the city tonight.

"So, what now?" Taryn plops against Berry, who has staked his claim to a corner. The bear lifts his head, huffs, and then lays back down.

"We should go find Michael and the other heroes while we have time. I doubt there's much else for us to do until the leaders finish meeting."

Taryn groans. "Man, I just got comfortable."

I reach out to Michael, and he responds with their location a few minutes later. The Puzzling Peacock has become home base to the heroes and a few of the challengers who decided to hang around.

"Yo, Pressley." Taryn guides Berry over to the death knight once we're about to leave. "As long as your manticore doesn't eat other people's pets, I've got the hookup for a nice stable in the city. Breebis is the best around." He looks at the manticore with a worried expression. The undead mount sits like a statue at the back of the tent. "She won't eat them, will she?"

A sigh rattles inside the death knight's helm. "For the third time, she does not attack unless ordered. But if you ask me that again, we might test her fondness for bear meat."

I fake a cough to keep from laughing. Dorothy isn't as considerate, and her laughter rings out.

"Come on, don't be like that. I was just making sure." Taryn crosses his arms. "I thought you might want someone to clean her up so she doesn't smell like death before the big battle. But I guess I was wrong."

"She smells like death because she's dead," I mutter under my breath loud enough for Dorothy to hear.

Dorothy leans in, whispering in my ear. "Shh, let him keep digging."

As if it was a premonition, Taryn keeps going. "I trust you. It's just, well..." He puts a hand to his mouth and speaks in a hushed voice. "She's scary looking, and I've heard the stories."

"You know what?" Pressley grabs the manticore's reins. "She could use a bath. It's not like she earned the name Beast Killer or anything. What's the worst that could happen?"

Taryn's eyes go wide. "Wait, maybe this was a—"

I squeeze Taryn's shoulder and usher him along. "Don't worry, bro. They'll be fine."

When we arrive at the gate, several guards stand sentry, barring our entry. There are still the occasional stragglers leaving for the camps, and a few imps zip by carrying messages, but no one seems to be going back into the city.

"What's your business?" a gruff-sounding lizardfolk calls to us as we approach. His purple-scaled hand grips the spear by his side.

I offer him a smile. "We have a meeting at the Puzzling Peacock."

The guard taps the butt of his spear against the stone street. "Unfortunately, entry is barred unless you have permission from the council."

Pressley steps forward like he's about to say something, but Taryn extends an arm and blocks his way.

"Allow me." He clears his throat. "I know you're just doing your job, but we really need to get inside the city. You remember the attack on the arena? The one where a big, ugly, blue troll fought tooth and nail to send those sea orc scum back to where they came from. You remember him?" Taryn uses both hands to gesture at me like I'm a showpiece at the jewelry store. "He might stink a little, but he's the troll that's going to be on the front lines of this invasion along with all of the heroes he's been able to rally to the cause. And yeah, he might have a temper, but he's the same troll who managed to unite all five troll tribes, and who has spent every waking moment trying to bring the kingdoms together so that you and yours have a home to come back to. If you want us to have the best chance possible at winning this thing, then you should probably let us inside. Oh, and don't forget that he brought a godsdamned dragon to fight by your side."

"Er, yes, uh, well." The guard looks to the others for help, but they've already stepped aside. "Um, I guess, well, shit." He sighs and steps aside. "Just go."

I don't know if I've ever been so insulted and flattered at the same time. I keep my face straight until we pass and then give Taryn the biggest grin I can make. "Damn, T, you didn't have to do the poor guy like that."

We make a quick visit by the stables, which I'm certain is more of an excuse for Taryn to see Breebis than anything his pets might need. To my surprise, the gnomish stable master isn't fazed by the manticore's appearance.

After bowing to the creature, Breebis approaches cautiously and strokes the manticore's fur along her neck. "She's majestic. What's her name?"

Pressley's breath rattles in his helm before he answers. "She doesn't have one."

"Well, we'll just have to fix that, won't we?" Breebis scratches the manticore's chest. "A creature this renowned must have a name, undead or not."

Taryn raises a finger in the air. "I might have a suggest—"

"No." Pressley's voice booms before Taryn can finish the sentence. He turns to Breebis. "Name her what you wish."

Breebis beams as she leads the manticore into the stables, followed by Taryn's pets.

After we leave, Taryn sulks as we make our way to the Puzzling Peacock. When Limery perches on Pressley's shoulder, the death knight doesn't object. Whatever happened in the dungeon forged a true bond between the two.

Taryn increases his pace until he's beside Pressley. He huffs and finally speaks what's on his mind. "So you're just going to let her name your mount without issue, but you won't even let me make a suggestion?"

"I trust her. She has a calming presence."

Taryn rolls his eyes. "Oh, and I don't?"

"Do we really need to go over the names of your pets again?" Dorothy laughs. "I mean, come on. Berry. Jordy. Flubs. Ruby is okay, I guess. There's a ninety percent chance you were going to suggest calling the manticore 'Manty.'"

"I'm offended you would even think that." Taryn tries to defend himself, but his reddening cheeks tell another story.

In the outer boroughs, the atmosphere is much different from the first time we visited. Despite how many people currently reside outside the city walls, the streets are sparsely populated. There are no tourists, no cleanup crew keeping the city in pristine order, just the occasional, hurrying gnome or an imp zipping over the top of the buildings.

Pruxford has been preparing in earnest, and their citizens were already being armed before I left for Goldspire. I expect there is not much for them to do now but wait.

When we arrive at the Puzzling Peacock, there are only a handful of heroes downstairs. An old gnome bartender polishes mugs behind the counter. Despite the rooms being booked, this is the first time I've seen the place this empty. Light from some unseen source shines on Michael the paladin in the far corner. He sits at a table with two of the heroes I know the least about. Sam the monk leans back in his chair with his hood pulled over his eyes, his dirty feet resting on the table. Next to him, Scotty the sniper has an assortment of arrows with various tips and colored fletching laid out before him as he organizes his quiver. He nods to me before returning his attention to his arrows. Sam and Scotty were both in the Challenger's Tournament but I've never had a moment alone with either of them. They fought beside us against the sea orcs, and they are here now. That's all that matters.

Still, I can't fight the knot forming in my stomach as I wonder where everyone else is. I expected more.

"Where is everyone?" I ask, unable to hide the disappointment in my voice.

Michael walks over, extending his arm. As we clasp one another around the forearm, a shimmer of light passes over my body.

"Don't worry. Onera has her watchful eye on us." He smiles, and I swear his teeth sparkle for a moment. "Many of those from the Challenger's Tournament have chosen to join their kingdoms now that they've arrived, but they will still be fighting. They felt it would be best to empower their people. As for the others, Arty stopped by after I received your message and asked if anyone wanted to clear one more dungeon. The council has barred reentry into the city without permits for now, but the Adventurers Guild still has its portal stones. They should return within a few hours."

I let out a sigh of relief. "Thank goodness, I was beginning to think they'd all backed out."

If they're still trying to scrape up a little more experience this close to the battle, then they're truly committed.

Michael pats me on the back. "We are ready for a fight."

"Good. Judging by what I've seen outside the city, it's going to be a big one." I step aside so he can see Dorothy and Pressley. "I brought two more for the cause."

"May Onera's light shine on you." Michael's gaze lingers on Pressley before he looks at me and laughs. "You really are something if you managed to convince this one to fight with you. He had his pick of any alliance he wanted when we first arrived, and he turned down every one."

Pressley acknowledges the comment with a grunt before taking a seat at a nearby table.

"I guess he was just waiting for the right one." I chuckle. "Should we have a drink while we wait for the others? We can catch each other up in the meantime."

"Oh yes!" Limery is suddenly hovering next to us. "Limmy would like a drinks."

The bartender has dull-blue skin and streaks of gray in what used to be vibrant sapphire hair. He lingers for a moment after placing a pitcher and several mugs on the table. "Tonight, your drinks are on the house." His brow furrows, and he clenches his fists. "We lost good gnomes during the attack. I lost friends. Make the bastards pay for what they did."

Michael grabs the gnome's fist in his own. "We'll give them hell just for you, old-timer."

While we wait for the others to return, Taryn and I tell Michael, Sam, and Scotty about the forces outside the city and King Orso's plans of attack. The battle plan is certain to change once he convenes with the other leaders, but it beats twiddling our thumbs and gives us something to talk about.

Michael has been keeping tabs on everyone, so he's able to fill us in on their new abilities. One of the most interesting is Don's Nullification Zone. It allows the void mage to create an area around him where other abilities don't work, not only preventing any magic user who stands within the zone from casting but also blocking any magical projectiles once they reach him. Sam has unlocked a new dual ability called The Tortoise and the Hare, where he can either gain increased movement speed or form a protective shell that blocks a certain amount of damage. Scotty unlocked Barrage, which allows him to form up to twelve copies of whatever projectile he's firing, even mimicking their effects, though they do slightly less damage than the original.

We're deep in conversation, and Limery is deeper into his mug, when the door opens and heavy footsteps fall against the aged timber.

A familiar voice calls from behind, "Leave it to a troll to stop for a drink while we're all hard at work." Arty is covered in mud and blood, but the cyclops grins from ear to ear.

I stand to greet him, and he wraps his arms around me in a massive bear hug. "Good to see you again, Chod."

Behind him, the rest of our remaining crew filters into the room. Randy the rogue and Don the void mage. Arty's two brothers, Roddick and Reddick, as well as a half-dozen of their adventuring companions. Drizz'rt the golden-scaled assassin and Kazzandra the giant both chose to fight with us instead of their countryfolk.

While we lost a good number of challengers, this is more of the crowd I was expecting. Every one of them is at least a level or two higher than the last time I was here.

We all stand in silence for a moment before Taryn nudges me in the ribs. "This is your show. You better say something."

I clear my throat, and every eye falls on me. "I appreciate all of the work you've put in over the past week. It might be that a hard-earned level is the difference between life and death for some of us. Tomorrow, we face a threat unlike anything else we've experienced. Look around the room at those standing among you. We'll be the ones leading the charge, and it will be us that the rest of Mythos looks upon when they need the courage to press onward. So pour yourself a drink, and let's get to work."

33. BLESSED BE THE SLEEP

Twilight creeps across the Pruxford countryside by the time we return to camp. King Orso's tent is still empty, but I spot King Favian on the back of his griffin, talking to Chief Rizza across the road. Since the trolls volunteered to follow me into battle, I'll need to speak to her once I have a better idea of the roles the heroes will play in all of this.

All around, fires flicker among the campsites like hundreds of fireflies. By this time tomorrow, we'll already be in Mosstar. For many, this is the last night they'll see.

A thunderous sound rumbles from the direction of the gate. I sense Caustic's alertness and pull mana to my fingertips just before a stampede of centaurs appears down the road, a trail of dust following in their wake. I let the tingle of mana fade as Swift Thundercrest leads a herd of hundreds down the dirt road toward us. The herd's leader is built like a draft horse from the waist down, and his majestic silver beard and hair whips in the wind. Thannis, Daimun, and Sylvie follow close behind him, the ground quaking as they pass. A cloud of pink and purple celestial fairies surrounds the centaurs, their iridescent bodies shimmering in the fading light. Behind the trail of dust, some of the elder centaurs pull wagons loaded with supplies. They might not be as fast or as nimble as they once were, but they're still doing their part.

Swift leads the herd to a prairie just past the trolls on the opposite side of the road, where they run in a circle, trampling the overgrown grass. The centaurs shout and thrust their weapons overhead until Swift unleashes a deep yodel that cuts them off. They disperse and fall into perfect formation, their hooves thudding against the earth in unison several times before quiet settles over the camp.

I'll give it to Swift, he knows how to make an entrance. Aside from Pruxford's army, this is everyone.

The centaurs and fairies begin setting up camp when a notification flashes in the corner of my vision.

Regional Alert! *On behalf of Pruxford, Mistville, Antadale, Ellynmylly, Wandermere, and the Isle of Mythos, we commend those who have chosen to fight back against the encroaching darkness. Our combined forces have gathered, and battle plans have been drawn. Orders will be delivered by your leaders. Until then, make your peace and rest well. At dawn, Mythos goes to war.*

I swallow hard after reading the message. We're on the brink of a war that could destroy everything these people have ever known. How in the hell is anyone going to sleep tonight?

There's movement in my peripheral as the gate opens again and a convoy of emerald carriages exits the city. One stops by the Vanarian camp, where Kassidy the teleportation mage, and Warwick, captain of King Favian's kingsguard, emerge. I'm sure Warwick isn't happy that King Favian left on the back of his griffin without him.

More carriages pass by, carrying the leaders of Antadale, Ellynmylly, and Mistville. At the end of the convoy, two carriages stop outside of Seascape's camp. King Orso, Kurzol, and a few members of the kingsguard exit the carriages. King Orso waves to his people as he makes his way to the royal tent. There's no mirth or excitement to his features, only unreadable stone. Knowing what awaits, this can't be easy for a king who cares so much for his people.

He turns around at the entrance to the tent as if he's about to say something. A cavernous roar from the direction of the troll camp cuts him off. I turn to see every troll standing along the roadside, divided into their respective tribes. At the far end, Abo's head is tilted back as he bellows at the heavens. Birds flock from the trees, and the jowls of the desert troll stretch to their limit as his powerful lungs continue their sonorous barrage. His deep clamor echoes off the hills, seemingly never-ending.

Abo's roar finally relents, but Kronan steps forward before it completely fades, unleashing a roar of his own. Where the desert troll's was deep and resonant, the mountain troll's is violent, terrifying in its fury. It cleaves through the night like the snarl of a lion in the darkness just before it attacks.

All around me, canvas hisses like a den of snakes as dwarves and humans emerge from their tents to see what's happening.

Kronan's boisterous roar fades, immediately replaced by Gord's. The forest troll booms with guttural passion, and my hair stands on end as I feel my connection to the tribe through his intensity. Chief Laojin answers for the arctic trolls, his roar icy and raw, like the cutting bite of an unexpected cold snap. The next roar is softer, resembling the swell of the tide just before it crashes against the rocky coastline, as Imoko does his part for the seaside trolls.

As he finishes, a familiar sensation stirs within me, and my body tingles with electricity. The first time it kindled, I was only beginning to understand my place among the forest trolls. This time, a fervor passes through me and sparks along my bond with Caustic.

I answer the call of my brethren, startling the dwarves around me as my roar thunders with anger and desperation, a prayer that the trolls may survive what's coming, that Limery and everyone I care about will see better days. Somewhere in the darkness, Caustic cries out, his primal ferocity enough to quake the heavens.

When all five tribes join in together, it's like a volcano erupting. None of this was planned and yet it's like I know my part, like I always have.

The roars of hundreds of trolls fade, leaving behind a deafening silence. All across the camp, we sit in a soundless vacuum, no one uttering a word.

Gord steps forward and beats his chest, the hollow pounding like a cannon. A heartbeat later, Malak and the other guardian trolls do the same. The male mountain trolls mirror the action, followed by the arctic trolls, then the desert, and finally the seaside trolls. I make my way through the dwarven camp until I'm standing in the road. I'm with them, yet on my own. All at once, we slowly lower into half-squats, the muscles of our massive thighs rippling with the movement.

In perfect unison, we smack a palm against our leg, and it echoes through the night. I bring my second hand down on the opposite leg, followed by a thunderous stomp and a deafening roar.

There's a pause just before the higher-pitched roars of the female trolls join in. They step forward, taking their places beside the males and mirroring our sequence, their dance every bit as raw and powerful as our own. When it's finished, Chief Rizza lets out a yodel that echoes off the hills.

We pound our chests in unison, our drums of war, and something inside of me takes over as I become one with the trolls across from me. The sequence of stomps, slaps, and roars change but somehow, I don't miss a beat as the rhythm continues, a musical madness composed of flesh and bone as we do our tribal dance. Braids whip through the night like striking vipers, and the music of our bodies clears the wildlife for miles. I close my eyes, letting the vibrations wash over me, and then they end.

The silence that follows is all-consuming, and I feel the void creeping in. Across from me, a song erupts from Chief Rizza, and her golden eyes lock with my own. She sings a wordless hymn, a guttural cry that wails against the darkness with a melody of power and melancholy. A song of farewell to the world we know and the ones who may not see what comes after.

My body tingles as electricity sparks within, and the shouts of surprise all around tell me that I'm not alone. Shockwaves course through my veins, threatening to explode like lightning, and I clench my fists to hold onto the feeling for as long as I can. As quickly as the sensation came, it fades away, and several notifications flash across my vision.

Alert! You have been blessed by the forest trolls.

Alert! You have been blessed by the mountain trolls.

Alert! You have been blessed by the desert trolls.

Alert! You have been blessed by the arctic trolls.

Alert! You have been blessed by the seaside trolls.

For the longest time, no one moves, no one even speaks, basking in the moment of what we all witnessed. What I was a part of. I have no idea what the troll blessings will do, but one saved my life once. Maybe they will offer us some protection in a land of shadows.

"That was beautiful," Dorothy whispers from behind.

I'm not sure when she found me but when I turn around, she, Taryn, and Pressley are all there.

Limery comes flying out of nowhere like a meteor and wraps his tiny arms around my neck. "Chods made Limmy feels the lightnings."

"I didn't know you could do that." Taryn looks at me with a reverence I'm not sure I deserve. Dorothy does as well, maybe even Pressley too, but his jeweled eye gives nothing away.

"Me neither. It just kind of happened." I chuckle, patting Limery on the back. "Like I'd been waiting for this moment my entire life."

"Chod, Taryn." King Orso appears from behind a tent, his kingsguard trailing a few feet away. "May I have a word? There was a great deal of deliberation, but the Mythos Council has a plan for the heroes. I'd like to discuss it with you."

"Of course." Taryn bows.

I nod in agreement and then turn to Pressley and Dorothy. "We'll meet up with you after."

King Orso's molten eyes burn with intensity as he leads us into his royal pavilion. He ushers everyone else out before revealing the council's plan. It's bold, and the trolls will be putting themselves in danger if they choose to follow, but if we can pull this off, then there's a chance to save Mythos before too many people are hurt.

Taryn and I exchange glances once we leave the tent. Before we have a chance to talk about the plan, a soothing hum comes from the direction of the Antadale camp. I close my eyes and listen to the catfolk chant. There's a disconnect between what they're saying and what I'm hearing, so I remove my communication stone and store it away.

The chant builds, settling over the campsite like a warm embrace as hundreds of voices meld together. It reminds me of the Gregorian chants I listened to once for history class, both ominous and comforting at the same time. I don't need to understand the words to appreciate the effect as the tension in my shoulders lessens and even my anxiety seems to ebb. The chanting continues for about ten minutes, and when it ends, my eyes are heavy, and a new notification flashes in my vision.

Alert! You have been soothed by an Antadalian Chant. Rest without worry.

"Limmy is sleepies." The imp rests his head on my shoulder.

"Me too, buddy."

Taryn yawns. "We can talk in the morning." He pats me on the back.

Limery is fast asleep by the time we reach Pressley's tent. Even though the death knight might not need sleep, his helm rattles as he sits in the corner.

I curl up next to Limery and welcome the sweet oblivion.

34. MYTHOS GOES TO WAR

I wake up to the sound of wagons crunching along the dirt road. Even though it's still dark out, the camp bustles with activity. I stretch my arms overhead, feeling as refreshed as I ever have. There's no telling how many sleepless nights the catfolk saved with their chant.

Around the tent, the others stir awake as the effects of the sleep buff come to an end. Pressley is missing, but several of his minions stand sentry in the corner.

"Today's the day," I say to myself more than anyone as I pull back the flaps of the tent. Although torches burn across the camp, I don't need them to see with my nightvision. "Holy shit."

My mouth drops open once my gaze falls upon the massive contraptions being rolled out of the city. The gnomes are well-regarded as great tinkerers, but I had no idea they made such impressive weapons of war. They seem centuries ahead of what most other kingdoms have. A convoy of catapults, siege towers, ballistae, trebuchets, and battering rams flows from the city, interspersed with battalions of soldiers wearing armor that has a purple hue to it. I can't help but wonder how many of the soldiers are everyday citizens thrust into the conflict.

Limery lands on my shoulder, his body warmer than normal. The catfolk may have helped us sleep, but the nerves have returned in full force this morning.

All around, dwarves and humans bark out orders as camps are dismantled and soldiers head to their locations.

I let the tent flap fall close. "You all ready?"

Dorothy looks up from the dagger she's using to clean her fingernails and grins. "This is going to be fun."

I wish I shared her disposition. For her, she's about to experience an epic battle in the most realistic game she's ever played. For me, the stakes are real. Everything I've grown to care about is on the line.

Taryn pats Berry on the side and then climbs on the umber bear's back. He nods solemnly. "Let's end this."

I send a quick message to Michael, telling him where to meet us, and we head for the trolls. Kassidy is supposed to join us as well. The crux of the plan revolves around the teleportation mage.

At the edge of camp, we find Pressley standing by a pile of bones. Hundreds of bones in various shapes and sizes litter the area, and more fall from his satchel each time he shakes it. There must be enough pieces for over a hundred minions. Even though the dwarves know he's on our side, they give him a wide berth as they work.

"Question." Taryn raises a finger. "How exactly are we supposed to tell your minions apart from the ones we're about to fight?"

I hadn't even thought about that, but he makes a good point.

Pressley waves his hand, and the bones begin assembling themselves. "They'll be the ones not trying to kill you."

Dorothy laughs, but I'm not sure if he's joking or not. Taryn blinks a few times, seemingly unsure himself.

Pressley grunts and stops what he's doing, motioning for one of his minions to join him. The death knight points an armored finger at the skeleton's elbow joint, where a dark purple energy holds the bones together. "Look at their joints. It's not easily noticeable, but the infernal energy that powers their bodies is the same as mine. Though some may look similar, every necromancer has a unique energy source. Once we see Valmar's, it will be easier to tell them apart."

Dorothy grins as she unravels the shawl from around her neck and dangles it in the air. "You could always tie ribbons around them."

Pruxford's forces continue to file down the road, setting up position across from Antadale and next to the centaurs.

A streak of silver passes overhead as King Favian flies by on his griffin. There are so many moving pieces right now. I just need to focus on the task at hand.

"Meet me by the trolls." I reach out to Caustic through our bond.

"You meet me by the trolls. I am already here."

I roll my eyes and continue onward. Is this what I was like as a teenager? Who am I kidding? I was probably worse.

The trolls are up and about, equipping armor and testing their new weapons. Caustic casts an imposing figure at the back of the camp, where he stands on his hind legs with his wings spread wide. He's surrounded by the three wyrms and a host of goblins. The wyrms lower their heads to the ground like snakes in deference to the mighty dragon. Not that long ago, they were nearly the same size. Now, he's much bigger. Caustic lowers himself to all fours, dipping his head and sniffing each one in turn before allowing them to rise. He moves in our direction, the wyrms and goblins following.

The chiefs and many of the councilmembers are gathered together just outside the copse of trees. They wear a gamut of emotions as we approach. Chief Rizza's face is stoic, the picture of leadership that has united the trolls for a chance at a better life, even though it may cost them dearly. Then there are Gord and Brutus, who grin with the thirst for battle. Chief Laojin gazes contemplatively toward the other camps while Chief Lida of the seaside trolls keeps adjusting her grip on her staff. Kronan looks like he's ready to fight the first person who breathes wrong. And then there's Abo, one of the last of his kind, whose welcoming smile is at odds with his fearsome appearance.

Abo extends his arm. "We are ready for war."

I grip his massive forearm and squeeze. "Good, because there's been a change of plans."

Once the other heroes arrive, I gather the trolls to inform them of the council's strategy. For better or worse, we're together in this. Kassidy hasn't arrived yet, but I'd wager he's fitting in a final meal before the battle.

There's a mixed reaction from some, but Gord, Brutus, and Kronan are giddy with excitement. Their thirst for battle is matched only by the rogues, Randy and Drizz'rt. They ache for somewhere to unleash their fury, no matter how it comes.

After we all know our roles, I summon horrors as we get into formation, starting with the dreadbeasts since they won't decay outside of combat. As long as I have at least one of them active, it'll prevent the horrors from deteriorating as rapidly, so I'll be able to summon fifty percent more than I normally would.

There's a crack as a rift tears through the air and the Dreadbeast of Torment steps from the void. Murmurs of excitement and awe surround the appearance of the demonic canine the size of a giant wolf. Its thick, black fur blends into the darkness except for a trail of silver that runs down its spine and orange eyes that burn like embers just beneath a set of dangerous horns. Saliva drips from the dreadbeast's fangs as it takes its position by my side like a feral guard dog.

"Scaries." Limery's body warms against my shoulder.

I pat him on the leg. "Don't worry, bud. They're on our side."

Cheevus traipses over on the back of his mangy wolf. "This one likes." The goblin's eyes are full of greed, and he smiles devilishly.

The dreadbeast snarls when the wolf gets too close, and Cheevus lets out a surprised yelp. His wolf tucks its tail and whimpers.

"You might want to give him some space." I chuckle as the wolf slowly backs away.

Next, I summon a Dreadbeast of Despair. There's another crack, and the mighty black bison steps through a rift, majestic and terrifying in its appearance. Shadowy tendrils flare from its ebony fur, and two crimson horns curve upward from the side of its head. It's the biggest of my summons, large enough that I could ride it as a mount if I didn't have Caustic.

"Damn!" Taryn guides Berry to the opposite side of me, away from the dreadbeast. "You didn't tell me they were this badass."

I shrug. "What'd you expect with a name like that?"

The demonic bison blows a thick stream of smoke when Michael the paladin moves closer.

Don the void mage nods approvingly. "Nice."

Gord approaches the Dreadbeast of Torment without fear, Peacemaker slung across his broad shoulders. He kneels and extends his hand. "You will dine on the bones of our enemies tonight."

The dreadbeast lets out a low growl as it sniffs Gord's hand, but the brutish troll doesn't flinch. After a tense moment, the dreadbeast licks his knuckles. A smile tugs at my mouth. No matter what Gord faces, he does it without fear. I'm lucky to have him accompany me into battle.

I slap him on the shoulder, rattling his bone armor. "I can summon ten of these at a time. This one is yours."

He grins. "It would be my honor."

While everyone ogles the new dreadbeasts, I summon a round of horrors and wait for the short cooldown on the dreadbeasts to reset. Compared to their brethren, the horrors look like Chihuahuas standing next to Rottweilers. They have just as much fight and fervor, but for the first time, they look small. The Horror of Finesse circles the dreadbeasts with its spindly limbs, sniffing at the air. Even the Horror of Power, which was once my most terrifying summon with its stocky frame and dangerous tusks, only comes up to the dreadbeasts's knees. The rotund, furry Horror of Vitality is enamored with the Dreadbeast of Despair, grasping at the smoking tendrils that flare from its body.

The horrors might not be as big or as powerful on a one-to-one basis, but with every new summon, I grow stronger, gaining one percent damage and HP for each one active. Combined with my Warforged ability, I'm the perfect choice to lead the charge.

I continue summoning until my mana runs out. I've never run out of mana before, but the dreadbeast take a lot more to summon than the horrors. Luckily, I came prepared and have a nice supply of mana potions I picked up in Goldspire. I down one and continue summoning until I have ten of each dreadbeast and twenty of each horror, increasing my health and damage by eighty percent. The horrors scatter amongst the trolls and goblins, and I send one of each dreadbeast to accompany each of the chiefs.

Behind the trolls, Pressley holds the rear, mounted on the manticore with several hundred skeleton minions to each side of him.

Between the two of us, we have enough minions to form our own battalion.

A final carriage exits the city, and the gate closes. My heart rate quickens and I force myself to breathe. Even though we're an army that's tens of thousands strong, we're going into a hellscape where the dead will outnumber us. Not to mention whatever else lurks in the shadows.

I take another deep breath as the carriage passes by with Richard the cleric and several of the gnomish councilmembers inside. My gaze follows them until their carriage stops across from the Antadale camp where the rest of the Pruxford forces are stationed.

The air crackles like a staticky radio just before the voice of Dezmin Dreamwader, head of the gnomish council, booms all around us.

"Soon, the sun will rise across the countryside, bringing a new day to Pruxford. For all of you gathered here today, this is a new dawn for all of Mythos. There comes a time when we must make difficult decisions, when we must choose between what is right and what is easy. In Pruxford, we have taken the easy road for far too long, choosing to ignore a mounting threat even as it tested our borders. You know why this fight is necessary. At first light, portals will open, and our idle hands will take on the weapons of war. Fight without mercy. Fight for your lives. Fight for Mythos."

Cheers erupt across the countryside as weapons are thrust into the air, and the trumpeting elephants of Antadale bellow their challenge. The cheers fade, and a cacophony of voices blend together as each leader gives a speech of their own. The words of King Orso, King Favian, and Swift's all muffle together, but the trolls stand silent. Chief Rizza motions for me to join her.

I call for Caustic to join me through our bond and take my place next to the chief.

She looks at me expectantly. "You should be the one to send us off."

"No." I shake my head. "They might believe in me, but they followed you to this moment. *I* follow you." I take her hand in mine. "Because you put your faith in me when I didn't deserve it. You helped me see that there are things in this world worth fighting for besides myself. Let me fight for you now."

She nods, and her golden eyes sparkle with emotion as she squeezes my hand.

Caustic lands behind us with a thud and raises his head proudly as he looks over the trolls.

"I'll be back shortly." I give Chief Rizza's hand another squeeze before climbing onto the dragon's back. He pushes off and soon we're soaring over the biggest army I've ever seen.

Seven kingdoms stand side by side in formation. King Favian soars above his people on his griffin, an inspiring sight if I've ever seen one. The Vanarian forces are led by the royal soldiers and city guards, their blue capes draping over silver armor. Beside them, the dwarven army stands ready with hundreds of statuesque gargoyles in the rear.

The giant elephants take point for the catfolk, their white-and-gold banners waving proudly from the giant saddles atop the magnificent beasts. They trumpet as we fly by, and catfolk thrust their spears in the air. Further down, the giants of Ellynmylly push their catapults into position behind soldiers holding shields of a dozen hues. At the far end, the merfolk form several columns on each side of their wagons, and massive sea snakes slither through their ranks.

Caustic roars as he turns around, where the forces of Pruxford, Wandermere, and the trolls wait on the other side of the road. Pruxford's siege weapons are ready for war, and I spot a familiar caravan among their ranks. Three wagons emblazoned with a large red lion across the canvas.

I guess the Underground Circus is going to Mosstar.

Next to them, the Wandermere herd stands at attention, hooves shifting at the prospect of battle. Among the trolls, Chief Rizza sits on the back of her wyrm and pumps her fist into the air. There's a flurry of movement as the trolls answer in kind.

The first rays of sunlight begin to creep over the hills, and a cloaked figure joins Dezmin Dreamwader in front of the Pruxford forces.

Richard pulls back his hood and drops to his knees. The air suddenly grows thick and humid, and static sets my hair on end. I watch the cleric with fascination as a red aura surrounds his body. The air crackles with energy, and red lightning strikes all around us. Caustic roars as he dives to rejoin our kin.

Lightning crashes as we descend, and thunder rumbles as the night sky burns crimson. Along the road, jagged fissures tear through reality as rifts appear. They splinter and fracture, growing larger as a swirl of silver and black forms within. Unlike the viewing portal we witnessed at the council, we're unable to see what waits on the other side.

Smoke rises from Richard's prone form, and the black chain that hangs from his neck glows molten red. Thunder crashes again, reverberating through my chest as the portals stabilize.

Silence settles across Pruxford, and I dismount Caustic to take my position next to Taryn and Dorothy.

"Where's Kassidy?" I look around for the teleportation mage but still don't see him. None of this works without him.

Taryn points over his shoulder. Kassidy sits on the back of the manticore behind Pressley with a pastry in one hand and the other wrapped around the death knight. He waves the pastry in my direction.

"That's as good a place as any, I suppose. Everyone ready?"

Taryn nods, and Dorothy smirks as she spins a blade in her palm. Limery perches on my shoulder, his claws digging into my skin, and all around me trolls march toward the portal as drums beat in the distance.

"I'll find you when it is time." Caustic's anticipation vibrates through me as his voice growls in my head.

A powerful gust sweeps across us as the dragon flies off. He's the first one to disappear through the portal, followed by a stampede of horrors and dreadbeasts. All around me, trolls, humans, dwarves, gnomes, and a myriad of races from across Mythos march through the portals.

I equip Destroyer and lift it in the air. *"Let's give them hell."*

35. EVERYONE HAS A PLAN UNTIL THEY GET PUNCHED IN THE MOUTH

The portal empties us into Mosstar, where dark clouds blot out the sky, leaving the kingdom in a state of perpetual twilight. A sulfuric stench permeates the air as I look across the wasteland. We're positioned to the far left of Mythos's forces, maybe half a mile from the outer wall. There's a sea of fog where the terrain dips slightly that stands between us and the horde of undead protecting the city.

Limery scrunches his nose. "This place is stinkies."

The smell is going to be the least of our problems, but I keep that thought to myself.

My gaze falls upon the city, and I swallow hard. It's bigger than I expected, easily the size of Vanaria. An eerie glow comes from within, drawing my eye toward the green flames that burn atop four colossal towers surrounding the keep. An obsidian spire rises from its center, shimmering like a beacon as it reflects the fiery towers.

I force my eyes away from the keep to take in the rest of the city. Only a smattering of windows glow across the elven stronghold.

They have no idea we're coming. Maybe we can end this before they know what's happening.

Our forces continue to exit the chaos portals, and I feel Caustic's presence as a shadow moves through the clouds overhead.

"Do you see anything?" I ask him.

"The city is quiet for now. We must hurry." The uneasiness in his voice sets my nerves on edge.

Steadfast, we march toward the city walls. I summon new horrors as the older ones expire. Unlike the dreadbeasts, they'll continue to decay until I engage in combat. I glance at the rage bar in the corner of my vision. It's dangerously low, but I haven't had a chance to replenish it since my fight with Dorothy. That leaves me about thirty seconds of Cold Rage before it runs out. Once I start smashing heads, that won't be a problem.

Something snaps behind us. When I turn around, the portals have vanished. There's nothing but a barren landscape covered in fog to one side and a forest of dark trees to the other. Despite my nightvision, there's a shroud hanging over the forest that I can't penetrate.

We're trapped here now. Our only way out is if we take the city and open the Mosstar portal.

"We have been spotted!" Caustic roars in my mind.

No sooner do I hear the words before the spire in the heart of the city flares a toxic green. Limery grows warm against my shoulder as the fiery towers surrounding the keep burn higher, and pyres erupt around the battlements. Figures move atop the city wall, and outside, a wave of chartreuse energy passes through the undead as they stir awake. If that's the color of their joints, then it'll be easy enough to tell them apart from Pressley's minions.

Michael the paladin drops to one knee, a golden aura surrounding him. It pulses, and a wave of energy passes over everyone in his immediate vicinity.

Alert! *You have been blessed by Onera. Deal increased damage against undead and take reduced damage from undead attacks for the next thirty minutes.*

Not bad. I'm even more glad he's on our side now.

We continue our steady march—a battalion of trolls, horrors, heroes, and undead. Even if Valmar knows we're here, it will take time for him to mobilize the rest of his forces. If we can push through the undead, we have a shot to overtake him before he can call in reinforcements.

"What's that?" Taryn points to the far right, where a blur of purple and yellow darts across the fog in front of the merfolk army.

Tozzet, the tidal mage from the tournament, propels himself on a low-hanging wave until he's nearly a hundred yards ahead of everyone else. He glides like a surfer until the wave suddenly dissipates, and he vanishes beneath the fog.

This wasn't part of the plan. *What the hell is he up to?*

A blue aura swells beneath the fog, and the mist constricts like it's being sucked into a vacuum. A glowing blue vortex circles the area where Tozzet disappeared as the particles merge into raging water, swirling like a miniature hurricane. The vortex grows higher, its spout swaying to the point that it might topple as the mage tries to contain it. Suddenly, it whips forward as the merfolk channels the fog into a crashing wave.

Chief Lida runs ahead, gathering fog around her as she mimics the merfolk. Down the line, two water mages from Seascape and another from Antadale do the same.

Tozzet's wave gathers momentum as it tears through the fog and collides with the undead. They scatter like flotsam as the wave passes through the horde and crashes into the outer wall. Water and bones splash a hundred feet in the air before settling into puddles across the battlefield.

Four more waves follow, less powerful, but enough to clear our visibility between here and the outer wall, knocking down more of the undead in the process.

Scattered bodies and detached bones lay motionless, the first casualties of the battle. I wonder if having so many undead means that each one is less powerful, but then all at once, they stir, rising from the muddy earth in haunting unison. They charge toward us silently, their battle-cry composed of thousands of bones that clack together like the chattering teeth of gods.

An avalanche of white descends from the city as more bodies pour from the far side.

"We make for the wall!" I roar above the chaos. "That is our only objective!"

We have our mission, and that's all that matters. If we don't succeed, then the whole plan is doomed.

Caustic descends from the clouds, his emerald scales reflecting the eldritch light of the city as he dives low, breathing out a stream of toxic gas. Dense green fog settles among the undead, a splash of color among a field of white, but it does little to damage their fleshless bodies.

Out of the corner of my eye, the fiery tips of the Ellynmylly archers sparkle against the darkness like fireflies as they raise their bows skyward. The arrows loose, streaming against the night, and my heart stutters as I wait for them to land.

The flaming arrows hit Caustic's gas with a thunderous explosion, and hundreds of skeletons are blown apart. Shards of white rain down upon the battle-field, and Caustic dives again, unleashing another stream of gas. Moments later, arrows fall like shooting stars into another bombastic blast.

Relief floods through me for a moment, but it's quickly squelched by the blood-curdling screams coming from behind us.

"Oh, noes." Limery's body flares with heat, so intense that I grimace.

The pain radiating through my shoulder is the least of my concerns once I notice the source of his distress. The shrouded trees of the forest are nothing more than skeletal branches, and above them, a swarm of darkness moves across the twilight sky. What I thought were leaves are actually giant bats, and they're flying toward us, their wings flapping like erratic sails.

Nearby, Scotty the sniper readies his bow. The weapon is slender and nearly as tall as he is. He nocks an arrow and as he pulls back, tendrils of white energy coil up and down the arrow's shaft. His face strains from the effort as the energy builds until it glows blinding white. He releases the arrow, and it splits into twelve copies as he activates Barrage. The arrows connect with a dozen massive bats, and chains of arcane energy wrap around their bodies. They plummet to the ground, but hundreds more flitter out from the forest.

I ready Destroyer for their attack, but the bats fly straight over us. Their eyes are set on Caustic as he continues to breathe gas upon the battlefield.

King Orso is quick to react, and the gargoyles take flight, but the bats reach Caustic first, tearing at his scales with claws and fangs. The dragon is undeterred by their attacks. He snaps a bat in half with his massive jaws, and entrails rain upon the undead. He rips the wing off another with his claws.

He's only swarmed for a moment before the gargoyles join him and chunks of flesh and stone start falling from the sky.

"Are you okay?" I reach out to Caustic through our bond.

"Do not worry about me." He rips another bat in half and tosses it aside. *"Make for the wall."*

Behind us, Pressley's minions swarm the fallen bats, with the trolls helping to finish them off. Malak crushes skulls with his golden hammer, and Abo wreaks havoc with a morning star that looks more like a baton in his large hand.

Nearby, Yashi shoots arrows from the back of her wyrm. Even though her aim is true, she's having little effect against the massive creatures. The bats fly past, arrows protruding from their wings and bodies. She manages to hit one in the eye, and the critical hit drops it like a brick.

Giant icicles soar skyward, ripping massive holes in the bat wings as Senzala calls upon the power of her totem.

Scotty continues to launch arrows into the sky with unnatural speed, dropping bats in droves with his magical arrows. He hits one with a combustible arrow, and it ignites the sky like a fiery meteor. Another stuck with an ice arrow plummets to the ground, its body smashing into thousands of shards upon impact.

Horrors and minions swarm the creatures as they fall. Several bats besiege a lone gargoyle, breaking a wing from its body, and it falls like an anchor straight toward Chief Lida.

I scream her name, but she doesn't hear me as she shoots darts of ice from a water pouch around her waist. There's nothing I can do but watch as the gargoyle plummets toward her.

Seconds before she meets her fate, a brilliant blue portal forms just above her head, swallowing the gargoyle and spitting it out of a second portal onto the approaching undead.

Thank god for Kassidy.

The sky is pure chaos as bats, gargoyles, and a dragon fight among the clouds. Below, imps and fairies dart across the battlefield, their synergy of fairy dust and fire evident in the pink and purple explosions that thunder around us.

A Dreadbeast of Torment growls by my side, eager to attack as its paws dance up and down. *Not yet.* The dreadbeasts have strict orders to defend those they're stationed with, and the undead army is almost upon us.

I set my gaze on the approaching enemies and squeeze Limery's foot. "Stay safe. If you need to fly away, you do it."

"Yous stay safes toos, Chods." Flames crackle in his palms.

I activate Cold Rage as I rush toward the horde of undead, side by side with Gord and Chief Rizza. My metallic skin shimmers, and I catch Gord grinning out of the corner of my eye. Michael buffs us with another blessing as the Dreadbeasts of Despair charge ahead, and the demonic bison bulldoze through the first line of skeletons like bowling pins. I swing Destroyer in an upward arc and bones go flying. The passive from Ram Rage sends a wave of energy that knocks back more skeletons as all hell breaks loose. The Dreadbeasts of Torment attack like feral wolves, crushing bones in their powerful jaws, and my rage meter rises as I hammer my way through the undead. Their rusted weapons and bony hands screech against my hardened skin as fireballs blaze around me from Limery and Jira. Up close, I notice the green tint to their joints but in the chaos, it'll be easy to confuse them with Pressley's. I summon horrors between hits, exploiting the buff from Horror of Power to deal double damage, and the Horrors of Vitality slow the surrounding undead enough to give us an edge.

Gord shatters bones as he cleaves through three undead with a single swipe. To my right, Chief Rizza's wyrm rips the head off another. Explosions rumble in the distance, and thunder roars in several directions. Everything happens so fast that I can only keep track of what's going on in my immediate vicinity.

I smash like a troll possessed and feel a gravitational pull as a ball of black energy sails past my shoulder into the horde of undead. It expands like a dying star before collapsing in on itself and pulling several dozen enemies into the void as it snuffs out of existence. Lightning crashes nearby, followed by a stream of sizzling moonlight as Taryn wreaks his own brand of havoc, his powers amplified against the undead. I hear Berry's roar as I smash through skeletons and turn to see Taryn in the midst of battle, the bear Imbued to twice its normal size. Lightning strikes, stunning a handful of undead in place just before Jordy rams into them and sends bones clattering.

With full stacks of Inferno, my warhammer glows a vibrant red, charring bone with each hit. Noxious odors linger on the battlefield from magic and the undead.

I activate Sweeping Slash and Concussive Force, stacking their effects to clear a path forward. The blow knocks a host of bodies backward, and two shadowy forms pass by as Randy and Drizz'rt dart into the fray. The two rogues fight back to back, surrounded by undead, and their bodies move in a blur as they slice through bone like it's butter.

An arrow hits my shoulder with a clink, followed by a host of cries as arrows pepper our location. Archers line the battlements, their silhouettes outlined by the green glow of the city as they fire without worry of injuring their own forces.

A seaside troll takes an arrow to the neck and collapses. Tormara snarls as she rips one from her arm.

"Archers!" I reach out to Caustic and a moment later, his body soars above the castle walls. "Limery, help him!" I point toward the diving dragon, and Limery dashes away.

The imp moves across the battlefield like a speeding bullet, and there's a thunderous explosion as his fireball ignites Caustic's gas. Bodies tumble from the high walls, but the structure withstands the blast. The attack will buy us some time but it won't be long before reinforcements take their places. We need to keep pushing.

A lone wail echoes from behind us, drawing my attention. Before I turn around, hundreds more join in. Their cries carry like the sirens that blare before a dangerous storm. The amplified howls drown out the clamor of weapons and the roars of beasts and monsters, and my eyes follow the sound to the top of the barren hillside where a new enemy awaits. Hundreds of large, fur-covered humanoids tilt their heads back and howl, setting my hair on end.

Fuck. Nobody said anything about werewolves.

Our battalion is the closest to the hillside, and it looks like we're about to be fighting on two fronts.

A rusty sword slams against my shoulder from behind, shrieking as it grates against my Warforged body. I turn just in time to see a black-and-red axe whistle through the air as Brutus decapitates the skeleton attacker.

"Watch your back," he growls, the joy of battle radiating in his eyes as they fall upon our new challengers.

The werewolves drop to all fours and storm down the hillside. Hundreds descend like a landslide, and even from here, I can see the blazing red eyes and matching aura that surrounds their deadly claws. I saw this once before when we fought the gnolls. They're in some kind of rage or pack frenzy.

Brutus grabs Kronan by the arm, turning the mountain troll to face the werewolves. Kronan's eyes widen, and then he looks over his shoulder toward the city wall.

"Rizza!" he bellows and somehow his voice carries across the carnage.

Chief Rizza looks at him from the back of her wyrm, and Kronan points toward the werewolves. A fierce frown spreads across her features, and I see the understanding in her eyes as she turns the wyrm to face the hill.

Michael pushes past me, his spotless silver armor pulsing with golden energy. I grab his arm. "Can you buy us a minute against the undead?"

He takes in the charging werewolves, glances at the undead, and nods. "By Onera's might." He raises his shield into the air, and it blazes with holy light. "Heroes, on me!"

The paladin slams his shield into the ground and a wave of brilliant energy shoots out in front of him, knocking the undead back a good twenty feet. Sam the monk appears at his side and lowers into a fighting stance. His arms move in a practiced motion, and colorful energy trails each movement like the strokes of a paintbrush. A brown aura rises from the earth, morphing into a herd of ethereal buffalo.

I turn my attention back to the werewolves and hear the stampede of hooves before bones clatter behind us.

Chief Rizza extends her sword, Trollbreaker blocking me from joining the fight against the werewolves. She meets my gaze, shaking her head. "The trolls will guard the rear. Lead the heroes to the wall."

Dammit! I want to argue, to stay and fight beside my kin, but I know she's right. This isn't how it was supposed to go. We were supposed to have the element of surprise but somehow, we're the ones caught off guard and forced to adapt.

"Trolls!" Her voice rings with authority. "We have a new challenge!"

Gord steps up beside me, his shoulders covered in a layer of bone dust. He wears a maniacal grin as he takes in the new challengers. When he beats his chest, something pulses within his eyes.

"Guardians! Rage with me against the darkness!" His skin sizzles, and steam radiates from his body as he unleashes a battle-cry that rivals Caustic in its ferocity.

All around us, the other male trolls answer his call. Abo joins his side. The massive desert troll is covered with cuts and missing a few fingers, but he stands tall. Steam emanates from his shoulders, and when he roars, his wounds begin to stitch themselves together.

Gord taps Peacemaker against my chest with a metallic clink. "Take care of yourself, brother. I'll see you on the other side."

His muscles bulge, and the guardian trolls rage in unison.

"Give 'em hell." I raise Destroyer in the air. "Heroes, with me! We've got a castle to storm."

We fight our way forward, a battalion of horrors and heroes. Behind us, trolls clash against werewolves amidst a maelstrom of roars, snarls, yelps, and battle-cries as they give us a fighting chance at reaching our target.

Ahead of me, three Dreadbeasts of Despair charge in an arrowhead formation, bulldozing through the skeleton army. The demonic bison have lost nearly half of their HP but with my high Constitution, it's far from worrisome.

Above us, Caustic and the gargoyles continue to battle the frenzy of bats among the clouds. Portals dot the skyline as Kassidy keeps the falling gargoyles from crushing our forces.

I fall back, letting Michael lead the attack as I search for the teleportation mage. I find him on the back of the manticore, his gaze focused on the skies as he searches for stone to redirect. Pressley swings his sword from the back of his mount while the manticore tears through the undead with her dangerous claws.

"How close do we need to be to the wall?" I shout at Kassidy as I smash a skeleton and its bones explode into dust.

The teleportation mage glances past me. "To move all of you, we need to close half the distance."

"Get ready, then. I've got a plan."

I search for Limery and find him hovering between Taryn and Dorothy. Taryn's Moonbeam sizzles against the undead, disintegrating their bones, and Dorothy wields a dagger in each hand, rivaling Randy and Drizz'rt with her fighting prowess as she cuts through our enemies.

"Taryn, cast Strong Wind on my horrors." I pull my last vial of Boom Dust from my inventory and throw it into the horde. "Limery, fireball!"

The imp tracks the vial as it arcs through the air, throwing a fireball that ignites the explosive mixture of fairy dust at just the right moment. It explodes like a bomb, dismembering undead and leaving a crater about twenty feet wide. I send my horrors forward, their smaller bodies worming between the legs of the undead directly in front of us.

Once they're in position, I cast Kamikaze, and the horrors detonate, dropping my bonus HP and damage by a sharp margin but clearing a path toward the wall.

"Push forward!" I shout.

A swirling blue portal hovers a few feet off the ground where the crater is. My dreadbeasts lead the way, with Michael the paladin and Don the void mage right behind them.

I stop in front of the portal, fighting back the horde from closing off our path. Pressley's minions join me, holding back the undead so the others can pass. Sam and Scotty leap into the swirl of blue energy, followed by Randy and Drizz'rt. I summon more horrors every chance I get to replace the ones I lost. Arty, his brothers, Kazzandra, and several adventurers rush past. The cyclops has a gash on his shoulder, painting his chiseled bicep a vibrant red, and several broken arrows protrude from the giant's back.

A massive stone wall forms across from me, crushing undead and creating a barrier as Taryn and Dorothy come bounding my way. Some of the skeletons spill around the wall and into the crater, falling through the portal.

"Hurry!" I yell as I activate Sweeping Slash, knocking back a host of skeletons.

Taryn and Berry pass through the portal, followed by Jordy, Ruby, and Dorothy.

"I'll be right behind you," I tell Limery, and he disappears.

Everyone is through but Kassidy and Pressley. The manticore hovers above the battlefield, allowing Kassidy to maintain his focus while the death knight shoots dark energy into the undead.

An arrow lodges in Kassidy's stomach, and the portal falters, shrinking in size as blood pools around the wound to his abdomen. The teleportation mage grimaces, holding a hand to his midsection and redoubling his focus until the portal returns to its original size.

"Pressley, let's go!" I shout.

Blood seeps through Kassidy's fingers. I don't know how much longer he'll be able to hold on. The manticore lands beside me, and Pressley's minions fight against the horde as he dismounts.

"You go. They need me out here."

"We need you!" I argue, but then I take in the rest of the battle for the first time. None of the other kingdoms have pushed close to the wall. Dead elephants litter the landscape like giant boulders, and many of the gnomish siege weapons are swarmed by undead like ants on a piece of candy. The merfolks' wagons are cracked, broken, and emptied. All the while, the undead continue to funnel from the far side of the city. There's no telling how the trolls are faring against the werewolves.

Our only hope is ending Valmar so that all of this stops.

"What can you do against this? You're one man."

Pressley pulls a vial that glows bright pink from his satchel. The Potion of Reincarnation that we looted in the Glossop Forest. "Go save Mythos. Let me do my part."

Kassidy coughs, blood pouring down his chin. "You have to go now."

Pressley downs the vial of pink liquid, and his body begins to morph. The last thing I see as I jump through the portal is a two-story-tall death knight drawing his sword.

36. BLAZE OF GLORY

Pressley's bones thickened and elongated as the Potion of Reincarnation coursed through him, transforming his body by epic proportions. Increased stats jolted his system, and his bones vibrated with the power. A shiver passed through the death knight, his entire being tingling with unspent energy so intense that it pushed back the cold that always lingered. Enchanted armor and weapons adapted to his changing body until the death knight stood so tall he could see the boots of the elves stationed on the outer wall. Arrows clinked off his helm, about as bothersome as gnats. He was a titan, a goliath, a mountain of death.

Pressley stared at the empty vial in his hand. It had morphed alongside him and was now the size of a boulder. He read the potion's description a final time.

Legendary Item. Potion of Reincarnation. *(Only usable by heroes.) User gains increased size and doubles all stats for the duration of the potion. Health drains with each step. When user's health reaches zero, their character is randomly re-rolled to level 1.*

A new health bar appeared across Pressley's vision next to a timer that ticked down from ten minutes. Every step the death knight took would deplete his health, and when his HP reached zero, he'd be rerolled into a new level-one character. A new race, a new class, and he'd have no choice in either. The timer was there to prevent him from hunkering down in one place in an attempt to hold onto such god-like power.

He laughed to himself. When he'd first read over the potion's effects, they had sounded awesome. Doubling his stats would double his power. But he'd been wrong. Doubling his stats amplified his power exponentially. This was as close to being a god in this world as he could come.

For the majority of his time in Mythos, Pressley had cared about one thing—acquiring power. Through hard work and devotion, he'd achieved his goal, and now he was throwing it all away. When the potion ended, everything he'd worked toward would fade away with his current body. Every choice he'd made and every bit of power he'd accrued would soon be for nothing.

No, that wasn't true. He was making it count for something right now. He'd be able to tell Eva that when the fate of Mythos was on the line, he'd stood for something. She'd learn what kind of man her father had always wanted to be. Strong. Powerful. A man of honor. And though he'd been selfish too many times in his life, this was proof that he could be selfless.

He was going to lose everything he'd worked toward, but he'd gained something that would endure. As much as he hated to admit it, he'd made a few friends in this world. Sacrifice was a part of friendship.

Now was his chance to go out in a blaze of glory so that the name of Pressley Allen would be revered across Mythos forever.

The timer ticked down, and he surveyed the battlefield. Below, his minions pushed back Mosstar's undead, hacking against bone with new fervor empowered by the death knight's increased stats. When he looked at his minions, they carried an aura of undeath that only he could see. It would have been much easier for his allies if they could tell the distinction as easily. In the dim light of the shadowlands, they'd be hard pressed to notice much of a difference between the two undead. He wouldn't hold it against anyone if a few fell to friendly fire.

Further away, the forces of Mythos were being overwhelmed. The merfolk's convoy of wagons was nothing more than kindling, and the siege engines of the gnomes had been overrun by skeletons, making them useless obstacles that prevented advancement. Bodies littered the battlefield, mixed among the broken bones of the undead. Magic flared across the landscape as waves crashed, fires blazed, and earth shifted at the whim of powerful mages. Fairies and imps darted through the chaos, leaving pastel explosions in their wake. King Orso fought side by side with his kingsguard and clerics, a myriad of auras flashing with each attack. They held back wave after wave of undead, but their positioning in the center of the battle meant there was no respite. King Favian rode his griffin above the battlefield, offering aid where he could among the maelstrom of bats and gargoyles that remained. He stooped low to pull a blood-covered giant fighting for her life from a swarm of undead. Skeletons clung to the giant's legs as she rose into the air, falling away like insects in a stiff breeze.

Despite all the powerful magic Mythos had brought, there was no escape from the wave of death that flowed from around the city. Thousands upon thousands of skeletons fought without tiring and marched fearlessly even as their forces crumbled around them. They had no desires of their own, no self-preservation, only the unceasing determination to fight.

Unlike the dead, the werewolves attacked with the coordinated tactics of a pack, tearing through the ranks of Mythos's less-skilled fighters. Giant spiders and hobgoblins had joined the fray, descending from the forest along with monstrous creatures cloaked in shadow. Everywhere Pressley looked, the situation was dire. Only the trolls held their own, but he could see the bodies of many among the dead. They fought with a fury of those who had nothing to lose. Pressley knew better, though. Chod had made sure of that. The trolls had everything to lose, and still, they raged.

He'd make sure their efforts weren't in vain. He raised his arm, aiming Blood-strike at a pack of werewolves. After charging a fraction of his HP into the attack, he released, and a bolt of red energy shot across the battlefield like liquid lightning. It exploded upon impact, tearing through werewolf bodies and giving the trolls an edge to push their attack.

Pressley threw the giant potion bottle into the horde of undead, angling his throw as he let go. Earth sprayed from the impact as the massive bottle skipped like a rock on water, crushing hundreds of enemies as it bounced across the battlefield.

With all of his stats doubled, he might be the most powerful person in Mythos for the next few minutes. He needed to cause as much destruction as possible with what time remained.

Pressley's health depleted by a sliver as he took a step, crushing undead beneath his boot with a satisfying crunch. He cast Unhallowed Ground to his right, and the earth sizzled like acid beneath his newfound power, rotting away the bodies of skeletons that passed into the area of effect. Their bodies melted like chocolate on a hot day, leaving behind a cream-colored gelatinous puddle.

While Pressley focused on the enemies on the ground, his manticore terrorized the skies alongside Caustic, showing why she'd earned the name Winged Fright. She ripped through bats with a vengeance, empowered by the death knight's increased stats. The bats' numbers had dwindled, but there were still hundreds of them, and they were powerful enough to break the stone bodies of the gargoyles when attacking together.

Caustic descended from the clouds, crushing a bat with his powerful jaws and spitting the mangled corpse onto the horde below. The dragon hovered in front of Pressley for a moment, roaring at the death knight.

"Don't worry. I'm on it." Pressley crushed more undead beneath his boots, and the dragon turned, soaring above the clouds to surprise his next victim.

Pressley cast Pestilence over the area directly in front of him. Dozens of undead decayed rapidly, crumpling to the ground as their bones were ravaged by disease.

The timer continued to tick down, along with Pressley's health as he took another step. One way or another, he was running out of time. He activated Frost Reaper, the new ability he'd unlocked in the manticore's dungeon, and a thick layer of frost coated his armor and trailed down his blade. As he moved across the battle-field, frost spread out from beneath his boots, slowing the undead in the death knight's immediate vicinity. He slashed his sword with enough force that it left a frozen trench in the earth. Skeletons sailed through the air with the arc of his blade, and Lifesteal replenished some of the HP he'd lost. If not for the timer, he might have one of the few classes that could counter the potion's adverse effect.

But nothing was ever that easy.

Pressley hacked through undead as he moved across the battlefield, leaving frozen channels and gaping holes of destruction from Pestilence and Unhallowed Ground in his wake.

The invasion had gone on long enough for forces inside the city to rally to its defense. Boulders and burning pitch launched at the death knight from catapults behind the walls. Pressley canceled Frost Reaper and cast Blight of the Undead, summoning a deafening buzz of insects that swarmed his colossal body, shielding him from the projectiles as he moved across the battlefield.

More undead focused their attack upon the towering menace, and skeletons piled around his feet, climbing over one another like a mound of ants. They fell from his legs with each thunderous step as he made his way toward Seascape's forces. Pressley slashed his sword through the air, swatting bats like they were flies, and fired Bloodstrike into the enemies attacking at the rear. His HP was at fifty percent by the time he found King Orso.

The king wielded his warhammer with unforgiving authority, shattering bones and tearing undead limb from limb. Pressley cast Unhallowed Ground, forming a barrier in front of the king and giving him a moment of respite.

The death knight canceled Blight of the Undead as he knelt, crushing enemies beneath the weight of his giant knee. "Chod has breached the wall. I don't have long in this form, but I should be able to offer you a fighting chance if you can rally your troops."

King Orso nodded, raising his warhammer into the air. "We will not fail."

The death knight stood, his gaze settling on the city. A green aura pulsed from the keep like a toxic heartbeat. Somewhere inside the walls, Chod was fighting his way to stop its beating.

Pressley activated Bone Detector, and his vision flooded with white. He grinned beneath his helm. *I can't believe I'm about to do this.*

His helm rumbled like thunder as he laughed. "This one's for you, you son of a bitch."

He sheathed his sword and cast Lifesteal with both hands. Purple energy shot into the horde of undead, the massive damage output refilling his HP completely. It was a good thing, because he'd need every last bit for what came next.

The earth shuddered as Pressley cast Summon Undead, and his health plummeted into the red as thousands of bones reassembled themselves under his control. The timer ticked down to less than a minute, and he ordered his minions into position while he waited on the cooldown to cast Lifesteal again.

Though his body blazed with energy, he took a deep breath, finding that sense of cold he'd grown accustomed to. Closing his eyes, he embraced the chill as he waited for his daughter's face to appear in the void. In the emptiness, he found comfort as her outline began to take shape, and deep within his core, he felt a spark of warmth.

Pressley opened his eyes, using Lifesteal to replenish his health a final time before he poured everything he had into Corpse Explosion.

Eva smiled at him, and then the world went black.

37. ANGEL OF DEATH

Kassidy's portal releases me inside the city walls, where dead elves lie across the cobbled streets. Randy and Drizz'rt wipe blood from their daggers, and Arty grimaces as he downs a health potion. The cyclops sighs as the wound on his shoulder starts to close.

We've cleared our first obstacle by making it past the wall, but the mission is far from over. Mosstar is a city of shadows, but I get the feeling that it always wasn't that way. The green flames from the keep give life to the gloom, where the dark streets are at odds with the beautiful architecture. Each building flows into the next with curves and ornamentations, and skeletal trees grow from within them. I can only imagine how beautiful this city was before darkness overtook it.

"This area is clear for now, but we need to get moving." Michael shines like a beacon in the center of the group. The effect adds to his paladin aesthetic, but it's terrible for sneaking through a city. That's the precise reason why I haven't summoned Pharos yet.

"Any way you can tone that down a bit?" I wave my hands up and down, gesturing at his entire being.

Dorothy scoffs. "Believe me, we already tried. He's a permanent glowstick."

Michael narrows his eyes at Dorothy. "Onera prefers I walk in the light, even among the shadows."

I suppress a laugh and focus on our situation. Kassidy portaled us into the left corner of the city, far from the action around the gate. After taking an arrow to the stomach, I hope he's okay, but I push the thought from my mind, along with my concern for everyone still fighting outside the city walls. There will be a time for that but for now, I need to be focused.

I peek around the corner and see elves rushing through the streets. They move chaotically. Some head toward the gate and others climb the battlements. Despite how dire the situation may seem outside the walls, we managed to catch the city off guard. Things could be a lot worse.

Feet patter down a nearby alley as an elf emerges from a side street, almost running past us before sliding to a halt. His eyes go wide as he takes us in, and he opens his mouth to scream.

An arrow lodges in the elf's throat before he has a chance, leaving him croaking as he gasps for air. Blood trickles through his fingers as he clutches his neck, panic in his eyes. Scotty approaches and jerks the arrow free in a swift motion. Blood spurts from the wound as the elf falls to the street.

I doubt that will be the last elf we run into, so I summon more horrors and feel the comforting grip of Destroyer against my palm. "You guys ready?"

What's left of our party of heroes focuses on me. Taryn, Dorothy, Randy, Don, Michael, Drizz'rt, Sam, Scotty, Kazzandra, Arty and his two brothers, Roddick and Reddick, and two more adventurers. For the life of me, I can't recall their names. One of them is Orin or Dorin, and I think the other one was something stupid like Matt. Regardless, I'm glad they're here.

"We've made it past the undead, but there's still a city of elves between us and our objective." I raise my warhammer and point it toward the keep. "Taryn, you have the amulet?"

Taryn reaches into his cloak, lifting a silver chain that holds an amulet set with an iridescent stone. It glimmers in the twilight. He scratches Berry behind the ears and then slides off the umber bear's back, where Jordy gently rams his head into Taryn's side.

My best friend looks up at me with eyes full of worry. "Keep them safe."

I squeeze his shoulder, and we both know that's a promise I can't make. "I'll do my best."

Taryn buffs us with Strong Wind, and then there's a burst of feathers as he transforms into a small red bird. He's almost invisible underneath the twilight sky, and if King Orso's theory holds true, the Amulet of Undetection will protect him from Valmar's gaze as well.

Half of my dreadbeasts are still outside the wall fighting alongside the trolls. I take the fact that they're still alive as a good sign. The ones still with me lead the way as we hurry about the perimeter, doing our best to cling to the shadows. With the attack concentrated around the gate, the streets are strangely empty. As we move further away from the sounds of battle, the chatter of the undead creep over the wall.

More than once I see a head disappear behind twitching curtains, and I can't help but wonder which side these people would fall on were they given a choice.

I reach out to Caustic for an update on the battle. *"How are the forces holding up?"*

There's a moment before he responds. *"I have taken many lives but the advance has stalled. Reinforcements have attacked from the forest, and elves fire upon us from the walls. The dead one fights with the strength of a dragon, but I do not know if it will be enough."*

A knot forms in my stomach. This is exactly what we didn't want to happen.

. . .

Incoming Message (Taryn): *Two streets ahead on your left. Group of six.*

I relay Taryn's message to the others, and we approach with caution. The soldiers turn the corner with swords and spears raised, and unlike the last elf, they don't seem surprised to see us. Randy, Drizz'rt, and Dorothy use Shadow Step in almost perfect synchronicity, appearing behind the elves and slitting the throats of the three at the back. Michael raises his sword. It beams with golden light, blinding the three remaining elves, while Don casts a void spear that extends outward and skewers two of them.

The lone elf turns to run, but Dorothy is waiting with a vicious snarl and plunges her blade into his neck.

I give them a look of surprise. "Have you guys been practicing behind my back?"

She looks from Randy to Drizz'rt and grins. "Great minds, I guess."

Incoming Message (Taryn): *Someone knows you're here. Three units moving from the north. Two more on your rear. Do you need me to come down?*

Message (Chod): *Stay where you are. We need your eyes in the sky.*

"Get ready for a fight. They know we're here." I summon another horror and turn my attention in the direction we came from.

My Dreadbeasts of Torment sniff at the air, and a low growl rumbles in their chests. Their bison brethren paw their hooves against the cobblestone, smoke pouring from their nostrils.

We split our forces in half and position ourselves back to back as we wait for our assailants. Taryn calls out enemy positions and intel, and since the non-heroes aren't capable of party chat, I relay it to the others. With aerial advantage, we pick off the enemies before they know what's happening.

"How the hell do they know we're here?" Randy pulls a dagger from a dead elf and flicks the blood into the street.

Dorothy nods in Michael's direction. "Could be the walking nightlight we have with us?"

I don't know if it's the stress of the situation or what, but Michael's gallant facade finally cracks.

He slams his shield into the ground and stares daggers at Dorothy. "I'm getting really tired of your little quips."

"Oh, is that so?" She spins her daggers in her palms. "You want to go, big guy?"

I step between them with my arms raised, and dreadbeasts flank me on both sides. "Guys, we're on the same side here. It doesn't matter how they know we're here. What matters is we get to the keep. Now, let's—"

The air distorts behind Michael as the fabric of reality tears, a sight I've become all too familiar with recently. Before I have a chance to call out, a blade pierces from the darkness, stabbing the paladin in the back of the neck. The sword rips through his throat, and his knees buckle as the divine light fades. A moment later, his body vanishes, leaving a pile of armor on the ground.

Someone cackles from within the portal, and heat radiates from Limery as his claws dig into my shoulder. The void stretches, and three figures step from the darkness. Ethan French, the warlock, is the first to emerge, his tattooed body held aloft by phantom wings. His dreadlocks float in the air like he's weightless, and a dark aura surrounds his body. He wears a sleeveless black robe that reveals the silver tattoos glowing against his dark skin. He's flanked by his two companions, Otis Wiggins the barbarian and Kevin Harris the sorcerer.

Otis grins as he rests his massive double-edged axe on his shoulder. He wears a black vest trimmed in white fur, and with his bald head and bushy beard, he's a prototypical movie villain. It's assholes like him that give barbarians a bad name. He's a mindless tool—the kind where if I gave him a penny for his thoughts, I'd get change back.

Opposite Otis, Kevin wears a wicked grin as he surveys our group. Ethan has power and Otis has brawn, but the sorcerer is a tactician. I know from experience how dangerous his Arcane Chains can be, and his robe is strapped with vials in a myriad of hues. I'm sure there are some powerful potions within his arsenal.

We'll need to end this before he has a chance to use them. Taryn sends a message, but I dismiss it. My complete attention is focused on the situation in front of us.

Don steps toward our assailants. "What are you idiots playing at?"

"Us?" Otis laughs. "We're not the ones pretending to be heroes."

"That's probably because you lost your imagination the tenth time your mother dropped you on your head." Randy joins the void mage's side. "I've seen zombies with more brains than you."

Otis lifts his axe from his shoulder and sneers. "I'll show you brains when I spill yours in the street."

He takes a step, but a shadowy hand reaches from the portal and pulls him back.

Ethan lowers himself until he's hovering a foot above the street. "Give us the troll and you can all go home safe and sound. No one else needs to get hurt."

Don takes another step forward. "That's not going to happen."

Ethan chuckles, but there's no mirth in it. "You're willing to die for him?"

"I'm willing to fight beside him because he's a lot more likable than you three assholes." Don doesn't wait to make the first move, clapping his hands together and sending a wave of energy pulsing from his body. His Nullification Zone expands, closing the portal and severing the shadowy hand in the process. It dissipates into a fine mist, and the warlock's wings vanish. Ethan falls to the ground.

Behind him, Otis tumbles over backward from the weight of his axe as Don's spell disables everyone's abilities in the immediate vicinity of the void mage. I don't know if it's because I'm too far away or if Cold Rage is protecting me, but my Warforged body doesn't falter.

"Get out of here!" Don yells. "We'll handle these fucks."

Randy moves slower than I'm used to seeing, but he's still quick enough to get the job done as he stabs Ethan in the shoulder. Drizz'rt doesn't need his speed, choosing to stick a dagger in Kevin's chest from ten feet away.

"Come on, let's go!" Dorothy pulls me by the forearm before I have a chance to join the fight.

Limery and I follow her down the side alley trailed by horrors, dreadbeasts, and Taryn's pets. There's a moment of panic as I search for Flubs, but then I notice a gelatinous green layer covering Berry's saddle. Good. They're all here.

We pass several streets and then an explosion rumbles outside the walls.

Limery looks over his shoulder. "What was thats?"

I reach out to Caustic with the same question. *What the hell was that?*

He doesn't answer, and three elves appear in front of us. My Dreadbeasts of Despair trample them to the ground at full speed, and the Dreadbeasts of Torment finish the job. They may be wearing armor, but these are definitely not soldiers.

"This way." Dorothy points down a street that runs perpendicular to the keep.

I shake my head, gesturing toward the towering structure ahead of us. "The keep is that way."

"Trust me. The keep will be heavily guarded, and my marauder class helps navigate ruins. There's a hidden tunnel a few streets over that leads straight under the castle."

"Okay, let's hurry." My mind drifts back to the explosion. The longer we take, the more danger everyone is in. *Caustic?* I reach out to him again as we follow Dorothy.

"The dead one sacrificed himself. The tide turns in our favor. I will join you shortly."

Before I have a chance to respond, Taryn sends a message.

Incoming Message (Taryn): *What's going on down there? The castle is the other way.*

My mind is pulling me in a dozen directions when I need to stay on the task at hand. As much as I want to ask about Don and the others, it can wait.

Message (Chod): *Dorothy says there's a hidden tunnel a few streets over.*

Incoming Message (Taryn): *Watch out. There's a group at the end of the street.*

• • •

I catch up with Dorothy and extend an arm, signaling for us to slow down as we approach the corner.

She nods, letting me and my summons take the lead.

When I turn the corner, my blood boils at the sight of Jude and Glenn surrounded by an escort of elves. Jude has cleaned up a bit since our run-in outside of Boneholde. The shaggy-haired fighter has new leather armor accented with green thread and a host of glittering daggers strapped to his chest and thighs.

"I knew we'd meet again." He licks his lips as he takes in my appearance. "As much as I dislike you, I've got to admit that bringing an army this big into the shadowlands just to die takes some troll-sized balls."

Glenn laughs, but it doesn't reach his soulless eyes. For the first time, he wears a set of pristine armor that isn't composed of mismatched pieces. His plate mail is solid black, fitting for the kind of sadistic asshole he is, and he holds an obsidian sword with a shimmering golden hilt.

His expressionless eyes meet mine. "I'm glad to see you again. I should thank you for making my job easier. Once we finish you, the rest of the trolls will be child's play."

My grip tightens around Destroyer, and mana blazes at my fingertips. I've killed them both before, and I can do it again.

"I wouldn't do that if I were you." Dorothy's frigid tone sets the hair at the back of my neck on end.

"Chods." There's a desperation in Limery's voice that freezes every cell in my body, and my heart sinks into the pit of my stomach.

I turn around, and Dorothy has Limery held against her chest, a dagger pressed to his throat.

"Please..." I search for words as Destroyer falls from my grip, but I can only repeat the same word again. "Please. Dorothy, please."

Her blue eyes flare orange, the same as the day we fought outside the trials, and her visage shifts as her mouth twists into a sinister smile. Cracks form along her face as her pallid white skin flakes away, revealing a deathly charcoal complexion. Her golden locks fade to a dull silver and when I analyze her, her class description has changed.

Dorothy Jordan
> _Level 33_
> _Revenant_
> _Elf_

Icy dread settles inside of me. She played me. All this time, I thought I had made amends, but she was just waiting for me to let my guard down. She knows I care about Limery more than anything in the world and she's going to use him to hurt me.

"Ethan was right. You are way too trusting." She presses the blade into Limery's throat until he whimpers, and beads of red sprout along the blade's edge.

"Please." I repeat again as panic flares in my chest. I try to fight against the soul-crushing dread so that I can find a way out of this, but it presses in on me from every angle, like I'm in the trials all over again. "I'll do anything, just please, don't hurt him."

"*What is happening!*" Caustic's voice rumbles in my mind. He must sense my distress through our bond.

"I bet you would. Anything to save your precious little Limmy." She laughs. "Too bad, Chad. You're not talking your way out of this one. I told you that I came here to make you pay. Turns out you pissed off a lot more people than just me. They were right, though. You do have a hero complex. I knew that if I was patient, if I played along, then my opportunity would come." She laughs again. "You should see the look on your face. Priceless." Her smile fades. "It'd make a great meme."

"You don't have to do this." I hold my hands up. "Let him go. You can take me instead. I won't fight it."

"You don't get it, do you?" She lets out an exasperated sigh. "You have no say here. There's no out. The only way this ends is in immeasurable pain for you. Then maybe you'll understand what it's like to be helpless while your world crumbles around you."

"Dorothy..." I step toward her, and her grip on the dagger tightens. Red trickles down Limery's neck, freezing me in place. "Why are you doing this?"

"Why? Don't be stupid. You know why." Her voice is strangely calm as she holds Limery's life in her hands. "You think I would just forgive and forget, Chad? That isn't how this works. It's cute that you care for him so much. Maybe I'd be sympathetic if you weren't such an asshole, but you ruined my life, and now I'm going to cause you as much pain as you caused me."

She pulls the dagger across Limery's throat, and his bulbous yellow eyes widen in shock just before my world comes crashing down around me. His head hangs limp, and a loud ringing fills my ears, blocking out everything. It can't end like this. It just can't. I pray to whatever god will listen as I shove the Angel of Death Brandy into the mouth of my closest dreadbeast and cast Sacrifice.

The demonic wolf explodes in a shower of shadows and gore. Then nothing. The ringing in my ears amplifies as I realize I failed. I promised to walk through hell for Limery and in the end, it was me who got him killed.

If not for me, Dorothy wouldn't be here.

She lets Limery's lifeless body fall from her grip like he means nothing, and anger flares in my core, a volcano ready to erupt. His body is inches from the street when time stops. For a brief moment, nothing moves, and then the world moves in reverse as the Angel of Death Brandy takes effect. Time rewinds for two seconds.

Limery's corpse floats back into Dorothy's arms, and blood surges into his small frame, allowing the dagger to seal it back inside.

"What the—" Dorothy blinks, unsure of what just happened.

"Go molten!" I shout.

Dorothy is too slow to react as Limery's body transforms into molten lava, melting the blade pressed against his neck. His eyes blaze white, and the flames surrounding his body turn blue as he burns hotter than ever, so hot that he incinerates Dorothy's arm up to the elbow and scorches her chest and face.

She recoils, her vest smoldering as her screams of anguish cut through the ringing in my ears. Limery darts past me, his face pure hatred as he collides with Jude in mid-air. The imp's small arms clench around Jude's throat, and Limery ignites his fire shield. A circle of heat surrounds him, and Jude's face blisters before turning to saggy mush that melts off the bone.

Glenn turns to run, but I throw Destroyer at him with all my might. It clanks against his armor, knocking him to the ground. Red feathers explode in front of him as Taryn appears, pinning the psychopath's arms by his side with the vines from his Sapling Staff.

Taryn kneels beside Glenn. "This one's for Stompy," he whispers before plunging his shadow blade into the man's skull.

I turn my attention back to Dorothy, who stands there in shock, looking at her stump of an arm.

"How?" she mumbles, and there's a far-off look in her eyes as a shadow descends upon her.

Caustic's jaws wrap around the revenant, severing her body in half with a powerful bite. He lands in front of me, a deep rumble emanating from his chest.

"I told you I do not trust her."

"I know." I should never have doubted a dragon's instincts.

Limery extinguishes his flames as he wraps his arms around my neck. He trembles against my body, and I fight back tears as I hold him tight.

"I'm sorry, buddy." I came so close to truly losing him.

"Limmy was scareds." He sniffles. "But Chods saves Limmy."

Taryn kicks a piece of Glenn's armor across the street. "I wonder where they're respawning."

"If I had to guess, it can't be too far."

"Dorothy, man..." Taryn shakes his head. "What a piece of work."

I try not to think about it. Unpacking what just happened is a rabbit hole for another time.

"We need to end this while we have a chance." Our plan has gone to shit, but my gaze falls on the obsidian tower in the center of the keep, sparking an idea. "You mind if I borrow the amulet? Maybe your cloak, too?"

Taryn follows my gaze. "What's the plan?"

"The others still need help. Take Limery and my horrors with you." I pick up Destroyer and sling it over my shoulder as I climb upon Caustic. "It's time for me to smash some shit."

38. THE KING OF EVIL

Caustic and I fly above the twilight city. I summon a Horror of Finesse from atop the dragon's back, and the gangly blue creature watches me with a look of betrayal as it plummets toward the earth. I cast Sacrifice, buffing my stats, before summoning the next horror in the rotation.

Far below, the outer gate has fallen. Mythos's forces push through the undead and into the city, clashing with the elves waiting on the other side. The keep will be surrounded within the hour, and Valmar will be forced to make his last stand. There's no telling how many will die trying to take down the wizard.

Unless I do something about it.

"Do you think this will work?" I ask Caustic.

"There is a chance." The dragon's muscles flex as he climbs higher, taking us above the clouds. *"It is foolish to fight without me by your side."*

Gotta love his unfiltered honesty. If I had only listened to him when it came to Dorothy.

"For this to work, I need the element of surprise."

"If you survive, that will be the surprise." He huffs.

Dragons aren't exactly known for their comforting pep talks, but he's not wrong. There's a good chance that this goes sideways. Relying on a castle map that hasn't been updated in over four hundred years isn't the most intelligent decision. And then there's the assumption that Valmar would be—

"This should suffice." Caustic interrupts my thoughts, and as much as he may try to conceal it, I can sense the worry in his tone.

I lean to the side and gulp as I look at the city below. From this high, even the elephants seem like ants. Of all the stupid things I've done during my time in Mythos, this might be the dumbest. I take a deep breath and fill my lungs with confidence.

"I'll be fine. No matter what happens, remember that I'll respawn. Focus on helping the others take the city." I pat Caustic on the back. *"He's never going to see this coming."*

I release my grip and slide from the dragon's back, summoning a surprised horror that flails wildly before Sacrifice snuffs it out of existence. For a moment, I enjoy the cool wind against my body, then I equip the three items that make up the Regeneration Triad as my body plummets toward the earth like a falling meteor.

I read over their stats one final time to ensure that this is just dumb and not suicide.

Item. Renewal Spear. *Capable of holding life aura equivalent to 500 HP. The Renewal Spear gathers aura passively while equipped and can steal health from enemies during battle. Life aura may be absorbed by the wielder at any time.* **Bonus:** *When paired with Regeneration Stone and Shield of Vigor, user will be granted a ten-foot aura that provides 20% increased regeneration for companions within its radius.*

Item. Shield of Vigor. *Increases HP by 30%.* **Bonus:** *When paired with Regeneration Stone and Renewal Spear, user will be granted a ten-foot aura that provides 20% increased regeneration for companions within its radius.*

Item. Regeneration Stone. *Increases health regeneration by 20%.* **Bonus:** *When paired with Shield of Vigor and Renewal Spear, user will be granted a ten-foot aura that provides 20% increased regeneration for companions within its radius.*

Notice! Complete Set: Regeneration Triad. *While wearing all three pieces of the Regeneration Triad, user will be granted a ten-foot aura that provides 20% increased regeneration for companions within its radius.*

Good. The thirty percent HP buff will help with the impact, and the health regeneration should keep me clinging to life if I've severely underestimated how strong my Warforged body is.

The Amulet of Undetection whips in the air as I fall, clinking against the side of my metallic head. I shift the angle of the shield to adjust my trajectory, using the four blazing green flames as my personal runway lights. The keep comes into detail far quicker than I expect, and the terror of what's about to happen finally settles in.

Is tenfold Constitution enough to save an idiot who essentially just went skydiving without a parachute? *Just breathe.* I'm Warforged. I could bellyflop in the middle of the street and still survive.

I hope.

I pull the shield against my chest and tighten my grip on the spear, squinting for the last few seconds as I fall toward what should be the throne room. Unlike in the movies, there's no slow-motion impact as I crash through the ceiling. No heroic moment where the walls explode, and me and Valmar rise from the rubble, lone survivors, as dust settles all around us.

Instead, I pierce through the roof of the keep like a speeding bullet, leaving a hole barely bigger than my body as I smash into the floor like a wrecking ball. My health drops by half from the impact, even with the thirty percent buff, and a deep metallic thrum echoes through my bones.

The room spins as I crawl to my feet among the cracked marble that surrounds a troll-shaped indentation. I can sense Caustic speaking to me, but the words swirl within the maelstrom of my addled brain.

A modicum of dust flits across the room, not nearly as heroic as I imagined, and I'm uncertain whether I'm seeing stars or if the tiny particles are sparkling in the torchlight. The hole in the ceiling casts a stream of green light from the fiery towers that reflects upon my metallic skin, reminding me of my first days in Mythos.

I chuckle to myself at the irony.

My vision finally settles, and I take in the rest of the room. Torches line the walls, burning with the same eerie green as the towers, and dozens of armored undead stand sentry around the room. Unlike the skeletons outside the city, these haven't been ravaged by the elements. Dried skin still covers their bones, and wispy hair hangs about their shoulders. They wear fine, polished armor and seem unfazed by my presence. Either the amulet is doing its job or Valmar is unthreatened by my sudden appearance.

He sits upon an obsidian throne at least twenty feet away, watching me with a curious expression. I missed by a long shot.

The infamous dark wizard is nothing like I expected. He has a menacing look about him, but for a necromancer, he's kind of handsome, with his chiseled jawline and his thick hair slicked back to fall over his shoulders. His skin is the dull gray of the undead, but he reminds me more of a vampire than some decrepit-looking lich. There's a suppleness to his flesh that other undead don't have, and his intense eyes burn similarly to Dorothy's.

"I'll give you credit, troll. You have been a constant thorn in my side." His mouth curls at the edge. "I admire your resolve."

I step out of the crater, stone crushing beneath my feet. "Yeah, well, I thought you'd be taller."

He laughs as he stands from his throne. His boots clack against the marble as he approaches nonchalantly. "Of all the outworlders, you show a surprising amount of promise. Join me and the world can be yours, for you and your trolls. You can make a new name for trollkind in your image."

He stops about three paces in front of me.

"Is that what you did?" I shift my gaze to the undead standing on each side of me. "We're in a city of elves and yet you're surrounded by the dead."

His eye twitches. "I'm surrounded by loyal soldiers. Every one of them swore an oath to protect me in their first life and the next."

I think I've found a sore spot, so I press onward. "And what about your citizens? For a city this big, it's awfully sparse. How many of your people are you marching to their deaths?"

"What would an outworlder know of our struggles?" He scoffs, and his eyes narrow. "You may call me a villain but tell me, where were the heroes when Mosstar's luscious lands slowly fell to the darkness? Where were the kingdoms that prospered when our soil turned to ash? When we begged for aid, who answered?" He shakes his head in disgust. "No one. Left alone, it was our fate to be consumed, but we refused. When the light offered no aid, we embraced the darkness. We allied ourselves with it, and I made it our power. Funny how they noticed us then, fearing what they did not understand, even though it was their inaction that forced us down this path." He tilts back his head and laughs. "If that makes me a villain, then crown me the king of evil."

Judging by the throne, someone already has.

"You killed innocent people," I argue.

"I did what was necessary to save *my* people. You of all people should understand this." His eyes blaze like embers. "You've seen what lurks beyond our city walls. This is no place for the elves. Not anymore. Once we were branded enemies, our only refuge was to take it by force. For four hundred years, I've watched my people waste away in the darkness. For four hundred years, I've added them to my ranks so that one day, we could start anew."

"That's not going to happen." I feel the cold metal of the spear against my fingers and wonder which of us has the faster reflexes. "We've breached the wall. Soon, the city will be overrun."

"The walls may fall, the city may surrender, but this is not the end for Valmar Worren or Mosstar. You may have caught me unprepared, but my forces are spread far and wide. Darkness can never be truly extinguished because it is merely the absence of light. It's always there, even when you can't see it."

I take a step forward, pointing my spear at him. "You're not leaving this city."

"Have it your way." He sighs like a teacher who's heard one too many excuses. "If you won't fight by my side, then you will fight for me. And after I raise your body, I'll use it to kill those you've sworn to protect. How many do you think will die at your hands?"

"That will never happen." I summon Pharos. The spirit guide bursts to life in front of me and charges at Valmar. The necromancer recoils from the ethereal light, and I plant the spear in his chest. Armor rattles as the undead charge from around the room. I summon a Dreadbeast of Torment, and the wolf lunges at the closest guard, tackling it to the ground.

Valmar snarls with a ferocity that could have come from Caustic as he pushes the spear deeper into his chest until the pressure releases and it juts through his back. He lunges, climbing up the spear's shaft and burying it deeper until his cold hands wrap around my arms and squeeze like vice grips. My increased Constitution does nothing to stop the ice-cold dread that courses through my body as frost forms along the necromancer's hands. His eyes rage with fury as ice spreads along my metallic skin and my health drops with each passing moment.

I let go of the spear and bring my arms up and outward, forcing Valmar to release his grip. Metal screams as swords and spears spark against my body. My dreadbeast yelps, and I summon its bison kin along with horrors to provide a distraction for the undead.

The spear skewering Valmar is an afterthought as the necromancer unleashes his rage. A black aura surrounds his hands as he fires a bolt of black energy. The first goes over my shoulder, blasting a hole in the far wall big enough to drive a bus through. The second bolt catches me in the chest, knocking me into the wall. My

Warforged body absorbs the impact, and I crawl to my feet. My health is down to twenty percent as I equip Destroyer and charge Valmar.

He cracks his neck, stalking toward me like the predator he is. An explosion thunders from outside the keep as he casts a spell, and a wave of energy flares through the necromancer's body. His undead guard rushes toward me, and I imbue my next attack with Concussive Force, punching the closest minion with enough power that its breastplate warps around my fist as it goes flying into the others like a bowling ball. I fight my way through his minions, smashing the ancient bodies until their armor clamors against the floor.

I swing Destroyer at Valmar, and he raises a fist to meet the head of my warhammer. His knuckles take the blow like an anvil, refusing to give under the force of my full power. Energy recoils down the weapon and through my body as I go flying backward.

What the hell was that? He must have an ability similar to Sacrifice that siphons power from his undead. And he has a lot of undead.

Valmar pounces across the room with superhuman speed, landing on top of me before I even hit the ground. His fists thrum as he punches my Warforged body. Marble cracks beneath my backside with each hit.

I summon a Horror of Power and swing blindly, hoping to connect with any part of the terror I'm facing. Valmar swats my fist away and clamps his hand around my throat, his icy grip crystallizing upon my metallic skin. I expected him to be more powerful than me, but I never thought he'd be stronger.

I never should have come alone.

Bright light flares behind the necromancer as Pharos rams into his backside. Valmar hisses at the spirit guide's presence. He rolls to the side and tosses me across the room like I weigh nothing.

I slam into a column, which cracks under the force of the impact. Valmar sets his gaze on Pharos, and his hands hum with dark power followed by an explosion that rocks the throne room as shards of darkness erupt from inside the frost goat. Void spikes protrude from Pharos's spirit, and his body dims before he vanishes into mist.

Valmar growls as his attention returns to me. There are no quips, no monologues, just unbridled anger that burns within his eyes.

A black bolt of energy crashes inches in front of me, sending exploding marble clinking against my chest. I scurry back and hear the familiar whir of a portal as something clasps around my midsection. Giant demonic fingers cinch around me, sending chills through my body as they hold me in place. Whatever being this is, it's far stronger than I am. I might not be susceptible to stuns or slows while I'm raging, but it does nothing to prevent me from being physically restrained by something stronger.

Valmar's face is expressionless as he kneels before me, the spear skewering his upper body scraping against the floor. He takes my chin in his long, slender fingers and looks into my eyes as if searching for something.

"You could have had everything." He cradles my chin, shaking his head in disappointment.

I hear the frost crackling along his fingers before the frigid cold settles in my jaw. Unable to move, I sit there helplessly as my health drops. When my HP dips below ten percent, my increased regeneration kicks in and holds the drain at bay.

Valmar smiles. "Tricky little troll."

His free hand blasts me in the chest, and my vision darkens at the edges as pain surges through my metal body. He blasts me again, and it's like my nerves are on fire. The third time, my body screams, and everything goes black.

39. SURVIVORS

The blackness fades, and I respawn in the crater I created when I crashed through the ceiling. I always assumed I would miss smashing Valmar like a pancake, but it made for a nice distraction while I set my spawn point.

I have full health and all my items, thanks to the Revive Potion.

Across the room, a black aura shrouds Valmar as the necromancer leans over a doppelgänger of my body. The Renewal Spear still protrudes from his chest and back, nothing more than a hindrance as he works.

With the Amulet of Undetection, neither Valmar nor his minions have any idea that I'm here. On top of that, I had the wherewithal to borrow Taryn's Cloak of Silence. I equip the cloak, muting my footsteps as I sneak across the throne room.

If this plan doesn't work, I'm going to be immensely fucked once Valmar discovers my trickery. He'll be able to spawn camp me back to level one, and there'll be nothing I can do about it.

The necromancer's body hums with energy as dark tendrils flow from his hands toward my lifeless corpse. They hover around the doppelgänger, unable to permeate the illusion.

Valmar grunts, and the tendrils fade as he shakes out his hands. "This isn't right."

Because it's not real, dumbass.

When I'm a few feet behind him, I activate Return to Sender and the enchanted stone triggers, ripping the Renewal Spear from Valmar's body and returning it to my hand. I plunge the weapon into the back of Valmar's skull and activate the life aura stored inside the spear, the anathema to his undead being. His head explodes like a grenade of dark matter. The torches extinguish, leaving me in darkness as a gust of cool air escapes through the ceiling. All around the room, armor clatters against the floor as his minions collapse, robbed of their energy source. The eerie glow surrounding the keep is gone. Whatever magic powered the fiery towers left with Valmar.

Caustic's voice is once again clear in my mind. *"The dead have fallen, and the elves have surrendered. I'm coming to find you."*

Emotion swells within me, and I drop to my knees. The Renewal Spear falls from my grasp, clanging against the marble floor, and a hollow ring echoes through the empty throne room.

Valmar's gone. Mosstar has surrendered. The war is over.

We survived. Not only that, but against all odds, we managed to win.

I'm sitting on the steps to the keep, deep in thought, when Caustic arrives.

For some reason, I can't stop thinking about what Valmar said. Did his rise to power happen because the elves were left to fend for themselves? And what happens to the elves, and Mosstar for that matter, now that Valmar is gone? I was so intent on ending the threat he presented that I never took a minute to think about what would come after. We saved the trolls. We saved Mythos. Valmar is no more. But what about the elves who will face the consequences of his actions?

We may have won the battle, but the work is just beginning.

The dragon huffs, and his golden eyes bore into me. *"You saved many lives today."*

I stroke his golden beard. *"We did."*

Caustic preens at the compliment, flexing his wings.

I let out a long sigh and cancel Cold Rage. The metallic sheen fades from my body, leaving me as a light blue troll, a ghost in the twilight.

Taryn and the other heroes arrive soon after. Limery darts toward me, nearly knocking me over as he wraps his arms around me.

"We dids its, Chods!" He grins. "We beats the bad mans."

I hug him back, grateful for the little guy more than ever. I came so close to losing him, and I still can't shake the image of his body tumbling toward the ground. With Dorothy and the others out there, will they try again to get their revenge? None of them know about the program's status, so I hope that they bide their time and we're all pulled from the game before they can hurt anyone else.

Even though they look a little worse for the wear, there are plenty of smiles to go around as the others catch up.

Scotty takes a seat on the steps, closing his eyes as he leans back and rests his elbows. I don't blame him. After today, we all need a long rest and a strong drink. The physical taxation of battle is nothing compared to the mental toll. Drizz'rt's golden scales are covered in crimson. Whether the blood belongs to him or someone else, there's no telling. Probably a little of both. Arty carries one of his brothers on his shoulder, and Don, Sam, Randy, Kazzandra, and one of the adventurers are nowhere to be seen.

"What happened?" I ask.

Taryn climbs down from Berry, inspecting me for injuries. "We got there just as Ethan summoned some kind of demon through his portal. Randy got the worst of it, and then Kazzandra put an axe in Ethan's head. He died, but the demon didn't fade away. In the chaos, we all forgot that he still had a Revive Potion from the tournament. Ethan showed back up and took out Don, and then Sam took one of Kevin's potions to the face. We got them in the end, though. No idea where their spawn point is, but I'm sure they'll find us." When he's satisfied that I'm not hurt, Taryn takes a seat beside me. "We lost Borin and Kazzandra, but Arty says we shouldn't mourn them, that there's no greater honor for an adventurer than to die with a weapon in their hand. He wants us to drink to their names. Roddick is still unconscious but he should come around soon."

Borin. The man died fighting beside us, and I never knew his name. Kazzandra could have fought alongside her kin, and yet she chose to stay with us.

Taryn glances past me in the direction of the keep. "Looks like your stupid plan worked."

I chuckle. "Looks like it."

Taryn raises a brow. "Then why don't you seem happy?"

"I am. At least part of me is." I stand up when I see the rest of our forces making their way up the main avenue, King Favian leading the way on his griffin. "We did what we came for. We saved Mythos. If you told me this would be the outcome a week ago, I'd have been ecstatic. But I don't know, man. Even though this is a victory, I don't know that we won."

Arty sets his brother gently on the steps before placing a massive hand on my shoulder. He gives me a sad smile, his lone eye blinking a few times. "That's the thing. There are no winners in war, only survivors."

After recounting my fight with Valmar, the clerics cleanse the necromancer's body to ensure that he's truly dead. I stay out of the way while the leaders deal with the aftermath. Deciding what's next for the elves and Mosstar will be no easy task.

My days here are numbered, so I leave the discussions to those who will be here to see it through. Many leaders wear the scars of battle. From the shredded fins and mangled scales of the merfolk to the blood-soaked fur of the Antadalians, they've paid for this victory in blood. Some more than others. Swift leaves bloody hoof-marks with each step, the centaur's legs a mess of cuts and gashes. Despite the noticeable limp, he smiles at me as he passes.

I wait for the trolls to arrive, but they never come, so I set off in search of my people. Limery stays with Caustic and Taryn. They'd all follow me, but I need a few moments to myself to process everything that has happened.

Hundreds of despondent elves line the city streets, forced to sit and wait while the fate of everything they know rests in the hands of leaders they've never met. In the aftermath of battle, I notice their gaunt faces and pale skin for the first time. They may wear armor, but these are no warriors.

With the dead no longer a threat, it won't take a large force to police the city. But there's still the worry of what lurks beyond its borders. Bats and werewolves were only some of the terrors residing in the shadowlands, and there's no telling what they'll do when they learn Valmar is gone.

I pass the Mosstar portal, where some of our forces have begun their journey home. For the average citizen who took up arms to defend their way of life, their duty has been fulfilled.

When the broken gate comes into view, I stop in my tracks. Beyond the city's border, a sea of white spreads across the landscape. Hundreds of thousands of bones cover the land like a blanket of snow.

Outside, I find the trolls among those gathering the bodies of the dead. My heart sinks when I see a line of green, blue, and purple corpses.

I find Chief Rizza leaning over the body of a fallen forest troll. Malak. He was a gentle guardian with a curious soul, always the first to laugh and the last to anger. Next to him, Yashi and Ismora lie hand in hand, the body of Yashi's wyrm stretched above them. I kneel next to Rizza and place a hand on her shoulder.

"I'm sorry," I whisper.

"They made their choice." Her golden eyes glisten. "We all did. Their names will not be forgotten."

I spot Chief Laojin, Senzala, and several more arctic trolls breaking apart some of the siege weapons to create a pyre.

A loud wail draws my attention to a group of goblins gathered around the body of a mountain troll. Cheevus has his hands wrapped around Kronan's feet, tears cutting streaks through the bone dust that covers his cheeks.

Kronan looks more peaceful than he ever did in life. His jaw is relaxed, and a warhammer rests across his chest, hiding the grievous wound that took him from the world. A handful of goblins lay beside him.

Cheevus howls as he buries his face against Kronan's feet.

"How did he fall?" I ask.

Cheevus sniffles as he looks at me. "Kronan protects Cheevus, protects goblins with his life." Fresh tears pour from his eyes.

"He was a good troll." We may have gotten off on the wrong foot, but I counted him as a friend in the end.

I walk among the dead, some I knew well, others I only ever saw in passing. I find Gord loading bodies into a wagon. I recognize one of the seaside trolls lying between the corpses of two dwarves. Gord's bone armor hangs in tatters, and cuts run across his legs and arms. His good tusk is broken at the tip, the bright white enamel contrasting against his forest-green skin.

"If you wanted them to match, you could have just asked me." I offer him a half-smile in my lame attempt to lighten the mood. "I would have done it for free."

Gord chuckles, but there's a sadness in his eyes, one I feel all too well. "Many say that young trolls are born with a thirst for battle. They say that violence is in our blood." He grabs the handle of the wagon, lifts it, and then lets it rest. His lip trembles before he speaks. "I used to believe it but standing here today, I would consider myself a lucky troll if I never fought again."

His body heaves, and I rush forward to embrace him. He squeezes me hard as a grief-wracked roar pours from the depths of his soul. I hold him tight, feeling the waves of emotion pass through the body of this so-called monster.

He swallows hard and lets out a shaky breath. "Enough of that. There is much to do."

"Mind if I give you a hand?"

He nods, grabbing the wagon and pulling it forward. Bones crunch beneath the wheels until Gord stops again, and I help him load more bodies into the wagon. An arctic troll. A human. Two dwarves. On and on we work until I lose track of time. He could do it alone, but there's a comfort in the company.

We work in silence, honoring the dead in the simplest way we know how, by being useful.

40. CURTAIN CALL

Three days later.

Taryn and I sit at the edge of a crystal-blue lake, basking in the afternoon sun. Ducks quack as a gentle breeze blows across the water, disturbing the reflection of the lush forest on the opposite side. Ruby snores softly at Taryn's feet, and the sounds of birds chirping and insects trilling play her the perfect lullaby. To our left, Tormara leans against her outstretched wyrm as she watches the young trolls play in the shallow water.

"This is heaven." Taryn crosses his arms behind his head and closes his eyes.

After everything that's happened, it's pretty damn close.

There's movement to our right as Limery swings on a rope hanging from a tall tree at the lake's edge. "Cannonballs!" he yells as he lets go and his tiny frame curls into a ball. He sinks into the lake, sending a splash of water that wakes Berry from a pleasant nap.

"I can't believe you taught him that." I grin at Taryn. "He's going to be insufferable."

"Who are you kidding?" Taryn sits up, pulling his knees to his chest. "He's always been insufferable."

"Cannonball!" Leo zooms through the air, barely touching the rope as he launches himself at his brother, sending a wave crashing into Limery's face.

They both cackle as they splash water at one another.

I lean back, propping myself on my elbows, and my gaze drifts up the hillside to the left, where Tawdrybluff Castle looms over the surrounding valley. My castle, and yet I'll only ever spend two nights in it.

Limery laughs maniacally as he flies over to the rope and flings himself into the lake again. I smile at the fun-loving imp as he swims across the water like a spindly-legged frog. It's high time he has the chance to enjoy himself and just be a kid with his brother.

He's not the only one whose life is changing. Yesterday, I sat down with Chief Rizza and the council, explaining that I'd be leaving soon, most likely never to return. I gave the trolls my items, my gold, and the deed to the castle. Caustic will be around to watch over them, after he attends to a personal matter in Wandermere. The dwarven countryside will be perfect for a green dragon.

I think the days of the tribes living in isolation are over. At the very least, they've agreed to yearly councils. While they all have their ancestral homelands, Tawdrybluff is home to a massive forest. I hope that one day it's filled with trolls from all over.

Valery says we'll all be pulled from the game tonight. While I wish we had longer, I'm grateful to have had a couple of days to just enjoy my time here. No monsters. No fighting. No quests. Just peace and quiet. I can't think of a better ending than that.

There's been no sign of Jude, Glenn, Dorothy, or the others since the battle. I imagine they're together licking their wounds and preparing their next plot. Joke's on them, though. They lost, and Mythos is destined for brighter days.

I wonder if they'll wish they'd done things differently once we're all back in the real world.

"I'm going to miss this place." Taryn plays with Flubs, and the slime oozes from one hand to the other. "Any idea what you're going to do once we're back?"

"Honestly, it's been about the last thing on my mind." I guess I'll have to catch up with my parents at some point. When I first came here, they were on my mind a lot. I was pissed at them for their absence in my life, and I let that resentment fester until it reared its ugly head in ways I'm not proud of. Sitting here now, I can't recall the last time they crossed my mind. Whether it's because of the rehabilitative effects of the program or I've finally learned to take responsibility for my actions, a giant weight has been lifted from my shoulders. I roll over on my side to face Taryn. "I just want to enjoy tonight."

He raises an imaginary mug. "Cheers to that."

A twig snaps behind us as footsteps approach, and I look over my shoulder to see Senzala walking down the path.

The arctic troll shaman waggles her brows and flashes me a mischievous smile. "It's time."

Senzala and I walk side-by-side as we arrive at the courtyard, where a bonfire roars and embers swirl through the twilight sky like fireflies. Tawdrybluff Castle is more rustic than Seascape, its exterior composed of thick blocks of rough granite. It's an imposing fortress with a courtyard that marries spartan architecture with natural landscaping. Vines crawl along thick wooden trellises, and several towering trees grow between the rows of stone tiles, tall enough to view from the castle's highest windows.

If the trolls were to ever build a castle, I imagine it would look something like this.

The celebrations are underway, and many dwarves from the surrounding areas have come to enjoy the festivities with their new troll neighbors. Casks of ale and wine flow like a river as dwarves and trolls share laughs and drinks like old friends. After what they've endured, this generation will be bonded for life. Perhaps the next will grow up in a world where a friendship between the two is no longer an anomaly.

A smoky aroma lingers in the air from giant slabs of meat roasting on spits around the courtyard. A dwarven celebration might not be complete without ale, but a troll revelry requires something to sink your tusks into. Drums mirror the heartbeat of the tribe as one of the young trolls takes a dwarf by the hand and leads her into the drum circle. Elder trolls and dwarves laugh as the younglings dance, stomping and flailing their arms with abandon.

This is my last evening in Mythos, and I have no idea how I can say a proper good-bye to everyone here. So many of those before me have played an integral role in the troll I've become. For a moment, I just stand there and take them all in.

On the far side of the courtyard, Gord and Chief Rizza lean against a balustrade overlooking the lake below.

Limery flies straight to the ale, grabbing mugs for himself and Leo. Their mother and father are perched atop one of the trellises with several of their kin. Lillith shakes her head as Limery downs the first mug like an impish frat boy. Bazel just shrugs. Limery is going to be a handful now that he's not following me into dangerous situations. Once the heroes are gone, he might be one of the strongest beings on the Isle. I wouldn't be surprised if he's the most famous imp to ever live, when all is said and done.

Senzala squeezes my hand, bringing me back to the moment. "Go on, say your good-byes. Just promise to save me a dance before the night is over."

I grin, feeling the warmth of her hand against mine. "As long as you show me the steps."

As I'm making my way through the crowded courtyard, I come across a gnome sitting by himself beneath one of the large oaks. His rose-colored hair and dusty-pink skin stick out like a sore thumb among the trolls and dwarves. He leans against the trunk with a book in one hand and a mug of wine in the other.

"You're a long way from Pruxford," I joke.

Pressley looks up from his book and rolls his eyes. "You should leave the jokes to the dwarf." His voice is high-pitched and nasally, the complete opposite end of the spectrum from when he was a death knight.

"Hey now, no need to be hostile." I grin as I crouch down beside him. "I'm glad you're here. What's it like being level one again?"

"It's weird." He takes a sip of his wine. "I feel weak."

"You're anything but weak. Look around you." I gesture at the full courtyard. "None of us would be here if it weren't for you."

"Oh, I'm not mad about it. This is the first time I've rested since I've been here. It's been nice to take a load off." He lifts the book he's reading. "I know I shouldn't be surprised, but did you know that every book in the library has an actual story in it? I've read three already, and I'm hoping to finish this one before the night's over. It's about a blood mage who retires and opens a tavern. Kind of nice to read about something where the fate of the world isn't on the line."

"I can't argue with that." I extend my arm, and he bumps his fist against mine. "Enjoy your book."

If Pressley can find some solace in the mundane, I'm confident anyone can.

I take a moment to say good-bye to as many trolls as I can. Jira and his tiny phoenix. Tormara. Guilda, the village elder. Jojin and Watu, who seem a bit lost without Malak around to lighten the mood.

Near the bonfire, I find Brutus surrounded by a group of goblins. He holds a massive rack of ribs in his hands, and Kronan's warhammer rests by his side. Cheevus sits next to the massive troll, and his mangy wolf stares at the ribs with ravenous desire.

I guess the goblins have found a new leader to follow. Of all their options, they picked the troll most likely to punt them into the lake for staring at him the wrong way. Then again, they've never seemed too concerned with their treatment as long as it's by someone or something stronger than they are.

To my surprise, Brutus breaks off a rib and hands it to Cheevus. Then one by one, he offers a piece to the wolf and the rest of the goblins.

"What's going on here?" I ask.

"Sharing a meal with some mighty warriors." Brutus grins as he offers me his last rib. I take it, sinking my teeth into the smoky meat. "I believe I finally understand what Kronan learned that day on the mountain. Power alone does not make one strong and following another is not a sign of weakness. To be a leader, one must know when to show strength and when to rely on the wisdom of others." He looks at the goblins as they devour their bones. "But above all, the tribe is at its greatest when we have a community."

I nearly choke on the rib when he says the last part. "How much have you had to drink?"

"So far?" He laughs. "Not nearly enough."

My brain is still reeling at Brutus's evolution when I finally make my way over to Gord and Chief Rizza. They stare out at the lake as the last rays of sunlight vanish beyond the trees.

"Aren't you two a couple of wallflowers."

Gord turns around. "I was wondering when you'd make your way up here." He lifts his mug in my direction. "To finally getting rid of you."

Good to know our moment outside of Mosstar hasn't changed his sense of humor.

"Gord." Chief Rizza gives him the same reproachful look she might offer to a mischievous child.

"He knows I don't mean it." Gord takes a swig from his mug and then slaps me on the shoulder. "In truth, the tribe will not be the same without you."

"I will hear none of that." There's an edge to Rizza's voice when she speaks. Her golden eyes meet mine, and her face softens along with her tone. "Whether in Mythos or elsewhere, Chod will always be a member of the tribe. Nothing will ever change that."

I gaze up at the stars, blinking back tears. There will be a time for that dam to break but not now, because once I start, I'm not sure I'll be able to stop. For now, I want to celebrate one last night with my friends, with my brothers and sisters, with my tribe.

Even though my sentence may be ending, the story of the trolls is just beginning.

EPILOGUE

Four months later.

Taryn and I sit on a bench in Central Park, eating hotdogs from a street vendor. There's a chill in the air as squirrels scurry through the bushes, stashing away acorns beneath trees tinged with orange. Soon, fall will stake its claim to the city, followed by the cold discontent of a New York winter.

I pull my jacket a little tighter, remembering the time I walked barefoot up a snow-covered mountain wearing nothing but a loincloth.

Taryn shoves the hotdog into his mouth, devouring half of it with one bite. He moans as mustard drips into his scruffy beard. "This is good," he says with a full mouth.

He's been growing the beard for a couple of months now, but it's nothing like the one he had in Mythos. Whenever he sends me a text or we talk on the phone, I still picture the short, stocky dwarf on the other side, not this mountain of a man sitting beside me.

I give him a mock grimace. "At least no one can say you don't feed the creature latched to your face."

Taryn rolls his eyes. "Come on. It's not that bad."

"Trust me, T." I laugh. "It's worse. I mean, it looks like you walked into a barber shop, swept the floor, and decided you'd rather glue someone else's hair to your face than actually grow a beard."

Taryn's mouth hangs open, and he places a hand over his chest. "Chod, I am wounded."

He still calls me that sometimes. Every time he does, it takes me back to Mythos, and I can't help wondering what all of my friends are up to.

Are Limery and Leo going on adventures together? Are the trolls sleeping in the castle, or are they more comfortable in the forest behind it? And Caustic, what does a young dragon do with all of his free time when he's not saving the world?

Taryn shoves the rest of the hotdog in his mouth and pulls up the sleeve of his sweatshirt. "Bro, I can't believe I didn't show you yet. Check this out." He grins as he lifts his wrist, revealing a fresh tattoo of a cat skeleton covered in slime. "Pretty sick, right?"

"Nice!" I lean in for a closer look. "What is that, four now?"

"Yep, Jordy is the only one left, but I can't decide where I want to put it. This one is cool, though. The green ink glows in the dark."

"No shit?" I raise my brows incredulously. "That's pretty cool."

We were out of the game a couple of weeks when Taryn decided he wanted to honor Stompy with a carrot tattoo over his heart. Not long after that, he got a bear head on the opposite side of his chest, followed by a ruby on his left wrist. It warms my heart to know I'm not the only one who still thinks about them.

Since we've been back, Taryn has re-enrolled in community college. With all of the money he made testing the rehab project, he'll be able to transfer to a university in the spring.

I can't say I've been quite as productive. I've felt a bit lost, to be honest, so I took some time to... I don't really know. There's been an emptiness in my life that I haven't been able to fill. Dad offered me a job working with him, but I turned it down. That's the last place I want to be.

While I figure things out, I try to keep myself busy. I read a lot. I've started running. I go to the gym, something I never thought I'd say, but without the nanites keeping me in shape, I've got to do something to keep this amazing body I've been given. It's been three months since we logged out, and the one thing I haven't thought about is gaming.

My phone vibrates, and I pull it from my jacket pocket, frowning at the unknown number flashing on the screen.

"Who is it?" Taryn raises a brow.

I shrug, showing him the phone.

He reaches for the phone, but I pull it back. "You're not gonna answer it?"

"Do you answer unknown numbers? It's probably a scam. I'm not exactly Mr. Popular, you know?" I place the phone back in my pocket and wait for it to quit vibrating.

"Eva, get back here!" a deep voice calls just as a young girl with curly black hair comes running down the path. She stops in front of us, where two squirrels are fighting over a piece of dirt-covered pizza crust beneath a tree.

"Daddy, look!" She grins, pointing at the critters. "They're hungry."

Her father smiles as he catches up, resting a hand on her shoulder. "How about we let them eat in peace? Your mother will kill me if we're late to the museum."

I watch them as they leave hand-in-hand. There's something vaguely familiar about the man, but I can't put my finger on it.

Taryn leans forward, his attention focused on the two squirrels. "My money's on the one with the fluffy tail."

My pocket vibrates again. Another unknown number.

"Come on, bro. It's either important, or they're very dedicated. Just see who it is."

What the hell? It's not like I have much else going on. I tap the screen. "Hello?"

"Chad?"

I almost drop the phone at the familiar sound of the woman's voice on the other end. "Yeah, uh, yeah, it's me."

I can hear the smile in Valery's voice when she speaks. "It's been a while. How would you like to take a vacation to Mythos?"

The End

ACKNOWLEDGMENTS

Congratulations! *You have finished* Sentenced to Troll.
    +1 stat point to distribute.
    +1 review to leave.
    6 of 6 completed. Reward: Isn't making it to the end a reward in itself?
    No? In that case, I'd like to officially welcome you as a member of the troll tribe.

Thank you for reading *Sentenced to Troll!* If you enjoyed your time in Mythos, please consider rating, reviewing, and sharing your thoughts on social media. Word of mouth is the best way to support indie authors like myself.

If you're looking for more books similar to my own, check out LitRPG Books.

ACKNOWLEDGMENTS

Congratulations! *You have finished* Sentenced to Troll.
    +1 stat point to distribute.
    +1 review to leave.
    6 of 6 completed. Reward: Isn't making it to the end a reward in itself?
    No? In that case, I'd like to officially welcome you as a member of the troll tribe.

Thank you for reading *Sentenced to Troll!* If you enjoyed your time in Mythos, please consider rating, reviewing, and sharing your thoughts on social media. Word of mouth is the best way to support indie authors like myself.

If you're looking for more books similar to my own, check out LitRPG Books.

ABOUT THE AUTHOR

S.L. Rowland is a cozy fantasy and LitRPG author known for crafting immersive worlds filled with adventure, heart, and a touch of humor. A lifelong gamer and fantasy enthusiast, he draws inspiration from tabletop RPGs, video games, and the fantastical. When he's not writing, he enjoys weightlifting, hiking with his Shiba Inu, and enduring the heartbreak of being an Atlanta sports fan.

SLRowland.com

Patreon-For signed paperbacks, advanced chapters, exclusive short stories, art, merch, and more.

Newsletter: For updates on new releases, sales, and behind the scenes content!

Email: slrowlandauthor@gmail.com

Find out more at https://linktr.ee/SLRowland

ALSO BY S.L. ROWLAND

Tales of Aedrea

Cursed Cocktails

Sword & Thistle

The Halfling's Harvest

There Be Dragons Here

Pangea Online

Pangea Online: Death and Axes

Pangea Online 2: Magic and Mayhem

Pangea Online 3: Vials and Tribulations

Sentenced to Troll 1-6

Path to Villainy: An NPC Kobold's Tale

Collected Editions

Pangea Online: The Complete Trilogy

Sentenced to Troll Compendium: Books 1-3

Sentenced to Troll Compendium 2: Books 4-6